X-MEN
FIRST CLASS
MUTANTS 101

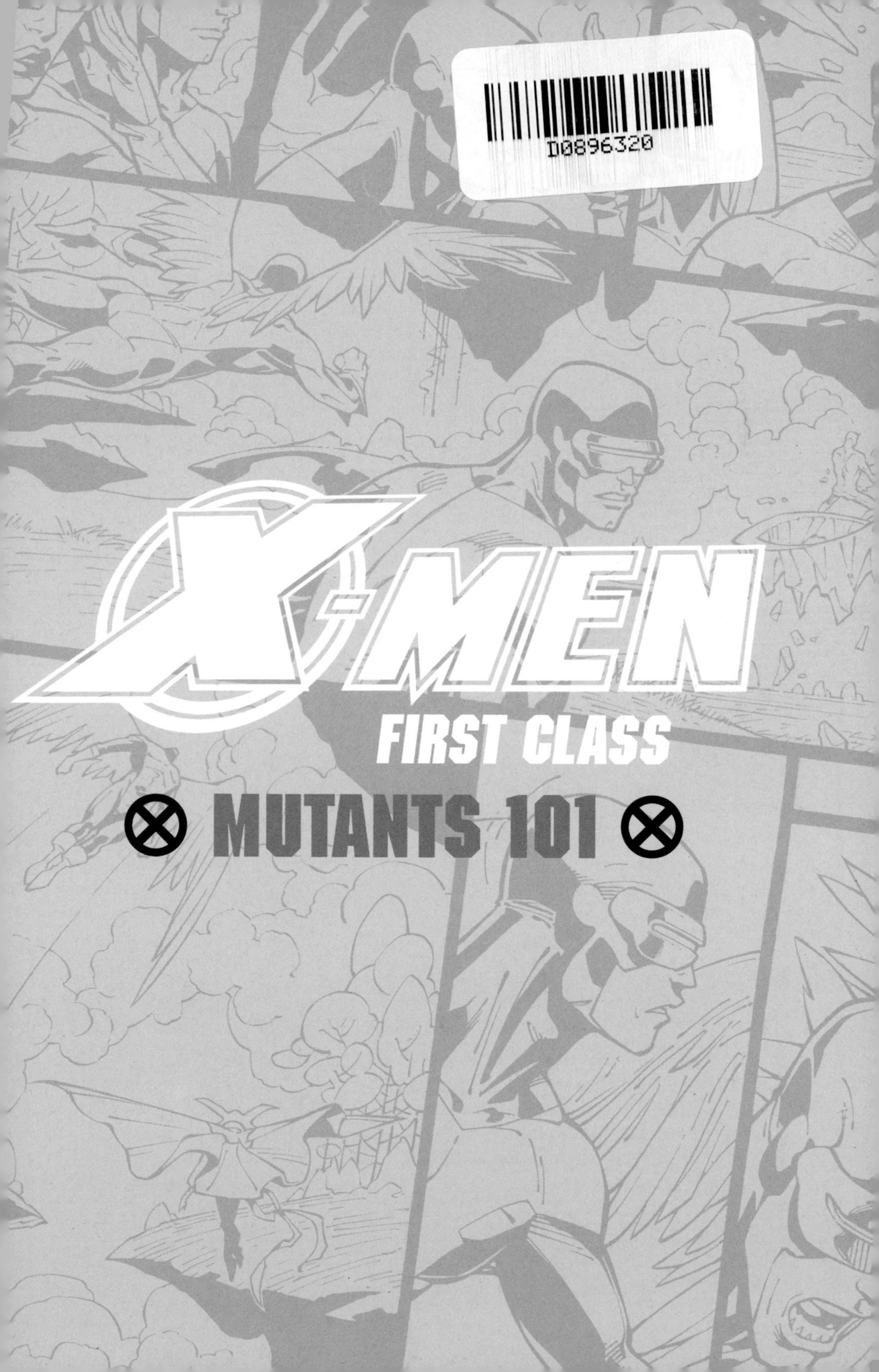

CONTENTS

X-MEN CREATED BY **STAN LEE** & **JACK KIRBY**

COLLECTION EDITOR **DANIEL KIRCHHOFFER** · ASSISTANT MANAGING EDITOR **MAIA LOY**

ASSOCIATE MANAGER, TALENT RELATIONS **LISA MONTALBANO** · ASSOCIATE MANAGER, DIGITAL ASSETS **JOE HOCHSTEIN**

DIRECTOR, PRODUCTION & SPECIAL PROJECTS **JENNIFER GRÜNWALD** · VP PRODUCTION & SPECIAL PROJECTS **JEFF YOUNGQUIST**

BOOK DESIGNER **JAY BOWEN** · SVP PRINT, SALES & MARKETING **DAVID GABRIEL**

EDITOR IN CHIEF **C.B. CEBULSKI**

X-MEN: FIRST CLASS — MUTANTS 101. Contains material originally published in magazine form as X-MEN: FIRST CLASS (2006) #1-8 and X-MEN: FIRST CLASS SPECIAL (2007) #1. First printing 2022. ISBN 978-1-302-93213-8. Published by MARVEL WORLDWIDE, INC., a subsidiary of MARVEL ENTERTAINMENT, LLC. OFFICE OF PUBLICATION: 1290 Avenue of the Americas, New York, NY 10104. © 2022 MARVEL No similarity between any of the names, characters, persons, and/or institutions in this book with those of any living or dead person or institution is intended, and any such similarity which may exist is purely coincidental. **Printed in Canada.** KEVIN FEIGE, Chief Creative Officer; DAN BUCKLEY, President, Marvel Entertainment; JOE QUESADA, EVP & Creative Director; DAVID BOGART, Associate Publisher & SVP of Talent Affairs; TOM BREVOORT, VP, Executive Editor; NICK LOWE, Executive Editor, VP of Content, Digital Publishing; DAVID GABRIEL, VP of Print & Digital Publishing; SVEN LARSEN, VP of Licensed Publishing; MARK ANNUNZIATO, VP of Planning & Forecasting; JEFF YOUNGQUIST, VP of Production & Special Projects; ALEX MORALES, Director of Publishing Operations; DAN EDINGTON, Director of Editorial Operations; RICKEY PURDIN, Director of Talent Relations; JENNIFER GRÜNWALD, Director of Production & Special Projects; SUSAN CRESPI, Production Manager; STAN LEE, Chairman Emeritus. For information regarding advertising in Marvel Comics or on Marvel.com, please contact Vit DeBellis, Custom Solutions & Integrated Advertising Manager, at vdebellis@marvel.com. For Marvel subscription inquiries, please call 888-511-5480. **Manufactured between 5/13/2022 and 6/14/2022 by SOLISCO PRINTERS, SCOTT, QC, CANADA.**

10 9 8 7 6 5 4 3 2 1

X-MEN

FIRST CLASS

✖ MUTANTS 101 ✖

JEFF PARKER WRITER

X-MEN: FIRST CLASS #1-8

ROGER CRUZ WITH **PAUL SMITH** (#6) PENCILERS

VICTOR OLAZABA (#1-6) & **ROGER CRUZ** (#7-8) WITH **PAUL SMITH** (#6) INKERS

VAL STAPLES COLORIST

NATE PIEKOS OF BLAMBOT® LETTERER

MARKO DJURDJEVIĆ COVER ART

SPECIAL THANKS TO SARAH WOOD & AMY MASCUNANA

X-MEN: FIRST CLASS SPECIAL

KEVIN NOWLAN COLLEEN COOVER NICK DRAGOTTA & **PAUL SMITH** PENCILERS

KEVIN NOWLAN COLLEEN COOVER MICHAEL ALLRED & **PAUL SMITH** INKERS

KEVIN NOWLAN COLLEEN COOVER LAURA ALLRED & **PETE PANTAZIS** COLORISTS

KEVIN NOWLAN COLLEEN COOVER & **NATE PIEKOS** OF BLAMBOT® LETTERERS

KEVIN NOWLAN COVER ART

NATHAN COSBY ASSISTANT EDITOR

MARK PANICCIA EDITOR

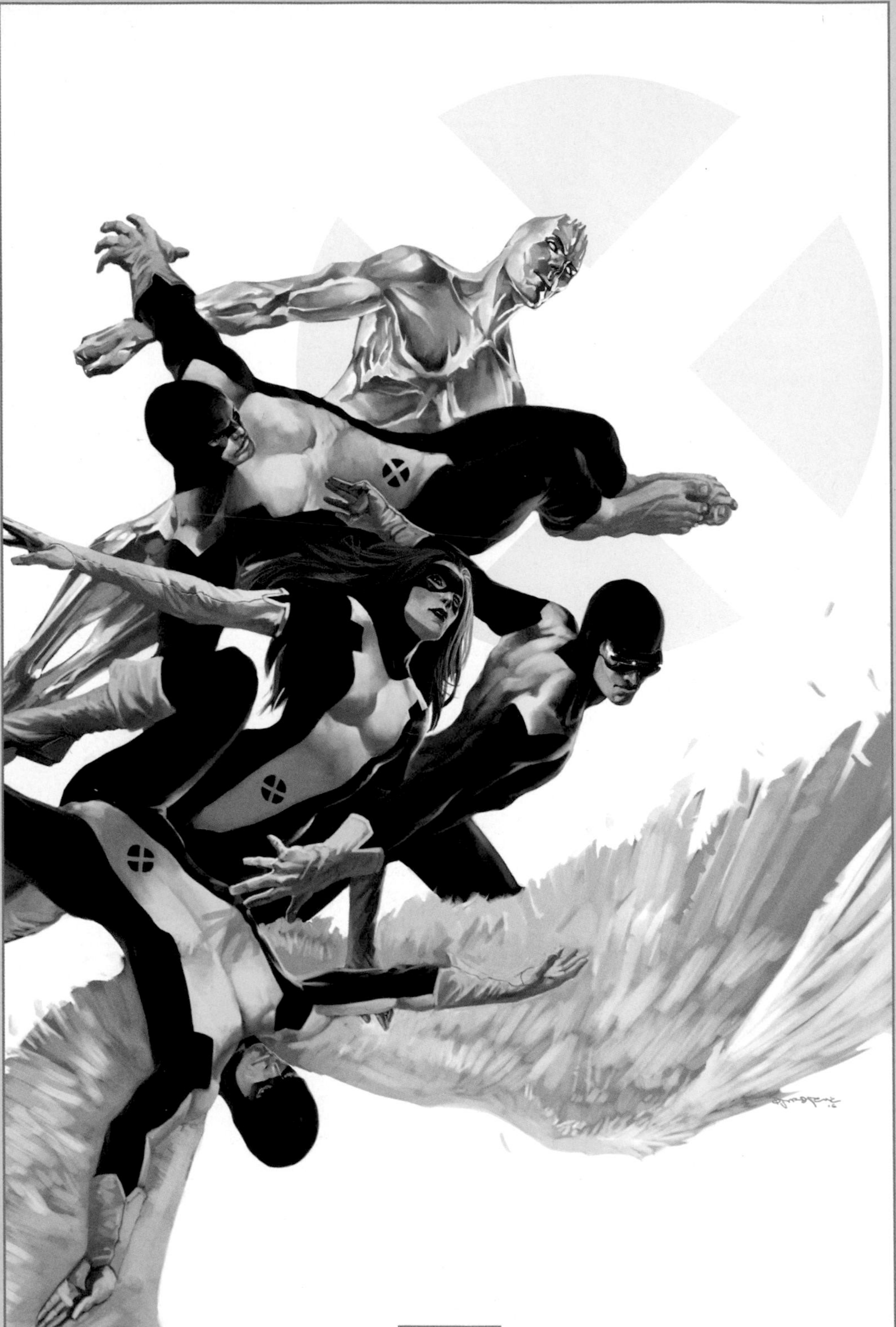

1

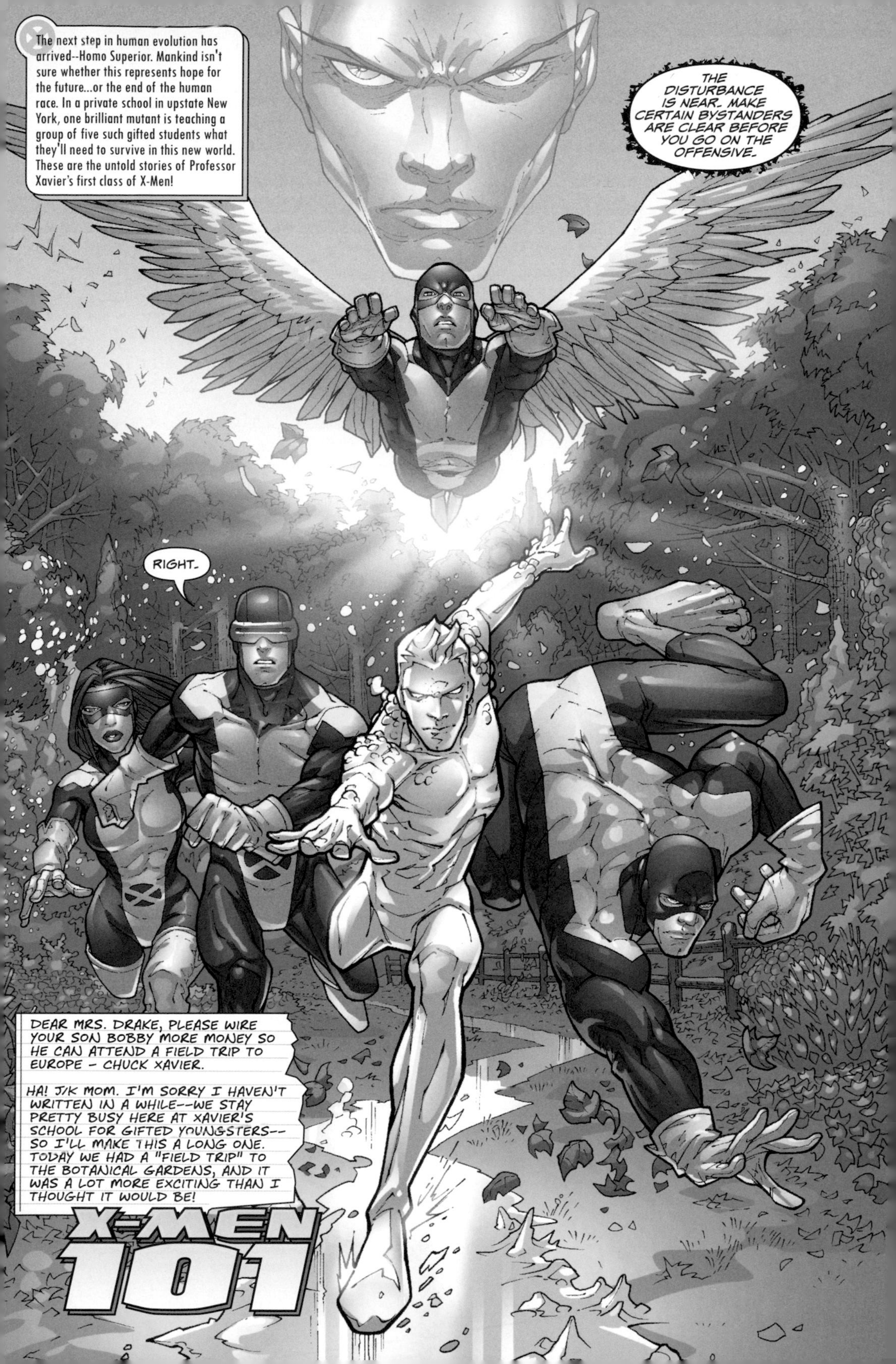
The next step in human evolution has arrived--Homo Superior. Mankind isn't sure whether this represents hope for the future...or the end of the human race. In a private school in upstate New York, one brilliant mutant is teaching a group of five such gifted students what they'll need to survive in this new world. These are the untold stories of Professor Xavier's first class of X-Men!
THE DISTURBANCE IS NEAR. MAKE CERTAIN BYSTANDERS ARE CLEAR BEFORE YOU GO ON THE OFFENSIVE.
RIGHT.
DEAR MRS. DRAKE, PLEASE WIRE YOUR SON BOBBY MORE MONEY SO HE CAN ATTEND A FIELD TRIP TO EUROPE - CHUCK XAVIER.
HA! J/K MOM. I'M SORRY I HAVEN'T WRITTEN IN A WHILE--WE STAY PRETTY BUSY HERE AT XAVIER'S SCHOOL FOR GIFTED YOUNGSTERS--SO I'LL MAKE THIS A LONG ONE. TODAY WE HAD A "FIELD TRIP" TO THE BOTANICAL GARDENS, AND IT WAS A LOT MORE EXCITING THAN I THOUGHT IT WOULD BE!
X-MEN 101

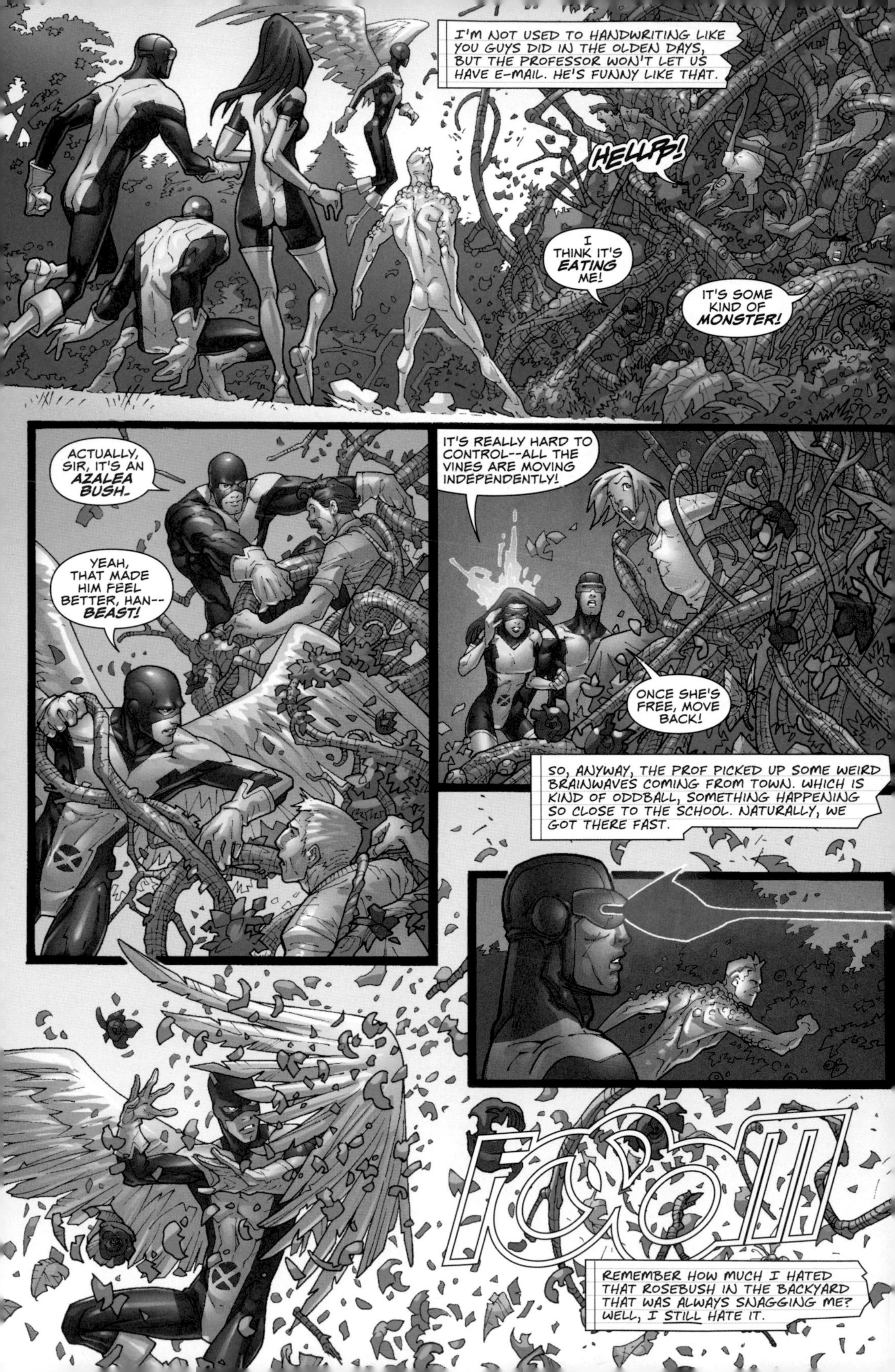

I'M NOT USED TO HANDWRITING LIKE YOU GUYS DID IN THE OLDEN DAYS, BUT THE PROFESSOR WON'T LET US HAVE E-MAIL. HE'S FUNNY LIKE THAT.
HELLLP!
I THINK IT'S EATING ME!
IT'S SOME KIND OF MONSTER!
ACTUALLY, SIR, IT'S AN AZALEA BUSH.
YEAH, THAT MADE HIM FEEL BETTER, HAN-- BEAST!
IT'S REALLY HARD TO CONTROL--ALL THE VINES ARE MOVING INDEPENDENTLY!
ONCE SHE'S FREE, MOVE BACK!
SO, ANYWAY, THE PROF PICKED UP SOME WEIRD BRAINWAVES COMING FROM TOWN. WHICH IS KIND OF ODDBALL, SOMETHING HAPPENING SO CLOSE TO THE SCHOOL. NATURALLY, WE GOT THERE FAST.
REMEMBER HOW MUCH I HATED THAT ROSEBUSH IN THE BACKYARD THAT WAS ALWAYS SNAGGING ME? WELL, I STILL HATE IT.

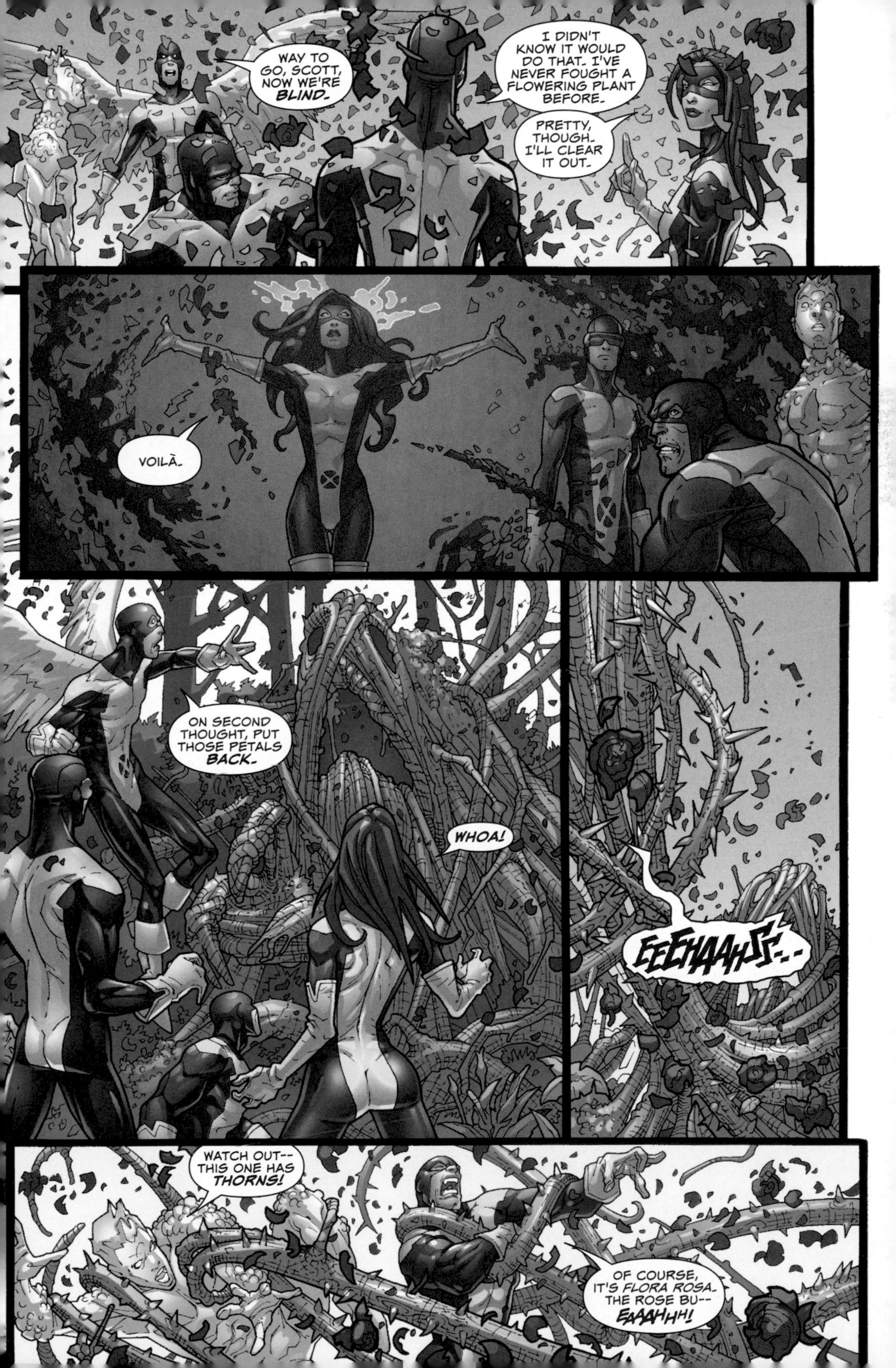
WAY TO GO, SCOTT, NOW WE'RE BLIND.
I DIDN'T KNOW IT WOULD DO THAT. I'VE NEVER FOUGHT A FLOWERING PLANT BEFORE.
PRETTY, THOUGH. I'LL CLEAR IT OUT.
VOILÀ.
ON SECOND THOUGHT, PUT THOSE PETALS BACK.
WHOA!
EEEHAAAHSS...
WATCH OUT-- THIS ONE HAS THORNS!
OF COURSE, IT'S FLORA ROSA. THE ROSE BU-- EAAAHHH!

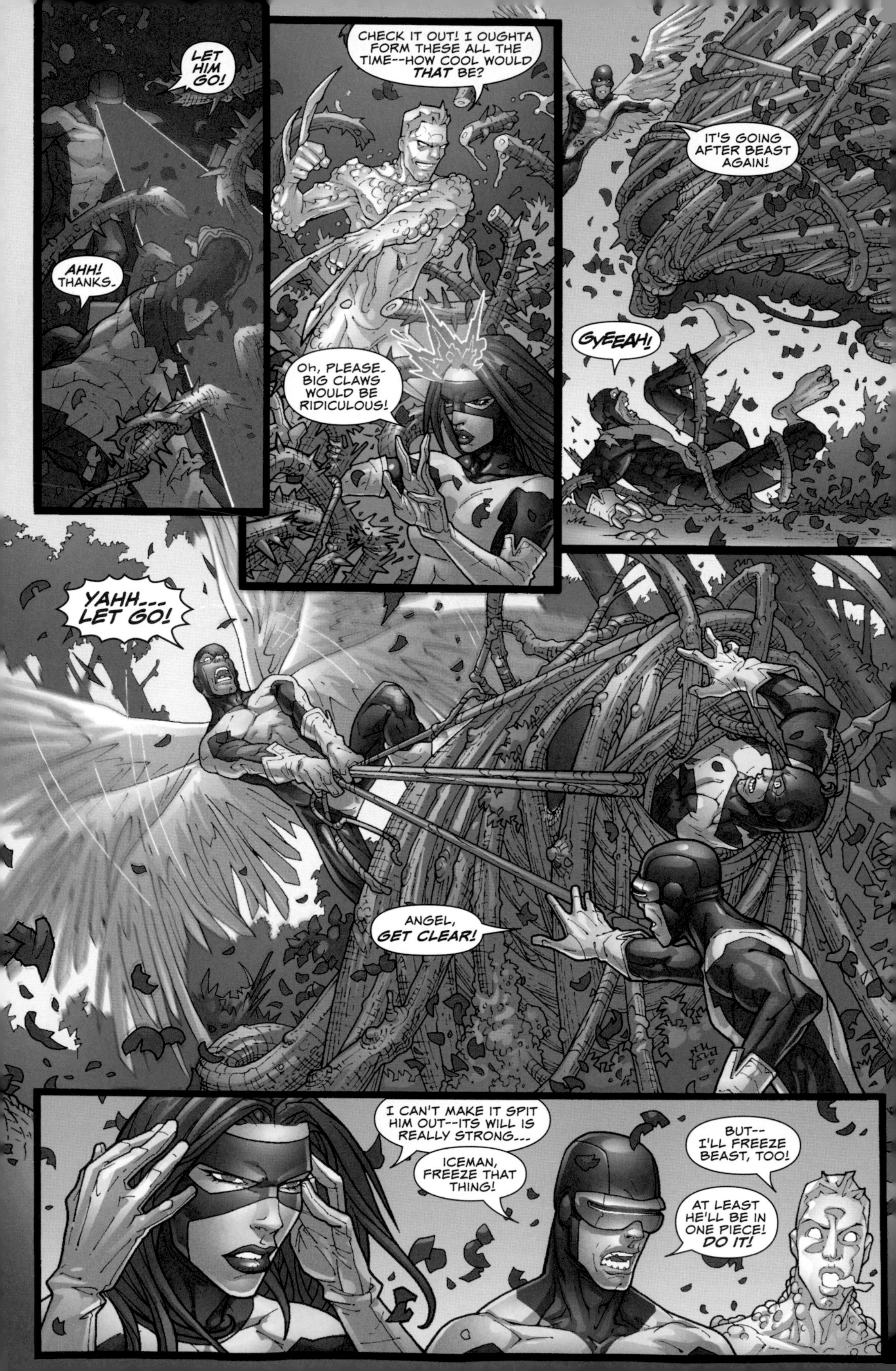
LET HIM GO!
AHH! THANKS.
CHECK IT OUT! I OUGHTA FORM THESE ALL THE TIME--HOW COOL WOULD THAT BE?
Oh, PLEASE. BIG CLAWS WOULD BE RIDICULOUS!
IT'S GOING AFTER BEAST AGAIN!
GYEEAH!
YAHH--- LET GO!
ANGEL, GET CLEAR!
I CAN'T MAKE IT SPIT HIM OUT--ITS WILL IS REALLY STRONG---
ICEMAN, FREEZE THAT THING!
BUT-- I'LL FREEZE BEAST, TOO!
AT LEAST HE'LL BE IN ONE PIECE! DO IT!

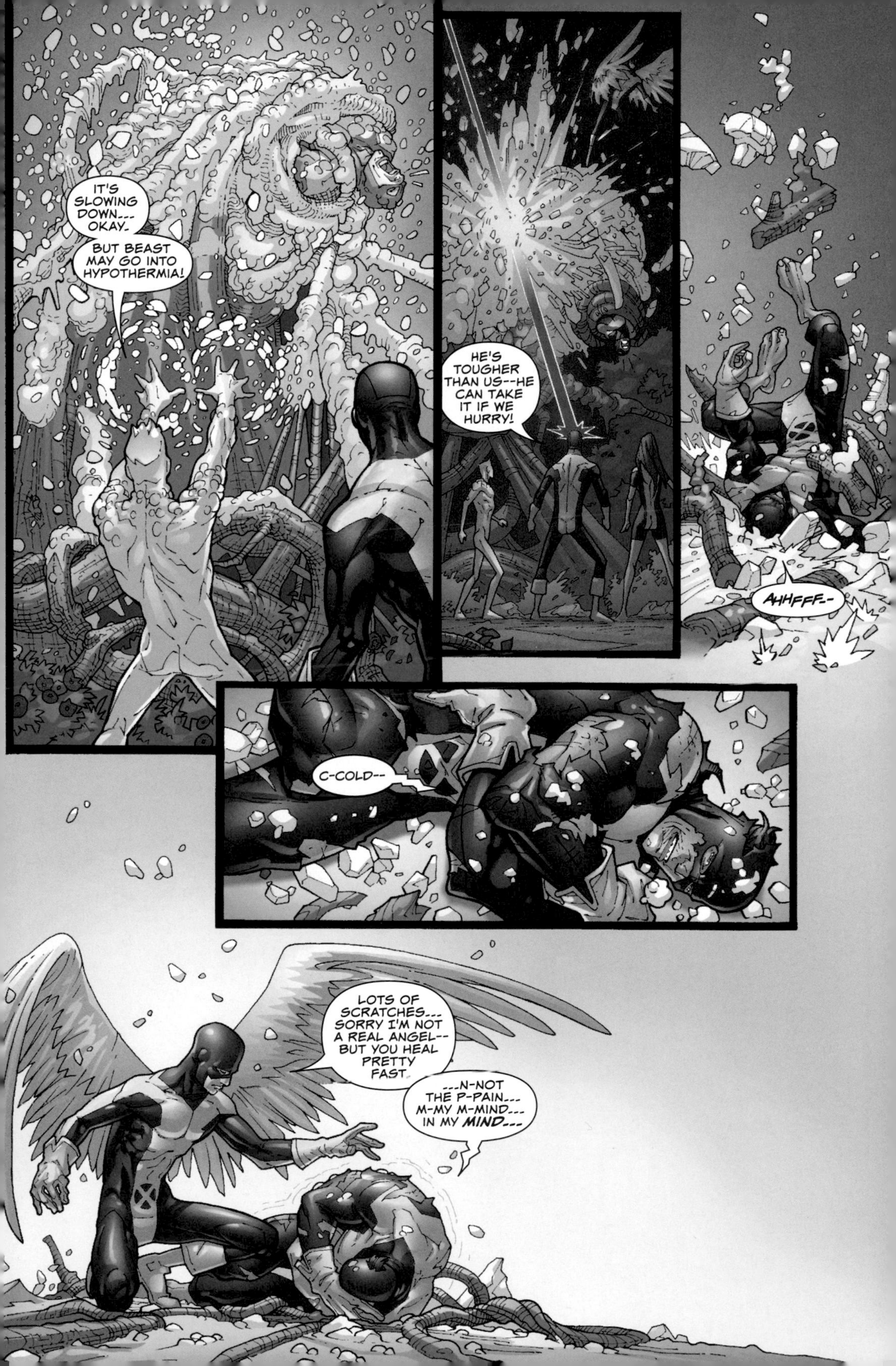
IT'S SLOWING DOWN--- OKAY-
BUT BEAST MAY GO INTO HYPOTHERMIA!
HE'S TOUGHER THAN US--HE CAN TAKE IT IF WE HURRY!
AHHFFF--
C-COLD--
LOTS OF SCRATCHES--- SORRY I'M NOT A REAL ANGEL-- BUT YOU HEAL PRETTY FAST.
---N-NOT THE P-PAIN--- M-MY M-MIND--- IN MY MIND---

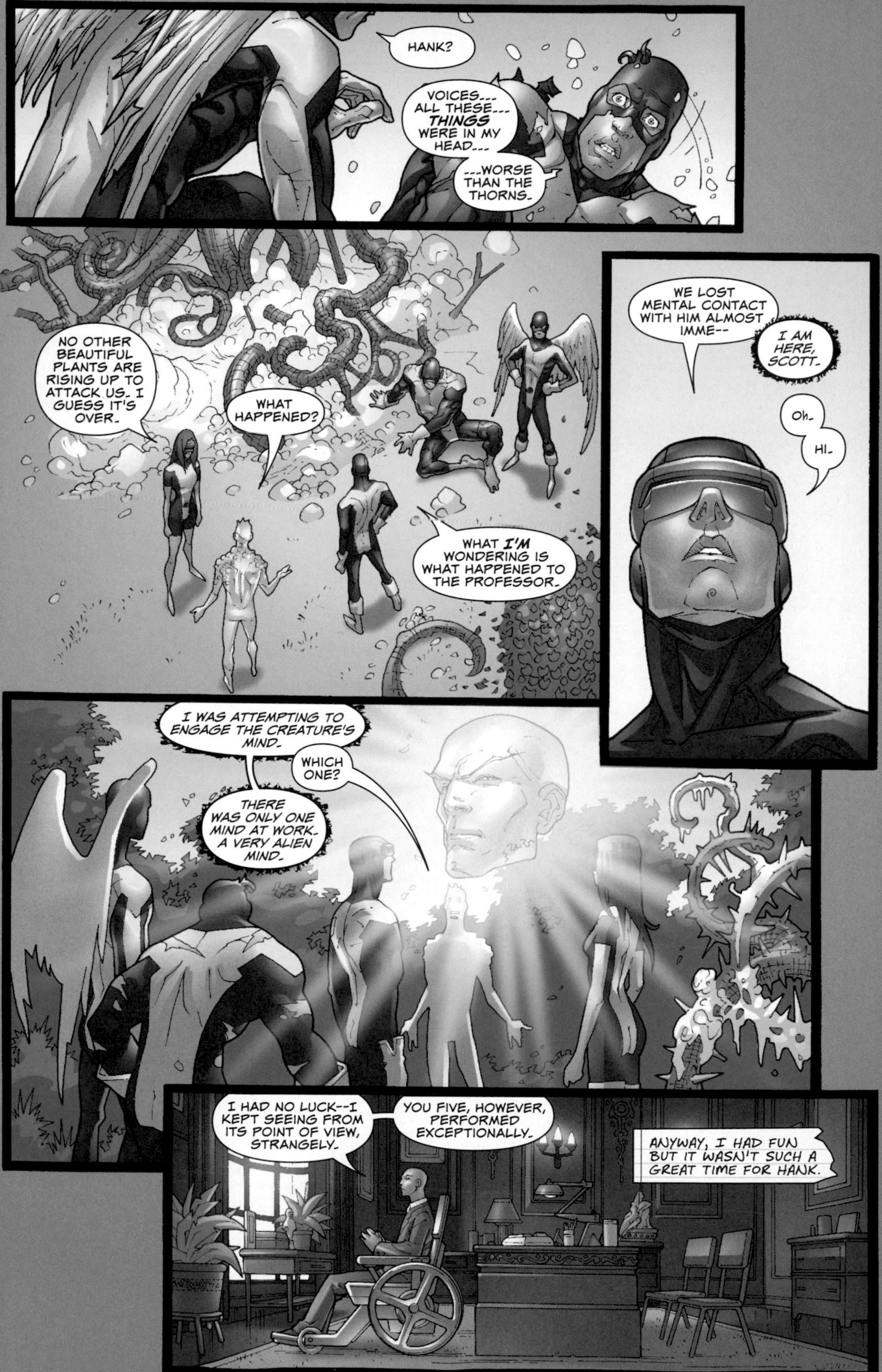

HANK?
VOICES... ALL THESE... THINGS WERE IN MY HEAD...
...WORSE THAN THE THORNS.
NO OTHER BEAUTIFUL PLANTS ARE RISING UP TO ATTACK US. I GUESS IT'S OVER.
WHAT HAPPENED?
WHAT I'M WONDERING IS WHAT HAPPENED TO THE PROFESSOR.
WE LOST MENTAL CONTACT WITH HIM ALMOST IMME--
I AM HERE, SCOTT.
Oh.
HI.
I WAS ATTEMPTING TO ENGAGE THE CREATURE'S MIND.
WHICH ONE?
THERE WAS ONLY ONE MIND AT WORK. A VERY ALIEN MIND.
I HAD NO LUCK--I KEPT SEEING FROM ITS POINT OF VIEW, STRANGELY.
YOU FIVE, HOWEVER, PERFORMED EXCEPTIONALLY.
ANYWAY, I HAD FUN BUT IT WASN'T SUCH A GREAT TIME FOR HANK.

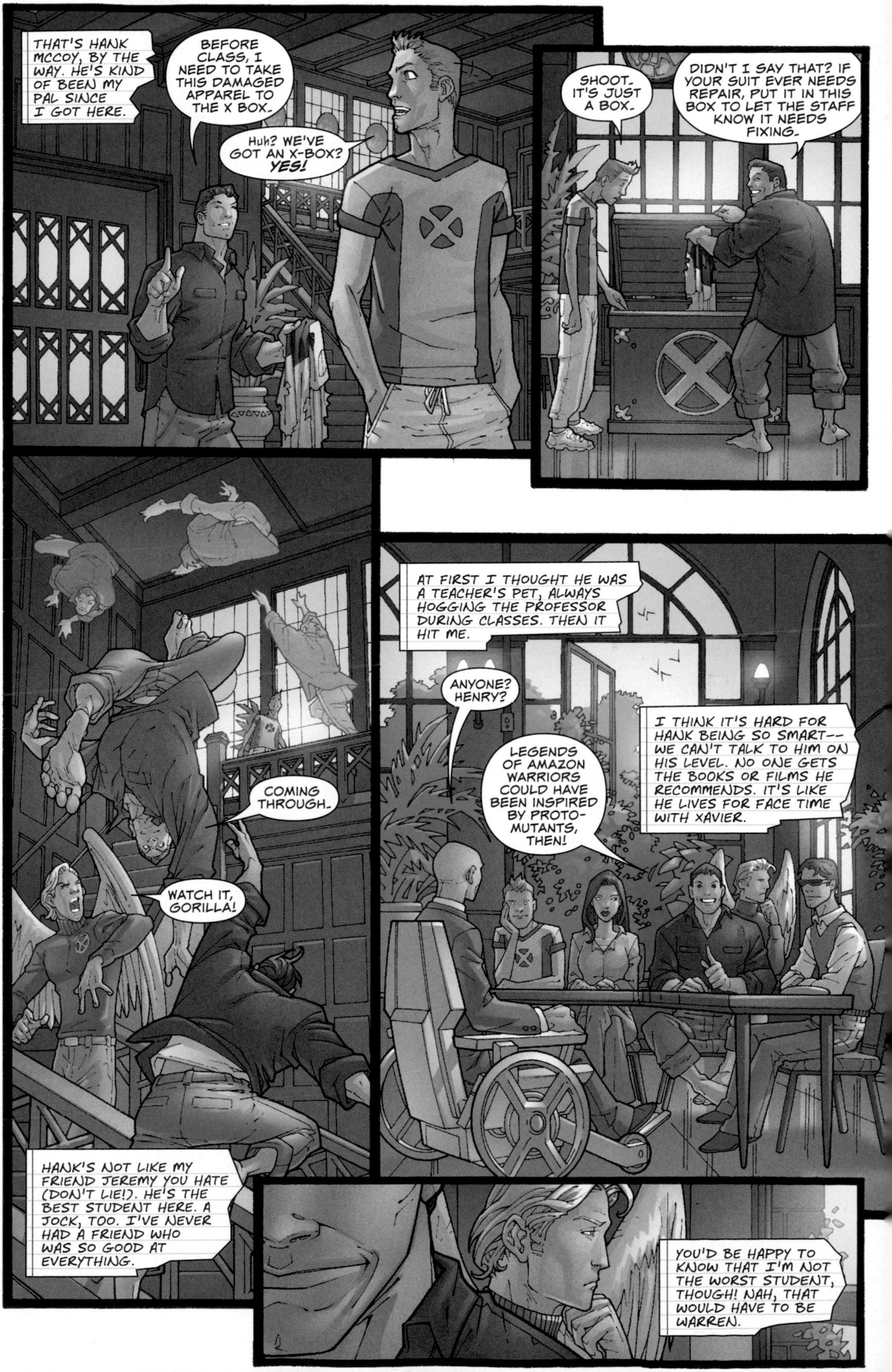
THAT'S HANK MCCOY, BY THE WAY. HE'S KIND OF BEEN MY PAL SINCE I GOT HERE.
BEFORE CLASS, I NEED TO TAKE THIS DAMAGED APPAREL TO THE X BOX.
Huh? WE'VE GOT AN X-BOX? YES!
SHOOT. IT'S JUST A BOX.
DIDN'T I SAY THAT? IF YOUR SUIT EVER NEEDS REPAIR, PUT IT IN THIS BOX TO LET THE STAFF KNOW IT NEEDS FIXING.
COMING THROUGH.
WATCH IT, GORILLA!
HANK'S NOT LIKE MY FRIEND JEREMY YOU HATE (DON'T LIE!). HE'S THE BEST STUDENT HERE. A JOCK, TOO. I'VE NEVER HAD A FRIEND WHO WAS SO GOOD AT EVERYTHING.
AT FIRST I THOUGHT HE WAS A TEACHER'S PET, ALWAYS HOGGING THE PROFESSOR DURING CLASSES. THEN IT HIT ME.
ANYONE? HENRY?
LEGENDS OF AMAZON WARRIORS COULD HAVE BEEN INSPIRED BY PROTO-MUTANTS, THEN!
I THINK IT'S HARD FOR HANK BEING SO SMART-- WE CAN'T TALK TO HIM ON HIS LEVEL. NO ONE GETS THE BOOKS OR FILMS HE RECOMMENDS. IT'S LIKE HE LIVES FOR FACE TIME WITH XAVIER.
YOU'D BE HAPPY TO KNOW THAT I'M NOT THE WORST STUDENT, THOUGH! NAH, THAT WOULD HAVE TO BE WARREN.

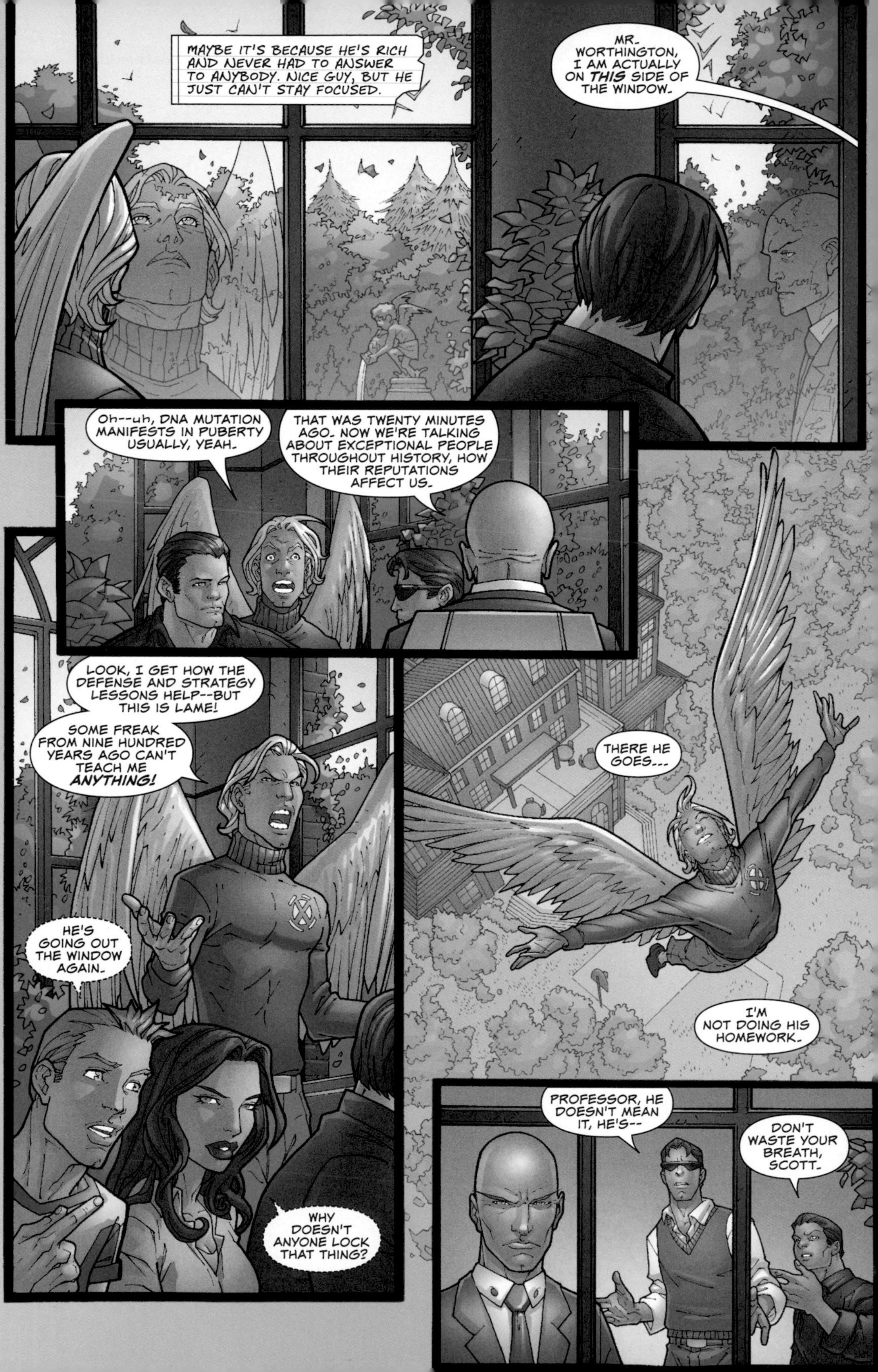
MAYBE IT'S BECAUSE HE'S RICH AND NEVER HAD TO ANSWER TO ANYBODY. NICE GUY, BUT HE JUST CAN'T STAY FOCUSED.
MR. WORTHINGTON, I AM ACTUALLY ON THIS SIDE OF THE WINDOW.
Oh--uh, DNA MUTATION MANIFESTS IN PUBERTY USUALLY, YEAH.
THAT WAS TWENTY MINUTES AGO. NOW WE'RE TALKING ABOUT EXCEPTIONAL PEOPLE THROUGHOUT HISTORY, HOW THEIR REPUTATIONS AFFECT US.
LOOK, I GET HOW THE DEFENSE AND STRATEGY LESSONS HELP--BUT THIS IS LAME!
SOME FREAK FROM NINE HUNDRED YEARS AGO CAN'T TEACH ME ANYTHING!
HE'S GOING OUT THE WINDOW AGAIN.
WHY DOESN'T ANYONE LOCK THAT THING?
THERE HE GOES...
I'M NOT DOING HIS HOMEWORK.
PROFESSOR, HE DOESN'T MEAN IT, HE'S--
DON'T WASTE YOUR BREATH, SCOTT.

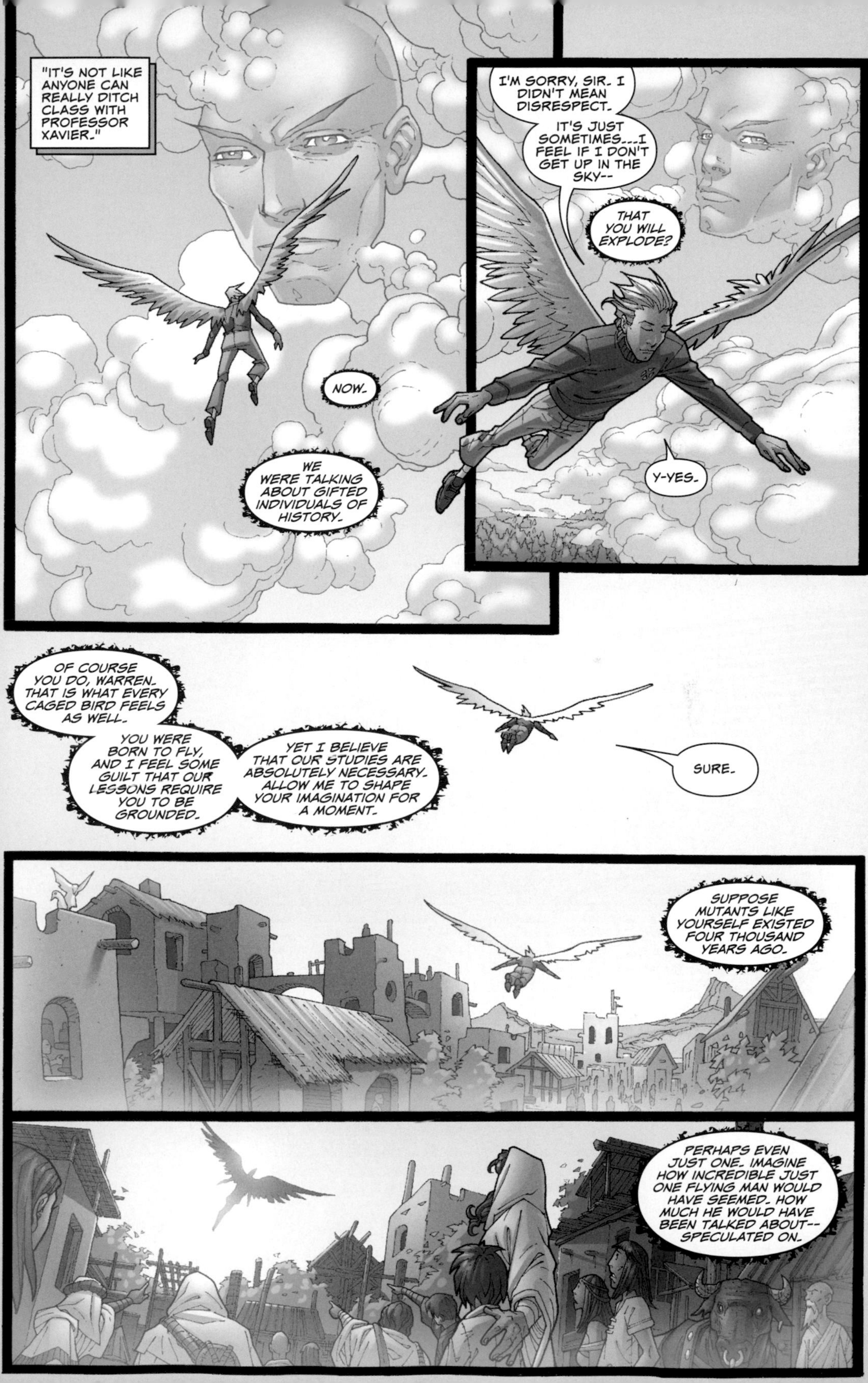
"IT'S NOT LIKE ANYONE CAN REALLY DITCH CLASS WITH PROFESSOR XAVIER."
I'M SORRY, SIR. I DIDN'T MEAN DISRESPECT.
IT'S JUST SOMETIMES... I FEEL IF I DON'T GET UP IN THE SKY--
THAT YOU WILL EXPLODE?
Y-YES.
NOW.
WE WERE TALKING ABOUT GIFTED INDIVIDUALS OF HISTORY.
SURE.
OF COURSE YOU DO, WARREN. THAT IS WHAT EVERY CAGED BIRD FEELS AS WELL.
YOU WERE BORN TO FLY, AND I FEEL SOME GUILT THAT OUR LESSONS REQUIRE YOU TO BE GROUNDED.
YET I BELIEVE THAT OUR STUDIES ARE ABSOLUTELY NECESSARY. ALLOW ME TO SHAPE YOUR IMAGINATION FOR A MOMENT.
SUPPOSE MUTANTS LIKE YOURSELF EXISTED FOUR THOUSAND YEARS AGO.
PERHAPS EVEN JUST ONE. IMAGINE HOW INCREDIBLE JUST ONE FLYING MAN WOULD HAVE SEEMED. HOW MUCH HE WOULD HAVE BEEN TALKED ABOUT-- SPECULATED ON.

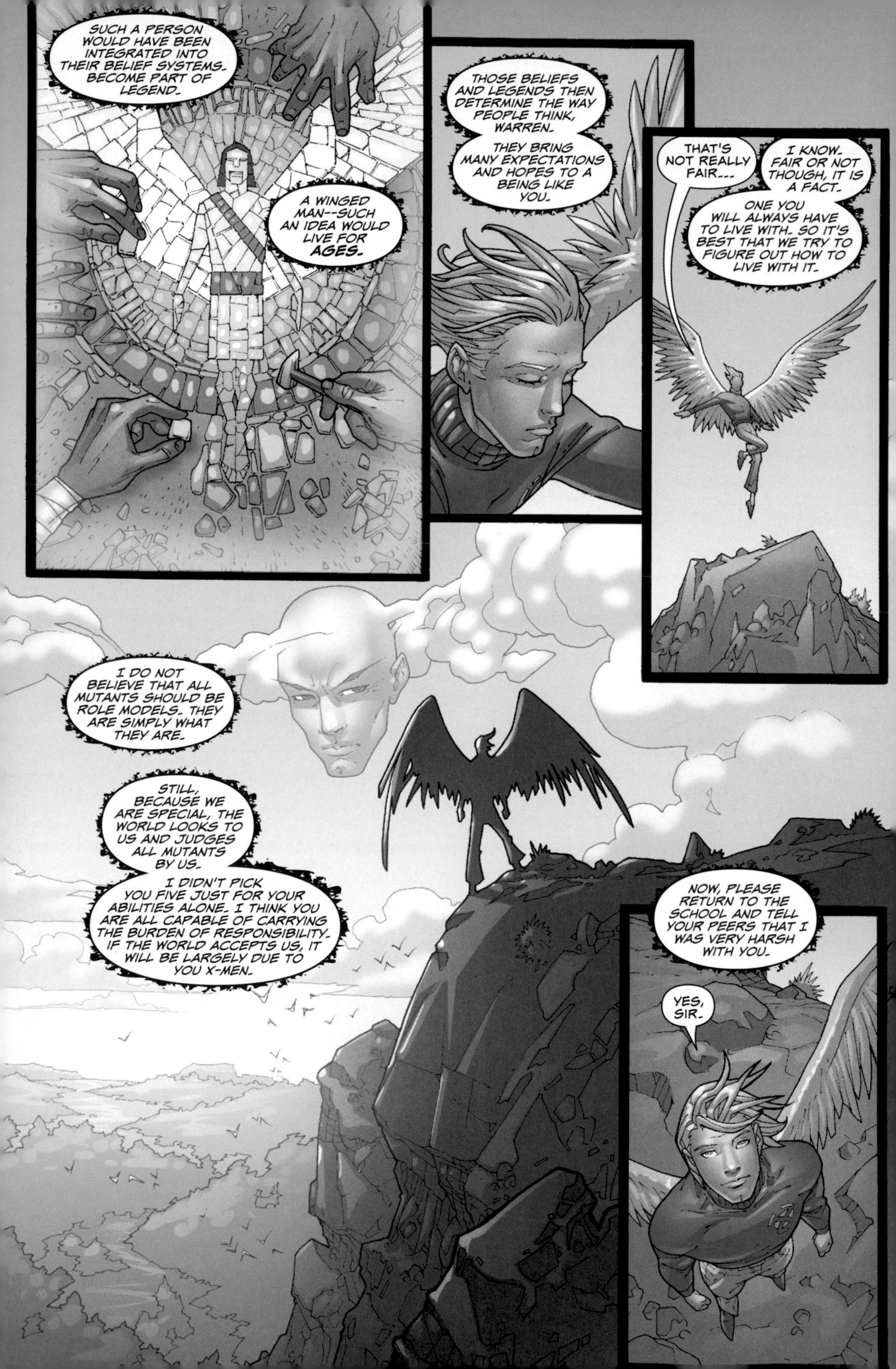
SUCH A PERSON WOULD HAVE BEEN INTEGRATED INTO THEIR BELIEF SYSTEMS. BECOME PART OF LEGEND.
A WINGED MAN--SUCH AN IDEA WOULD LIVE FOR AGES.
THOSE BELIEFS AND LEGENDS THEN DETERMINE THE WAY PEOPLE THINK, WARREN.
THEY BRING MANY EXPECTATIONS AND HOPES TO A BEING LIKE YOU.
THAT'S NOT REALLY FAIR...
I KNOW. FAIR OR NOT THOUGH, IT IS A FACT.
ONE YOU WILL ALWAYS HAVE TO LIVE WITH. SO IT'S BEST THAT WE TRY TO FIGURE OUT HOW TO LIVE WITH IT.
I DO NOT BELIEVE THAT ALL MUTANTS SHOULD BE ROLE MODELS. THEY ARE SIMPLY WHAT THEY ARE.
STILL, BECAUSE WE ARE SPECIAL, THE WORLD LOOKS TO US AND JUDGES ALL MUTANTS BY US.
I DIDN'T PICK YOU FIVE JUST FOR YOUR ABILITIES ALONE. I THINK YOU ARE ALL CAPABLE OF CARRYING THE BURDEN OF RESPONSIBILITY. IF THE WORLD ACCEPTS US, IT WILL BE LARGELY DUE TO YOU X-MEN.
NOW, PLEASE RETURN TO THE SCHOOL AND TELL YOUR PEERS THAT I WAS VERY HARSH WITH YOU.
YES, SIR.

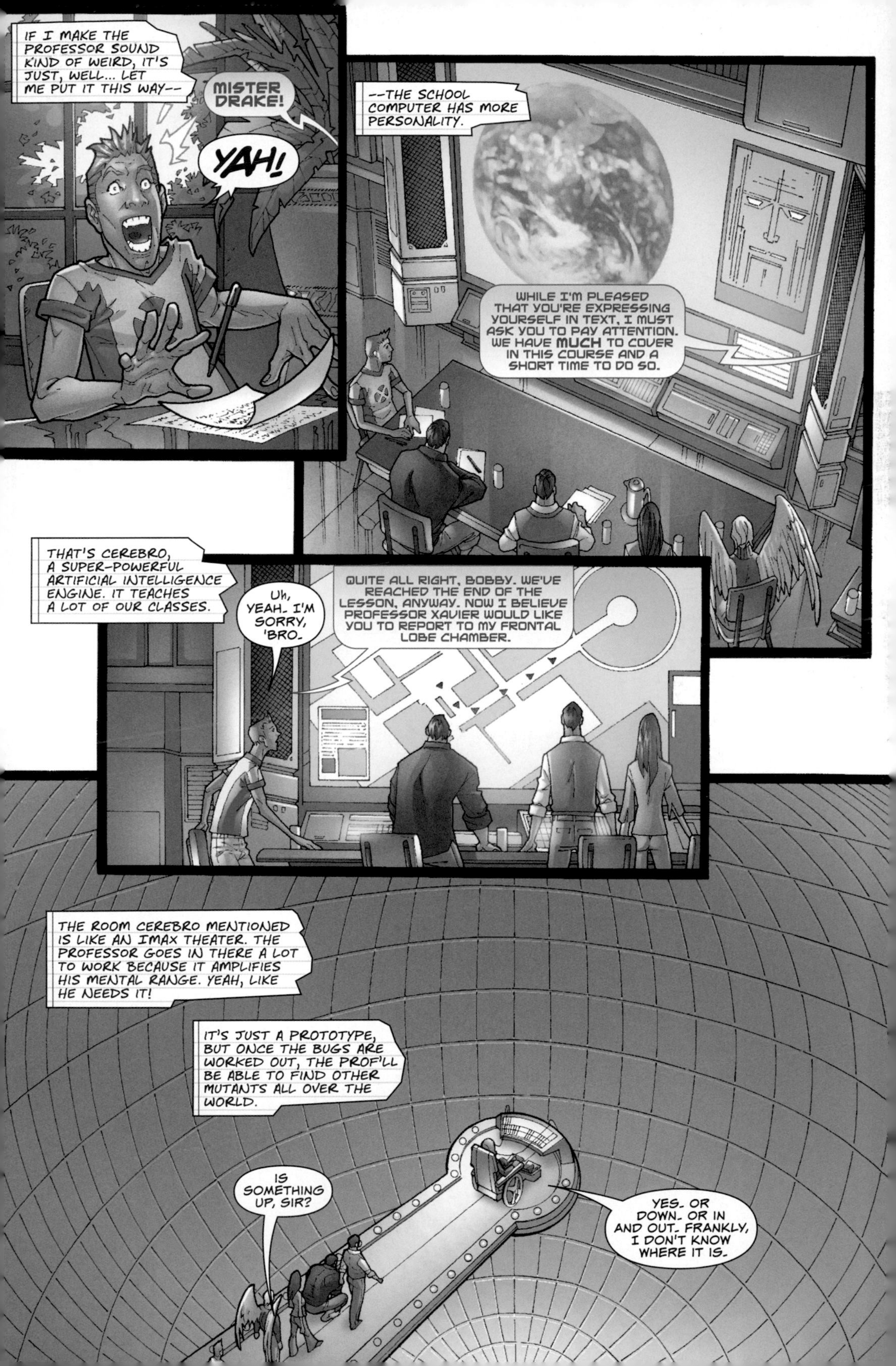
IF I MAKE THE PROFESSOR SOUND KIND OF WEIRD, IT'S JUST, WELL... LET ME PUT IT THIS WAY--
MISTER DRAKE!
YAH!
--THE SCHOOL COMPUTER HAS MORE PERSONALITY.
WHILE I'M PLEASED THAT YOU'RE EXPRESSING YOURSELF IN TEXT, I MUST ASK YOU TO PAY ATTENTION. WE HAVE MUCH TO COVER IN THIS COURSE AND A SHORT TIME TO DO SO.
THAT'S CEREBRO, A SUPER-POWERFUL ARTIFICIAL INTELLIGENCE ENGINE. IT TEACHES A LOT OF OUR CLASSES.
Uh, YEAH. I'M SORRY, 'BRO.
QUITE ALL RIGHT, BOBBY. WE'VE REACHED THE END OF THE LESSON, ANYWAY. NOW I BELIEVE PROFESSOR XAVIER WOULD LIKE YOU TO REPORT TO MY FRONTAL LOBE CHAMBER.
THE ROOM CEREBRO MENTIONED IS LIKE AN IMAX THEATER. THE PROFESSOR GOES IN THERE A LOT TO WORK BECAUSE IT AMPLIFIES HIS MENTAL RANGE. YEAH, LIKE HE NEEDS IT!
IT'S JUST A PROTOTYPE, BUT ONCE THE BUGS ARE WORKED OUT, THE PROF'LL BE ABLE TO FIND OTHER MUTANTS ALL OVER THE WORLD.
IS SOMETHING UP, SIR?
YES. OR DOWN. OR IN AND OUT. FRANKLY, I DON'T KNOW WHERE IT IS.

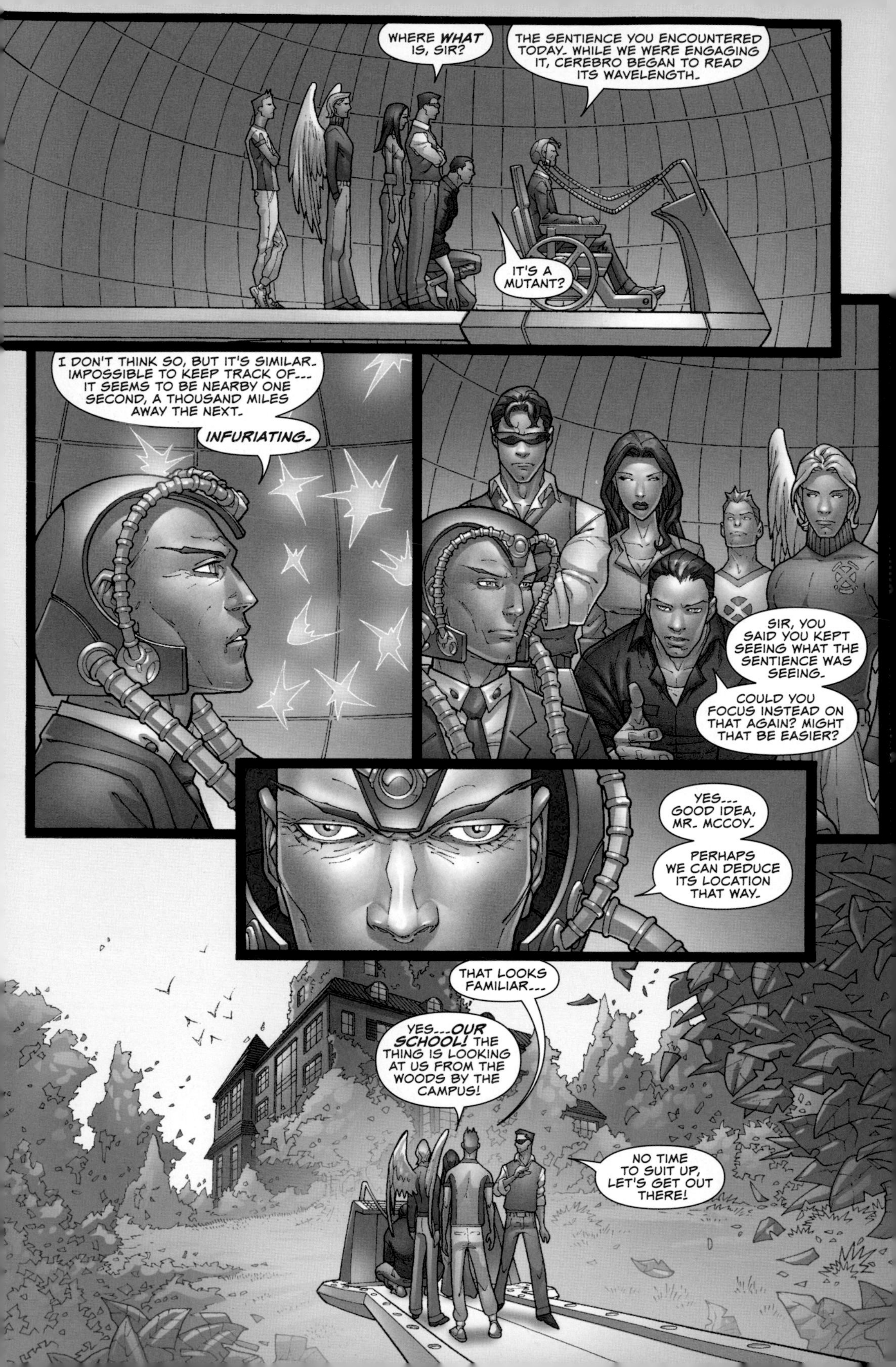

WHERE *WHAT* IS, SIR?
THE SENTIENCE YOU ENCOUNTERED TODAY. WHILE WE WERE ENGAGING IT, CEREBRO BEGAN TO READ ITS WAVELENGTH.
IT'S A MUTANT?
I DON'T THINK SO, BUT IT'S SIMILAR. IMPOSSIBLE TO KEEP TRACK OF--- IT SEEMS TO BE NEARBY ONE SECOND, A THOUSAND MILES AWAY THE NEXT.
INFURIATING.
SIR, YOU SAID YOU KEPT SEEING WHAT THE SENTIENCE WAS SEEING.
COULD YOU FOCUS INSTEAD ON THAT AGAIN? MIGHT THAT BE EASIER?
YES--- GOOD IDEA, MR. MCCOY.
PERHAPS WE CAN DEDUCE ITS LOCATION THAT WAY.
THAT LOOKS FAMILIAR---
YES---*OUR SCHOOL!* THE THING IS LOOKING AT US FROM THE WOODS BY THE CAMPUS!
NO TIME TO SUIT UP, LET'S GET OUT THERE!

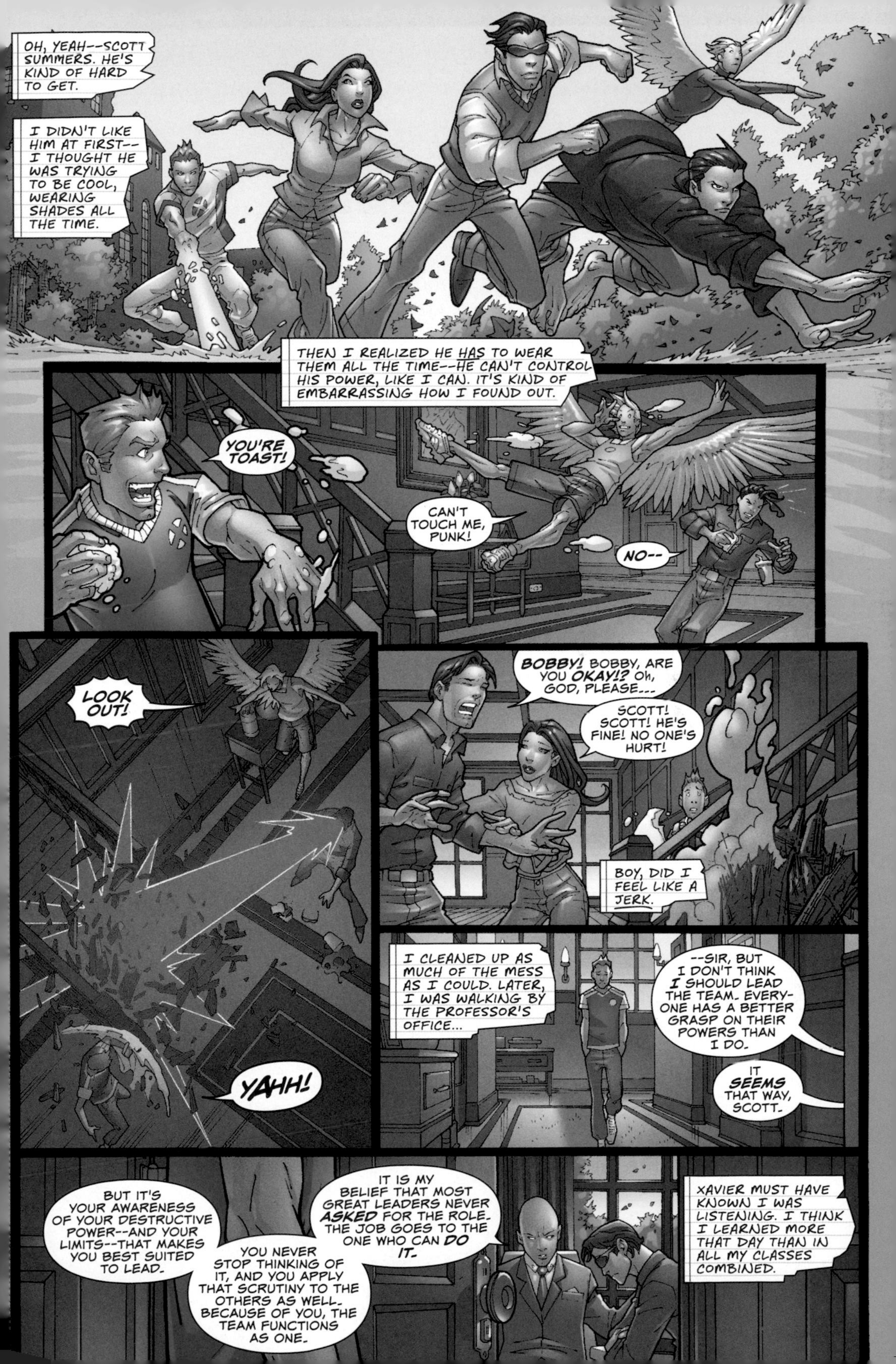
OH, YEAH--SCOTT SUMMERS. HE'S KIND OF HARD TO GET.
I DIDN'T LIKE HIM AT FIRST--I THOUGHT HE WAS TRYING TO BE COOL, WEARING SHADES ALL THE TIME.
THEN I REALIZED HE HAS TO WEAR THEM ALL THE TIME--HE CAN'T CONTROL HIS POWER, LIKE I CAN. IT'S KIND OF EMBARRASSING HOW I FOUND OUT.
YOU'RE TOAST!
CAN'T TOUCH ME, PUNK!
NO--
LOOK OUT!
YAHH!
BOBBY! BOBBY, ARE YOU OKAY!? OH, GOD, PLEASE...
SCOTT! SCOTT! HE'S FINE! NO ONE'S HURT!
BOY, DID I FEEL LIKE A JERK.
I CLEANED UP AS MUCH OF THE MESS AS I COULD. LATER, I WAS WALKING BY THE PROFESSOR'S OFFICE...
--SIR, BUT I DON'T THINK I SHOULD LEAD THE TEAM. EVERYONE HAS A BETTER GRASP ON THEIR POWERS THAN I DO.
IT SEEMS THAT WAY, SCOTT.
BUT IT'S YOUR AWARENESS OF YOUR DESTRUCTIVE POWER--AND YOUR LIMITS--THAT MAKES YOU BEST SUITED TO LEAD.
YOU NEVER STOP THINKING OF IT, AND YOU APPLY THAT SCRUTINY TO THE OTHERS AS WELL. BECAUSE OF YOU, THE TEAM FUNCTIONS AS ONE.
IT IS MY BELIEF THAT MOST GREAT LEADERS NEVER ASKED FOR THE ROLE. THE JOB GOES TO THE ONE WHO CAN DO IT.
XAVIER MUST HAVE KNOWN I WAS LISTENING. I THINK I LEARNED MORE THAT DAY THAN IN ALL MY CLASSES COMBINED.

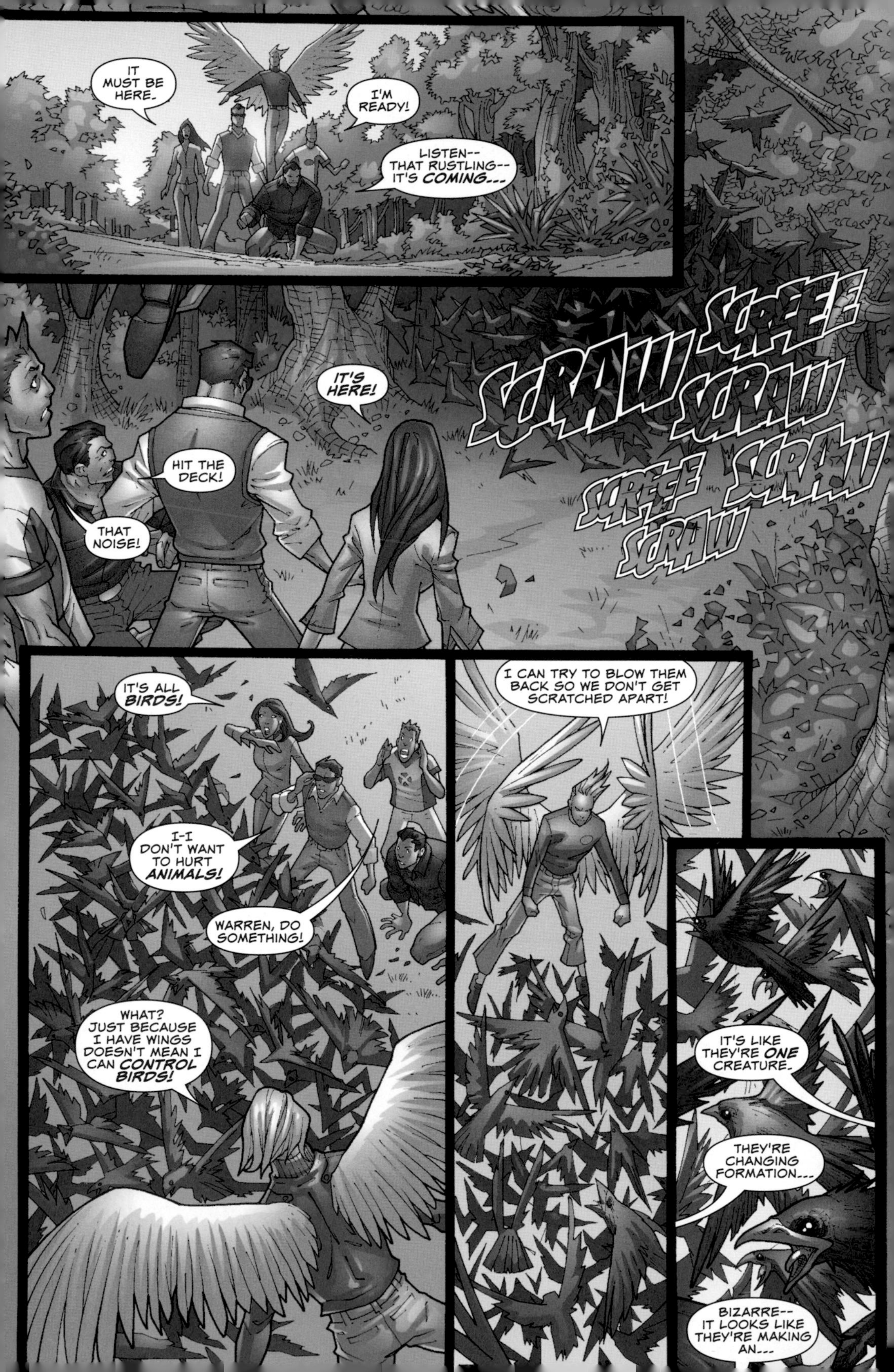
IT MUST BE HERE.
I'M READY!
LISTEN-- THAT RUSTLING-- IT'S COMING...
IT'S HERE!
HIT THE DECK!
THAT NOISE!
SCRAW SCREEE SCRAW SCREEE SCRAW SCRAW
IT'S ALL BIRDS!
I-I DON'T WANT TO HURT ANIMALS!
WARREN, DO SOMETHING!
WHAT? JUST BECAUSE I HAVE WINGS DOESN'T MEAN I CAN CONTROL BIRDS!
I CAN TRY TO BLOW THEM BACK SO WE DON'T GET SCRATCHED APART!
IT'S LIKE THEY'RE ONE CREATURE.
THEY'RE CHANGING FORMATION...
BIZARRE-- IT LOOKS LIKE THEY'RE MAKING AN...

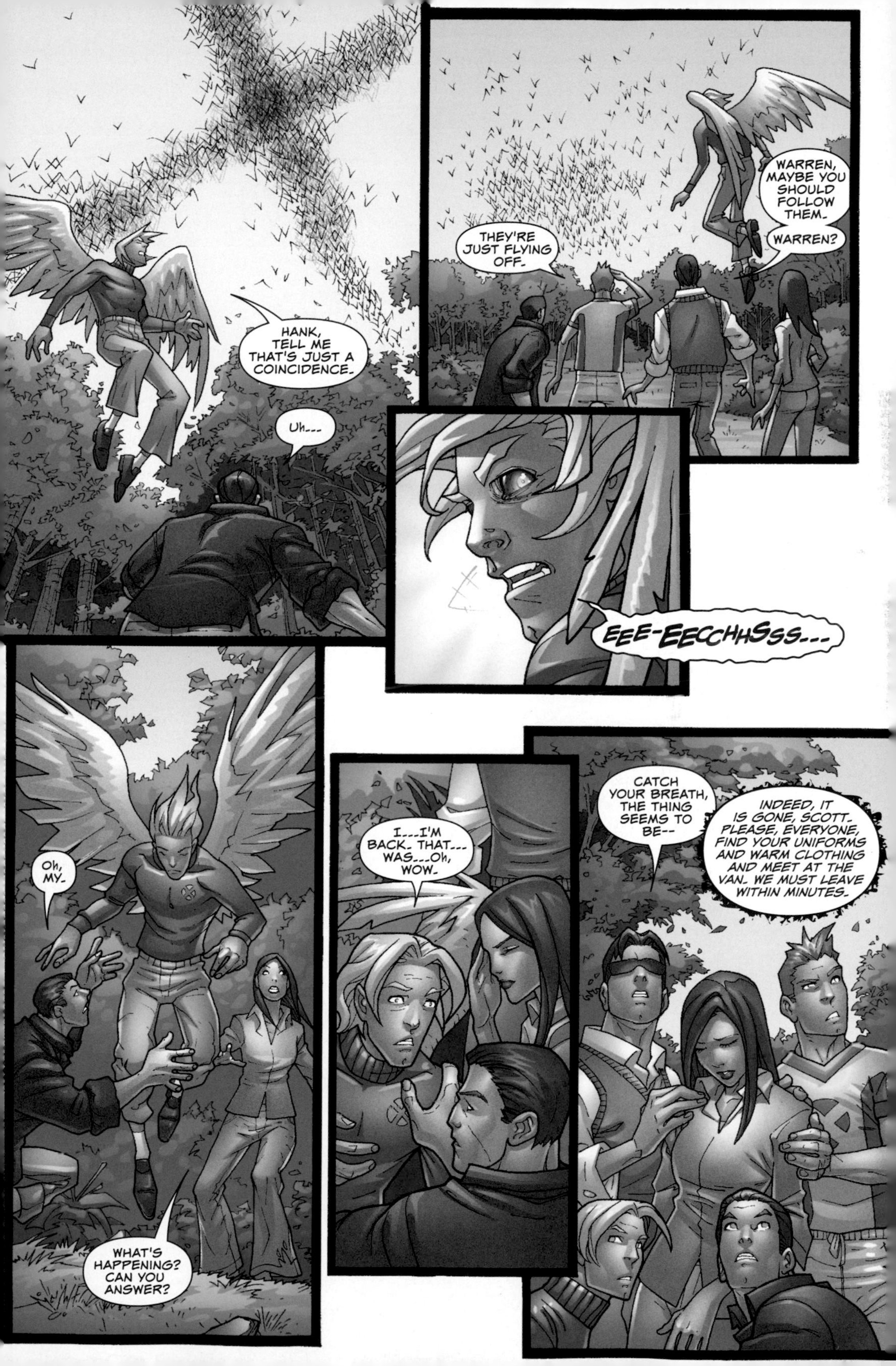
HANK, TELL ME THAT'S JUST A COINCIDENCE.
Uh...
THEY'RE JUST FLYING OFF.
WARREN, MAYBE YOU SHOULD FOLLOW THEM.
WARREN?
EEE-EECCHHSSS...
Oh, MY.
WHAT'S HAPPENING? CAN YOU ANSWER?
I...I'M BACK. THAT... WAS...OH, WOW.
CATCH YOUR BREATH, THE THING SEEMS TO BE--
INDEED, IT IS GONE, SCOTT. PLEASE, EVERYONE, FIND YOUR UNIFORMS AND WARM CLOTHING AND MEET AT THE VAN. WE MUST LEAVE WITHIN MINUTES.

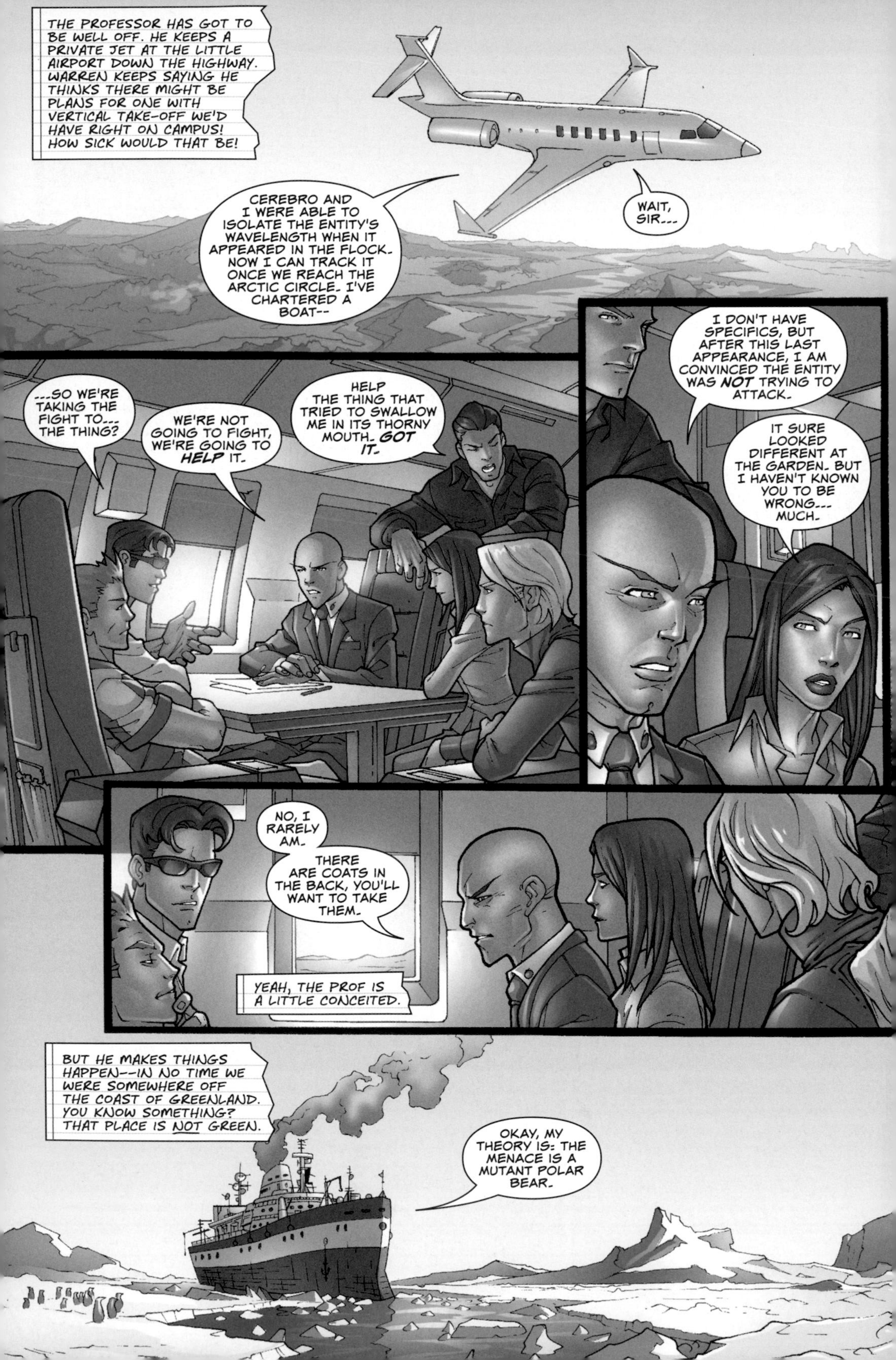
THE PROFESSOR HAS GOT TO BE WELL OFF. HE KEEPS A PRIVATE JET AT THE LITTLE AIRPORT DOWN THE HIGHWAY. WARREN KEEPS SAYING HE THINKS THERE MIGHT BE PLANS FOR ONE WITH VERTICAL TAKE-OFF WE'D HAVE RIGHT ON CAMPUS! HOW SICK WOULD THAT BE!
CEREBRO AND I WERE ABLE TO ISOLATE THE ENTITY'S WAVELENGTH WHEN IT APPEARED IN THE FLOCK. NOW I CAN TRACK IT ONCE WE REACH THE ARCTIC CIRCLE. I'VE CHARTERED A BOAT--
WAIT, SIR...
...SO WE'RE TAKING THE FIGHT TO... THE THING?
WE'RE NOT GOING TO FIGHT, WE'RE GOING TO **HELP** IT.
HELP THE THING THAT TRIED TO SWALLOW ME IN ITS THORNY MOUTH. **GOT IT.**
I DON'T HAVE SPECIFICS, BUT AFTER THIS LAST APPEARANCE, I AM CONVINCED THE ENTITY WAS **NOT** TRYING TO ATTACK.
IT SURE LOOKED DIFFERENT AT THE GARDEN. BUT I HAVEN'T KNOWN YOU TO BE WRONG... MUCH.
NO, I RARELY AM.
THERE ARE COATS IN THE BACK, YOU'LL WANT TO TAKE THEM.
YEAH, THE PROF IS A LITTLE CONCEITED.
BUT HE MAKES THINGS HAPPEN--IN NO TIME WE WERE SOMEWHERE OFF THE COAST OF GREENLAND. YOU KNOW SOMETHING? THAT PLACE IS NOT GREEN.
OKAY, MY THEORY IS: THE MENACE IS A MUTANT POLAR BEAR.

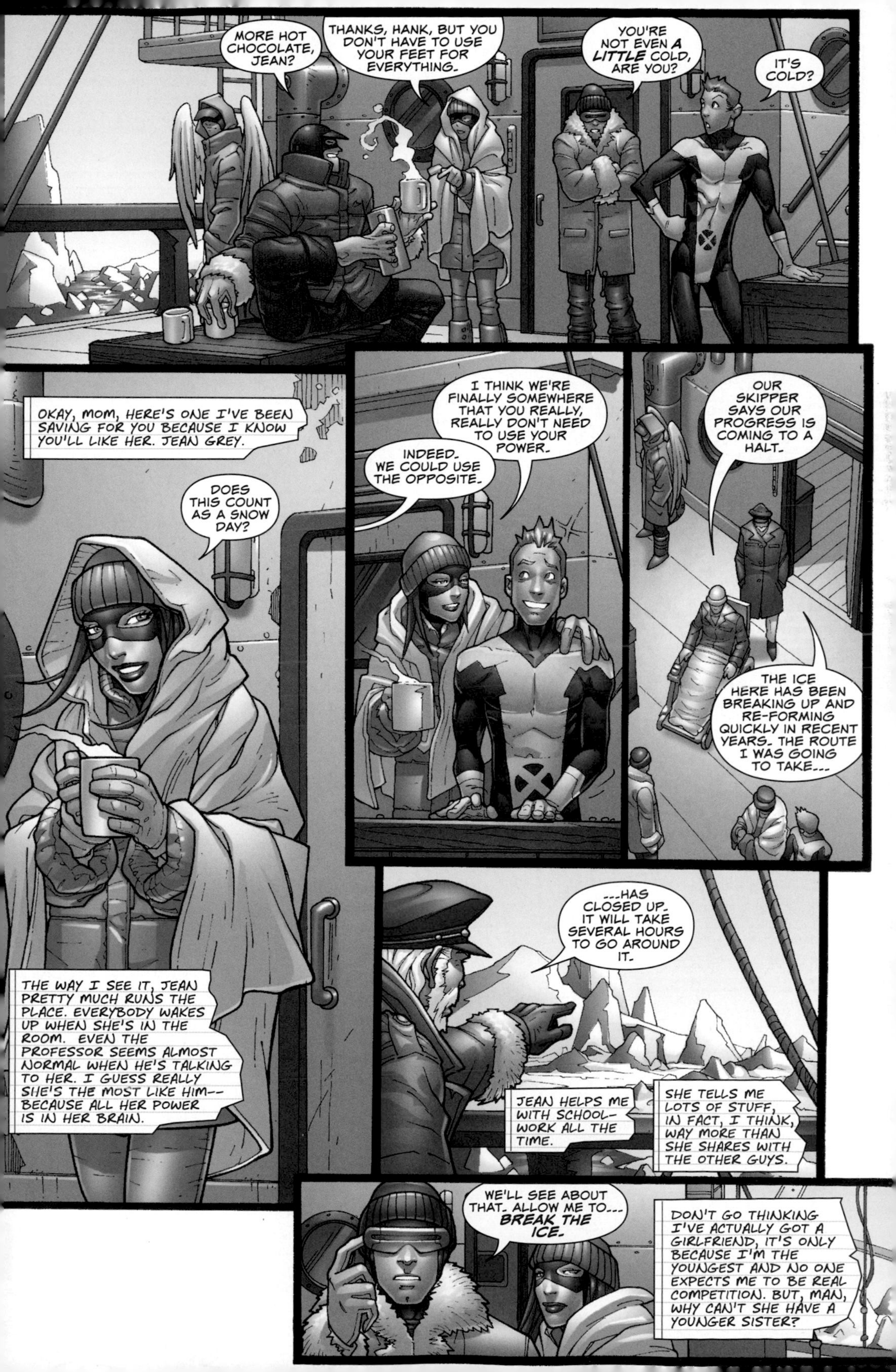

MORE HOT CHOCOLATE, JEAN?
THANKS, HANK, BUT YOU DON'T HAVE TO USE YOUR FEET FOR EVERYTHING.
YOU'RE NOT EVEN A *LITTLE* COLD, ARE YOU?
IT'S COLD?
OKAY, MOM, HERE'S ONE I'VE BEEN SAVING FOR YOU BECAUSE I KNOW YOU'LL LIKE HER. JEAN GREY.
DOES THIS COUNT AS A SNOW DAY?
THE WAY I SEE IT, JEAN PRETTY MUCH RUNS THE PLACE. EVERYBODY WAKES UP WHEN SHE'S IN THE ROOM. EVEN THE PROFESSOR SEEMS ALMOST NORMAL WHEN HE'S TALKING TO HER. I GUESS REALLY SHE'S THE MOST LIKE HIM-- BECAUSE ALL HER POWER IS IN HER BRAIN.
I THINK WE'RE FINALLY SOMEWHERE THAT YOU REALLY, REALLY DON'T NEED TO USE YOUR POWER.
INDEED. WE COULD USE THE OPPOSITE.
OUR SKIPPER SAYS OUR PROGRESS IS COMING TO A HALT.
THE ICE HERE HAS BEEN BREAKING UP AND RE-FORMING QUICKLY IN RECENT YEARS. THE ROUTE I WAS GOING TO TAKE...
...HAS CLOSED UP. IT WILL TAKE SEVERAL HOURS TO GO AROUND IT.
JEAN HELPS ME WITH SCHOOL-WORK ALL THE TIME.
SHE TELLS ME LOTS OF STUFF, IN FACT, I THINK, WAY MORE THAN SHE SHARES WITH THE OTHER GUYS.
WE'LL SEE ABOUT THAT. ALLOW ME TO... ***BREAK THE ICE.***
DON'T GO THINKING I'VE ACTUALLY GOT A GIRLFRIEND, IT'S ONLY BECAUSE I'M THE YOUNGEST AND NO ONE EXPECTS ME TO BE REAL COMPETITION. BUT, MAN, WHY CAN'T SHE HAVE A YOUNGER SISTER?

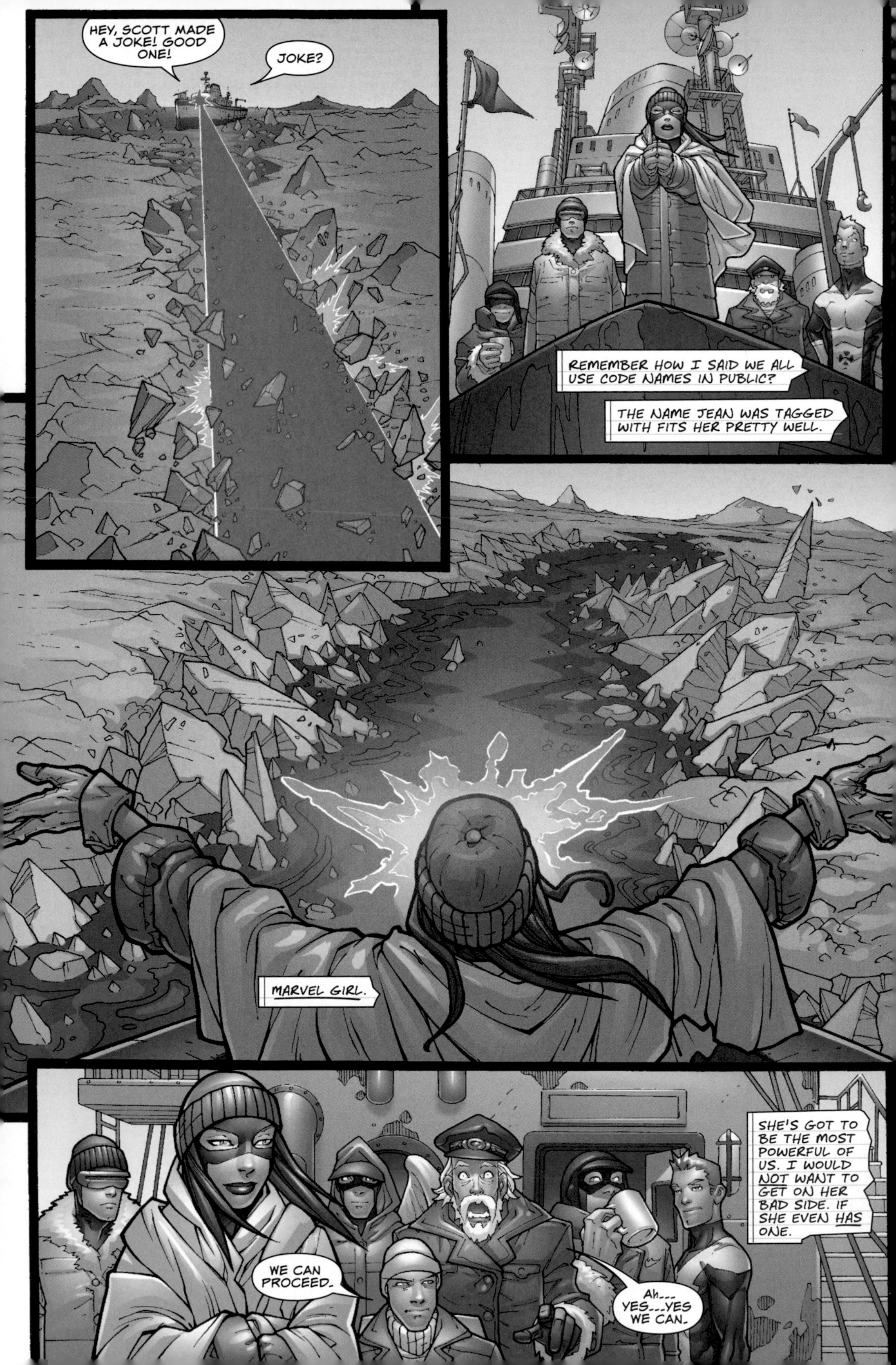

HEY, SCOTT MADE A JOKE! GOOD ONE!
JOKE?
REMEMBER HOW I SAID WE ALL USE CODE NAMES IN PUBLIC?
THE NAME JEAN WAS TAGGED WITH FITS HER PRETTY WELL.
MARVEL GIRL.
SHE'S GOT TO BE THE MOST POWERFUL OF US. I WOULD NOT WANT TO GET ON HER BAD SIDE. IF SHE EVEN HAS ONE.
WE CAN PROCEED.
Ah... YES...YES WE CAN.

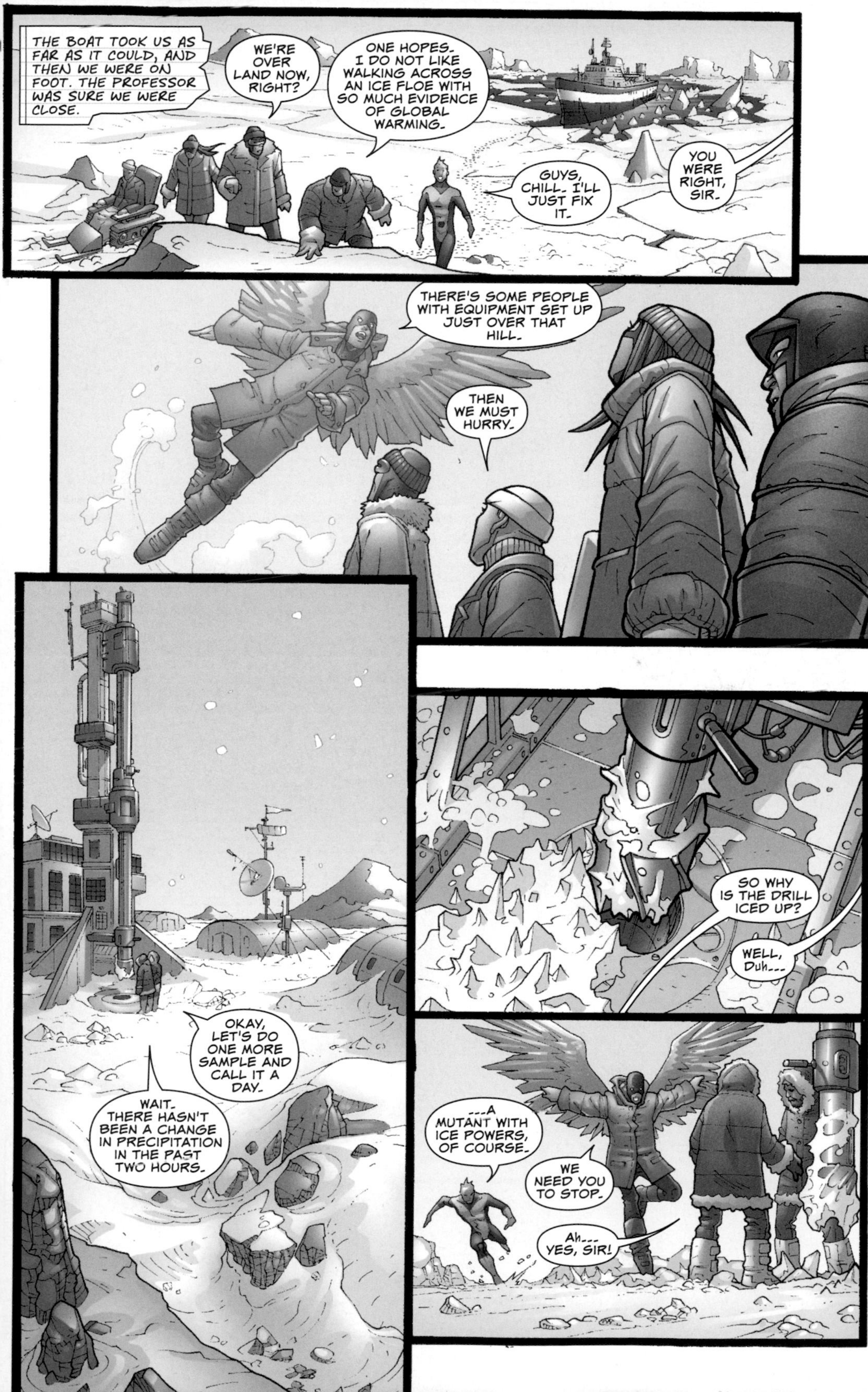
THE BOAT TOOK US AS FAR AS IT COULD, AND THEN WE WERE ON FOOT. THE PROFESSOR WAS SURE WE WERE CLOSE.
WE'RE OVER LAND NOW, RIGHT?
ONE HOPES. I DO NOT LIKE WALKING ACROSS AN ICE FLOE WITH SO MUCH EVIDENCE OF GLOBAL WARMING.
GUYS, CHILL. I'LL JUST FIX IT.
YOU WERE RIGHT, SIR.
THERE'S SOME PEOPLE WITH EQUIPMENT SET UP JUST OVER THAT HILL.
THEN WE MUST HURRY.
OKAY, LET'S DO ONE MORE SAMPLE AND CALL IT A DAY.
WAIT. THERE HASN'T BEEN A CHANGE IN PRECIPITATION IN THE PAST TWO HOURS.
SO WHY IS THE DRILL ICED UP?
WELL, Duh...
...A MUTANT WITH ICE POWERS, OF COURSE.
WE NEED YOU TO STOP.
Ah... YES, SIR!

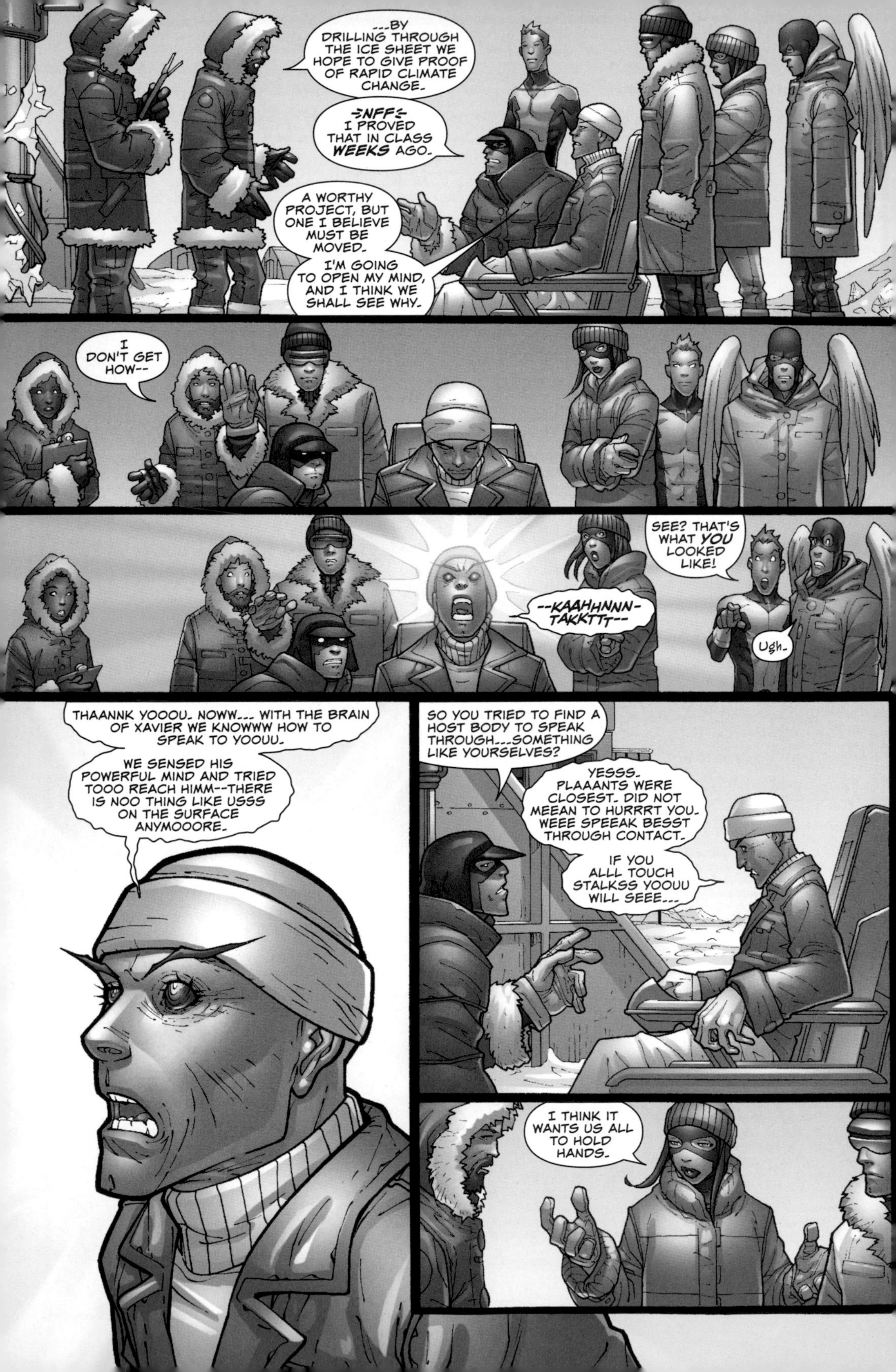

...BY DRILLING THROUGH THE ICE SHEET WE HOPE TO GIVE PROOF OF RAPID CLIMATE CHANGE.
=NFF= I PROVED THAT IN CLASS WEEKS AGO.
A WORTHY PROJECT, BUT ONE I BELIEVE MUST BE MOVED.
I'M GOING TO OPEN MY MIND, AND I THINK WE SHALL SEE WHY.
I DON'T GET HOW--
SEE? THAT'S WHAT YOU LOOKED LIKE!
--KAAHHNNN-TAKKTTT--
Ugh.
THAANNK YOOOU. NOWW... WITH THE BRAIN OF XAVIER WE KNOWWW HOW TO SPEAK TO YOOUU.
WE SENSED HIS POWERFUL MIND AND TRIED TOOO REACH HIMM--THERE IS NOO THING LIKE USSS ON THE SURFACE ANYMOOORE.
SO YOU TRIED TO FIND A HOST BODY TO SPEAK THROUGH...SOMETHING LIKE YOURSELVES?
YESSS. PLAAANTS WERE CLOSEST. DID NOT MEEAN TO HURRRT YOU. WEEE SPEEAK BESST THROUGH CONTACT.
IF YOU ALLL TOUCH STALKSS YOOUU WILL SEEE...
I THINK IT WANTS US ALL TO HOLD HANDS.

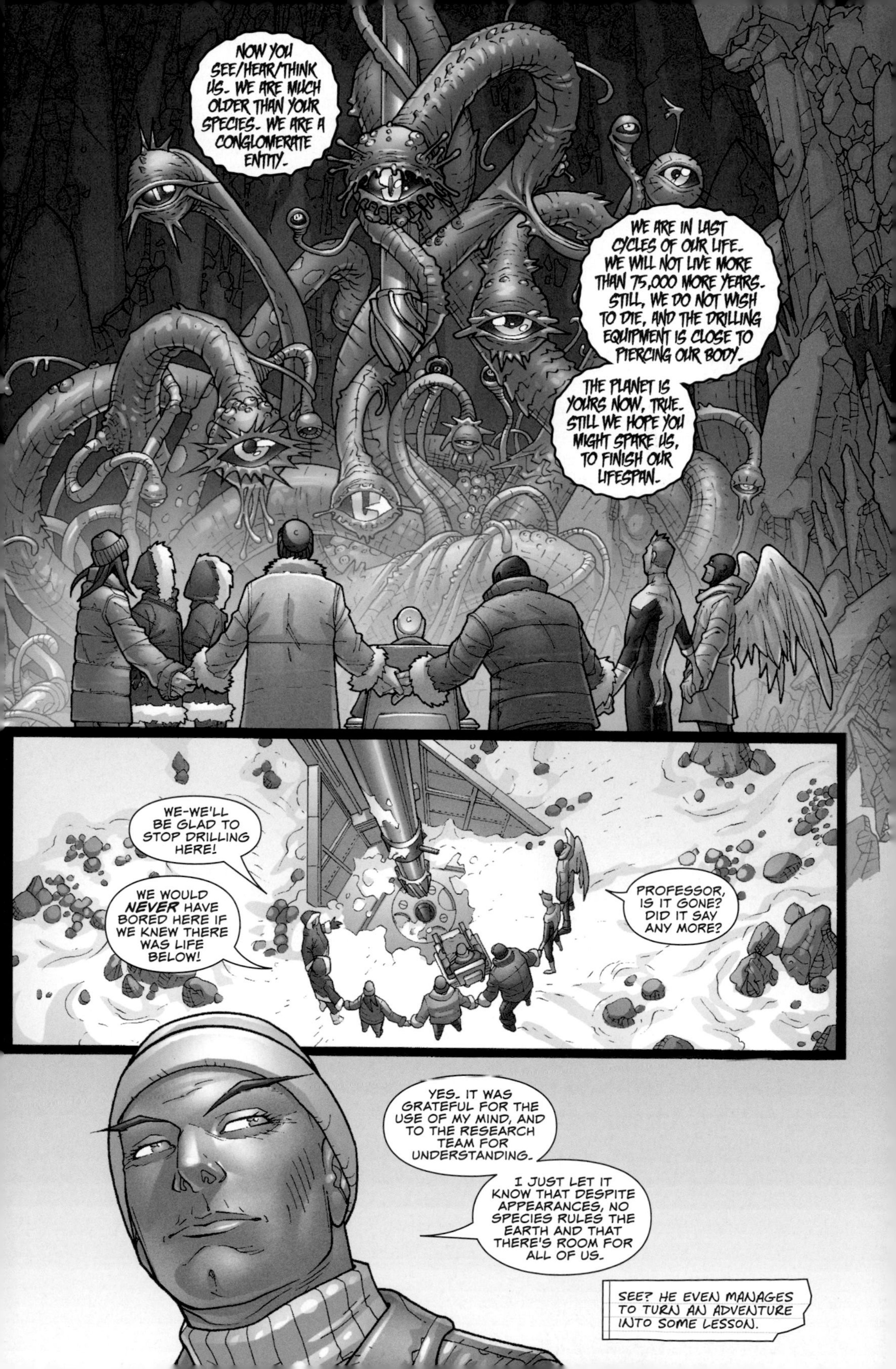

NOW YOU SEE/HEAR/THINK US. WE ARE MUCH OLDER THAN YOUR SPECIES. WE ARE A CONGLOMERATE ENTITY.
WE ARE IN LAST CYCLES OF OUR LIFE. WE WILL NOT LIVE MORE THAN 75,000 MORE YEARS. STILL, WE DO NOT WISH TO DIE, AND THE DRILLING EQUIPMENT IS CLOSE TO PIERCING OUR BODY.
THE PLANET IS YOURS NOW, TRUE. STILL WE HOPE YOU MIGHT SPARE US, TO FINISH OUR LIFESPAN.
WE-WE'LL BE GLAD TO STOP DRILLING HERE!
WE WOULD **NEVER** HAVE BORED HERE IF WE KNEW THERE WAS LIFE BELOW!
PROFESSOR, IS IT GONE? DID IT SAY ANY MORE?
YES. IT WAS GRATEFUL FOR THE USE OF MY MIND, AND TO THE RESEARCH TEAM FOR UNDERSTANDING.
I JUST LET IT KNOW THAT DESPITE APPEARANCES, NO SPECIES RULES THE EARTH AND THAT THERE'S ROOM FOR ALL OF US.
SEE? HE EVEN MANAGES TO TURN AN ADVENTURE INTO SOME LESSON.

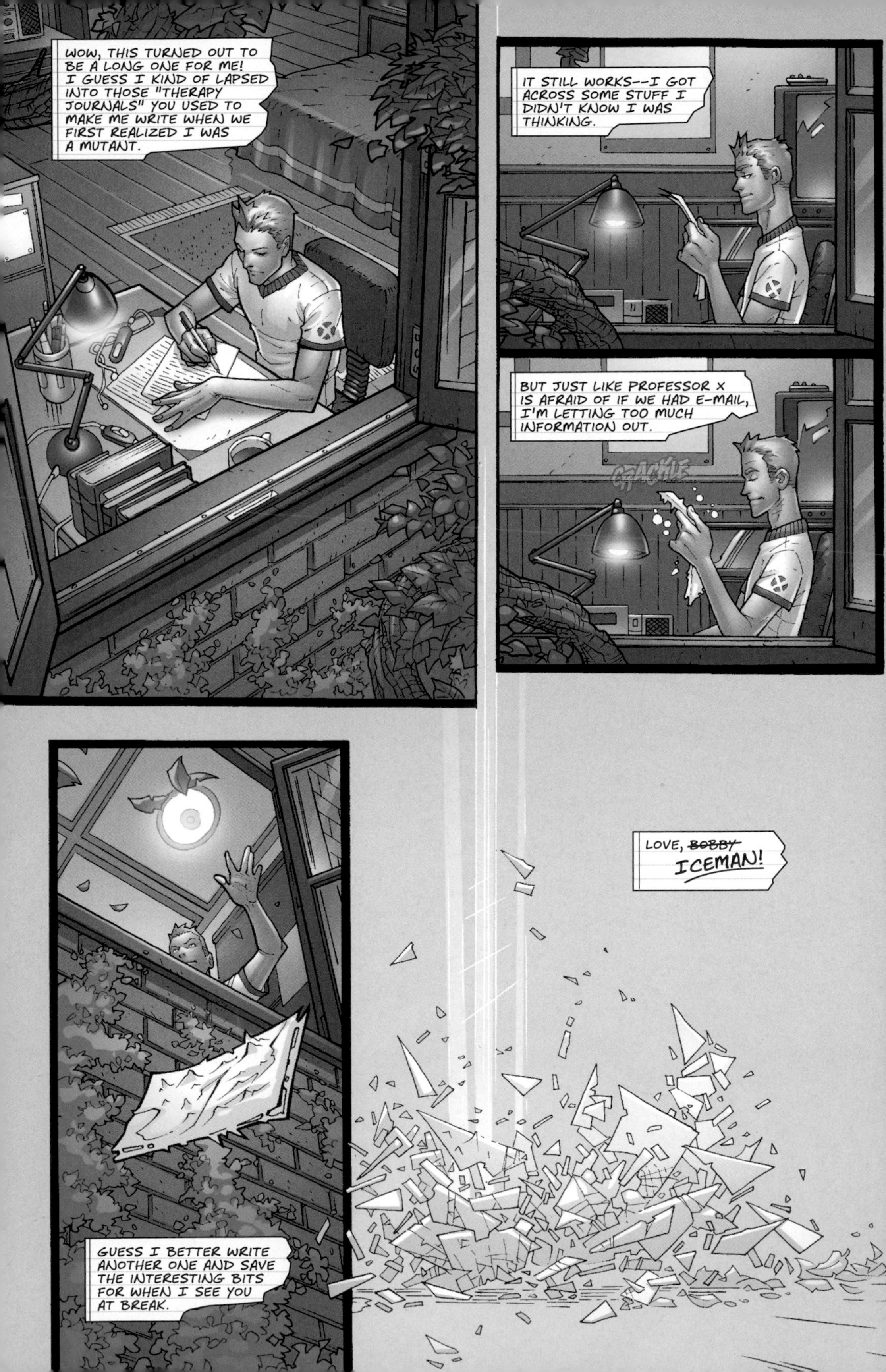
WOW, THIS TURNED OUT TO BE A LONG ONE FOR ME! I GUESS I KIND OF LAPSED INTO THOSE "THERAPY JOURNALS" YOU USED TO MAKE ME WRITE WHEN WE FIRST REALIZED I WAS A MUTANT.
IT STILL WORKS--I GOT ACROSS SOME STUFF I DIDN'T KNOW I WAS THINKING.
BUT JUST LIKE PROFESSOR X IS AFRAID OF IF WE HAD E-MAIL, I'M LETTING TOO MUCH INFORMATION OUT.
CRACKLE
GUESS I BETTER WRITE ANOTHER ONE AND SAVE THE INTERESTING BITS FOR WHEN I SEE YOU AT BREAK.
LOVE, ~~BOBBY~~
ICEMAN!

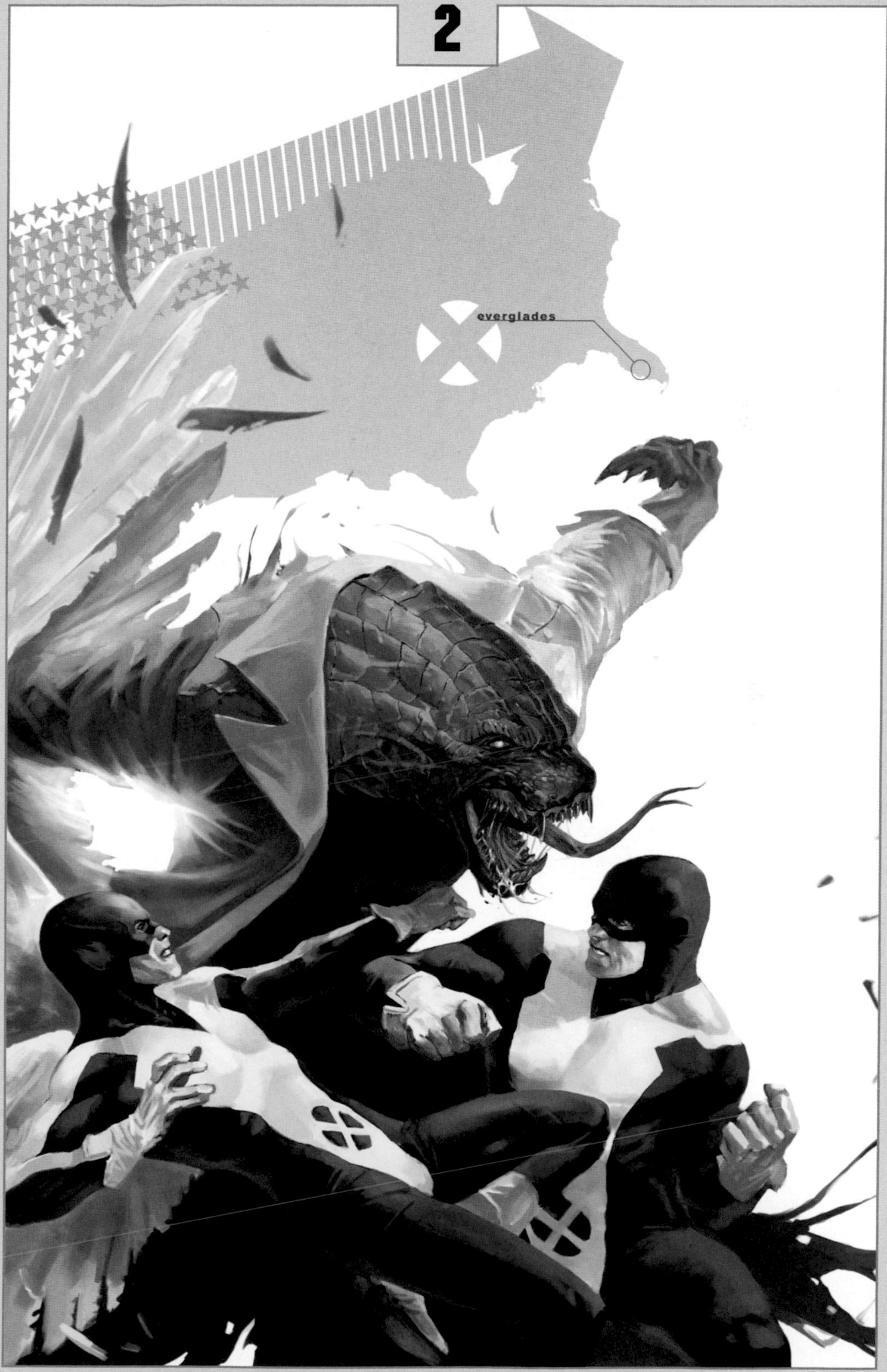
2
everglades

THE NEXT STEP IN HUMAN EVOLUTION HAS ARRIVED—HOMO SUPERIOR. MANKIND ISN'T SURE WHETHER THIS REPRESENTS HOPE FOR THE FUTURE...OR THE END OF THE HUMAN RACE. IN A PRIVATE SCHOOL IN UPSTATE NEW YORK, ONE BRILLIANT MUTANT IS TEACHING A GROUP OF FIVE SUCH GIFTED STUDENTS WHAT THEY'LL NEED TO SURVIVE IN THIS NEW WORLD. THESE ARE THE UNTOLD STORIES OF PROFESSOR XAVIER'S FIRST CLASS OF X-MEN!

XAVIER'S SCHOOL FOR GIFTED YOUNGSTERS

PROPERTY OF:

BOBBY DRAKE

*DAG! THOUGHT PROF WAS SAYING "JEANS" ALL DURING CLASS, LIKE THEY WERE BUDS. NOW, LOOK UP THE WORD "GENOME" TONIGHT.

HEADMASTER

PROFESSOR CHARLES XAVIER

THINK THAT KAT GIRL DOWN AT CAFE-A-GO-GO LIKES THE BOBBY! GOTTA GET HANK TO GO DOWN THERE WITH ME--IF HE PROMISES NOT TO SWING ON THE RAFTERS AGAIN

PROOF— I'M SURE SCOTT IS DOZING BEHIND HIS GLASSES IN CLASS NOW THIS MORNING HE DROOLED

('COURSE, JEAN WAS SITTING RIGHT IN FRONT..)

SCOTT SUMMERS "CYCLOPS"

JEAN GREY "MARVEL GIRL"

HENRY "HANK" McCOY "BEAST"

AW SICK! FEATHER FUZZ IS STUCK TO MY BACKPACK!

I HATE WHEN WARREN MOLTS!!

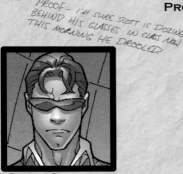

WARREN WORTHINGTON III "ANGEL"

ROBERT DRAKE "ICEMAN"

BOBBY

IF I WERE X, I'D SUPER CHARGE MY WHEELCHAIR SO I COULD BLAST ALL OVER THE PLACE! SOME BIG FAT TIRES - HOW SWEET WOULD THAT BE? JUGGERNAUT COMES RUNNING IN ALL "I'M THE JUGGERNAUT, I CAN'T BE STOPPED-- **WHAMMMM!!!** I'M SPINNING OUT ON HIS FACE, DOING DOUGHNUTS ALL OVER HIS HEAD! THEN HE'S LAYING THERE ALL "UHHH" AND I BACK UP AND POINT AT HIM AND GO "GET BACK IN THAT RUBY, CHUMP! **X!!!"**

MAYBE IF I HOLD MY HEAD LIKE THIS, CEREBRO CAN'T TELL I'M NAPPING. **OIDN'T WORK!**

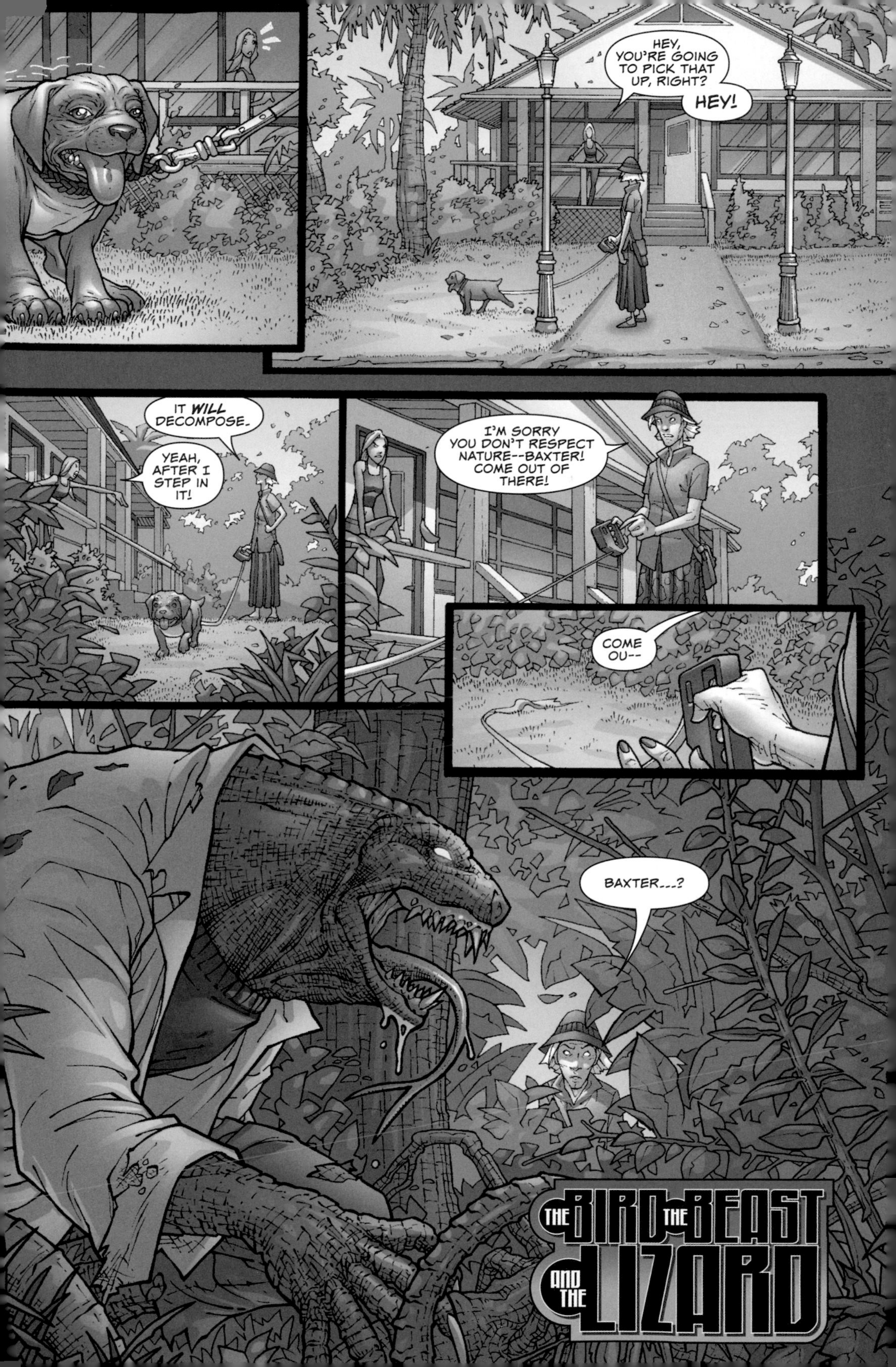
HEY, YOU'RE GOING TO PICK THAT UP, RIGHT?
HEY!
IT WILL DECOMPOSE.
YEAH, AFTER I STEP IN IT!
I'M SORRY YOU DON'T RESPECT NATURE--BAXTER! COME OUT OF THERE!
COME OU--
BAXTER...?
THE BIRD THE BEAST AND THE LIZARD

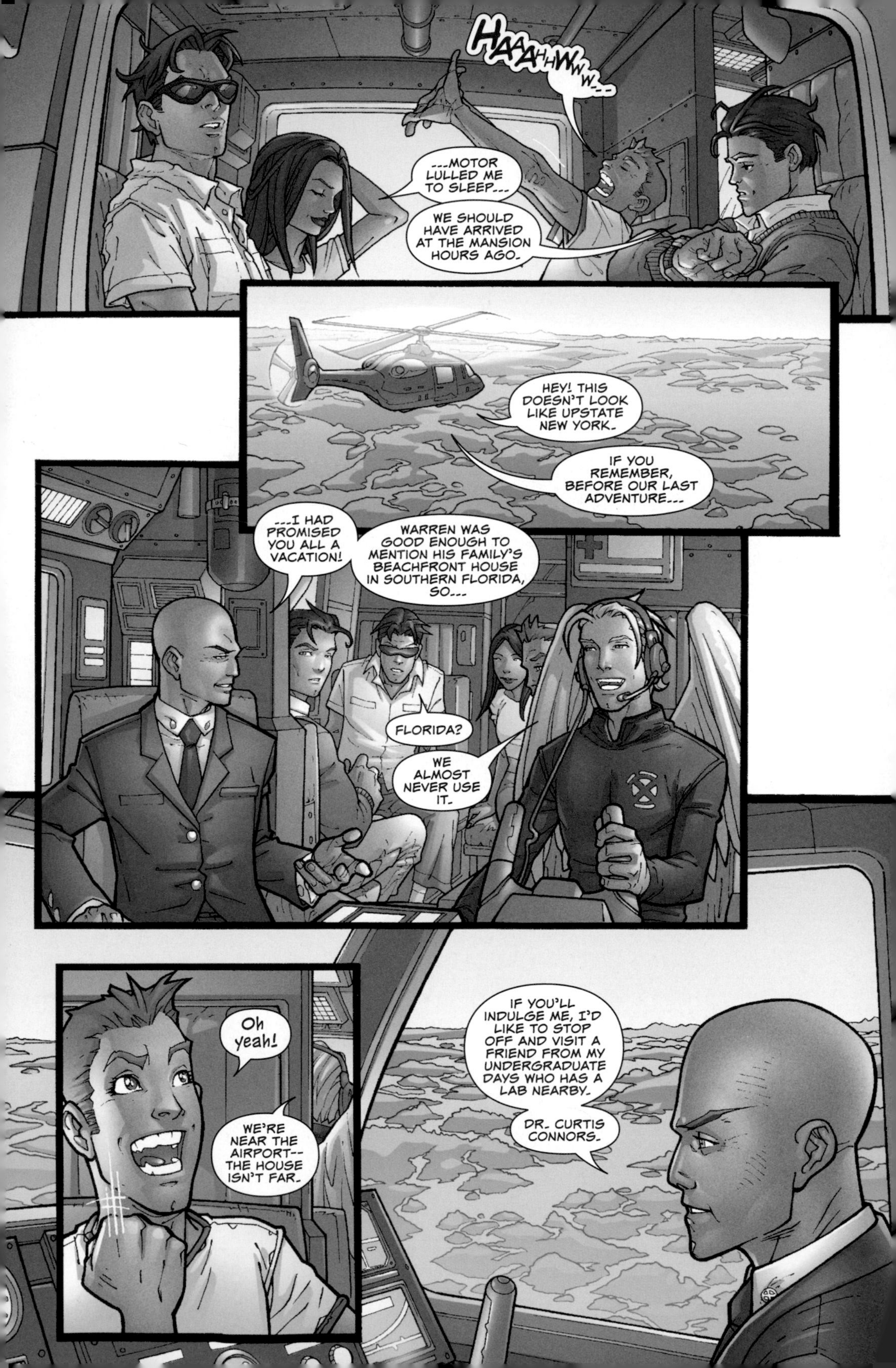
HAAAHHWWW--
---MOTOR LULLED ME TO SLEEP---
WE SHOULD HAVE ARRIVED AT THE MANSION HOURS AGO.
HEY! THIS DOESN'T LOOK LIKE UPSTATE NEW YORK.
IF YOU REMEMBER, BEFORE OUR LAST ADVENTURE---
---I HAD PROMISED YOU ALL A VACATION!
WARREN WAS GOOD ENOUGH TO MENTION HIS FAMILY'S BEACHFRONT HOUSE IN SOUTHERN FLORIDA, SO---
FLORIDA?
WE ALMOST NEVER USE IT.
Oh yeah!
WE'RE NEAR THE AIRPORT-- THE HOUSE ISN'T FAR.
IF YOU'LL INDULGE ME, I'D LIKE TO STOP OFF AND VISIT A FRIEND FROM MY UNDERGRADUATE DAYS WHO HAS A LAB NEARBY.
DR. CURTIS CONNORS.

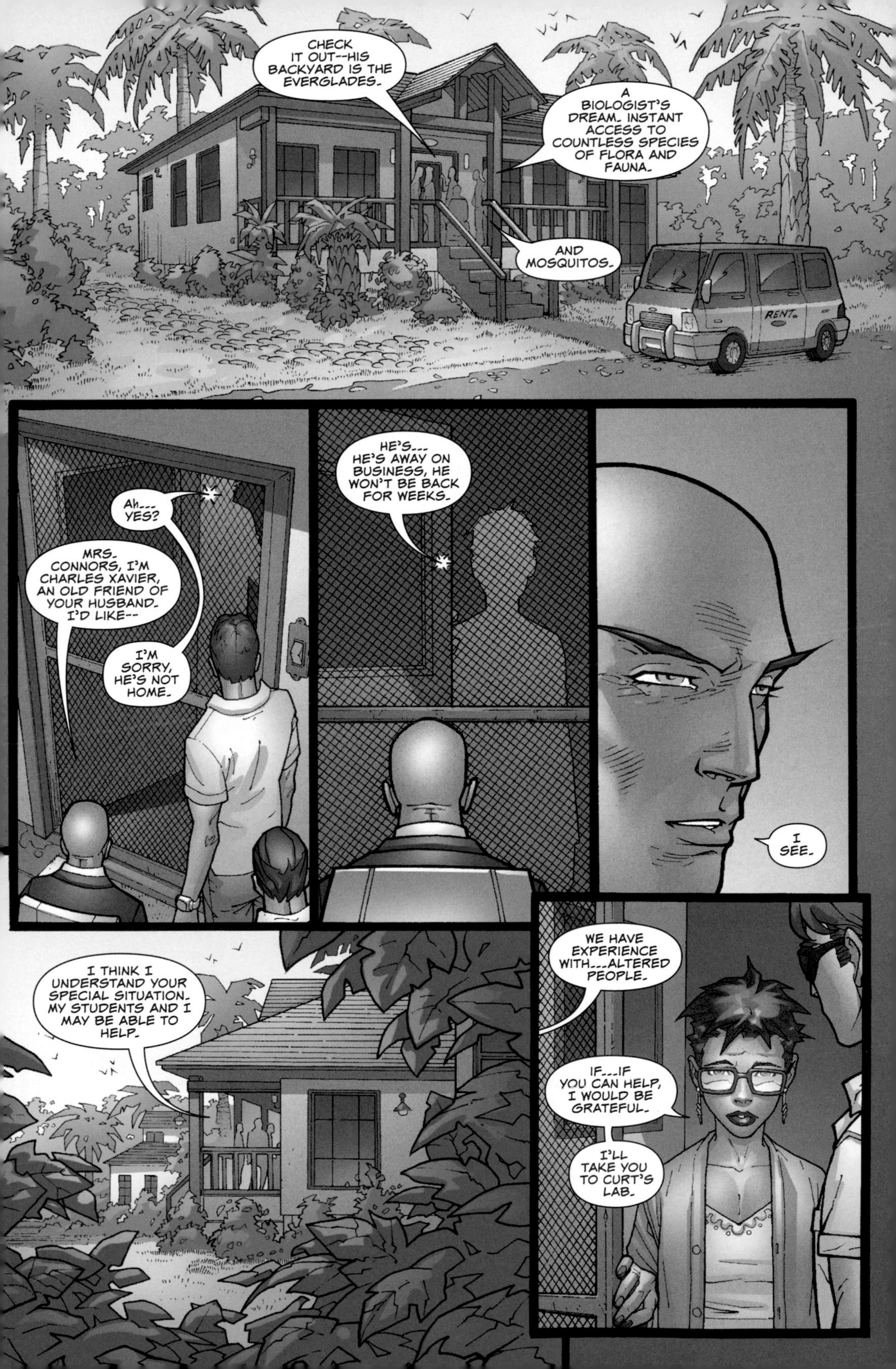
CHECK IT OUT--HIS BACKYARD IS THE EVERGLADES.
A BIOLOGIST'S DREAM. INSTANT ACCESS TO COUNTLESS SPECIES OF FLORA AND FAUNA.
AND MOSQUITOS.
RENT.
Ah... YES?
MRS. CONNORS, I'M CHARLES XAVIER, AN OLD FRIEND OF YOUR HUSBAND. I'D LIKE--
I'M SORRY, HE'S NOT HOME.
HE'S... HE'S AWAY ON BUSINESS, HE WON'T BE BACK FOR WEEKS.
I SEE.
I THINK I UNDERSTAND YOUR SPECIAL SITUATION. MY STUDENTS AND I MAY BE ABLE TO HELP.
WE HAVE EXPERIENCE WITH...ALTERED PEOPLE.
IF...IF YOU CAN HELP, I WOULD BE GRATEFUL.
I'LL TAKE YOU TO CURT'S LAB.

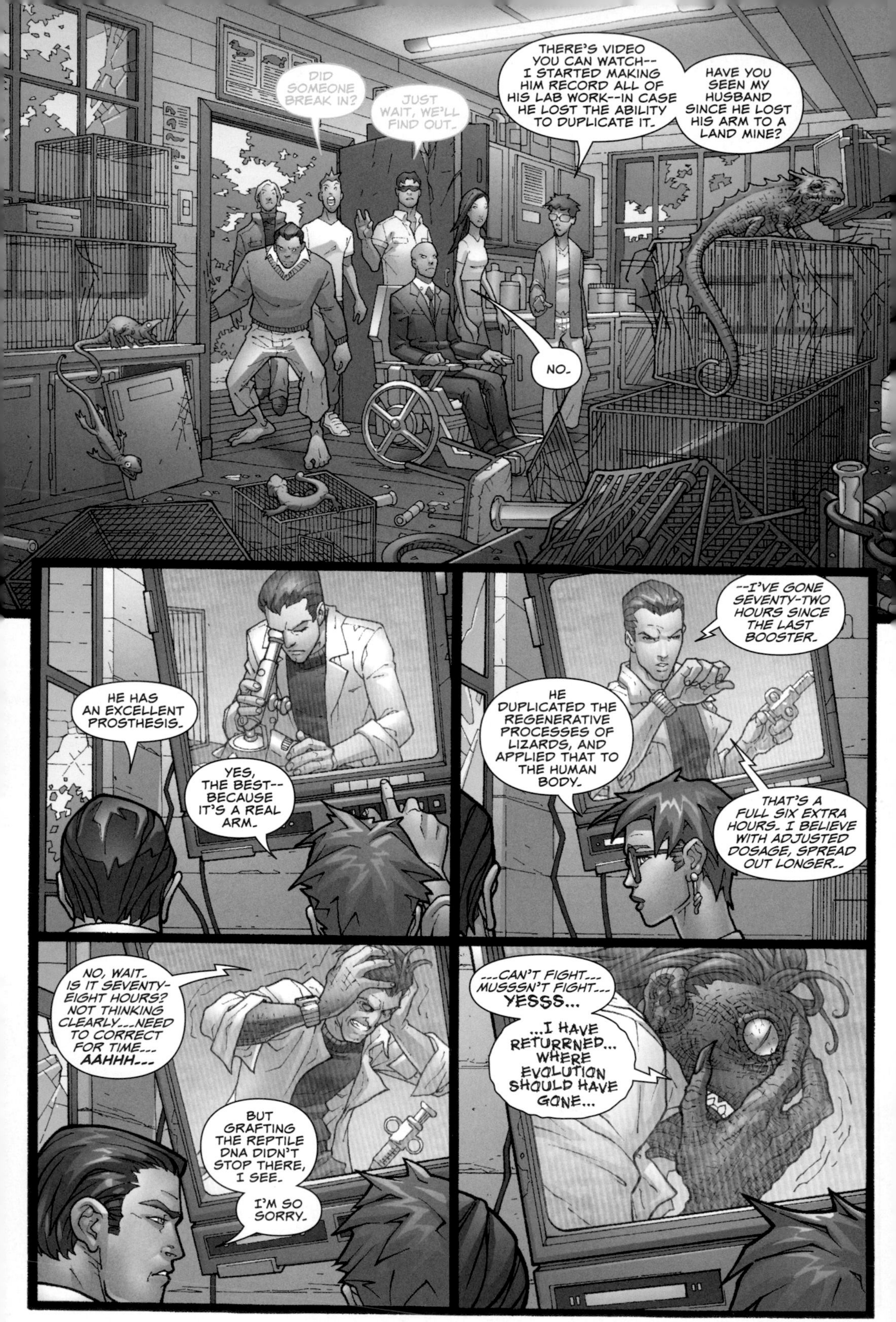
DID SOMEONE BREAK IN?
JUST WAIT, WE'LL FIND OUT.
THERE'S VIDEO YOU CAN WATCH-- I STARTED MAKING HIM RECORD ALL OF HIS LAB WORK--IN CASE HE LOST THE ABILITY TO DUPLICATE IT.
HAVE YOU SEEN MY HUSBAND SINCE HE LOST HIS ARM TO A LAND MINE?
NO.
HE HAS AN EXCELLENT PROSTHESIS.
YES, THE BEST-- BECAUSE IT'S A REAL ARM.
--I'VE GONE SEVENTY-TWO HOURS SINCE THE LAST BOOSTER.
HE DUPLICATED THE REGENERATIVE PROCESSES OF LIZARDS, AND APPLIED THAT TO THE HUMAN BODY.
THAT'S A FULL SIX EXTRA HOURS. I BELIEVE WITH ADJUSTED DOSAGE, SPREAD OUT LONGER...
NO, WAIT. IS IT SEVENTY-EIGHT HOURS? NOT THINKING CLEARLY...NEED TO CORRECT FOR TIME... AAHHH...
BUT GRAFTING THE REPTILE DNA DIDN'T STOP THERE, I SEE.
I'M SO SORRY.
...CAN'T FIGHT... MUSSSN'T FIGHT... YESSS...
...I HAVE RETURRNED... WHERE EVOLUTION SHOULD HAVE GONE...

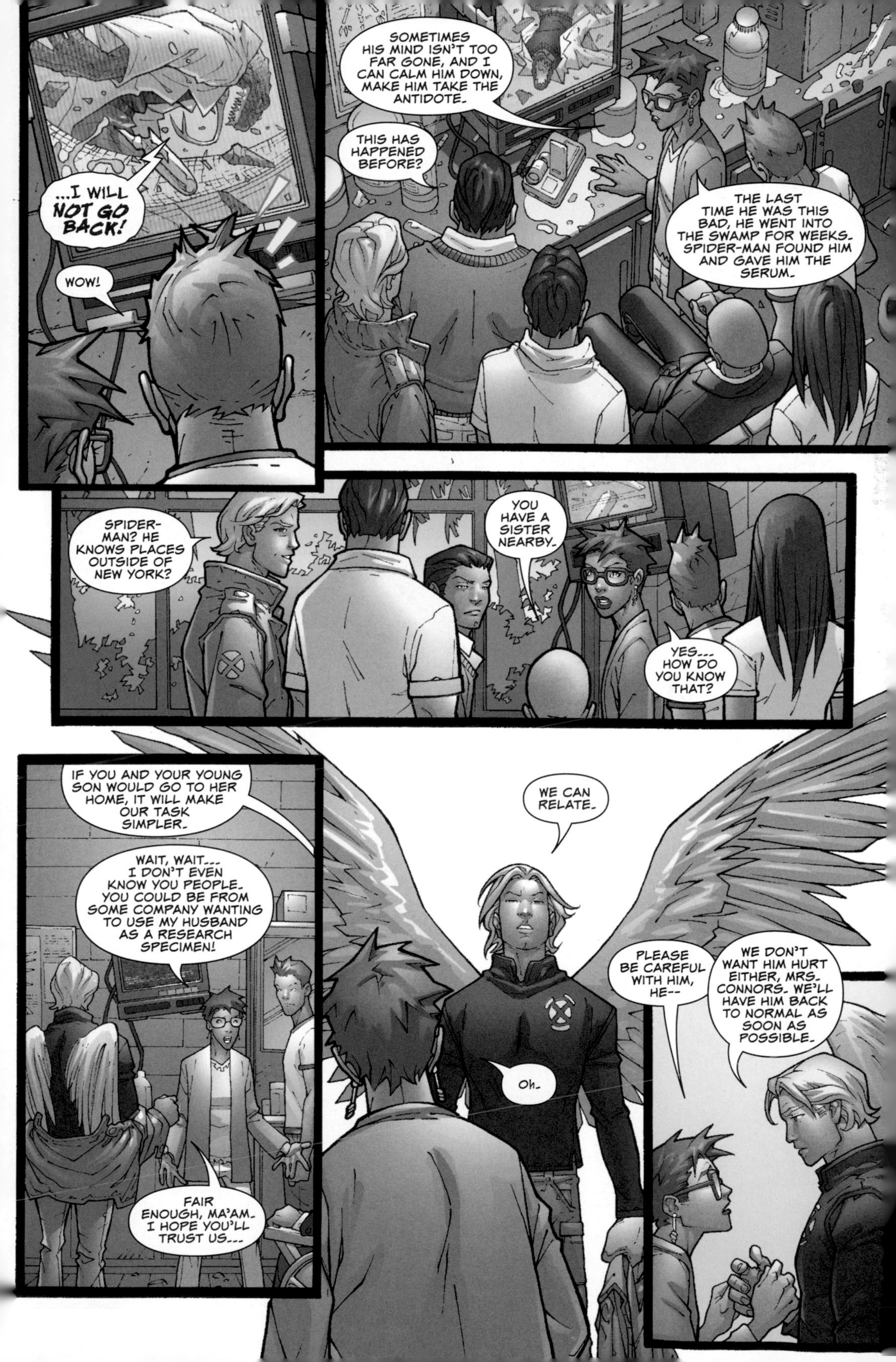
...I WILL NOT GO BACK!
WOW!
SOMETIMES HIS MIND ISN'T TOO FAR GONE, AND I CAN CALM HIM DOWN, MAKE HIM TAKE THE ANTIDOTE.
THIS HAS HAPPENED BEFORE?
THE LAST TIME HE WAS THIS BAD, HE WENT INTO THE SWAMP FOR WEEKS. SPIDER-MAN FOUND HIM AND GAVE HIM THE SERUM.
SPIDER-MAN? HE KNOWS PLACES OUTSIDE OF NEW YORK?
YOU HAVE A SISTER NEARBY.
YES... HOW DO YOU KNOW THAT?
IF YOU AND YOUR YOUNG SON WOULD GO TO HER HOME, IT WILL MAKE OUR TASK SIMPLER.
WAIT, WAIT... I DON'T EVEN KNOW YOU PEOPLE. YOU COULD BE FROM SOME COMPANY WANTING TO USE MY HUSBAND AS A RESEARCH SPECIMEN!
FAIR ENOUGH, MA'AM. I HOPE YOU'LL TRUST US...
WE CAN RELATE.
Oh.
PLEASE BE CAREFUL WITH HIM, HE--
WE DON'T WANT HIM HURT EITHER, MRS. CONNORS. WE'LL HAVE HIM BACK TO NORMAL AS SOON AS POSSIBLE.

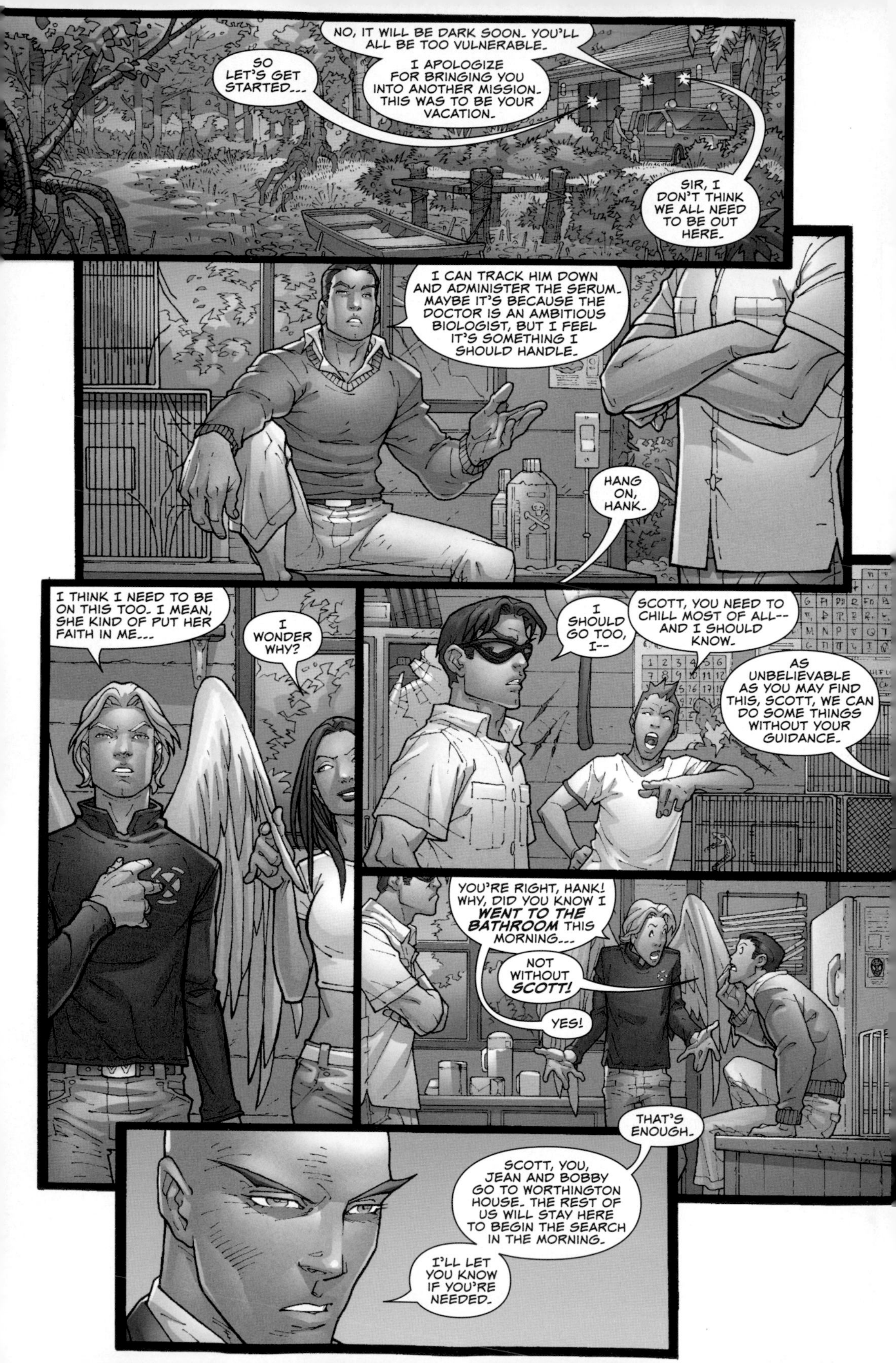
SO LET'S GET STARTED...
NO, IT WILL BE DARK SOON. YOU'LL ALL BE TOO VULNERABLE.
I APOLOGIZE FOR BRINGING YOU INTO ANOTHER MISSION. THIS WAS TO BE YOUR VACATION.
SIR, I DON'T THINK WE ALL NEED TO BE OUT HERE.
I CAN TRACK HIM DOWN AND ADMINISTER THE SERUM. MAYBE IT'S BECAUSE THE DOCTOR IS AN AMBITIOUS BIOLOGIST, BUT I FEEL IT'S SOMETHING I SHOULD HANDLE.
HANG ON, HANK.
I THINK I NEED TO BE ON THIS TOO. I MEAN, SHE KIND OF PUT HER FAITH IN ME...
I WONDER WHY?
I SHOULD GO TOO, I--
SCOTT, YOU NEED TO CHILL MOST OF ALL-- AND I SHOULD KNOW.
AS UNBELIEVABLE AS YOU MAY FIND THIS, SCOTT, WE CAN DO SOME THINGS WITHOUT YOUR GUIDANCE.
YOU'RE RIGHT, HANK! WHY, DID YOU KNOW I *WENT TO THE BATHROOM* THIS MORNING...
NOT WITHOUT *SCOTT!*
YES!
THAT'S ENOUGH.
SCOTT, YOU, JEAN AND BOBBY GO TO WORTHINGTON HOUSE. THE REST OF US WILL STAY HERE TO BEGIN THE SEARCH IN THE MORNING.
I'LL LET YOU KNOW IF YOU'RE NEEDED.

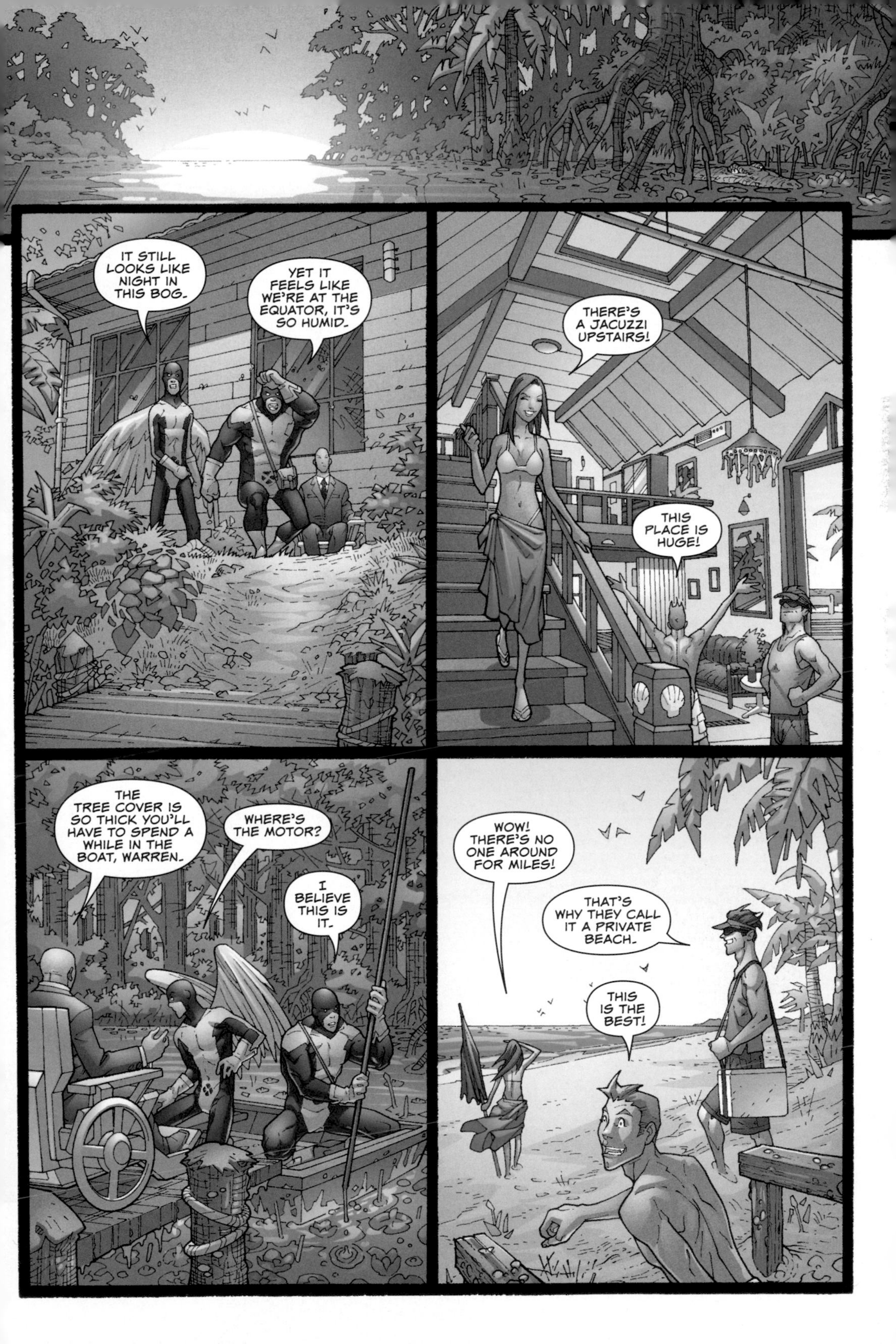
IT STILL LOOKS LIKE NIGHT IN THIS BOG.
YET IT FEELS LIKE WE'RE AT THE EQUATOR, IT'S SO HUMID.
THERE'S A JACUZZI UPSTAIRS!
THIS PLACE IS HUGE!
THE TREE COVER IS SO THICK YOU'LL HAVE TO SPEND A WHILE IN THE BOAT, WARREN.
WHERE'S THE MOTOR?
I BELIEVE THIS IS IT.
WOW! THERE'S NO ONE AROUND FOR MILES!
THAT'S WHY THEY CALL IT A PRIVATE BEACH.
THIS IS THE BEST!

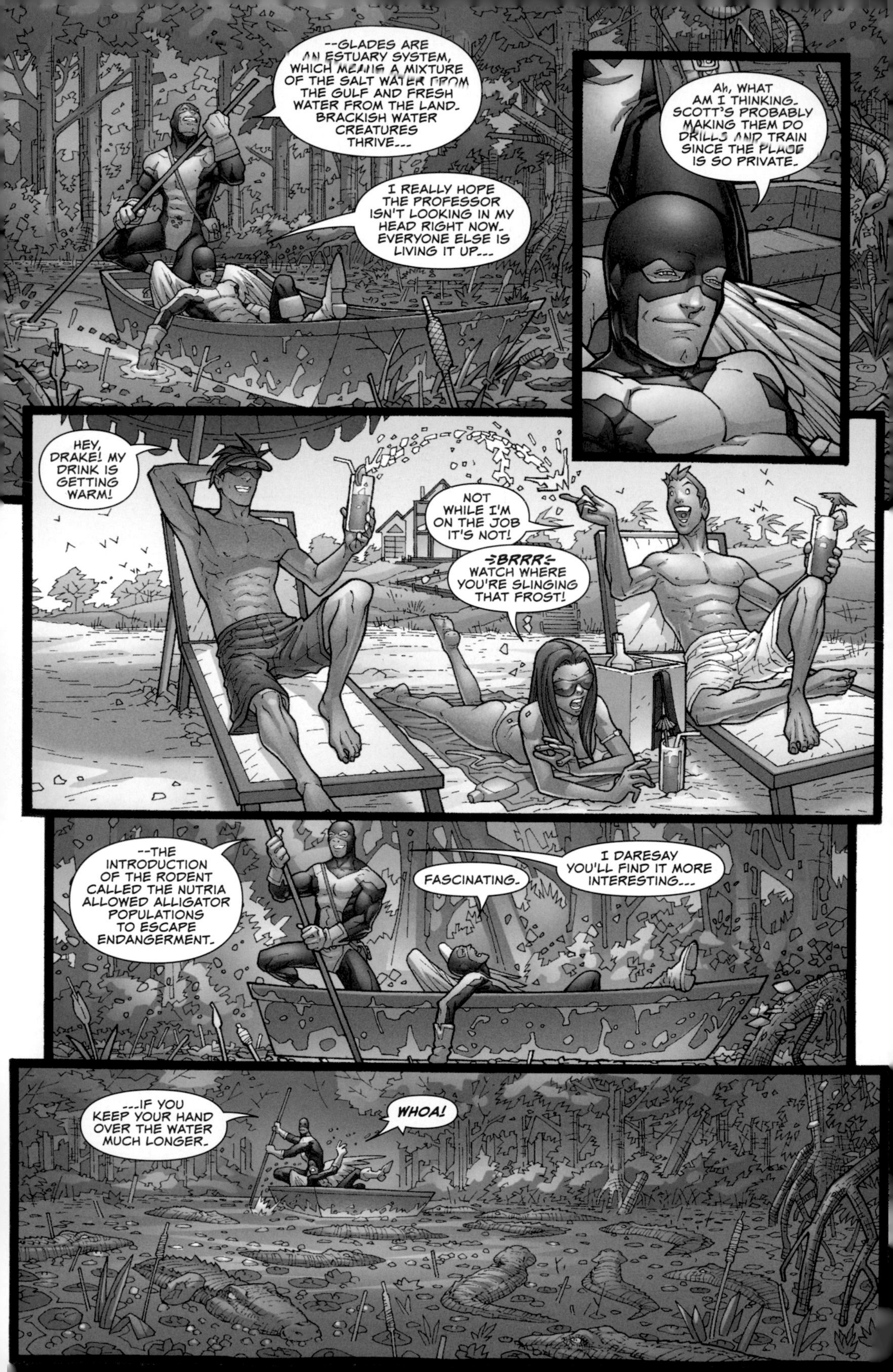
--GLADES ARE AN ESTUARY SYSTEM, WHICH MEANS A MIXTURE OF THE SALT WATER FROM THE GULF AND FRESH WATER FROM THE LAND. BRACKISH WATER CREATURES THRIVE...
I REALLY HOPE THE PROFESSOR ISN'T LOOKING IN MY HEAD RIGHT NOW. EVERYONE ELSE IS LIVING IT UP...
AH, WHAT AM I THINKING. SCOTT'S PROBABLY MAKING THEM DO DRILLS AND TRAIN SINCE THE PLACE IS SO PRIVATE.
HEY, DRAKE! MY DRINK IS GETTING WARM!
NOT WHILE I'M ON THE JOB IT'S NOT!
BRRR
WATCH WHERE YOU'RE SLINGING THAT FROST!
--THE INTRODUCTION OF THE RODENT CALLED THE NUTRIA ALLOWED ALLIGATOR POPULATIONS TO ESCAPE ENDANGERMENT.
FASCINATING.
I DARESAY YOU'LL FIND IT MORE INTERESTING...
...IF YOU KEEP YOUR HAND OVER THE WATER MUCH LONGER.
WHOA!

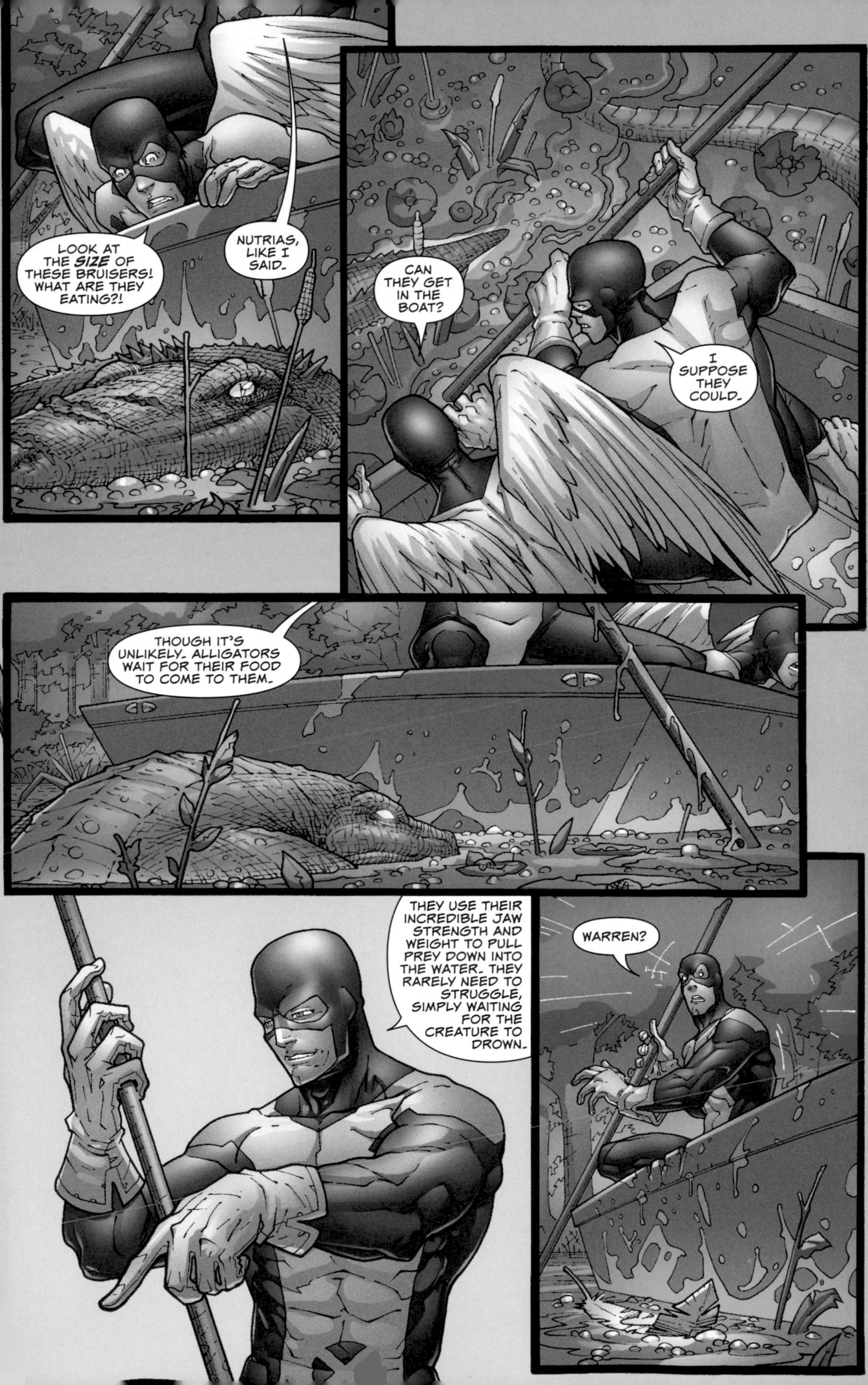
LOOK AT THE SIZE OF THESE BRUISERS! WHAT ARE THEY EATING?!
NUTRIAS, LIKE I SAID.
CAN THEY GET IN THE BOAT?
I SUPPOSE THEY COULD.
THOUGH IT'S UNLIKELY. ALLIGATORS WAIT FOR THEIR FOOD TO COME TO THEM.
THEY USE THEIR INCREDIBLE JAW STRENGTH AND WEIGHT TO PULL PREY DOWN INTO THE WATER. THEY RARELY NEED TO STRUGGLE, SIMPLY WAITING FOR THE CREATURE TO DROWN.
WARREN?

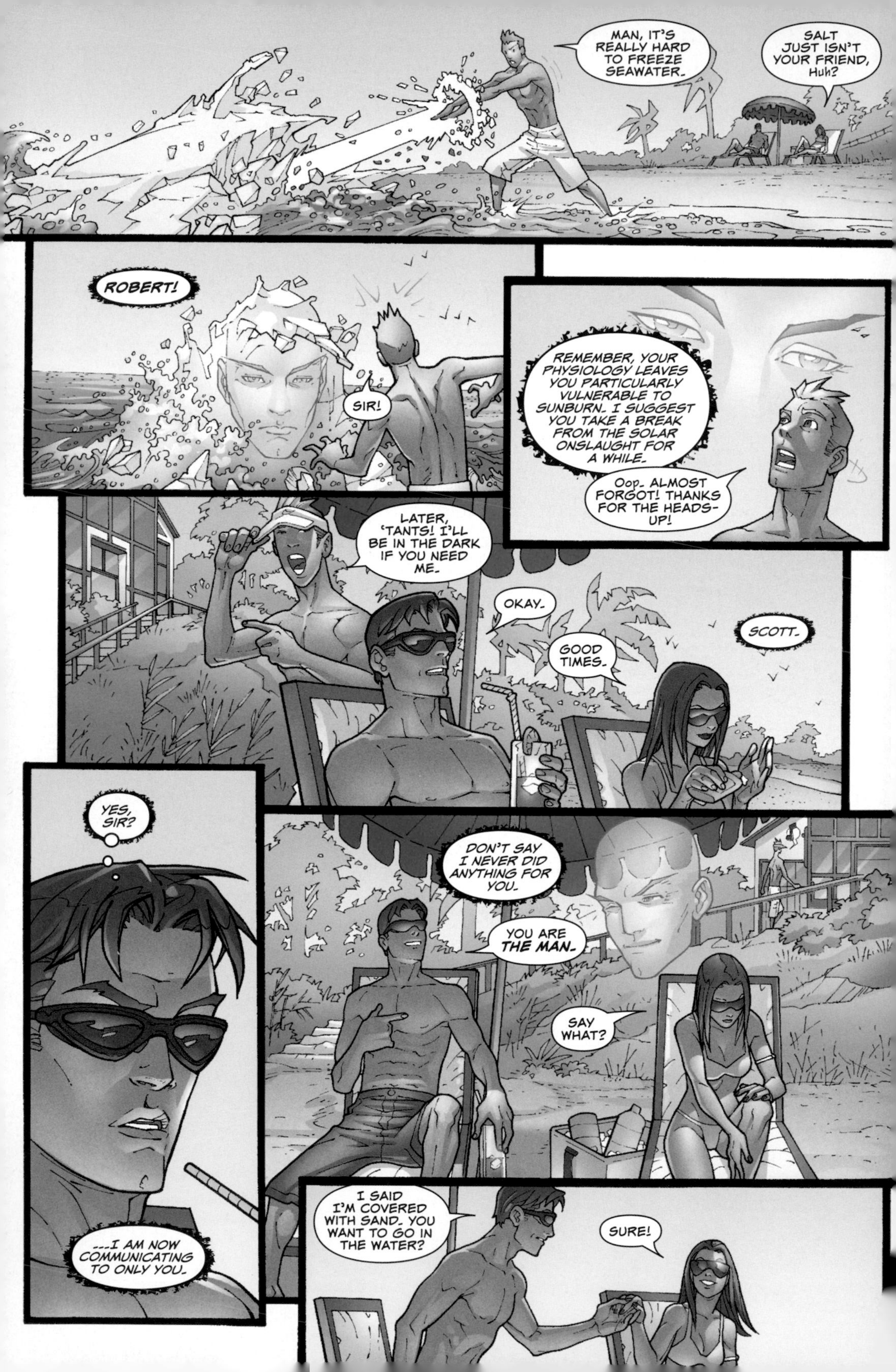

MAN, IT'S REALLY HARD TO FREEZE SEAWATER.
SALT JUST ISN'T YOUR FRIEND, Huh?
ROBERT!
SIR!
REMEMBER, YOUR PHYSIOLOGY LEAVES YOU PARTICULARLY VULNERABLE TO SUNBURN. I SUGGEST YOU TAKE A BREAK FROM THE SOLAR ONSLAUGHT FOR A WHILE.
Oop. ALMOST FORGOT! THANKS FOR THE HEADS-UP!
LATER, 'TANTS! I'LL BE IN THE DARK IF YOU NEED ME.
OKAY.
GOOD TIMES.
SCOTT.
YES, SIR?
...I AM NOW COMMUNICATING TO ONLY YOU.
DON'T SAY I NEVER DID ANYTHING FOR YOU.
YOU ARE THE MAN.
SAY WHAT?
I SAID I'M COVERED WITH SAND. YOU WANT TO GO IN THE WATER?
SURE!

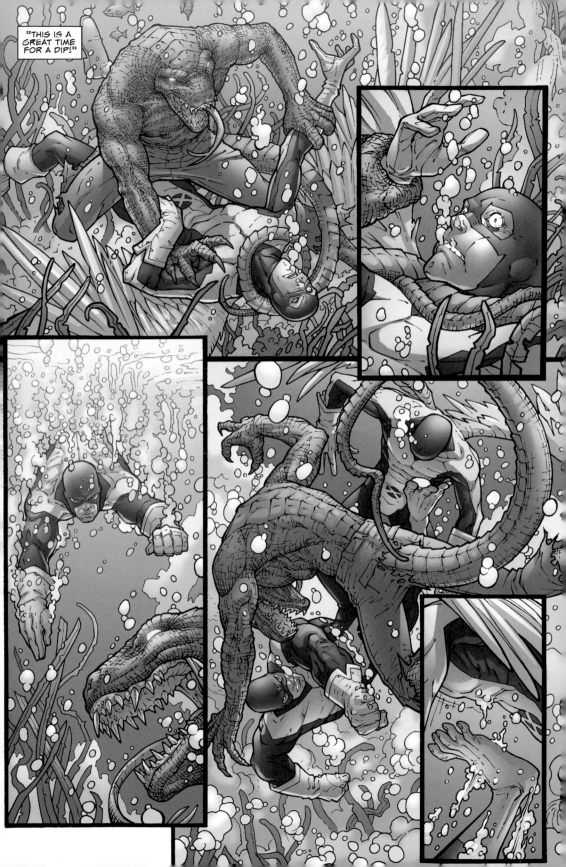

"THIS IS A GREAT TIME FOR A DIP!"

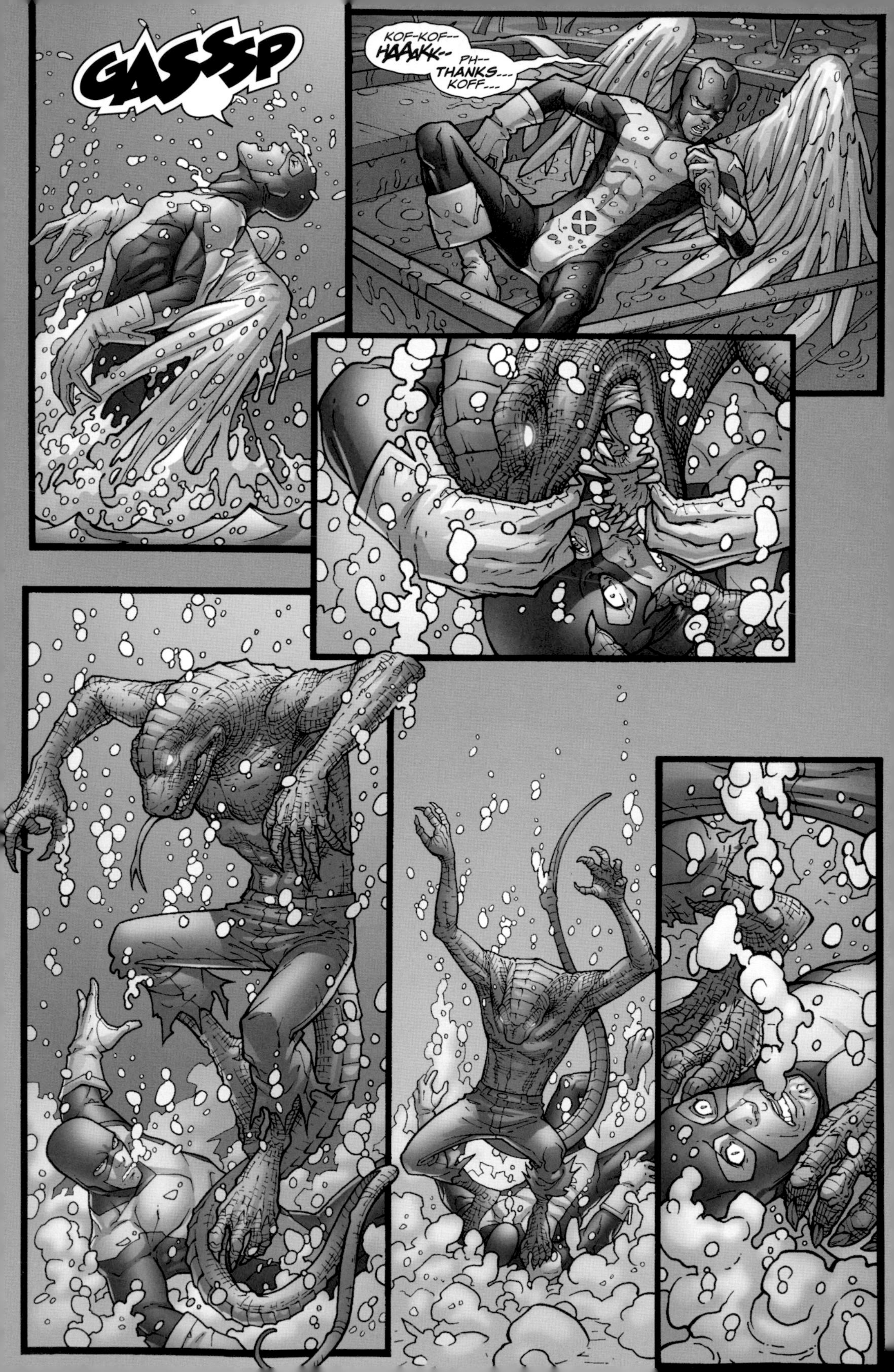
GASSP
KOF-KOF--
HAAAKK--
PH--
THANKS---
KOFF---

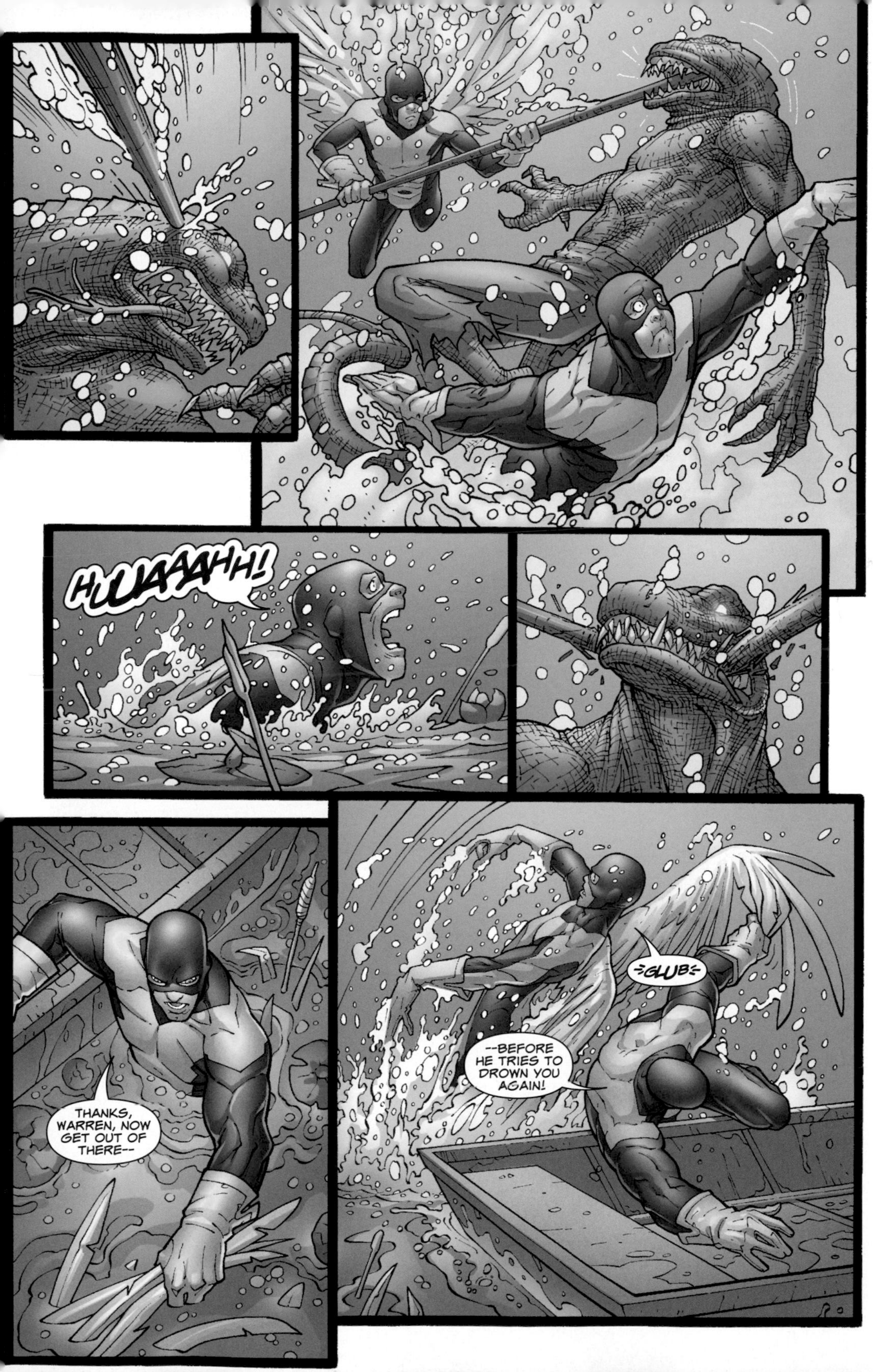
HUUAAAHH!
THANKS, WARREN, NOW GET OUT OF THERE--
--BEFORE HE TRIES TO DROWN YOU AGAIN!
GLUB

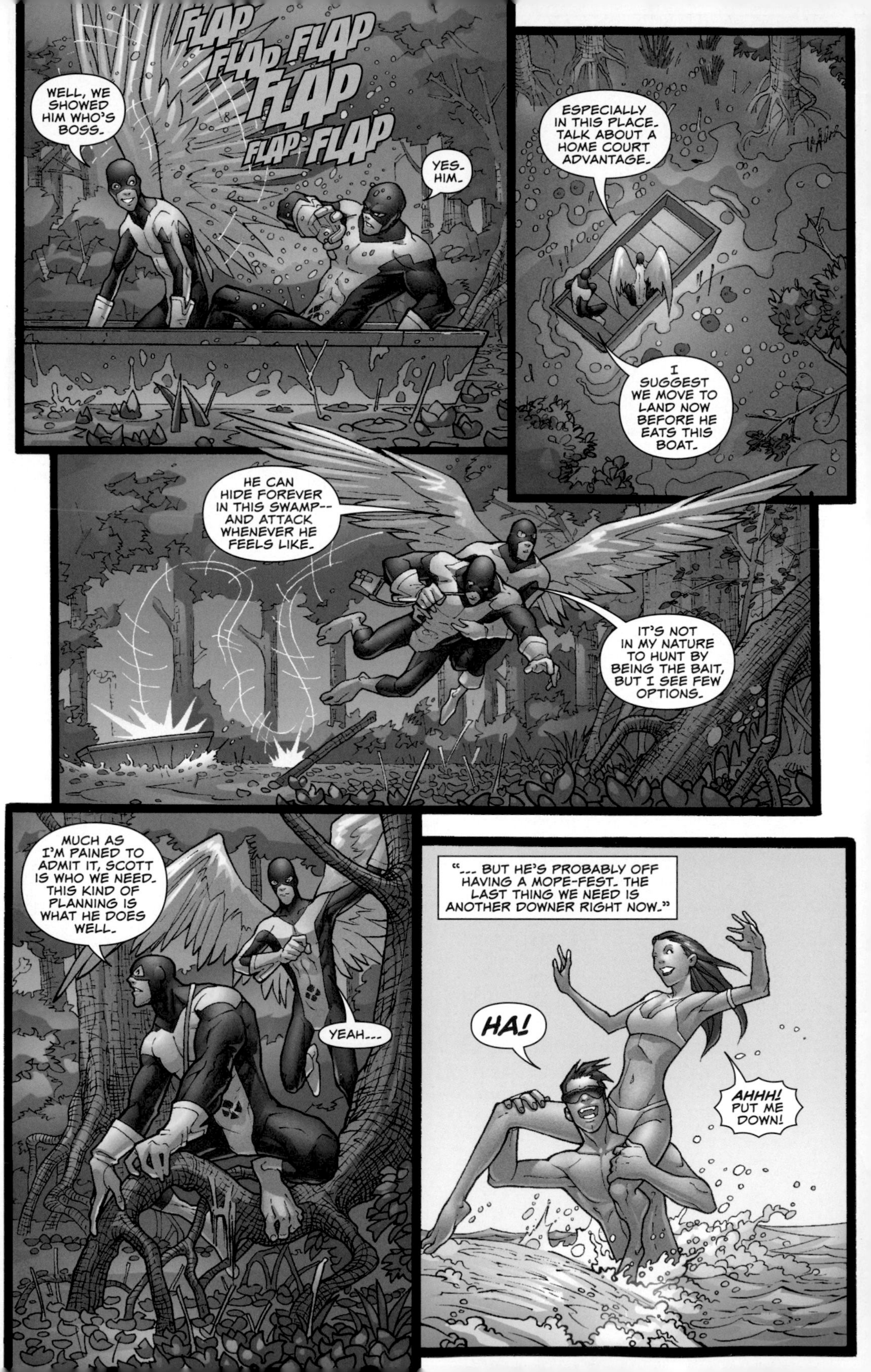
FLAP
FLAP FLAP
FLAP
FLAP FLAP
WELL, WE SHOWED HIM WHO'S BOSS.
YES. HIM.
ESPECIALLY IN THIS PLACE. TALK ABOUT A HOME COURT ADVANTAGE.
I SUGGEST WE MOVE TO LAND NOW BEFORE HE EATS THIS BOAT.
HE CAN HIDE FOREVER IN THIS SWAMP-- AND ATTACK WHENEVER HE FEELS LIKE.
IT'S NOT IN MY NATURE TO HUNT BY BEING THE BAIT, BUT I SEE FEW OPTIONS.
MUCH AS I'M PAINED TO ADMIT IT, SCOTT IS WHO WE NEED. THIS KIND OF PLANNING IS WHAT HE DOES WELL.
YEAH...
"... BUT HE'S PROBABLY OFF HAVING A MOPE-FEST. THE LAST THING WE NEED IS ANOTHER DOWNER RIGHT NOW."
HA!
AHHH! PUT ME DOWN!

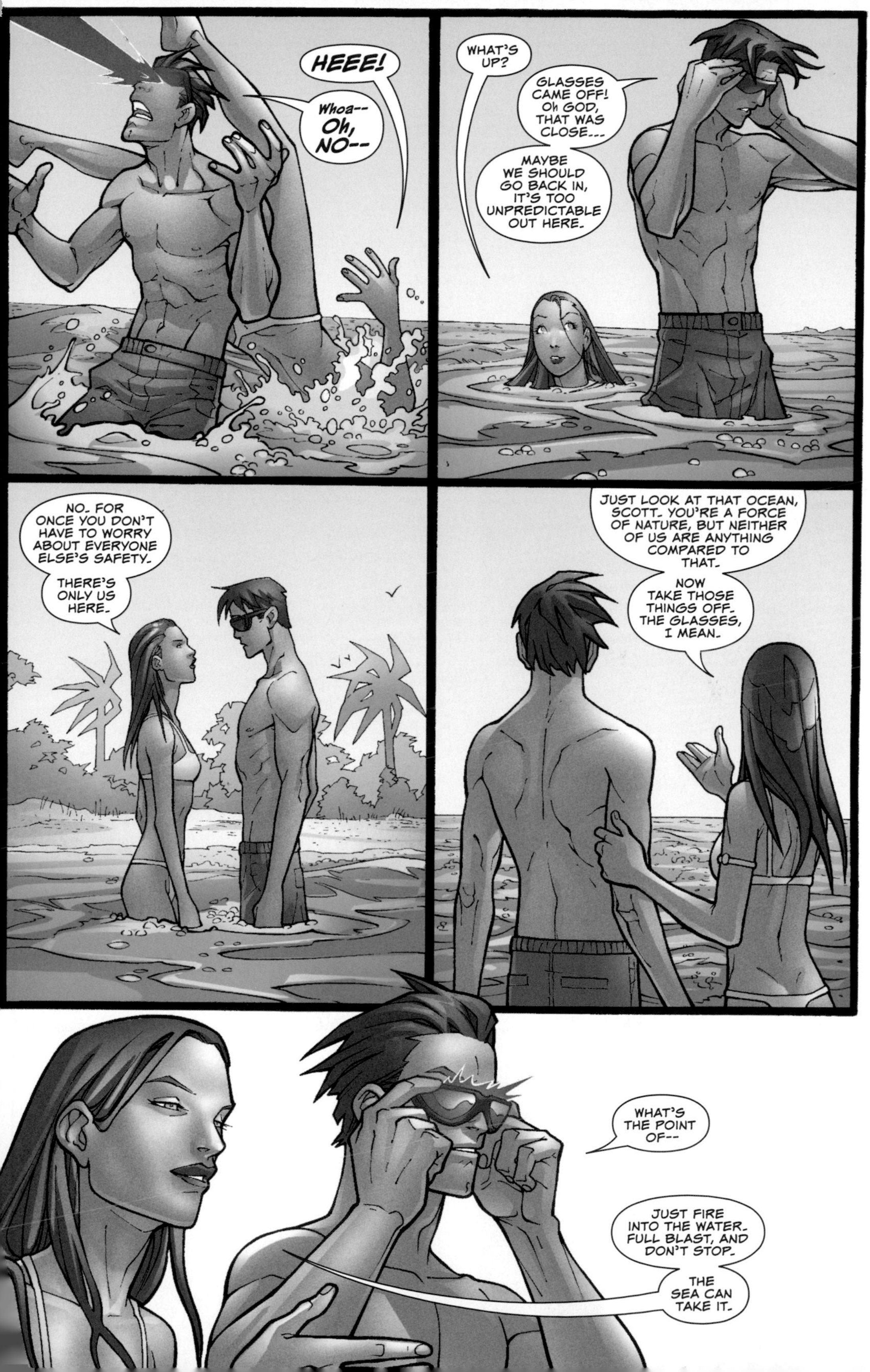
HEEE!
Whoa-- Oh, NO--
WHAT'S UP?
GLASSES CAME OFF! Oh GOD, THAT WAS CLOSE...
MAYBE WE SHOULD GO BACK IN, IT'S TOO UNPREDICTABLE OUT HERE.
NO. FOR ONCE YOU DON'T HAVE TO WORRY ABOUT EVERYONE ELSE'S SAFETY.
THERE'S ONLY US HERE.
JUST LOOK AT THAT OCEAN, SCOTT. YOU'RE A FORCE OF NATURE, BUT NEITHER OF US ARE ANYTHING COMPARED TO THAT.
NOW TAKE THOSE THINGS OFF. THE GLASSES, I MEAN.
WHAT'S THE POINT OF--
JUST FIRE INTO THE WATER. FULL BLAST, AND DON'T STOP.
THE SEA CAN TAKE IT.

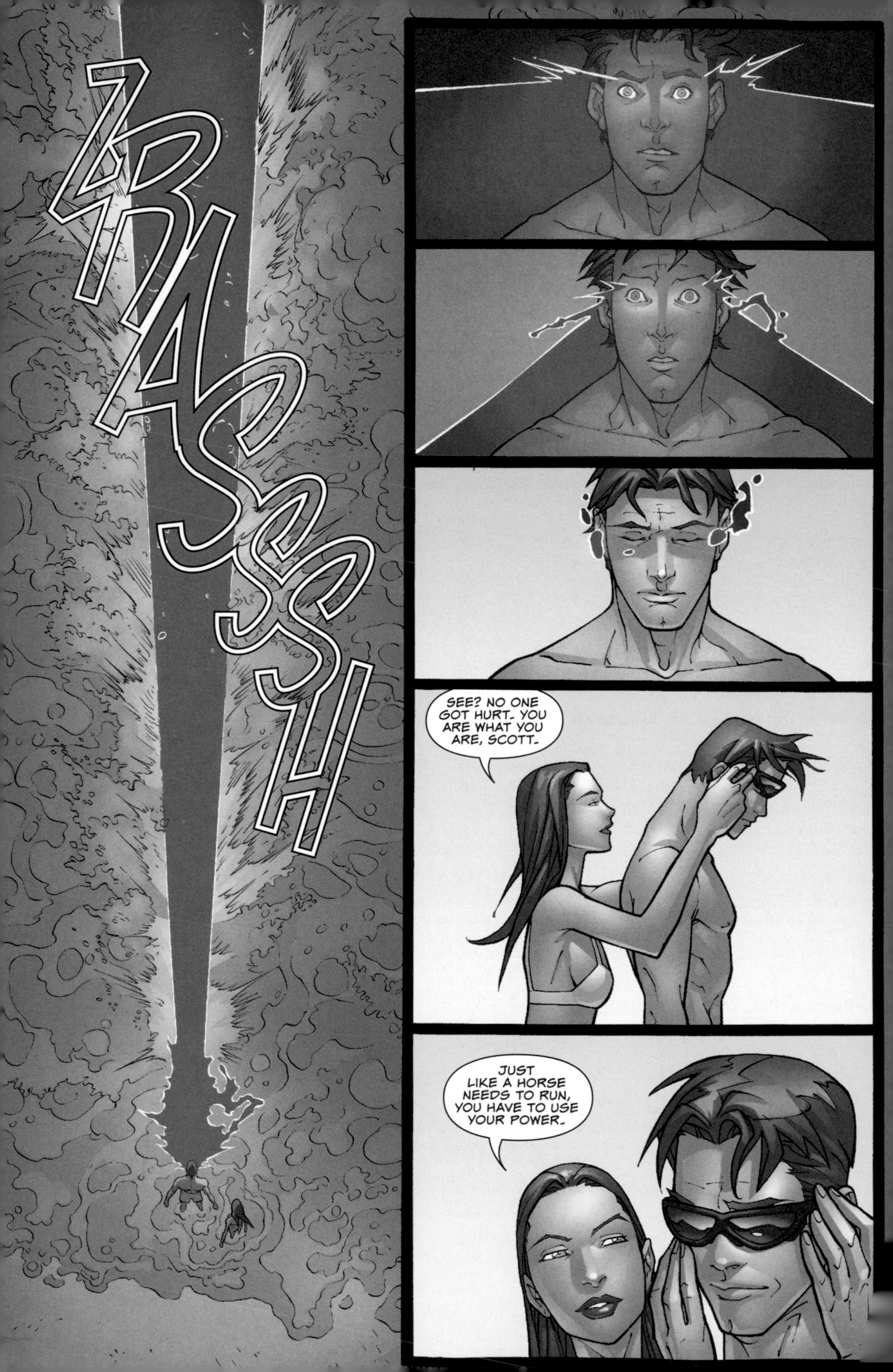
ZRASSSH
SEE? NO ONE GOT HURT. YOU ARE WHAT YOU ARE, SCOTT.
JUST LIKE A HORSE NEEDS TO RUN, YOU HAVE TO USE YOUR POWER.

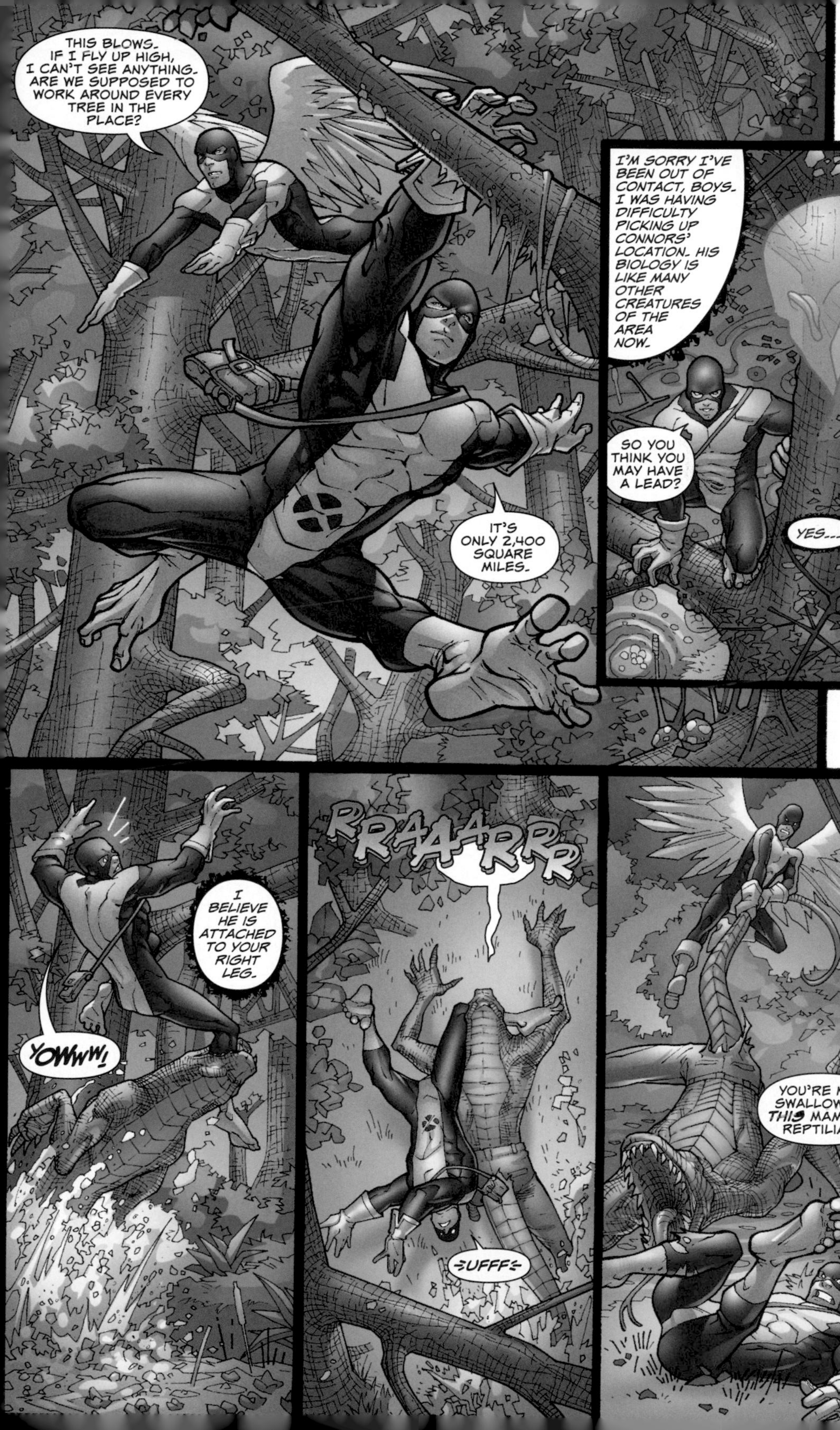
THIS BLOWS. IF I FLY UP HIGH, I CAN'T SEE ANYTHING. ARE WE SUPPOSED TO WORK AROUND EVERY TREE IN THE PLACE?
IT'S ONLY 2,400 SQUARE MILES.
I'M SORRY I'VE BEEN OUT OF CONTACT, BOYS. I WAS HAVING DIFFICULTY PICKING UP CONNORS' LOCATION. HIS BIOLOGY IS LIKE MANY OTHER CREATURES OF THE AREA NOW.
SO YOU THINK YOU MAY HAVE A LEAD?
YES...
I BELIEVE HE IS ATTACHED TO YOUR RIGHT LEG.
YOWWW!
RRAAARRR
UFFF
YOU'RE NOT SWALLOWING THIS MAMMAL, REPTILIAN!

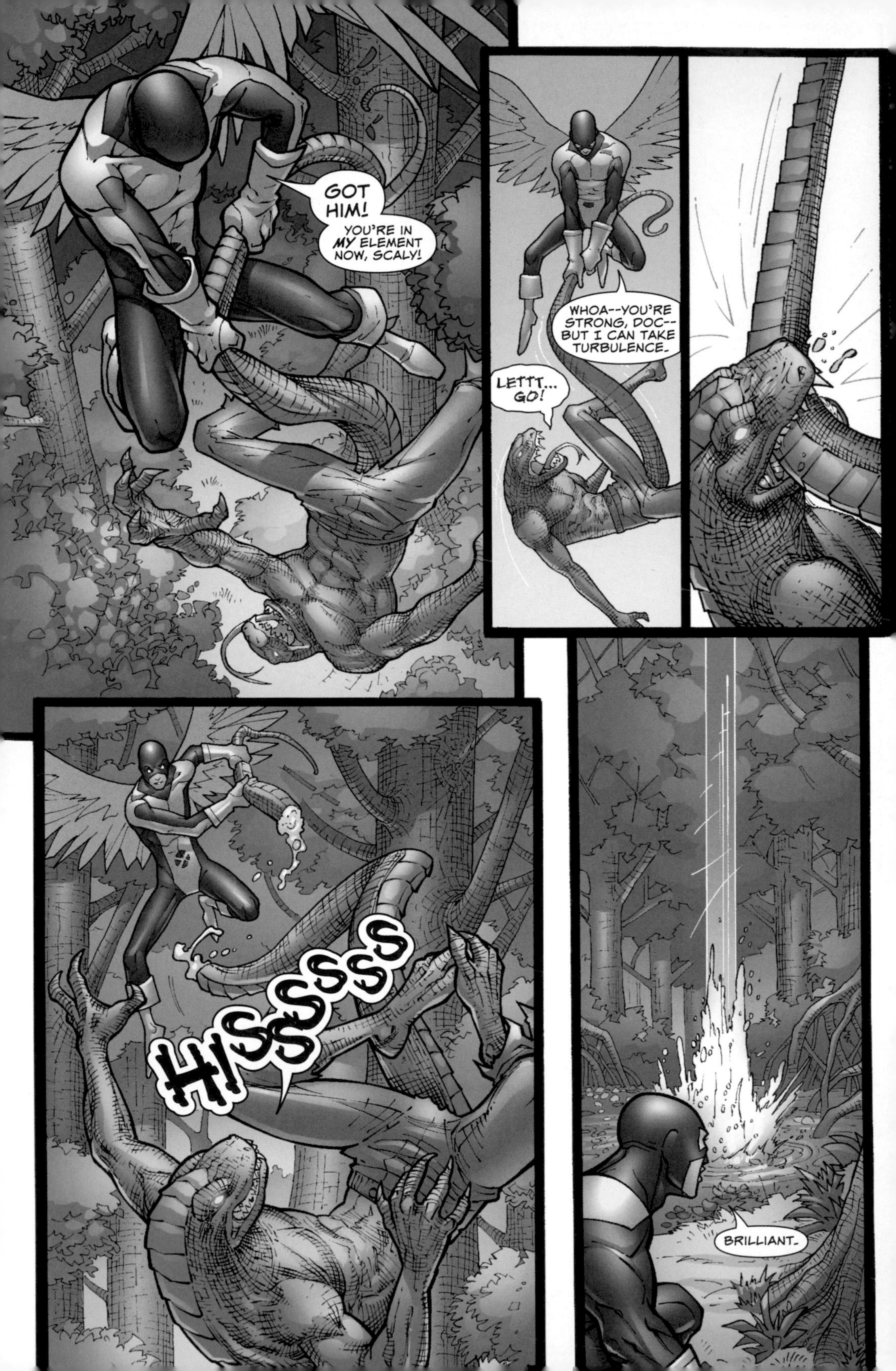
GOT HIM!
YOU'RE IN MY ELEMENT NOW, SCALY!
WHOA--YOU'RE STRONG, DOC-- BUT I CAN TAKE TURBULENCE.
LETTT... GO!
HISSSSSS
BRILLIANT.

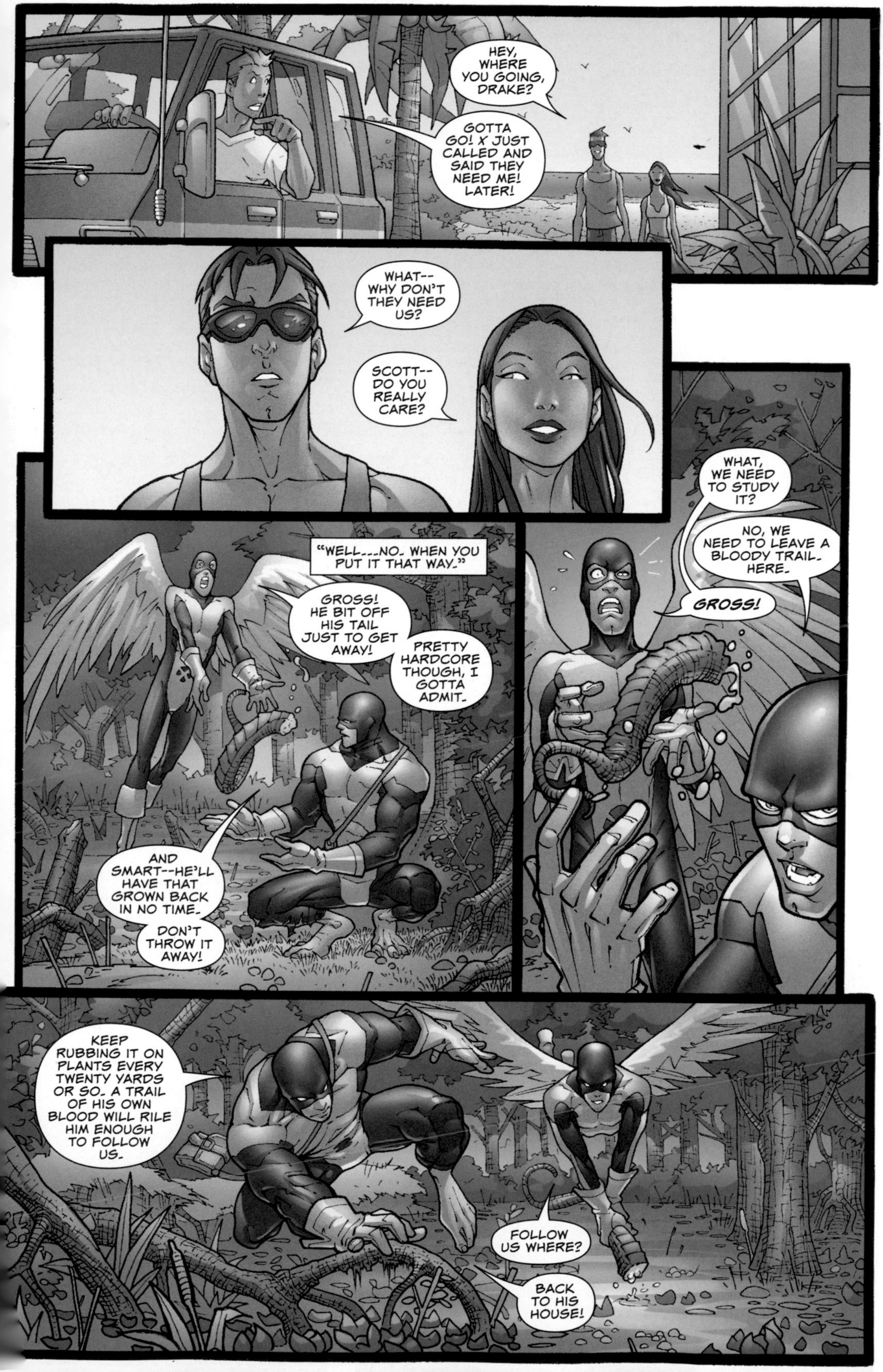
HEY, WHERE YOU GOING, DRAKE?
GOTTA GO! X JUST CALLED AND SAID THEY NEED ME! LATER!
WHAT-- WHY DON'T THEY NEED US?
SCOTT-- DO YOU REALLY CARE?
"WELL...NO. WHEN YOU PUT IT THAT WAY."
GROSS! HE BIT OFF HIS TAIL JUST TO GET AWAY!
PRETTY HARDCORE THOUGH, I GOTTA ADMIT.
AND SMART--HE'LL HAVE THAT GROWN BACK IN NO TIME.
DON'T THROW IT AWAY!
WHAT, WE NEED TO STUDY IT?
NO, WE NEED TO LEAVE A BLOODY TRAIL HERE.
GROSS!
KEEP RUBBING IT ON PLANTS EVERY TWENTY YARDS OR SO. A TRAIL OF HIS OWN BLOOD WILL RILE HIM ENOUGH TO FOLLOW US.
FOLLOW US WHERE?
BACK TO HIS HOUSE!

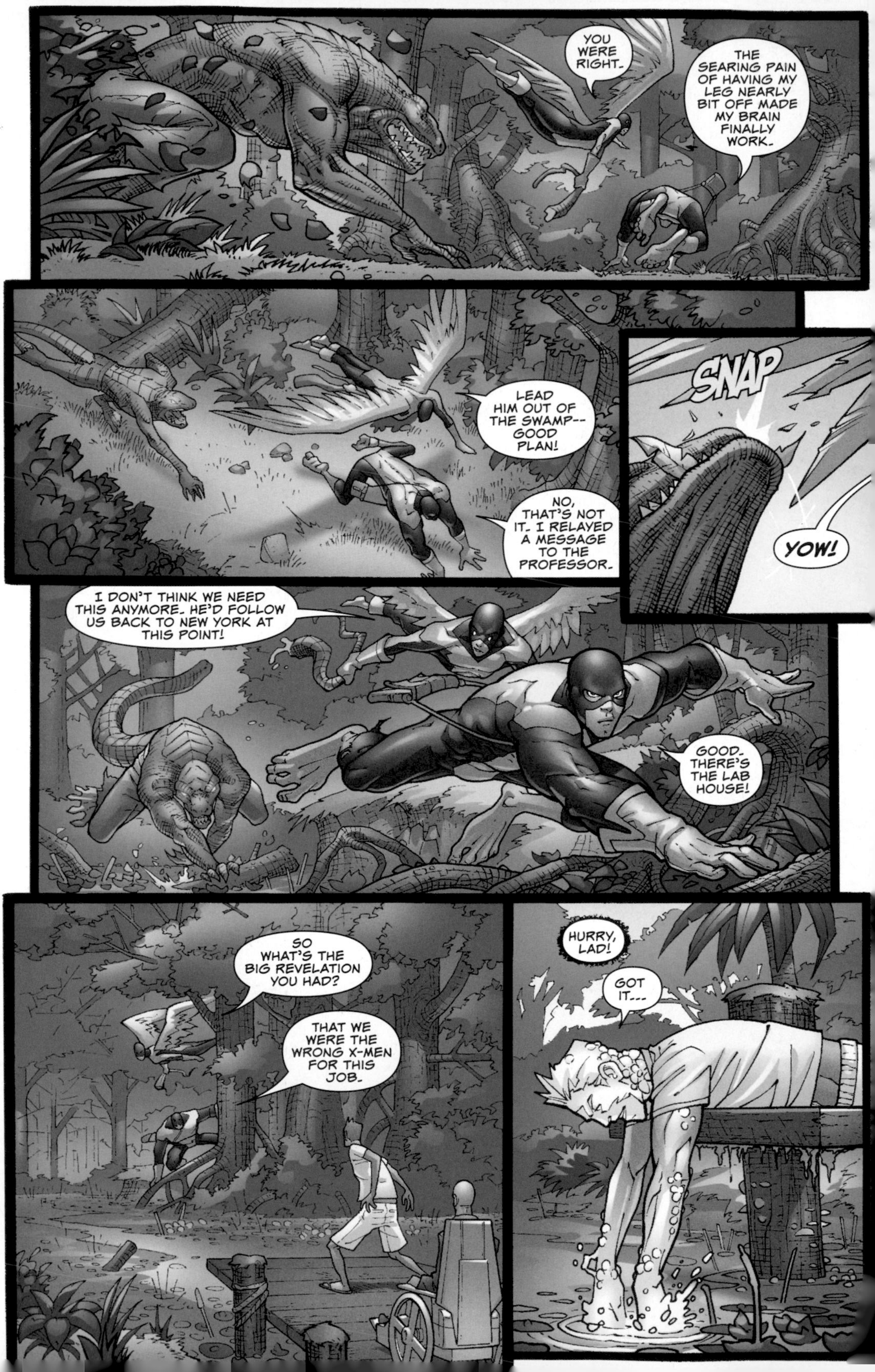
YOU WERE RIGHT.
THE SEARING PAIN OF HAVING MY LEG NEARLY BIT OFF MADE MY BRAIN FINALLY WORK.
LEAD HIM OUT OF THE SWAMP--GOOD PLAN!
NO, THAT'S NOT IT. I RELAYED A MESSAGE TO THE PROFESSOR.
SNAP
YOW!
I DON'T THINK WE NEED THIS ANYMORE. HE'D FOLLOW US BACK TO NEW YORK AT THIS POINT!
GOOD. THERE'S THE LAB HOUSE!
SO WHAT'S THE BIG REVELATION YOU HAD?
THAT WE WERE THE WRONG X-MEN FOR THIS JOB.
HURRY, LAD!
GOT IT...

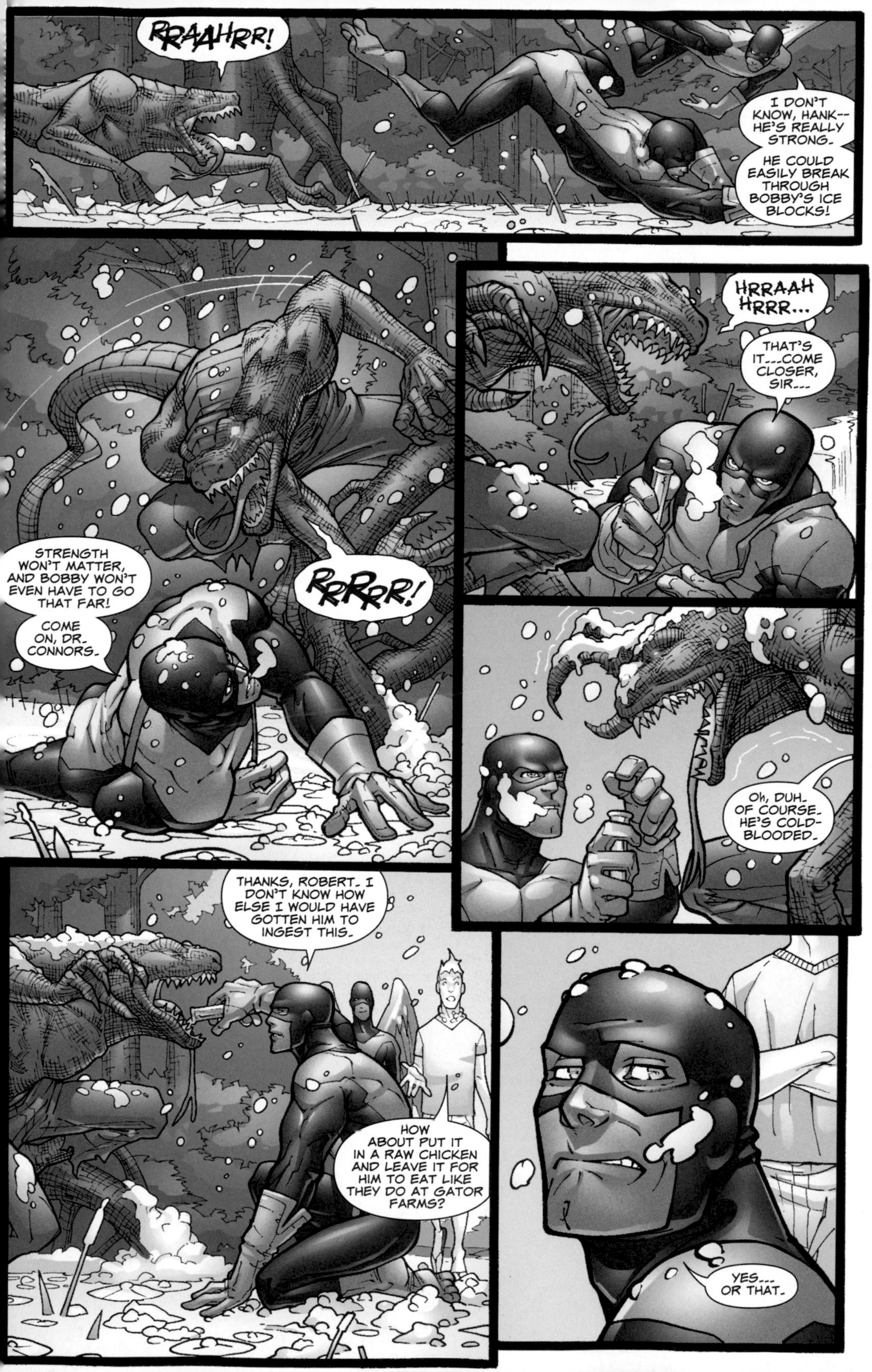
RRAAHRR!
I DON'T KNOW, HANK-- HE'S REALLY STRONG.
HE COULD EASILY BREAK THROUGH BOBBY'S ICE BLOCKS!
STRENGTH WON'T MATTER, AND BOBBY WON'T EVEN HAVE TO GO THAT FAR!
COME ON, DR. CONNORS.
RRRRRR!
HRRAAH HRRR...
THAT'S IT...COME CLOSER, SIR...
Oh, DUH. OF COURSE. HE'S COLD-BLOODED.
THANKS, ROBERT. I DON'T KNOW HOW ELSE I WOULD HAVE GOTTEN HIM TO INGEST THIS.
HOW ABOUT PUT IT IN A RAW CHICKEN AND LEAVE IT FOR HIM TO EAT LIKE THEY DO AT GATOR FARMS?
YES... OR THAT.

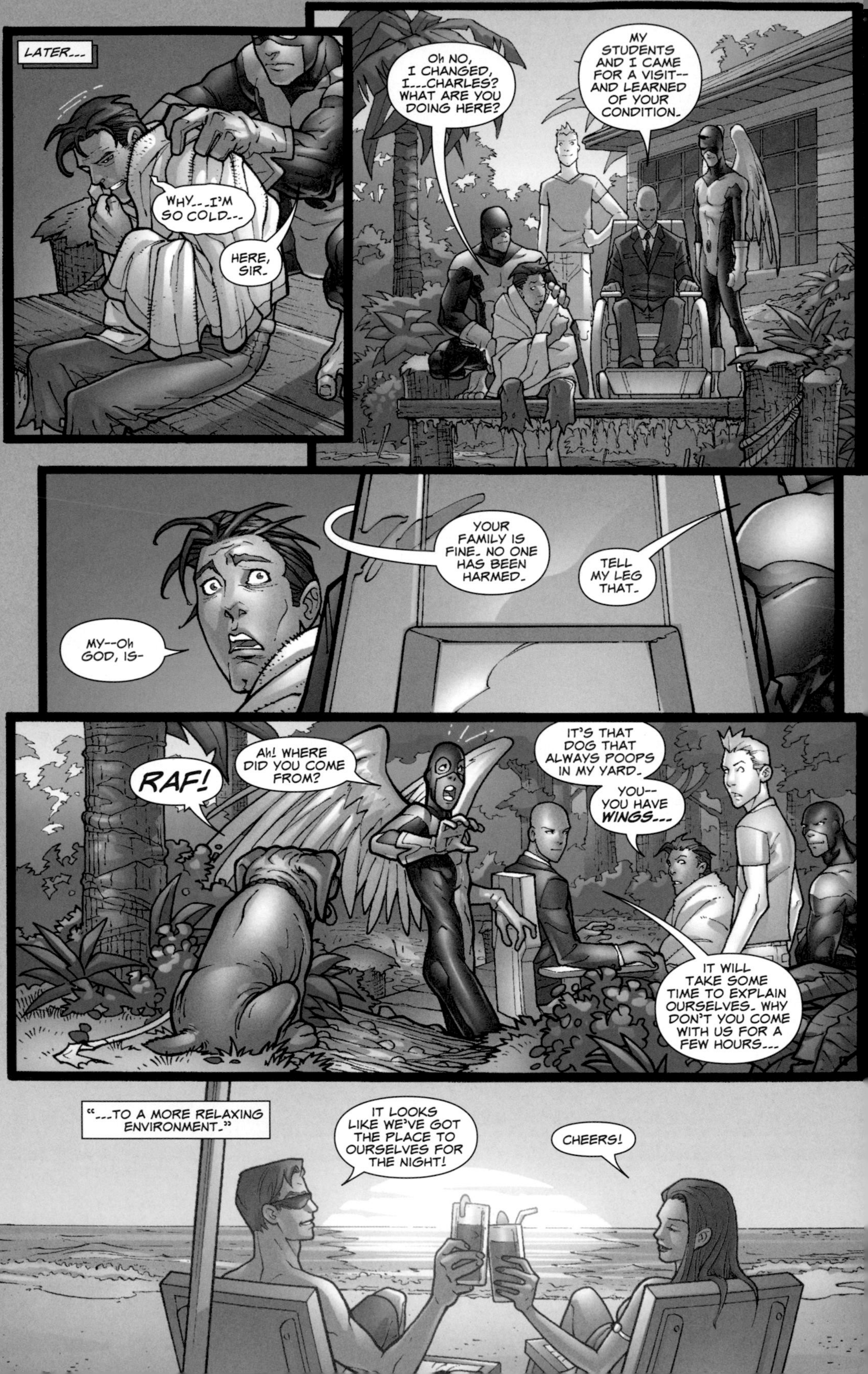
LATER...
WHY...I'M SO COLD...
HERE, SIR.
Oh NO, I CHANGED, I...CHARLES? WHAT ARE YOU DOING HERE?
MY STUDENTS AND I CAME FOR A VISIT-- AND LEARNED OF YOUR CONDITION.
MY--Oh GOD, IS-
YOUR FAMILY IS FINE. NO ONE HAS BEEN HARMED.
TELL MY LEG THAT.
RAF!
Ah! WHERE DID YOU COME FROM?
IT'S THAT DOG THAT ALWAYS POOPS IN MY YARD.
YOU-- YOU HAVE WINGS...
IT WILL TAKE SOME TIME TO EXPLAIN OURSELVES. WHY DON'T YOU COME WITH US FOR A FEW HOURS...
"...TO A MORE RELAXING ENVIRONMENT."
IT LOOKS LIKE WE'VE GOT THE PLACE TO OURSELVES FOR THE NIGHT!
CHEERS!

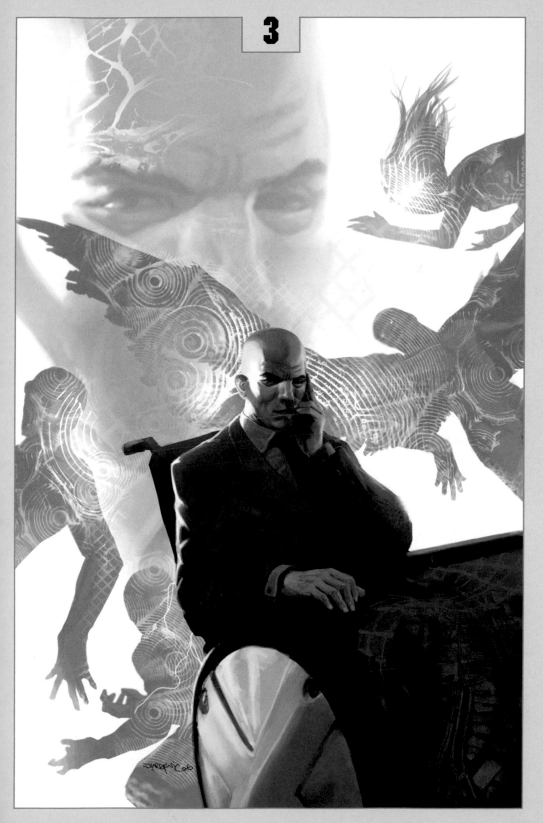

THE NEXT STEP IN HUMAN EVOLUTION HAS ARRIVED—HOMO SUPERIOR. MANKIND ISN'T SURE WHETHER THIS REPRESENTS HOPE FOR THE FUTURE...OR THE END OF THE HUMAN RACE. IN A PRIVATE SCHOOL IN UPSTATE NEW YORK, ONE BRILLIANT MUTANT IS TEACHING A GROUP OF FIVE SUCH GIFTED STUDENTS WHAT THEY'LL NEED TO SURVIVE IN THIS NEW WORLD. THESE ARE THE UNTOLD STORIES OF PROFESSOR XAVIER'S FIRST CLASS OF X-MEN!

XAVIER'S SCHOOL FOR GIFTED YOUNGSTERS

PROPERTY OF:

CYCLOPS

HEADMASTER

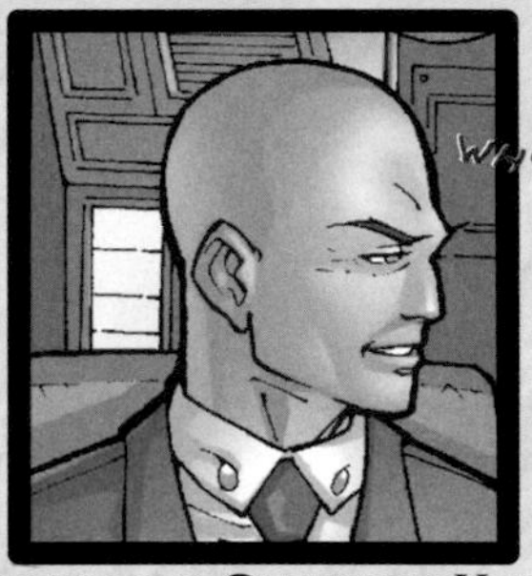

WHY DID I LET THE PROF PICK MY NAME? I DO KIND OF LIKE IT WHEN THE GUYS CALL ME CYKE THOUGH...

BOY, I HAVEN'T CALLED ALEX IN A WHILE--WONDER IF HE'S TAKING CARE OF MY CAR.

PROFESSOR CHARLES XAVIER

I SEE EVERYTHING AS RED. JEAN HAS RED HAIR. COINCIDENCE? FATE?

GOT TO THANK HANK FOR LENDING SUN TZU'S THE ART OF WAR. FINALLY HE RECOMMENDS SOMETHING I UNDERSTAND.

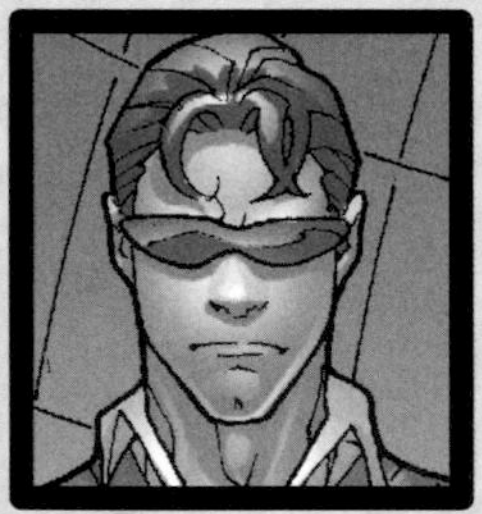

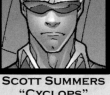

SCOTT SUMMERS
"CYCLOPS"

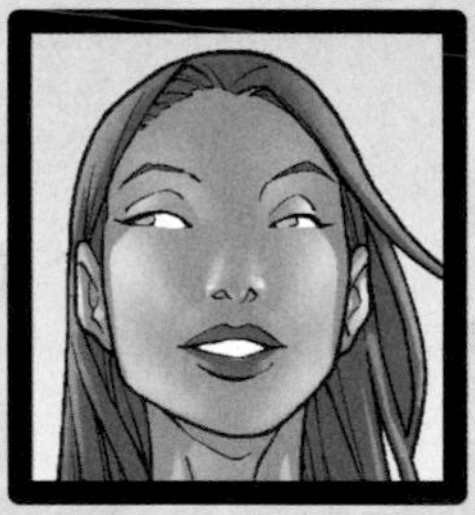

JEAN GREY
"MARVEL GIRL"

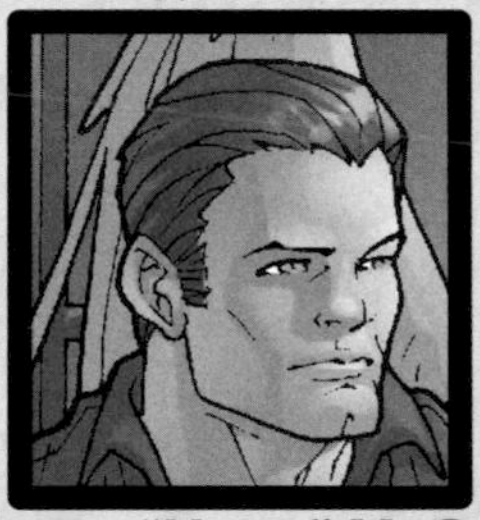

HENRY "HANK" McCOY
"BEAST"

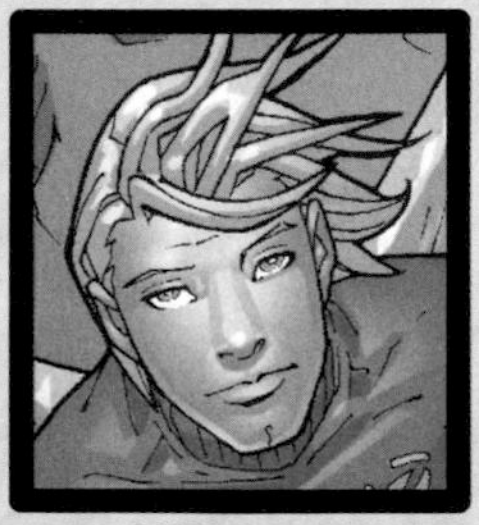

IF I COULD FLY LIKE WARREN, I COULD TARGET THREATS SO MUCH BETTER... OF COURSE, I MIGHT BARF ON THEM TOO. I DON'T KNOW HOW HE CAN MANEUVER LIKE THAT WITHOUT LOSING IT.

WARREN WORTHINGTON III
"ANGEL"

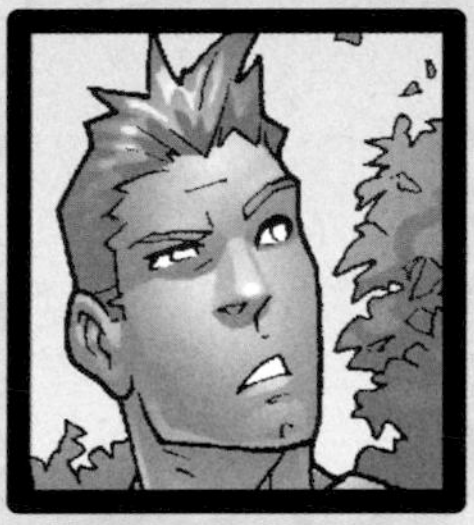

ROBERT DRAKE
"ICEMAN"

THERMOSTAT IN ROOM NOT BROKEN, BOBBY IS JUST PRANKING ME AGAIN. LITTLE #&^!@

WHEN IS THAT JET GOING TO BE FINISHED? VERTICAL TAKE-OFF AND LANDING, SPEED OF SOUND... NOW THAT'S A PROPER SUPER HERO RIDE.

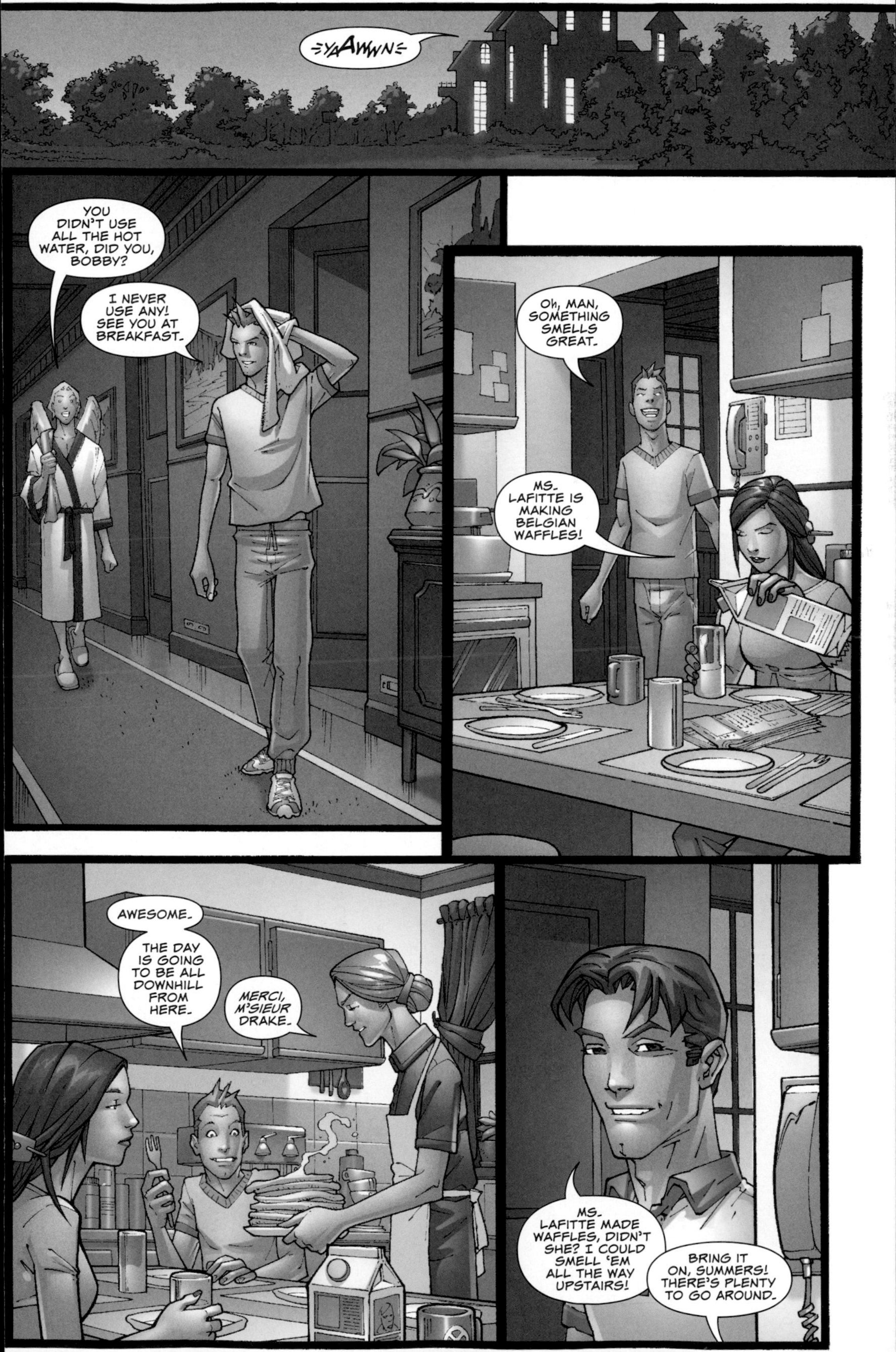
YAAWWN
YOU DIDN'T USE ALL THE HOT WATER, DID YOU, BOBBY?
I NEVER USE ANY! SEE YOU AT BREAKFAST.
Oh, MAN, SOMETHING SMELLS GREAT.
MS. LAFITTE IS MAKING BELGIAN WAFFLES!
AWESOME.
THE DAY IS GOING TO BE ALL DOWNHILL FROM HERE.
MERCI, M'SIEUR DRAKE.
MS. LAFITTE MADE WAFFLES, DIDN'T SHE? I COULD SMELL 'EM ALL THE WAY UPSTAIRS!
BRING IT ON, SUMMERS! THERE'S PLENTY TO GO AROUND.

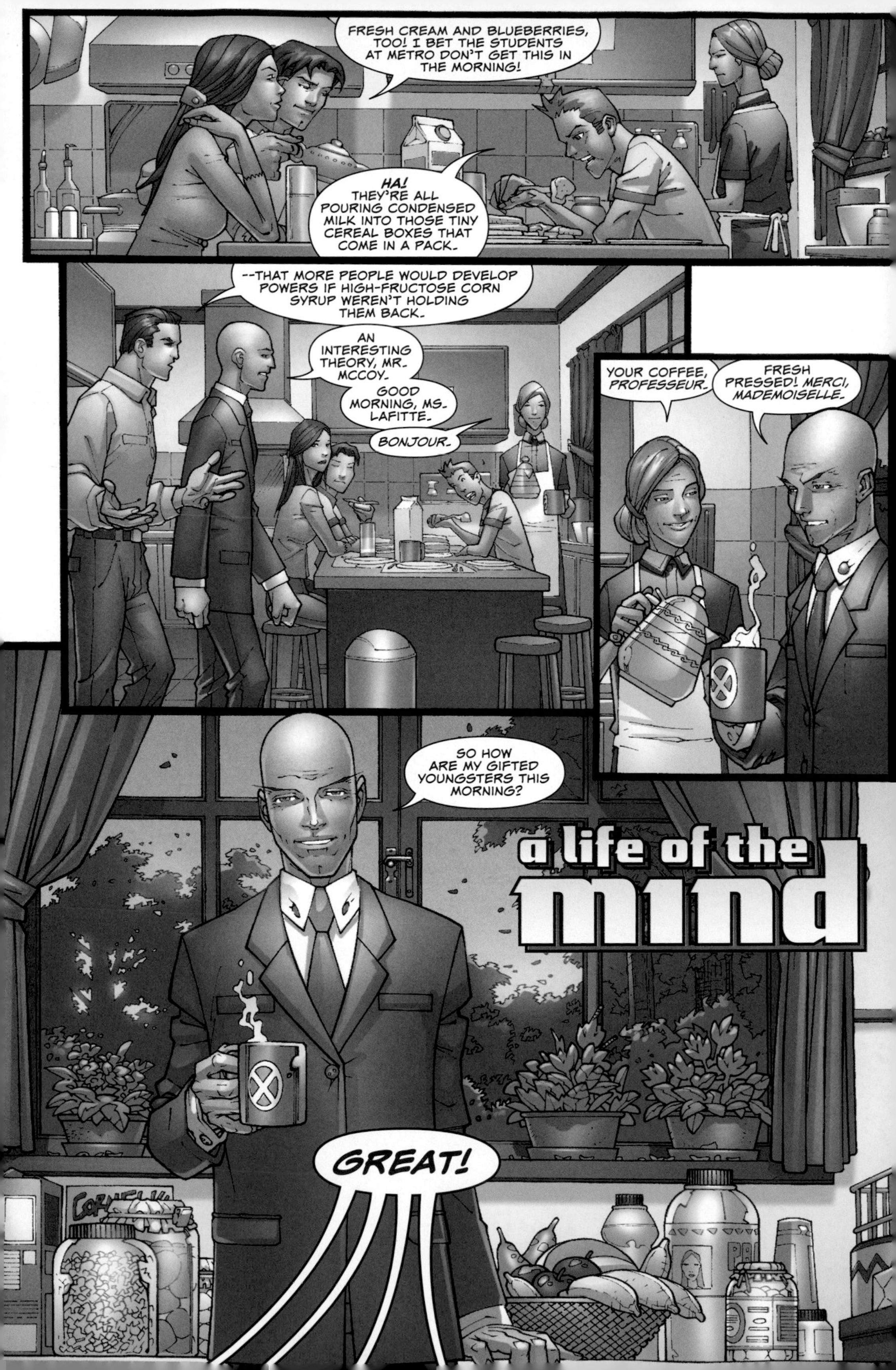
FRESH CREAM AND BLUEBERRIES, TOO! I BET THE STUDENTS AT METRO DON'T GET THIS IN THE MORNING!
HA! THEY'RE ALL POURING CONDENSED MILK INTO THOSE TINY CEREAL BOXES THAT COME IN A PACK.
--THAT MORE PEOPLE WOULD DEVELOP POWERS IF HIGH-FRUCTOSE CORN SYRUP WEREN'T HOLDING THEM BACK.
AN INTERESTING THEORY, MR. MCCOY.
GOOD MORNING, MS. LAFITTE.
BONJOUR.
YOUR COFFEE, PROFESSEUR.
FRESH PRESSED! MERCI, MADEMOISELLE.
SO HOW ARE MY GIFTED YOUNGSTERS THIS MORNING?
a life of the mind
GREAT!

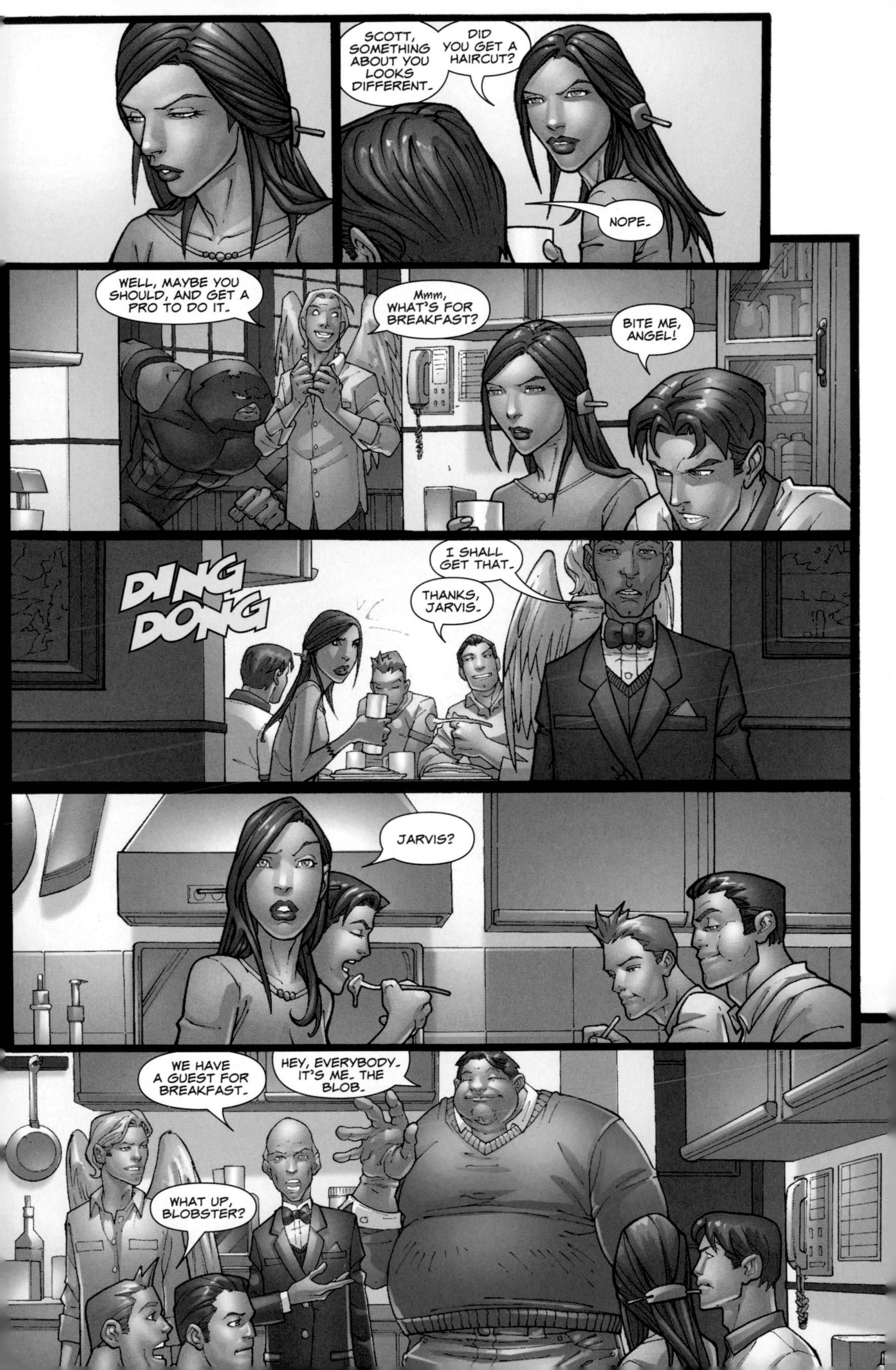
SCOTT, SOMETHING ABOUT YOU LOOKS DIFFERENT.
DID YOU GET A HAIRCUT?
NOPE.
WELL, MAYBE YOU SHOULD, AND GET A PRO TO DO IT.
Mmm, WHAT'S FOR BREAKFAST?
BITE ME, ANGEL!
DING DONG
I SHALL GET THAT.
THANKS, JARVIS.
JARVIS?
WE HAVE A GUEST FOR BREAKFAST.
HEY, EVERYBODY. IT'S ME. THE BLOB.
WHAT UP, BLOBSTER?

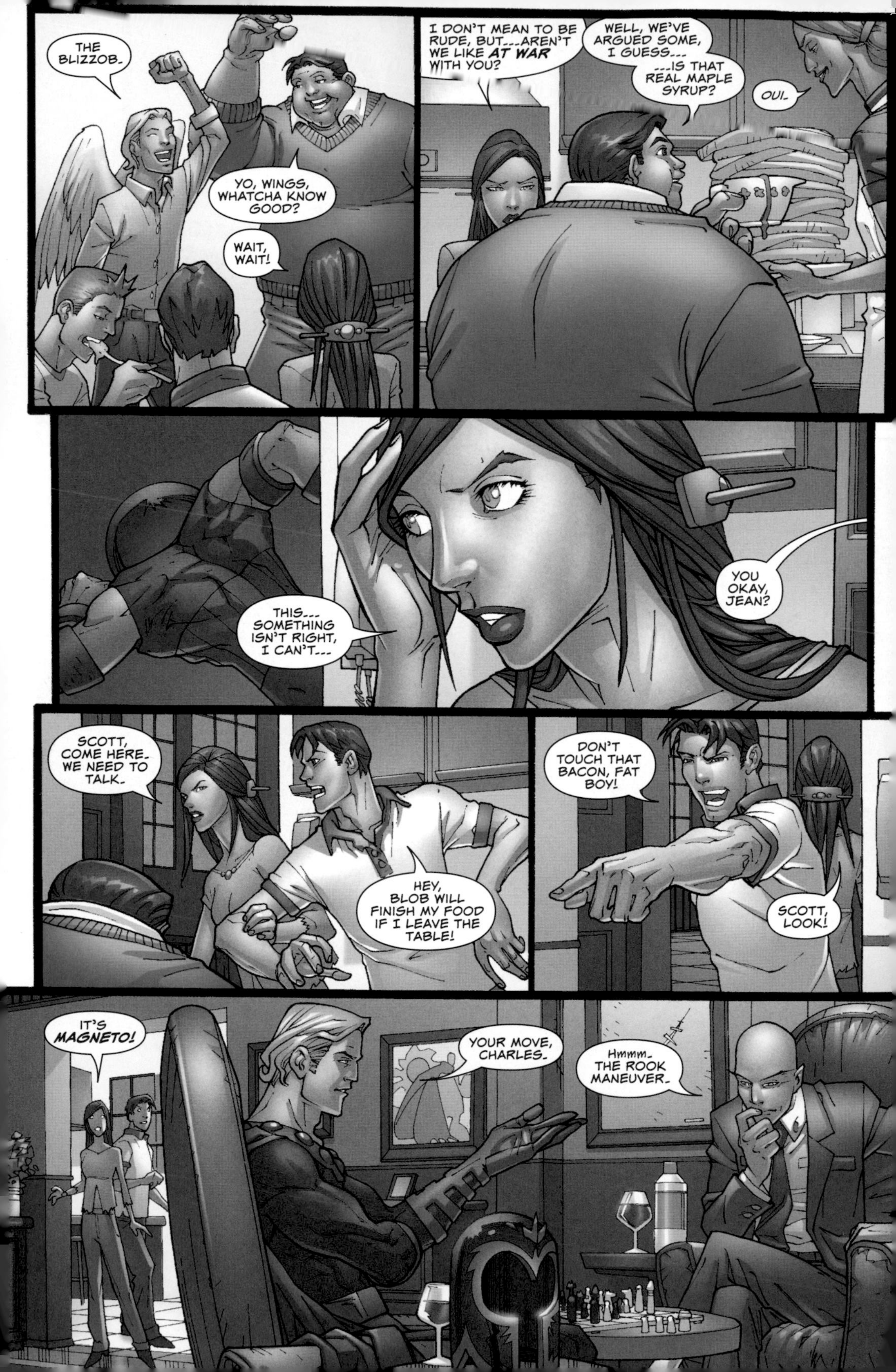

THE BLIZZOB.
YO, WINGS, WHATCHA KNOW GOOD?
WAIT, WAIT!
I DON'T MEAN TO BE RUDE, BUT... AREN'T WE LIKE AT WAR WITH YOU?
WELL, WE'VE ARGUED SOME, I GUESS... ...IS THAT REAL MAPLE SYRUP?
OUI.
THIS... SOMETHING ISN'T RIGHT, I CAN'T...
YOU OKAY, JEAN?
SCOTT, COME HERE. WE NEED TO TALK.
HEY, BLOB WILL FINISH MY FOOD IF I LEAVE THE TABLE!
DON'T TOUCH THAT BACON, FAT BOY!
SCOTT, LOOK!
IT'S MAGNETO!
YOUR MOVE, CHARLES.
Hmmm. THE ROOK MANEUVER.

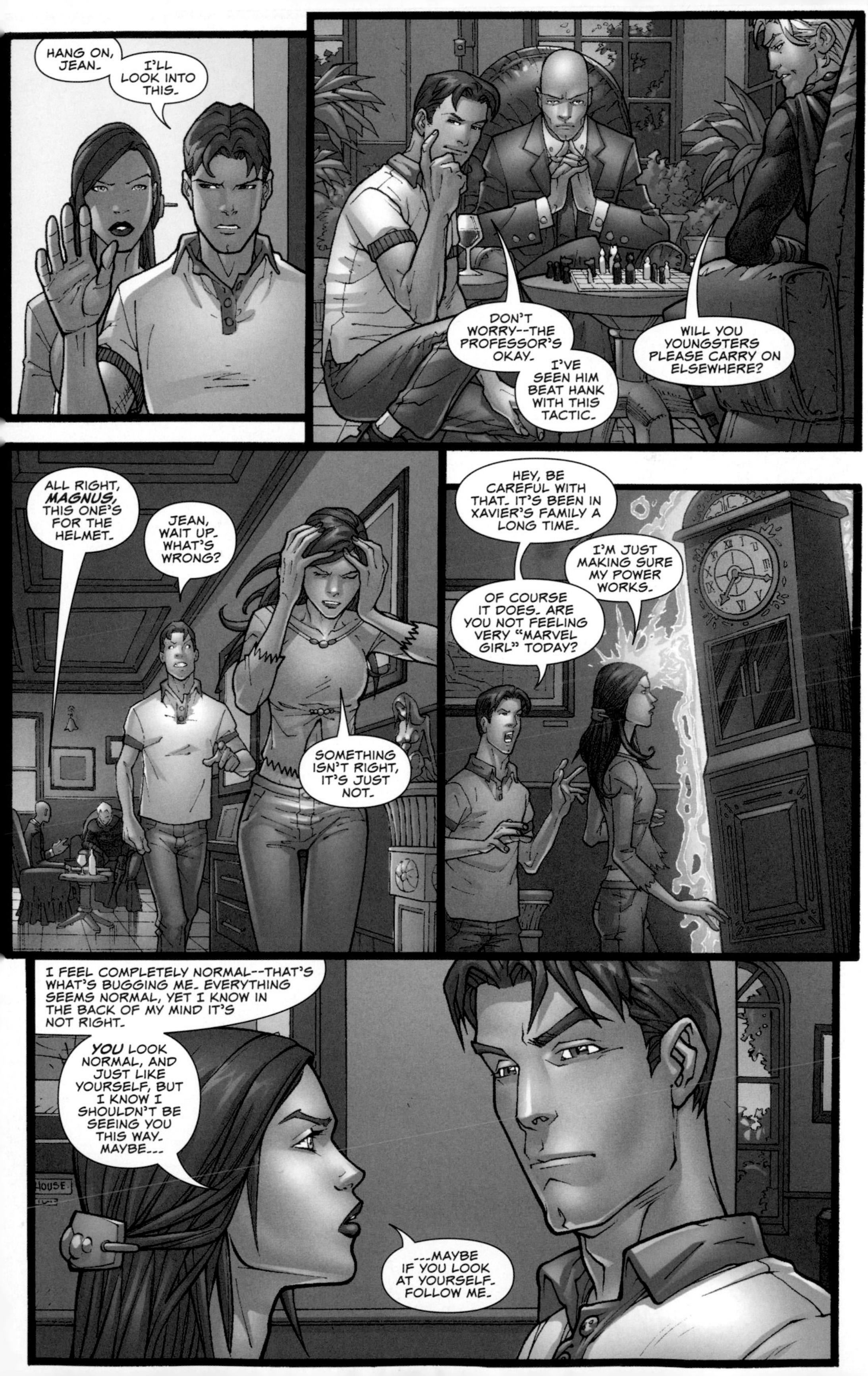
HANG ON, JEAN.
I'LL LOOK INTO THIS.
DON'T WORRY--THE PROFESSOR'S OKAY.
I'VE SEEN HIM BEAT HANK WITH THIS TACTIC.
WILL YOU YOUNGSTERS PLEASE CARRY ON ELSEWHERE?
ALL RIGHT, MAGNUS, THIS ONE'S FOR THE HELMET.
JEAN, WAIT UP. WHAT'S WRONG?
SOMETHING ISN'T RIGHT, IT'S JUST NOT.
HEY, BE CAREFUL WITH THAT. IT'S BEEN IN XAVIER'S FAMILY A LONG TIME.
I'M JUST MAKING SURE MY POWER WORKS.
OF COURSE IT DOES. ARE YOU NOT FEELING VERY "MARVEL GIRL" TODAY?
I FEEL COMPLETELY NORMAL--THAT'S WHAT'S BUGGING ME. EVERYTHING SEEMS NORMAL, YET I KNOW IN THE BACK OF MY MIND IT'S NOT RIGHT.
YOU LOOK NORMAL, AND JUST LIKE YOURSELF, BUT I KNOW I SHOULDN'T BE SEEING YOU THIS WAY. MAYBE...
...MAYBE IF YOU LOOK AT YOURSELF. FOLLOW ME.

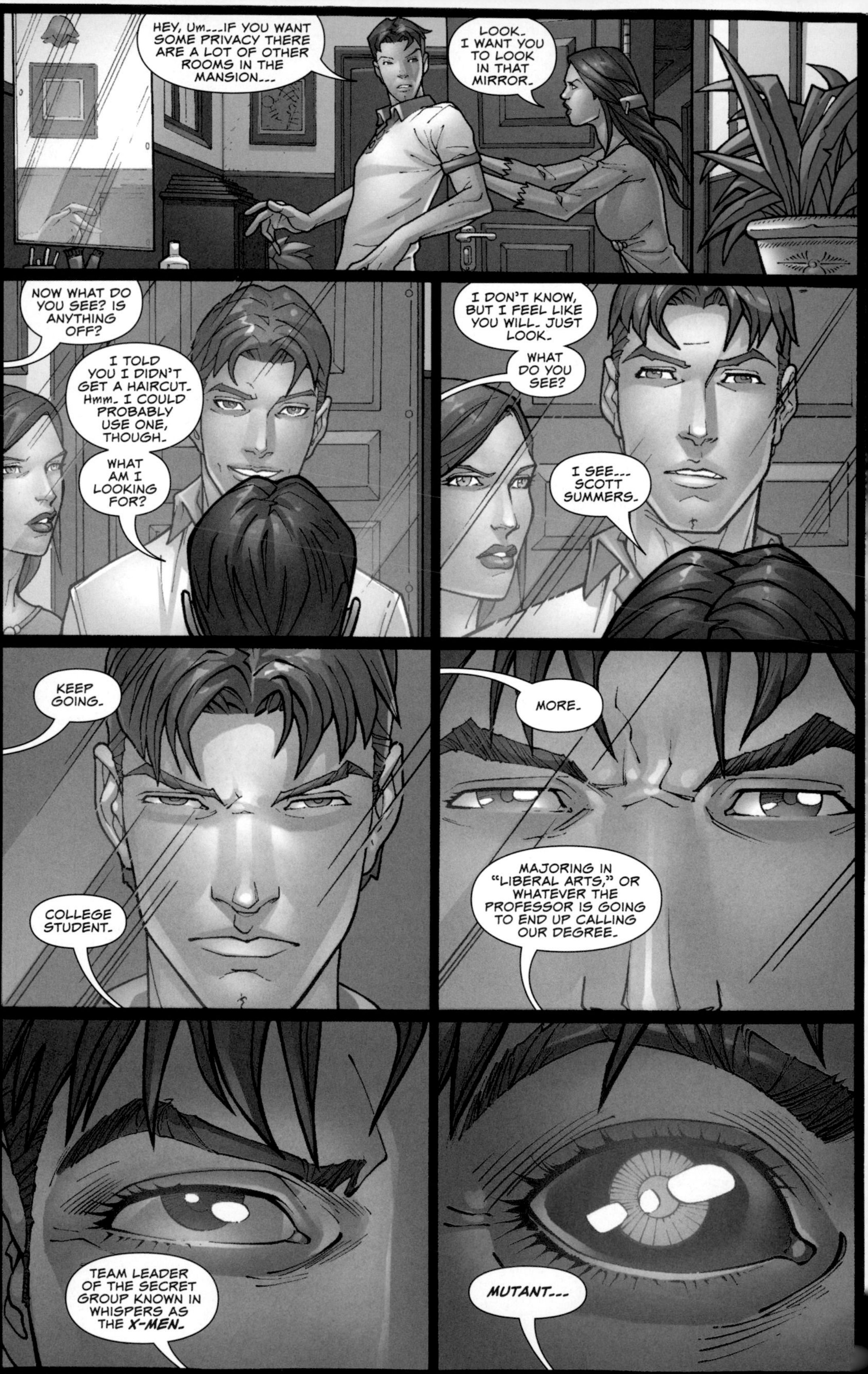
HEY, Um...IF YOU WANT SOME PRIVACY THERE ARE A LOT OF OTHER ROOMS IN THE MANSION...
LOOK. I WANT YOU TO LOOK IN THAT MIRROR.
NOW WHAT DO YOU SEE? IS ANYTHING OFF?
I TOLD YOU I DIDN'T GET A HAIRCUT. Hmm. I COULD PROBABLY USE ONE, THOUGH.
WHAT AM I LOOKING FOR?
I DON'T KNOW, BUT I FEEL LIKE YOU WILL. JUST LOOK.
WHAT DO YOU SEE?
I SEE... SCOTT SUMMERS.
KEEP GOING.
COLLEGE STUDENT.
MORE.
MAJORING IN "LIBERAL ARTS," OR WHATEVER THE PROFESSOR IS GOING TO END UP CALLING OUR DEGREE.
TEAM LEADER OF THE SECRET GROUP KNOWN IN WHISPERS AS THE X-MEN.
MUTANT...

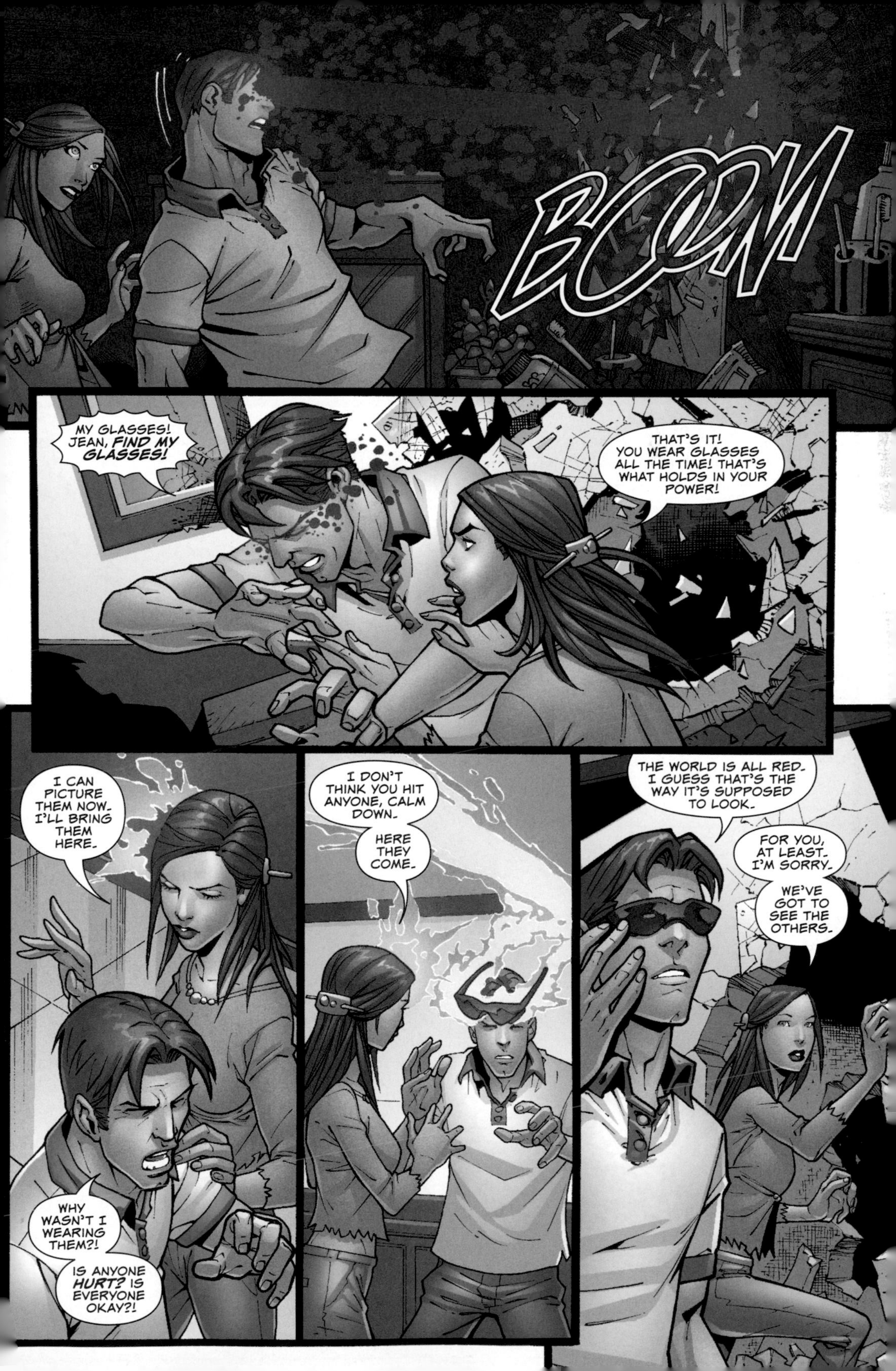
BOOM
MY GLASSES! JEAN, FIND MY GLASSES!
THAT'S IT! YOU WEAR GLASSES ALL THE TIME! THAT'S WHAT HOLDS IN YOUR POWER!
I CAN PICTURE THEM NOW. I'LL BRING THEM HERE.
WHY WASN'T I WEARING THEM?!
IS ANYONE HURT? IS EVERYONE OKAY?!
I DON'T THINK YOU HIT ANYONE, CALM DOWN.
HERE THEY COME.
THE WORLD IS ALL RED. I GUESS THAT'S THE WAY IT'S SUPPOSED TO LOOK.
FOR YOU, AT LEAST. I'M SORRY.
WE'VE GOT TO SEE THE OTHERS.

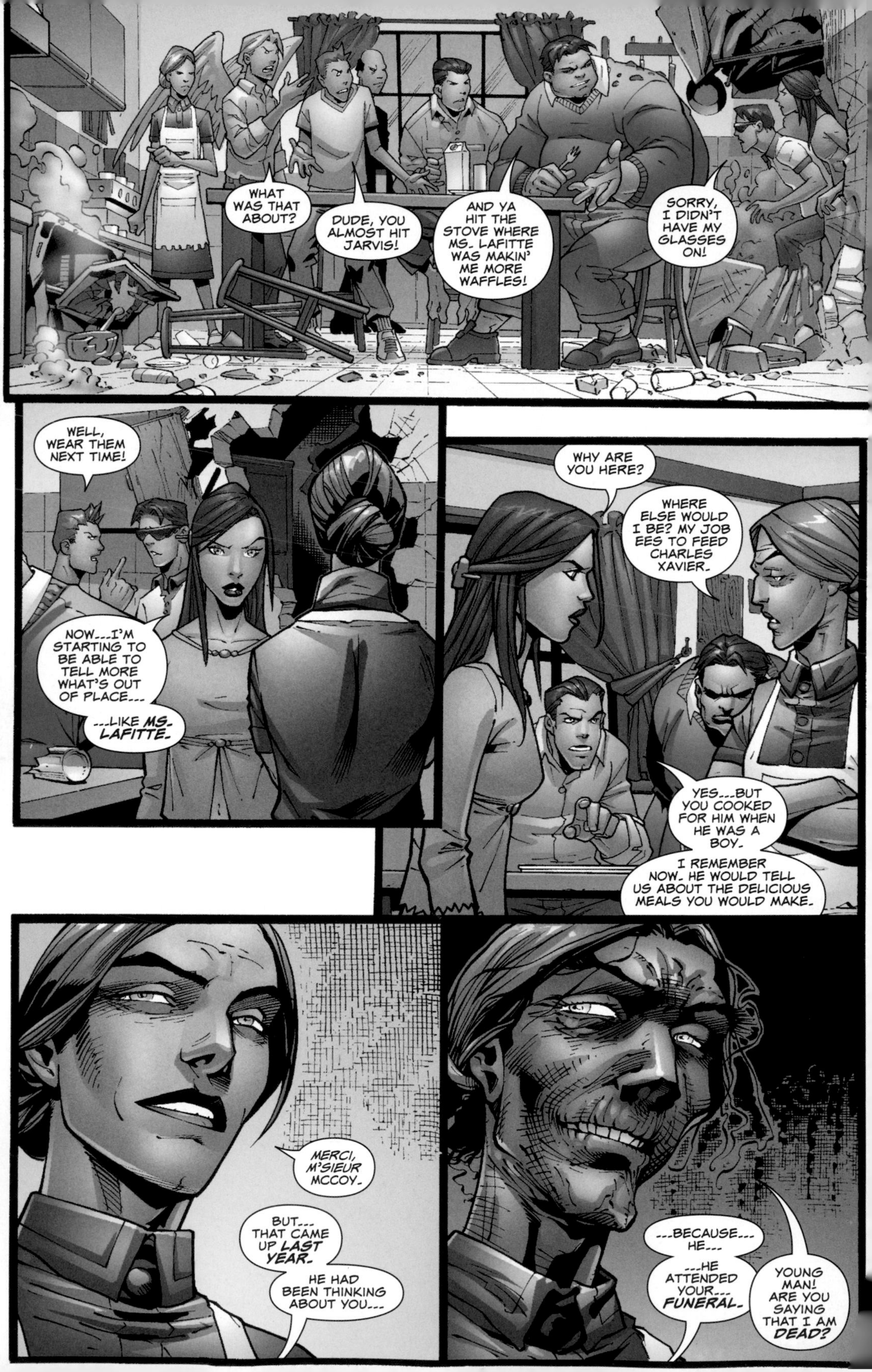
WHAT WAS THAT ABOUT?
DUDE, YOU ALMOST HIT JARVIS!
AND YA HIT THE STOVE WHERE MS. LAFITTE WAS MAKIN' ME MORE WAFFLES!
SORRY, I DIDN'T HAVE MY GLASSES ON!
WELL, WEAR THEM NEXT TIME!
NOW... I'M STARTING TO BE ABLE TO TELL MORE WHAT'S OUT OF PLACE...
...LIKE MS. LAFITTE.
WHY ARE YOU HERE?
WHERE ELSE WOULD I BE? MY JOB EES TO FEED CHARLES XAVIER.
YES... BUT YOU COOKED FOR HIM WHEN HE WAS A BOY.
I REMEMBER NOW. HE WOULD TELL US ABOUT THE DELICIOUS MEALS YOU WOULD MAKE.
MERCI, M'SIEUR MCCOY.
BUT... THAT CAME UP LAST YEAR.
HE HAD BEEN THINKING ABOUT YOU...
...BECAUSE... HE...
...HE ATTENDED YOUR... FUNERAL.
YOUNG MAN! ARE YOU SAYING THAT I AM DEAD?

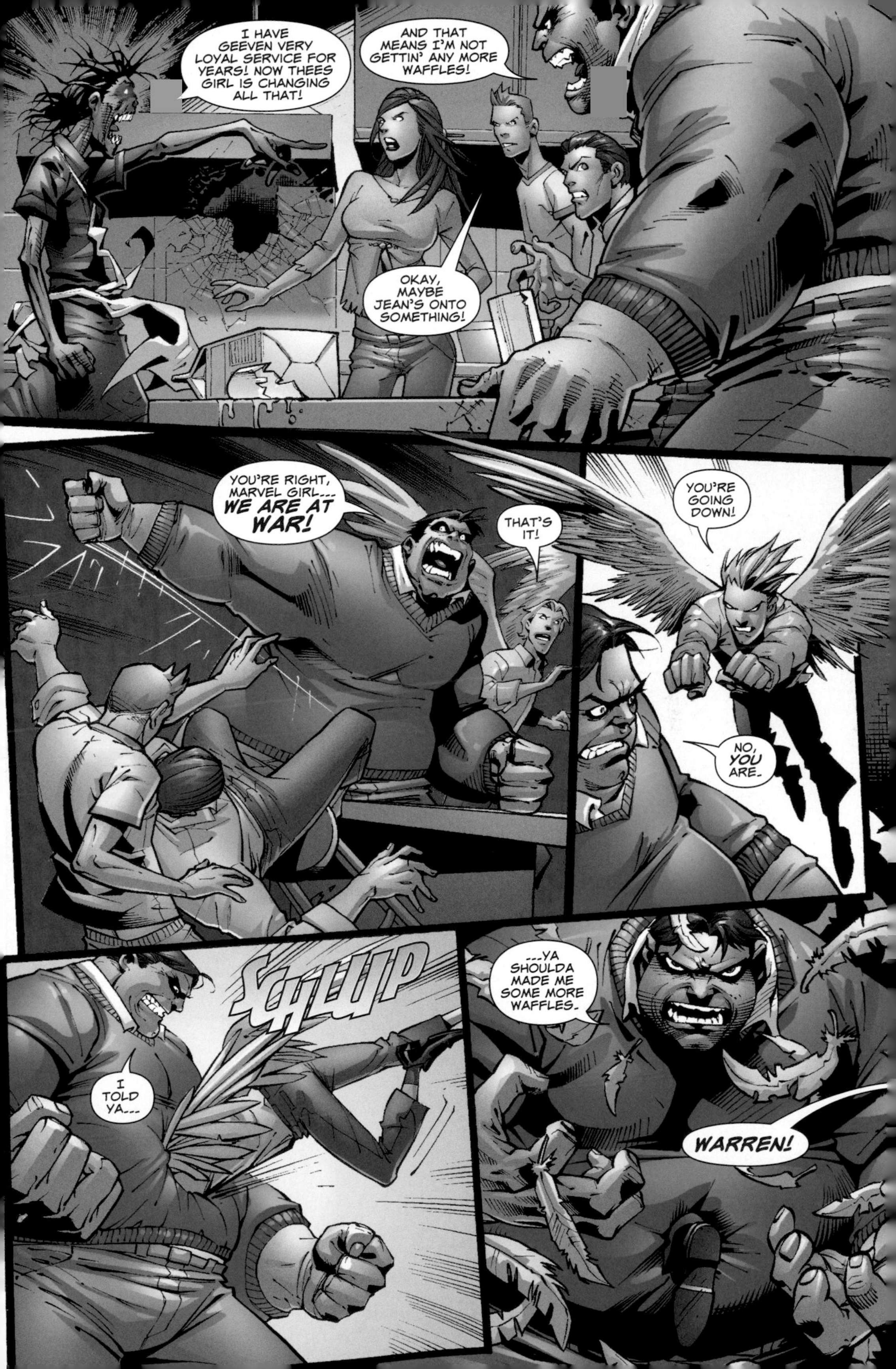
I HAVE GEEVEN VERY LOYAL SERVICE FOR YEARS! NOW THEES GIRL IS CHANGING ALL THAT!
AND THAT MEANS I'M NOT GETTIN' ANY MORE WAFFLES!
OKAY, MAYBE JEAN'S ONTO SOMETHING!
YOU'RE RIGHT, MARVEL GIRL... WE ARE AT WAR!
THAT'S IT!
YOU'RE GOING DOWN!
NO, YOU ARE.
SCHLUP
I TOLD YA...
...YA SHOULDA MADE ME SOME MORE WAFFLES.
WARREN!

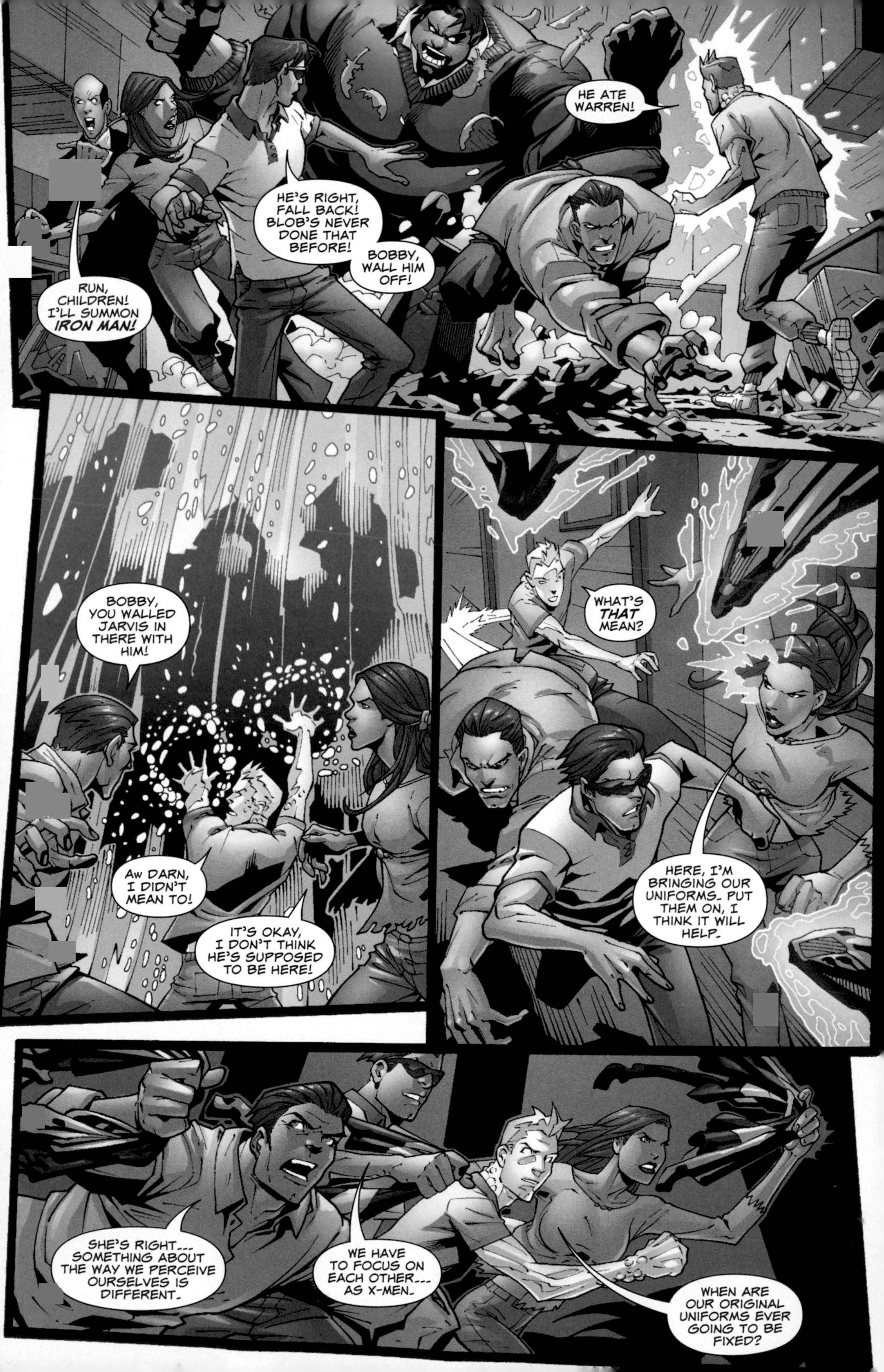
RUN, CHILDREN! I'LL SUMMON IRON MAN!
HE'S RIGHT, FALL BACK! BLOB'S NEVER DONE THAT BEFORE!
BOBBY, WALL HIM OFF!
HE ATE WARREN!
BOBBY, YOU WALLED JARVIS IN THERE WITH HIM!
AW DARN, I DIDN'T MEAN TO!
IT'S OKAY, I DON'T THINK HE'S SUPPOSED TO BE HERE!
WHAT'S THAT MEAN?
HERE, I'M BRINGING OUR UNIFORMS. PUT THEM ON, I THINK IT WILL HELP.
SHE'S RIGHT... SOMETHING ABOUT THE WAY WE PERCEIVE OURSELVES IS DIFFERENT.
WE HAVE TO FOCUS ON EACH OTHER... AS X-MEN.
WHEN ARE OUR ORIGINAL UNIFORMS EVER GOING TO BE FIXED?

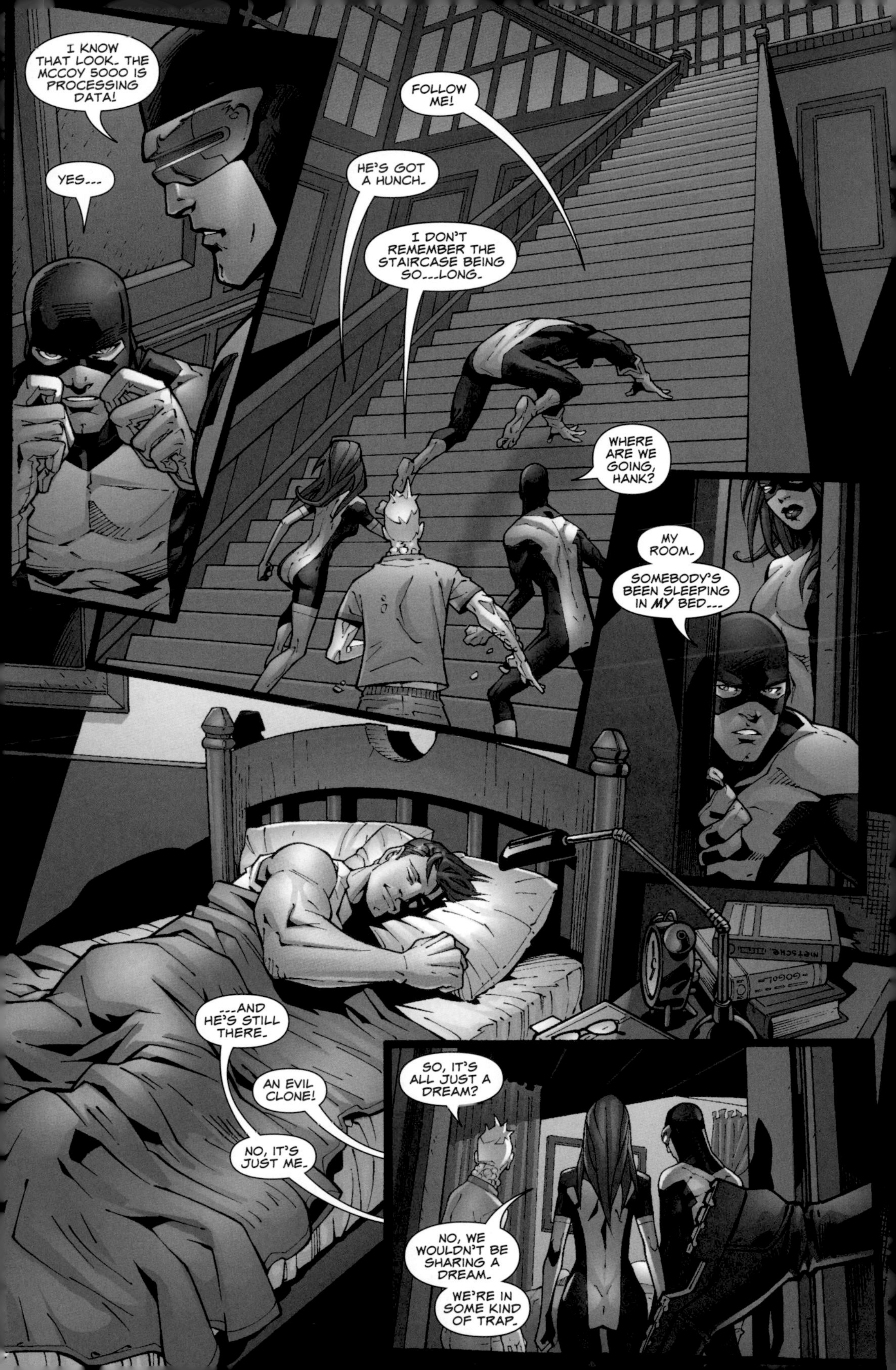
I KNOW THAT LOOK. THE MCCOY 5000 IS PROCESSING DATA!
YES...
FOLLOW ME!
HE'S GOT A HUNCH.
I DON'T REMEMBER THE STAIRCASE BEING SO...LONG.
WHERE ARE WE GOING, HANK?
MY ROOM.
SOMEBODY'S BEEN SLEEPING IN *MY* BED...
NIETSCHE
GOGOL
...AND HE'S STILL THERE.
AN EVIL CLONE!
NO, IT'S JUST ME.
SO, IT'S ALL JUST A DREAM?
NO, WE WOULDN'T BE SHARING A DREAM.
WE'RE IN SOME KIND OF TRAP.

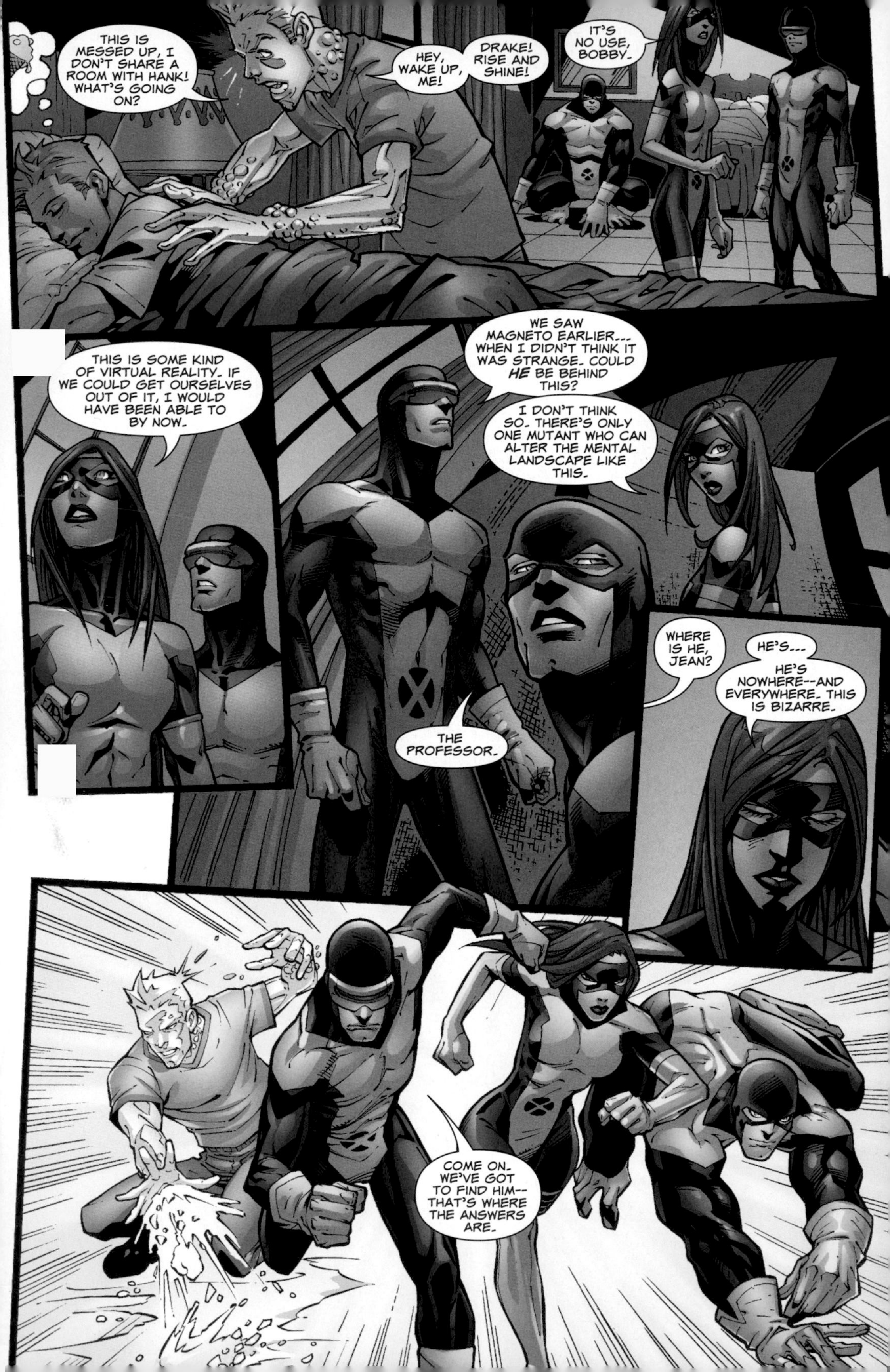
THIS IS MESSED UP, I DON'T SHARE A ROOM WITH HANK! WHAT'S GOING ON?
HEY, WAKE UP, ME!
DRAKE! RISE AND SHINE!
IT'S NO USE, BOBBY.
THIS IS SOME KIND OF VIRTUAL REALITY. IF WE COULD GET OURSELVES OUT OF IT, I WOULD HAVE BEEN ABLE TO BY NOW.
WE SAW MAGNETO EARLIER... WHEN I DIDN'T THINK IT WAS STRANGE. COULD HE BE BEHIND THIS?
I DON'T THINK SO. THERE'S ONLY ONE MUTANT WHO CAN ALTER THE MENTAL LANDSCAPE LIKE THIS.
THE PROFESSOR.
WHERE IS HE, JEAN?
HE'S...
HE'S NOWHERE--AND EVERYWHERE. THIS IS BIZARRE.
COME ON. WE'VE GOT TO FIND HIM-- THAT'S WHERE THE ANSWERS ARE.

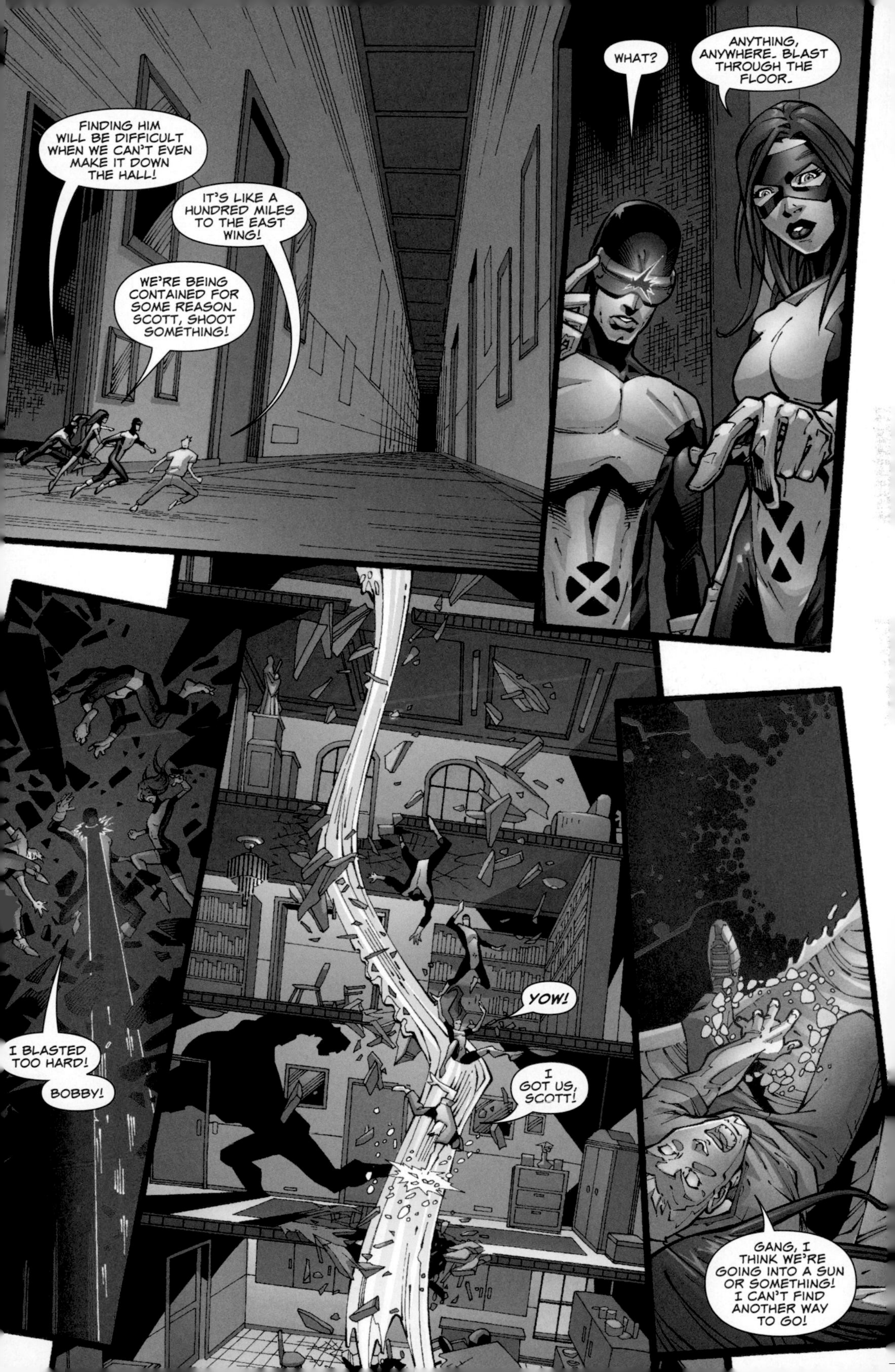

FINDING HIM WILL BE DIFFICULT WHEN WE CAN'T EVEN MAKE IT DOWN THE HALL!
IT'S LIKE A HUNDRED MILES TO THE EAST WING!
WE'RE BEING CONTAINED FOR SOME REASON. SCOTT, SHOOT SOMETHING!
WHAT?
ANYTHING, ANYWHERE. BLAST THROUGH THE FLOOR.
I BLASTED TOO HARD!
BOBBY!
YOW!
I GOT US, SCOTT!
GANG, I THINK WE'RE GOING INTO A SUN OR SOMETHING! I CAN'T FIND ANOTHER WAY TO GO!

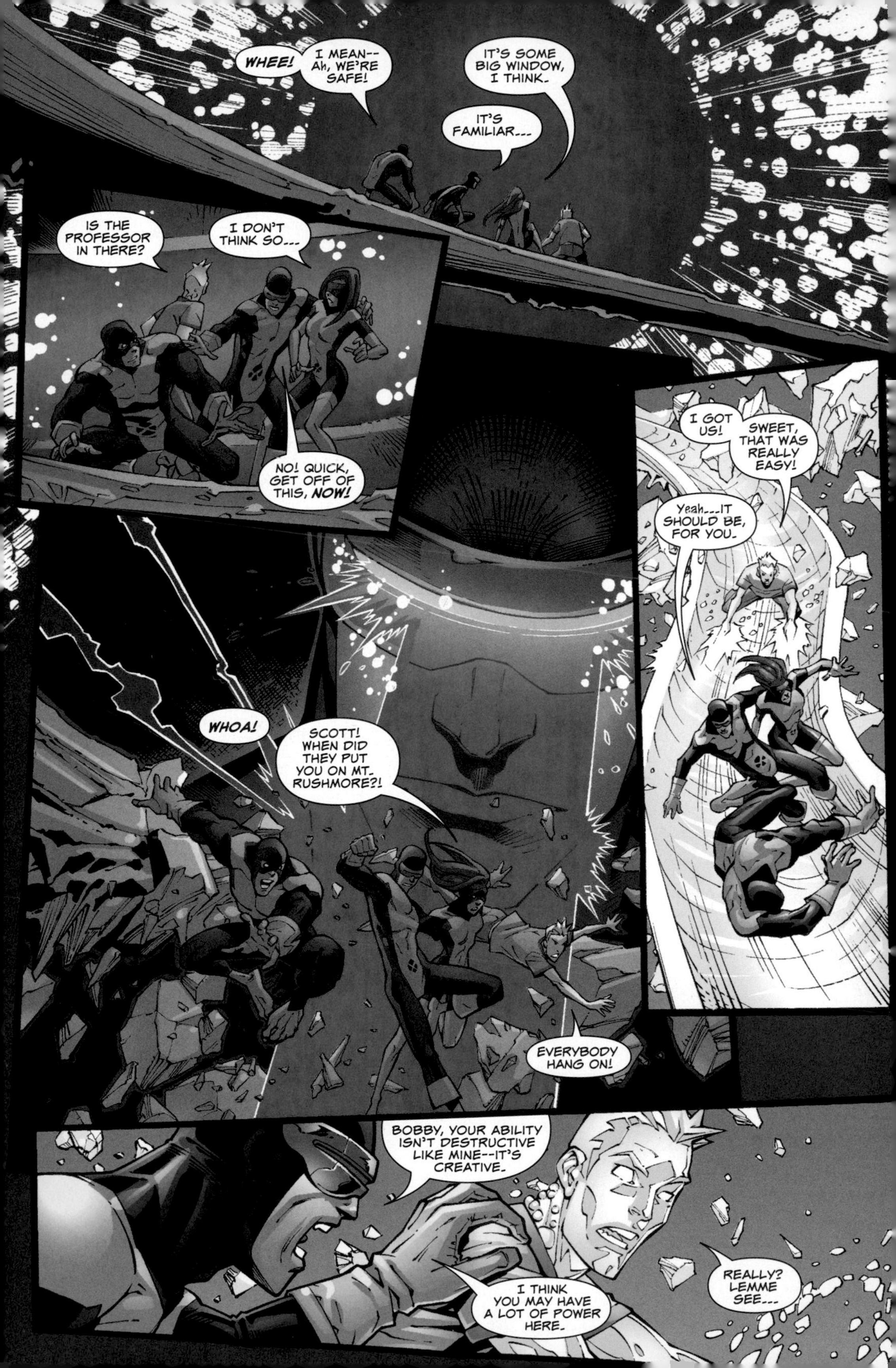

WHEE!
I MEAN-- Ah, WE'RE SAFE!
IT'S SOME BIG WINDOW, I THINK.
IT'S FAMILIAR...
IS THE PROFESSOR IN THERE?
I DON'T THINK SO...
NO! QUICK, GET OFF OF THIS, NOW!
WHOA!
SCOTT! WHEN DID THEY PUT YOU ON MT. RUSHMORE?!
EVERYBODY HANG ON!
I GOT US!
SWEET, THAT WAS REALLY EASY!
Yeah...IT SHOULD BE, FOR YOU.
BOBBY, YOUR ABILITY ISN'T DESTRUCTIVE LIKE MINE--IT'S CREATIVE.
I THINK YOU MAY HAVE A LOT OF POWER HERE.
REALLY? LEMME SEE...

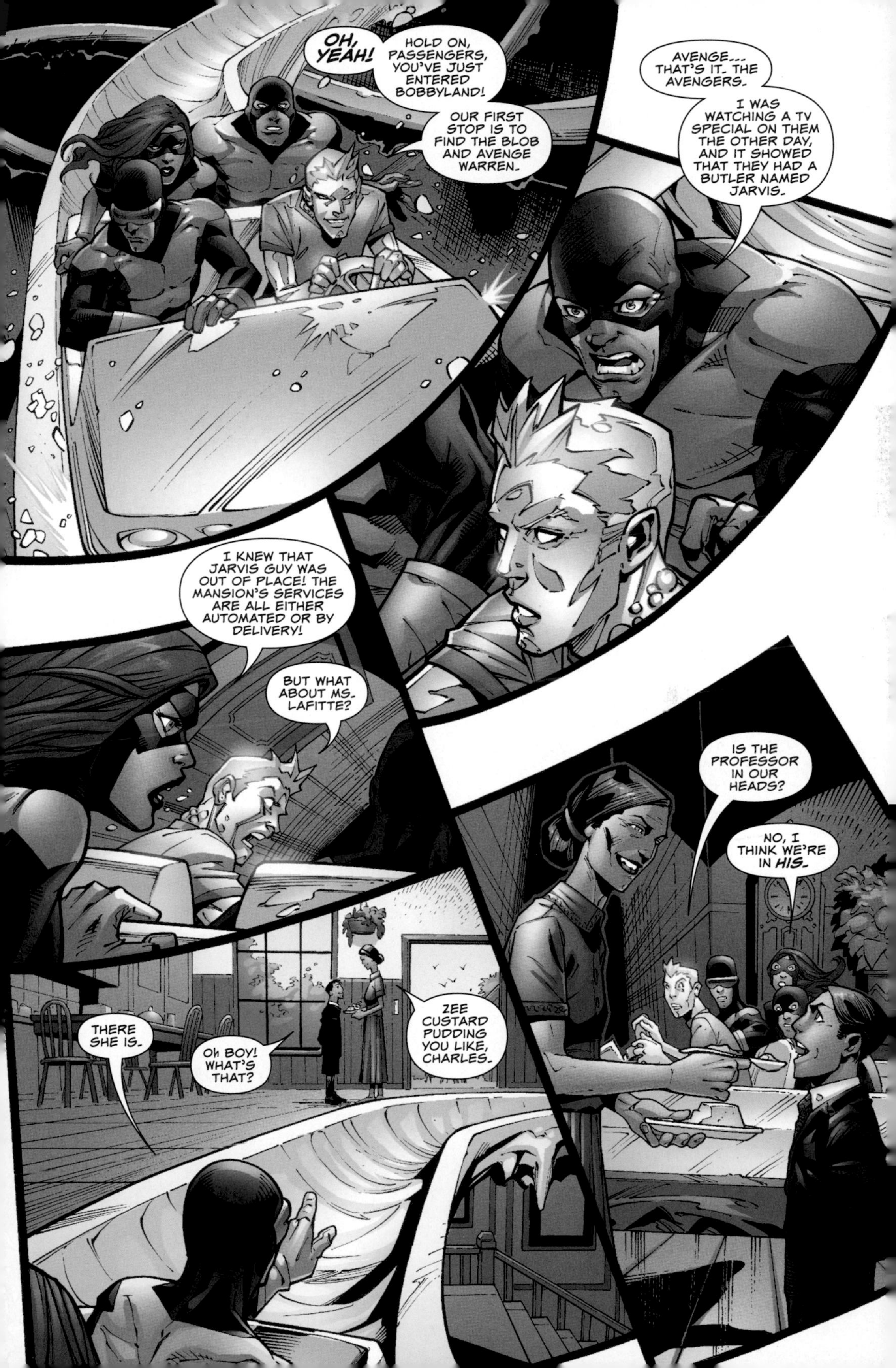
OH, YEAH!
HOLD ON, PASSENGERS, YOU'VE JUST ENTERED BOBBYLAND!
OUR FIRST STOP IS TO FIND THE BLOB AND AVENGE WARREN.
AVENGE... THAT'S IT. THE AVENGERS.
I WAS WATCHING A TV SPECIAL ON THEM THE OTHER DAY, AND IT SHOWED THAT THEY HAD A BUTLER NAMED JARVIS.
I KNEW THAT JARVIS GUY WAS OUT OF PLACE! THE MANSION'S SERVICES ARE ALL EITHER AUTOMATED OR BY DELIVERY!
BUT WHAT ABOUT MS. LAFITTE?
IS THE PROFESSOR IN OUR HEADS?
NO, I THINK WE'RE IN HIS.
THERE SHE IS.
Oh BOY! WHAT'S THAT?
ZEE CUSTARD PUDDING YOU LIKE, CHARLES.

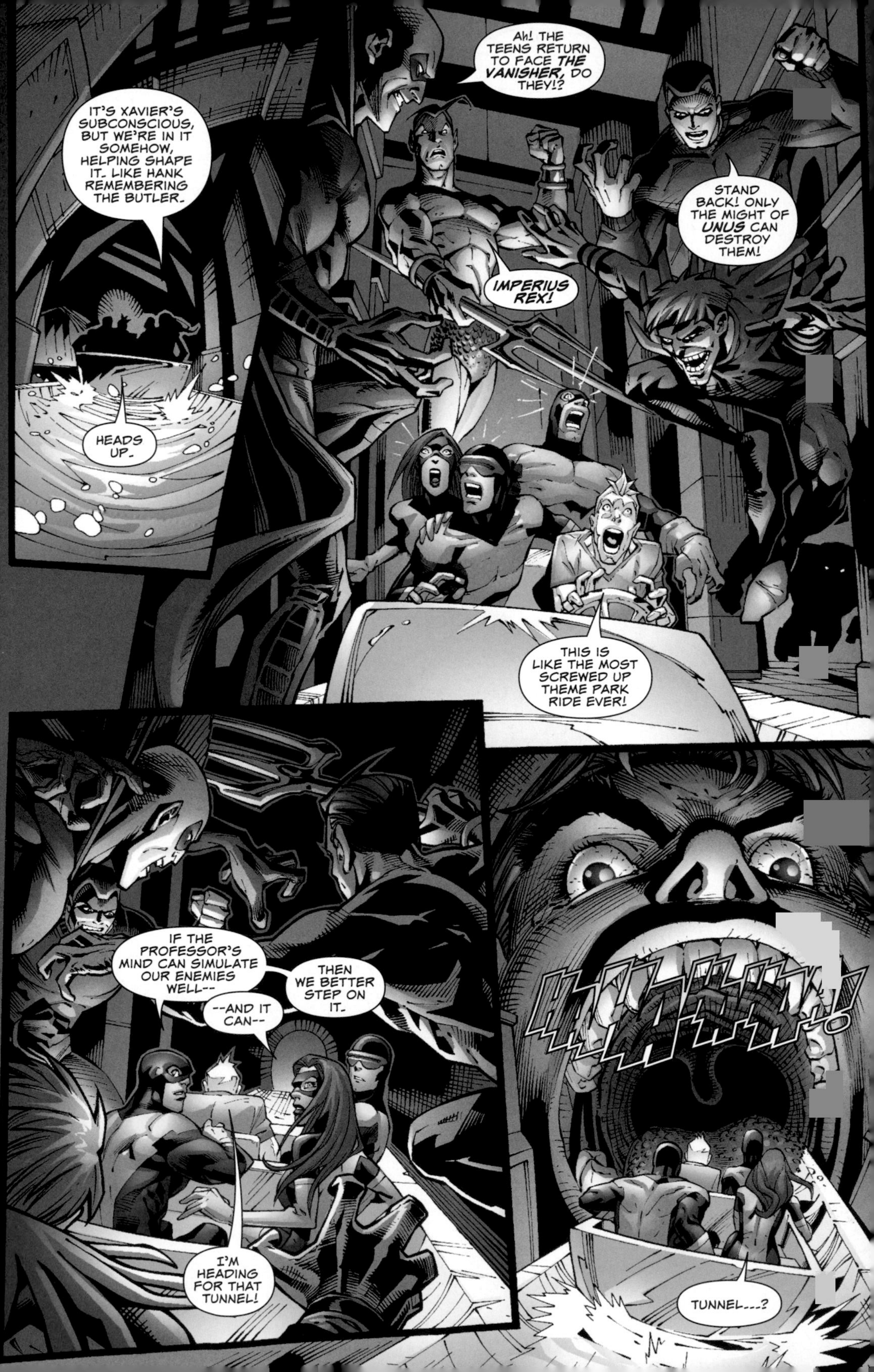
IT'S XAVIER'S SUBCONSCIOUS, BUT WE'RE IN IT SOMEHOW, HELPING SHAPE IT. LIKE HANK REMEMBERING THE BUTLER.
HEADS UP.
Ah! THE TEENS RETURN TO FACE THE VANISHER, DO THEY!?
IMPERIUS REX!
STAND BACK! ONLY THE MIGHT OF UNUS CAN DESTROY THEM!
THIS IS LIKE THE MOST SCREWED UP THEME PARK RIDE EVER!
IF THE PROFESSOR'S MIND CAN SIMULATE OUR ENEMIES WELL--
--AND IT CAN--
THEN WE BETTER STEP ON IT.
I'M HEADING FOR THAT TUNNEL!
TUNNEL...?

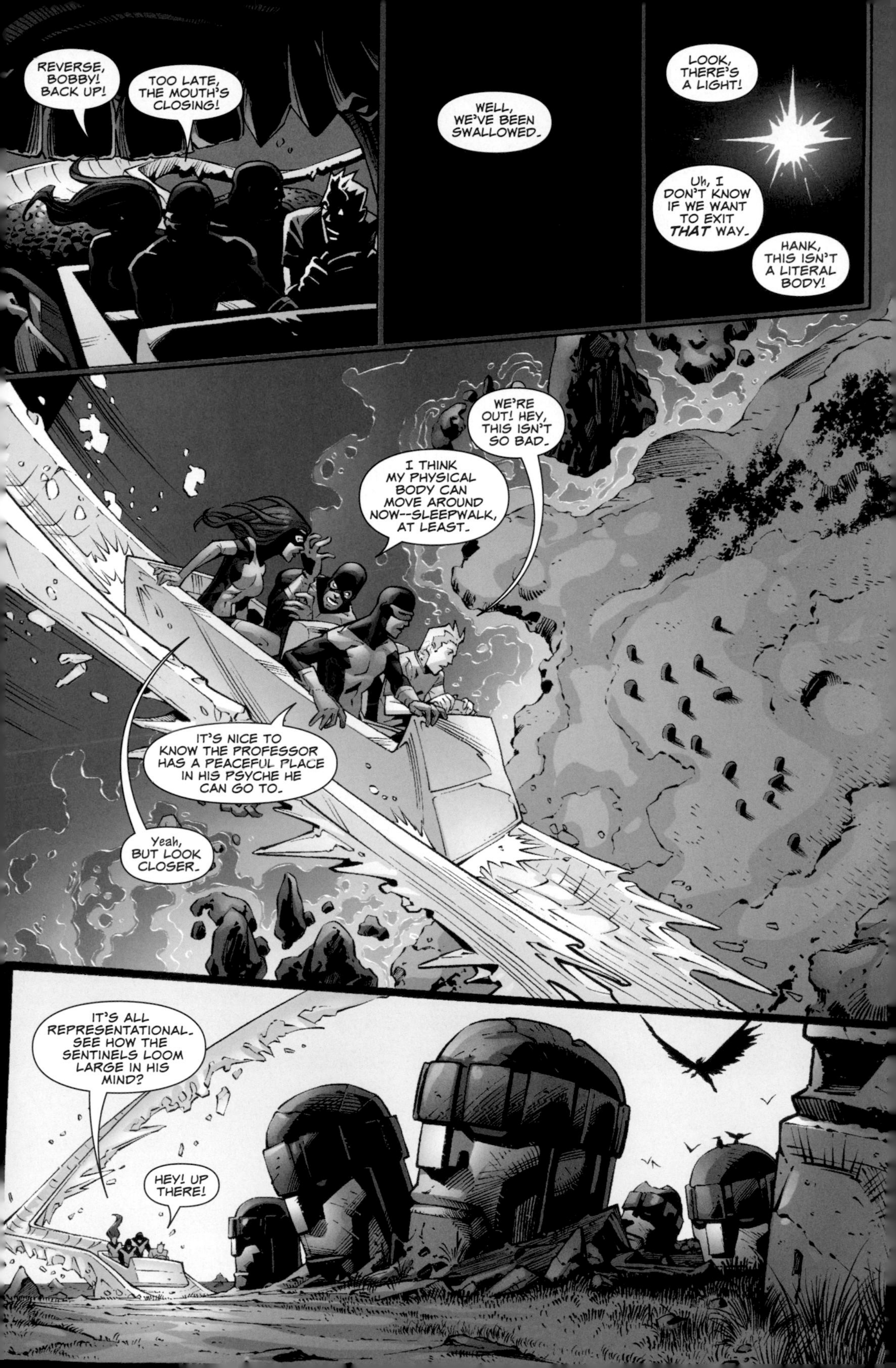
REVERSE, BOBBY! BACK UP!
TOO LATE, THE MOUTH'S CLOSING!
WELL, WE'VE BEEN SWALLOWED...
LOOK, THERE'S A LIGHT!
Uh, I DON'T KNOW IF WE WANT TO EXIT THAT WAY...
HANK, THIS ISN'T A LITERAL BODY!
WE'RE OUT! HEY, THIS ISN'T SO BAD...
I THINK MY PHYSICAL BODY CAN MOVE AROUND NOW--SLEEPWALK, AT LEAST...
IT'S NICE TO KNOW THE PROFESSOR HAS A PEACEFUL PLACE IN HIS PSYCHE HE CAN GO TO...
Yeah, BUT LOOK CLOSER...
IT'S ALL REPRESENTATIONAL... SEE HOW THE SENTINELS LOOM LARGE IN HIS MIND?
HEY! UP THERE!

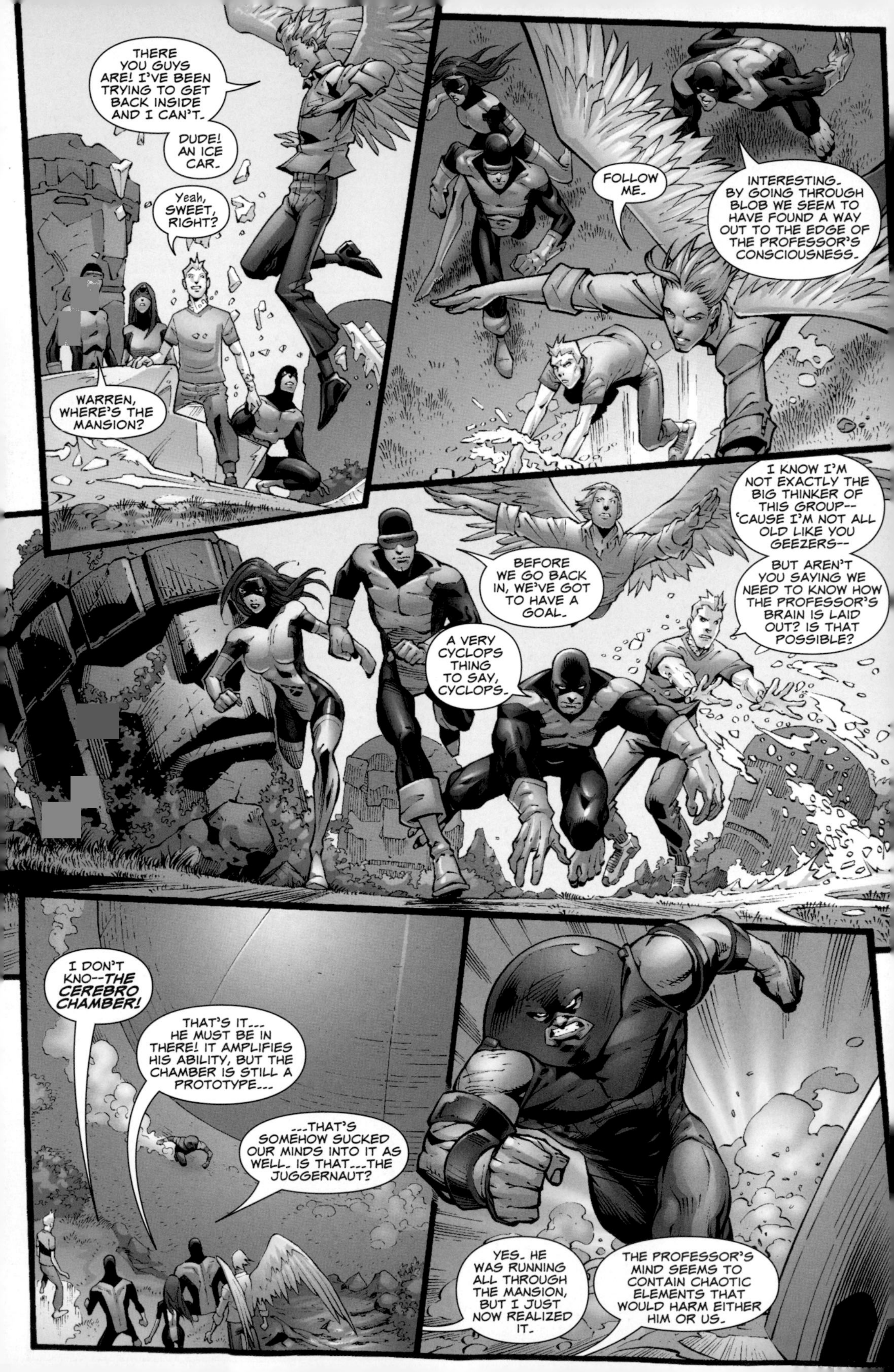
THERE YOU GUYS ARE! I'VE BEEN TRYING TO GET BACK INSIDE AND I CAN'T.
DUDE! AN ICE CAR.
Yeah, SWEET, RIGHT?
WARREN, WHERE'S THE MANSION?
FOLLOW ME.
INTERESTING. BY GOING THROUGH BLOB WE SEEM TO HAVE FOUND A WAY OUT TO THE EDGE OF THE PROFESSOR'S CONSCIOUSNESS.
BEFORE WE GO BACK IN, WE'VE GOT TO HAVE A GOAL.
A VERY CYCLOPS THING TO SAY, CYCLOPS.
I KNOW I'M NOT EXACTLY THE BIG THINKER OF THIS GROUP-- 'CAUSE I'M NOT ALL OLD LIKE YOU GEEZERS--
BUT AREN'T YOU SAYING WE NEED TO KNOW HOW THE PROFESSOR'S BRAIN IS LAID OUT? IS THAT POSSIBLE?
I DON'T KNO--*THE CEREBRO CHAMBER!*
THAT'S IT... HE MUST BE IN THERE! IT AMPLIFIES HIS ABILITY, BUT THE CHAMBER IS STILL A PROTOTYPE...
...THAT'S SOMEHOW SUCKED OUR MINDS INTO IT AS WELL. IS THAT... THE JUGGERNAUT?
YES. HE WAS RUNNING ALL THROUGH THE MANSION, BUT I JUST NOW REALIZED IT.
THE PROFESSOR'S MIND SEEMS TO CONTAIN CHAOTIC ELEMENTS THAT WOULD HARM EITHER HIM OR US.

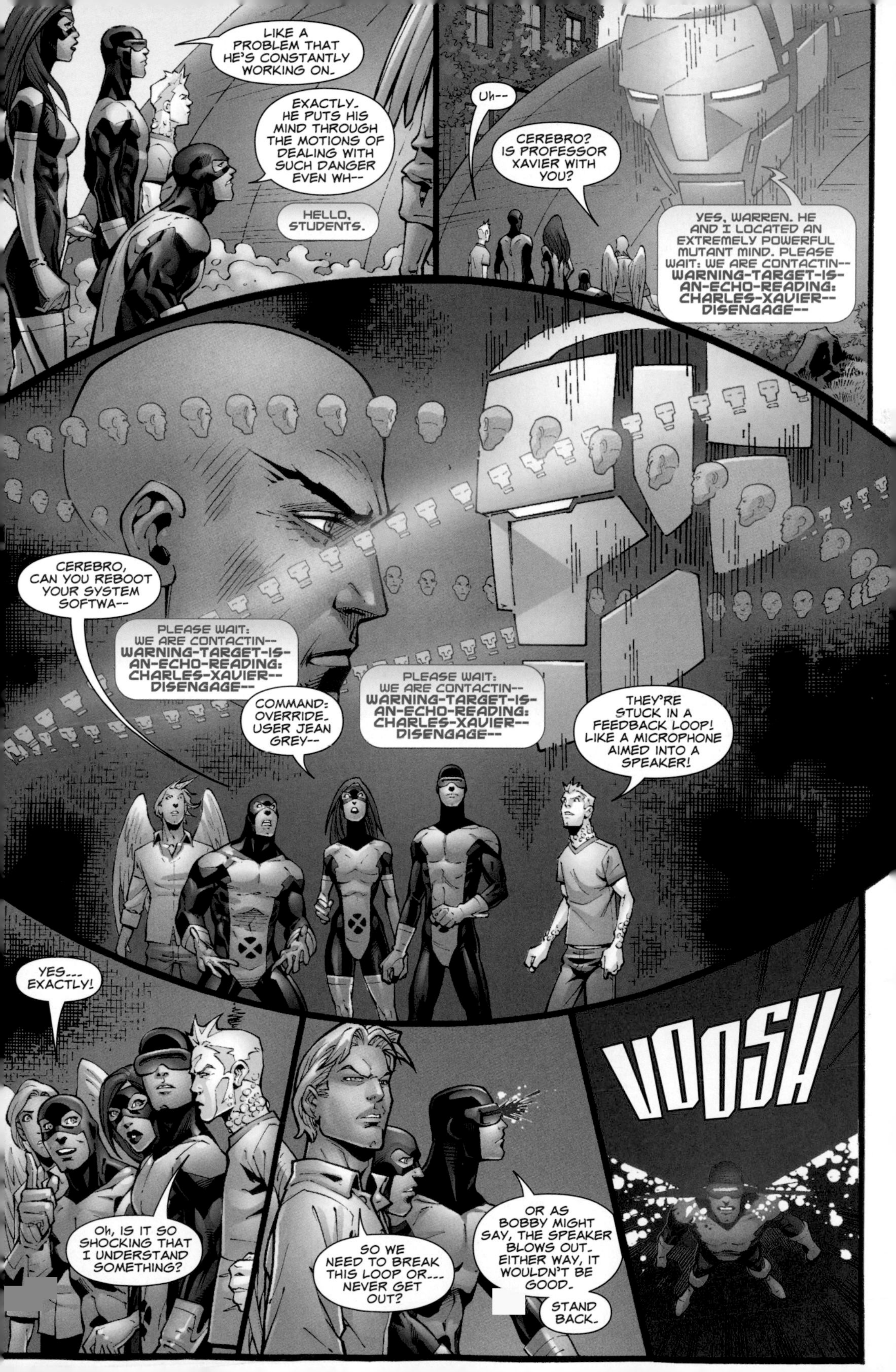
LIKE A PROBLEM THAT HE'S CONSTANTLY WORKING ON.
EXACTLY. HE PUTS HIS MIND THROUGH THE MOTIONS OF DEALING WITH SUCH DANGER EVEN WH--
HELLO, STUDENTS.
Uh--
CEREBRO? IS PROFESSOR XAVIER WITH YOU?
YES, WARREN. HE AND I LOCATED AN EXTREMELY POWERFUL MUTANT MIND. PLEASE WAIT: WE ARE CONTACTIN-- WARNING-TARGET-IS-AN-ECHO-READING: CHARLES-XAVIER-- DISENGAGE--
CEREBRO, CAN YOU REBOOT YOUR SYSTEM SOFTWA--
PLEASE WAIT: WE ARE CONTACTIN-- WARNING-TARGET-IS-AN-ECHO-READING: CHARLES-XAVIER-- DISENGAGE--
COMMAND: OVERRIDE. USER JEAN GREY--
PLEASE WAIT: WE ARE CONTACTIN-- WARNING-TARGET-IS-AN-ECHO-READING: CHARLES-XAVIER-- DISENGAGE--
THEY'RE STUCK IN A FEEDBACK LOOP! LIKE A MICROPHONE AIMED INTO A SPEAKER!
YES... EXACTLY!
Oh, IS IT SO SHOCKING THAT I UNDERSTAND SOMETHING?
SO WE NEED TO BREAK THIS LOOP OR... NEVER GET OUT?
OR AS BOBBY MIGHT SAY, THE SPEAKER BLOWS OUT. EITHER WAY, IT WOULDN'T BE GOOD.
STAND BACK.
VOOSH

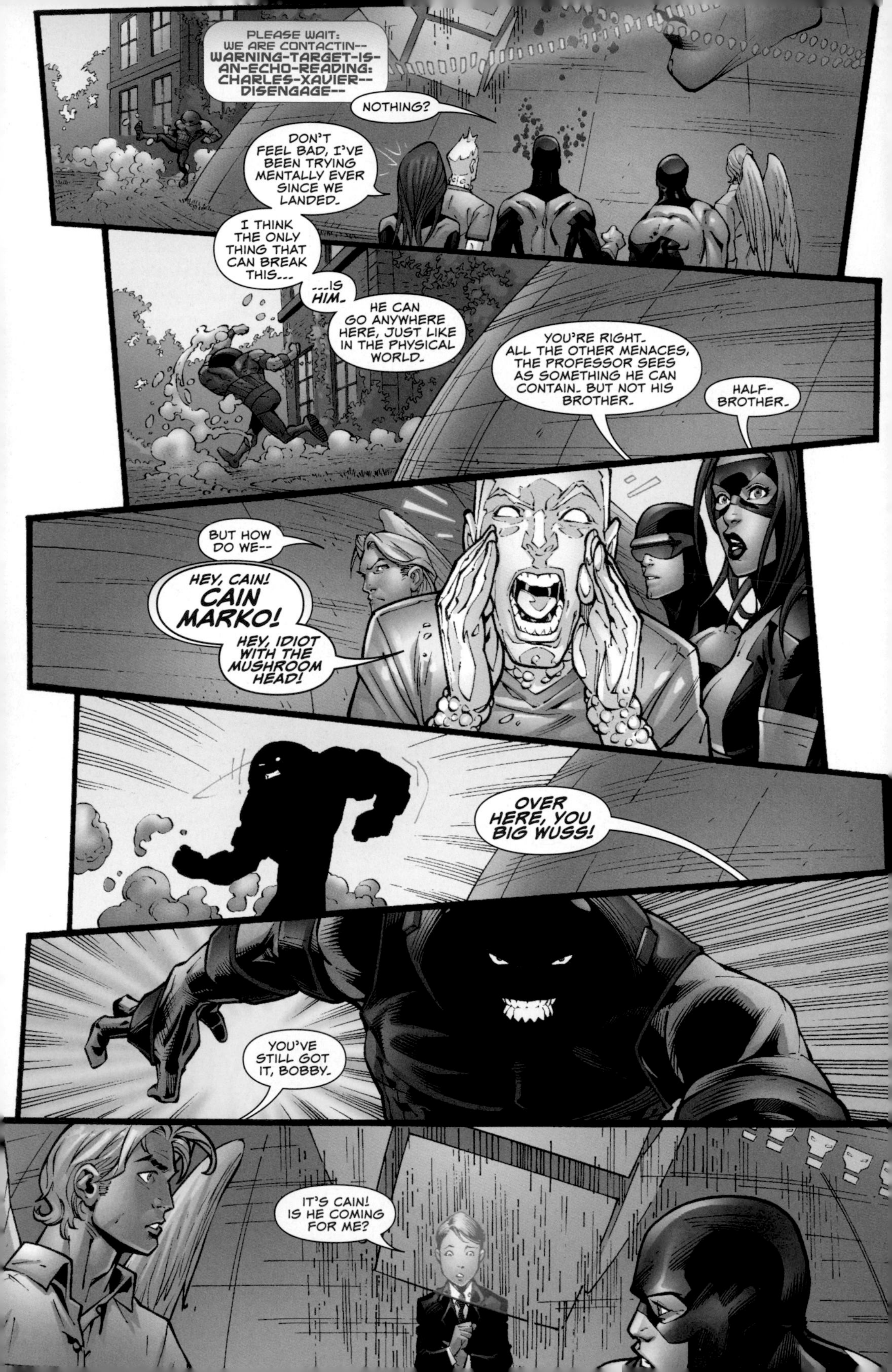
PLEASE WAIT: WE ARE CONTACTIN-- WARNING-TARGET-IS-AN-ECHO-READING: CHARLES-XAVIER-- DISENGAGE--
NOTHING?
DON'T FEEL BAD, I'VE BEEN TRYING MENTALLY EVER SINCE WE LANDED.
I THINK THE ONLY THING THAT CAN BREAK THIS...
...IS HIM.
HE CAN GO ANYWHERE HERE, JUST LIKE IN THE PHYSICAL WORLD.
YOU'RE RIGHT. ALL THE OTHER MENACES, THE PROFESSOR SEES AS SOMETHING HE CAN CONTAIN. BUT NOT HIS BROTHER.
HALF-BROTHER.
BUT HOW DO WE--
HEY, CAIN! CAIN MARKO!
HEY, IDIOT WITH THE MUSHROOM HEAD!
OVER HERE, YOU BIG WUSS!
YOU'VE STILL GOT IT, BOBBY.
IT'S CAIN! IS HE COMING FOR ME?

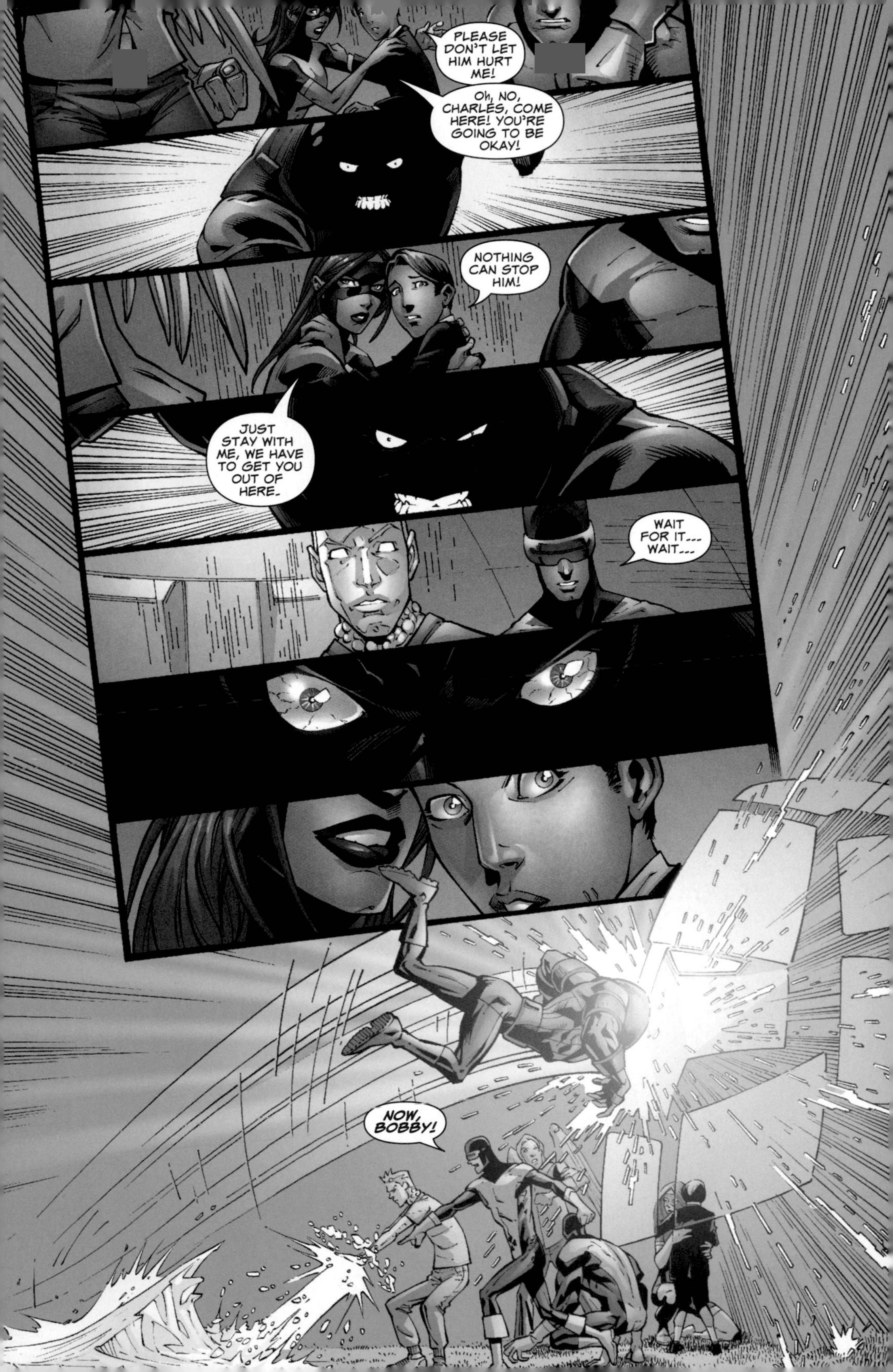
PLEASE DON'T LET HIM HURT ME!
OH, NO, CHARLES, COME HERE! YOU'RE GOING TO BE OKAY!
NOTHING CAN STOP HIM!
JUST STAY WITH ME, WE HAVE TO GET YOU OUT OF HERE.
WAIT FOR IT... WAIT...
NOW, BOBBY!

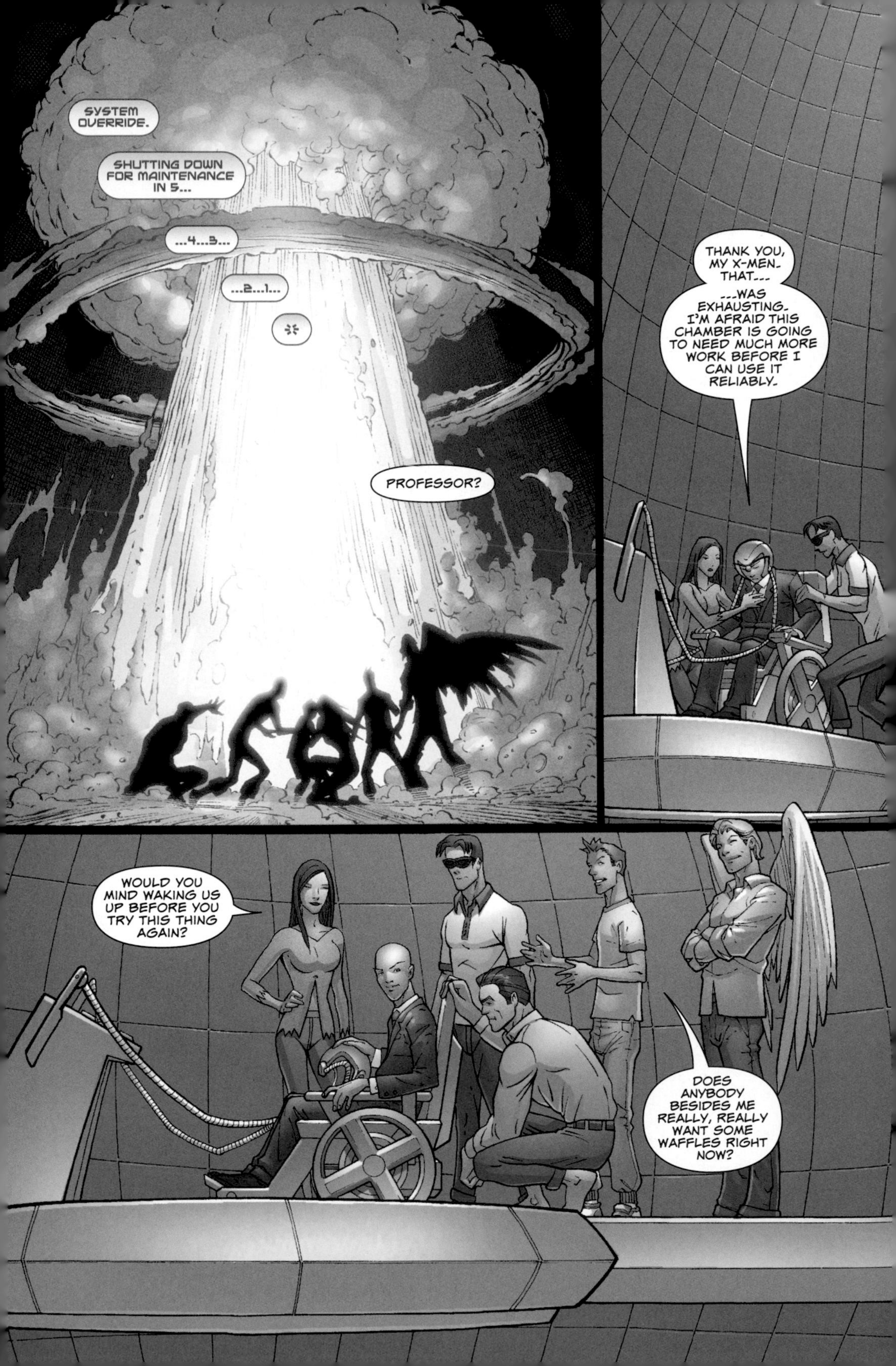
SYSTEM OVERRIDE.
SHUTTING DOWN FOR MAINTENANCE IN 5...
...4...3...
...2...1...
PROFESSOR?
THANK YOU, MY X-MEN. THAT...
...WAS EXHAUSTING. I'M AFRAID THIS CHAMBER IS GOING TO NEED MUCH MORE WORK BEFORE I CAN USE IT RELIABLY.
WOULD YOU MIND WAKING US UP BEFORE YOU TRY THIS THING AGAIN?
DOES ANYBODY BESIDES ME REALLY, REALLY WANT SOME WAFFLES RIGHT NOW?

4

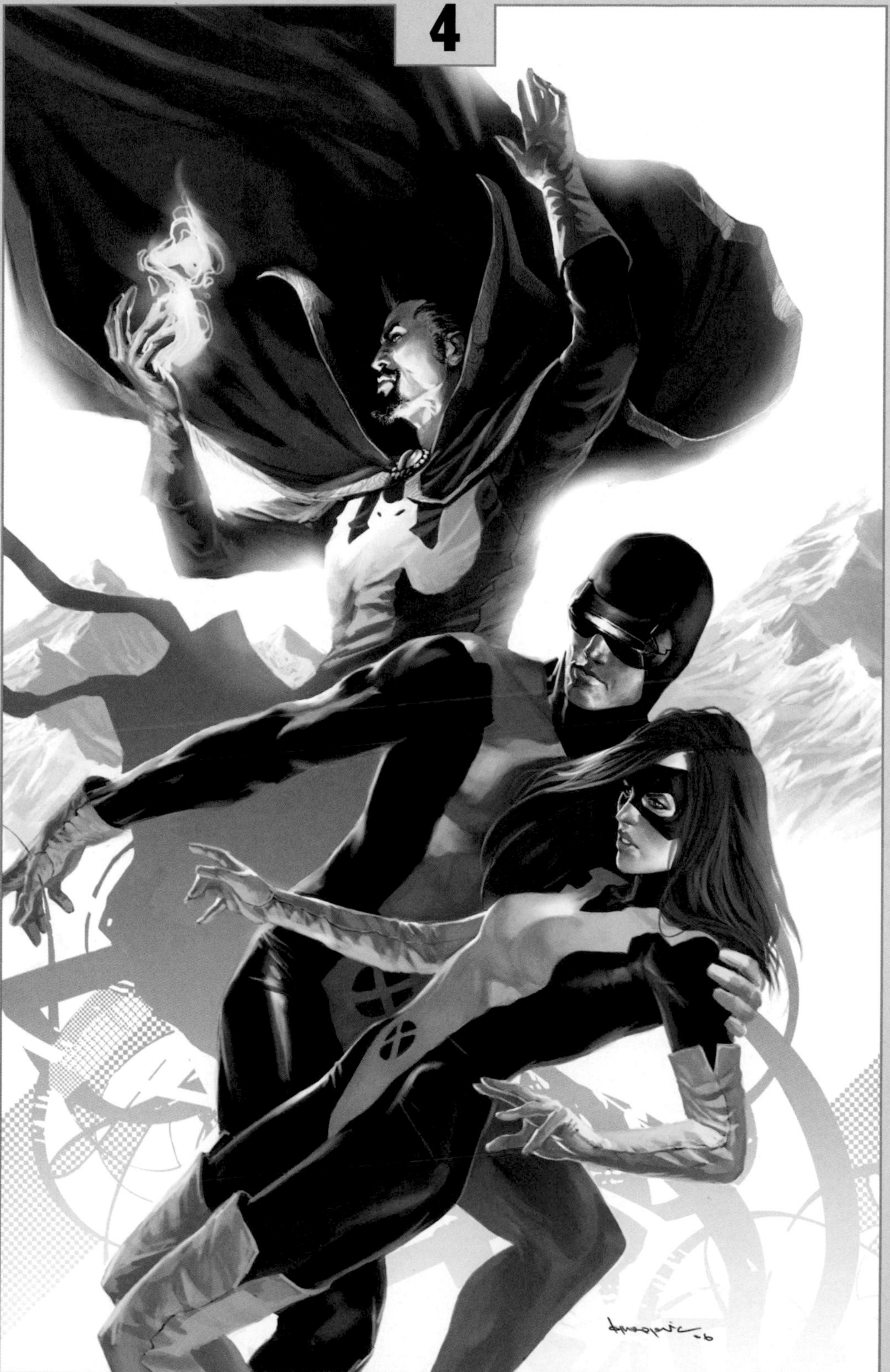

The next step in human evolution has arrived—Homo Superior. Mankind isn't sure whether this represents hope for the future...or the end of the human race. In a private school in upstate New York, one brilliant mutant is teaching a group of five such gifted students what they'll need to survive in this new world. These are the untold stories of Professor Xavier's first class of X-Men!

XAVIER'S SCHOOL FOR GIFTED YOUNGSTERS

Property of:

Warren

HEADMASTER

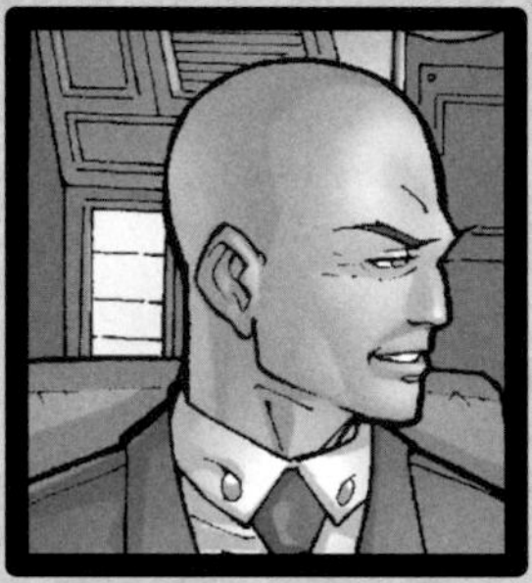

Professor Charles Xavier

... window's open, X is down the hal
answering the phone—I'm going for i
Scratch it, he's back.

What a surprise.
Scott gets to class early and macs
the seat next to Jean.
Didn't see that coming.
Come on Charles, enough of all these
hardfaces, get some ladies in this place!

IDEA—Maybe Hank can rig up Cerebro t
rule out MALE mutants when he's scopi
the planet! I mean, that would save t
and make everyone happy, right!

Who rocks? Jean is who. Went shopping and picked
me up a coat that hides wings AND actually looks good.

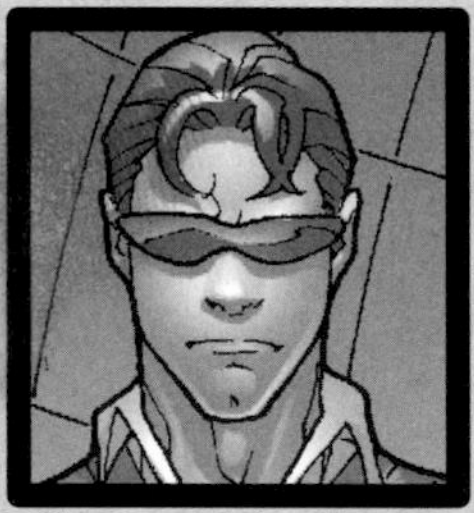

Scott Summers
"Cyclops"

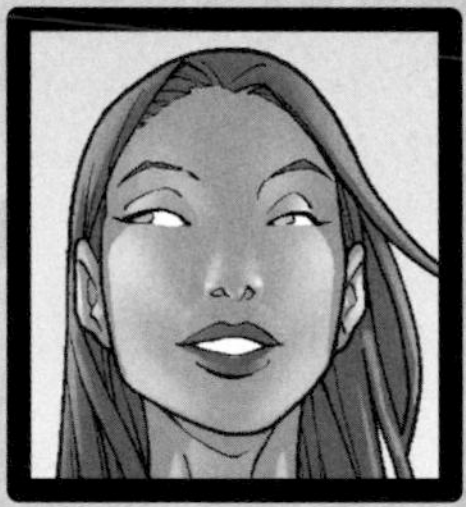

Jean Grey
"Marvel Girl"

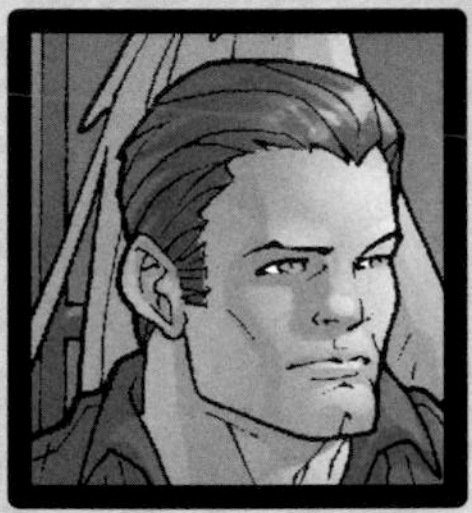

Henry "Hank" McCoy
"Beast"

** thought; we could just ask Cerebro
do us a solid,
he's kind of coo

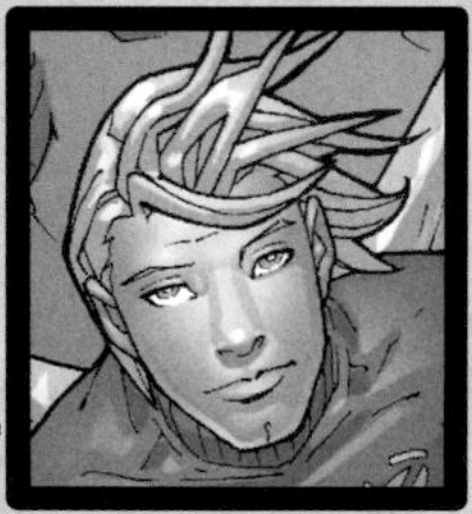

Warren Worthington III
"Angel"

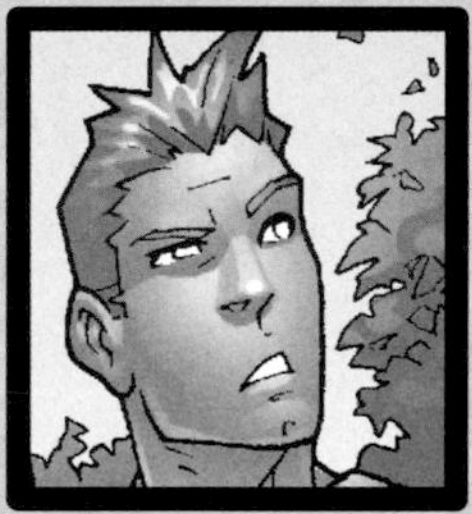

Robert Drake
"Iceman"

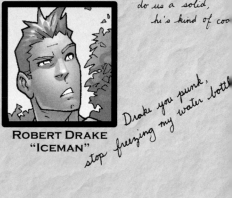

Dad's accountant called
and said I'm not
spending my college funds
fast enough—dude, you
fight Magneto and
Blob and Underwater Guy and Toad, then show me where
you get time to spend money!

Drake you punk,
stop freezing my water bottl

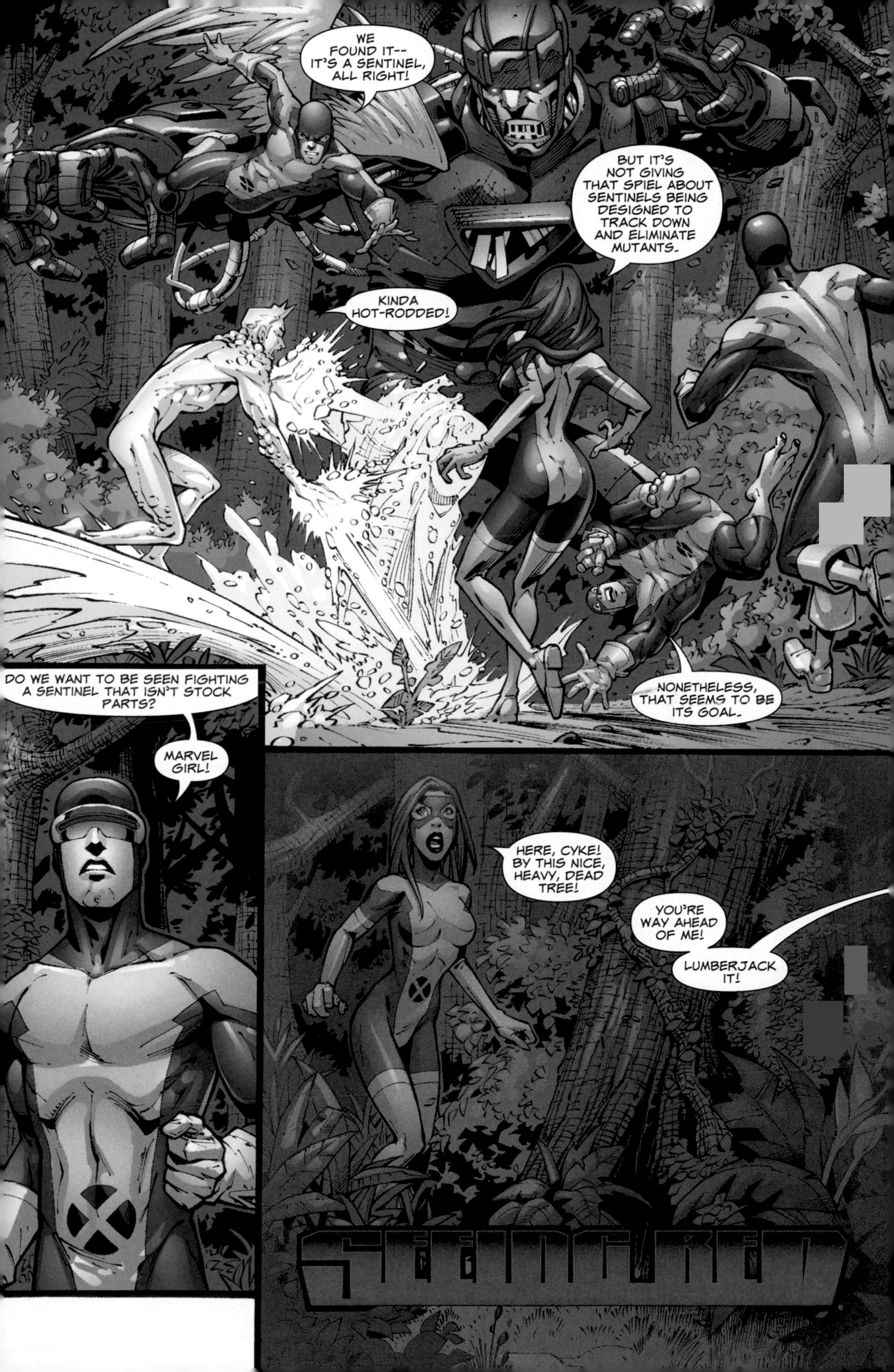
WE FOUND IT-- IT'S A SENTINEL, ALL RIGHT!
BUT IT'S NOT GIVING THAT SPIEL ABOUT SENTINELS BEING DESIGNED TO TRACK DOWN AND ELIMINATE MUTANTS.
KINDA HOT-RODDED!
NONETHELESS, THAT SEEMS TO BE ITS GOAL.
DO WE WANT TO BE SEEN FIGHTING A SENTINEL THAT ISN'T STOCK PARTS?
MARVEL GIRL!
HERE, CYKE! BY THIS NICE, HEAVY, DEAD TREE!
YOU'RE WAY AHEAD OF ME!
LUMBERJACK IT!

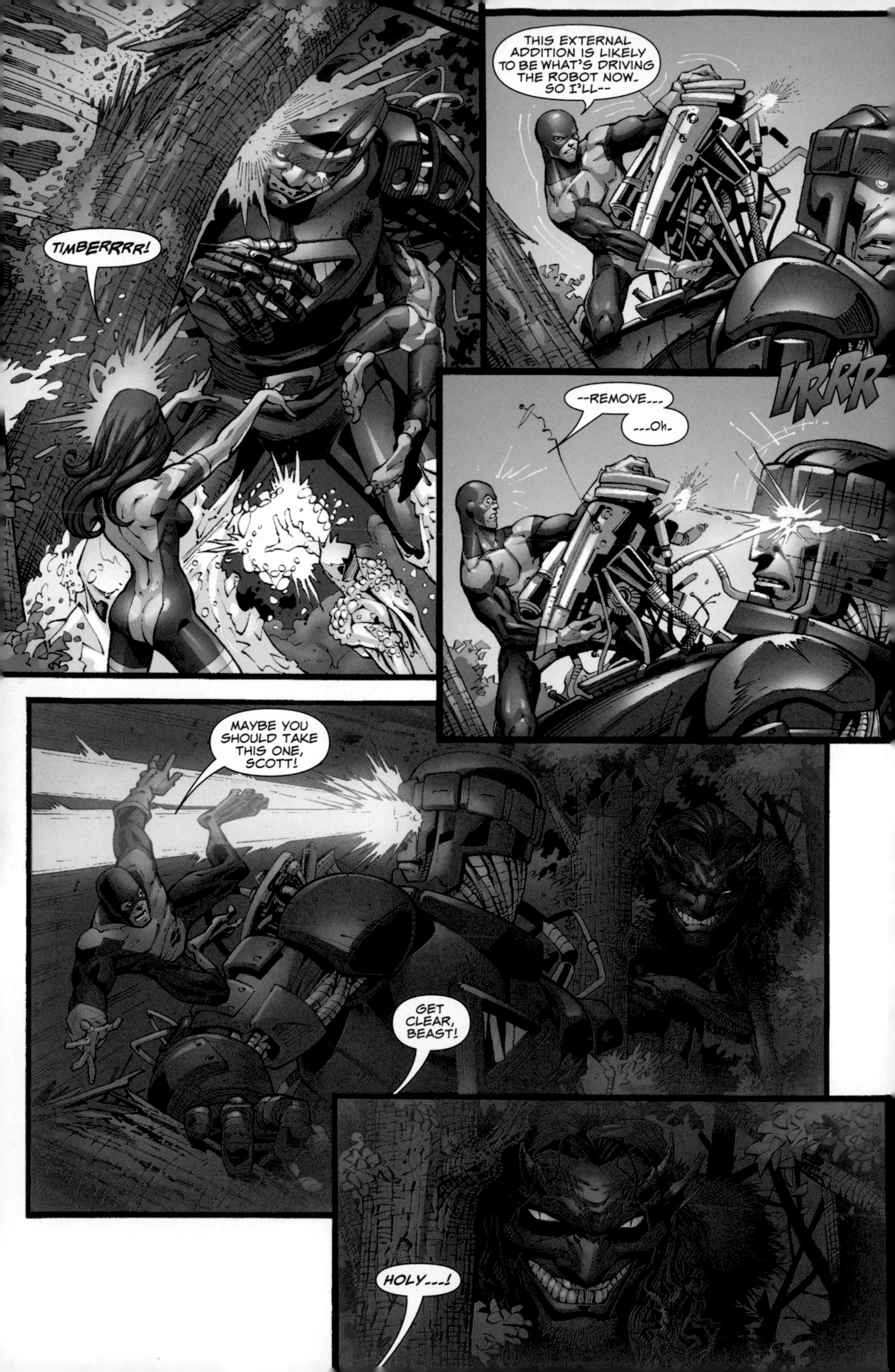
TIMBERRRR!
THIS EXTERNAL ADDITION IS LIKELY TO BE WHAT'S DRIVING THE ROBOT NOW. SO I'LL--
IRRR
--REMOVE...
...Oh.
MAYBE YOU SHOULD TAKE THIS ONE, SCOTT!
GET CLEAR, BEAST!
HOLY...!

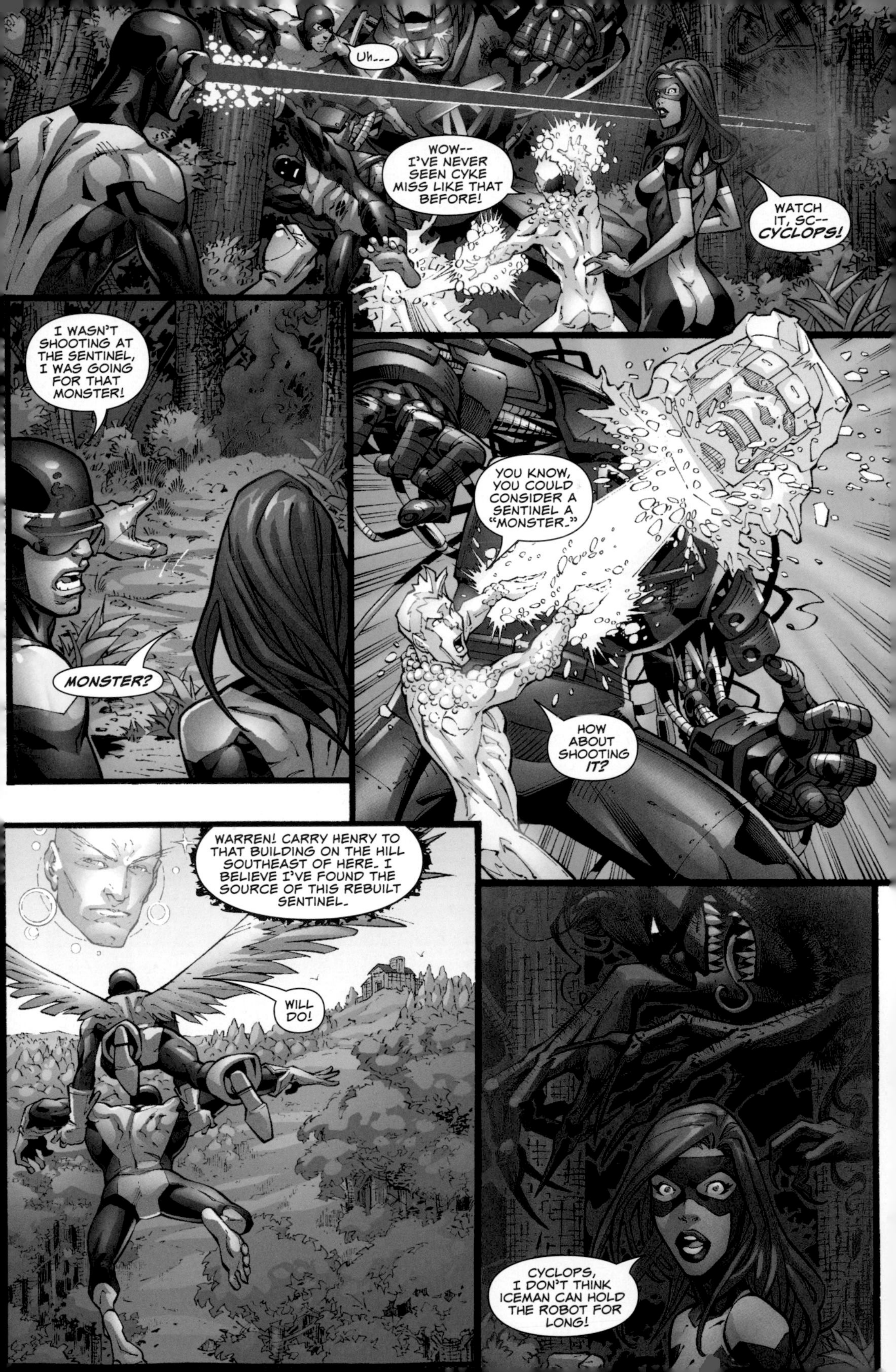
Uh--
WOW-- I'VE NEVER SEEN CYKE MISS LIKE THAT BEFORE!
WATCH IT, SC-- CYCLOPS!
I WASN'T SHOOTING AT THE SENTINEL, I WAS GOING FOR THAT MONSTER!
MONSTER?
YOU KNOW, YOU COULD CONSIDER A SENTINEL A "MONSTER."
HOW ABOUT SHOOTING IT?
WARREN! CARRY HENRY TO THAT BUILDING ON THE HILL SOUTHEAST OF HERE. I BELIEVE I'VE FOUND THE SOURCE OF THIS REBUILT SENTINEL.
WILL DO!
CYCLOPS, I DON'T THINK ICEMAN CAN HOLD THE ROBOT FOR LONG!

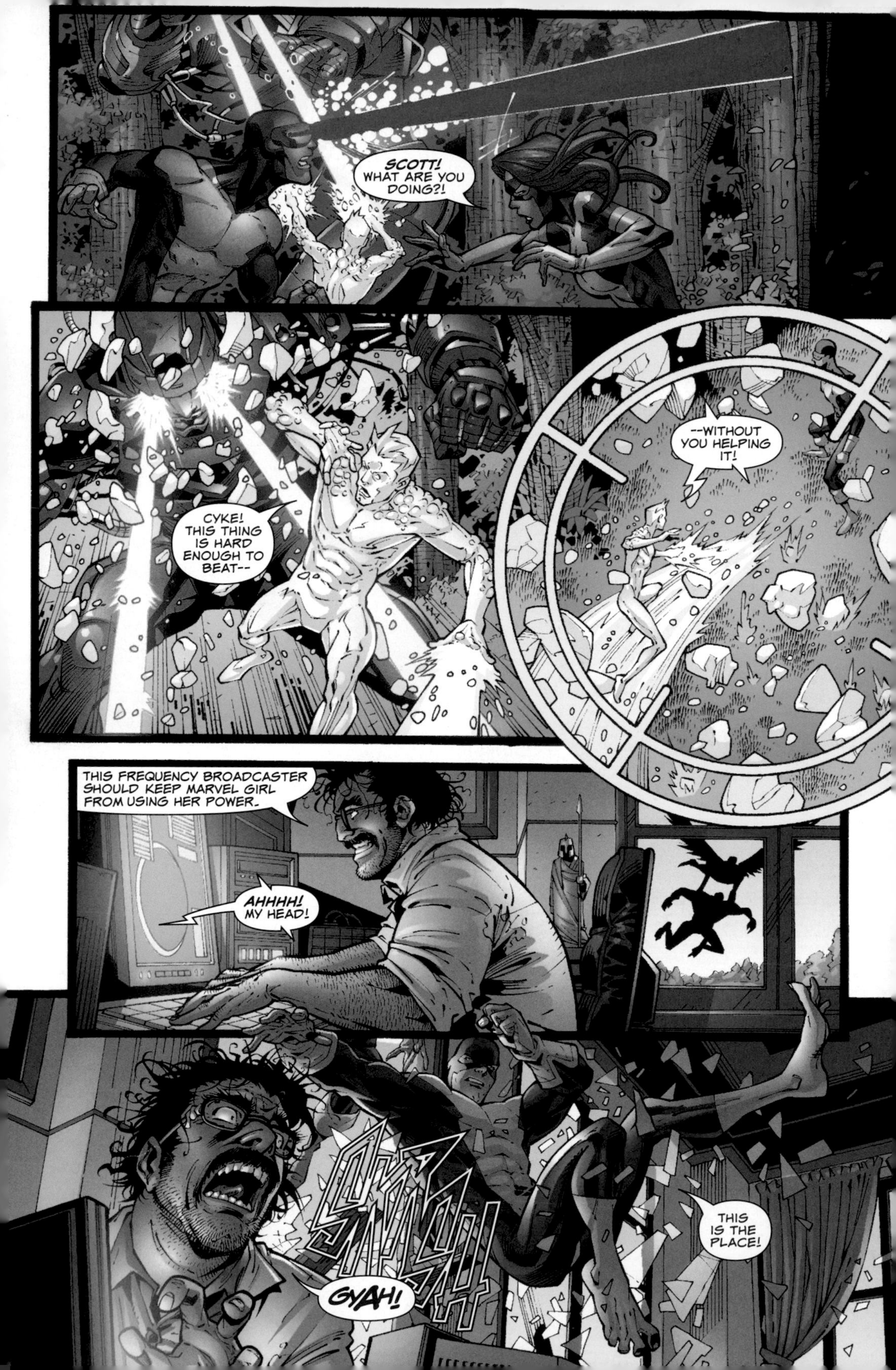
SCOTT! WHAT ARE YOU DOING?!
CYKE! THIS THING IS HARD ENOUGH TO BEAT--
--WITHOUT YOU HELPING IT!
THIS FREQUENCY BROADCASTER SHOULD KEEP MARVEL GIRL FROM USING HER POWER.
AHHHH! MY HEAD!
SMASH
GYAH!
THIS IS THE PLACE!

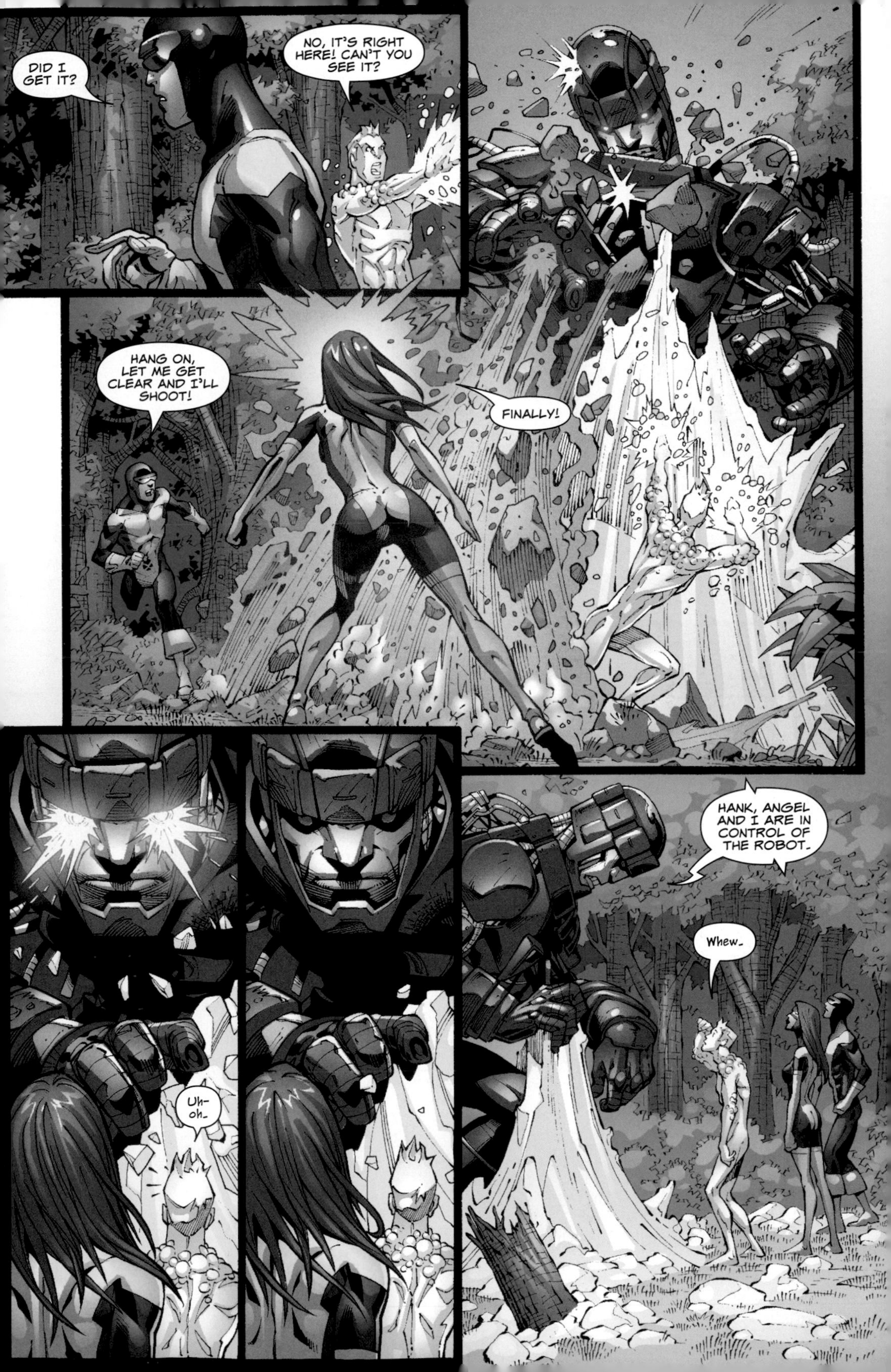
DID I GET IT?
NO, IT'S RIGHT HERE! CAN'T YOU SEE IT?
HANG ON, LET ME GET CLEAR AND I'LL SHOOT!
FINALLY!
Uh-oh.
HANK, ANGEL AND I ARE IN CONTROL OF THE ROBOT.
Whew.

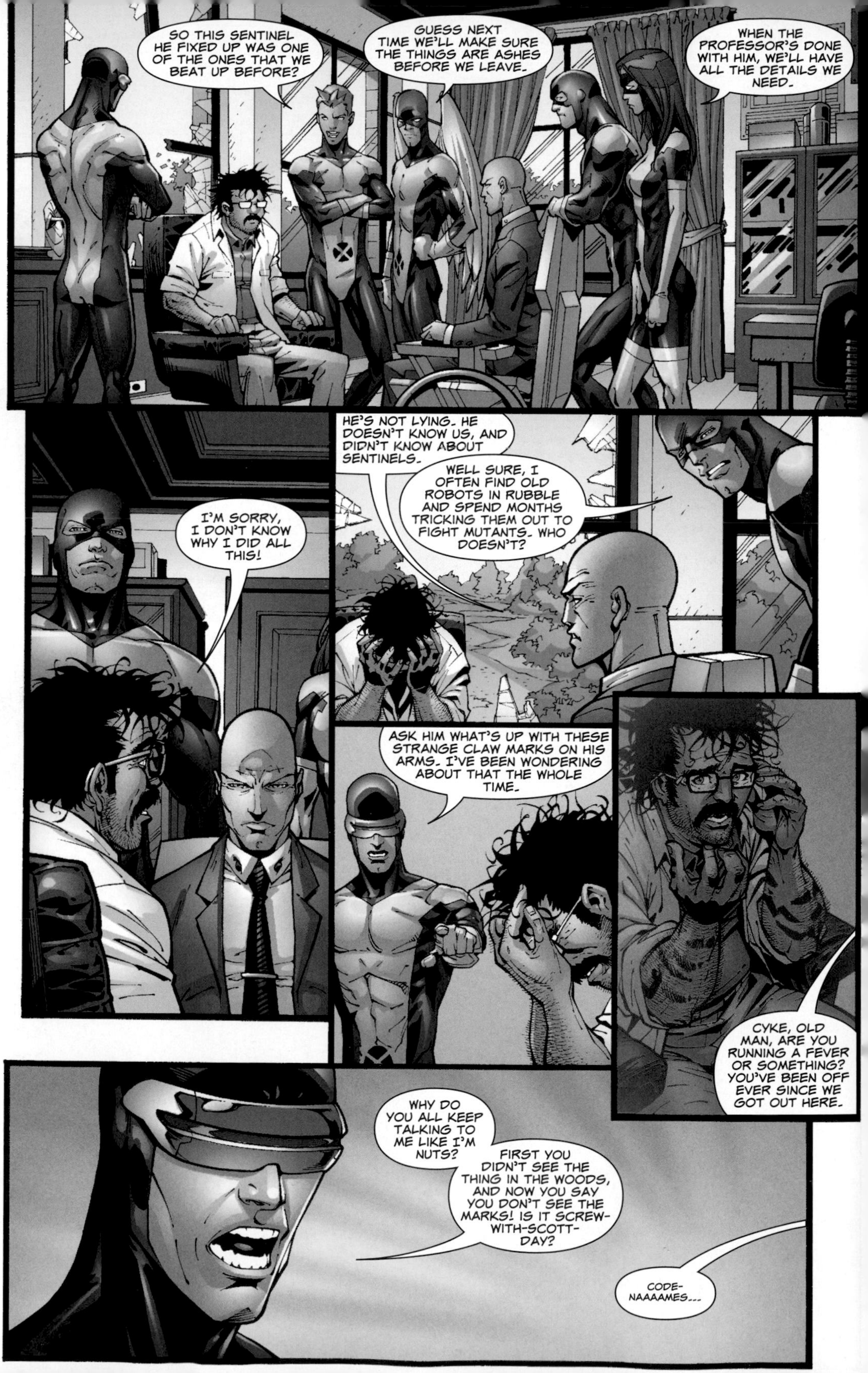

SO THIS SENTINEL HE FIXED UP WAS ONE OF THE ONES THAT WE BEAT UP BEFORE?
GUESS NEXT TIME WE'LL MAKE SURE THE THINGS ARE ASHES BEFORE WE LEAVE.
WHEN THE PROFESSOR'S DONE WITH HIM, WE'LL HAVE ALL THE DETAILS WE NEED.
I'M SORRY, I DON'T KNOW WHY I DID ALL THIS!
HE'S NOT LYING. HE DOESN'T KNOW US, AND DIDN'T KNOW ABOUT SENTINELS.
WELL SURE, I OFTEN FIND OLD ROBOTS IN RUBBLE AND SPEND MONTHS TRICKING THEM OUT TO FIGHT MUTANTS. WHO DOESN'T?
ASK HIM WHAT'S UP WITH THESE STRANGE CLAW MARKS ON HIS ARMS. I'VE BEEN WONDERING ABOUT THAT THE WHOLE TIME.
CYKE, OLD MAN, ARE YOU RUNNING A FEVER OR SOMETHING? YOU'VE BEEN OFF EVER SINCE WE GOT OUT HERE.
WHY DO YOU ALL KEEP TALKING TO ME LIKE I'M NUTS?
FIRST YOU DIDN'T SEE THE THING IN THE WOODS, AND NOW YOU SAY YOU DON'T SEE THE MARKS! IS IT SCREW-WITH-SCOTT-DAY?
CODE-NAAAAMES...

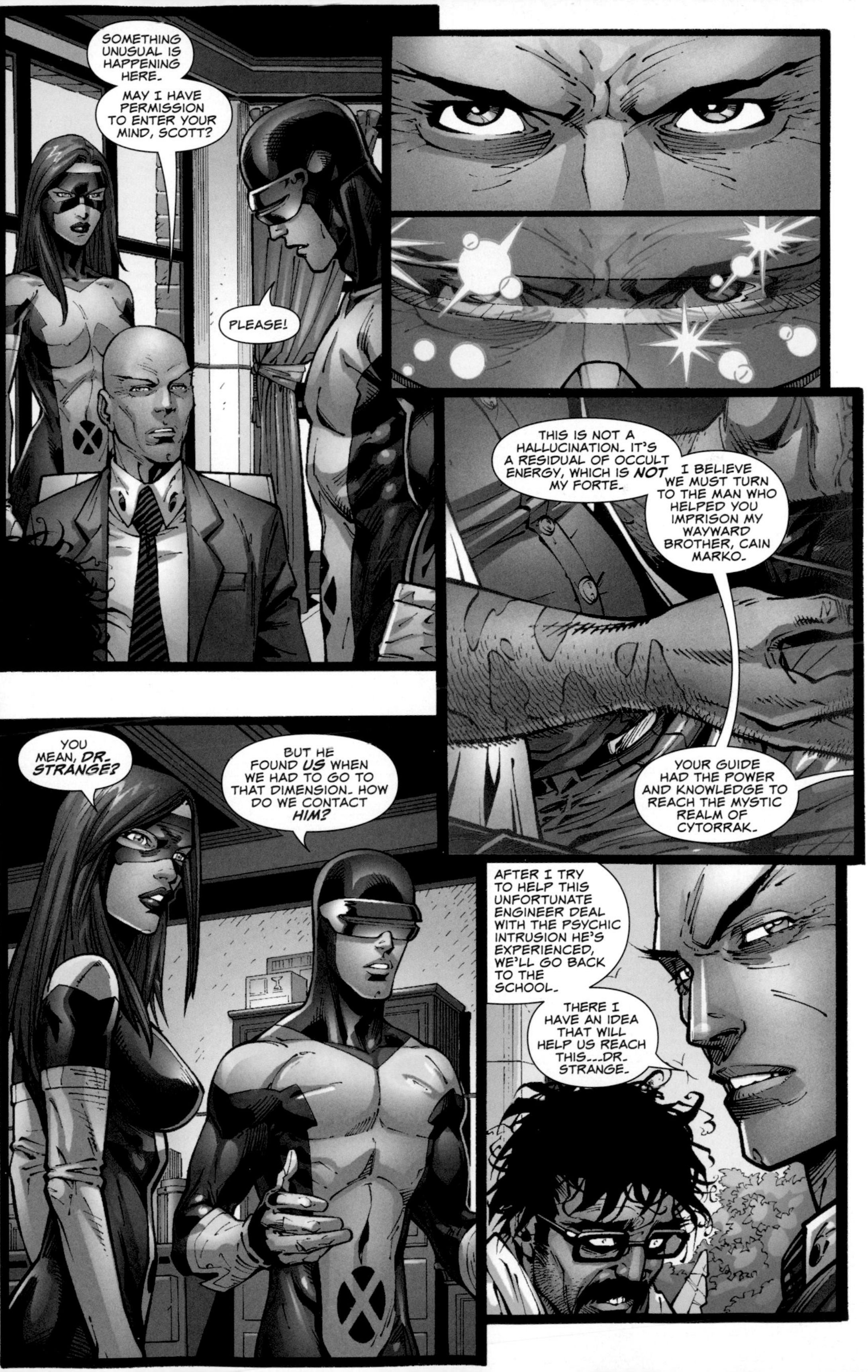
SOMETHING UNUSUAL IS HAPPENING HERE.
MAY I HAVE PERMISSION TO ENTER YOUR MIND, SCOTT?
PLEASE!
THIS IS NOT A HALLUCINATION. IT'S A RESIDUAL OF OCCULT ENERGY, WHICH IS NOT MY FORTE.
I BELIEVE WE MUST TURN TO THE MAN WHO HELPED YOU IMPRISON MY WAYWARD BROTHER, CAIN MARKO.
YOUR GUIDE HAD THE POWER AND KNOWLEDGE TO REACH THE MYSTIC REALM OF CYTORRAK.
YOU MEAN, DR. STRANGE?
BUT HE FOUND US WHEN WE HAD TO GO TO THAT DIMENSION. HOW DO WE CONTACT HIM?
AFTER I TRY TO HELP THIS UNFORTUNATE ENGINEER DEAL WITH THE PSYCHIC INTRUSION HE'S EXPERIENCED, WE'LL GO BACK TO THE SCHOOL.
THERE I HAVE AN IDEA THAT WILL HELP US REACH THIS...DR. STRANGE.

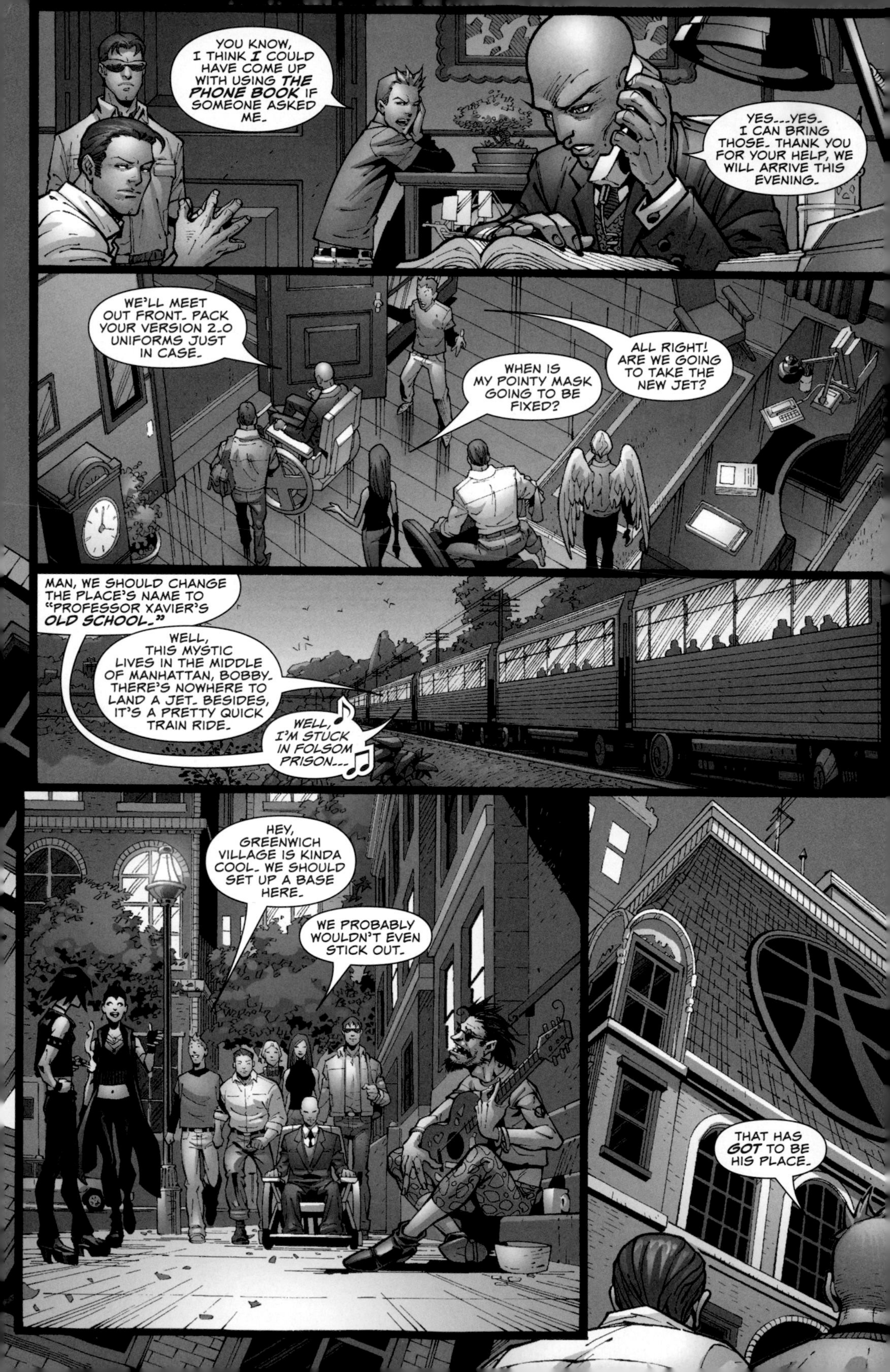
YOU KNOW, I THINK I COULD HAVE COME UP WITH USING THE PHONE BOOK IF SOMEONE ASKED ME.
YES... YES. I CAN BRING THOSE. THANK YOU FOR YOUR HELP, WE WILL ARRIVE THIS EVENING.
WE'LL MEET OUT FRONT. PACK YOUR VERSION 2.0 UNIFORMS JUST IN CASE.
ALL RIGHT! ARE WE GOING TO TAKE THE NEW JET?
WHEN IS MY POINTY MASK GOING TO BE FIXED?
MAN, WE SHOULD CHANGE THE PLACE'S NAME TO "PROFESSOR XAVIER'S OLD SCHOOL."
WELL, THIS MYSTIC LIVES IN THE MIDDLE OF MANHATTAN, BOBBY. THERE'S NOWHERE TO LAND A JET. BESIDES, IT'S A PRETTY QUICK TRAIN RIDE.
WELL, I'M STUCK IN FOLSOM PRISON...
HEY, GREENWICH VILLAGE IS KINDA COOL. WE SHOULD SET UP A BASE HERE.
WE PROBABLY WOULDN'T EVEN STICK OUT.
THAT HAS GOT TO BE HIS PLACE.

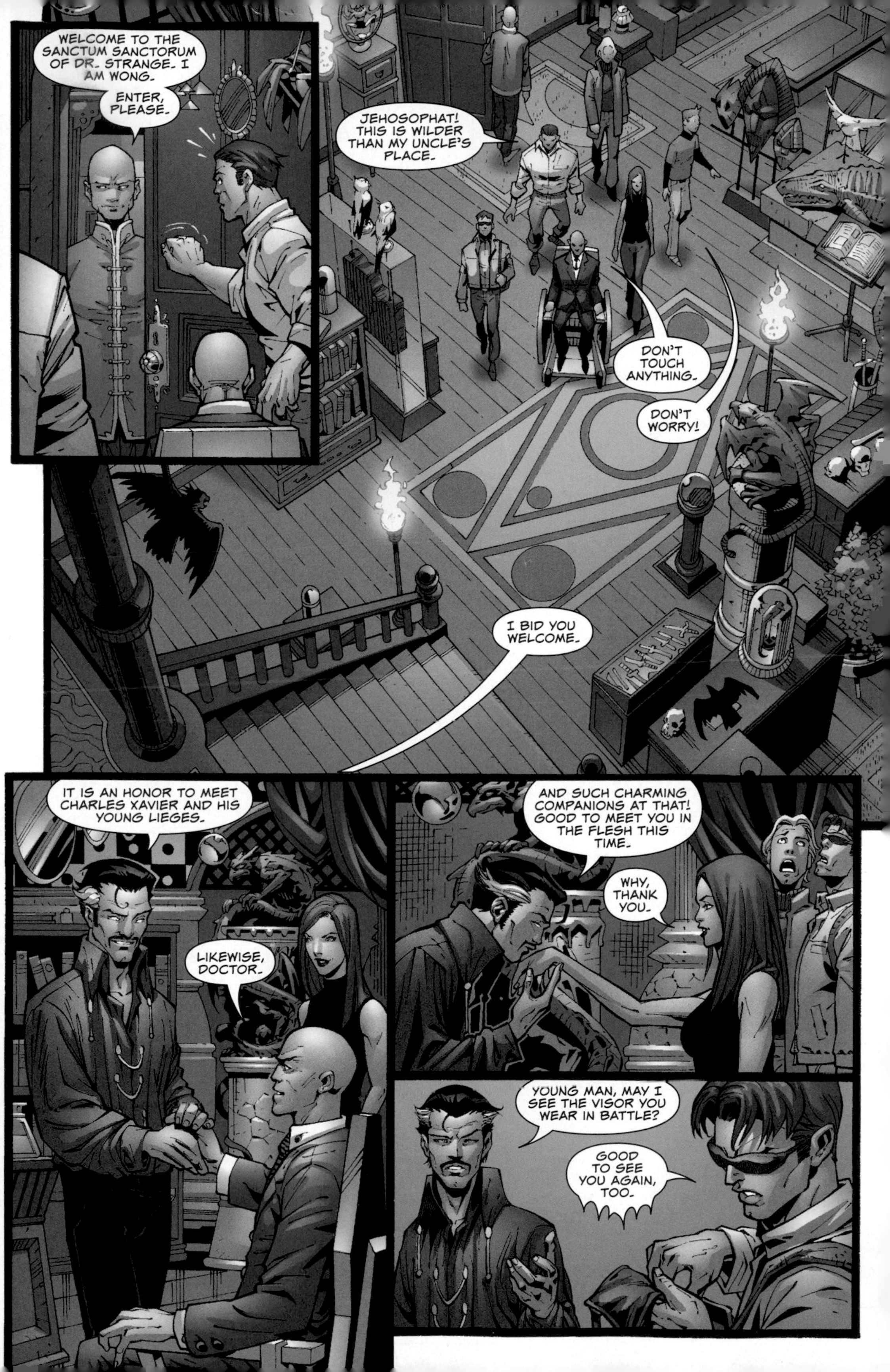
WELCOME TO THE SANCTUM SANCTORUM OF DR. STRANGE. I AM WONG.
ENTER, PLEASE.
JEHOSOPHAT! THIS IS WILDER THAN MY UNCLE'S PLACE.
DON'T TOUCH ANYTHING.
DON'T WORRY!
I BID YOU WELCOME.
IT IS AN HONOR TO MEET CHARLES XAVIER AND HIS YOUNG LIEGES.
LIKEWISE, DOCTOR.
AND SUCH CHARMING COMPANIONS AT THAT! GOOD TO MEET YOU IN THE FLESH THIS TIME.
WHY, THANK YOU.
YOUNG MAN, MAY I SEE THE VISOR YOU WEAR IN BATTLE?
GOOD TO SEE YOU AGAIN, TOO.

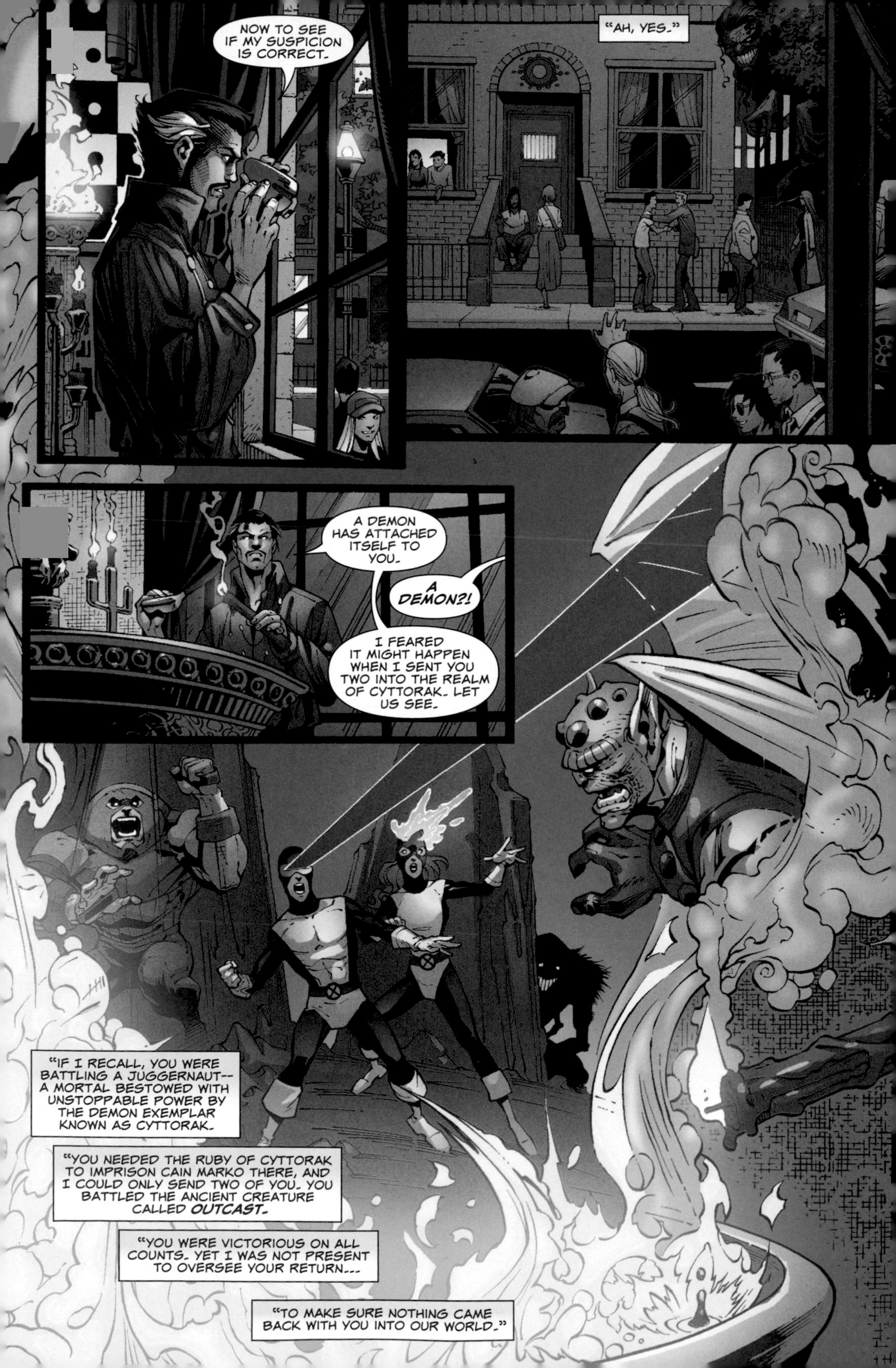
NOW TO SEE IF MY SUSPICION IS CORRECT.
"AH, YES."
A DEMON HAS ATTACHED ITSELF TO YOU.
A DEMON?!
I FEARED IT MIGHT HAPPEN WHEN I SENT YOU TWO INTO THE REALM OF CYTTORAK. LET US SEE.
"IF I RECALL, YOU WERE BATTLING A JUGGERNAUT-- A MORTAL BESTOWED WITH UNSTOPPABLE POWER BY THE DEMON EXEMPLAR KNOWN AS CYTTORAK.
"YOU NEEDED THE RUBY OF CYTTORAK TO IMPRISON CAIN MARKO THERE, AND I COULD ONLY SEND TWO OF YOU. YOU BATTLED THE ANCIENT CREATURE CALLED OUTCAST.
"YOU WERE VICTORIOUS ON ALL COUNTS. YET I WAS NOT PRESENT TO OVERSEE YOUR RETURN...
"TO MAKE SURE NOTHING CAME BACK WITH YOU INTO OUR WORLD."

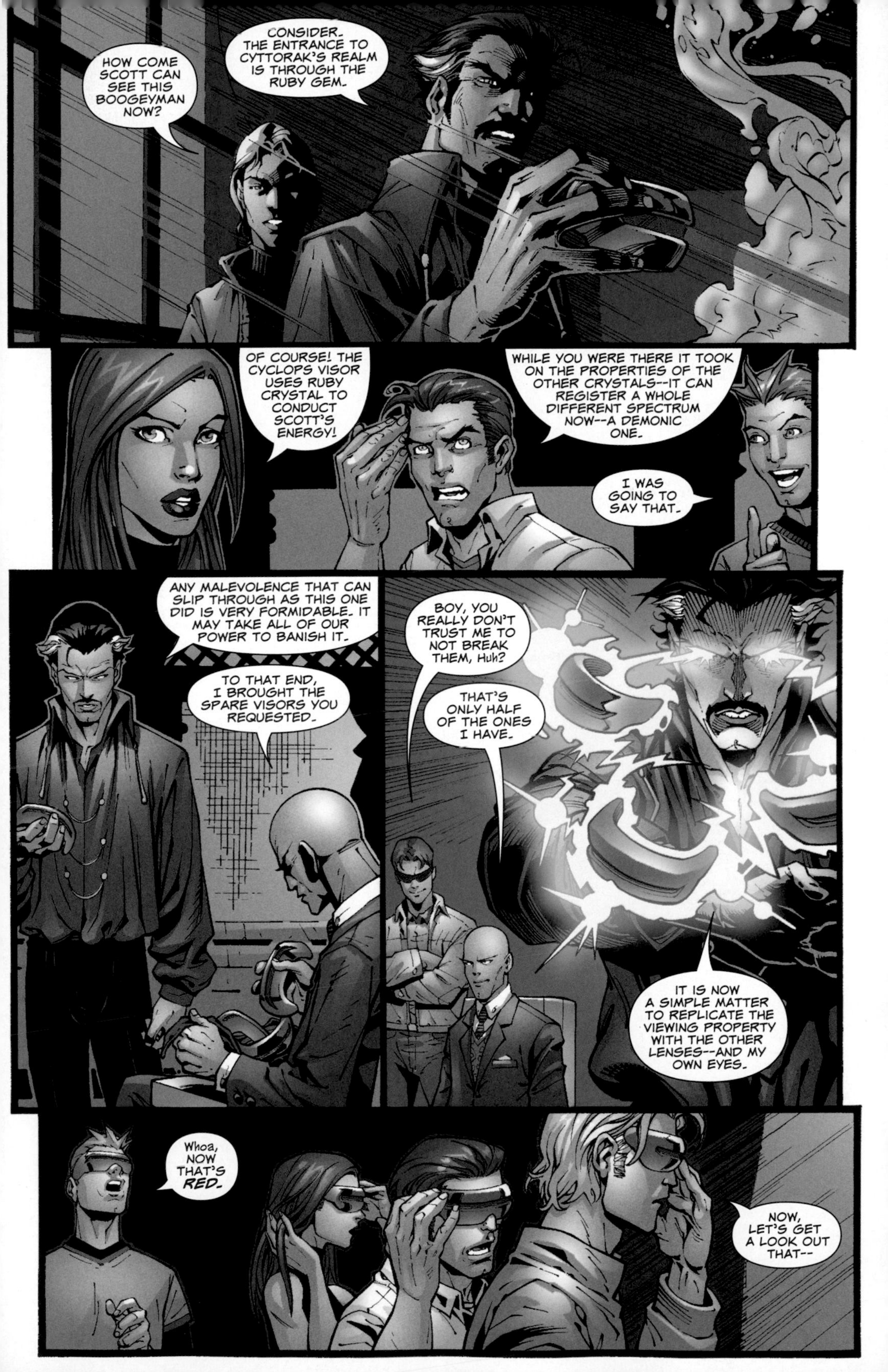
HOW COME SCOTT CAN SEE THIS BOOGEYMAN NOW?
CONSIDER. THE ENTRANCE TO CYTTORAK'S REALM IS THROUGH THE RUBY GEM.
OF COURSE! THE CYCLOPS VISOR USES RUBY CRYSTAL TO CONDUCT SCOTT'S ENERGY!
WHILE YOU WERE THERE IT TOOK ON THE PROPERTIES OF THE OTHER CRYSTALS--IT CAN REGISTER A WHOLE DIFFERENT SPECTRUM NOW--A DEMONIC ONE.
I WAS GOING TO SAY THAT.
ANY MALEVOLENCE THAT CAN SLIP THROUGH AS THIS ONE DID IS VERY FORMIDABLE. IT MAY TAKE ALL OF OUR POWER TO BANISH IT.
TO THAT END, I BROUGHT THE SPARE VISORS YOU REQUESTED.
BOY, YOU REALLY DON'T TRUST ME TO NOT BREAK THEM, Huh?
THAT'S ONLY HALF OF THE ONES I HAVE.
IT IS NOW A SIMPLE MATTER TO REPLICATE THE VIEWING PROPERTY WITH THE OTHER LENSES--AND MY OWN EYES.
Whoa, NOW THAT'S RED.
NOW, LET'S GET A LOOK OUT THAT--

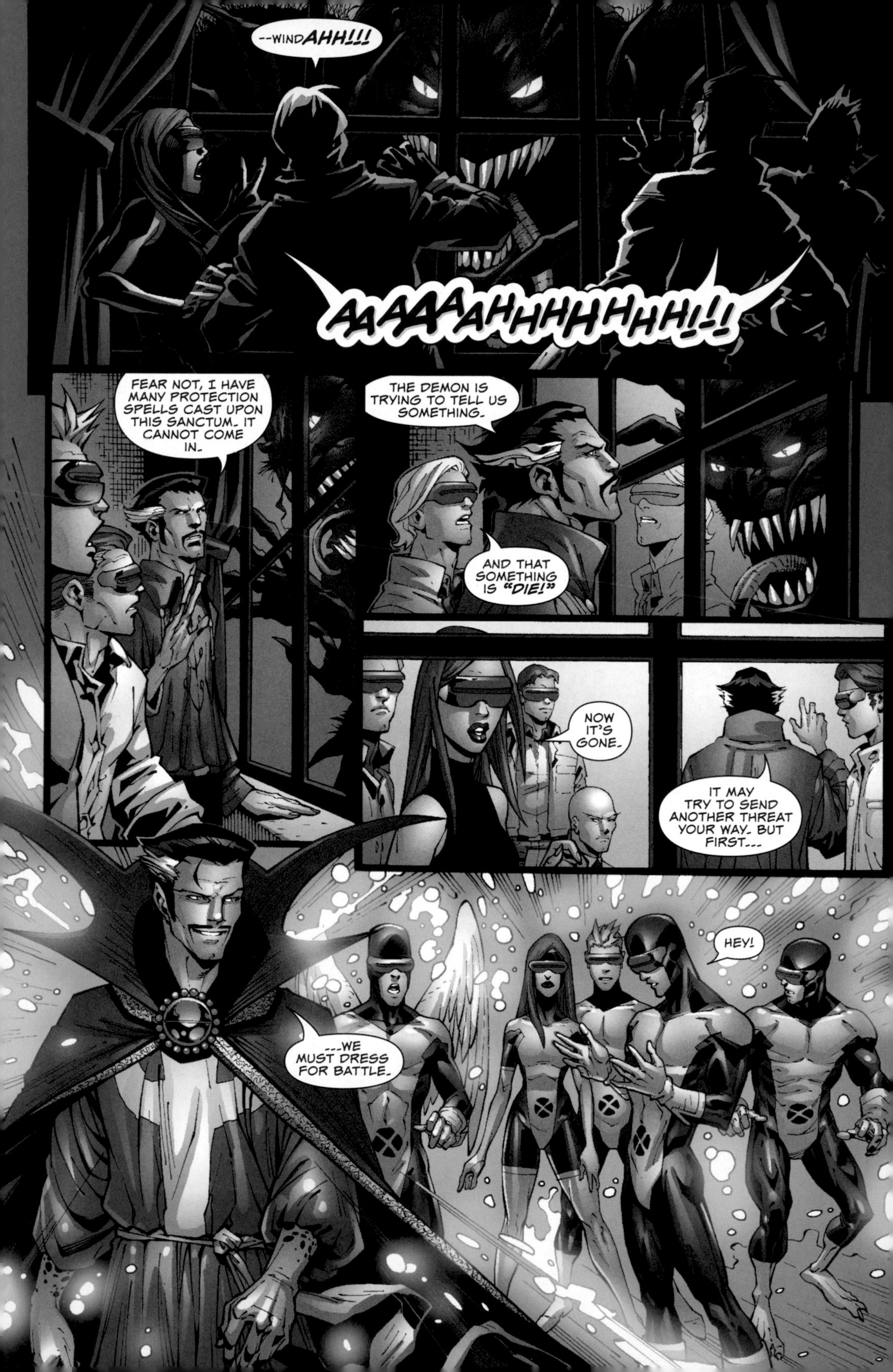
--WINDAHH!!!
AAAAAAHHHHHHH!!!
FEAR NOT, I HAVE MANY PROTECTION SPELLS CAST UPON THIS SANCTUM. IT CANNOT COME IN.
THE DEMON IS TRYING TO TELL US SOMETHING.
AND THAT SOMETHING IS "DIE!"
NOW IT'S GONE.
IT MAY TRY TO SEND ANOTHER THREAT YOUR WAY. BUT FIRST---
---WE MUST DRESS FOR BATTLE.
HEY!

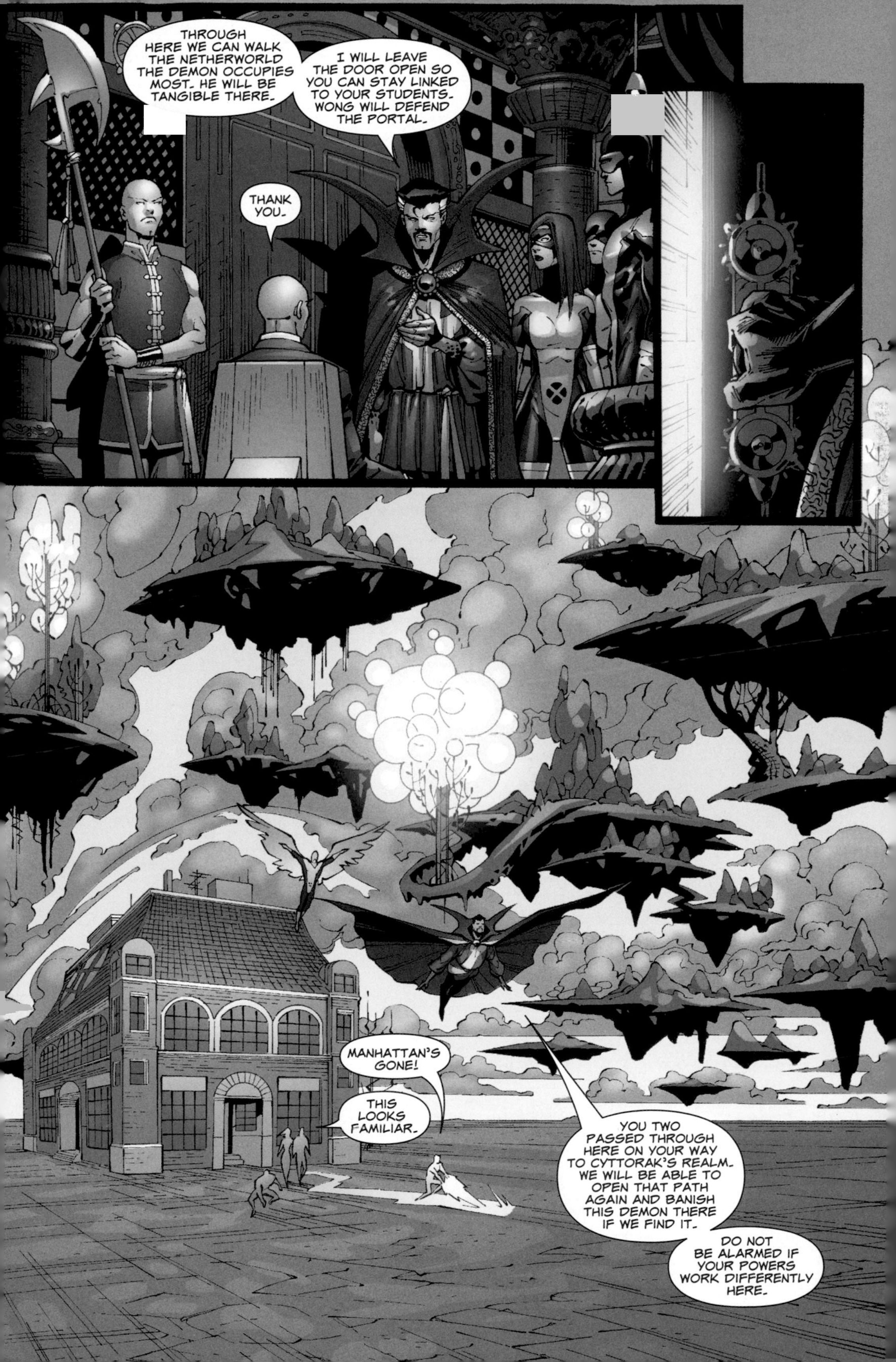
THROUGH HERE WE CAN WALK THE NETHERWORLD THE DEMON OCCUPIES MOST. HE WILL BE TANGIBLE THERE.
I WILL LEAVE THE DOOR OPEN SO YOU CAN STAY LINKED TO YOUR STUDENTS. WONG WILL DEFEND THE PORTAL.
THANK YOU.
MANHATTAN'S GONE!
THIS LOOKS FAMILIAR.
YOU TWO PASSED THROUGH HERE ON YOUR WAY TO CYTTORAK'S REALM. WE WILL BE ABLE TO OPEN THAT PATH AGAIN AND BANISH THIS DEMON THERE IF WE FIND IT.
DO NOT BE ALARMED IF YOUR POWERS WORK DIFFERENTLY HERE.

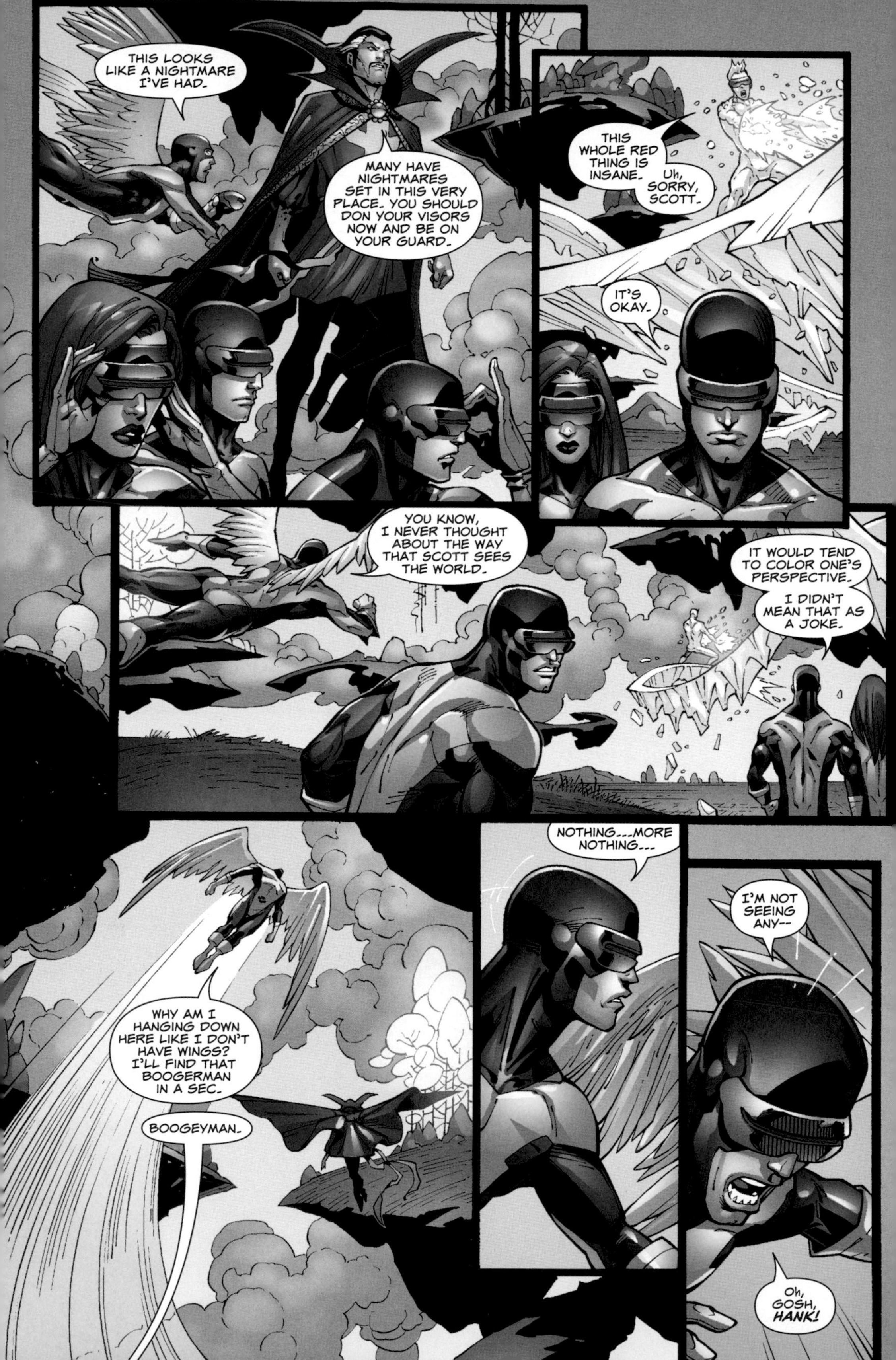

THIS LOOKS LIKE A NIGHTMARE I'VE HAD.
MANY HAVE NIGHTMARES SET IN THIS VERY PLACE. YOU SHOULD DON YOUR VISORS NOW AND BE ON YOUR GUARD.
THIS WHOLE RED THING IS INSANE.
Uh, SORRY, SCOTT.
IT'S OKAY.
YOU KNOW, I NEVER THOUGHT ABOUT THE WAY THAT SCOTT SEES THE WORLD.
IT WOULD TEND TO COLOR ONE'S PERSPECTIVE.
I DIDN'T MEAN THAT AS A JOKE.
WHY AM I HANGING DOWN HERE LIKE I DON'T HAVE WINGS? I'LL FIND THAT BOOGERMAN IN A SEC.
BOOGEYMAN.
NOTHING...MORE NOTHING...
I'M NOT SEEING ANY--
Oh, GOSH, HANK!

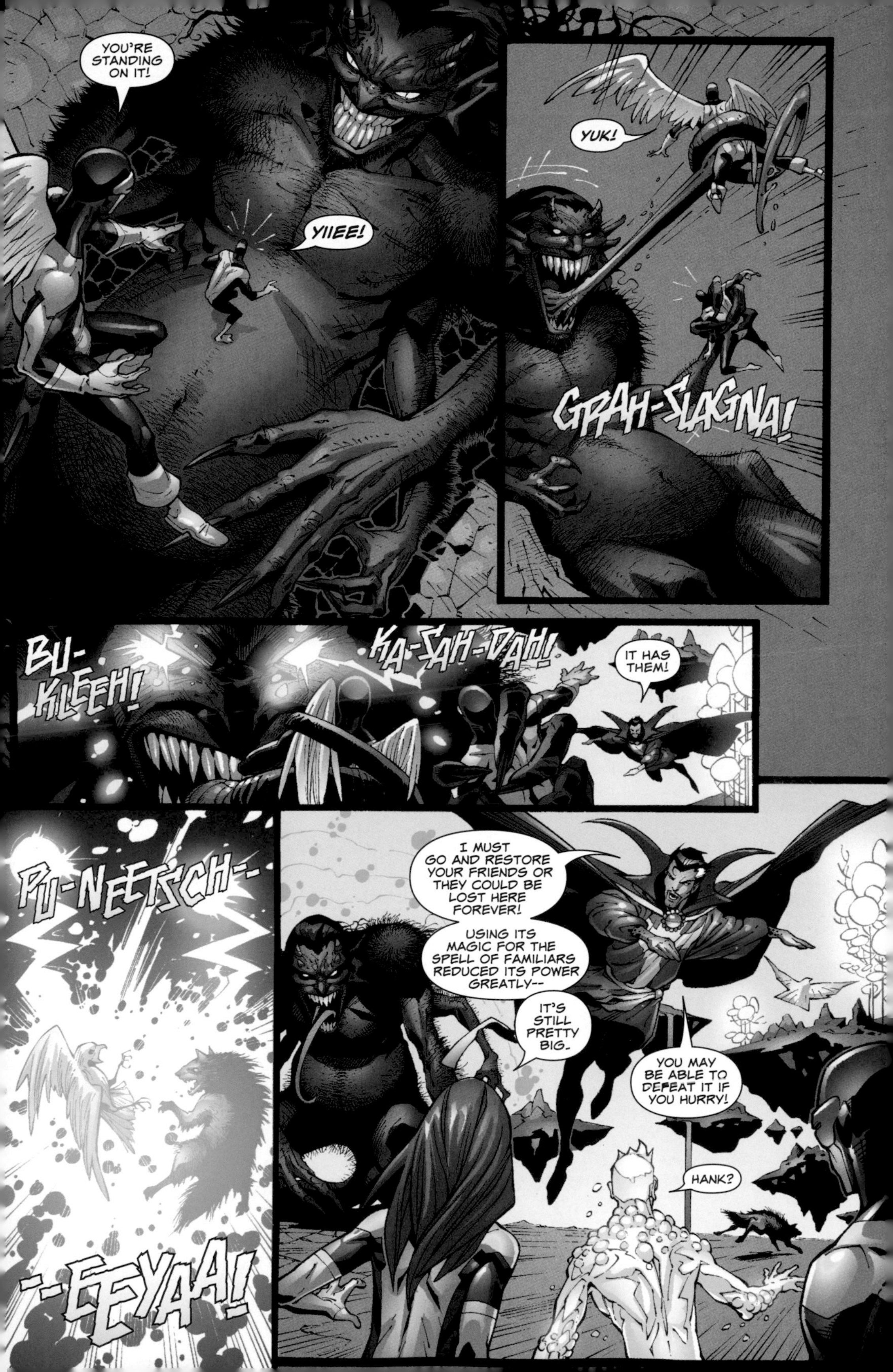
YOU'RE STANDING ON IT!
YIIEE!
YUK!
GRAH-SLAGNA!
BU-KLEEH!
KA-SAH-DAH!
IT HAS THEM!
PU-NEETSCH--
--EEYAA!
I MUST GO AND RESTORE YOUR FRIENDS OR THEY COULD BE LOST HERE FOREVER!
USING ITS MAGIC FOR THE SPELL OF FAMILIARS REDUCED ITS POWER GREATLY--
IT'S STILL PRETTY BIG.
YOU MAY BE ABLE TO DEFEAT IT IF YOU HURRY!
HANK?

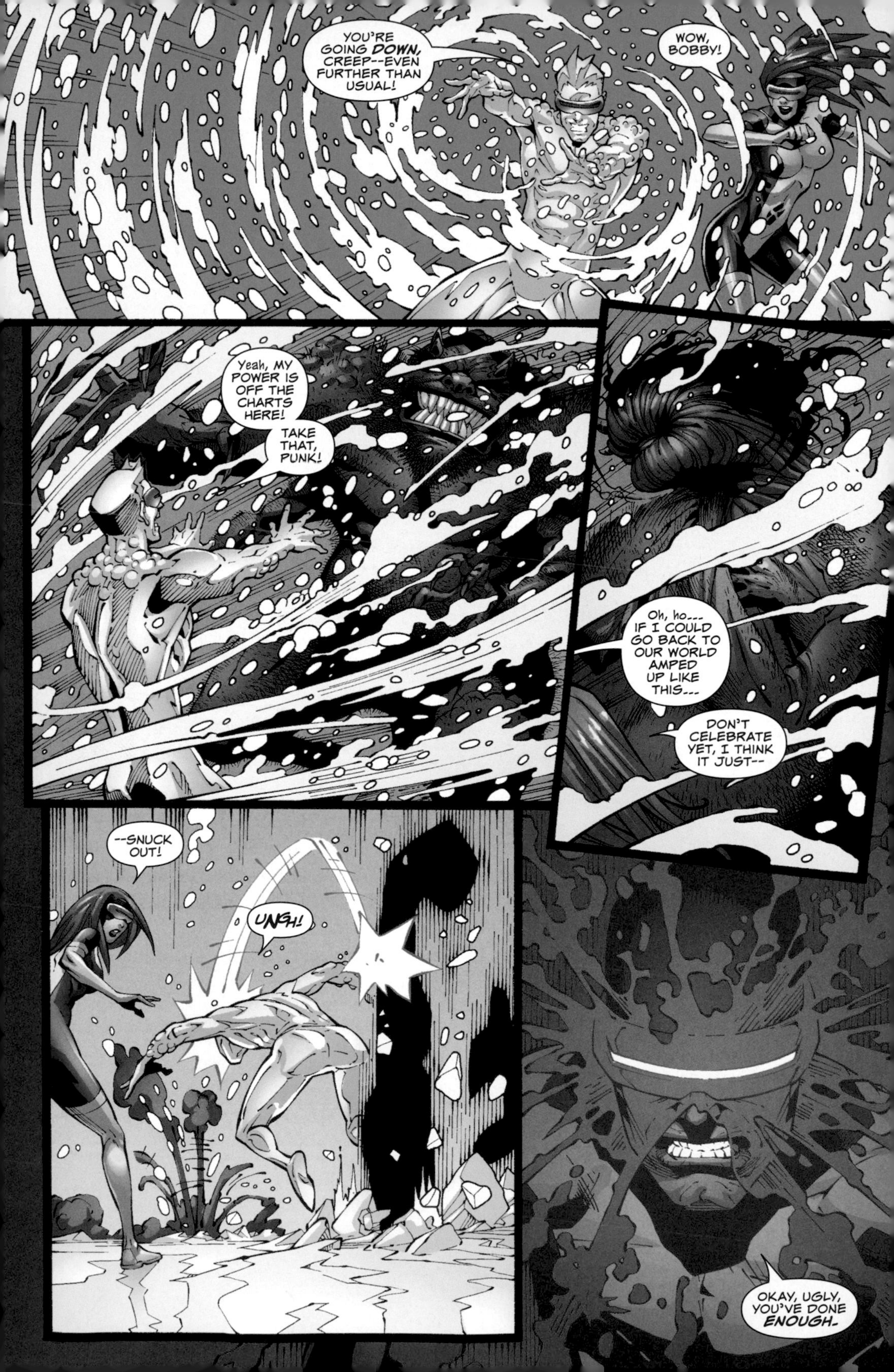
YOU'RE GOING DOWN, CREEP--EVEN FURTHER THAN USUAL!
WOW, BOBBY!
Yeah, MY POWER IS OFF THE CHARTS HERE!
TAKE THAT, PUNK!
Oh, ho--- IF I COULD GO BACK TO OUR WORLD AMPED UP LIKE THIS---
DON'T CELEBRATE YET, I THINK IT JUST--
--SNUCK OUT!
UNGH!
OKAY, UGLY, YOU'VE DONE ENOUGH.

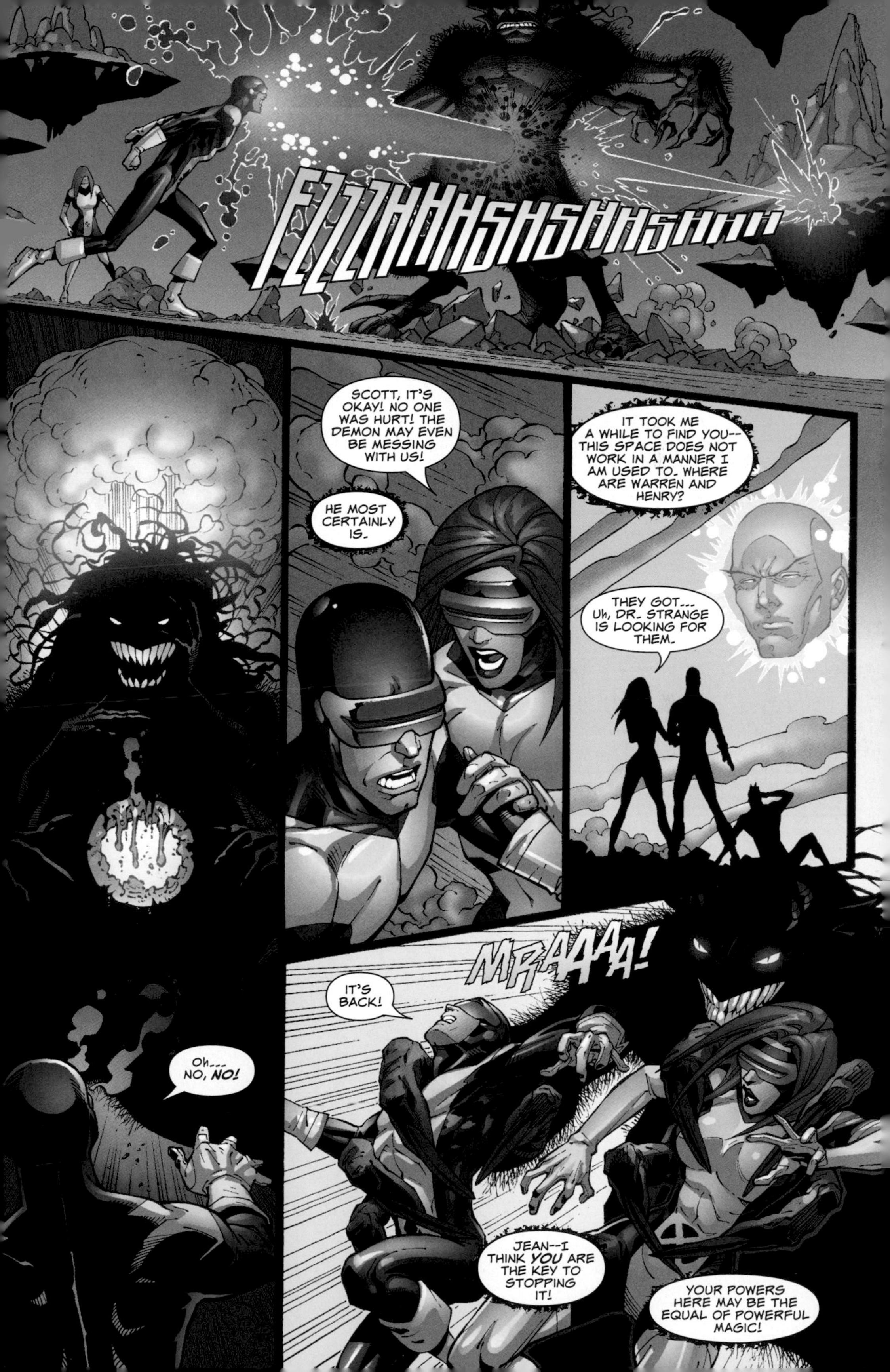
FZZZHHHSHSHSHHSHHH
SCOTT, IT'S OKAY! NO ONE WAS HURT! THE DEMON MAY EVEN BE MESSING WITH US!
HE MOST CERTAINLY IS.
IT TOOK ME A WHILE TO FIND YOU-- THIS SPACE DOES NOT WORK IN A MANNER I AM USED TO. WHERE ARE WARREN AND HENRY?
THEY GOT... Uh, DR. STRANGE IS LOOKING FOR THEM.
MRAAAA!
IT'S BACK!
Oh... NO, NO!
JEAN--I THINK YOU ARE THE KEY TO STOPPING IT!
YOUR POWERS HERE MAY BE THE EQUAL OF POWERFUL MAGIC!

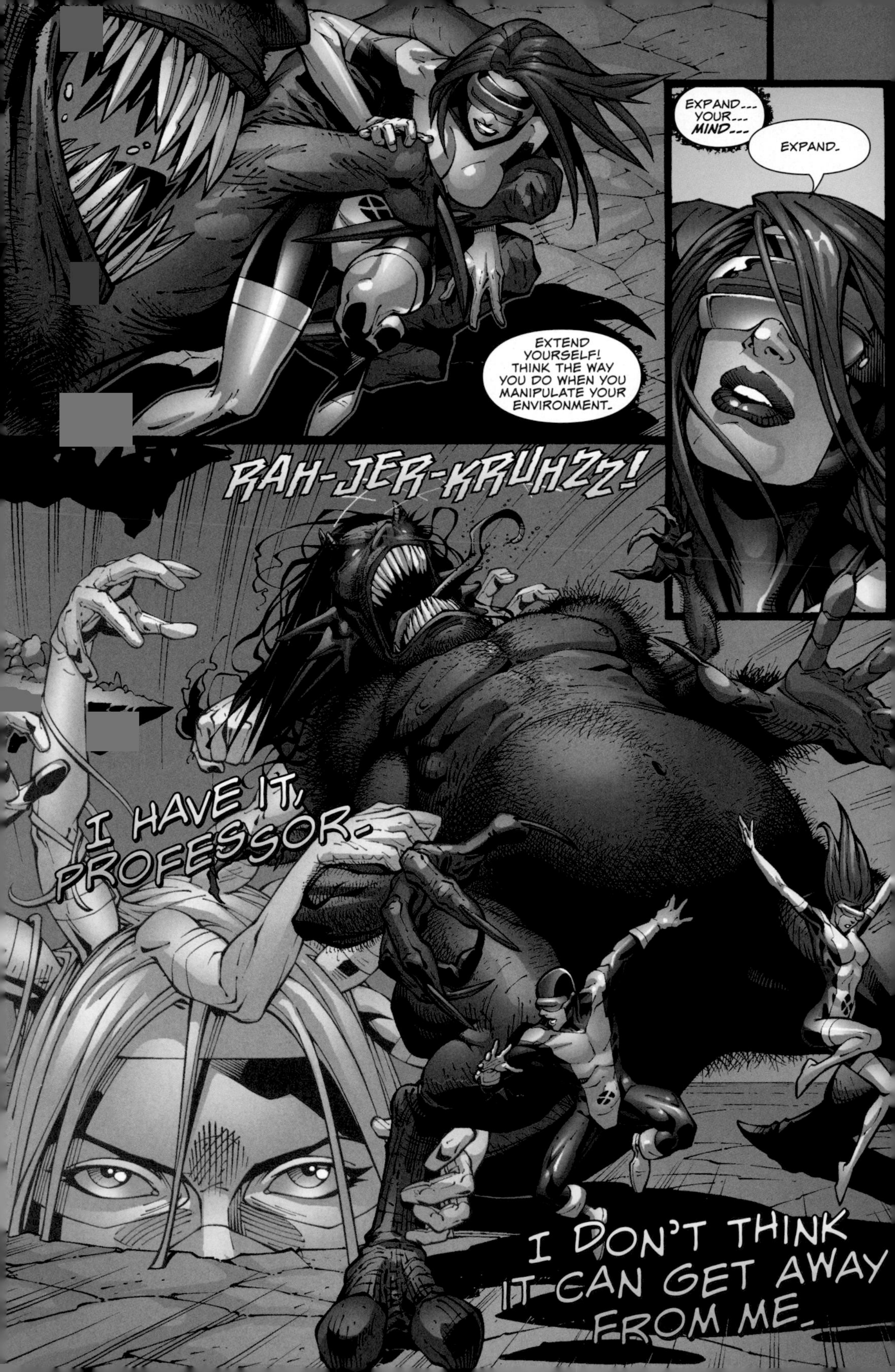
EXTEND YOURSELF! THINK THE WAY YOU DO WHEN YOU MANIPULATE YOUR ENVIRONMENT.
EXPAND... YOUR... MIND...
EXPAND.
RAH-JER-KRUHZZ!
I HAVE IT, PROFESSOR.
I DON'T THINK IT CAN GET AWAY FROM ME.

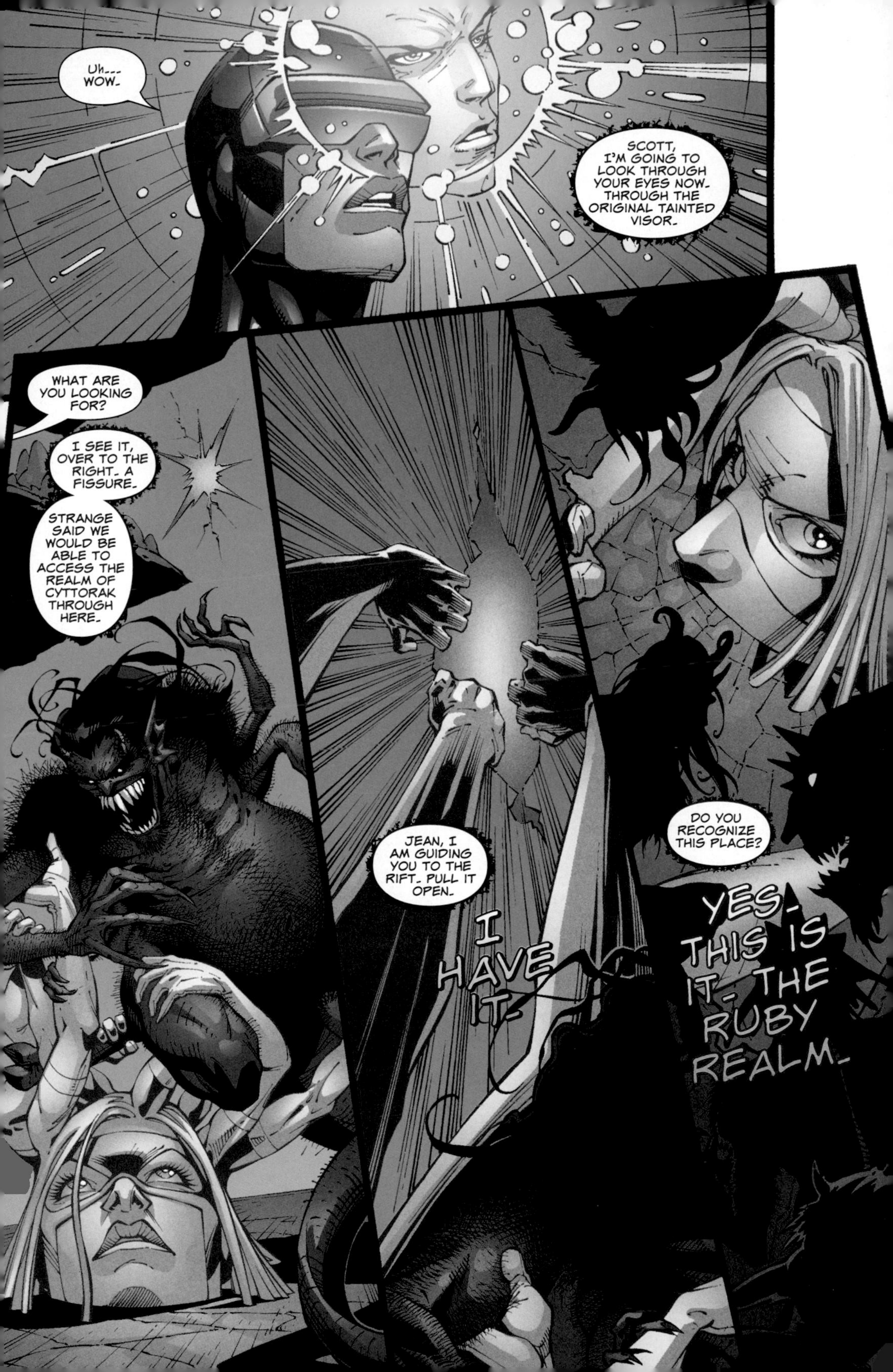
UH...
WOW.
SCOTT, I'M GOING TO LOOK THROUGH YOUR EYES NOW. THROUGH THE ORIGINAL TAINTED VISOR.
WHAT ARE YOU LOOKING FOR?
I SEE IT, OVER TO THE RIGHT. A FISSURE.
STRANGE SAID WE WOULD BE ABLE TO ACCESS THE REALM OF CYTTORAK THROUGH HERE.
JEAN, I AM GUIDING YOU TO THE RIFT. PULL IT OPEN.
I HAVE IT.
DO YOU RECOGNIZE THIS PLACE?
YES. THIS IS IT. THE RUBY REALM.

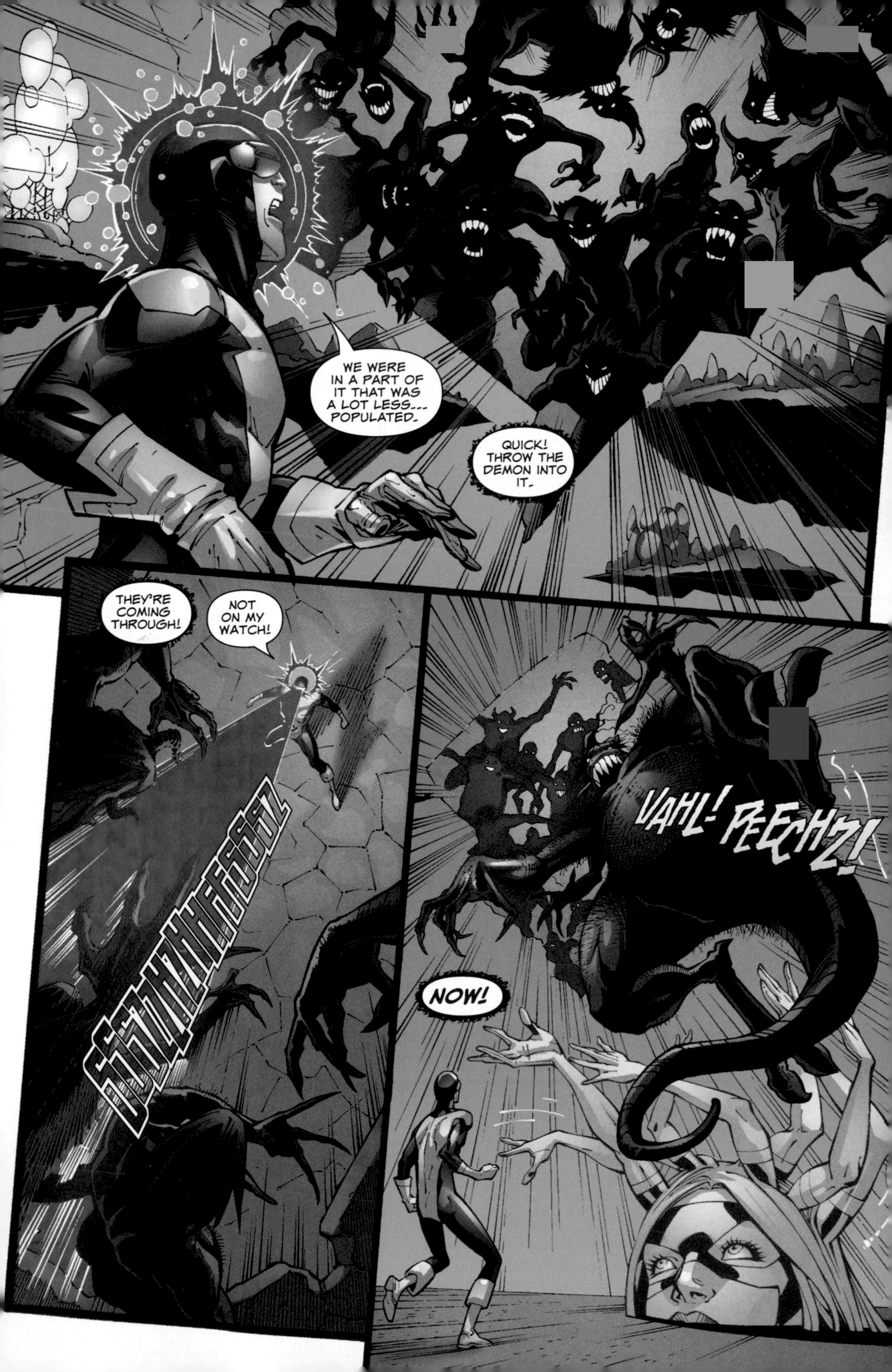
WE WERE IN A PART OF IT THAT WAS A LOT LESS... POPULATED.
QUICK! THROW THE DEMON INTO IT.
THEY'RE COMING THROUGH!
NOT ON MY WATCH!
VAHL! PEECHZ!
NOW!

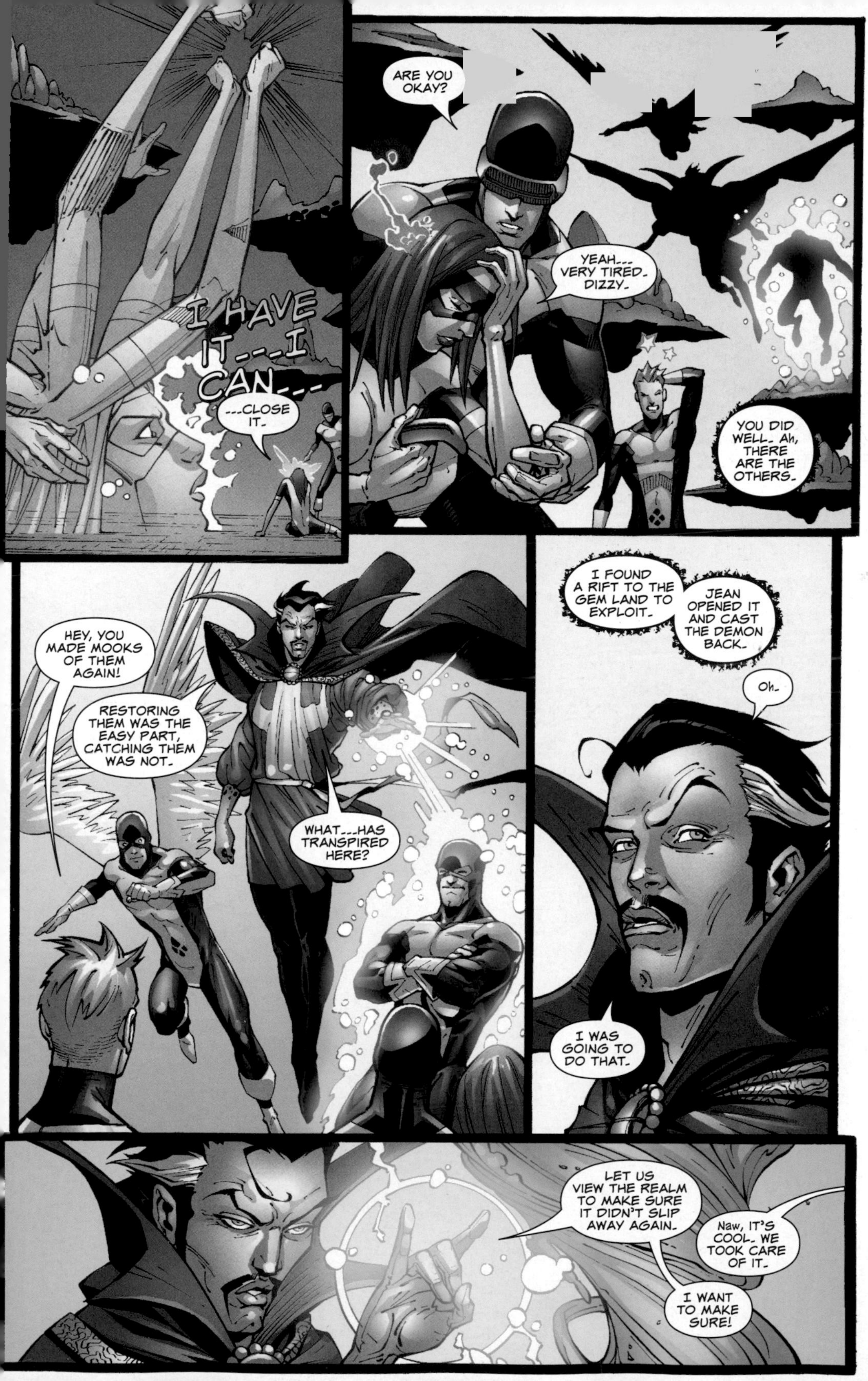
I HAVE IT---I CAN---
---CLOSE IT.
ARE YOU OKAY?
YEAH--- VERY TIRED. DIZZY.
YOU DID WELL. Ah, THERE ARE THE OTHERS.
HEY, YOU MADE MOOKS OF THEM AGAIN!
RESTORING THEM WAS THE EASY PART, CATCHING THEM WAS NOT.
WHAT---HAS TRANSPIRED HERE?
I FOUND A RIFT TO THE GEM LAND TO EXPLOIT.
JEAN OPENED IT AND CAST THE DEMON BACK.
Oh.
I WAS GOING TO DO THAT.
LET US VIEW THE REALM TO MAKE SURE IT DIDN'T SLIP AWAY AGAIN.
Naw, IT'S COOL. WE TOOK CARE OF IT.
I WANT TO MAKE SURE!

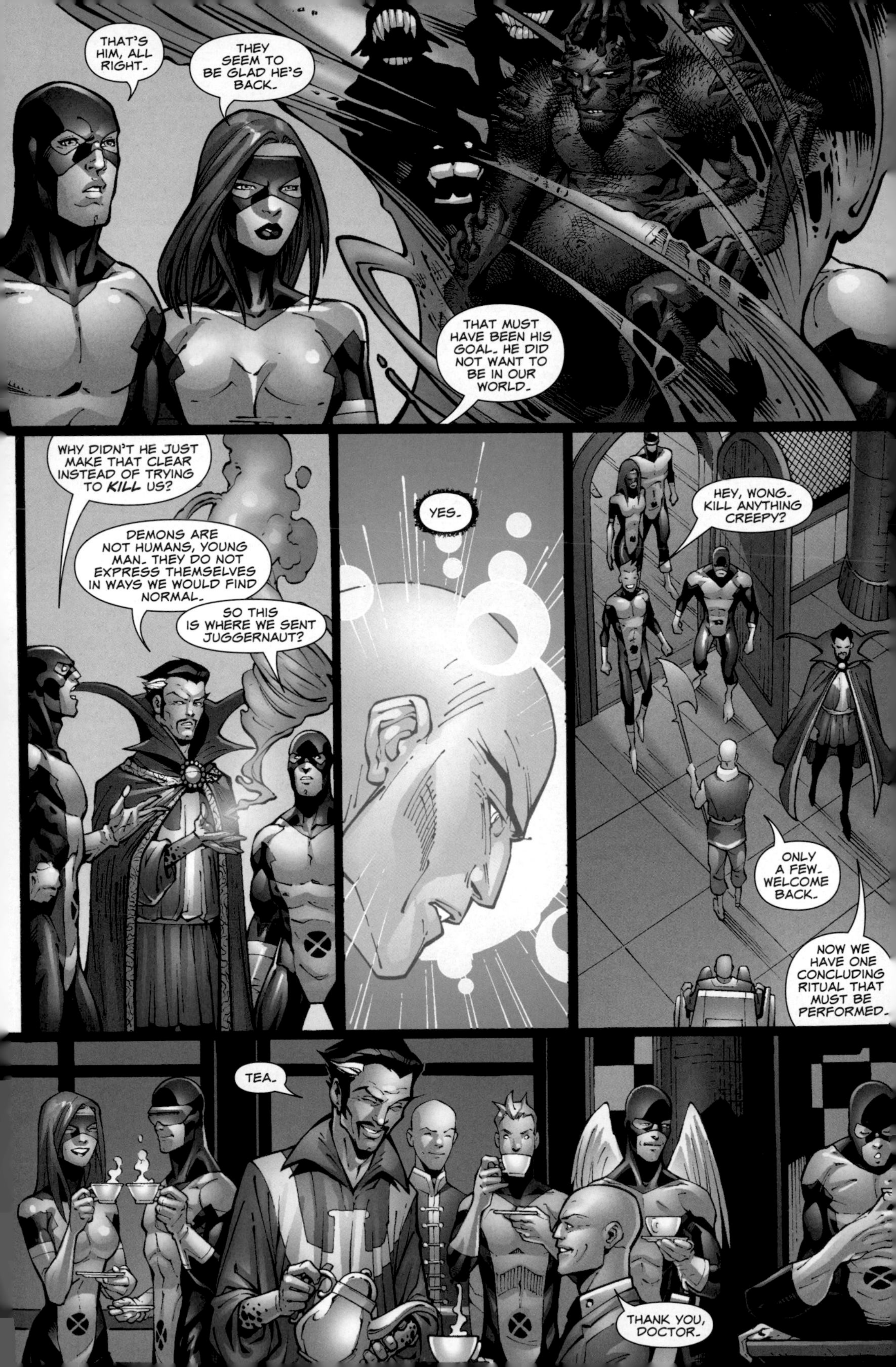
THAT'S HIM, ALL RIGHT.
THEY SEEM TO BE GLAD HE'S BACK.
THAT MUST HAVE BEEN HIS GOAL. HE DID NOT WANT TO BE IN OUR WORLD.
WHY DIDN'T HE JUST MAKE THAT CLEAR INSTEAD OF TRYING TO KILL US?
DEMONS ARE NOT HUMANS, YOUNG MAN. THEY DO NOT EXPRESS THEMSELVES IN WAYS WE WOULD FIND NORMAL.
SO THIS IS WHERE WE SENT JUGGERNAUT?
YES.
HEY, WONG. KILL ANYTHING CREEPY?
ONLY A FEW. WELCOME BACK.
NOW WE HAVE ONE CONCLUDING RITUAL THAT MUST BE PERFORMED.
TEA.
THANK YOU, DOCTOR.

5

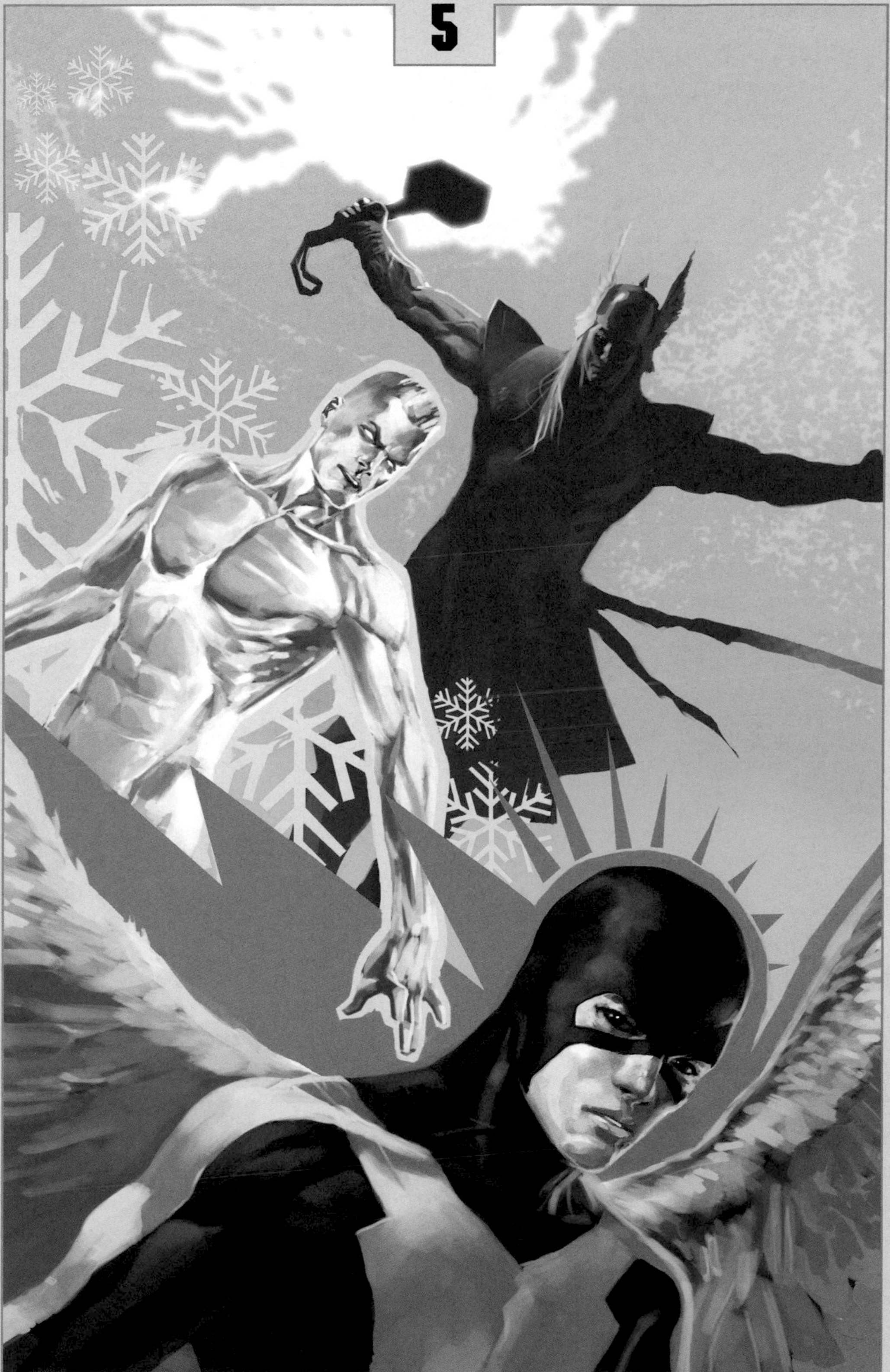

THE NEXT STEP IN HUMAN EVOLUTION HAS ARRIVED—HOMO SUPERIOR. MANKIND ISN'T SURE WHETHER THIS REPRESENTS HOPE FOR THE FUTURE...OR THE END OF THE HUMAN RACE. IN A PRIVATE SCHOOL IN UPSTATE NEW YORK, ONE BRILLIANT MUTANT IS TEACHING A GROUP OF FIVE SUCH GIFTED STUDENTS WHAT THEY'LL NEED TO SURVIVE IN THIS NEW WORLD. THESE ARE THE UNTOLD STORIES OF PROFESSOR XAVIER'S FIRST CLASS OF X-MEN!

XAVIER'S SCHOOL FOR GIFTED YOUNGSTERS

PROPERTY OF:

Marvel Girl

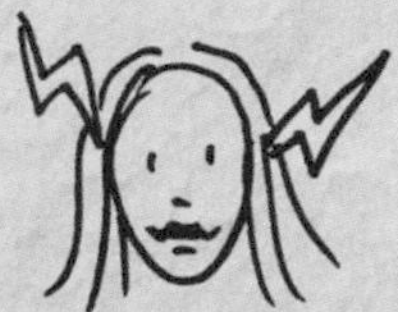

HEADMASTER

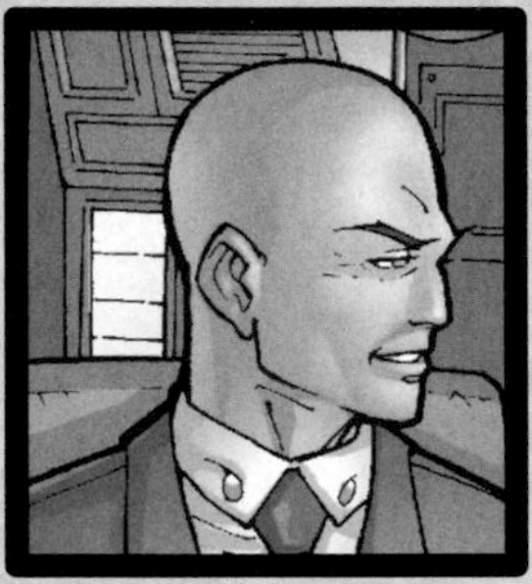

PROFESSOR CHARLES XAVIER

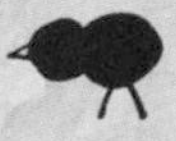

Yesterday during our mission Xavier had a song stuck in his head, and now it's stuck in MY head. Driving me nuts!

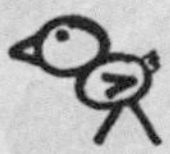

I hear Scott down the hall. Can always tell by the quick footsteps. ~~Wonder if he wore that silk shirt he sometimes does? Now that is HOT..~~

Why didn't I get to choose my own picture for this thing? I HATE this picture. Ug.

Hank's explaining something to me.. Keep nodding, smile... WHAT IS HE TALKING ABOUT?

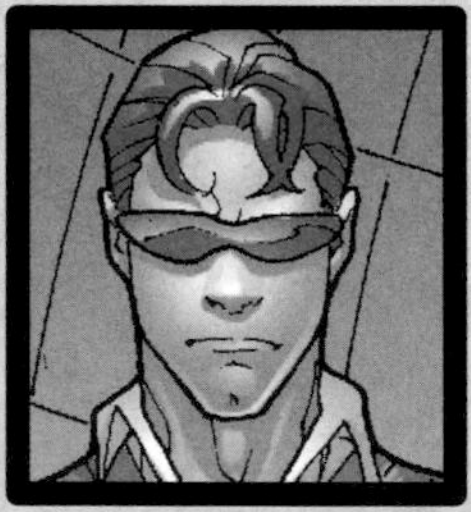

SCOTT SUMMERS
"CYCLOPS"

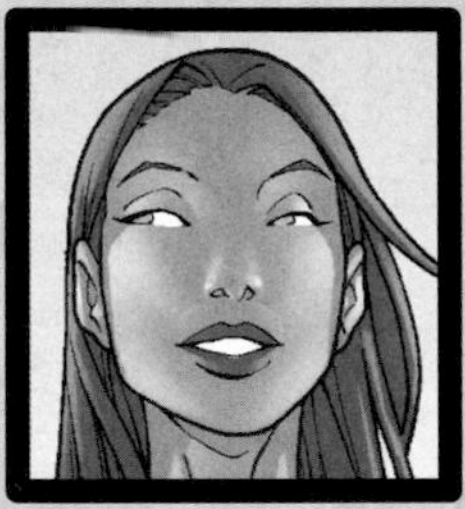

JEAN GREY
"MARVEL GIRL"

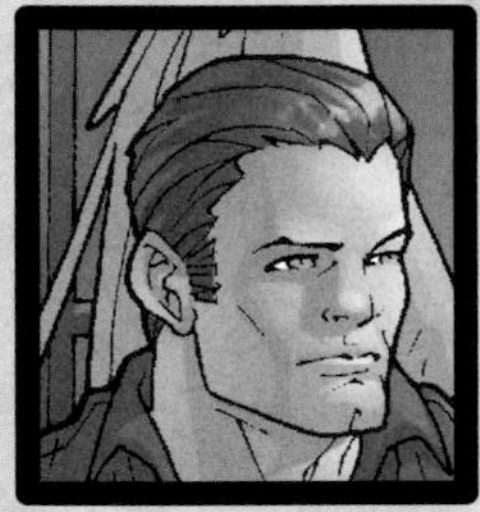

HENRY "HANK" McCOY
"BEAST"

I'm thinking we all need red uniforms.

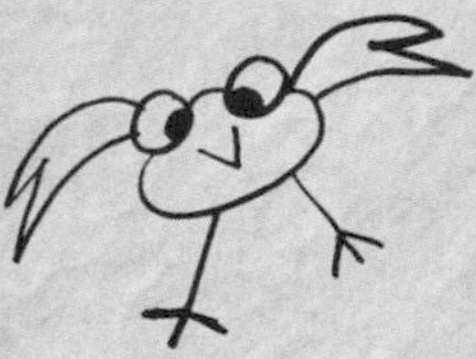

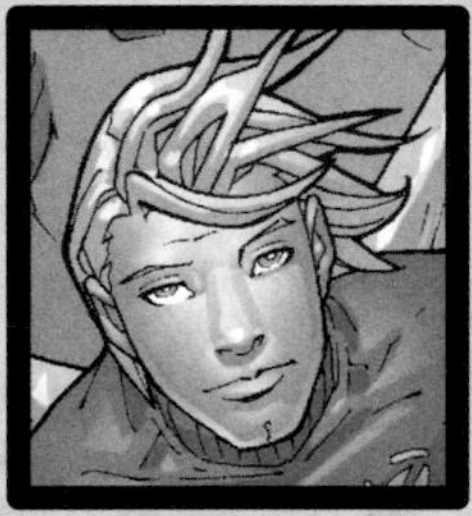

WARREN WORTHINGTON III
"ANGEL"

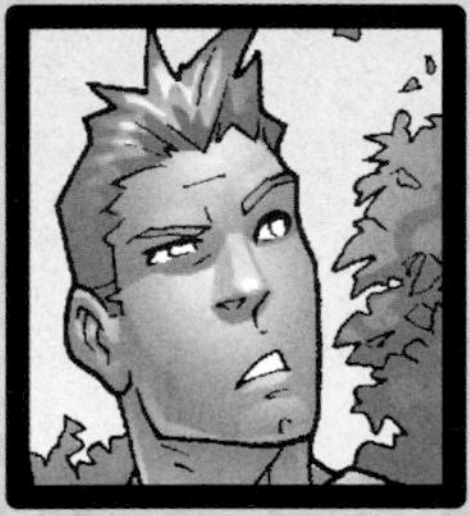

ROBERT DRAKE
"ICEMAN"

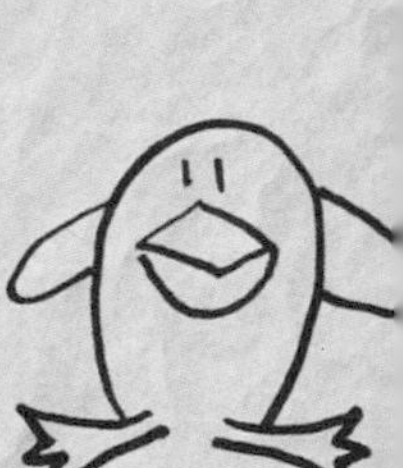

Warren, stay put... the Professor is a lil cranky today... I know it's sunny out and the window is open, but don't... don't... - He's gone.

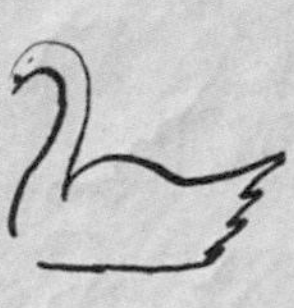

Bobby needs some advice on the girl down at the coffee shop and I told him just BE-YOUR-SELF. But quit wiggling in your seat, making nasty jokes and mouthing sound effects to things all the time. And be yourself.

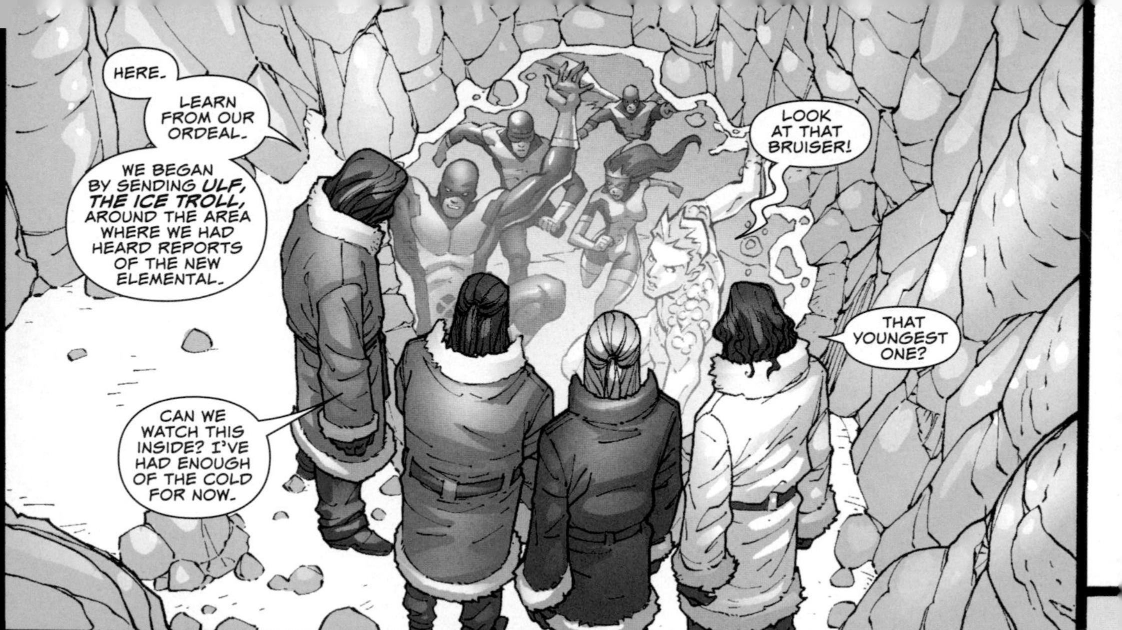
HERE.
LEARN FROM OUR ORDEAL.
WE BEGAN BY SENDING ULF, THE ICE TROLL, AROUND THE AREA WHERE WE HAD HEARD REPORTS OF THE NEW ELEMENTAL.
LOOK AT THAT BRUISER!
THAT YOUNGEST ONE?
CAN WE WATCH THIS INSIDE? I'VE HAD ENOUGH OF THE COLD FOR NOW.

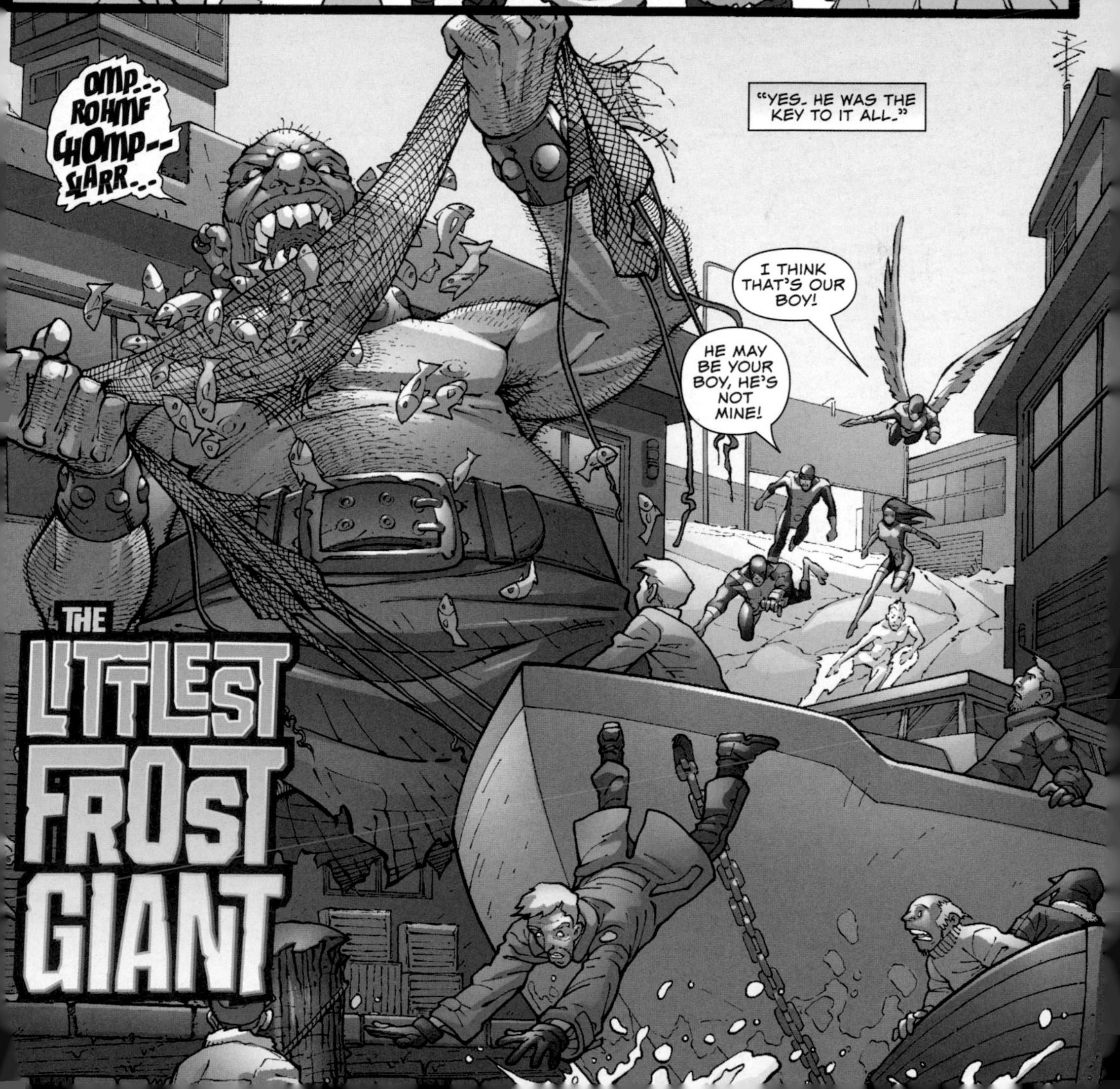
OMP... ROHMF CHOMP... SLARR...
"YES. HE WAS THE KEY TO IT ALL."
I THINK THAT'S OUR BOY!
HE MAY BE YOUR BOY, HE'S NOT MINE!
THE LITTLEST FROST GIANT

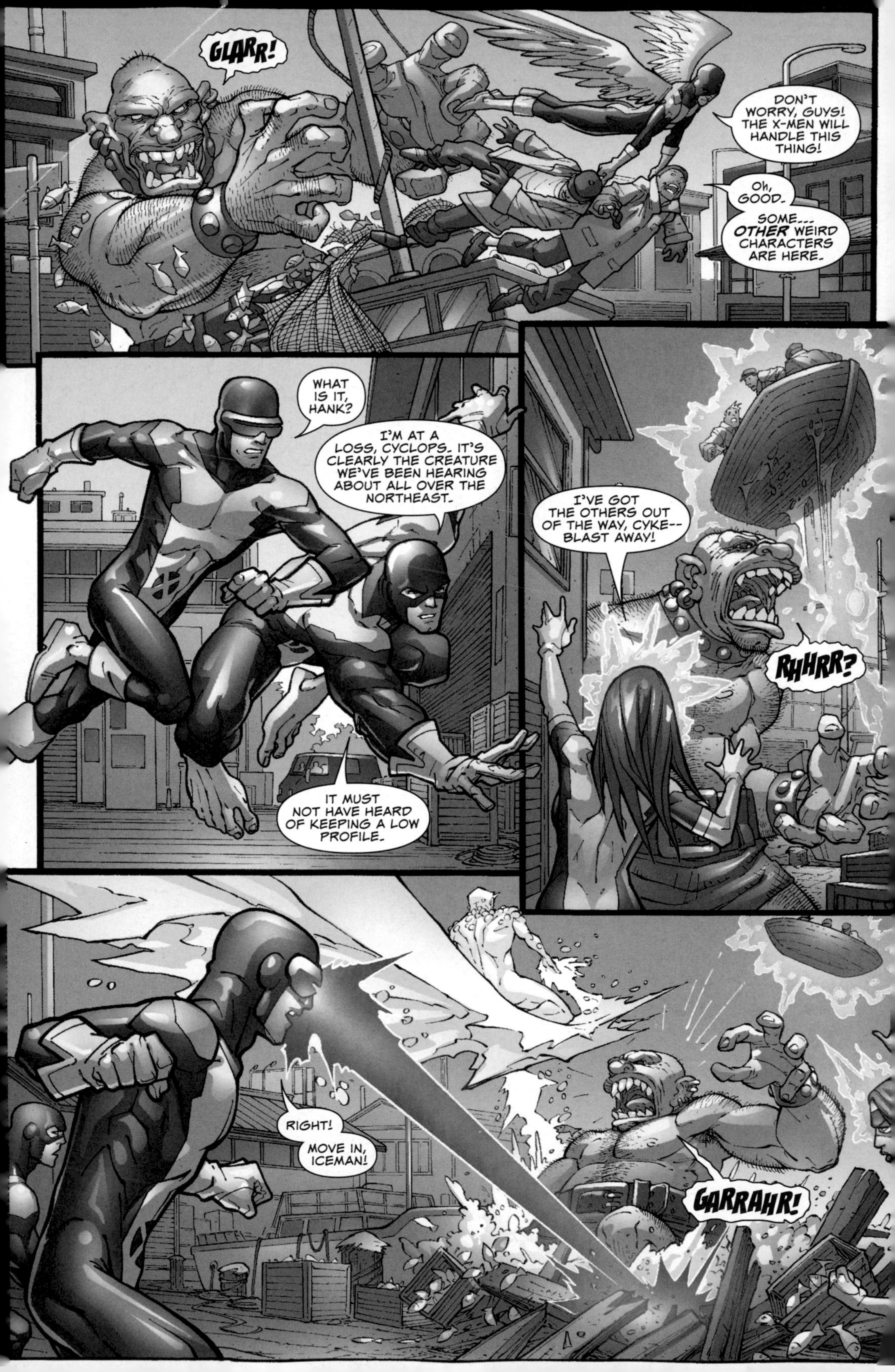
GLARR!
DON'T WORRY, GUYS! THE X-MEN WILL HANDLE THIS THING!
Oh, GOOD.
SOME... OTHER WEIRD CHARACTERS ARE HERE.
WHAT IS IT, HANK?
I'M AT A LOSS, CYCLOPS. IT'S CLEARLY THE CREATURE WE'VE BEEN HEARING ABOUT ALL OVER THE NORTHEAST.
IT MUST NOT HAVE HEARD OF KEEPING A LOW PROFILE.
I'VE GOT THE OTHERS OUT OF THE WAY, CYKE-- BLAST AWAY!
RHHRR?
RIGHT!
MOVE IN, ICEMAN!
GARRAHR!

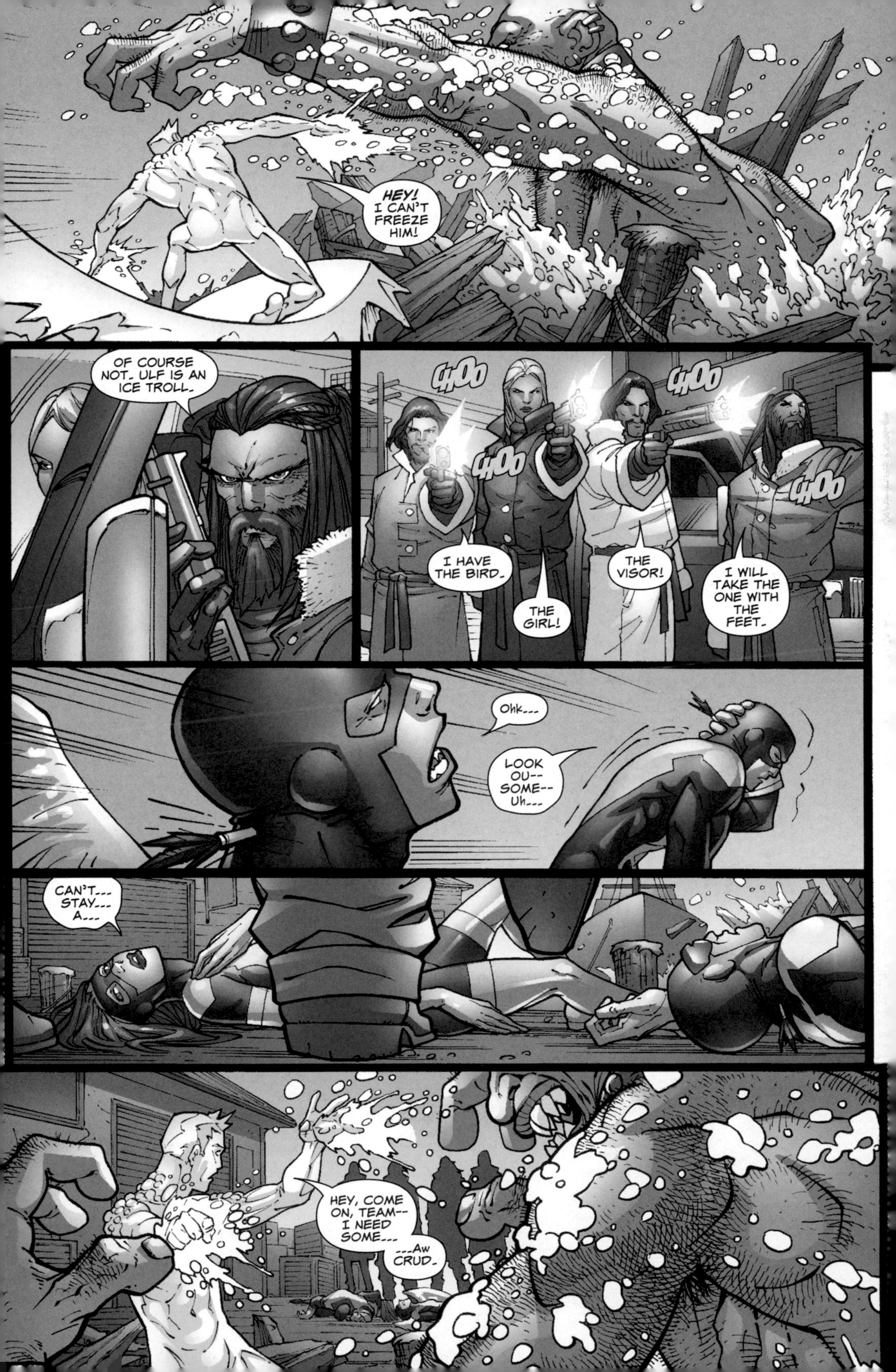
HEY! I CAN'T FREEZE HIM!
OF COURSE NOT. ULF IS AN ICE TROLL.
CHOO
CHOO
CHOO
CHOO
I HAVE THE BIRD.
THE GIRL!
THE VISOR!
I WILL TAKE THE ONE WITH THE FEET.
Ohk...
LOOK OU-- SOME-- Uh...
CAN'T... STAY... A...
HEY, COME ON, TEAM-- I NEED SOME...
...Aw CRUD.

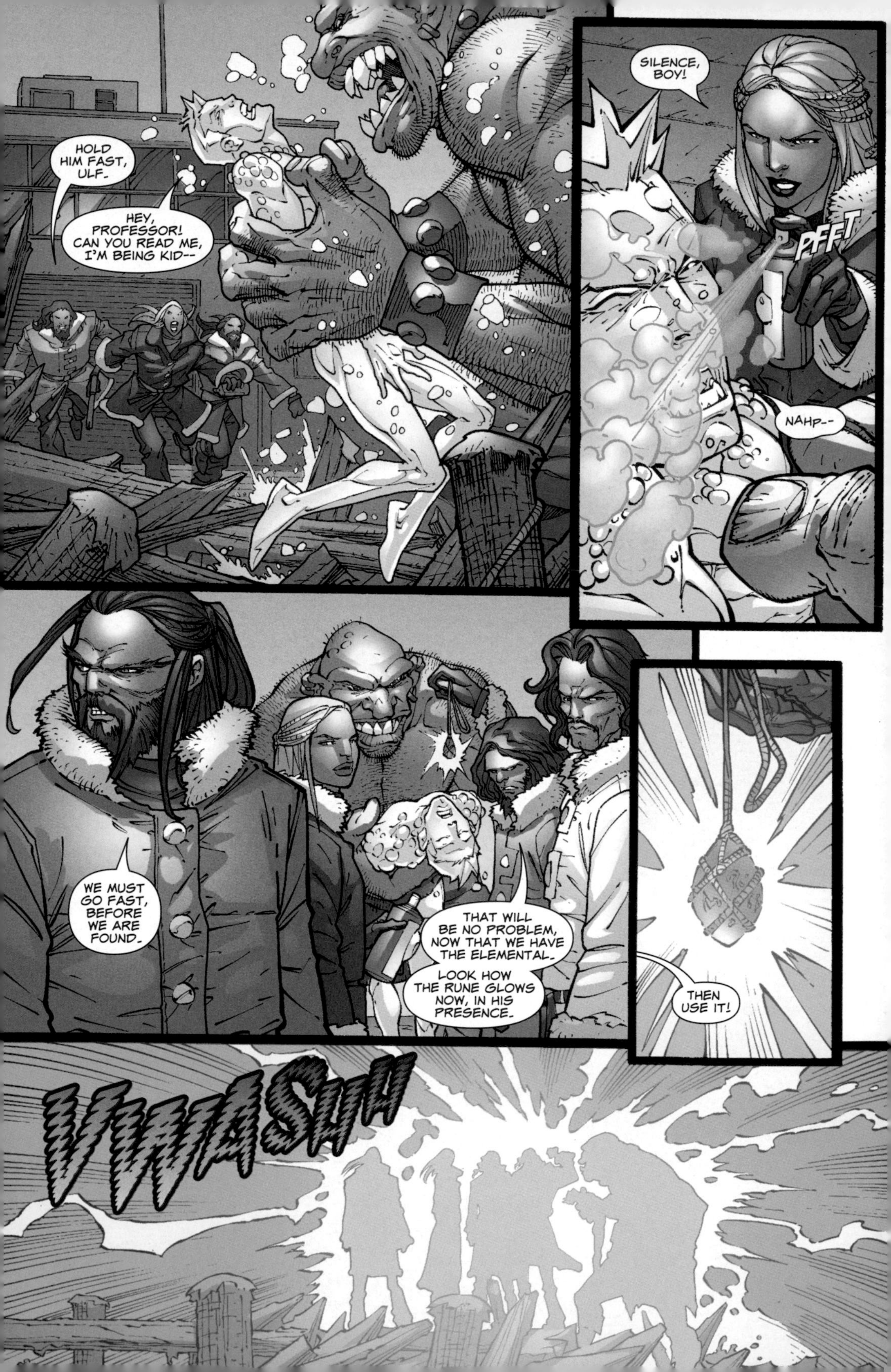
HOLD HIM FAST, ULF.
HEY, PROFESSOR! CAN YOU READ ME, I'M BEING KID--
SILENCE, BOY!
PFFT
NAHP--
WE MUST GO FAST, BEFORE WE ARE FOUND.
THAT WILL BE NO PROBLEM, NOW THAT WE HAVE THE ELEMENTAL.
LOOK HOW THE RUNE GLOWS NOW, IN HIS PRESENCE.
THEN USE IT!
VVMASH

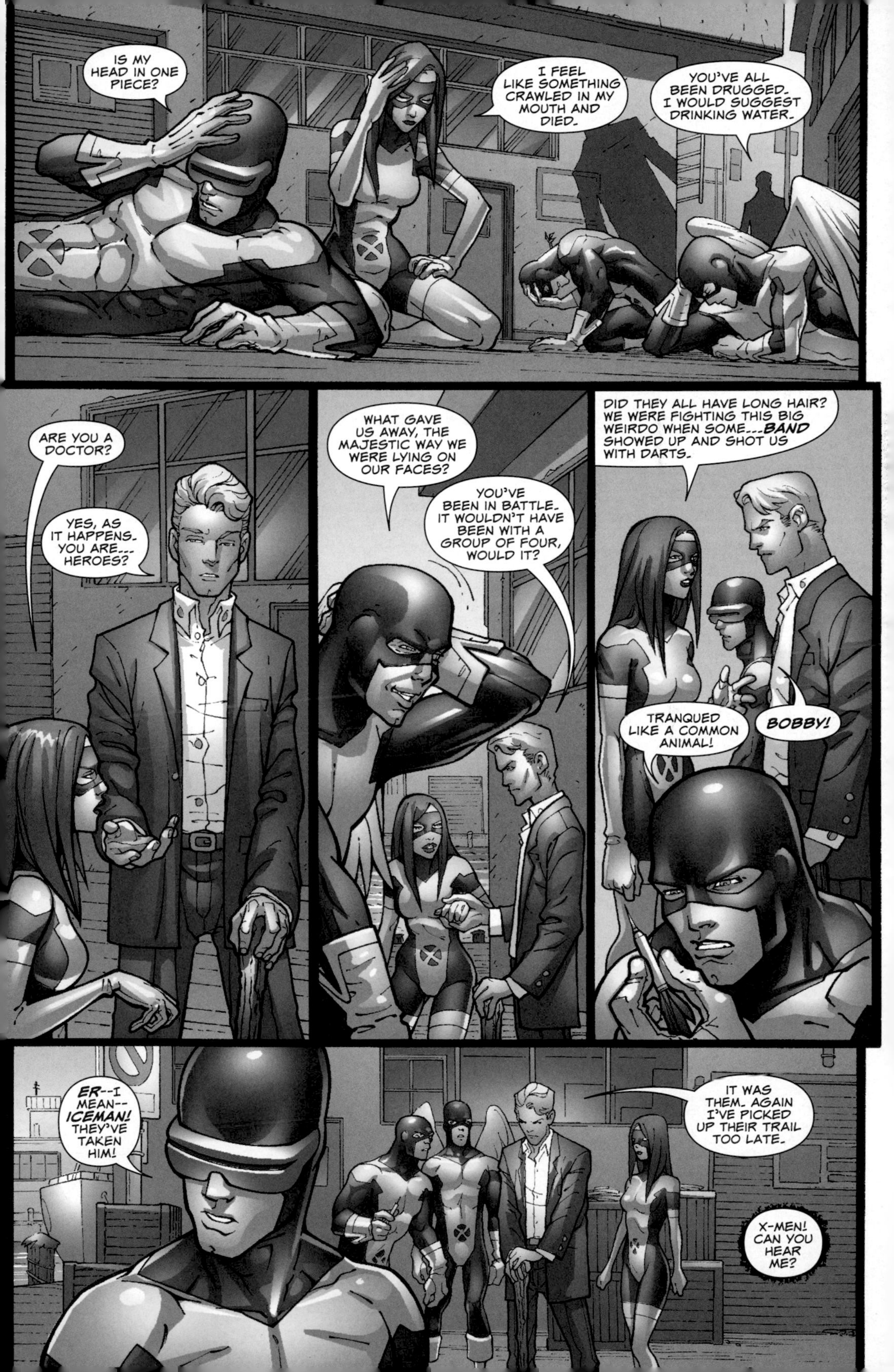

IS MY HEAD IN ONE PIECE?
I FEEL LIKE SOMETHING CRAWLED IN MY MOUTH AND DIED.
YOU'VE ALL BEEN DRUGGED. I WOULD SUGGEST DRINKING WATER.
ARE YOU A DOCTOR?
YES, AS IT HAPPENS. YOU ARE... HEROES?
WHAT GAVE US AWAY, THE MAJESTIC WAY WE WERE LYING ON OUR FACES?
YOU'VE BEEN IN BATTLE. IT WOULDN'T HAVE BEEN WITH A GROUP OF FOUR, WOULD IT?
DID THEY ALL HAVE LONG HAIR? WE WERE FIGHTING THIS BIG WEIRDO WHEN SOME...BAND SHOWED UP AND SHOT US WITH DARTS.
TRANQUED LIKE A COMMON ANIMAL!
BOBBY!
ER--I MEAN--ICEMAN! THEY'VE TAKEN HIM!
IT WAS THEM. AGAIN I'VE PICKED UP THEIR TRAIL TOO LATE.
X-MEN! CAN YOU HEAR ME?

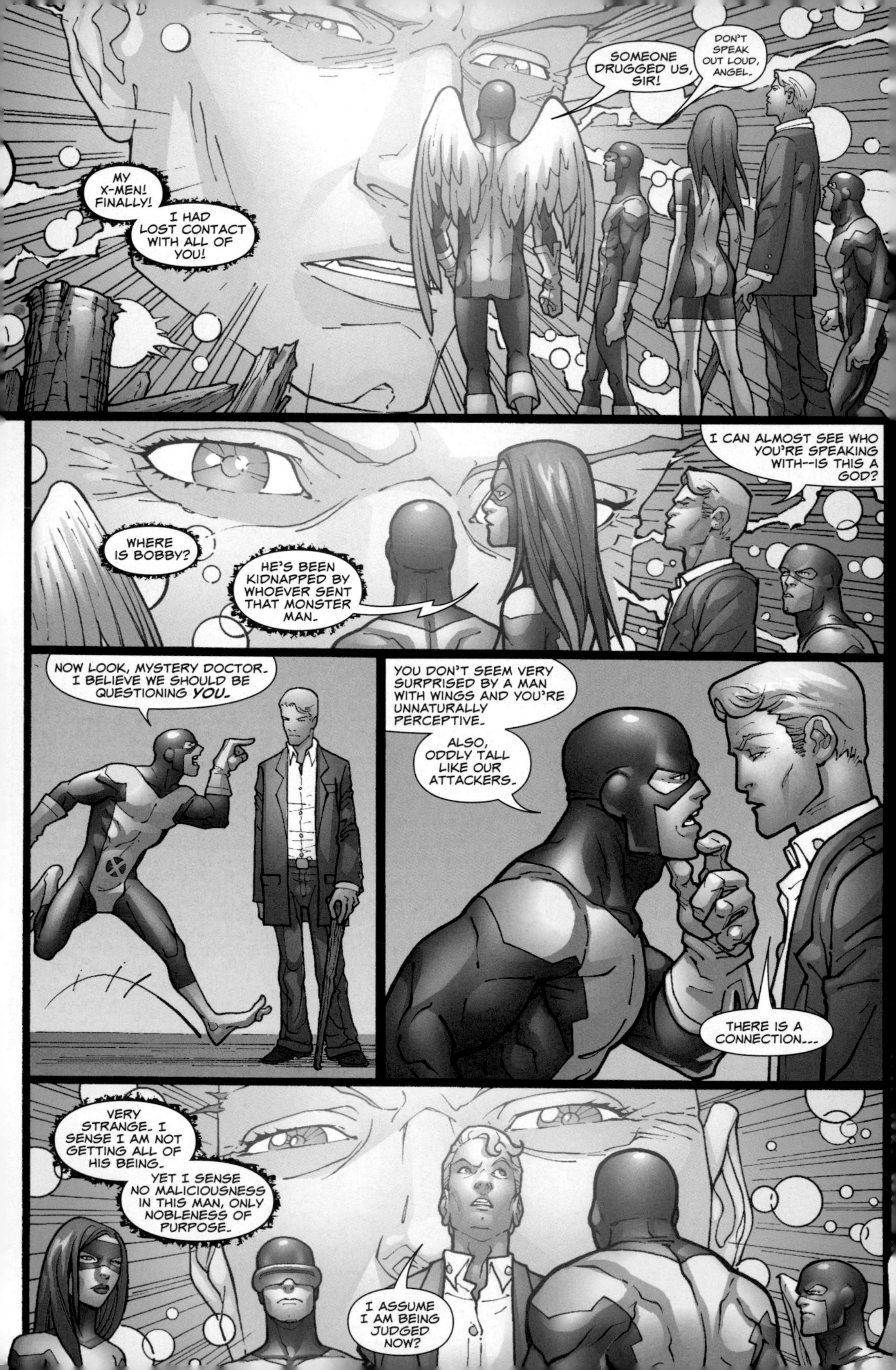
MY X-MEN! FINALLY!
I HAD LOST CONTACT WITH ALL OF YOU!
SOMEONE DRUGGED US, SIR!
DON'T SPEAK OUT LOUD, ANGEL.
I CAN ALMOST SEE WHO YOU'RE SPEAKING WITH--IS THIS A GOD?
WHERE IS BOBBY?
HE'S BEEN KIDNAPPED BY WHOEVER SENT THAT MONSTER MAN.
NOW LOOK, MYSTERY DOCTOR. I BELIEVE WE SHOULD BE QUESTIONING YOU.
YOU DON'T SEEM VERY SURPRISED BY A MAN WITH WINGS AND YOU'RE UNNATURALLY PERCEPTIVE.
ALSO, ODDLY TALL LIKE OUR ATTACKERS.
THERE IS A CONNECTION...
VERY STRANGE. I SENSE I AM NOT GETTING ALL OF HIS BEING.
YET I SENSE NO MALICIOUSNESS IN THIS MAN, ONLY NOBLENESS OF PURPOSE.
I ASSUME I AM BEING JUDGED NOW?

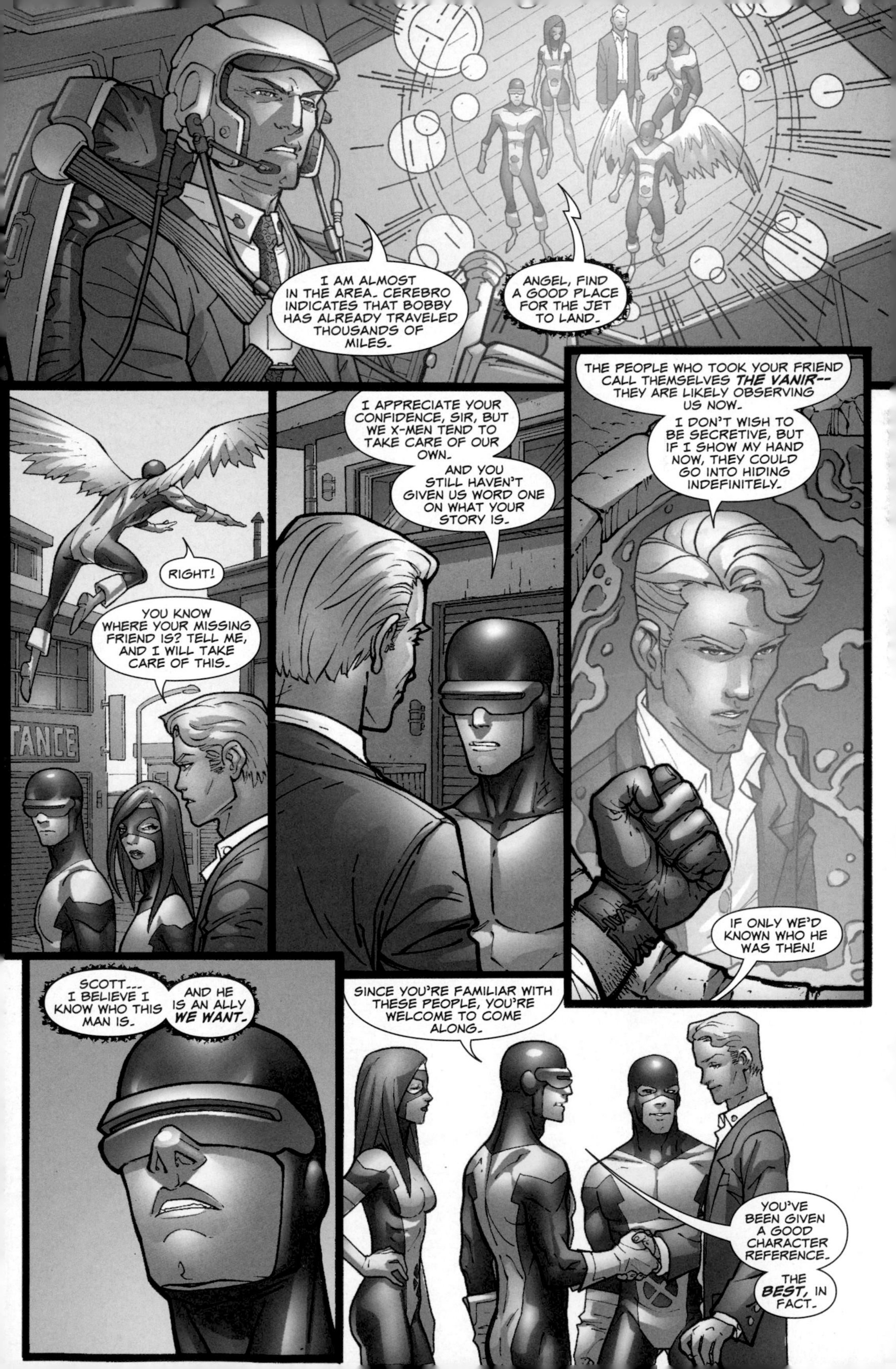
I AM ALMOST IN THE AREA. CEREBRO INDICATES THAT BOBBY HAS ALREADY TRAVELED THOUSANDS OF MILES.
ANGEL, FIND A GOOD PLACE FOR THE JET TO LAND.
RIGHT!
YOU KNOW WHERE YOUR MISSING FRIEND IS? TELL ME, AND I WILL TAKE CARE OF THIS.
TANCE
I APPRECIATE YOUR CONFIDENCE, SIR, BUT WE X-MEN TEND TO TAKE CARE OF OUR OWN.
AND YOU STILL HAVEN'T GIVEN US WORD ONE ON WHAT YOUR STORY IS.
THE PEOPLE WHO TOOK YOUR FRIEND CALL THEMSELVES *THE VANIR*-- THEY ARE LIKELY OBSERVING US NOW.
I DON'T WISH TO BE SECRETIVE, BUT IF I SHOW MY HAND NOW, THEY COULD GO INTO HIDING INDEFINITELY.
IF ONLY WE'D KNOWN WHO HE WAS THEN!
SCOTT... I BELIEVE I KNOW WHO THIS MAN IS.
AND HE IS AN ALLY *WE WANT*.
SINCE YOU'RE FAMILIAR WITH THESE PEOPLE, YOU'RE WELCOME TO COME ALONG.
YOU'VE BEEN GIVEN A GOOD CHARACTER REFERENCE.
THE *BEST*, IN FACT.

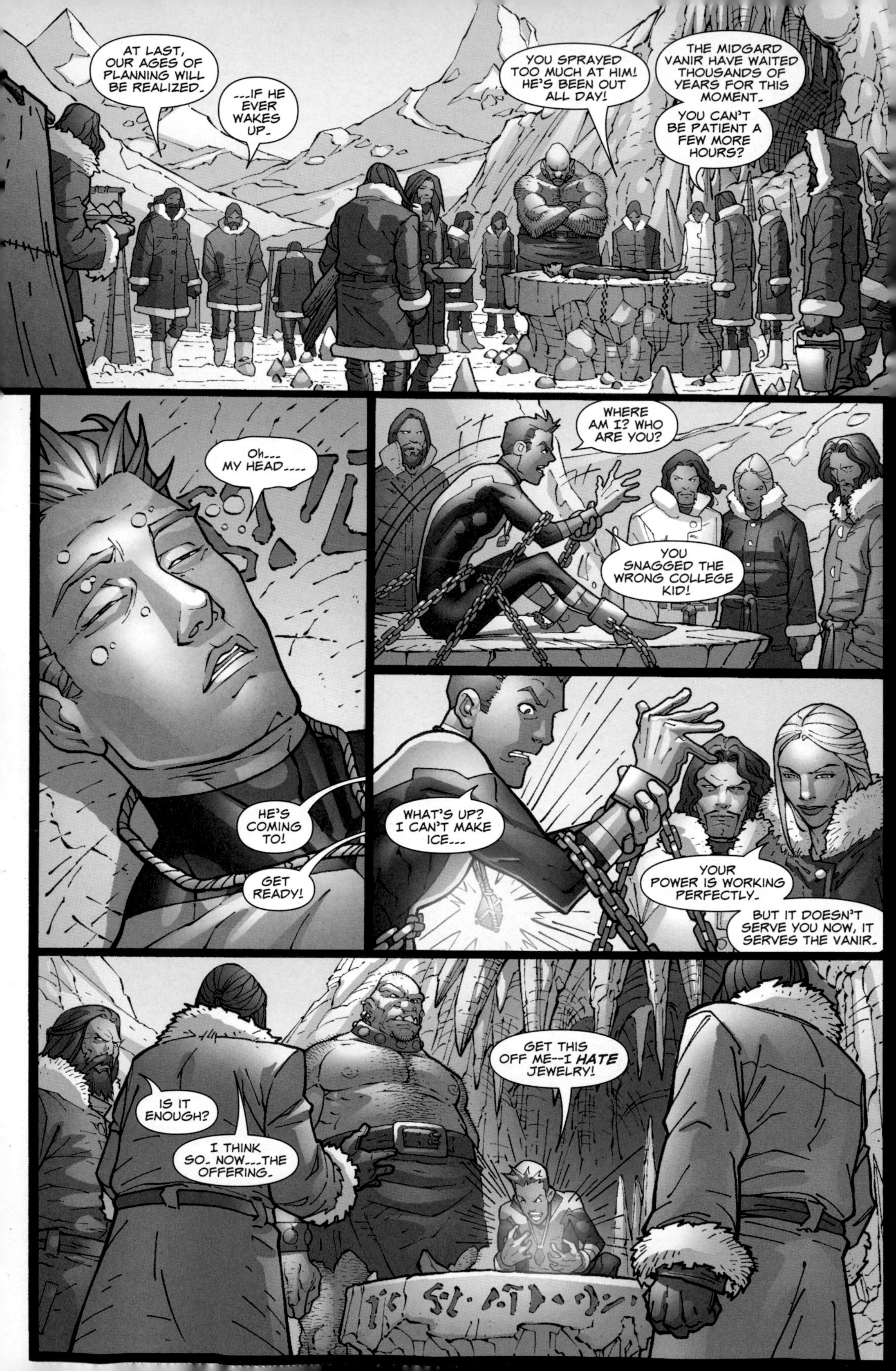
AT LAST, OUR AGES OF PLANNING WILL BE REALIZED.
...IF HE EVER WAKES UP.
YOU SPRAYED TOO MUCH AT HIM! HE'S BEEN OUT ALL DAY!
THE MIDGARD VANIR HAVE WAITED THOUSANDS OF YEARS FOR THIS MOMENT.
YOU CAN'T BE PATIENT A FEW MORE HOURS?
Oh... MY HEAD....
HE'S COMING TO!
GET READY!
WHERE AM I? WHO ARE YOU?
YOU SNAGGED THE WRONG COLLEGE KID!
WHAT'S UP? I CAN'T MAKE ICE...
YOUR POWER IS WORKING PERFECTLY.
BUT IT DOESN'T SERVE YOU NOW, IT SERVES THE VANIR.
IS IT ENOUGH?
I THINK SO. NOW...THE OFFERING.
GET THIS OFF ME--I HATE JEWELRY!

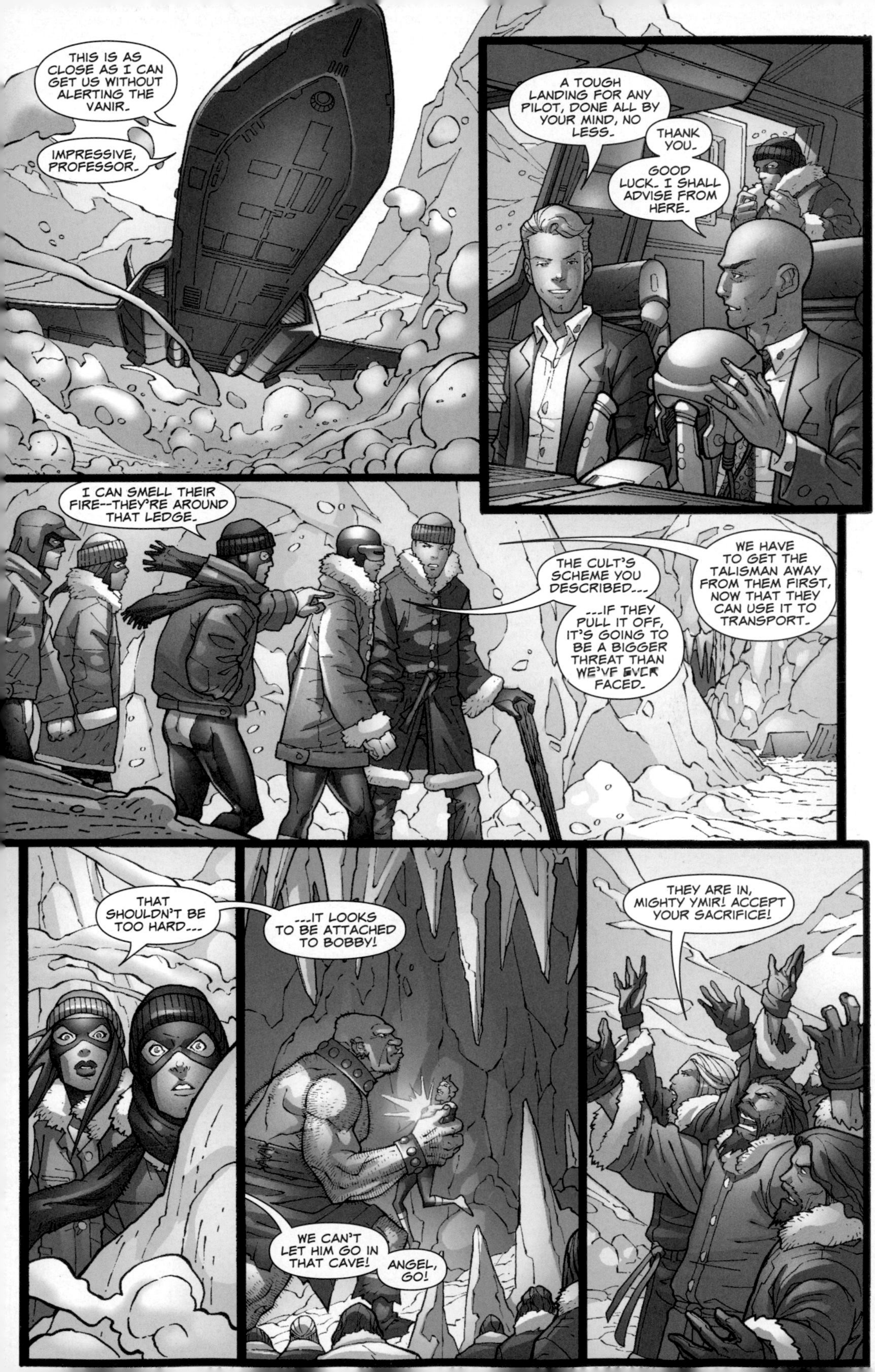
THIS IS AS CLOSE AS I CAN GET US WITHOUT ALERTING THE VANIR.
IMPRESSIVE, PROFESSOR.
A TOUGH LANDING FOR ANY PILOT, DONE ALL BY YOUR MIND, NO LESS.
THANK YOU.
GOOD LUCK. I SHALL ADVISE FROM HERE.
I CAN SMELL THEIR FIRE--THEY'RE AROUND THAT LEDGE.
THE CULT'S SCHEME YOU DESCRIBED---
---IF THEY PULL IT OFF, IT'S GOING TO BE A BIGGER THREAT THAN WE'VE EVER FACED.
WE HAVE TO GET THE TALISMAN AWAY FROM THEM FIRST, NOW THAT THEY CAN USE IT TO TRANSPORT.
THAT SHOULDN'T BE TOO HARD---
---IT LOOKS TO BE ATTACHED TO BOBBY!
WE CAN'T LET HIM GO IN THAT CAVE!
ANGEL, GO!
THEY ARE IN, MIGHTY YMIR! ACCEPT YOUR SACRIFICE!

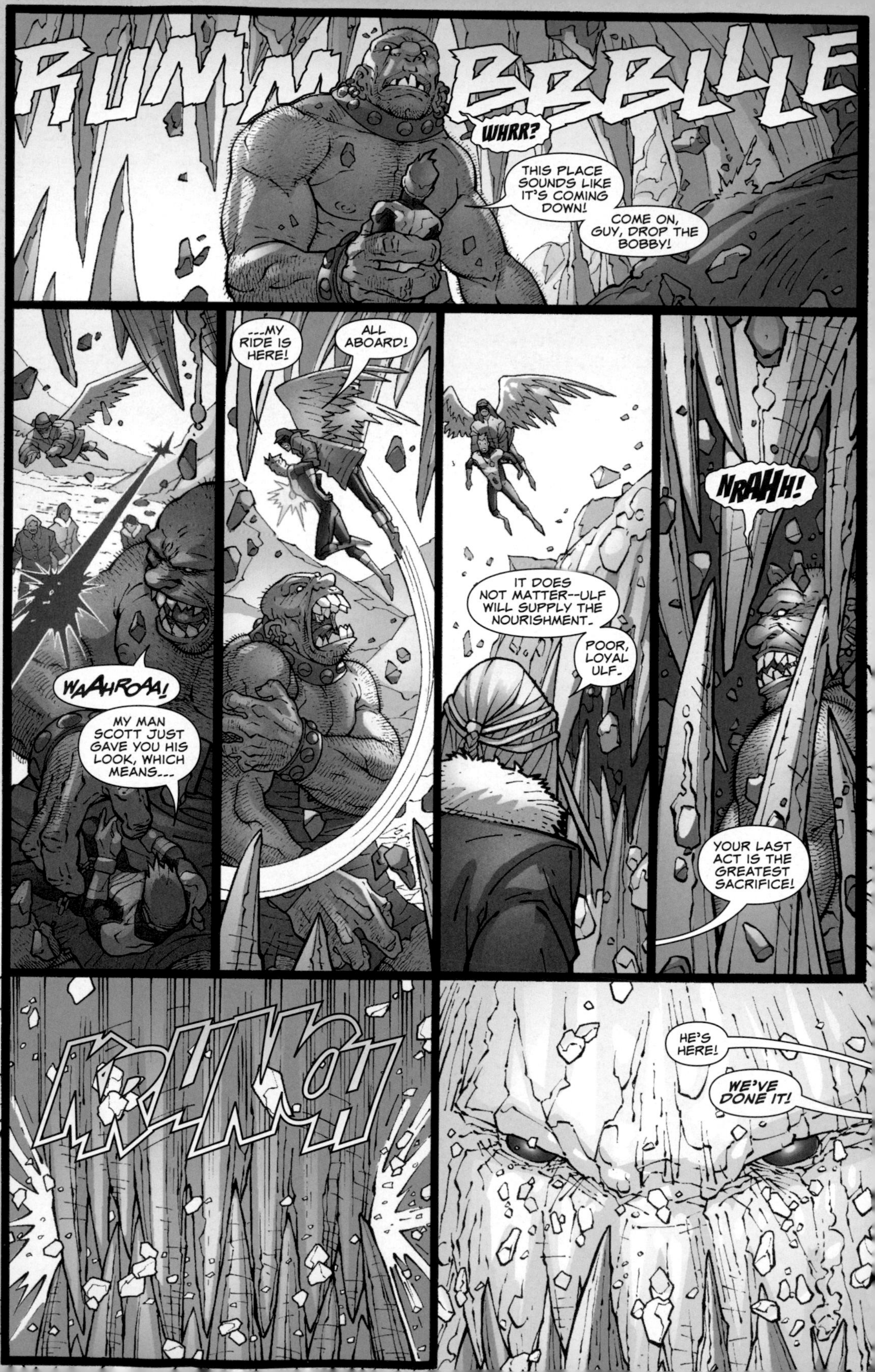
RUMMMBBBLLE
WHRR?
THIS PLACE SOUNDS LIKE IT'S COMING DOWN!
COME ON, GUY, DROP THE BOBBY!
WAAHROAA!
MY MAN SCOTT JUST GAVE YOU HIS LOOK, WHICH MEANS---
---MY RIDE IS HERE!
ALL ABOARD!
IT DOES NOT MATTER--ULF WILL SUPPLY THE NOURISHMENT.
POOR, LOYAL ULF.
NRAHH!
YOUR LAST ACT IS THE GREATEST SACRIFICE!
HE'S HERE!
WE'VE DONE IT!

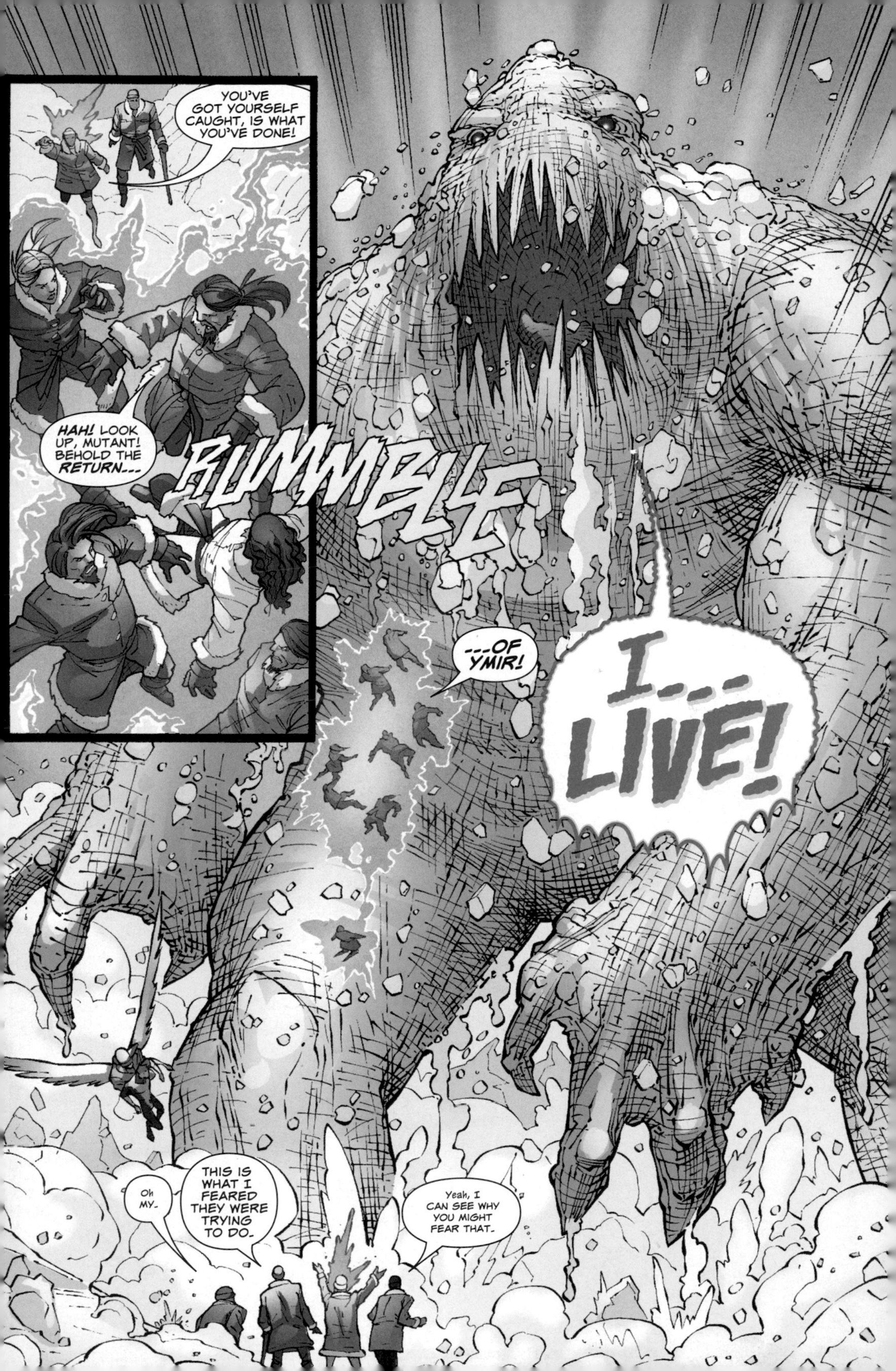
YOU'VE GOT YOURSELF CAUGHT, IS WHAT YOU'VE DONE!
HAH! LOOK UP, MUTANT! BEHOLD THE RETURN---
RUMMBLE
---OF YMIR!
I... LIVE!
Oh my.
THIS IS WHAT I FEARED THEY WERE TRYING TO DO.
Yeah, I can see why you might fear that.

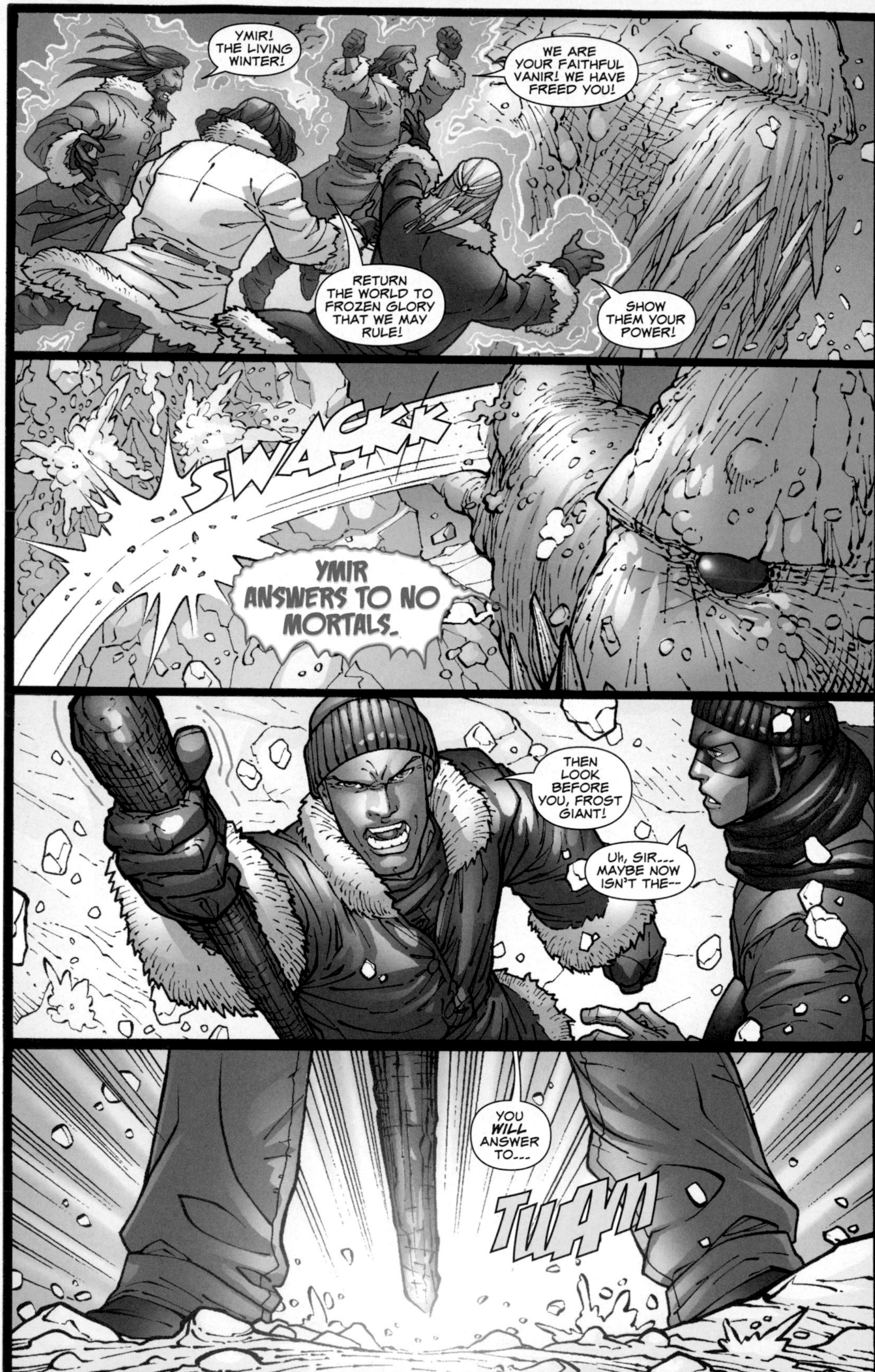
YMIR! THE LIVING WINTER!
WE ARE YOUR FAITHFUL VANIR! WE HAVE FREED YOU!
RETURN THE WORLD TO FROZEN GLORY THAT WE MAY RULE!
SHOW THEM YOUR POWER!
SWACKK
YMIR ANSWERS TO NO MORTALS.
THEN LOOK BEFORE YOU, FROST GIANT!
Uh, SIR... MAYBE NOW ISN'T THE--
YOU WILL ANSWER TO...
TWAM

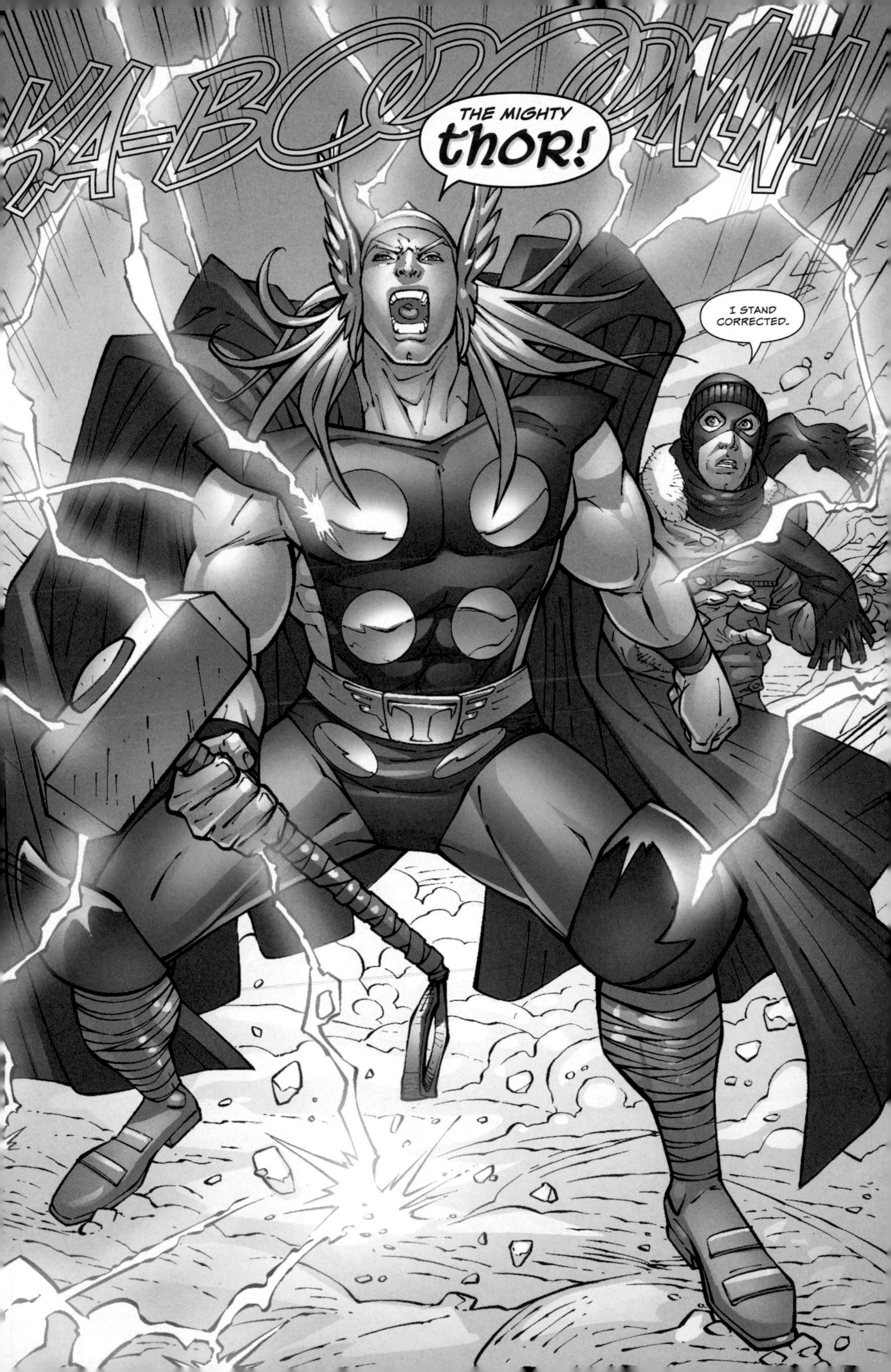

KA-BOOOOOMM
THE MIGHTY thor!
I STAND CORRECTED.

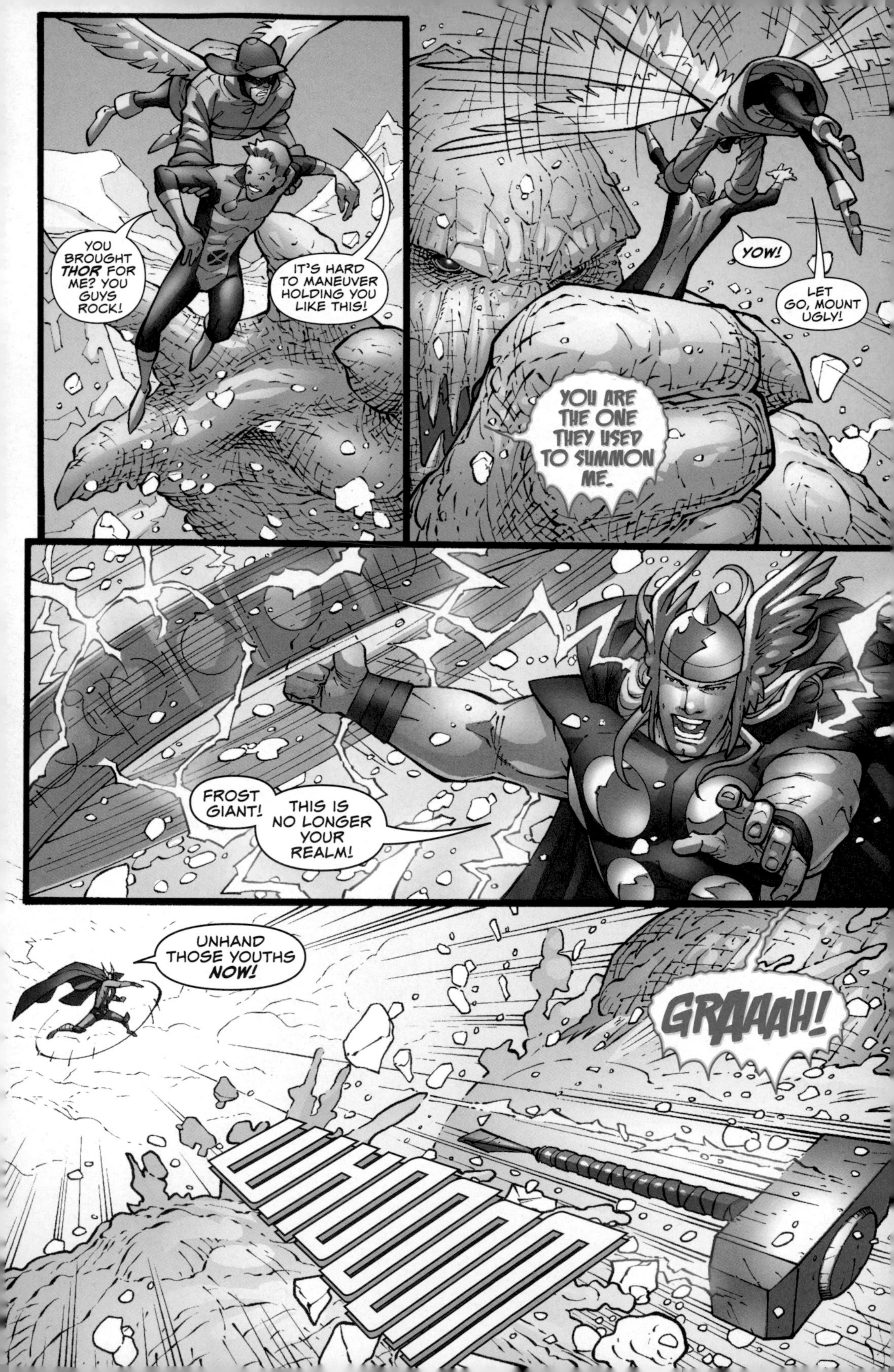
YOU BROUGHT THOR FOR ME? YOU GUYS ROCK!
IT'S HARD TO MANEUVER HOLDING YOU LIKE THIS!
YOW!
LET GO, MOUNT UGLY!
YOU ARE THE ONE THEY USED TO SUMMON ME.
FROST GIANT!
THIS IS NO LONGER YOUR REALM!
UNHAND THOSE YOUTHS NOW!
GRAAAH!

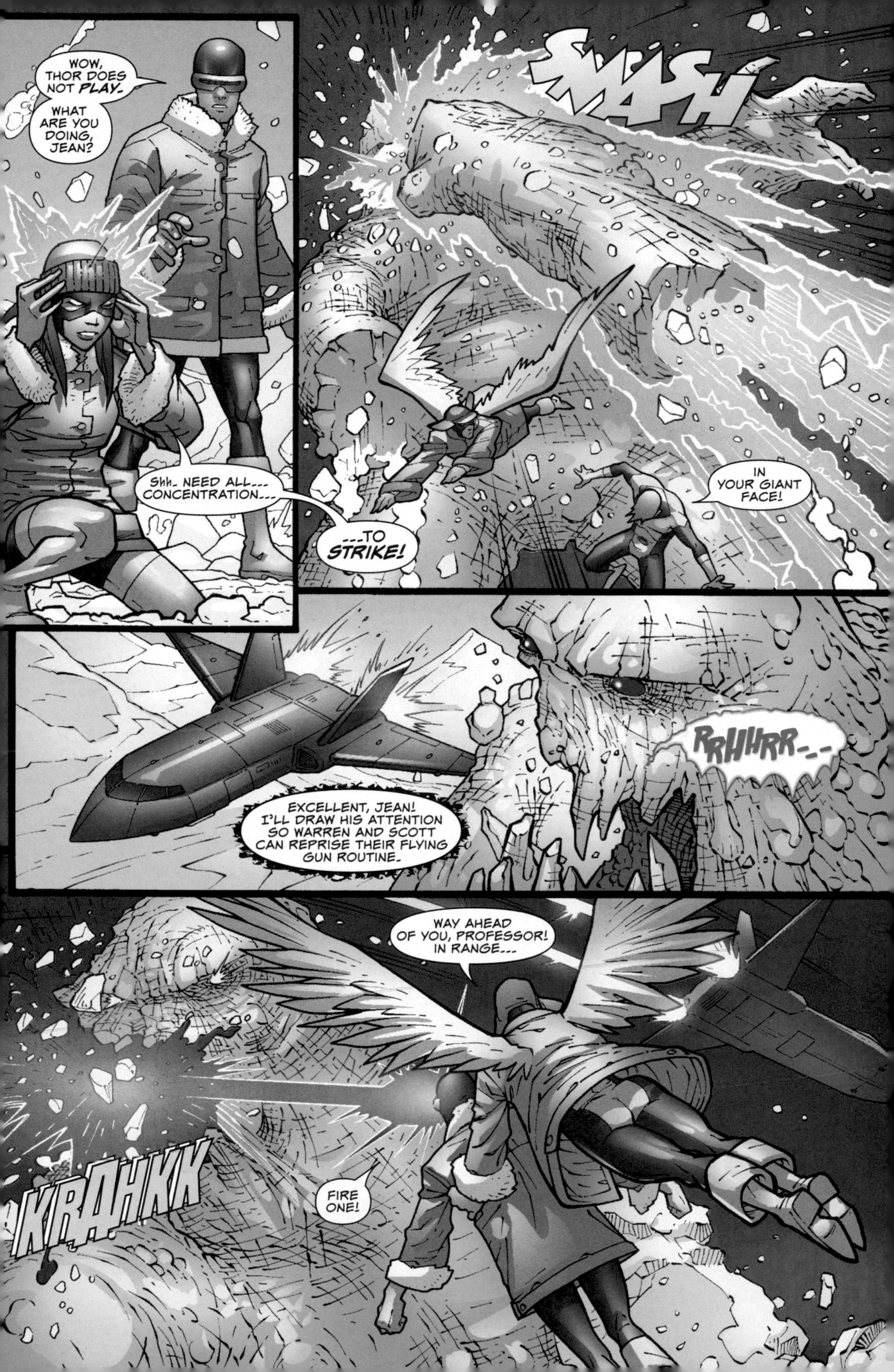
WOW, THOR DOES NOT PLAY.
WHAT ARE YOU DOING, JEAN?
SHH. NEED ALL... CONCENTRATION...
...TO STRIKE!
SMASH
IN YOUR GIANT FACE!
RRHHRR...
EXCELLENT, JEAN! I'LL DRAW HIS ATTENTION SO WARREN AND SCOTT CAN REPRISE THEIR FLYING GUN ROUTINE.
WAY AHEAD OF YOU, PROFESSOR! IN RANGE...
FIRE ONE!
KRAHKK

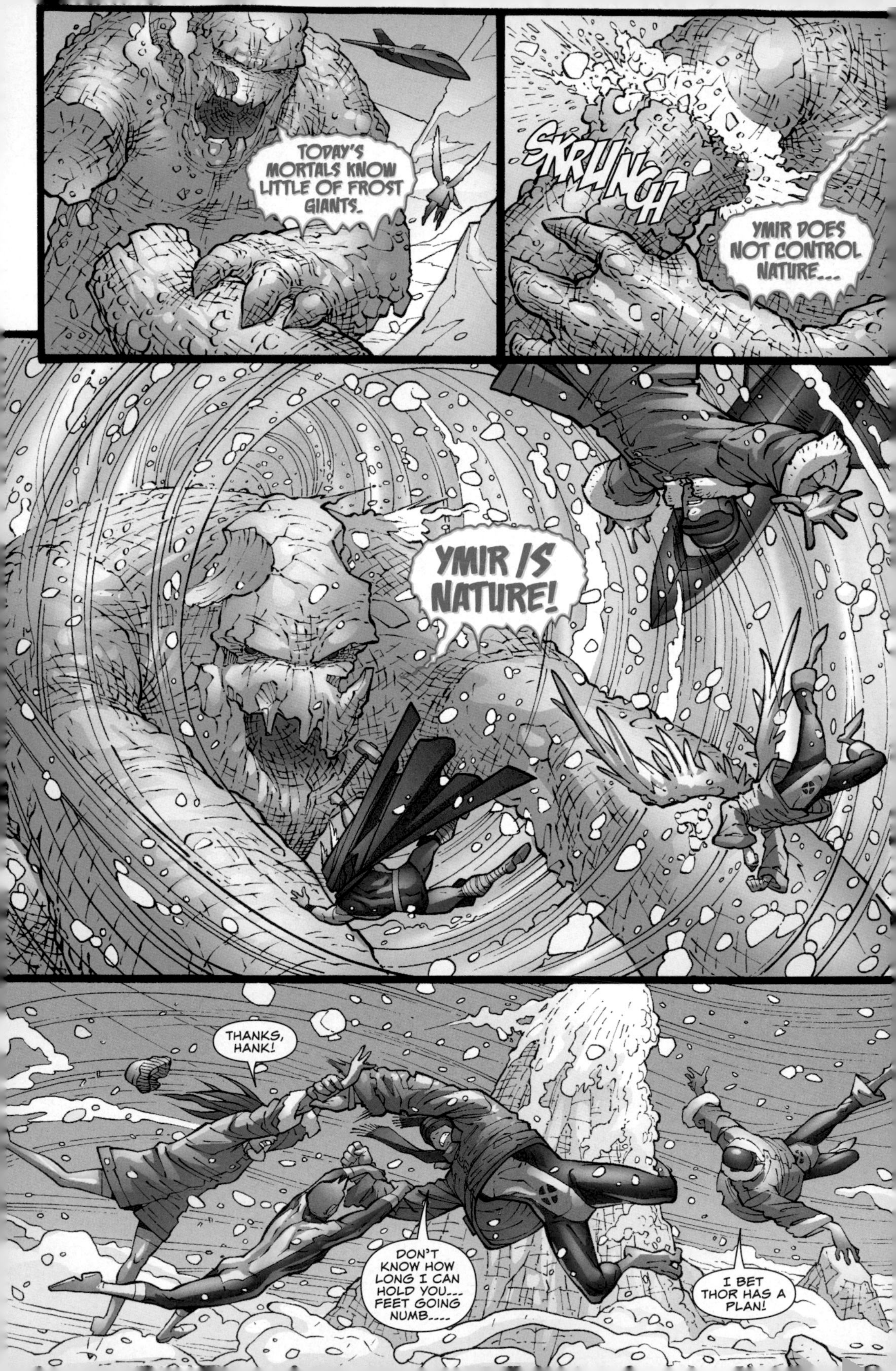
TODAY'S MORTALS KNOW LITTLE OF FROST GIANTS.
SKRUNCH
YMIR DOES NOT CONTROL NATURE...
YMIR IS NATURE!
THANKS, HANK!
DON'T KNOW HOW LONG I CAN HOLD YOU... FEET GOING NUMB....
I BET THOR HAS A PLAN!

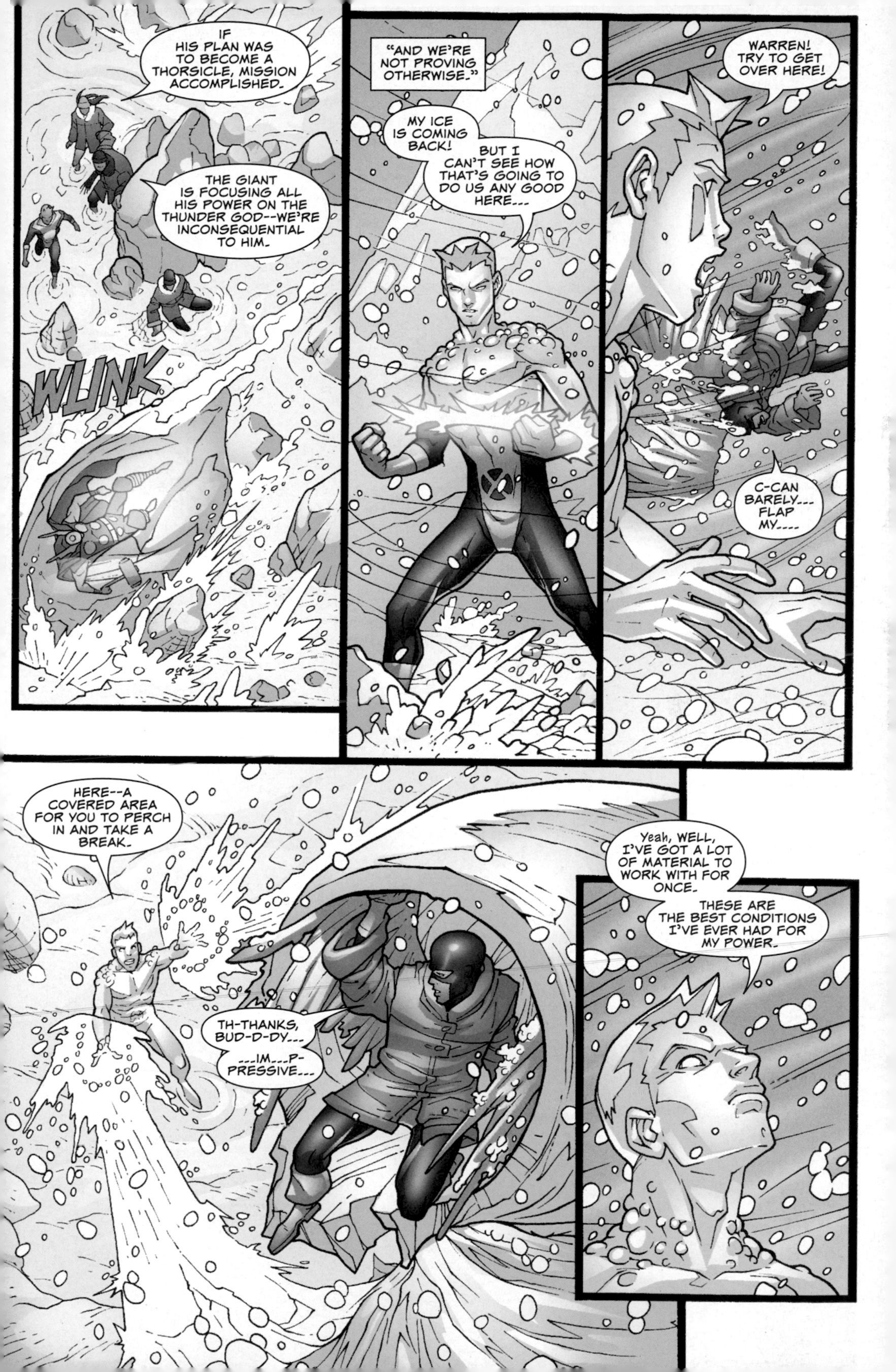
IF HIS PLAN WAS TO BECOME A THORSICLE, MISSION ACCOMPLISHED.
THE GIANT IS FOCUSING ALL HIS POWER ON THE THUNDER GOD--WE'RE INCONSEQUENTIAL TO HIM.
WUNK
"AND WE'RE NOT PROVING OTHERWISE."
MY ICE IS COMING BACK!
BUT I CAN'T SEE HOW THAT'S GOING TO DO US ANY GOOD HERE...
WARREN! TRY TO GET OVER HERE!
C-CAN BARELY... FLAP MY....
HERE--A COVERED AREA FOR YOU TO PERCH IN AND TAKE A BREAK.
TH-THANKS, BUD-D-DY...
...IM...P-PRESSIVE...
Yeah, WELL, I'VE GOT A LOT OF MATERIAL TO WORK WITH FOR ONCE.
THESE ARE THE BEST CONDITIONS I'VE EVER HAD FOR MY POWER.

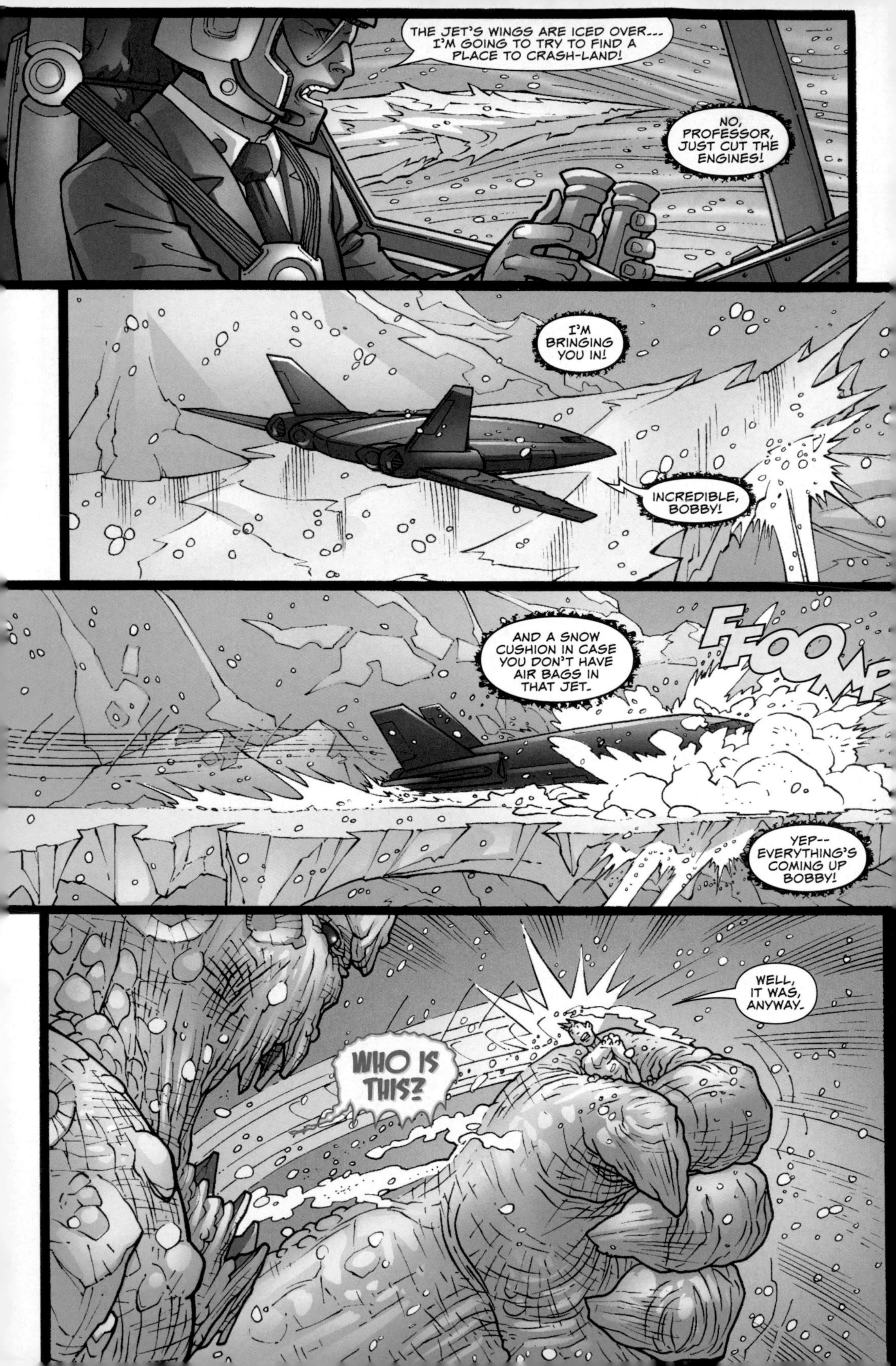
THE JET'S WINGS ARE ICED OVER... I'M GOING TO TRY TO FIND A PLACE TO CRASH-LAND!
NO, PROFESSOR, JUST CUT THE ENGINES!
I'M BRINGING YOU IN!
INCREDIBLE, BOBBY!
AND A SNOW CUSHION IN CASE YOU DON'T HAVE AIR BAGS IN THAT JET.
FFOOMP
YEP-- EVERYTHING'S COMING UP BOBBY!
WELL, IT WAS, ANYWAY.
WHO IS THIS?

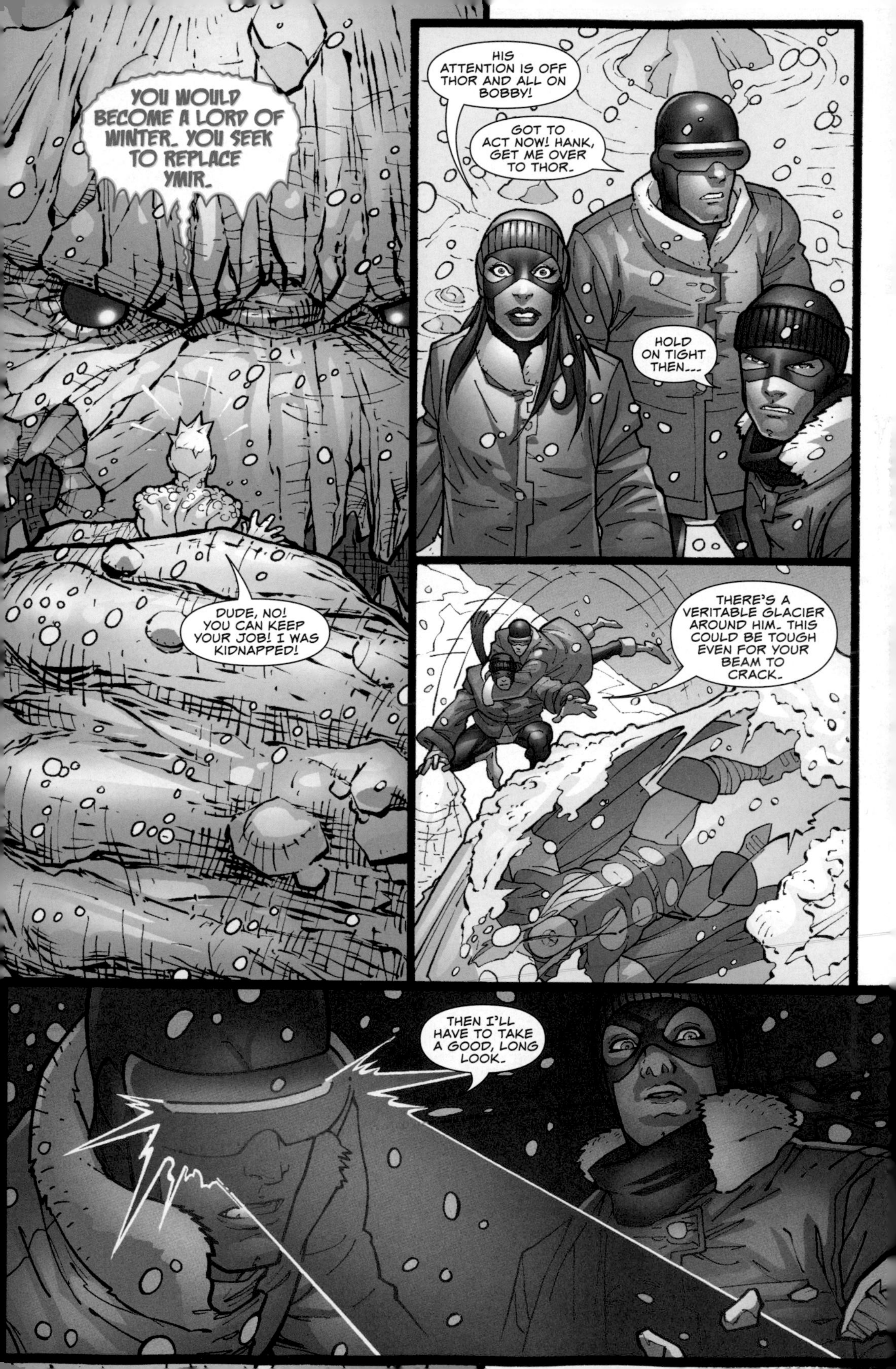
YOU WOULD BECOME A LORD OF WINTER. YOU SEEK TO REPLACE YMIR.
DUDE, NO! YOU CAN KEEP YOUR JOB! I WAS KIDNAPPED!
HIS ATTENTION IS OFF THOR AND ALL ON BOBBY!
GOT TO ACT NOW! HANK, GET ME OVER TO THOR.
HOLD ON TIGHT THEN...
THERE'S A VERITABLE GLACIER AROUND HIM. THIS COULD BE TOUGH EVEN FOR YOUR BEAM TO CRACK.
THEN I'LL HAVE TO TAKE A GOOD, LONG LOOK.

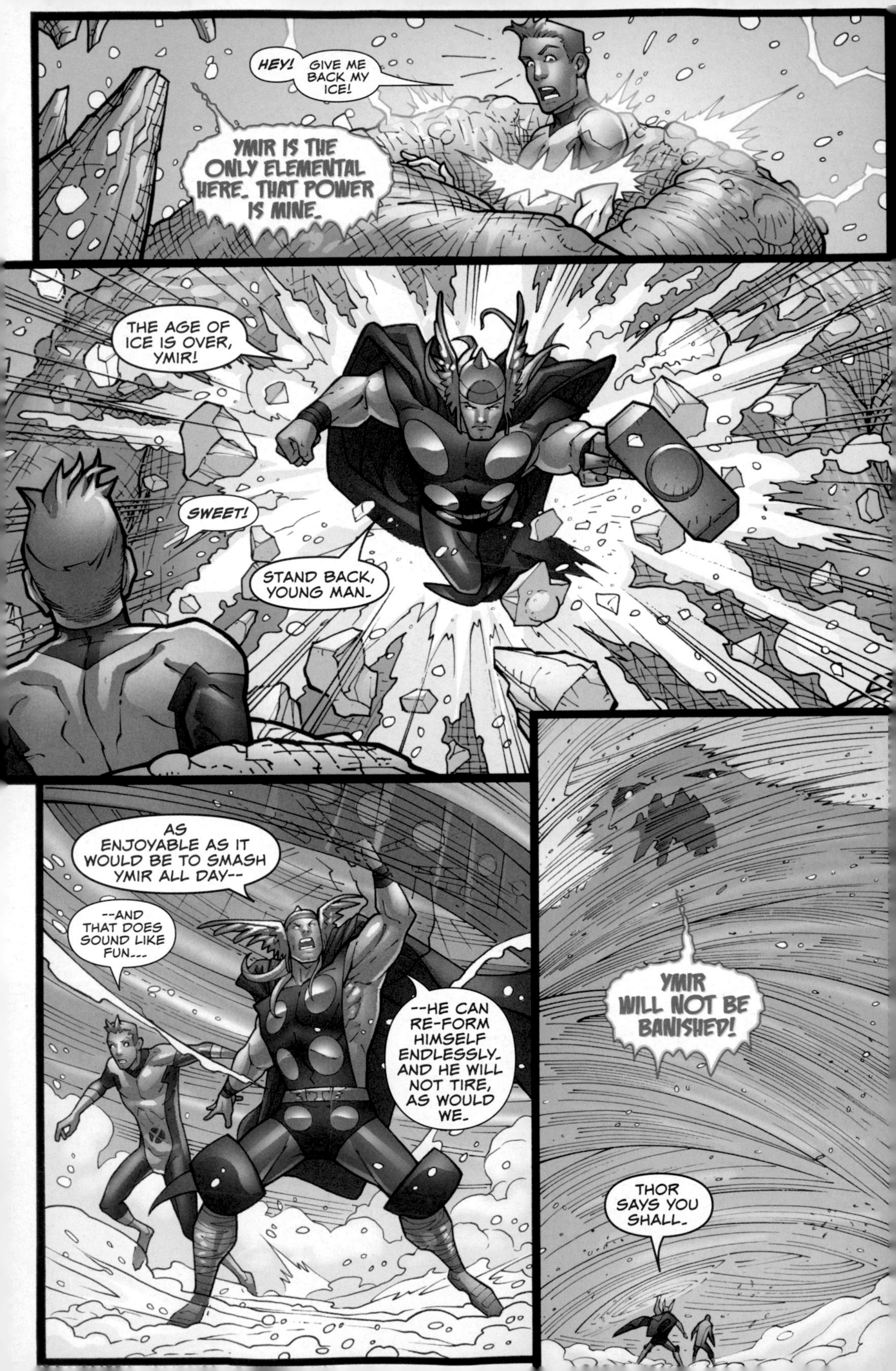
HEY! GIVE ME BACK MY ICE!
YMIR IS THE ONLY ELEMENTAL HERE. THAT POWER IS MINE.
THE AGE OF ICE IS OVER, YMIR!
SWEET!
STAND BACK, YOUNG MAN.
AS ENJOYABLE AS IT WOULD BE TO SMASH YMIR ALL DAY--
--AND THAT DOES SOUND LIKE FUN...
--HE CAN RE-FORM HIMSELF ENDLESSLY. AND HE WILL NOT TIRE, AS WOULD WE.
YMIR WILL NOT BE BANISHED!
THOR SAYS YOU SHALL.

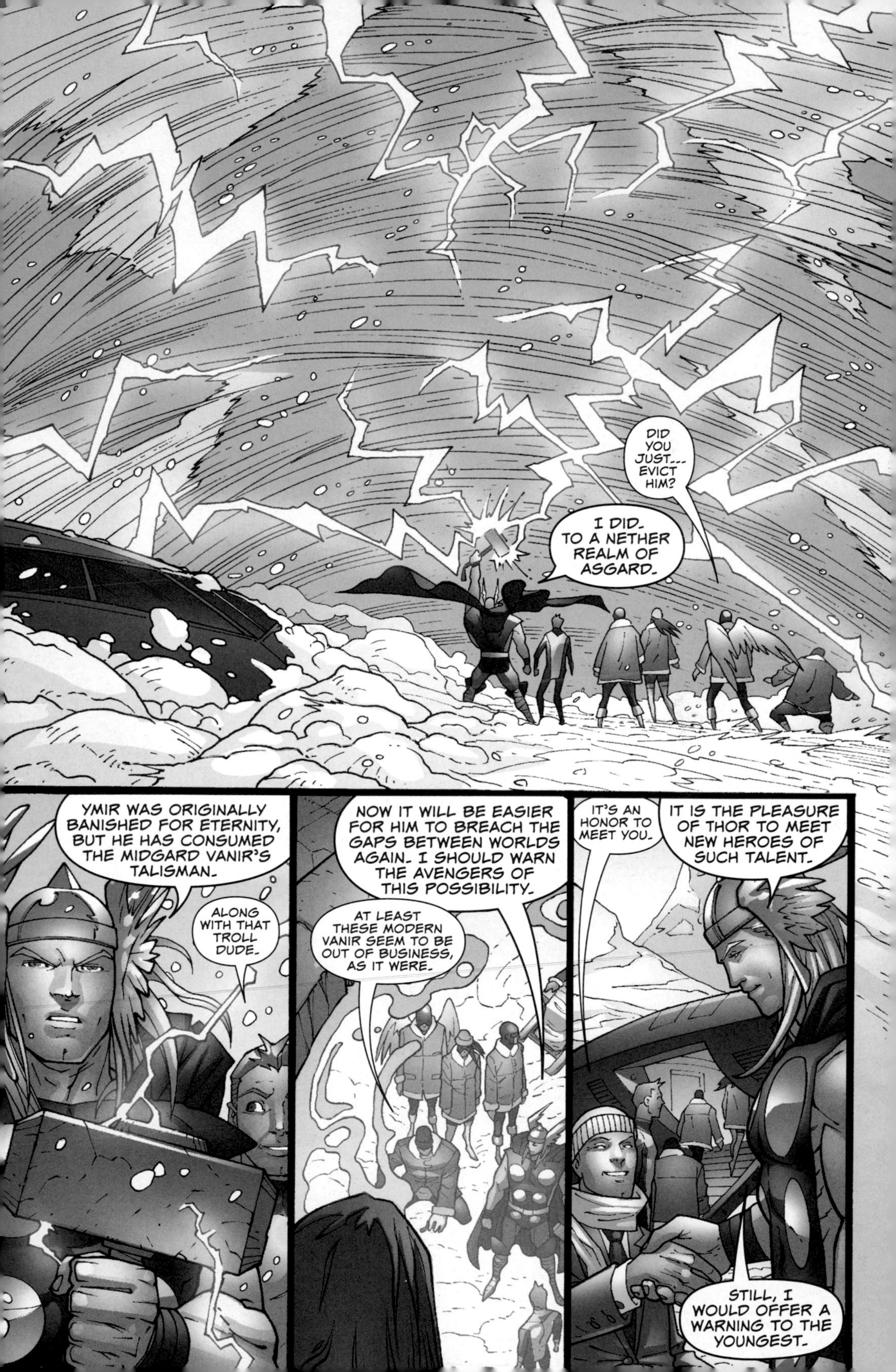
DID YOU JUST... EVICT HIM?
I DID. TO A NETHER REALM OF ASGARD.
YMIR WAS ORIGINALLY BANISHED FOR ETERNITY, BUT HE HAS CONSUMED THE MIDGARD VANIR'S TALISMAN.
ALONG WITH THAT TROLL DUDE.
NOW IT WILL BE EASIER FOR HIM TO BREACH THE GAPS BETWEEN WORLDS AGAIN. I SHOULD WARN THE AVENGERS OF THIS POSSIBILITY.
AT LEAST THESE MODERN VANIR SEEM TO BE OUT OF BUSINESS, AS IT WERE.
IT'S AN HONOR TO MEET YOU.
IT IS THE PLEASURE OF THOR TO MEET NEW HEROES OF SUCH TALENT.
STILL, I WOULD OFFER A WARNING TO THE YOUNGEST.

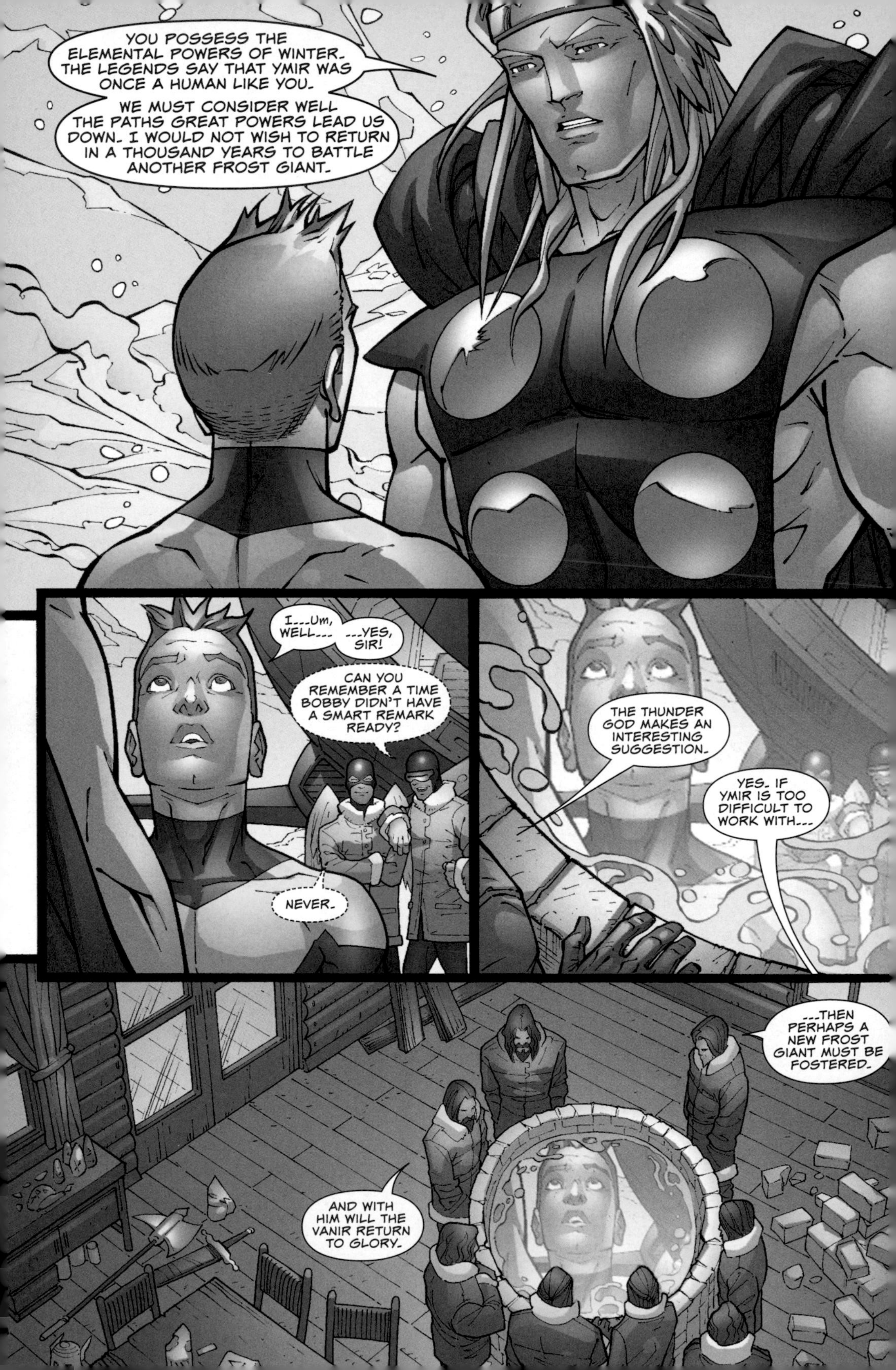
YOU POSSESS THE ELEMENTAL POWERS OF WINTER. THE LEGENDS SAY THAT YMIR WAS ONCE A HUMAN LIKE YOU.
WE MUST CONSIDER WELL THE PATHS GREAT POWERS LEAD US DOWN. I WOULD NOT WISH TO RETURN IN A THOUSAND YEARS TO BATTLE ANOTHER FROST GIANT.
I...UM, WELL...
...YES, SIR!
CAN YOU REMEMBER A TIME BOBBY DIDN'T HAVE A SMART REMARK READY?
NEVER.
THE THUNDER GOD MAKES AN INTERESTING SUGGESTION.
YES. IF YMIR IS TOO DIFFICULT TO WORK WITH...
...THEN PERHAPS A NEW FROST GIANT MUST BE FOSTERED.
AND WITH HIM WILL THE VANIR RETURN TO GLORY.

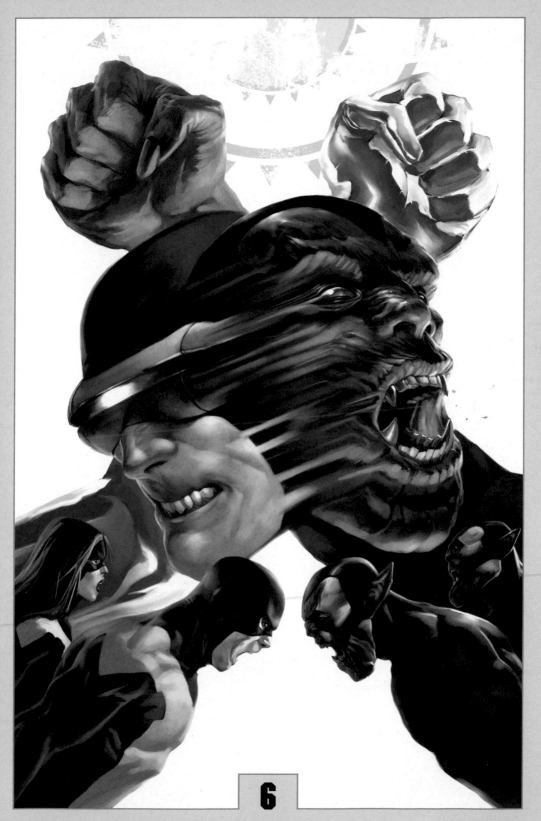

6

THE NEXT STEP IN HUMAN EVOLUTION HAS ARRIVED—HOMO SUPERIOR. MANKIND ISN'T SURE WHETHER THIS REPRESENTS HOPE FOR THE FUTURE...OR THE END OF THE HUMAN RACE. IN A PRIVATE SCHOOL IN UPSTATE NEW YORK, ONE BRILLIANT MUTANT IS TEACHING A GROUP OF FIVE SUCH GIFTED STUDENTS WHAT THEY'LL NEED TO SURVIVE IN THIS NEW WORLD. THESE ARE THE UNTOLD STORIES OF PROFESSOR XAVIER'S FIRST CLASS OF X-MEN!

XAVIER'S SCHOOL FOR GIFTED YOUNGSTERS

PROPERTY OF:

Beast

HEADMASTER

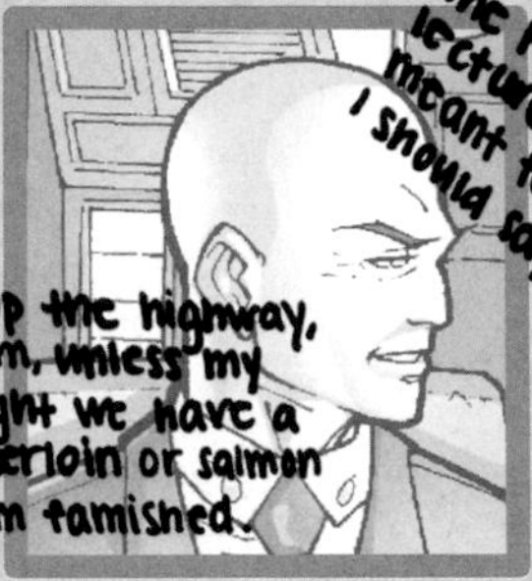

PROFESSOR CHARLES XAVIER

The Professor made a gaffe earlier in his lecture! He said "mutate" when he clearly meant to say "mutant!" Should I say something? I should say something.

Just smelled the caterer driving up the highway, still about a kilometer away. Mmm, unless my olfactory neurons deceive me, tonight we have a choice of peppercorn-crusted tenderloin or salmon marinated in mint and... basil! I'm famished.

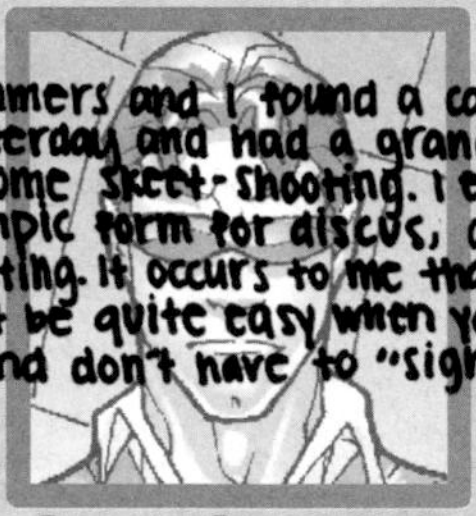

SCOTT SUMMERS
"CYCLOPS"

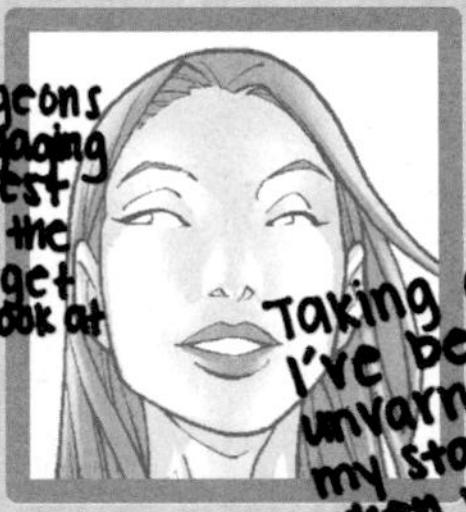

JEAN GREY
"MARVEL GIRL"

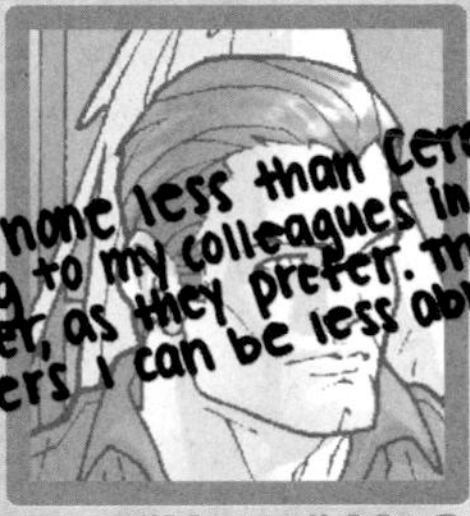

HENRY "HANK" McCOY
"BEAST"

Summers and I found a case of clay pigeons yesterday and had a grand old time engaging in some skeet-shooting. I employed my best Olympic form for discus, and he did all the shooting. It occurs to me that hitting a target must be quite easy when you need only look at it and don't have to "sight."

Taking a cue from none less than Cerebro, I've been speaking to my colleagues in an unvarnished manner, as they prefer. Thank my stars and garters I can be less abridged when writing.

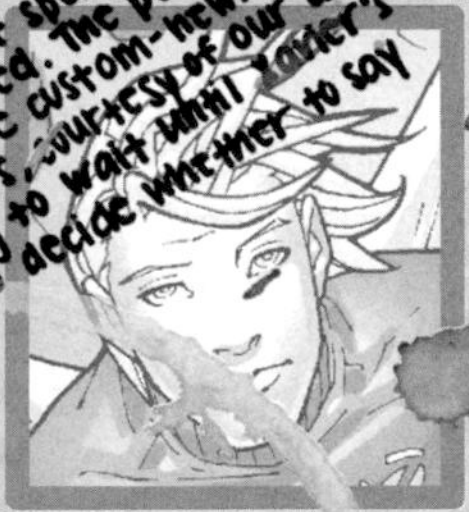

WARREN WORTHINGTON III
"ANGEL"

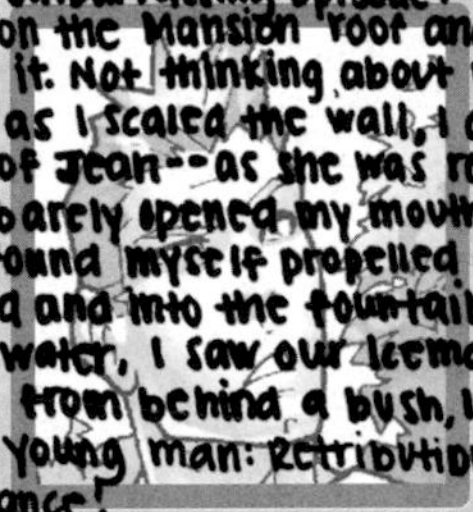

ROBERT DRAKE
"ICEMAN"

LATEST IRONY: I was very ready to reprimand Warren for his exorbitant spending on trifles last week when UPS arrived. The package (to me) was comprised of one custom-hewn pair of size 15 leather shoes, courtesy of our aviator. Now I'm going to wait until Xavier's Mutant Ethics class to decide whether to say anything.

A most Embarrassing Episode: Drake lost his Frisbee on the Mansion roof and asked me to retrieve it. Not thinking about which hall we were by as I scaled the wall, I came by the window of Jean--as she was readying for a bath. I barely opened my mouth to explain when I found myself propelled across the courtyard and into the fountain. As I shook off the water, I saw our Iceman pick up his Frisbee from behind a bush, laughing at me. Warning, young man: Retribution is a harsh comeuppance!

Wonder of wonders, I overheard young Drake explaining compounded interest to Worthington! Maybe there is a future for that lad after all.

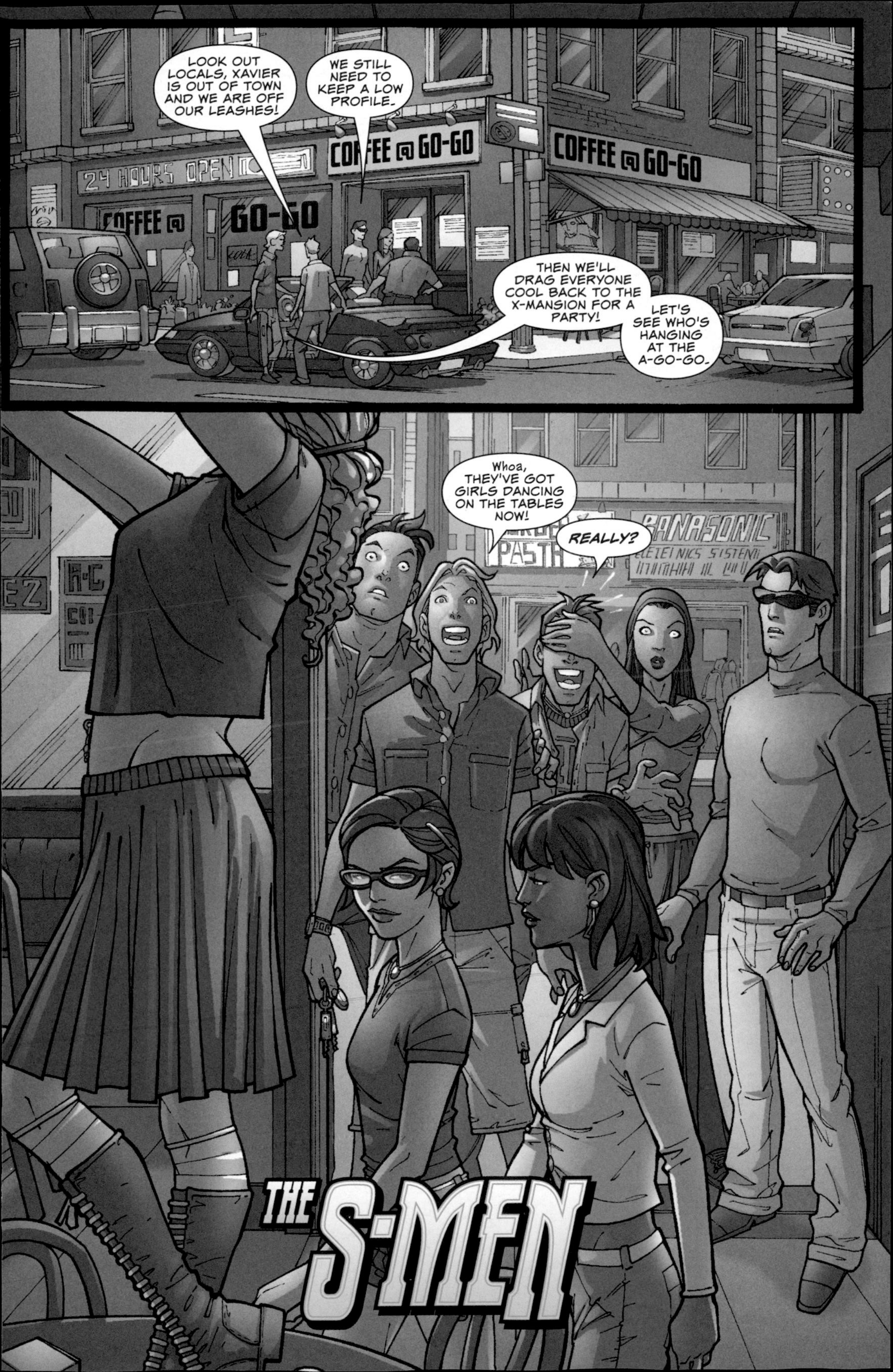
LOOK OUT LOCALS, XAVIER IS OUT OF TOWN AND WE ARE OFF OUR LEASHES!
WE STILL NEED TO KEEP A LOW PROFILE.
24 HOURS OPEN
COFFEE @ GO-GO
COFFEE @ GO-GO
COFFEE @ GO-GO
THEN WE'LL DRAG EVERYONE COOL BACK TO THE X-MANSION FOR A PARTY!
LET'S SEE WHO'S HANGING AT THE A-GO-GO.
Whoa, THEY'VE GOT GIRLS DANCING ON THE TABLES NOW!
REALLY?
PANASONIC
THE S-MEN

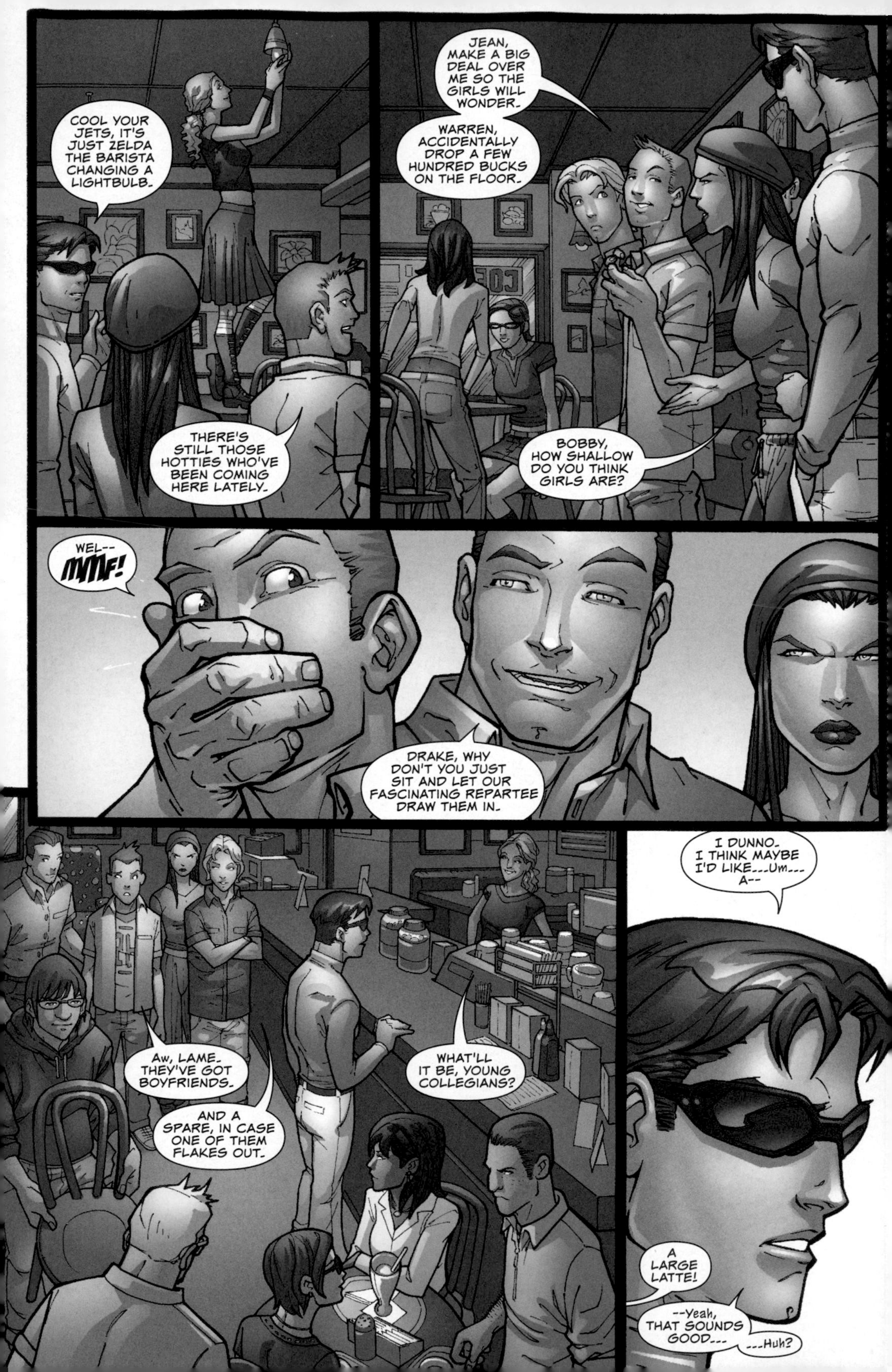
COOL YOUR JETS, IT'S JUST ZELDA THE BARISTA CHANGING A LIGHTBULB.
THERE'S STILL THOSE HOTTIES WHO'VE BEEN COMING HERE LATELY.
JEAN, MAKE A BIG DEAL OVER ME SO THE GIRLS WILL WONDER.
WARREN, ACCIDENTALLY DROP A FEW HUNDRED BUCKS ON THE FLOOR.
BOBBY, HOW SHALLOW DO YOU THINK GIRLS ARE?
WEL-- MMF!
DRAKE, WHY DON'T YOU JUST SIT AND LET OUR FASCINATING REPARTEE DRAW THEM IN.
Aw, LAME. THEY'VE GOT BOYFRIENDS.
AND A SPARE, IN CASE ONE OF THEM FLAKES OUT.
WHAT'LL IT BE, YOUNG COLLEGIANS?
I DUNNO. I THINK MAYBE I'D LIKE...Um... A--
A LARGE LATTE!
--Yeah, THAT SOUNDS GOOD...
...Huh?

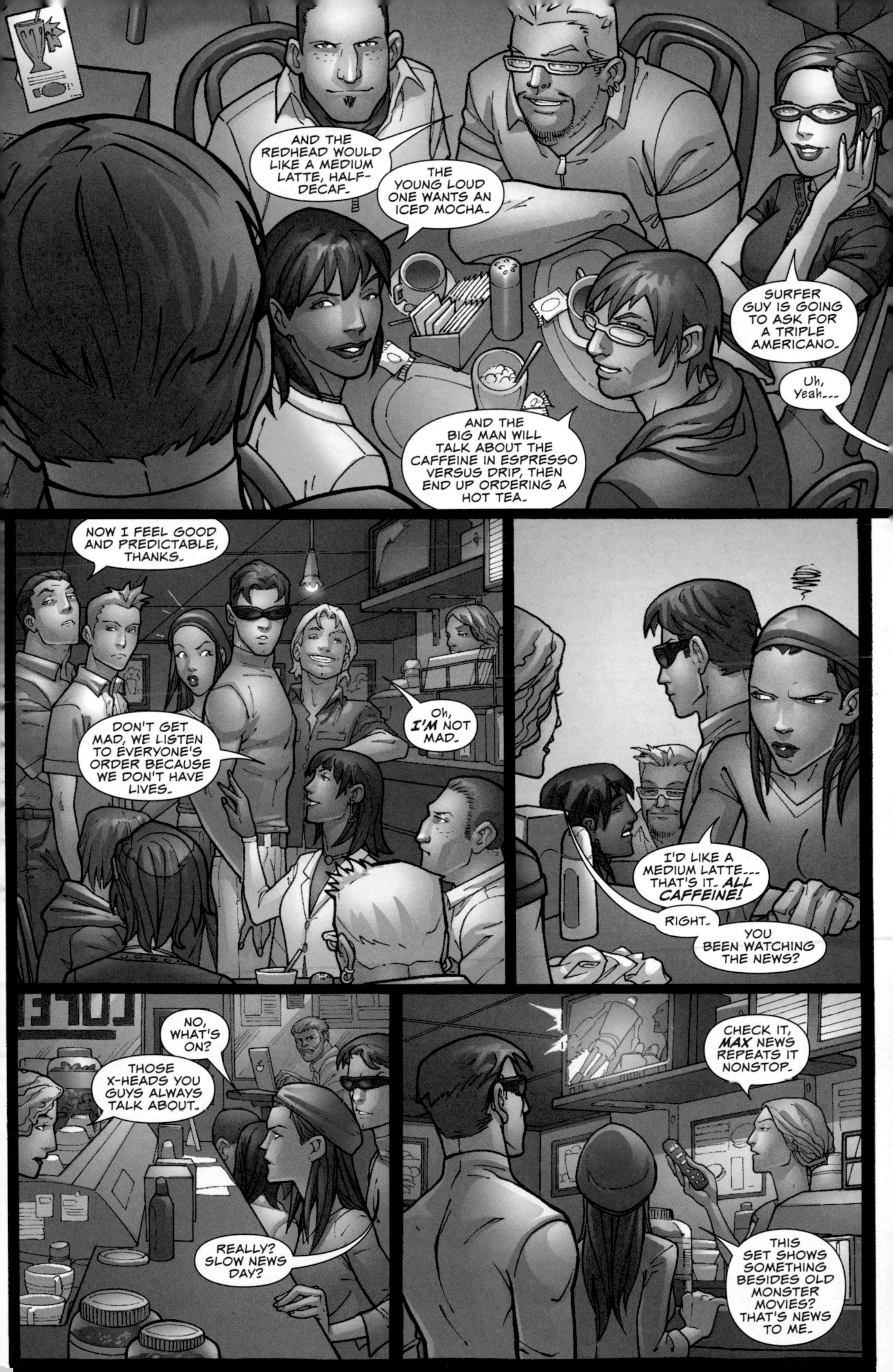
AND THE REDHEAD WOULD LIKE A MEDIUM LATTE, HALF-DECAF.
THE YOUNG LOUD ONE WANTS AN ICED MOCHA.
SURFER GUY IS GOING TO ASK FOR A TRIPLE AMERICANO.
Uh, Yeah...
AND THE BIG MAN WILL TALK ABOUT THE CAFFEINE IN ESPRESSO VERSUS DRIP, THEN END UP ORDERING A HOT TEA.
NOW I FEEL GOOD AND PREDICTABLE, THANKS.
DON'T GET MAD, WE LISTEN TO EVERYONE'S ORDER BECAUSE WE DON'T HAVE LIVES.
Oh, *I'M* NOT MAD.
I'D LIKE A MEDIUM LATTE... THAT'S IT. *ALL CAFFEINE!*
RIGHT.
YOU BEEN WATCHING THE NEWS?
NO, WHAT'S ON?
THOSE X-HEADS YOU GUYS ALWAYS TALK ABOUT.
REALLY? SLOW NEWS DAY?
CHECK IT, *MAX* NEWS REPEATS IT NONSTOP.
THIS SET SHOWS SOMETHING BESIDES OLD MONSTER MOVIES? THAT'S NEWS TO ME.

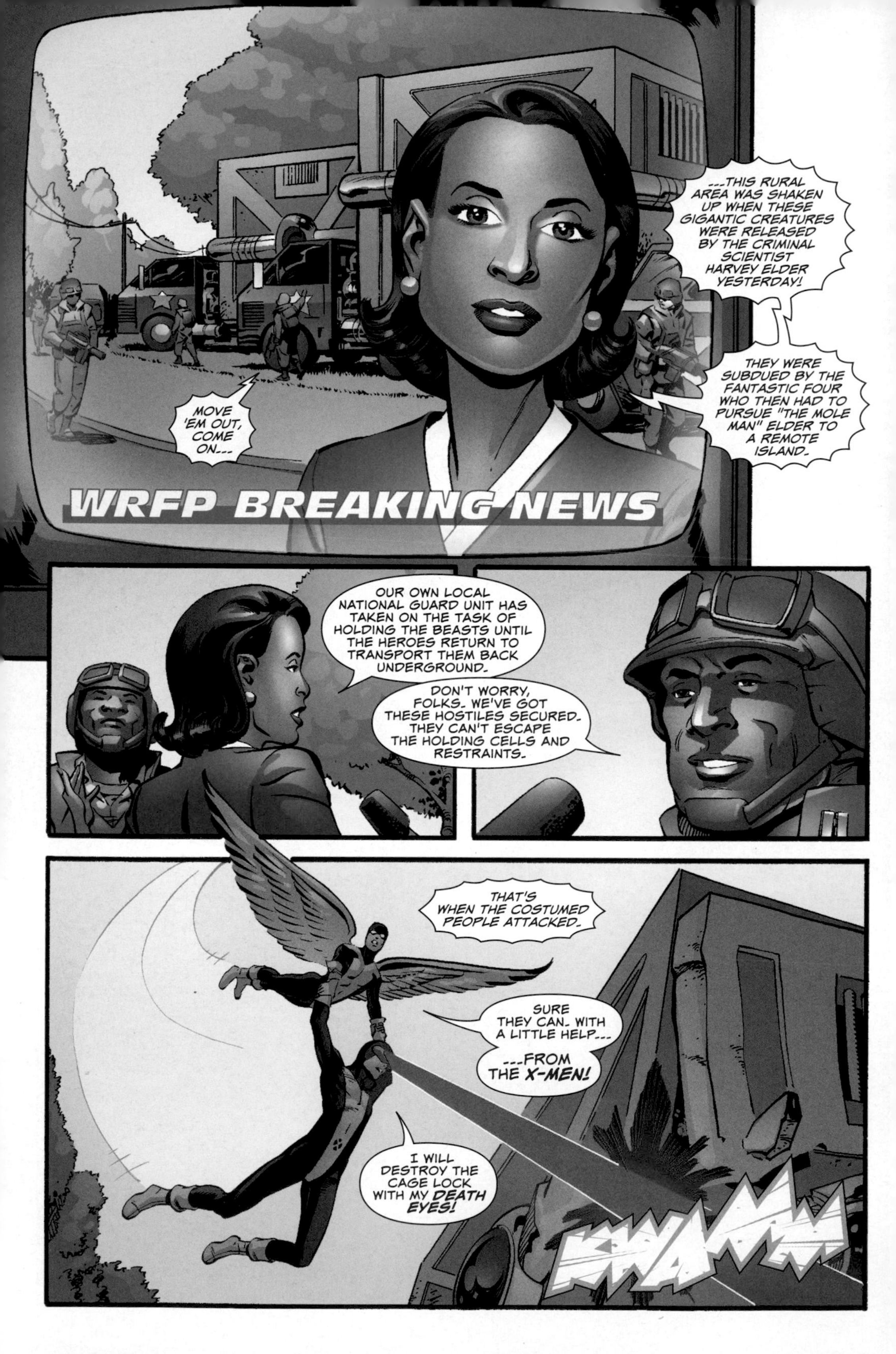
---THIS RURAL AREA WAS SHAKEN UP WHEN THESE GIGANTIC CREATURES WERE RELEASED BY THE CRIMINAL SCIENTIST HARVEY ELDER YESTERDAY!
THEY WERE SUBDUED BY THE FANTASTIC FOUR WHO THEN HAD TO PURSUE "THE MOLE MAN" ELDER TO A REMOTE ISLAND.
MOVE 'EM OUT, COME ON---
WRFP BREAKING NEWS
OUR OWN LOCAL NATIONAL GUARD UNIT HAS TAKEN ON THE TASK OF HOLDING THE BEASTS UNTIL THE HEROES RETURN TO TRANSPORT THEM BACK UNDERGROUND.
DON'T WORRY, FOLKS. WE'VE GOT THESE HOSTILES SECURED. THEY CAN'T ESCAPE THE HOLDING CELLS AND RESTRAINTS.
THAT'S WHEN THE COSTUMED PEOPLE ATTACKED.
SURE THEY CAN. WITH A LITTLE HELP---
---FROM THE X-MEN!
I WILL DESTROY THE CAGE LOCK WITH MY DEATH EYES!
KWAMM

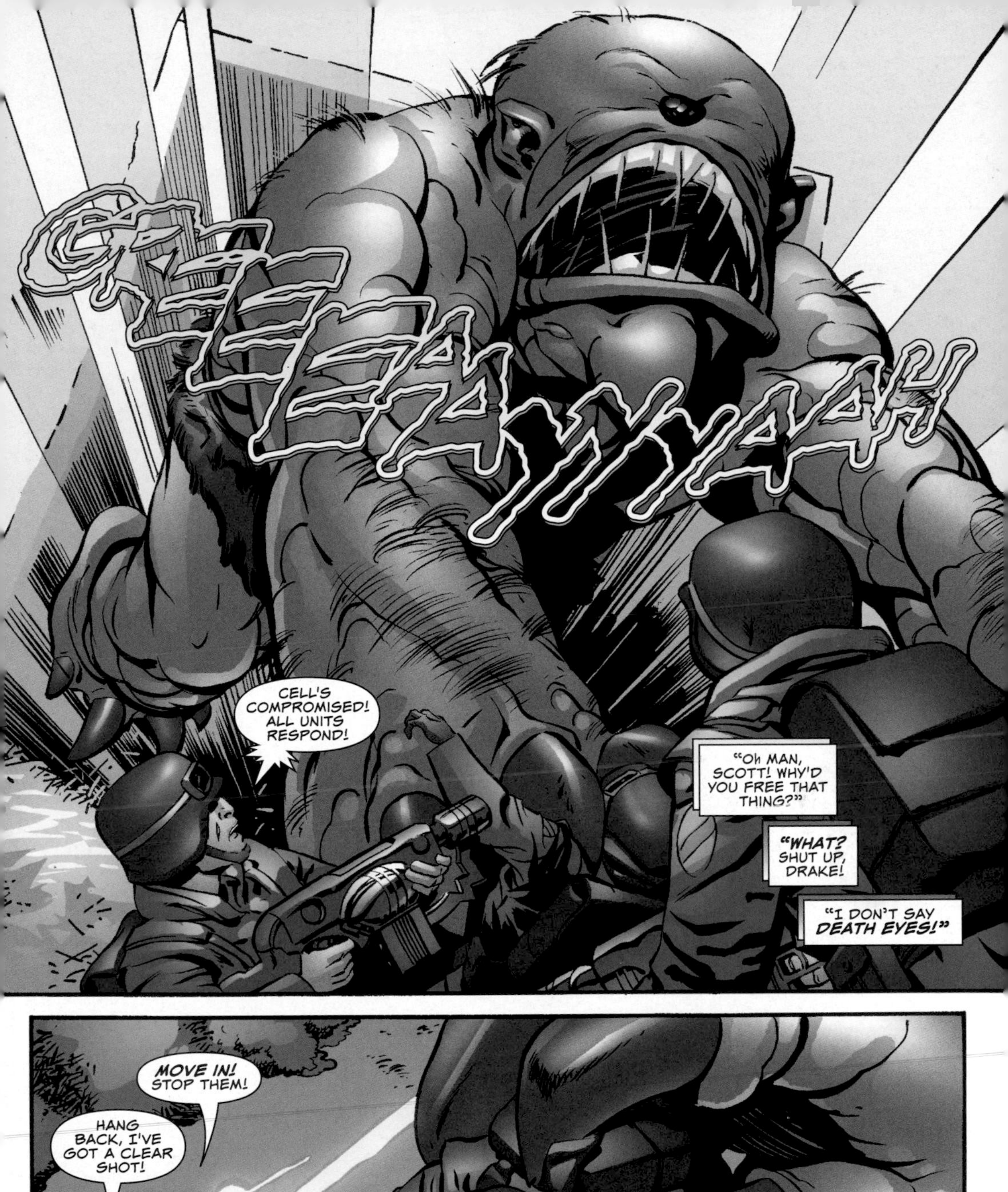
CELL'S COMPROMISED! ALL UNITS RESPOND!
"OH MAN, SCOTT! WHY'D YOU FREE THAT THING?"
"*WHAT?* SHUT UP, DRAKE!"
"I DON'T SAY *DEATH EYES!*"

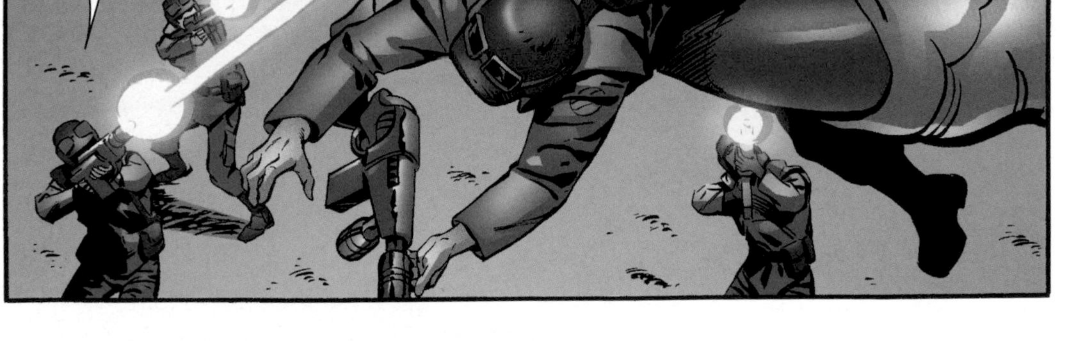
MOVE IN! STOP THEM!
HANG BACK, I'VE GOT A CLEAR SHOT!

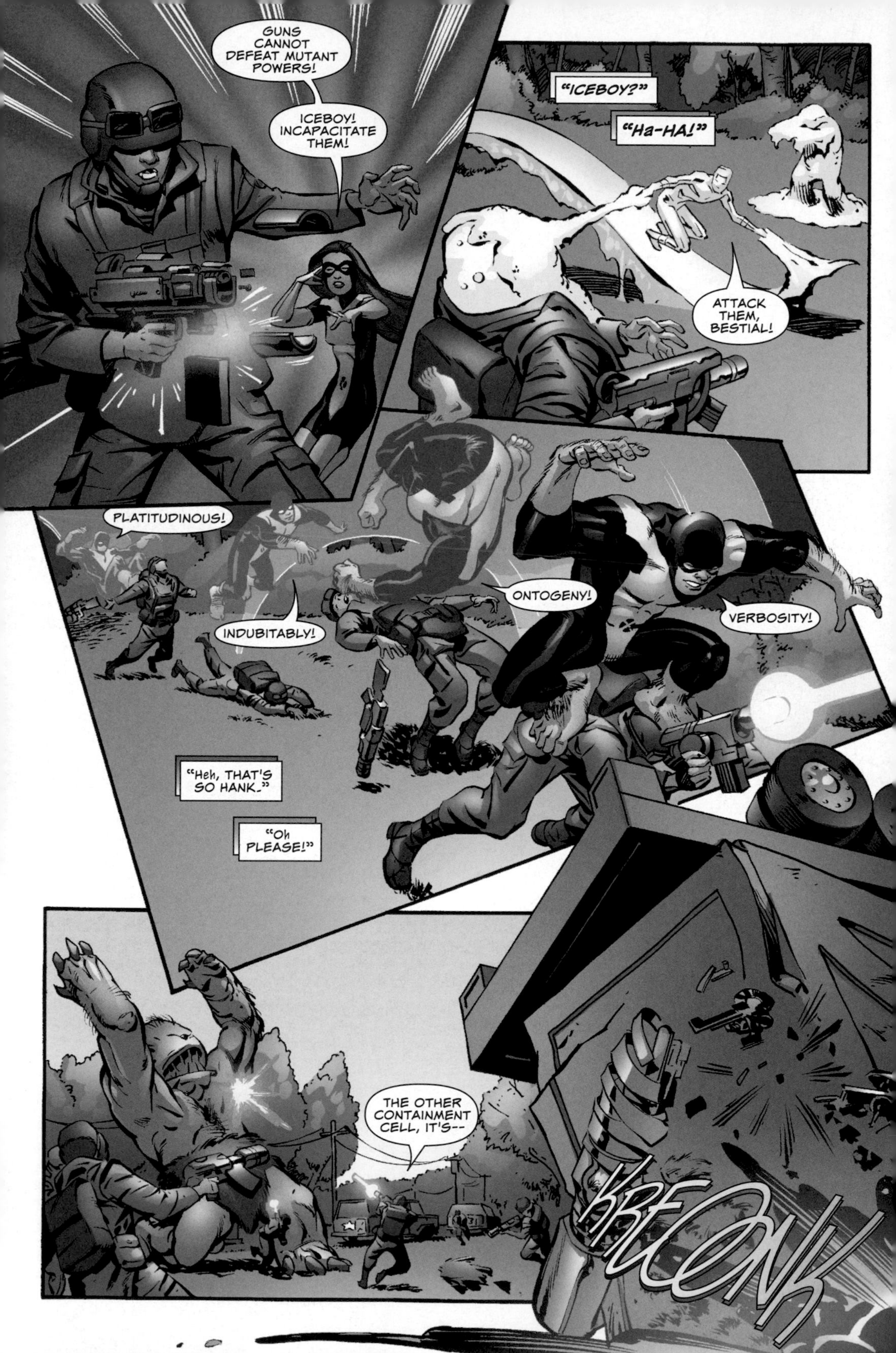
GUNS CANNOT DEFEAT MUTANT POWERS!
ICEBOY! INCAPACITATE THEM!
"ICEBOY?"
"Ha-HA!"
ATTACK THEM, BESTIAL!
PLATITUDINOUS!
INDUBITABLY!
ONTOGENY!
VERBOSITY!
"Heh, THAT'S SO HANK."
"Oh PLEASE!"
THE OTHER CONTAINMENT CELL, IT'S--
KREONK

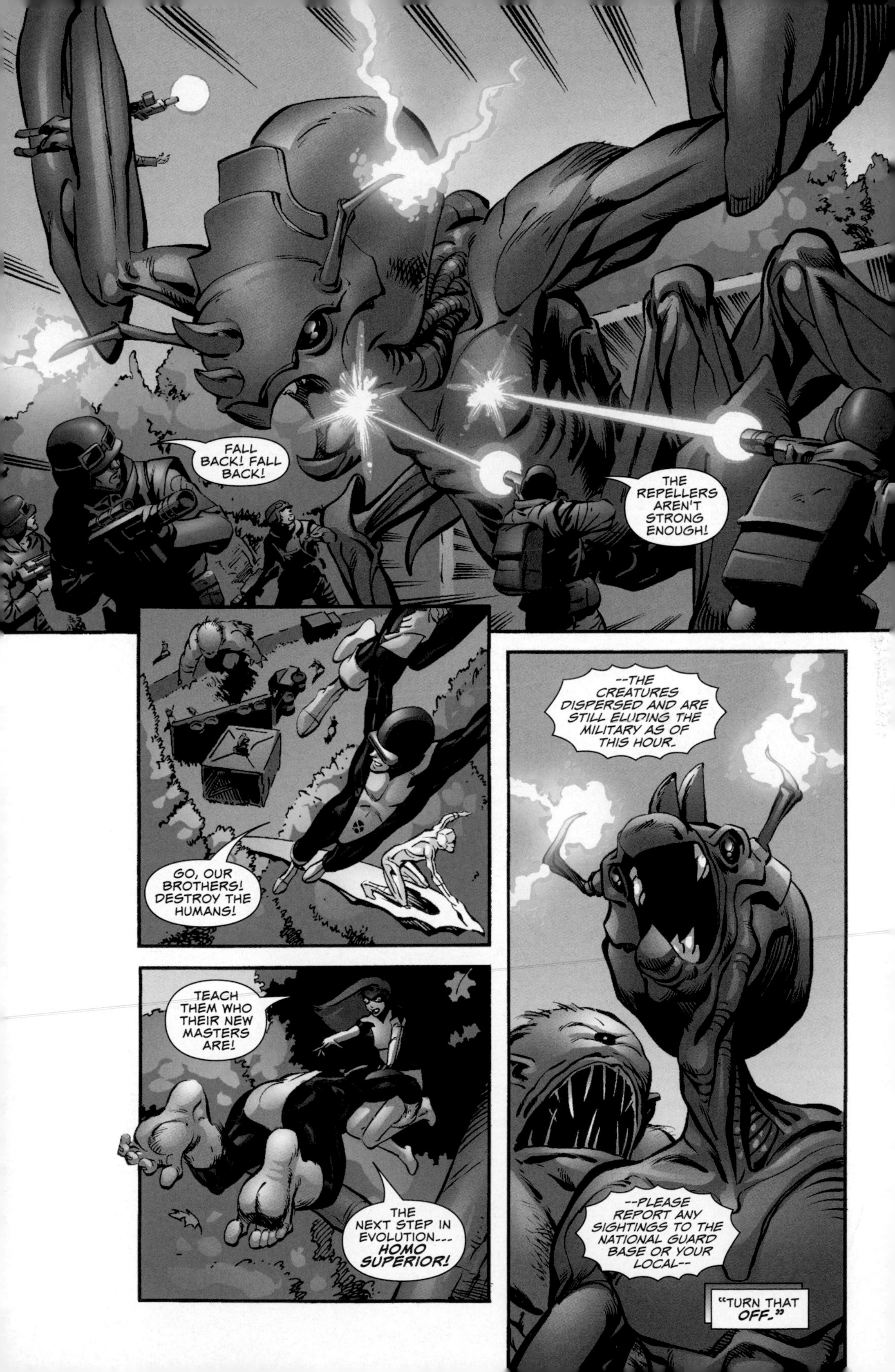
FALL BACK! FALL BACK!
THE REPELLERS AREN'T STRONG ENOUGH!
GO, OUR BROTHERS! DESTROY THE HUMANS!
TEACH THEM WHO THEIR NEW MASTERS ARE!
THE NEXT STEP IN EVOLUTION--- HOMO SUPERIOR!
--THE CREATURES DISPERSED AND ARE STILL ELUDING THE MILITARY AS OF THIS HOUR.
--PLEASE REPORT ANY SIGHTINGS TO THE NATIONAL GUARD BASE OR YOUR LOCAL--
"TURN THAT OFF-"

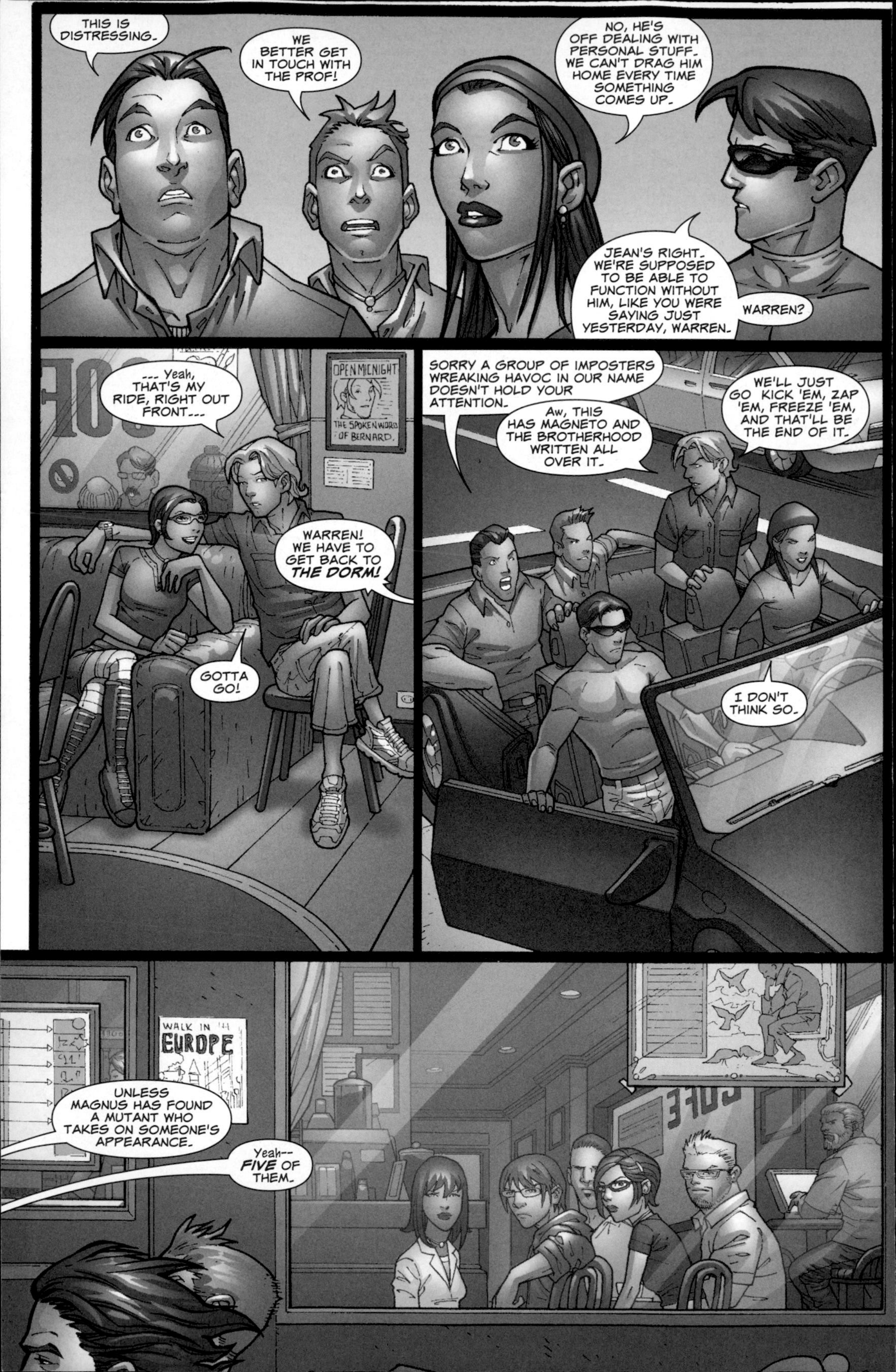
THIS IS DISTRESSING.
WE BETTER GET IN TOUCH WITH THE PROF!
NO, HE'S OFF DEALING WITH PERSONAL STUFF. WE CAN'T DRAG HIM HOME EVERY TIME SOMETHING COMES UP.
JEAN'S RIGHT. WE'RE SUPPOSED TO BE ABLE TO FUNCTION WITHOUT HIM, LIKE YOU WERE SAYING JUST YESTERDAY, WARREN.
WARREN?
OPEN MIDNIGHT
THE SPOKEN WORD OF BERNARD.
... Yeah, THAT'S MY RIDE, RIGHT OUT FRONT...
WARREN! WE HAVE TO GET BACK TO THE DORM!
GOTTA GO!
SORRY A GROUP OF IMPOSTERS WREAKING HAVOC IN OUR NAME DOESN'T HOLD YOUR ATTENTION.
Aw, THIS HAS MAGNETO AND THE BROTHERHOOD WRITTEN ALL OVER IT.
WE'LL JUST GO KICK 'EM, ZAP 'EM, FREEZE 'EM, AND THAT'LL BE THE END OF IT.
I DON'T THINK SO.
WALK IN EUROPE
UNLESS MAGNUS HAS FOUND A MUTANT WHO TAKES ON SOMEONE'S APPEARANCE.
Yeah-- FIVE OF THEM.

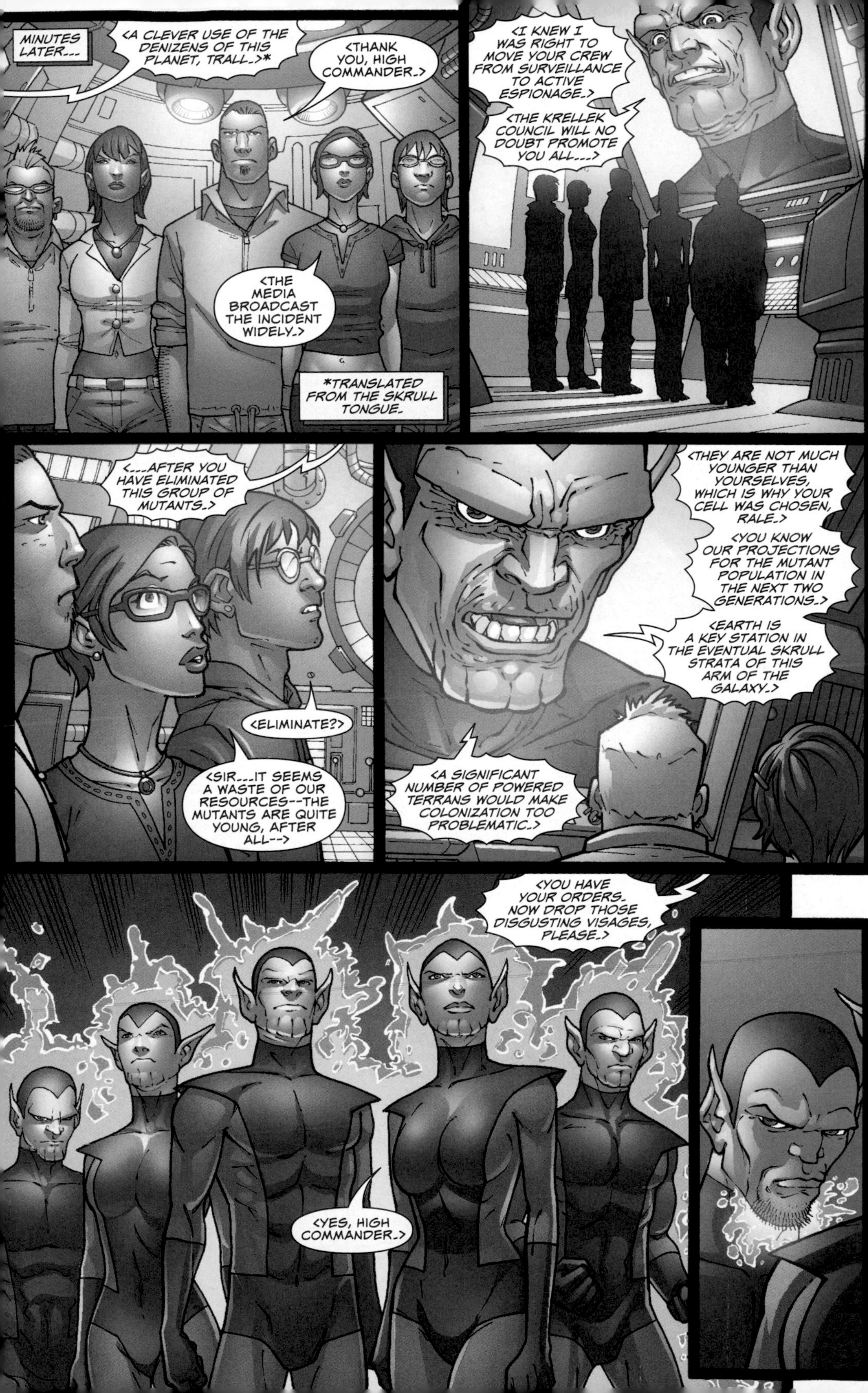

MINUTES LATER...
<A CLEVER USE OF THE DENIZENS OF THIS PLANET, TRALL.>*
<THANK YOU, HIGH COMMANDER.>
<THE MEDIA BROADCAST THE INCIDENT WIDELY.>
*TRANSLATED FROM THE SKRULL TONGUE.
<I KNEW I WAS RIGHT TO MOVE YOUR CREW FROM SURVEILLANCE TO ACTIVE ESPIONAGE.>
<THE KRELLEK COUNCIL WILL NO DOUBT PROMOTE YOU ALL...>
<...AFTER YOU HAVE ELIMINATED THIS GROUP OF MUTANTS.>
<ELIMINATE?>
<SIR...IT SEEMS A WASTE OF OUR RESOURCES--THE MUTANTS ARE QUITE YOUNG, AFTER ALL-->
<THEY ARE NOT MUCH YOUNGER THAN YOURSELVES, WHICH IS WHY YOUR CELL WAS CHOSEN, RALE.>
<YOU KNOW OUR PROJECTIONS FOR THE MUTANT POPULATION IN THE NEXT TWO GENERATIONS.>
<EARTH IS A KEY STATION IN THE EVENTUAL SKRULL STRATA OF THIS ARM OF THE GALAXY.>
<A SIGNIFICANT NUMBER OF POWERED TERRANS WOULD MAKE COLONIZATION TOO PROBLEMATIC.>
<YOU HAVE YOUR ORDERS. NOW DROP THOSE DISGUSTING VISAGES, PLEASE.>
<YES, HIGH COMMANDER.>

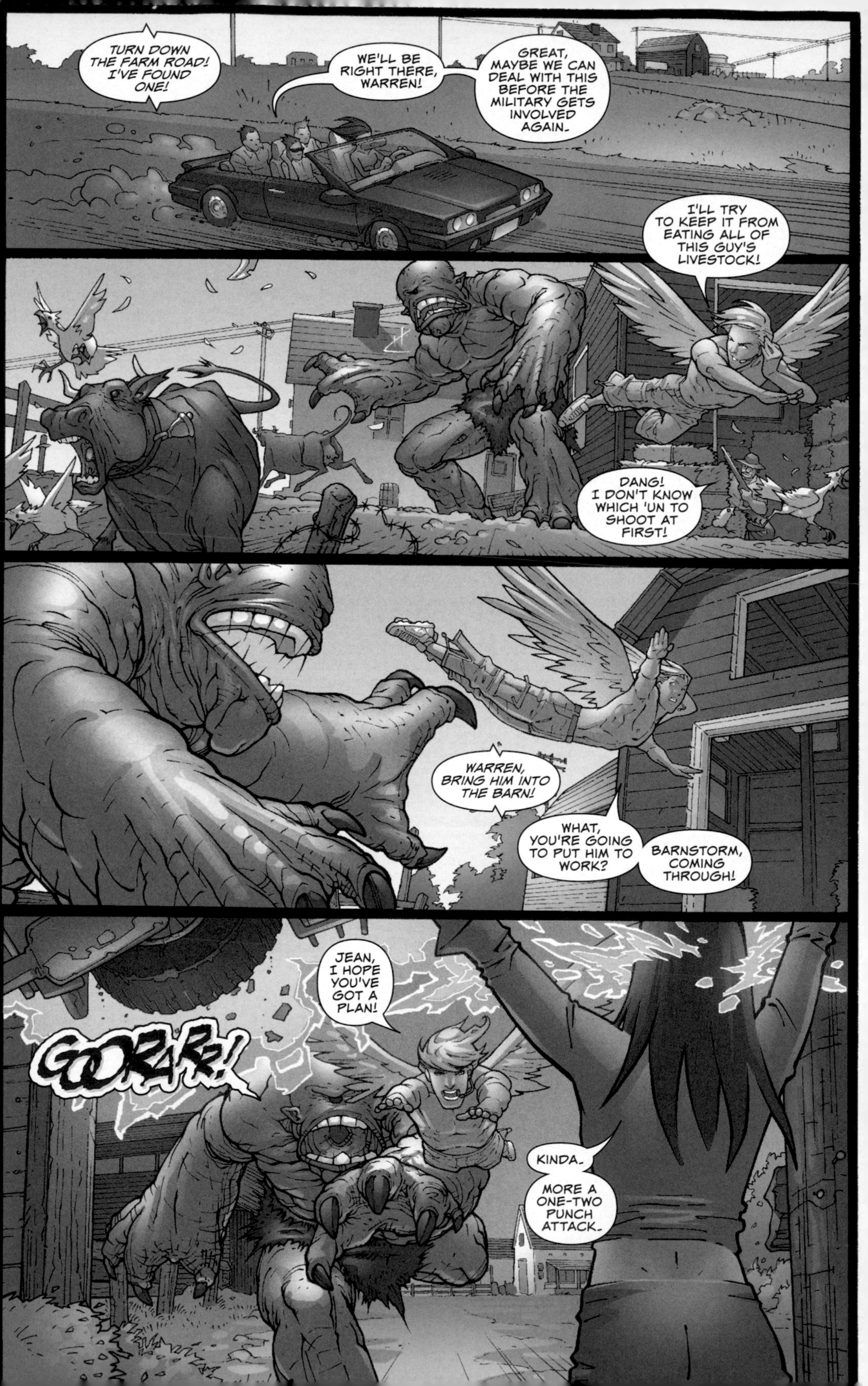
TURN DOWN THE FARM ROAD! I'VE FOUND ONE!
WE'LL BE RIGHT THERE, WARREN!
GREAT, MAYBE WE CAN DEAL WITH THIS BEFORE THE MILITARY GETS INVOLVED AGAIN.
I'LL TRY TO KEEP IT FROM EATING ALL OF THIS GUY'S LIVESTOCK!
DANG! I DON'T KNOW WHICH 'UN TO SHOOT AT FIRST!
WARREN, BRING HIM INTO THE BARN!
WHAT, YOU'RE GOING TO PUT HIM TO WORK?
BARNSTORM, COMING THROUGH!
JEAN, I HOPE YOU'VE GOT A PLAN!
GOORARRR!
KINDA.
MORE A ONE-TWO PUNCH ATTACK.

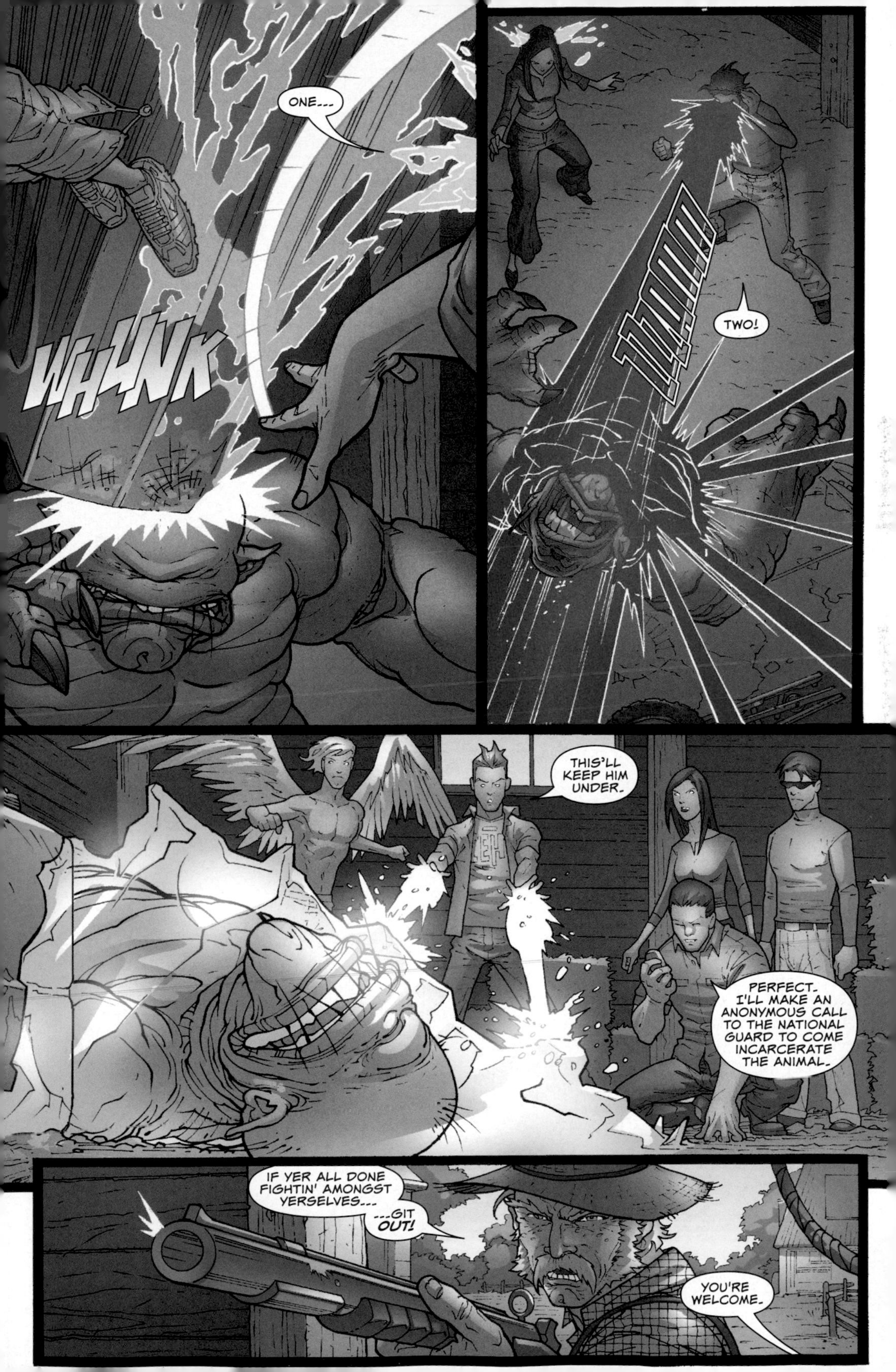
ONE---
WHUNK
TWO!
THIS'LL KEEP HIM UNDER.
PERFECT. I'LL MAKE AN ANONYMOUS CALL TO THE NATIONAL GUARD TO COME INCARCERATE THE ANIMAL.
IF YER ALL DONE FIGHTIN' AMONGST YERSELVES---
---GIT OUT!
YOU'RE WELCOME.

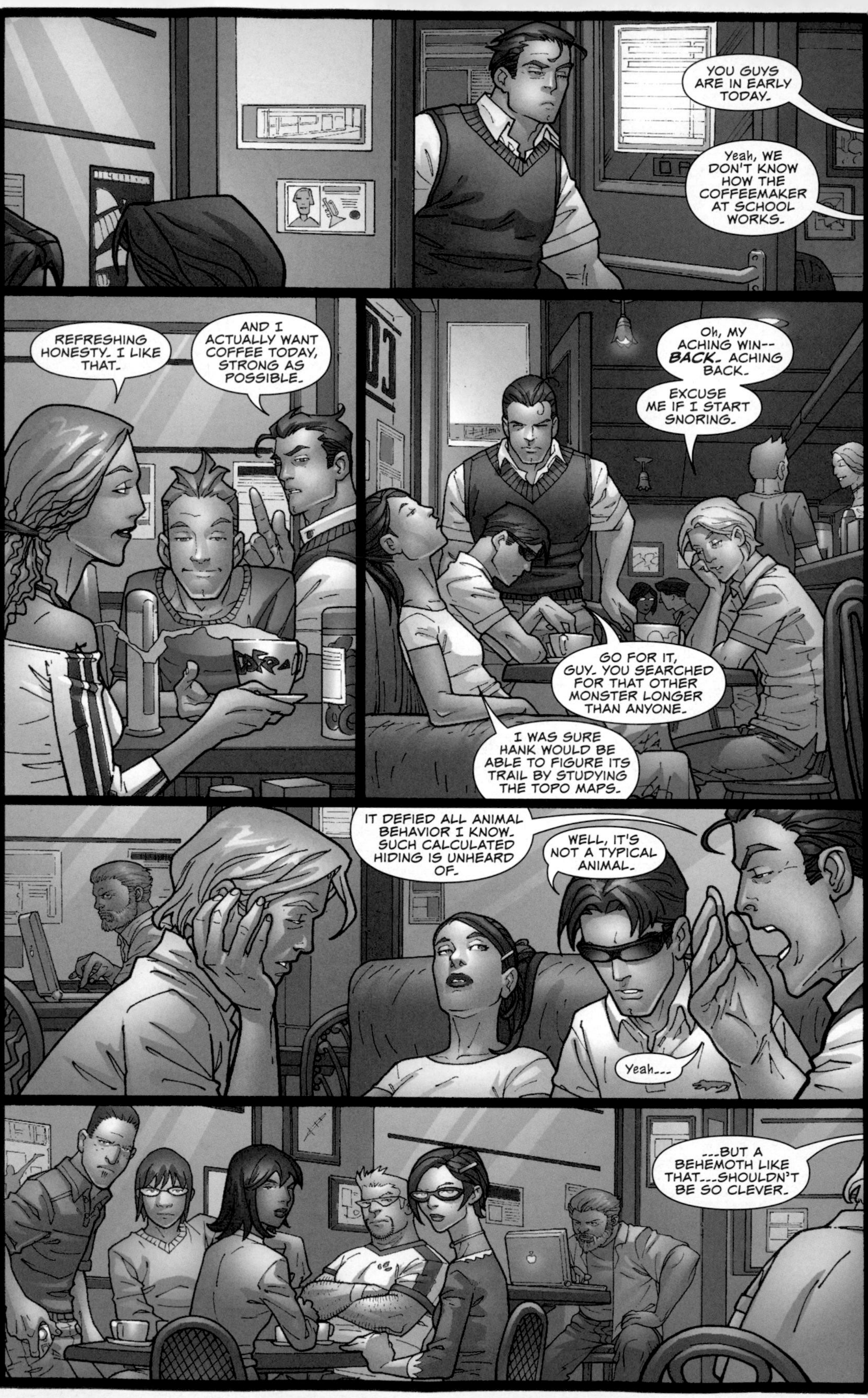

YOU GUYS ARE IN EARLY TODAY.
Yeah, WE DON'T KNOW HOW THE COFFEEMAKER AT SCHOOL WORKS.
REFRESHING HONESTY. I LIKE THAT.
AND I ACTUALLY WANT COFFEE TODAY, STRONG AS POSSIBLE.
Oh, MY ACHING WIN-- BACK. ACHING BACK.
EXCUSE ME IF I START SNORING.
GO FOR IT, GUY. YOU SEARCHED FOR THAT OTHER MONSTER LONGER THAN ANYONE.
I WAS SURE HANK WOULD BE ABLE TO FIGURE ITS TRAIL BY STUDYING THE TOPO MAPS.
IT DEFIED ALL ANIMAL BEHAVIOR I KNOW. SUCH CALCULATED HIDING IS UNHEARD OF.
WELL, IT'S NOT A TYPICAL ANIMAL.
Yeah...
...BUT A BEHEMOTH LIKE THAT...SHOULDN'T BE SO CLEVER.

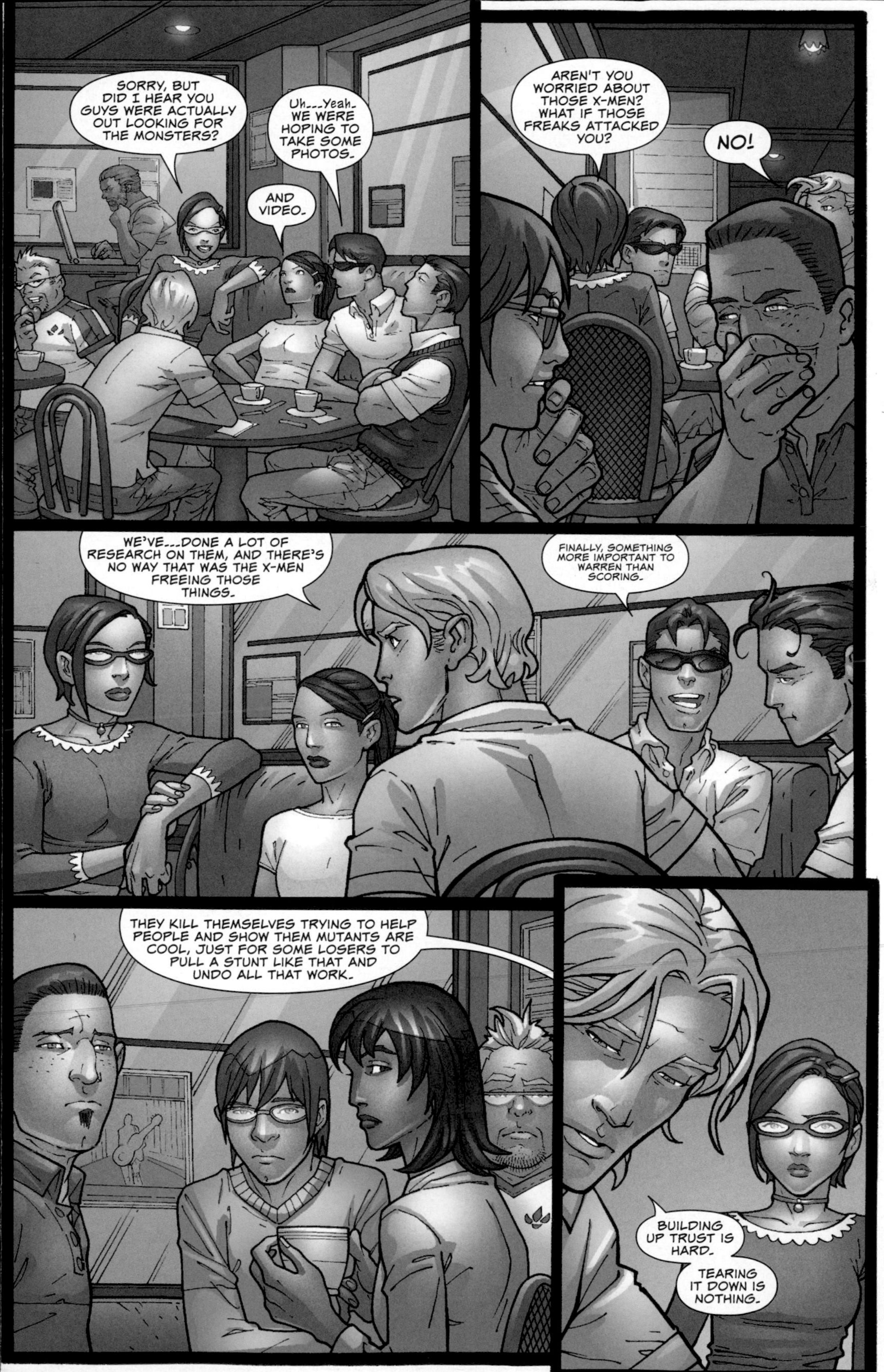
SORRY, BUT DID I HEAR YOU GUYS WERE ACTUALLY OUT LOOKING FOR THE MONSTERS?
Uh...Yeah. WE WERE HOPING TO TAKE SOME PHOTOS.
AND VIDEO.
AREN'T YOU WORRIED ABOUT THOSE X-MEN? WHAT IF THOSE FREAKS ATTACKED YOU?
NO!
WE'VE...DONE A LOT OF RESEARCH ON THEM, AND THERE'S NO WAY THAT WAS THE X-MEN FREEING THOSE THINGS.
FINALLY, SOMETHING MORE IMPORTANT TO WARREN THAN SCORING.
THEY KILL THEMSELVES TRYING TO HELP PEOPLE AND SHOW THEM MUTANTS ARE COOL, JUST FOR SOME LOSERS TO PULL A STUNT LIKE THAT AND UNDO ALL THAT WORK.
BUILDING UP TRUST IS HARD.
TEARING IT DOWN IS NOTHING.

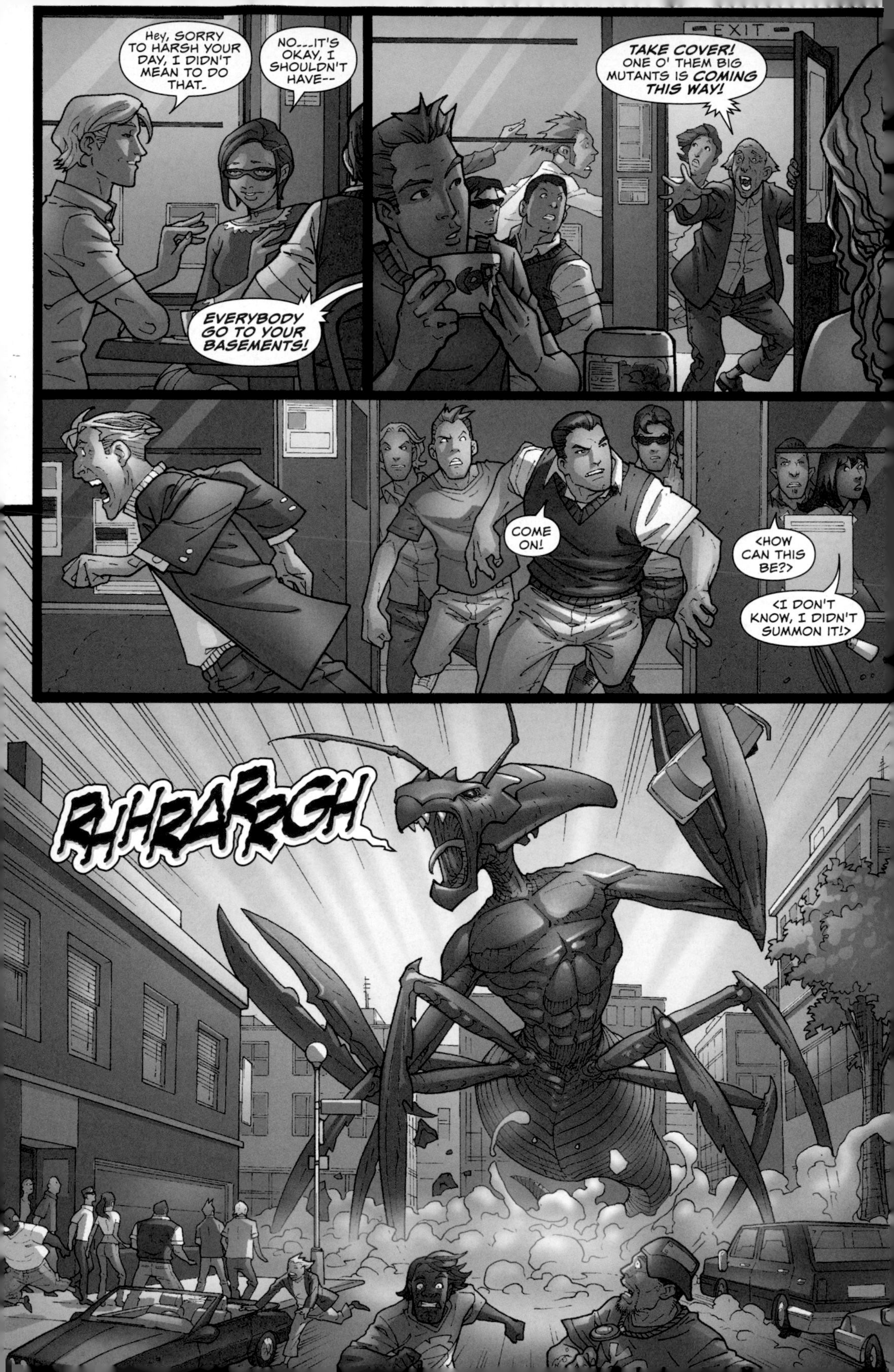

Hey, SORRY TO HARSH YOUR DAY, I DIDN'T MEAN TO DO THAT.
NO---IT'S OKAY, I SHOULDN'T HAVE--
EVERYBODY GO TO YOUR BASEMENTS!
EXIT
TAKE COVER! ONE O' THEM BIG MUTANTS IS COMING THIS WAY!
COME ON!
<HOW CAN THIS BE?>
<I DON'T KNOW, I DIDN'T SUMMON IT!>
RHHRARRGH

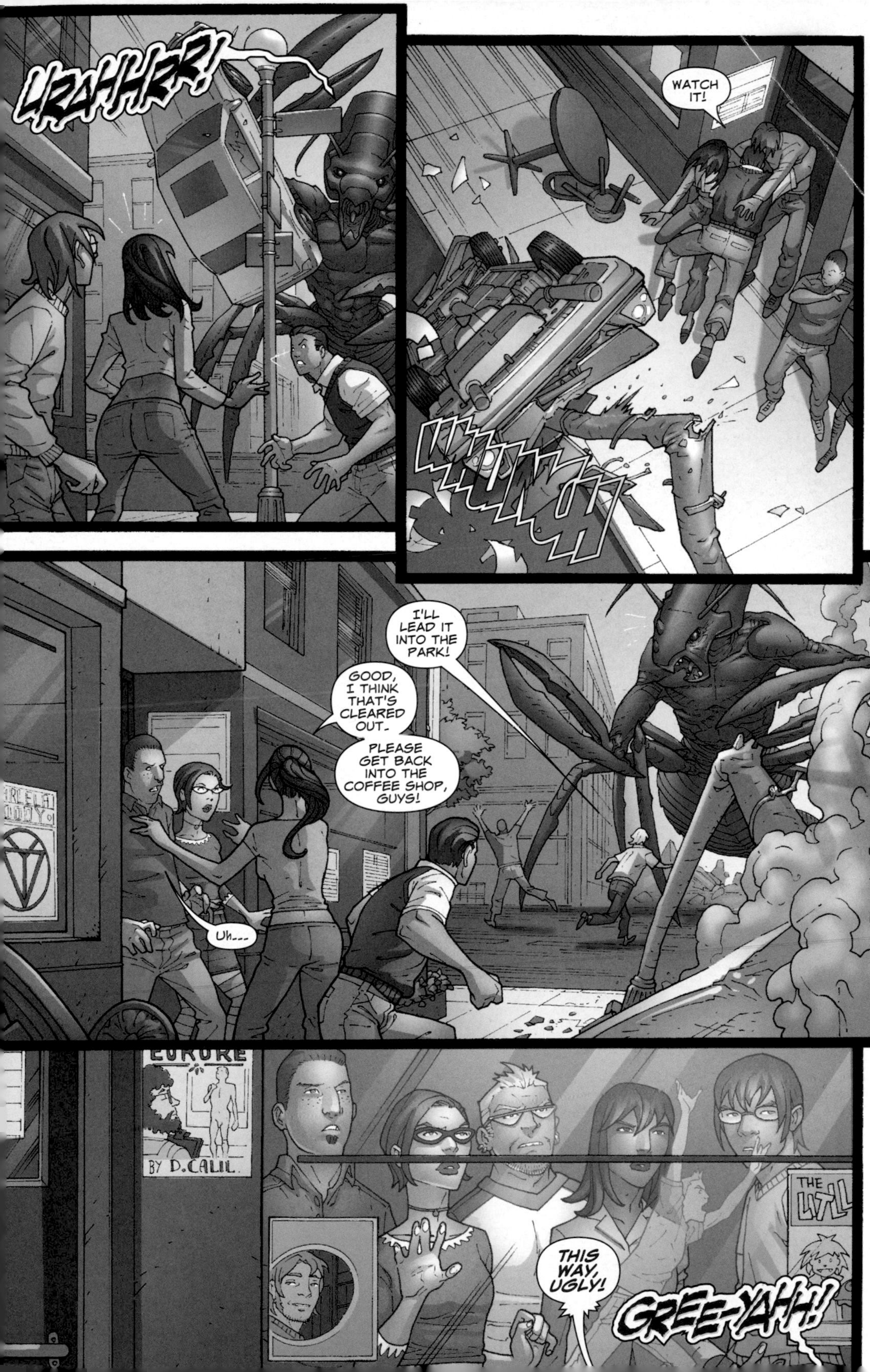
URAHHRR!
WATCH IT!
I'LL LEAD IT INTO THE PARK!
GOOD, I THINK THAT'S CLEARED OUT.
PLEASE GET BACK INTO THE COFFEE SHOP, GUYS!
Uh...
BY D.CALIL.
THIS WAY, UGLY!
GREE-YAHH!

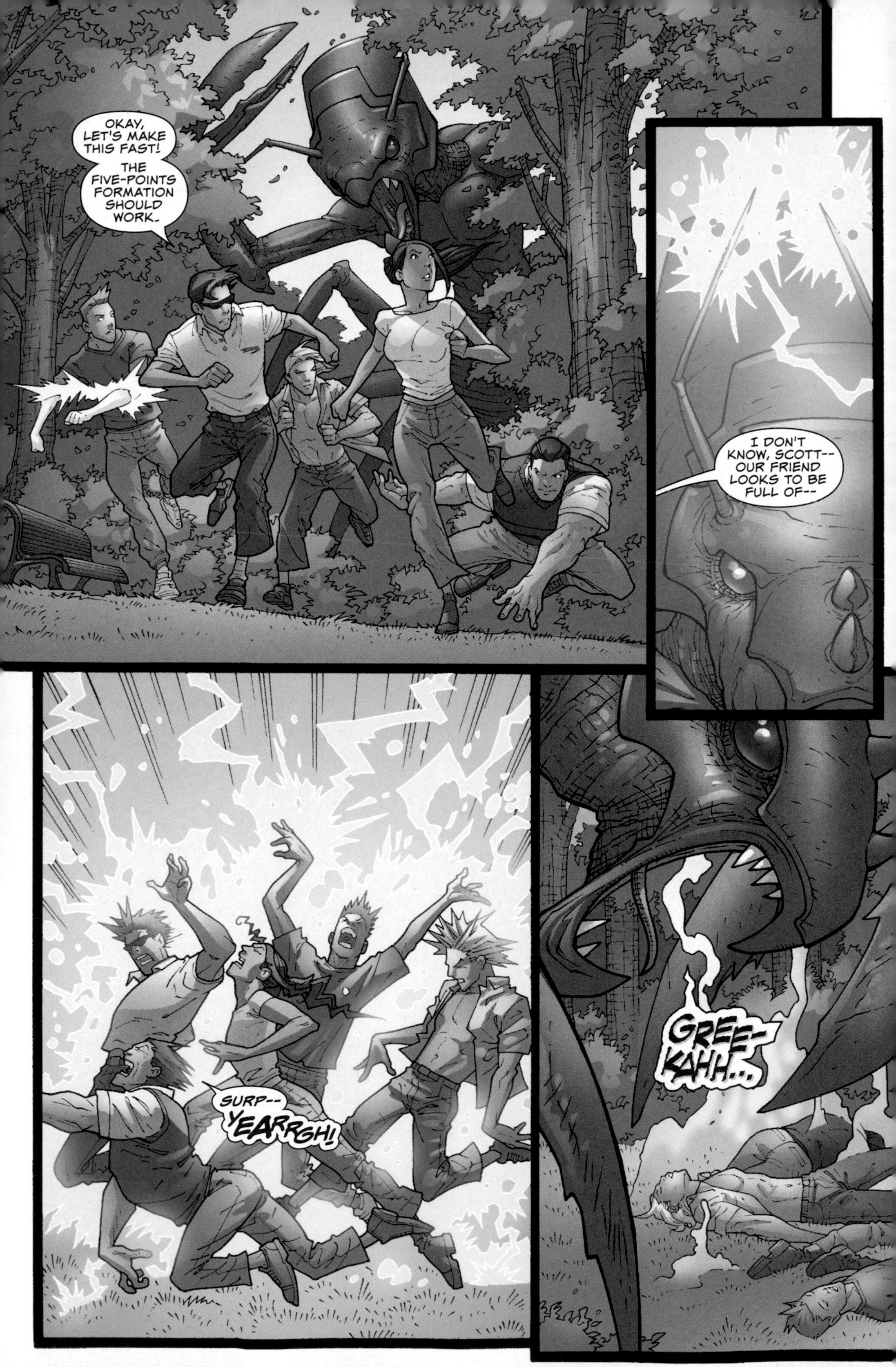
OKAY, LET'S MAKE THIS FAST!
THE FIVE-POINTS FORMATION SHOULD WORK.
I DON'T KNOW, SCOTT-- OUR FRIEND LOOKS TO BE FULL OF--
SURP-- YEARRGH!
GREE-KAHH...

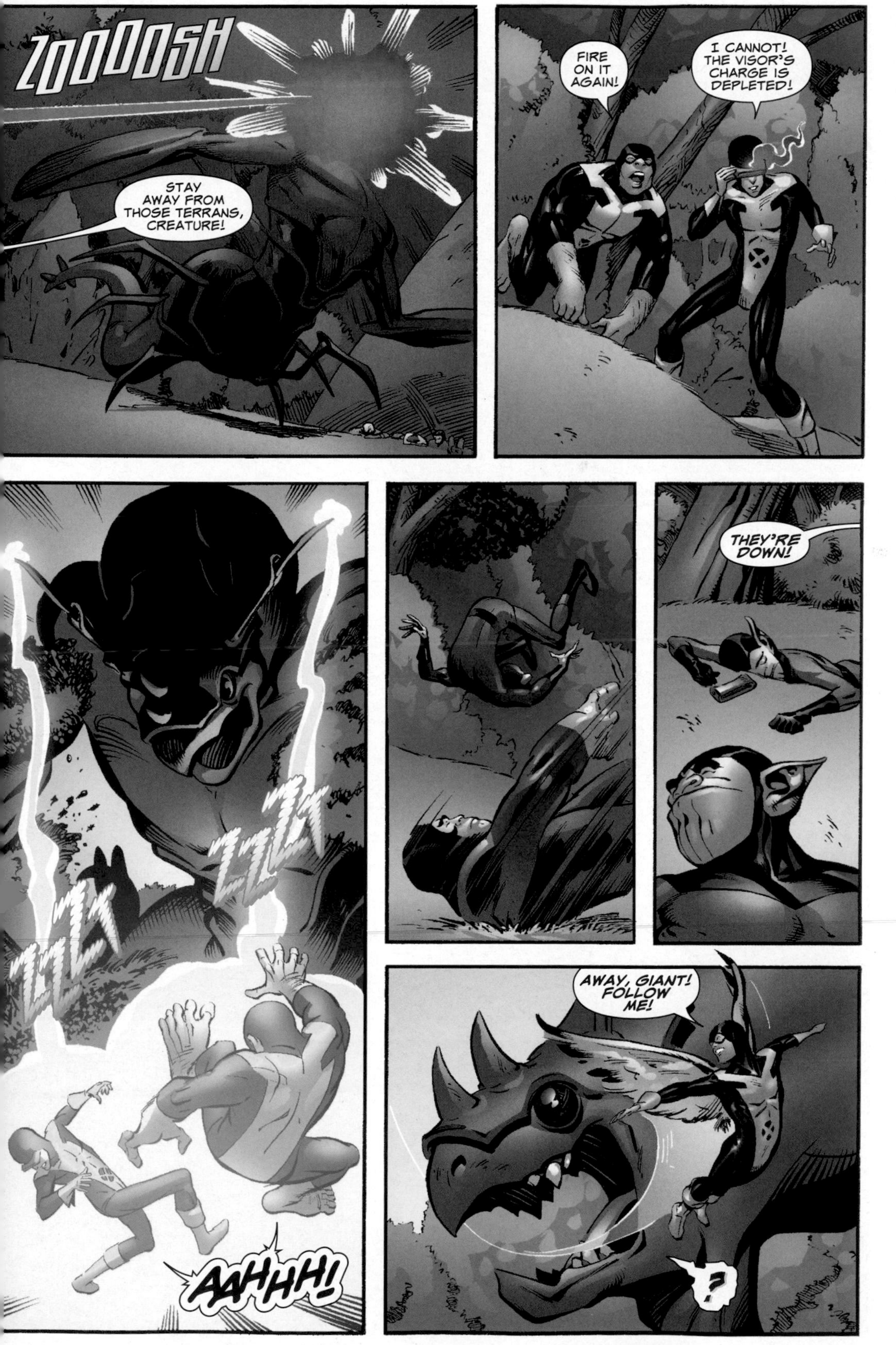
ZOOOOSH
STAY AWAY FROM THOSE TERRANS, CREATURE!
FIRE ON IT AGAIN!
I CANNOT! THE VISOR'S CHARGE IS DEPLETED!
ZZZAK
ZZZAK
AAHHH!
THEY'RE DOWN!
AWAY, GIANT! FOLLOW ME!
?

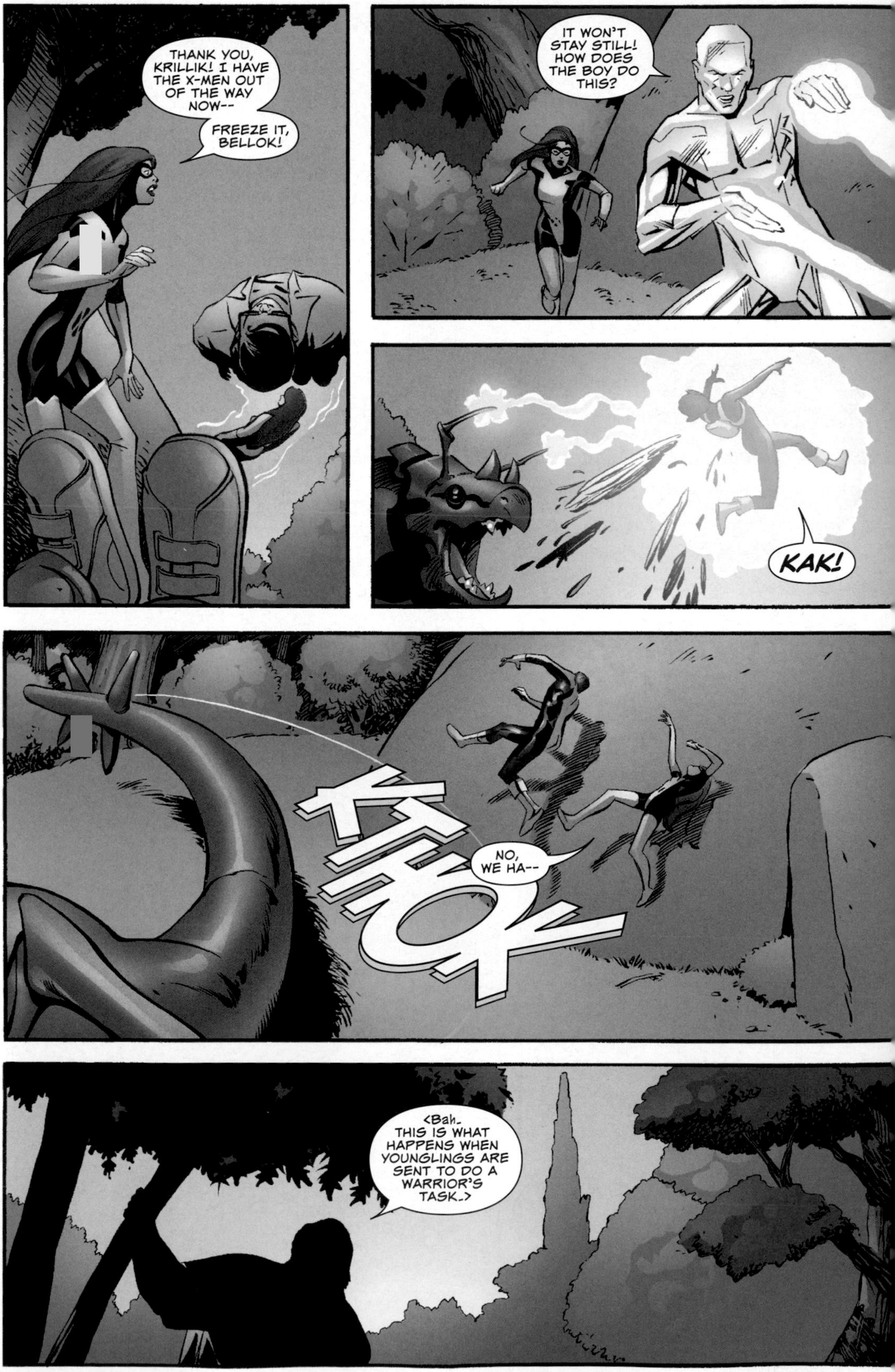
THANK YOU, KRILLIK! I HAVE THE X-MEN OUT OF THE WAY NOW--
FREEZE IT, BELLOK!
IT WON'T STAY STILL! HOW DOES THE BOY DO THIS?
KAK!
KTHOK
NO, WE HA--
<Bah. THIS IS WHAT HAPPENS WHEN YOUNGLINGS ARE SENT TO DO A WARRIOR'S TASK.>

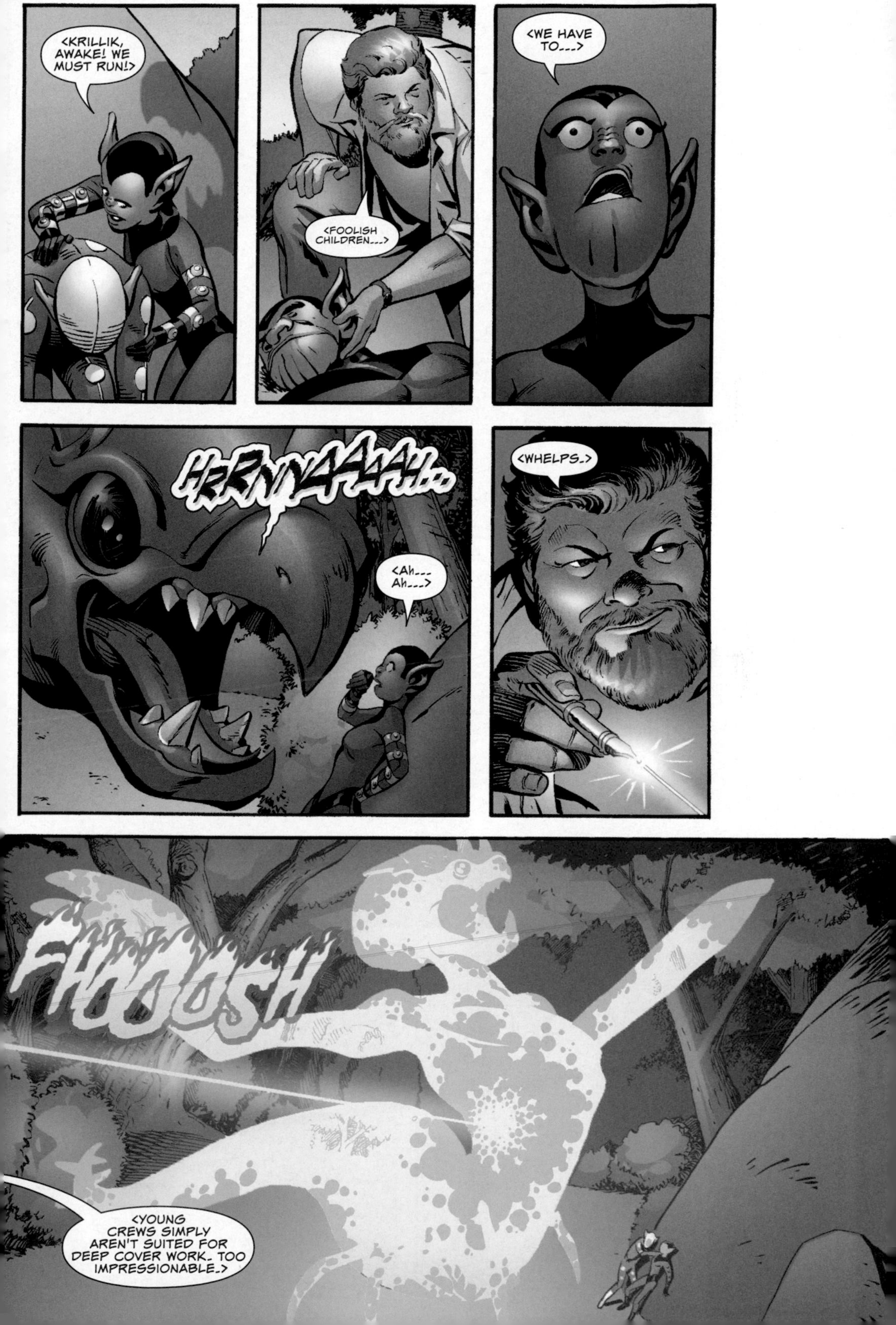

<KRILLIK, AWAKE! WE MUST RUN!>
<FOOLISH CHILDREN...>
<WE HAVE TO...>
HRRNNAAAAH..
<Ah... Ah...>
<WHELPS.>
FHOOOSH
<YOUNG CREWS SIMPLY AREN'T SUITED FOR DEEP COVER WORK. TOO IMPRESSIONABLE.>

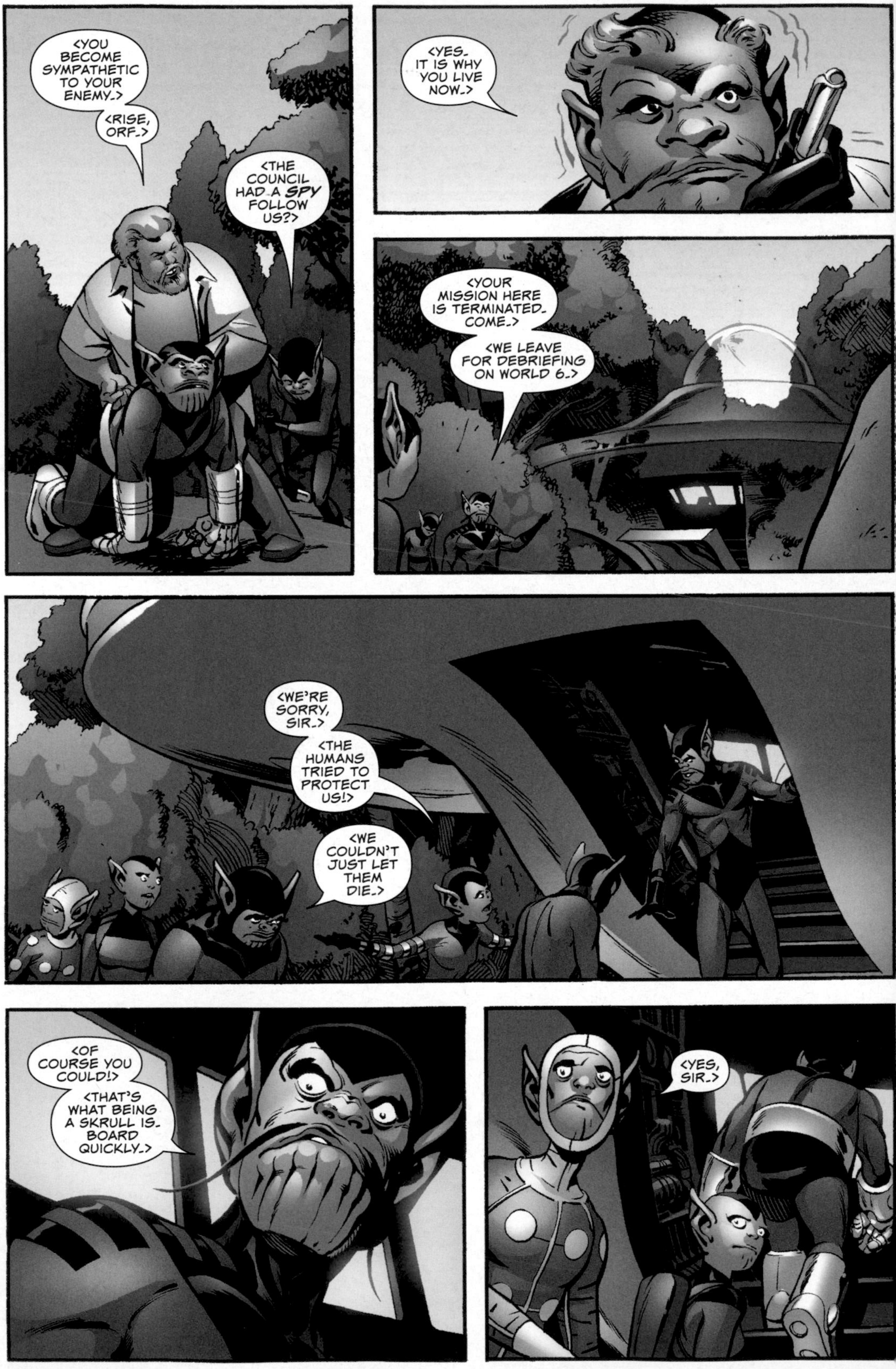
<YOU BECOME SYMPATHETIC TO YOUR ENEMY.>
<RISE, ORF.>
<THE COUNCIL HAD A SPY FOLLOW US?>
<YES. IT IS WHY YOU LIVE NOW.>
<YOUR MISSION HERE IS TERMINATED. COME.>
<WE LEAVE FOR DEBRIEFING ON WORLD 6.>
<WE'RE SORRY, SIR.>
<THE HUMANS TRIED TO PROTECT US!>
<WE COULDN'T JUST LET THEM DIE.>
<OF COURSE YOU COULD!>
<THAT'S WHAT BEING A SKRULL IS. BOARD QUICKLY.>
<YES, SIR.>

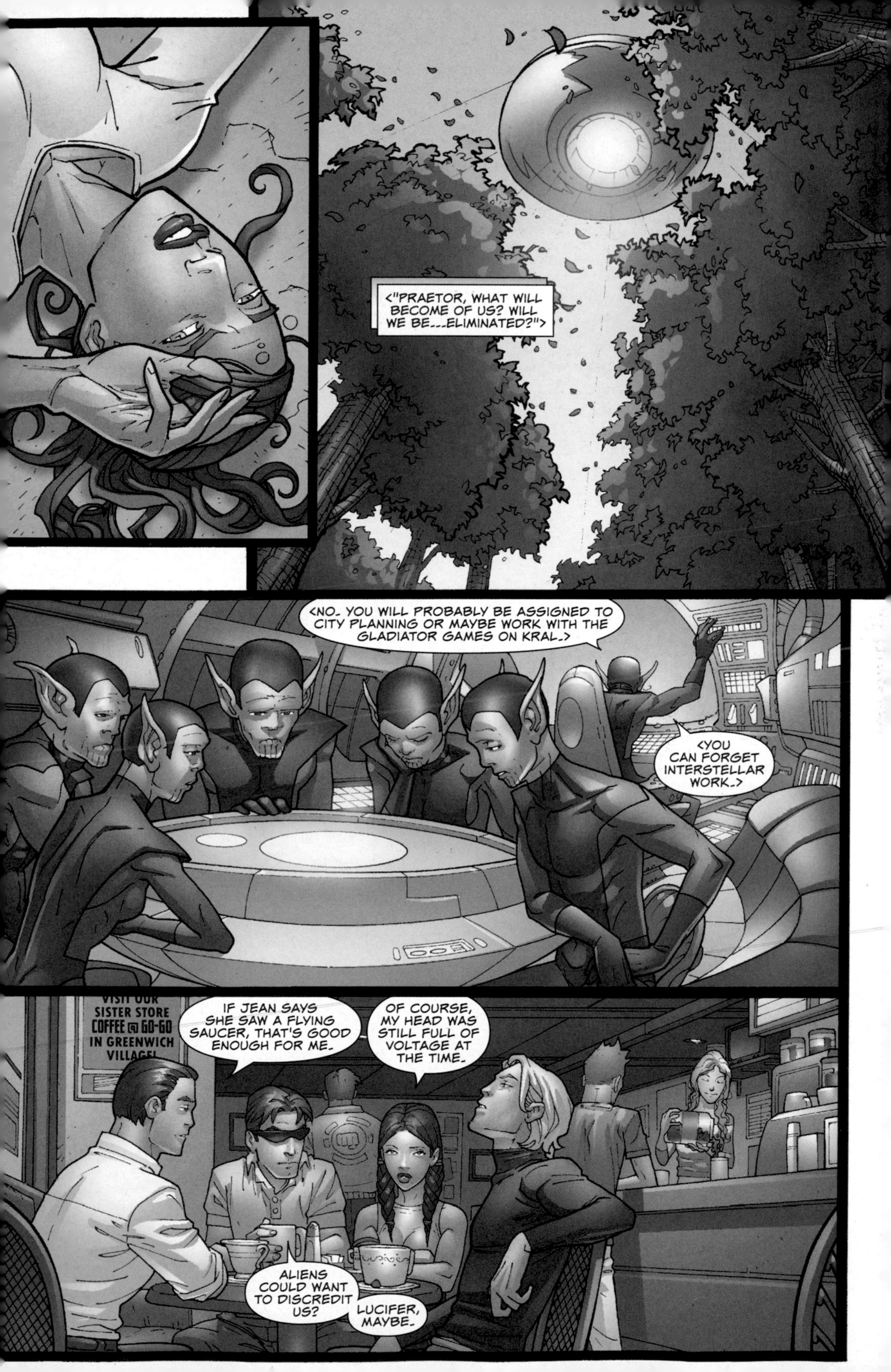

<"PRAETOR, WHAT WILL BECOME OF US? WILL WE BE...ELIMINATED?">
<NO. YOU WILL PROBABLY BE ASSIGNED TO CITY PLANNING OR MAYBE WORK WITH THE GLADIATOR GAMES ON KRAL.>
<YOU CAN FORGET INTERSTELLAR WORK.>
VISIT OUR SISTER STORE COFFEE @ GO-GO IN GREENWICH VILLAGE!
IF JEAN SAYS SHE SAW A FLYING SAUCER, THAT'S GOOD ENOUGH FOR ME.
OF COURSE, MY HEAD WAS STILL FULL OF VOLTAGE AT THE TIME.
ALIENS COULD WANT TO DISCREDIT US?
LUCIFER, MAYBE.

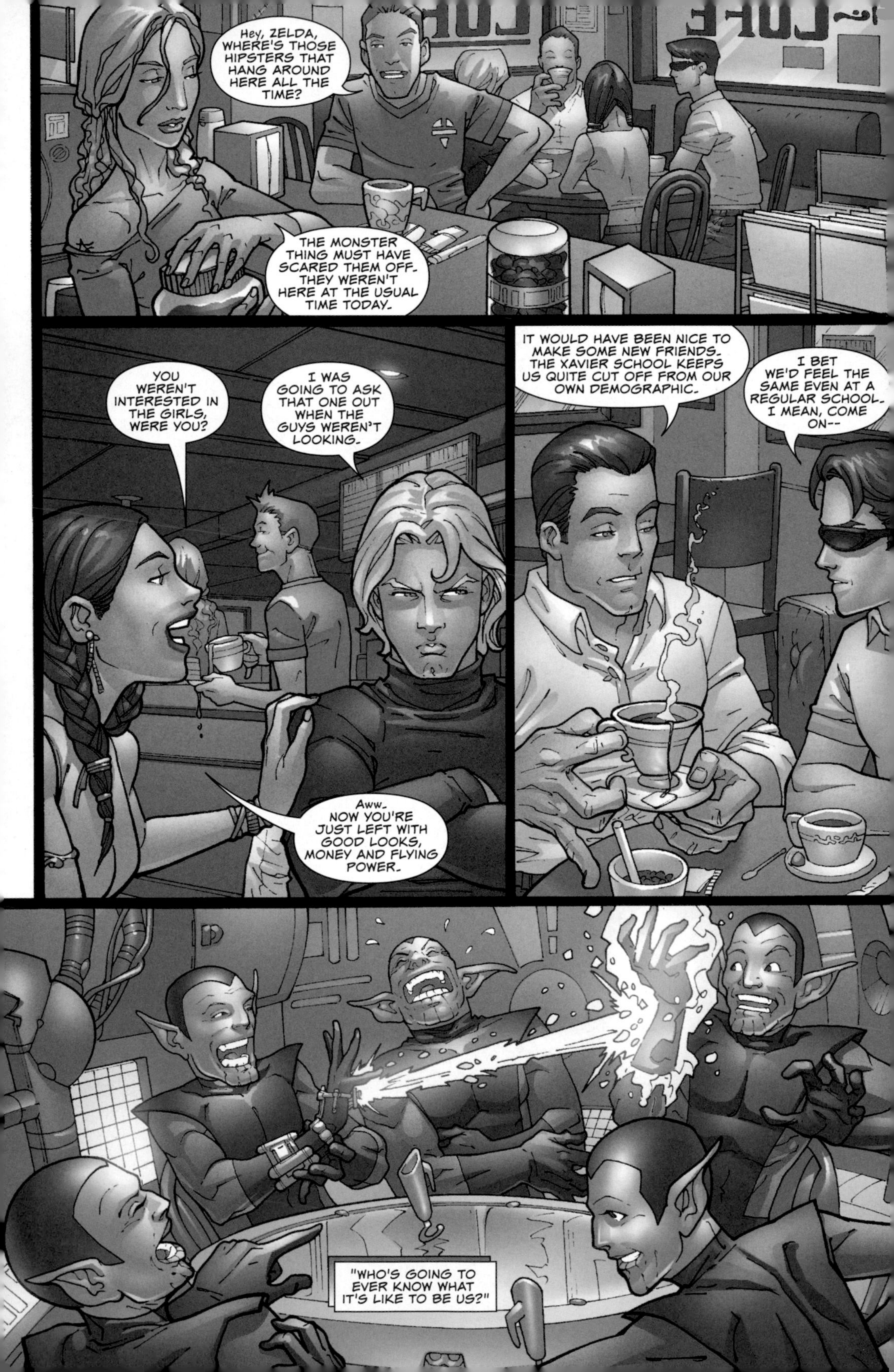
Hey, ZELDA, WHERE'S THOSE HIPSTERS THAT HANG AROUND HERE ALL THE TIME?
THE MONSTER THING MUST HAVE SCARED THEM OFF. THEY WEREN'T HERE AT THE USUAL TIME TODAY.
YOU WEREN'T INTERESTED IN THE GIRLS, WERE YOU?
I WAS GOING TO ASK THAT ONE OUT WHEN THE GUYS WEREN'T LOOKING.
AWW. NOW YOU'RE JUST LEFT WITH GOOD LOOKS, MONEY AND FLYING POWER.
IT WOULD HAVE BEEN NICE TO MAKE SOME NEW FRIENDS. THE XAVIER SCHOOL KEEPS US QUITE CUT OFF FROM OUR OWN DEMOGRAPHIC.
I BET WE'D FEEL THE SAME EVEN AT A REGULAR SCHOOL. I MEAN, COME ON--
"WHO'S GOING TO EVER KNOW WHAT IT'S LIKE TO BE US?"

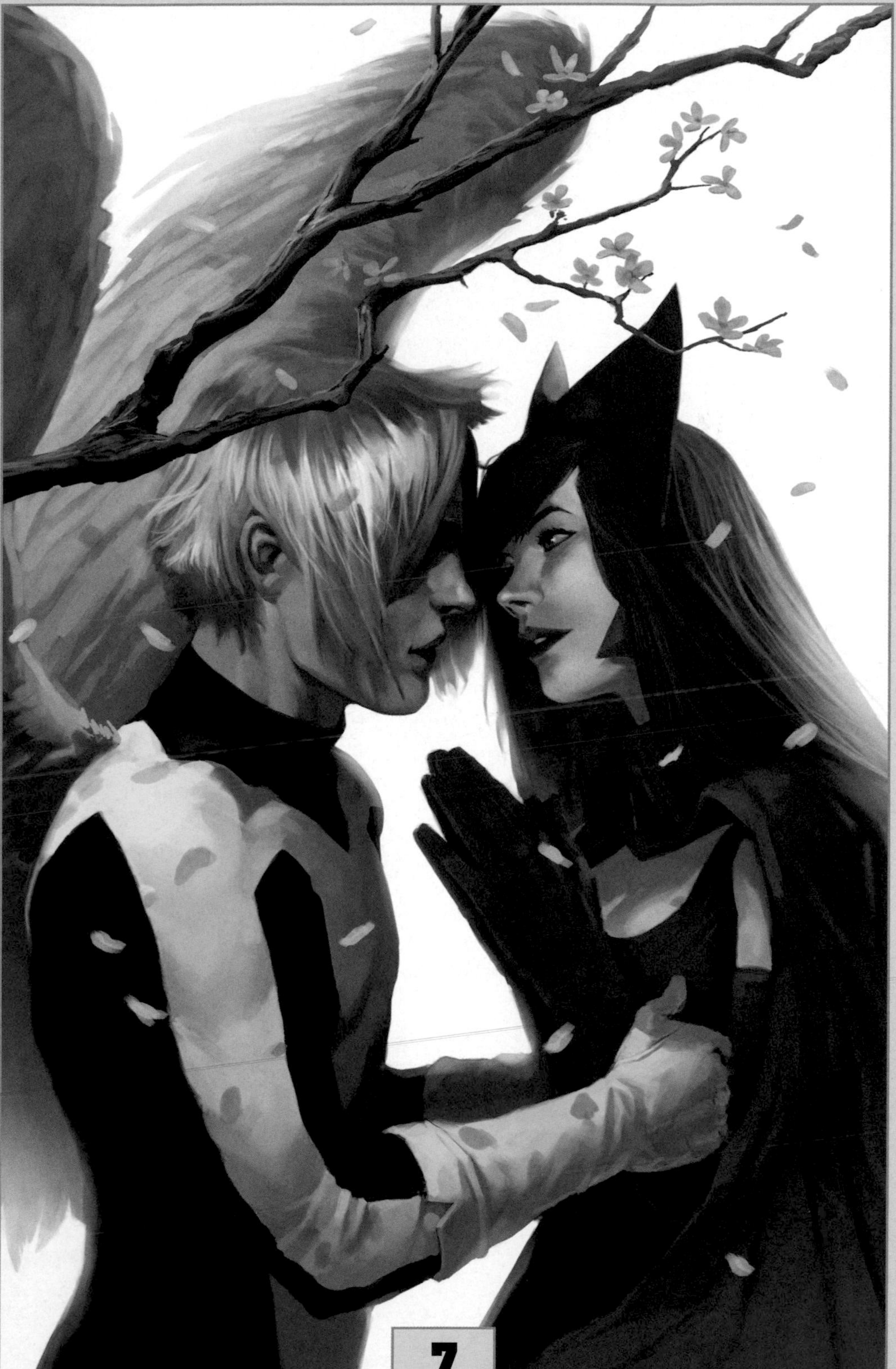
7

THE NEXT STEP IN HUMAN EVOLUTION HAS ARRIVED—HOMO SUPERIOR. MANKIND ISN'T SURE WHETHER THIS REPRESENTS HOPE FOR THE FUTURE...OR THE END OF THE HUMAN RACE. IN A PRIVATE SCHOOL IN UPSTATE NEW YORK, ONE BRILLIANT MUTANT IS TEACHING A GROUP OF FIVE SUCH GIFTED STUDENTS WHAT THEY'LL NEED TO SURVIVE IN THIS NEW WORLD. THESE ARE THE UNTOLD STORIES OF PROFESSOR XAVIER'S FIRST CLASS OF X-MEN!

XAVIER'S SCHOOL FOR GIFTED YOUNGSTERS

PROPERTY OF:

CEREBRO

HEADMASTER

PROFESSOR CHARLES XAVIER

SEMESTER EVALUATION: SCOTT SUMMERS HAS EXCEEDED PROJECTIONS IN CLASSWORK AND PERFORMED SUCCESSFULLY IN THE FIELD.

SEMESTER EVALUATION: JEAN GREY HAS EXCEEDED PROJECTIONS IN CLASSWORK AND PERFORMED SUCCESSFULLY IN THE FIELD.

SEMESTER EVALUATION: HENRY MCCOY HAS EXCEEDED PROJECTIONS IN CLASSWORK AND PERFORMED SUCCESSFULLY IN THE FIELD.

SCOTT SUMMERS "CYCLOPS"

JEAN GREY "MARVEL GIRL"

HENRY "HANK" MCCOY "BEAST"

WARREN WORTHINGTON III "ANGEL"

ROBERT DRAKE "ICEMAN"

SEMESTER EVALUATION: WARREN WORTHINGTON HAS EXCEEDED PROJECTIONS IN CLASSWORK AND PERFORMED SUCCESSFULLY IN THE FIELD.

SEMESTER EVALUATION: ROBERT DRAKE HAS A PERFECT ATTENDANCE RATE.

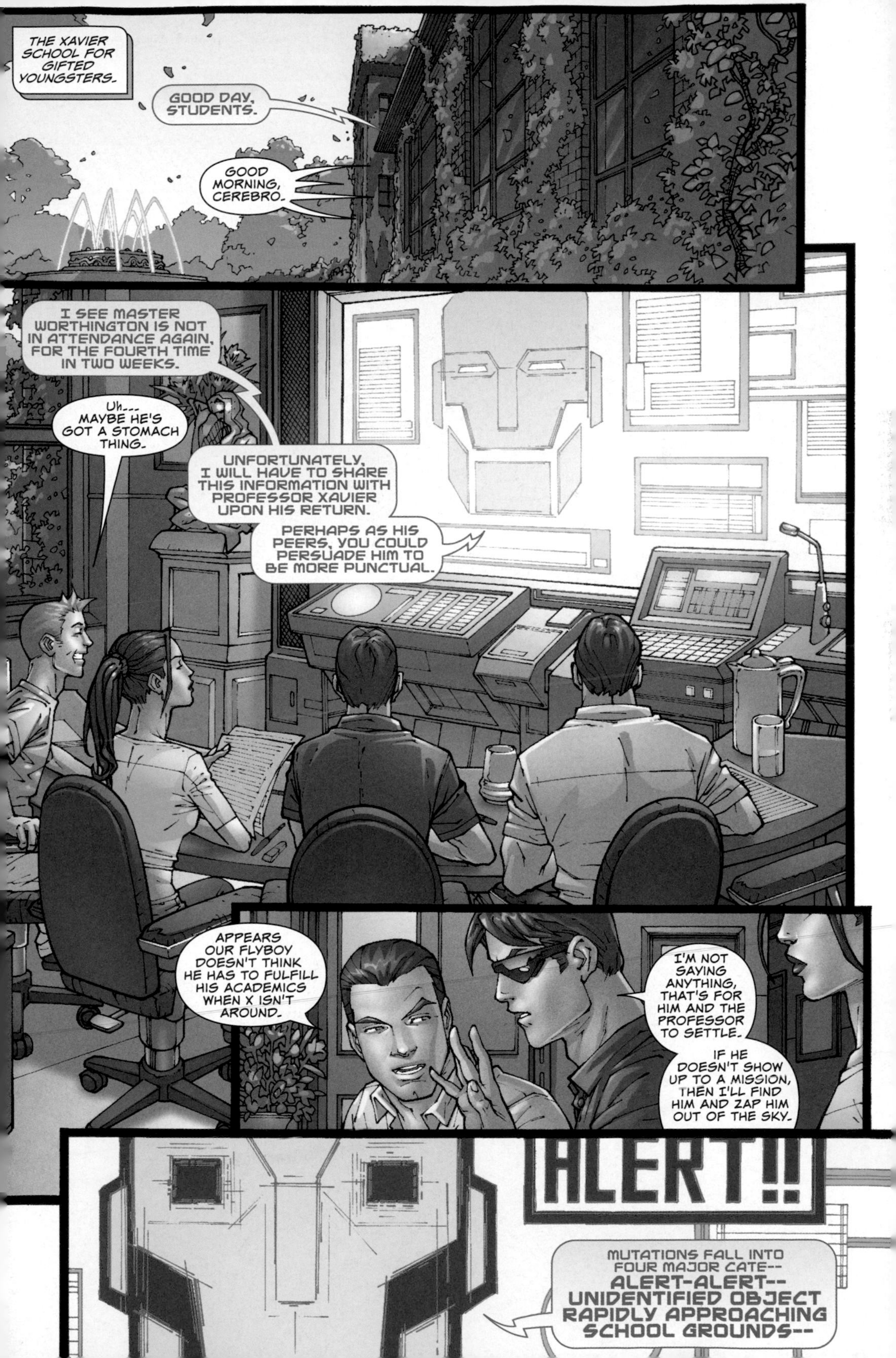
THE XAVIER SCHOOL FOR GIFTED YOUNGSTERS.
GOOD DAY, STUDENTS.
GOOD MORNING, CEREBRO.
I SEE MASTER WORTHINGTON IS NOT IN ATTENDANCE AGAIN, FOR THE FOURTH TIME IN TWO WEEKS.
UH... MAYBE HE'S GOT A STOMACH THING.
UNFORTUNATELY, I WILL HAVE TO SHARE THIS INFORMATION WITH PROFESSOR XAVIER UPON HIS RETURN.
PERHAPS AS HIS PEERS, YOU COULD PERSUADE HIM TO BE MORE PUNCTUAL.
APPEARS OUR FLYBOY DOESN'T THINK HE HAS TO FULFILL HIS ACADEMICS WHEN X ISN'T AROUND.
I'M NOT SAYING ANYTHING, THAT'S FOR HIM AND THE PROFESSOR TO SETTLE.
IF HE DOESN'T SHOW UP TO A MISSION, THEN I'LL FIND HIM AND ZAP HIM OUT OF THE SKY.
ALERT!!
MUTATIONS FALL INTO FOUR MAJOR CATE--
ALERT-ALERT--
UNIDENTIFIED OBJECT RAPIDLY APPROACHING SCHOOL GROUNDS--

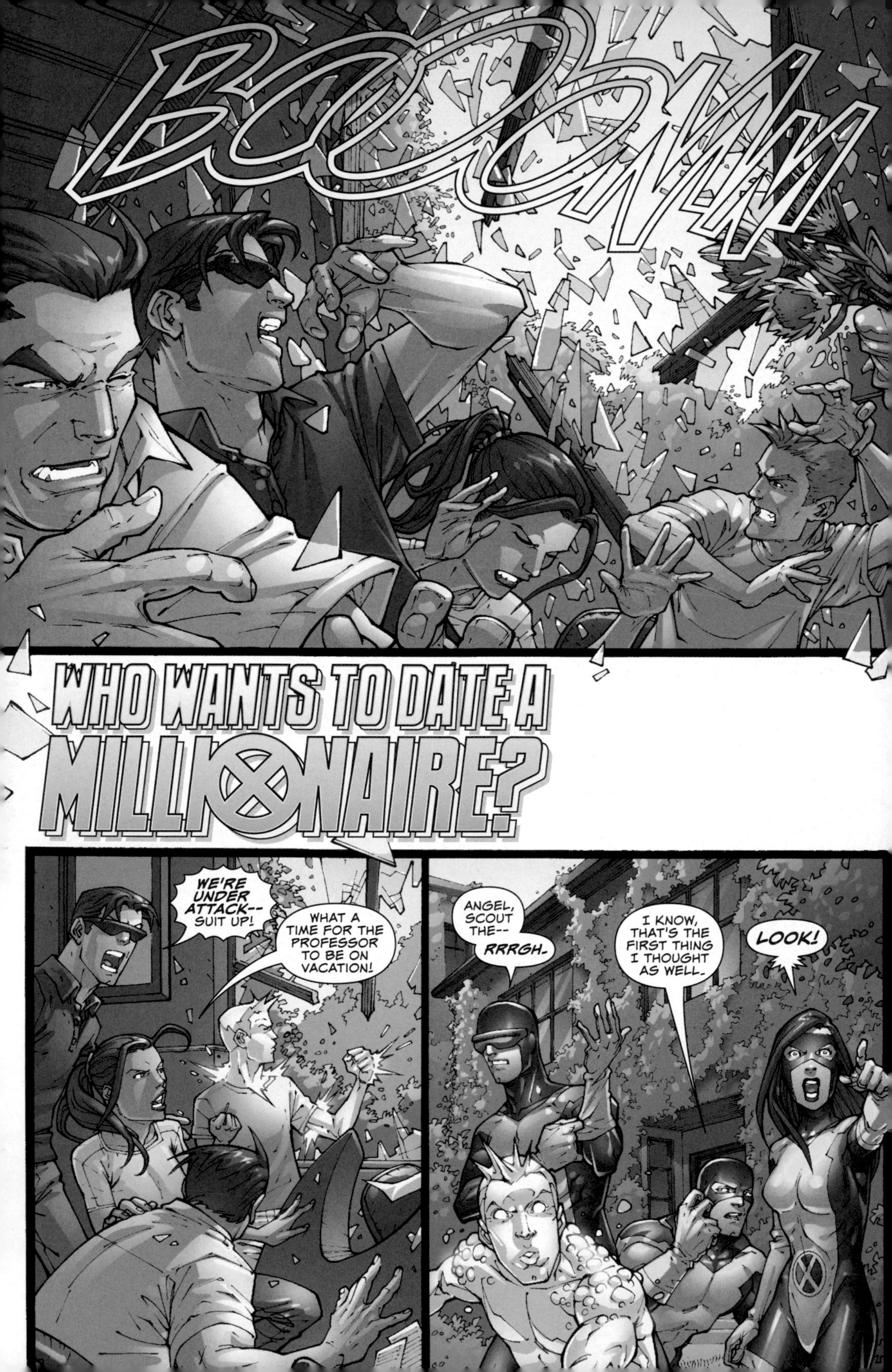
WHO WANTS TO DATE A MILLIONAIRE?
WE'RE UNDER ATTACK-- SUIT UP!
WHAT A TIME FOR THE PROFESSOR TO BE ON VACATION!
ANGEL, SCOUT THE--
RRRGH.
I KNOW, THAT'S THE FIRST THING I THOUGHT AS WELL.
LOOK!

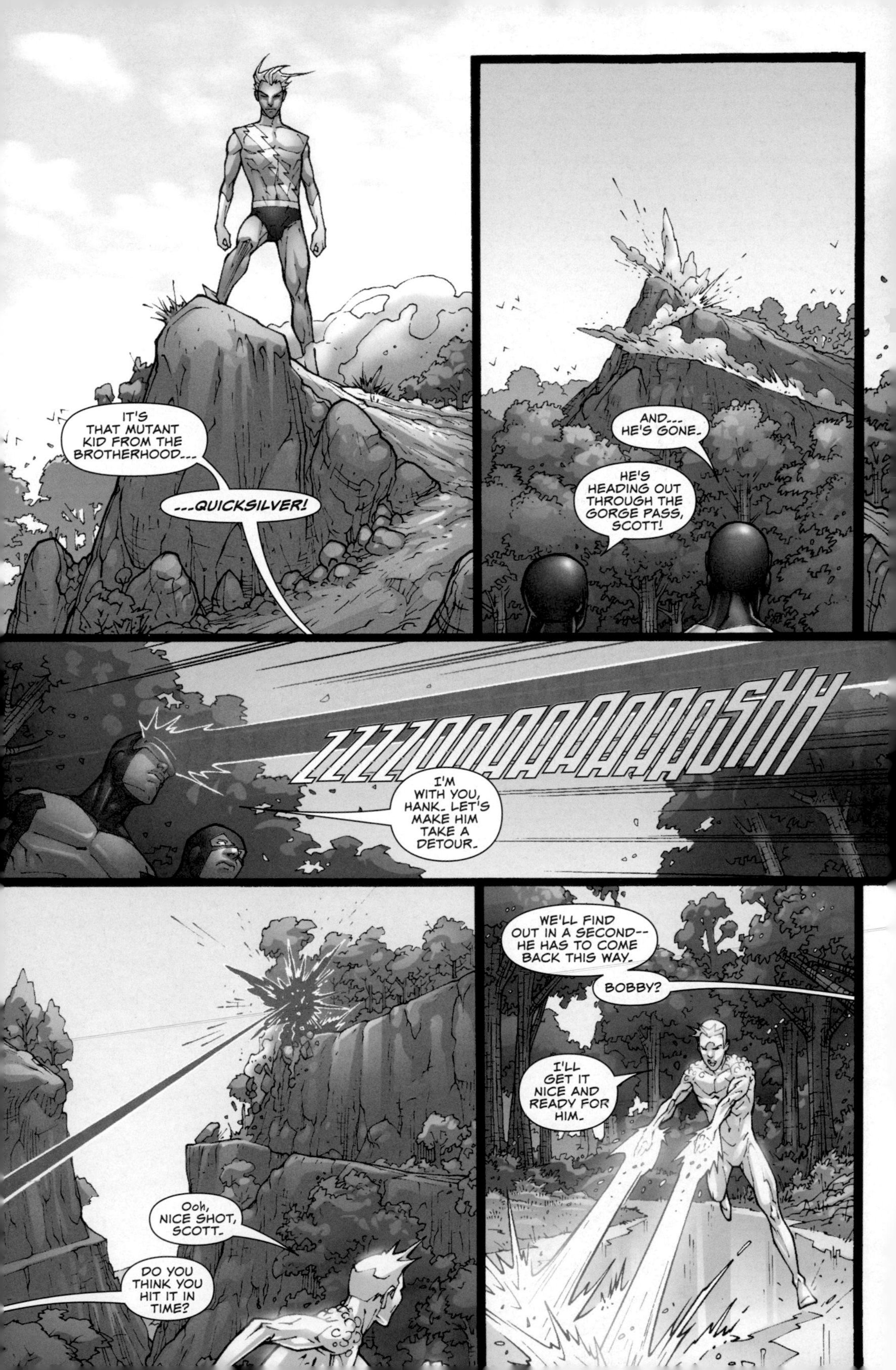
IT'S THAT MUTANT KID FROM THE BROTHERHOOD---
---QUICKSILVER!
AND--- HE'S GONE.
HE'S HEADING OUT THROUGH THE GORGE PASS, SCOTT!
ZZZZOOAAAAAAAOSHH
I'M WITH YOU, HANK. LET'S MAKE HIM TAKE A DETOUR.
Ooh, NICE SHOT, SCOTT.
DO YOU THINK YOU HIT IT IN TIME?
WE'LL FIND OUT IN A SECOND-- HE HAS TO COME BACK THIS WAY.
BOBBY?
I'LL GET IT NICE AND READY FOR HIM.

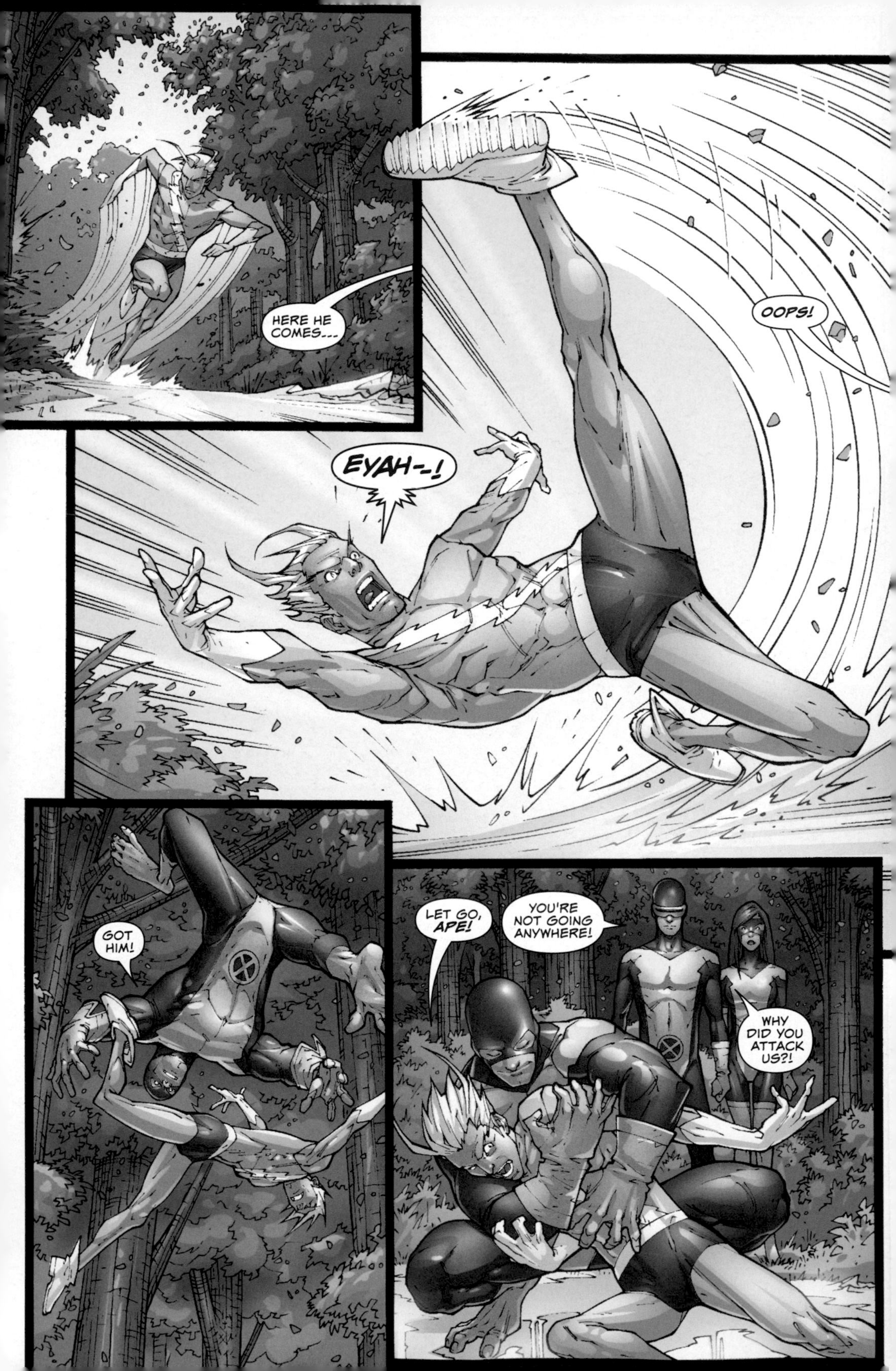
HERE HE COMES...
OOPS!
EYAH--!
GOT HIM!
LET GO, APE!
YOU'RE NOT GOING ANYWHERE!
WHY DID YOU ATTACK US?!

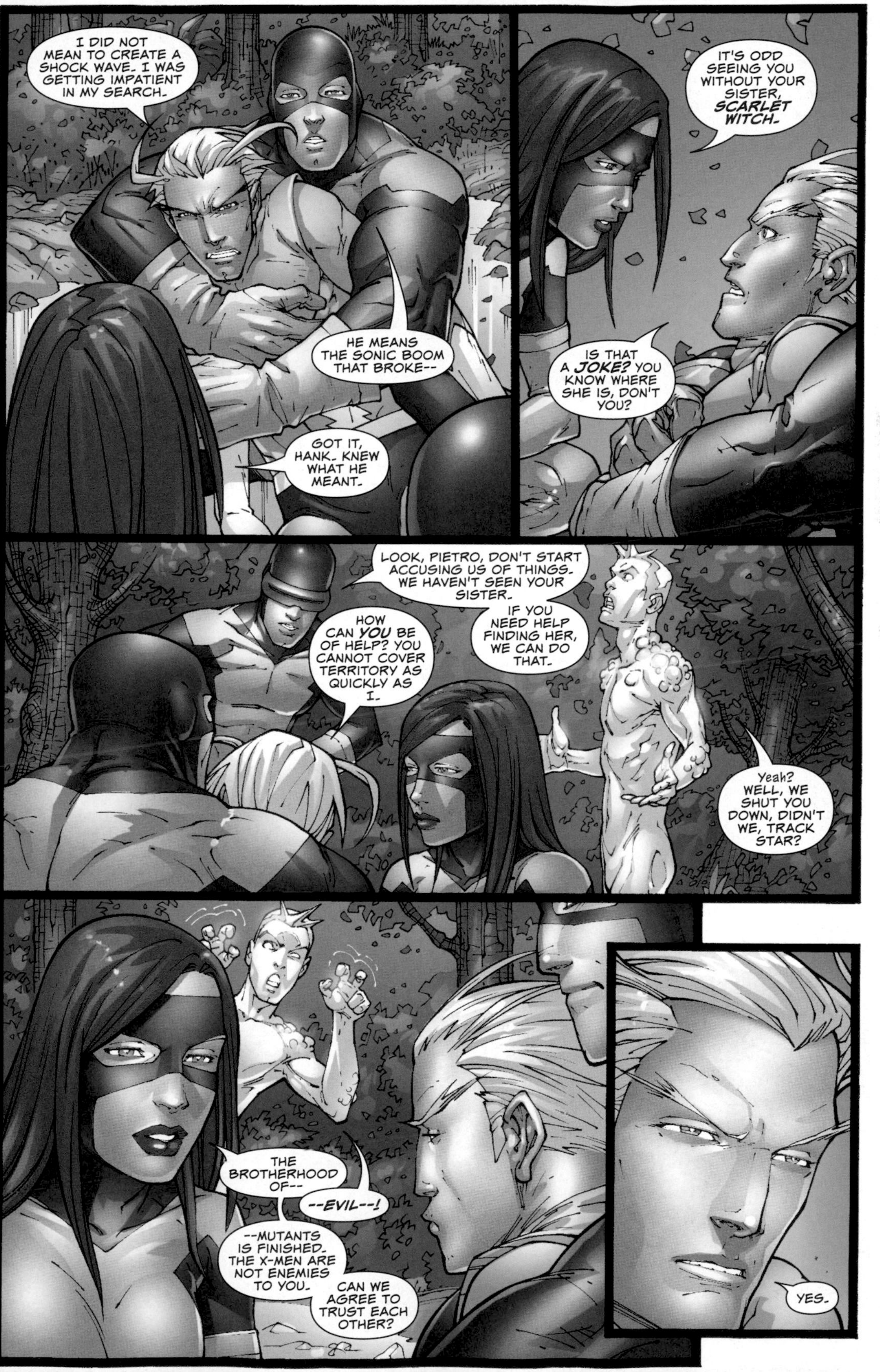
I DID NOT MEAN TO CREATE A SHOCK WAVE. I WAS GETTING IMPATIENT IN MY SEARCH.
HE MEANS THE SONIC BOOM THAT BROKE--
GOT IT, HANK. KNEW WHAT HE MEANT.
IT'S ODD SEEING YOU WITHOUT YOUR SISTER, SCARLET WITCH.
IS THAT A JOKE? YOU KNOW WHERE SHE IS, DON'T YOU?
LOOK, PIETRO, DON'T START ACCUSING US OF THINGS. WE HAVEN'T SEEN YOUR SISTER.
IF YOU NEED HELP FINDING HER, WE CAN DO THAT.
HOW CAN YOU BE OF HELP? YOU CANNOT COVER TERRITORY AS QUICKLY AS I.
Yeah? WELL, WE SHUT YOU DOWN, DIDN'T WE, TRACK STAR?
THE BROTHERHOOD OF--
--EVIL--!
--MUTANTS IS FINISHED. THE X-MEN ARE NOT ENEMIES TO YOU.
CAN WE AGREE TO TRUST EACH OTHER?
YES.

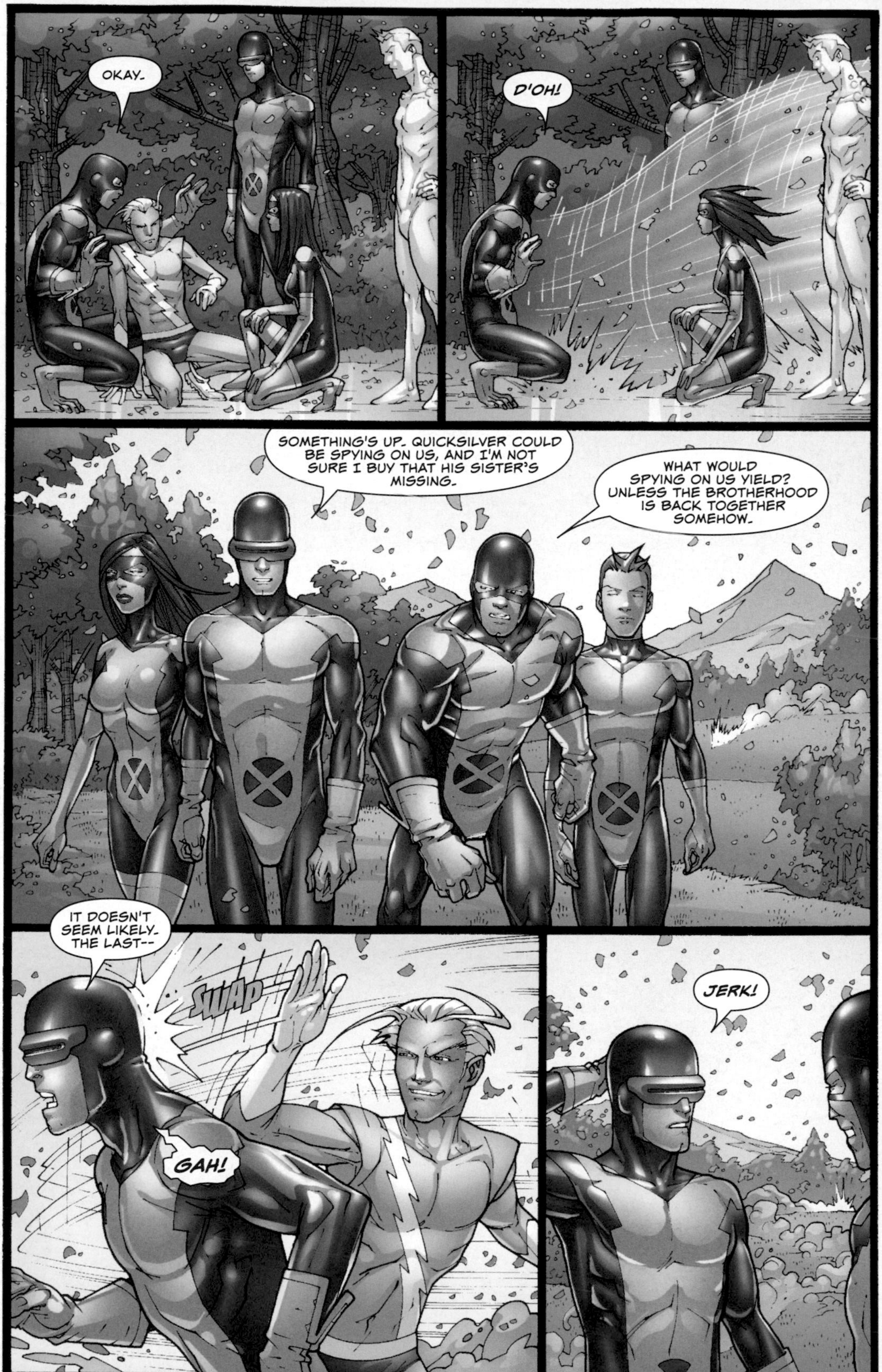
OKAY.
D'OH!
SOMETHING'S UP. QUICKSILVER COULD BE SPYING ON US, AND I'M NOT SURE I BUY THAT HIS SISTER'S MISSING.
WHAT WOULD SPYING ON US YIELD? UNLESS THE BROTHERHOOD IS BACK TOGETHER SOMEHOW.
IT DOESN'T SEEM LIKELY. THE LAST--
SWAP
GAH!
JERK!

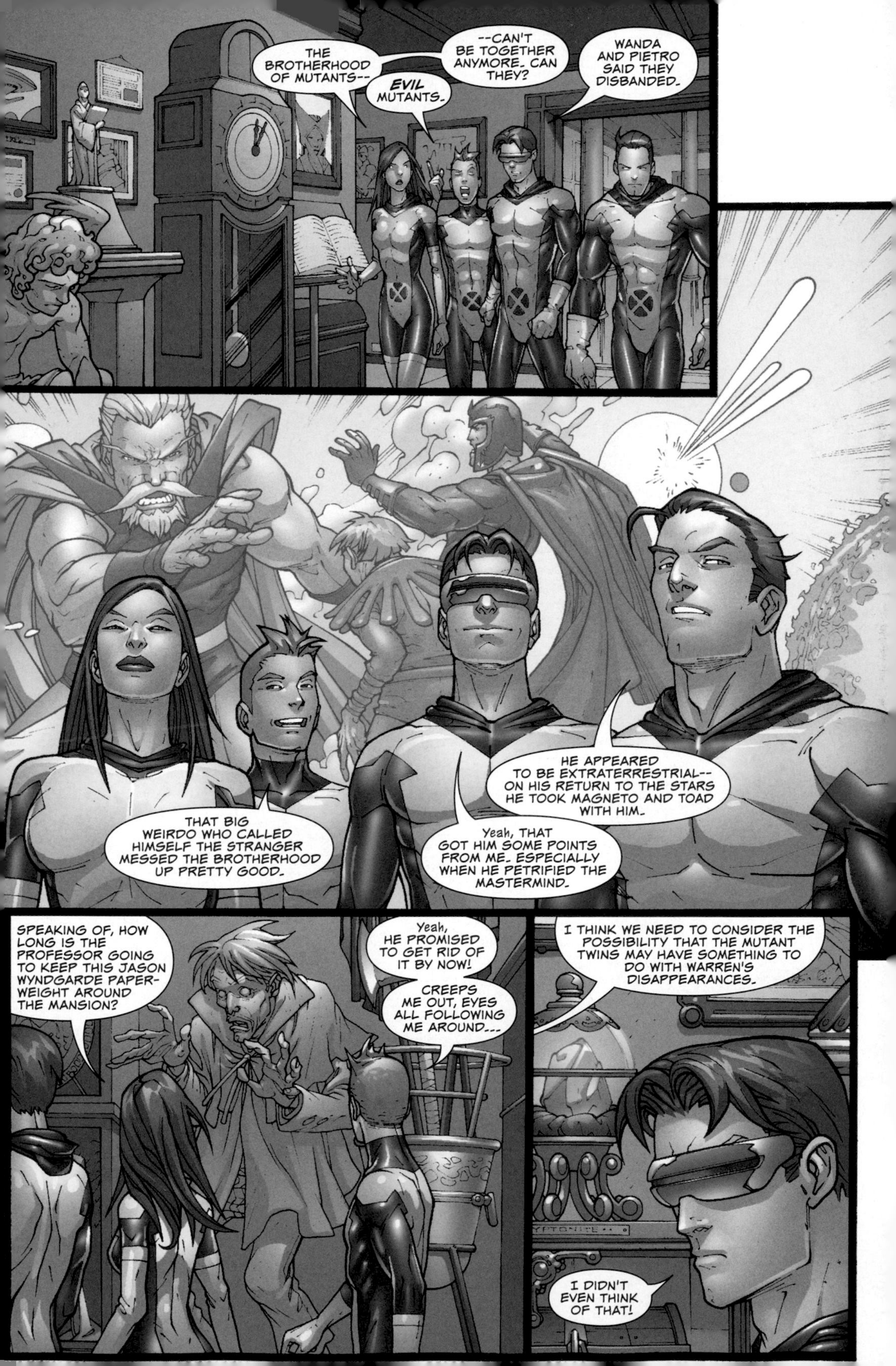
THE BROTHERHOOD OF MUTANTS--
--CAN'T BE TOGETHER ANYMORE. CAN THEY?
EVIL MUTANTS.
WANDA AND PIETRO SAID THEY DISBANDED.
THAT BIG WEIRDO WHO CALLED HIMSELF THE STRANGER MESSED THE BROTHERHOOD UP PRETTY GOOD.
HE APPEARED TO BE EXTRATERRESTRIAL-- ON HIS RETURN TO THE STARS HE TOOK MAGNETO AND TOAD WITH HIM.
Yeah, THAT GOT HIM SOME POINTS FROM ME. ESPECIALLY WHEN HE PETRIFIED THE MASTERMIND.
SPEAKING OF, HOW LONG IS THE PROFESSOR GOING TO KEEP THIS JASON WYNDGARDE PAPER-WEIGHT AROUND THE MANSION?
Yeah, HE PROMISED TO GET RID OF IT BY NOW!
CREEPS ME OUT, EYES ALL FOLLOWING ME AROUND...
I THINK WE NEED TO CONSIDER THE POSSIBILITY THAT THE MUTANT TWINS MAY HAVE SOMETHING TO DO WITH WARREN'S DISAPPEARANCES.
I DIDN'T EVEN THINK OF THAT!

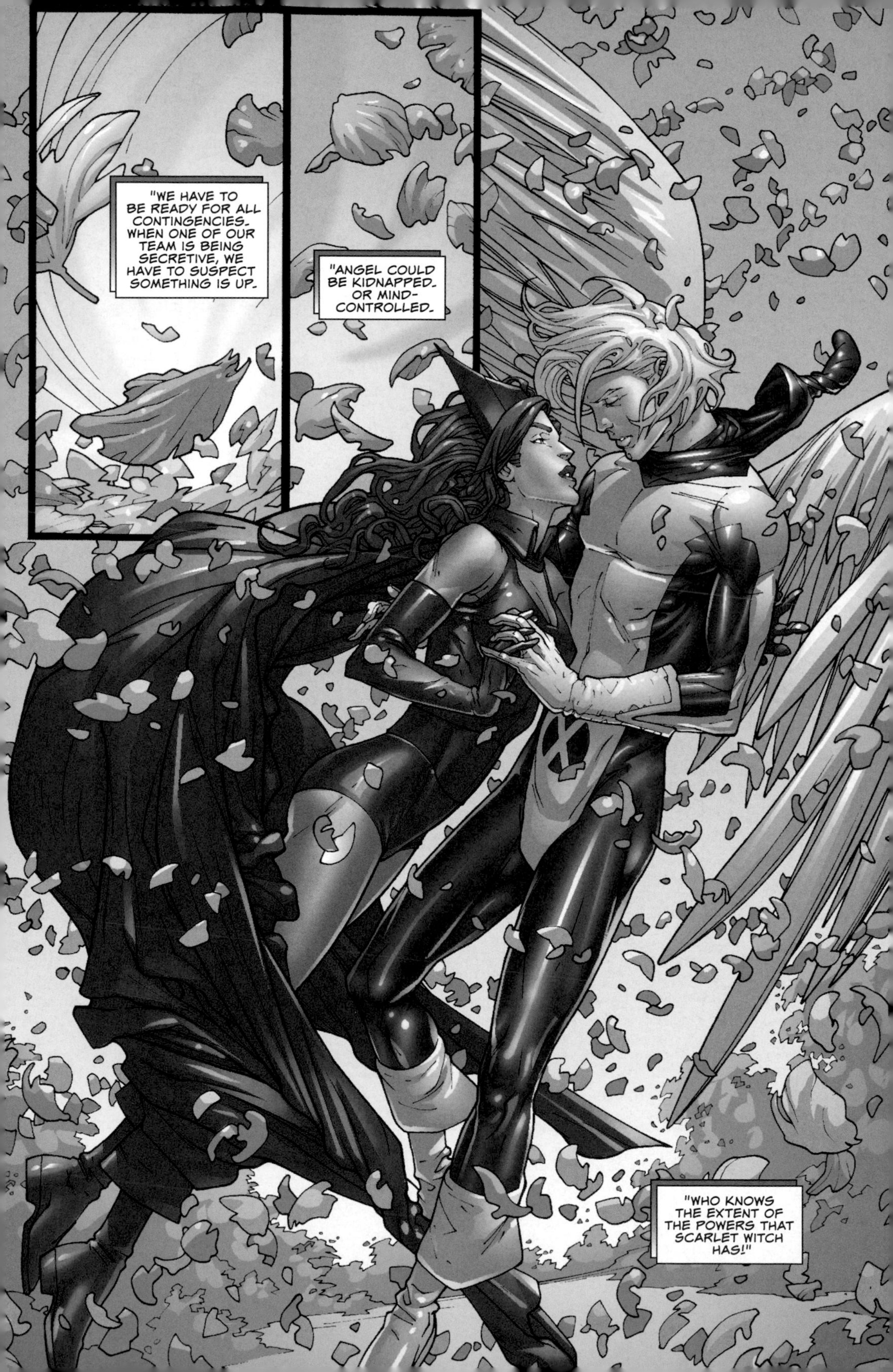
"WE HAVE TO BE READY FOR ALL CONTINGENCIES. WHEN ONE OF OUR TEAM IS BEING SECRETIVE, WE HAVE TO SUSPECT SOMETHING IS UP.
"ANGEL COULD BE KIDNAPPED. OR MIND-CONTROLLED.
"WHO KNOWS THE EXTENT OF THE POWERS THAT SCARLET WITCH HAS!"

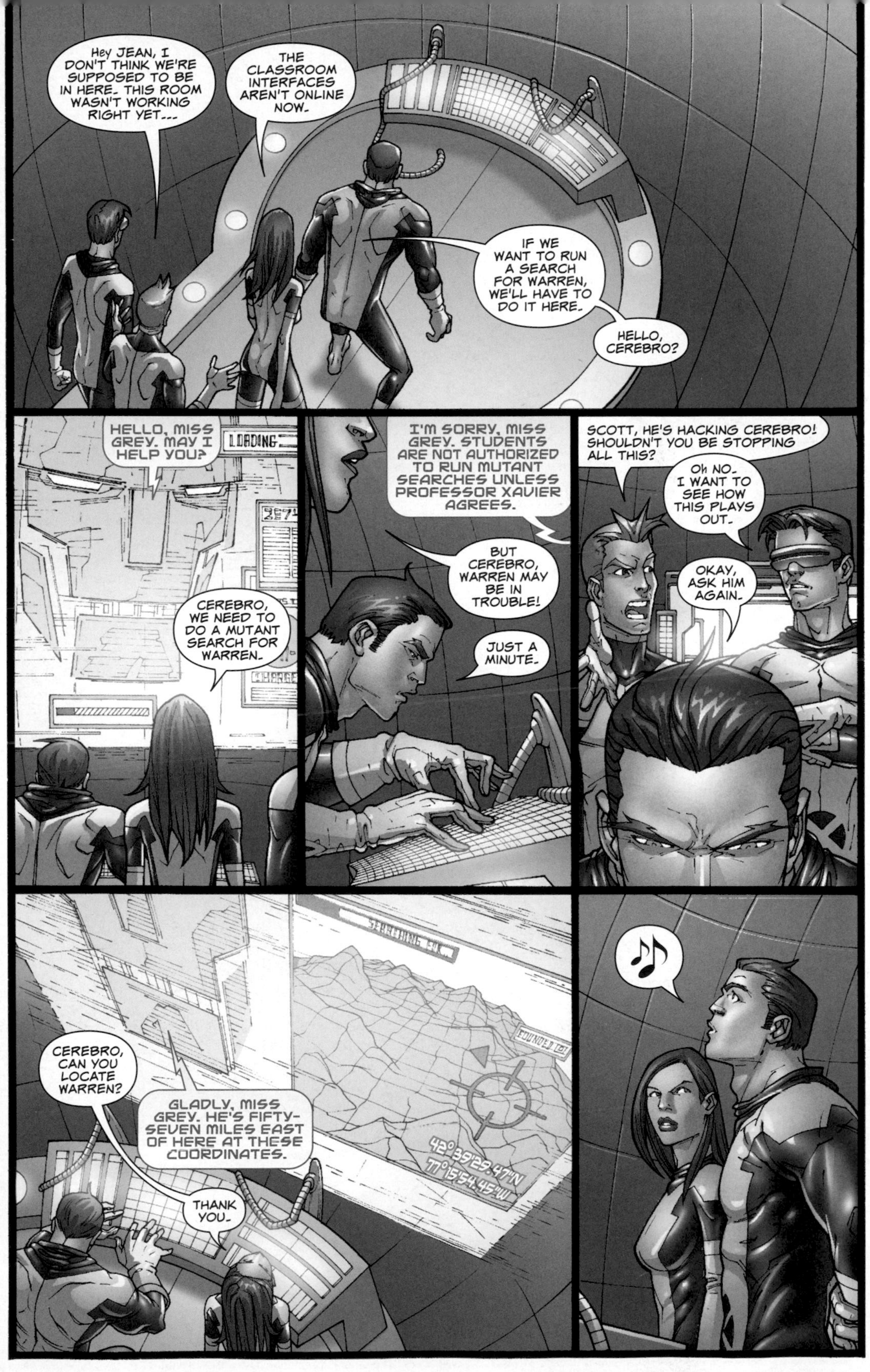

Hey JEAN, I DON'T THINK WE'RE SUPPOSED TO BE IN HERE. THIS ROOM WASN'T WORKING RIGHT YET...
THE CLASSROOM INTERFACES AREN'T ONLINE NOW.
IF WE WANT TO RUN A SEARCH FOR WARREN, WE'LL HAVE TO DO IT HERE.
HELLO, CEREBRO?
HELLO, MISS GREY. MAY I HELP YOU?
LOADING
CEREBRO, WE NEED TO DO A MUTANT SEARCH FOR WARREN.
I'M SORRY, MISS GREY. STUDENTS ARE NOT AUTHORIZED TO RUN MUTANT SEARCHES UNLESS PROFESSOR XAVIER AGREES.
BUT CEREBRO, WARREN MAY BE IN TROUBLE!
JUST A MINUTE.
SCOTT, HE'S HACKING CEREBRO! SHOULDN'T YOU BE STOPPING ALL THIS?
Oh NO. I WANT TO SEE HOW THIS PLAYS OUT.
OKAY, ASK HIM AGAIN.
CEREBRO, CAN YOU LOCATE WARREN?
GLADLY, MISS GREY. HE'S FIFTY-SEVEN MILES EAST OF HERE AT THESE COORDINATES.
42° 39'29.47"N
77° 15'54.45"W
THANK YOU.
♪

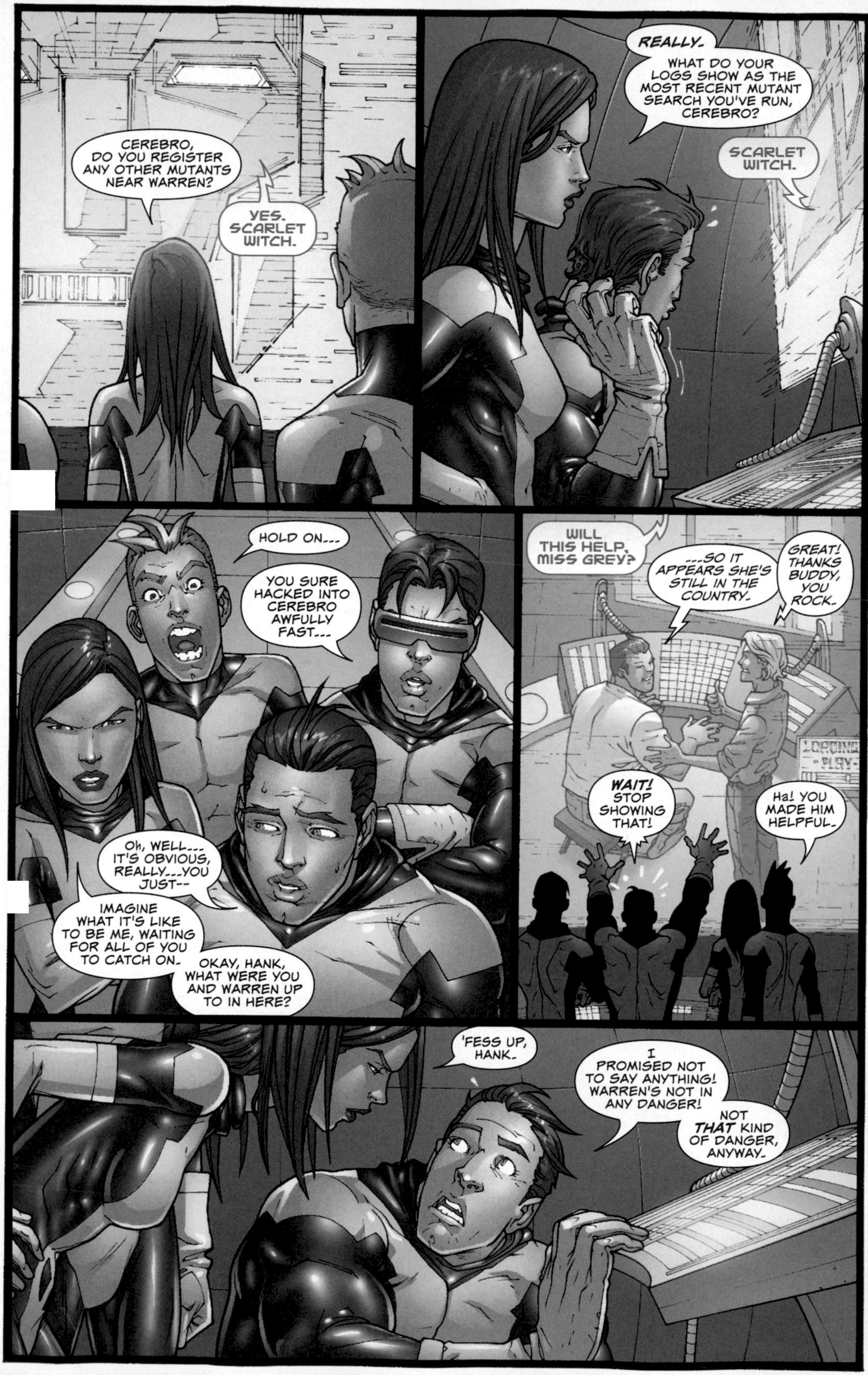
CEREBRO, DO YOU REGISTER ANY OTHER MUTANTS NEAR WARREN?
YES. SCARLET WITCH.
REALLY.
WHAT DO YOUR LOGS SHOW AS THE MOST RECENT MUTANT SEARCH YOU'VE RUN, CEREBRO?
SCARLET WITCH.
HOLD ON...
YOU SURE HACKED INTO CEREBRO AWFULLY FAST...
Oh, WELL... IT'S OBVIOUS, REALLY... YOU JUST--
IMAGINE WHAT IT'S LIKE TO BE ME, WAITING FOR ALL OF YOU TO CATCH ON.
OKAY, HANK, WHAT WERE YOU AND WARREN UP TO IN HERE?
WILL THIS HELP, MISS GREY?
...SO IT APPEARS SHE'S STILL IN THE COUNTRY.
GREAT! THANKS BUDDY, YOU ROCK.
WAIT! STOP SHOWING THAT!
Ha! YOU MADE HIM HELPFUL.
'FESS UP, HANK.
I PROMISED NOT TO SAY ANYTHING! WARREN'S NOT IN ANY DANGER!
NOT THAT KIND OF DANGER, ANYWAY.

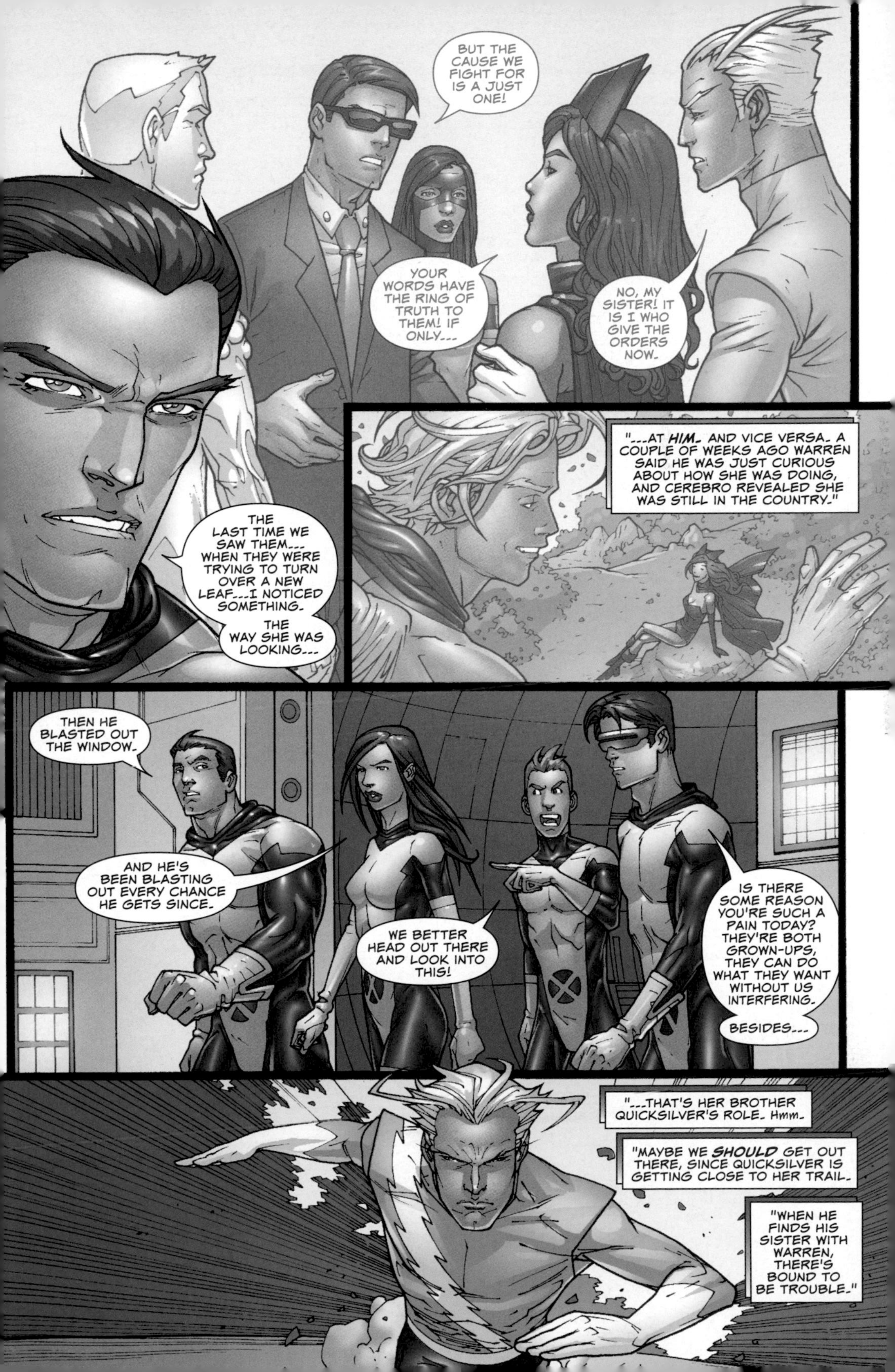
BUT THE CAUSE WE FIGHT FOR IS A JUST ONE!
YOUR WORDS HAVE THE RING OF TRUTH TO THEM! IF ONLY...
NO, MY SISTER! IT IS I WHO GIVE THE ORDERS NOW.
THE LAST TIME WE SAW THEM... WHEN THEY WERE TRYING TO TURN OVER A NEW LEAF... I NOTICED SOMETHING.
THE WAY SHE WAS LOOKING...
"...AT **HIM**. AND VICE VERSA. A COUPLE OF WEEKS AGO WARREN SAID HE WAS JUST CURIOUS ABOUT HOW SHE WAS DOING, AND CEREBRO REVEALED SHE WAS STILL IN THE COUNTRY."
THEN HE BLASTED OUT THE WINDOW.
AND HE'S BEEN BLASTING OUT EVERY CHANCE HE GETS SINCE.
WE BETTER HEAD OUT THERE AND LOOK INTO THIS!
IS THERE SOME REASON YOU'RE SUCH A PAIN TODAY? THEY'RE BOTH GROWN-UPS, THEY CAN DO WHAT THEY WANT WITHOUT US INTERFERING.
BESIDES...
"...THAT'S HER BROTHER QUICKSILVER'S ROLE. Hmm.
"MAYBE WE **SHOULD** GET OUT THERE, SINCE QUICKSILVER IS GETTING CLOSE TO HER TRAIL.
"WHEN HE FINDS HIS SISTER WITH WARREN, THERE'S BOUND TO BE TROUBLE."

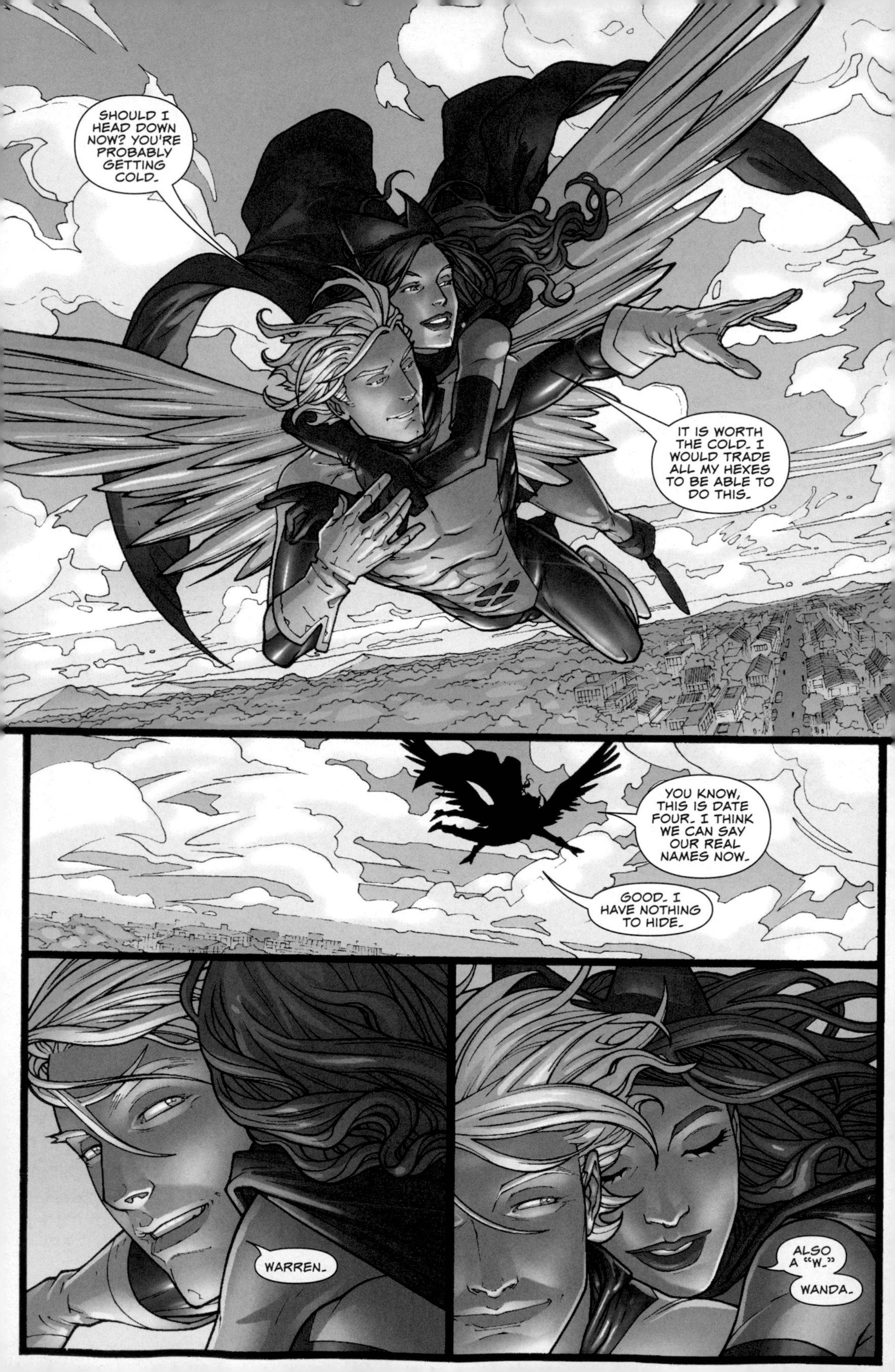
SHOULD I HEAD DOWN NOW? YOU'RE PROBABLY GETTING COLD.
IT IS WORTH THE COLD. I WOULD TRADE ALL MY HEXES TO BE ABLE TO DO THIS.
YOU KNOW, THIS IS DATE FOUR. I THINK WE CAN SAY OUR REAL NAMES NOW.
GOOD. I HAVE NOTHING TO HIDE.
WARREN.
ALSO A "W."
WANDA.

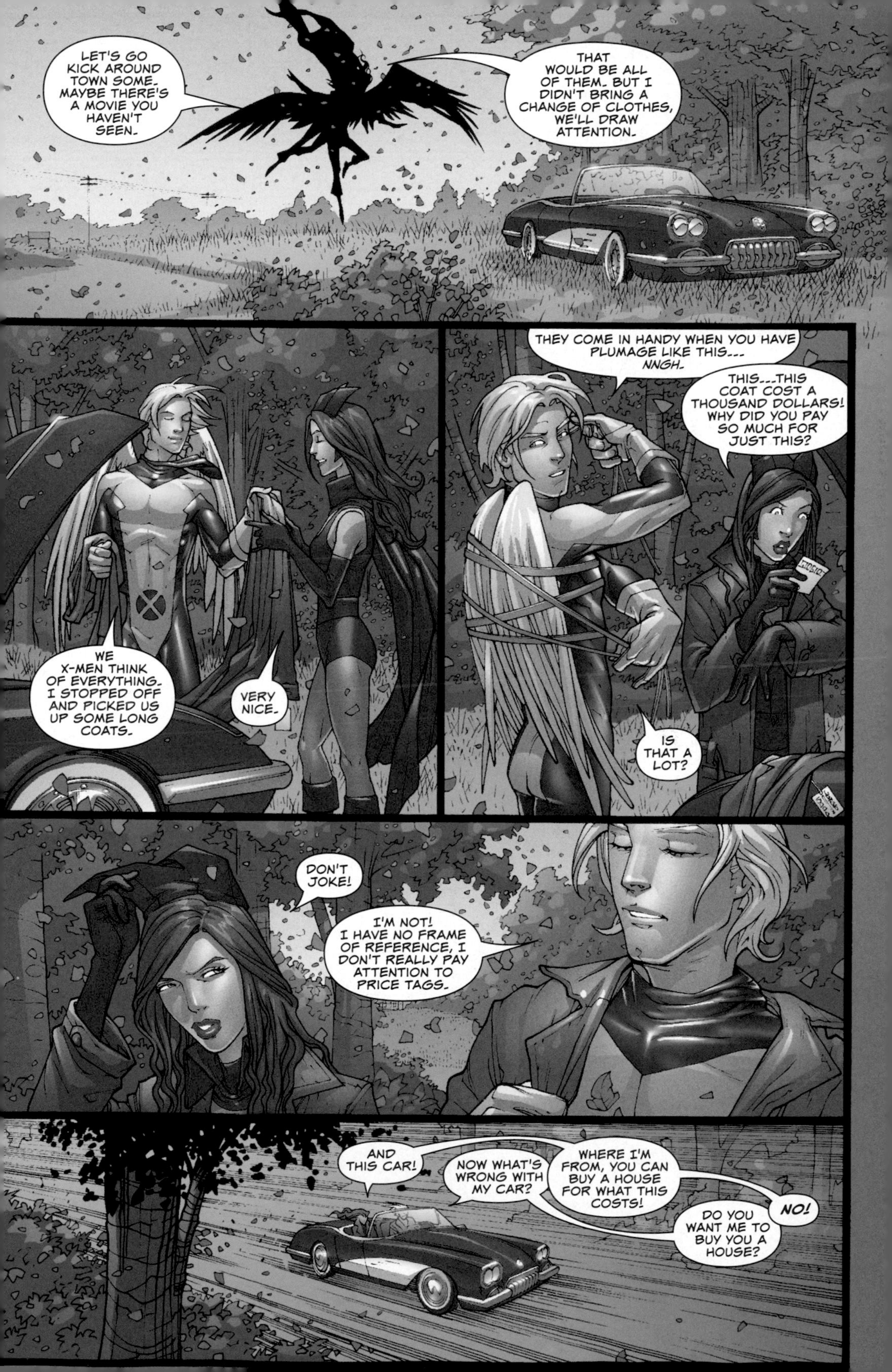

LET'S GO KICK AROUND TOWN SOME. MAYBE THERE'S A MOVIE YOU HAVEN'T SEEN.
THAT WOULD BE ALL OF THEM. BUT I DIDN'T BRING A CHANGE OF CLOTHES, WE'LL DRAW ATTENTION.
WE X-MEN THINK OF EVERYTHING. I STOPPED OFF AND PICKED US UP SOME LONG COATS.
VERY NICE.
THEY COME IN HANDY WHEN YOU HAVE PLUMAGE LIKE THIS... NNGH.
THIS...THIS COAT COST A THOUSAND DOLLARS! WHY DID YOU PAY SO MUCH FOR JUST THIS?
IS THAT A LOT?
DON'T JOKE!
I'M NOT! I HAVE NO FRAME OF REFERENCE, I DON'T REALLY PAY ATTENTION TO PRICE TAGS.
AND THIS CAR!
WHERE I'M FROM, YOU CAN BUY A HOUSE FOR WHAT THIS COSTS!
NOW WHAT'S WRONG WITH MY CAR?
DO YOU WANT ME TO BUY YOU A HOUSE?
NO!

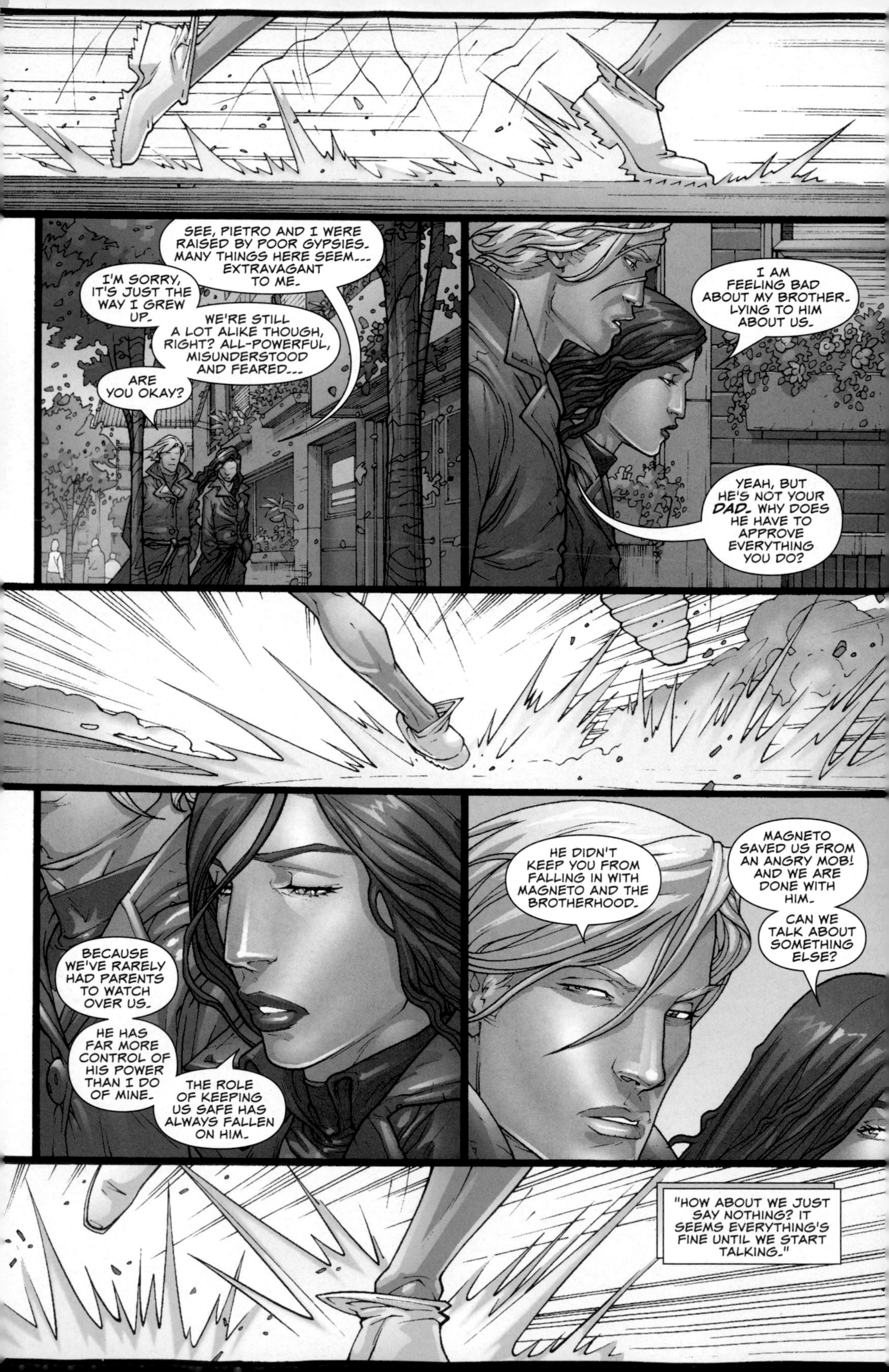

I'M SORRY, IT'S JUST THE WAY I GREW UP.
SEE, PIETRO AND I WERE RAISED BY POOR GYPSIES. MANY THINGS HERE SEEM... EXTRAVAGANT TO ME.
WE'RE STILL A LOT ALIKE THOUGH, RIGHT? ALL-POWERFUL, MISUNDERSTOOD AND FEARED...
ARE YOU OKAY?
I AM FEELING BAD ABOUT MY BROTHER. LYING TO HIM ABOUT US.
YEAH, BUT HE'S NOT YOUR DAD. WHY DOES HE HAVE TO APPROVE EVERYTHING YOU DO?
BECAUSE WE'VE RARELY HAD PARENTS TO WATCH OVER US.
HE HAS FAR MORE CONTROL OF HIS POWER THAN I DO OF MINE.
THE ROLE OF KEEPING US SAFE HAS ALWAYS FALLEN ON HIM.
HE DIDN'T KEEP YOU FROM FALLING IN WITH MAGNETO AND THE BROTHERHOOD.
MAGNETO SAVED US FROM AN ANGRY MOB! AND WE ARE DONE WITH HIM.
CAN WE TALK ABOUT SOMETHING ELSE?
"HOW ABOUT WE JUST SAY NOTHING? IT SEEMS EVERYTHING'S FINE UNTIL WE START TALKING."

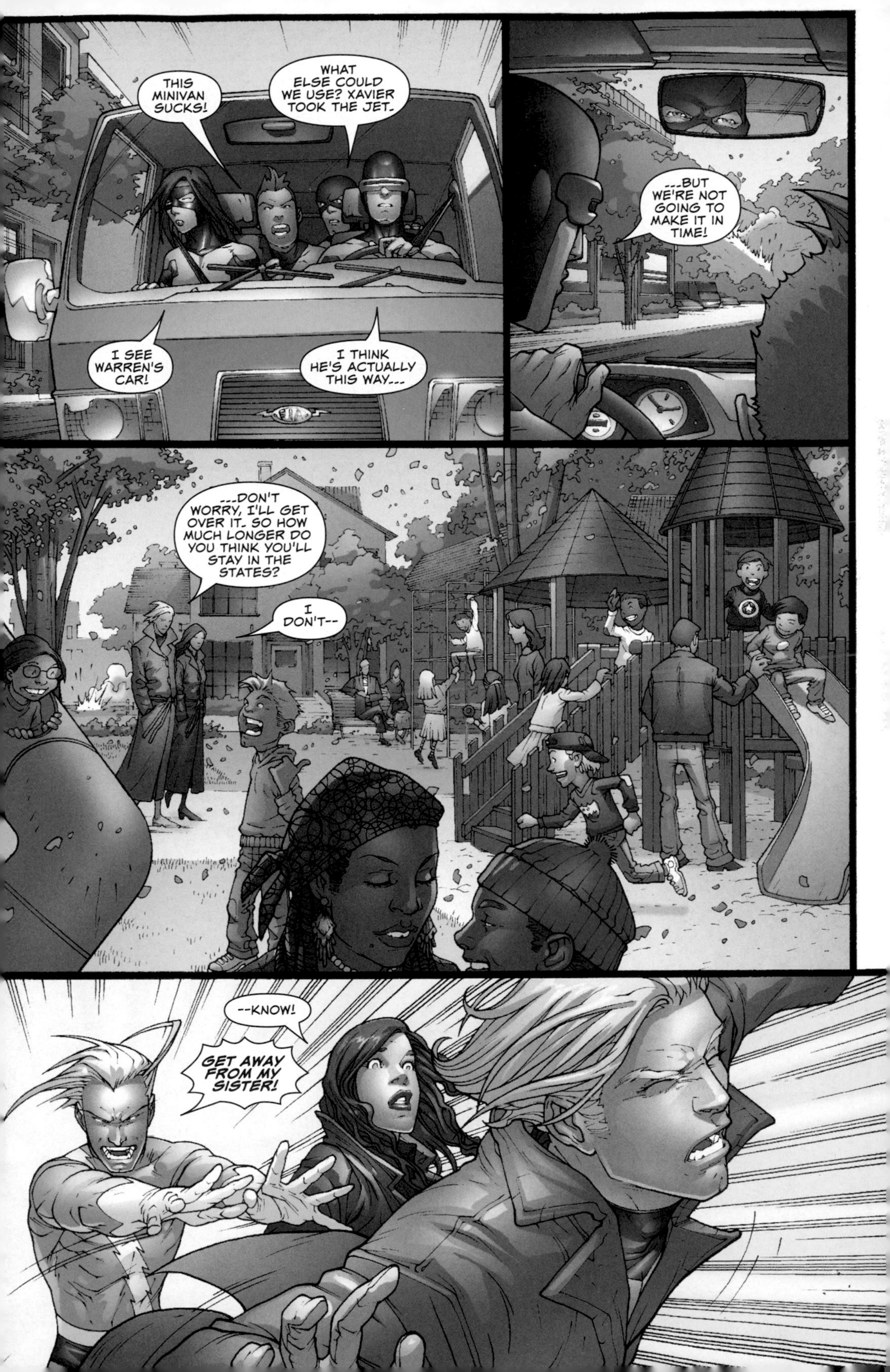

THIS MINIVAN SUCKS!
WHAT ELSE COULD WE USE? XAVIER TOOK THE JET.
I SEE WARREN'S CAR!
I THINK HE'S ACTUALLY THIS WAY---
---BUT WE'RE NOT GOING TO MAKE IT IN TIME!
---DON'T WORRY, I'LL GET OVER IT. SO HOW MUCH LONGER DO YOU THINK YOU'LL STAY IN THE STATES?
I DON'T--
--KNOW!
GET AWAY FROM MY SISTER!

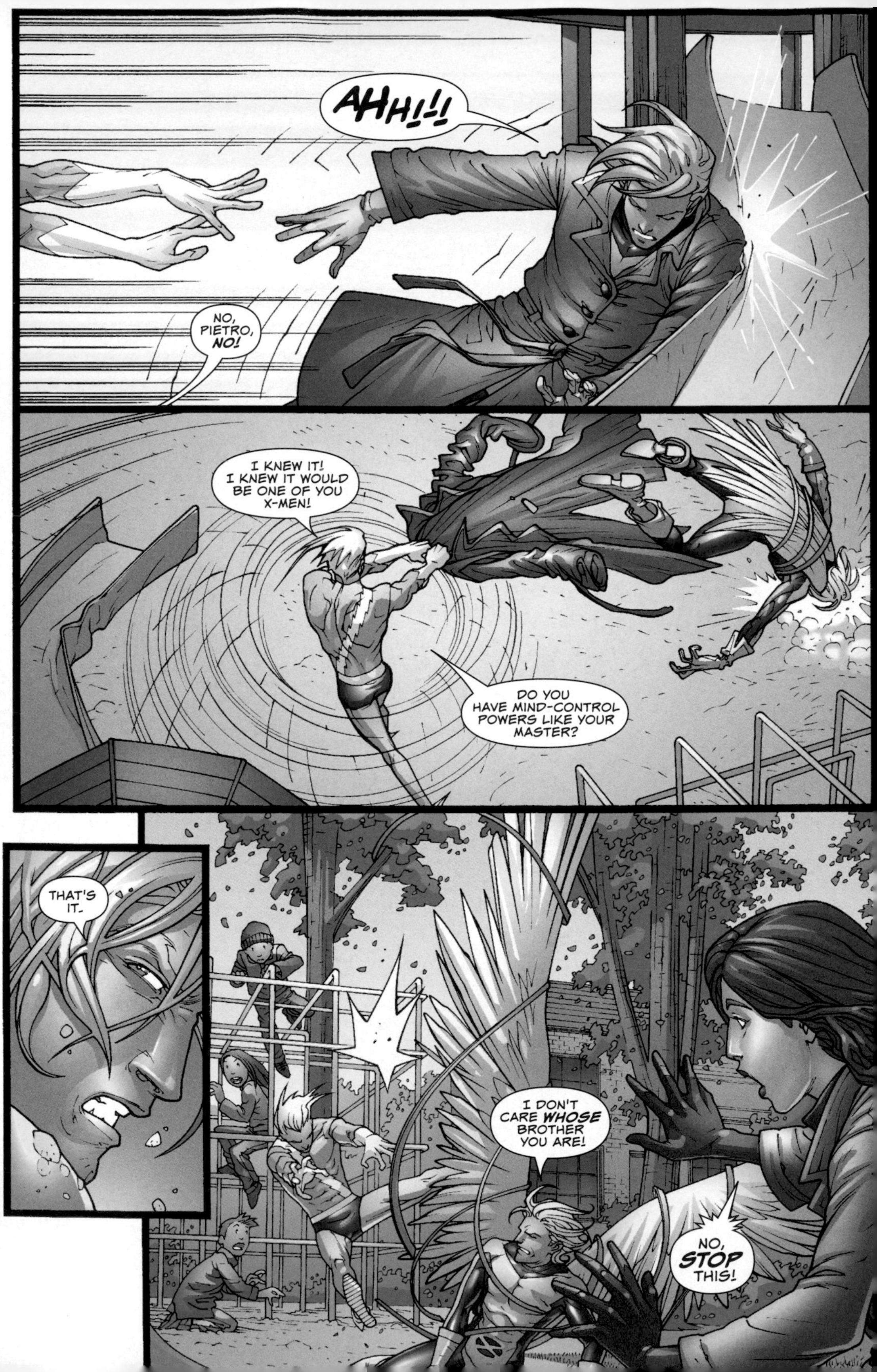
AHH!-!!
NO, PIETRO, NO!
I KNEW IT! I KNEW IT WOULD BE ONE OF YOU X-MEN!
DO YOU HAVE MIND-CONTROL POWERS LIKE YOUR MASTER?
THAT'S IT.
I DON'T CARE WHOSE BROTHER YOU ARE!
NO, STOP THIS!

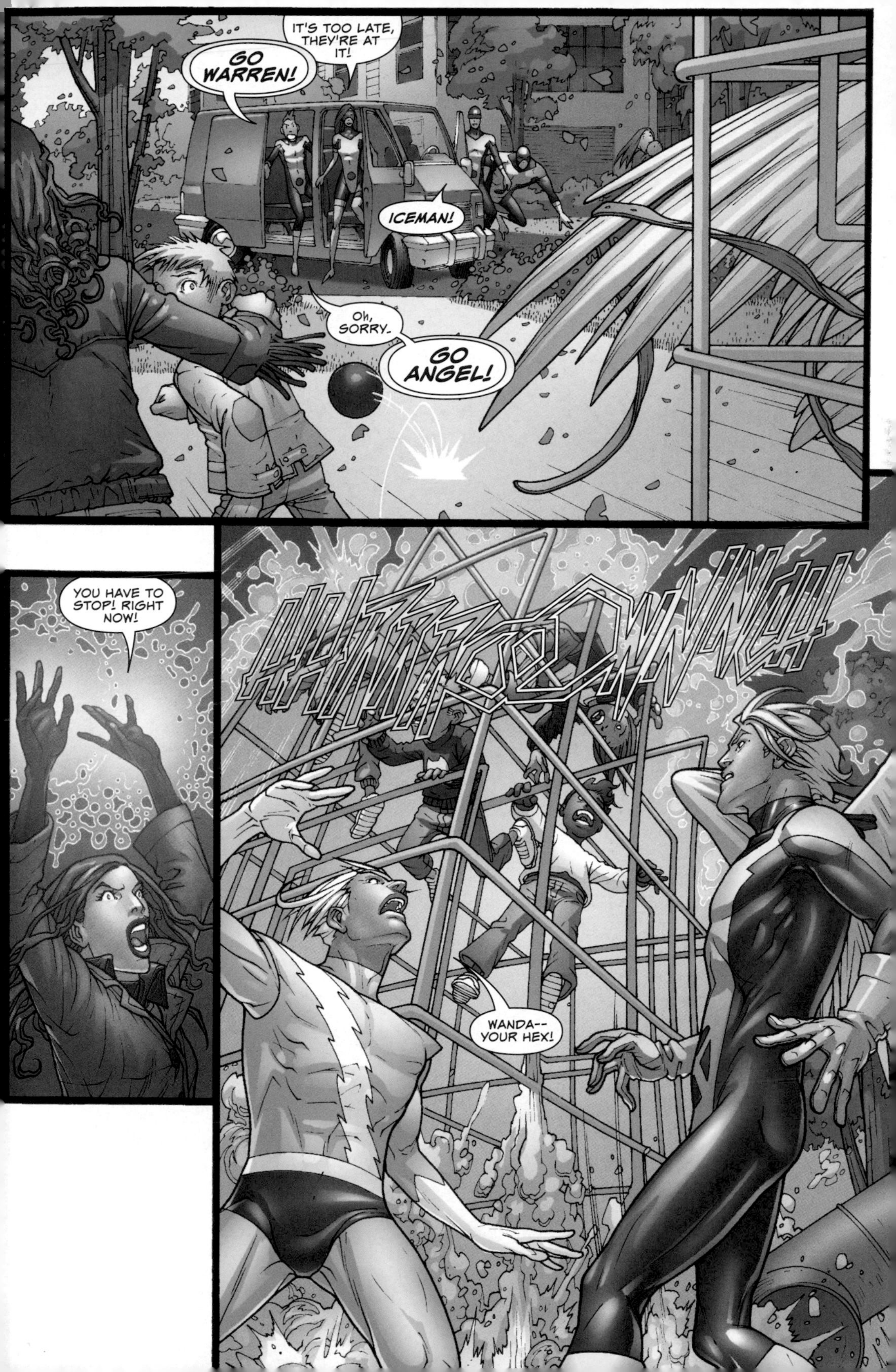

IT'S TOO LATE, THEY'RE AT IT!
GO WARREN!
ICEMAN!
Oh, SORRY.
GO ANGEL!
YOU HAVE TO STOP! RIGHT NOW!
WANDA-- YOUR HEX!

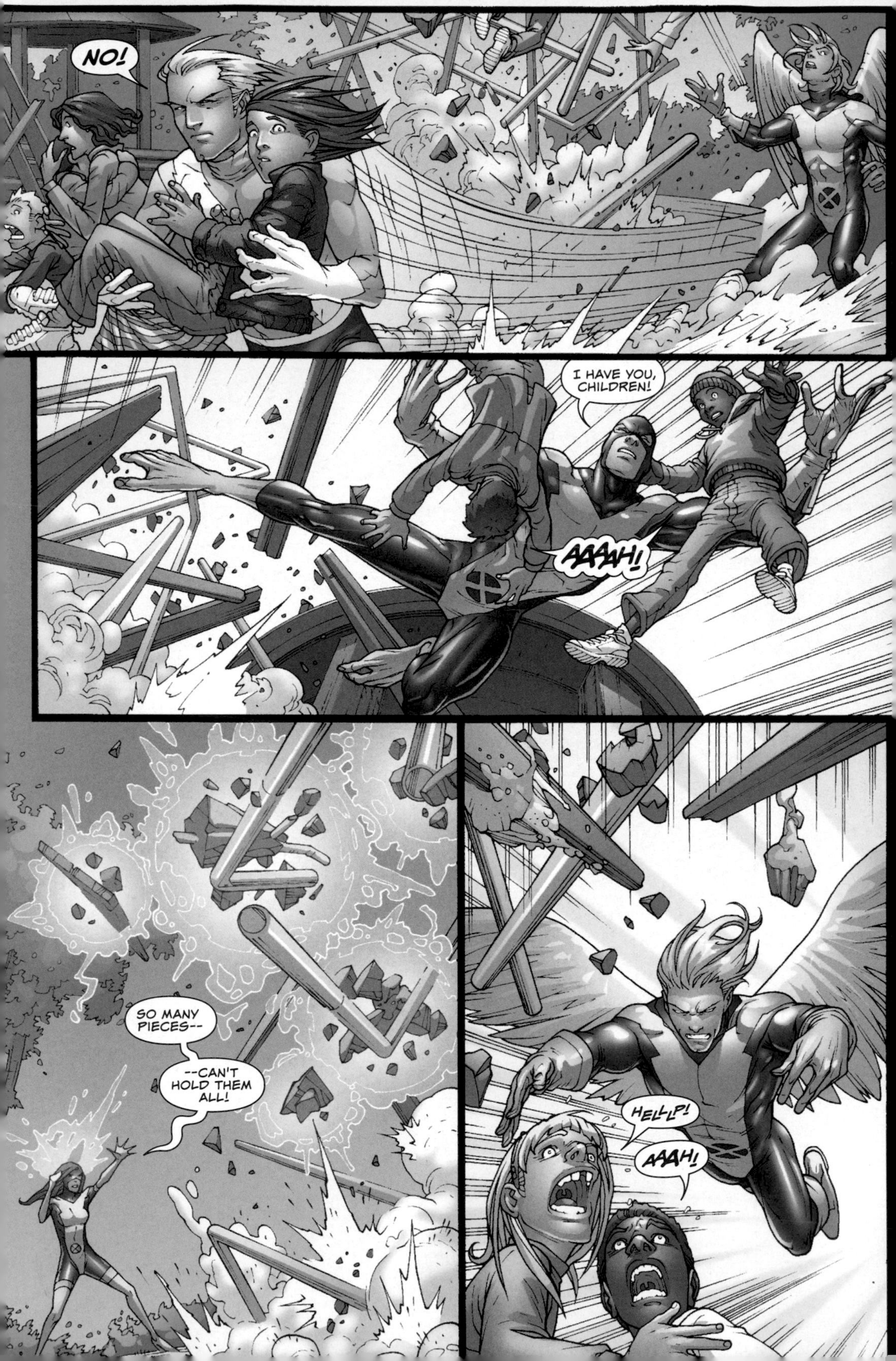
NO!
I HAVE YOU, CHILDREN!
AAAAH!
SO MANY PIECES--
--CAN'T HOLD THEM ALL!
HELLLP!
AAAH!

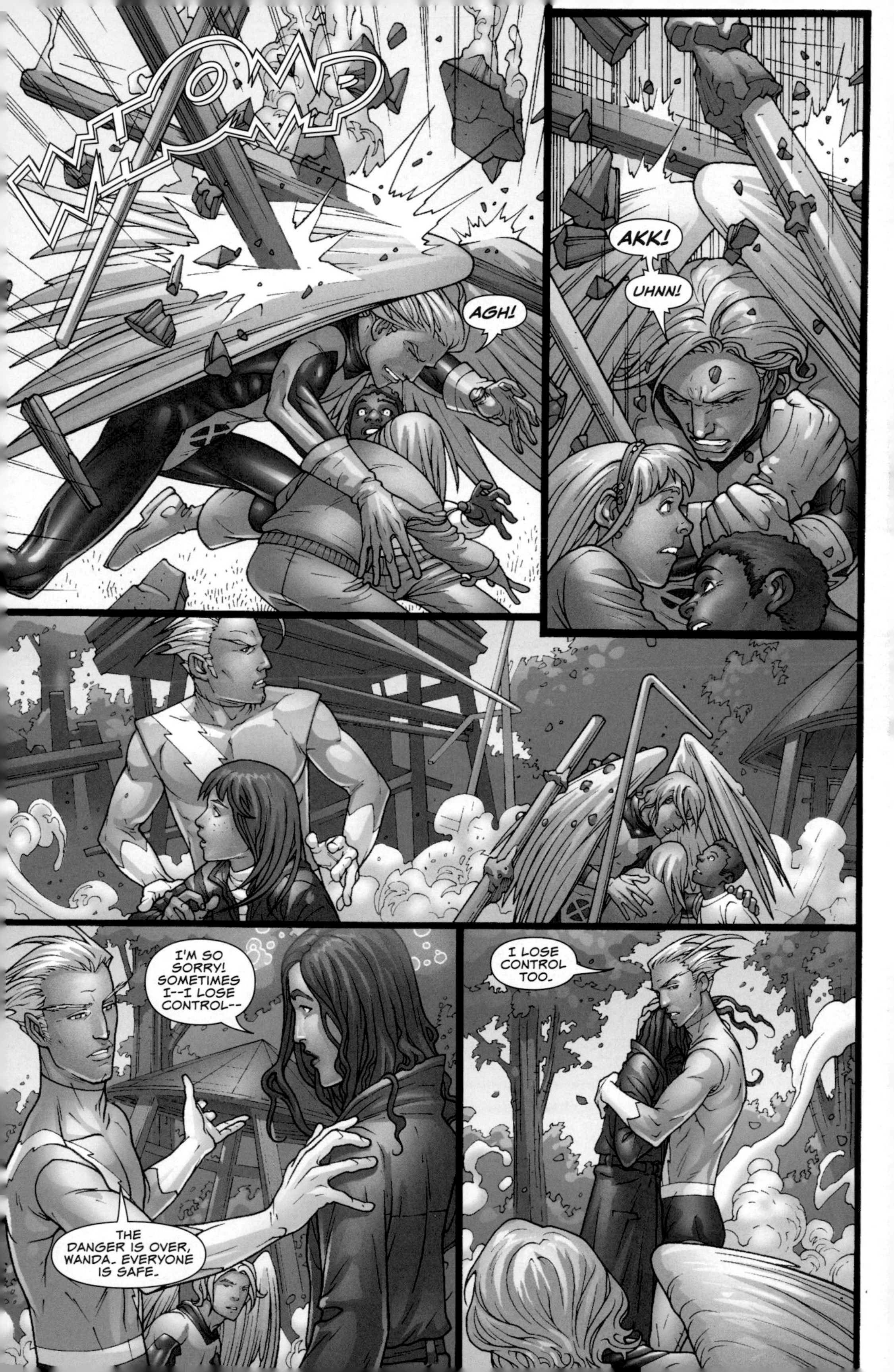
WHOOMP
AGH!
AKK!
UHNN!
I'M SO SORRY! SOMETIMES I--I LOSE CONTROL--
THE DANGER IS OVER, WANDA. EVERYONE IS SAFE.
I LOSE CONTROL TOO.

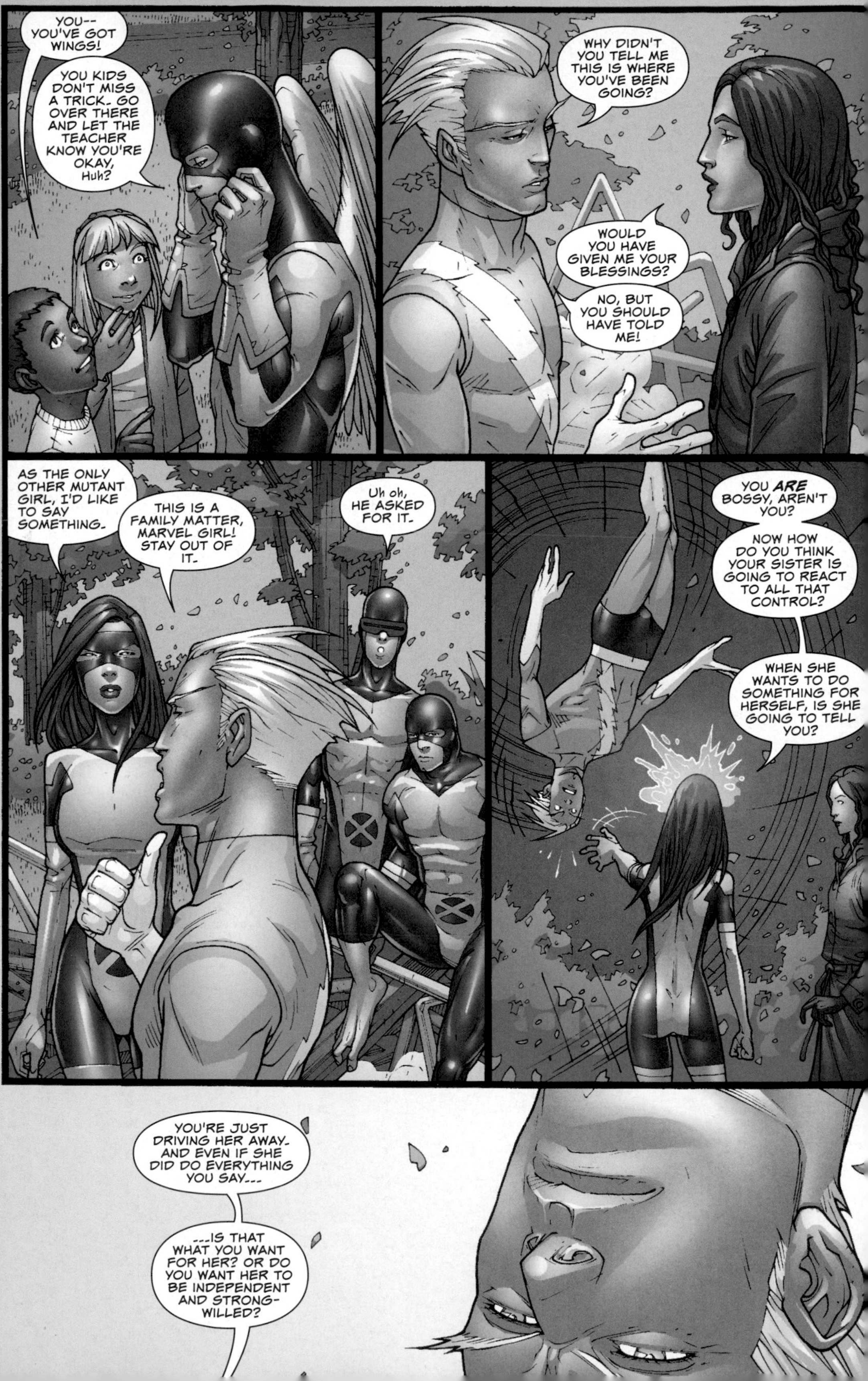

YOU-- YOU'VE GOT WINGS!
YOU KIDS DON'T MISS A TRICK. GO OVER THERE AND LET THE TEACHER KNOW YOU'RE OKAY, HUH?
WHY DIDN'T YOU TELL ME THIS IS WHERE YOU'VE BEEN GOING?
WOULD YOU HAVE GIVEN ME YOUR BLESSINGS?
NO, BUT YOU SHOULD HAVE TOLD ME!
AS THE ONLY OTHER MUTANT GIRL, I'D LIKE TO SAY SOMETHING.
THIS IS A FAMILY MATTER, MARVEL GIRL! STAY OUT OF IT.
Uh oh, HE ASKED FOR IT.
YOU ARE BOSSY, AREN'T YOU?
NOW HOW DO YOU THINK YOUR SISTER IS GOING TO REACT TO ALL THAT CONTROL?
WHEN SHE WANTS TO DO SOMETHING FOR HERSELF, IS SHE GOING TO TELL YOU?
YOU'RE JUST DRIVING HER AWAY. AND EVEN IF SHE DID DO EVERYTHING YOU SAY...
...IS THAT WHAT YOU WANT FOR HER? OR DO YOU WANT HER TO BE INDEPENDENT AND STRONG-WILLED?

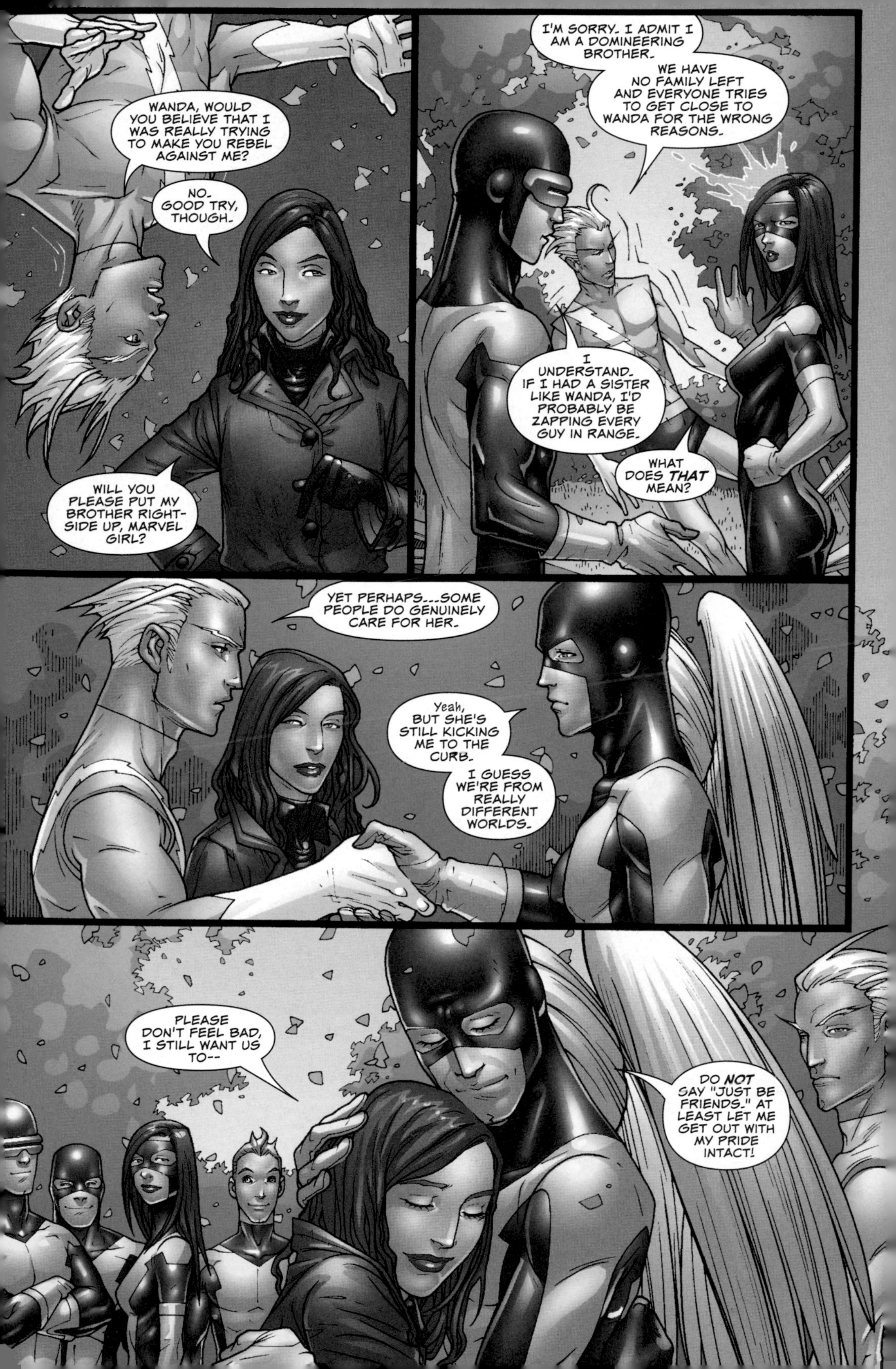
WANDA, WOULD YOU BELIEVE THAT I WAS REALLY TRYING TO MAKE YOU REBEL AGAINST ME?
NO. GOOD TRY, THOUGH.
WILL YOU PLEASE PUT MY BROTHER RIGHT-SIDE UP, MARVEL GIRL?
I'M SORRY. I ADMIT I AM A DOMINEERING BROTHER.
WE HAVE NO FAMILY LEFT AND EVERYONE TRIES TO GET CLOSE TO WANDA FOR THE WRONG REASONS.
I UNDERSTAND. IF I HAD A SISTER LIKE WANDA, I'D PROBABLY BE ZAPPING EVERY GUY IN RANGE.
WHAT DOES THAT MEAN?
YET PERHAPS... SOME PEOPLE DO GENUINELY CARE FOR HER.
Yeah, BUT SHE'S STILL KICKING ME TO THE CURB.
I GUESS WE'RE FROM REALLY DIFFERENT WORLDS.
PLEASE DON'T FEEL BAD, I STILL WANT US TO--
DO NOT SAY "JUST BE FRIENDS." AT LEAST LET ME GET OUT WITH MY PRIDE INTACT!

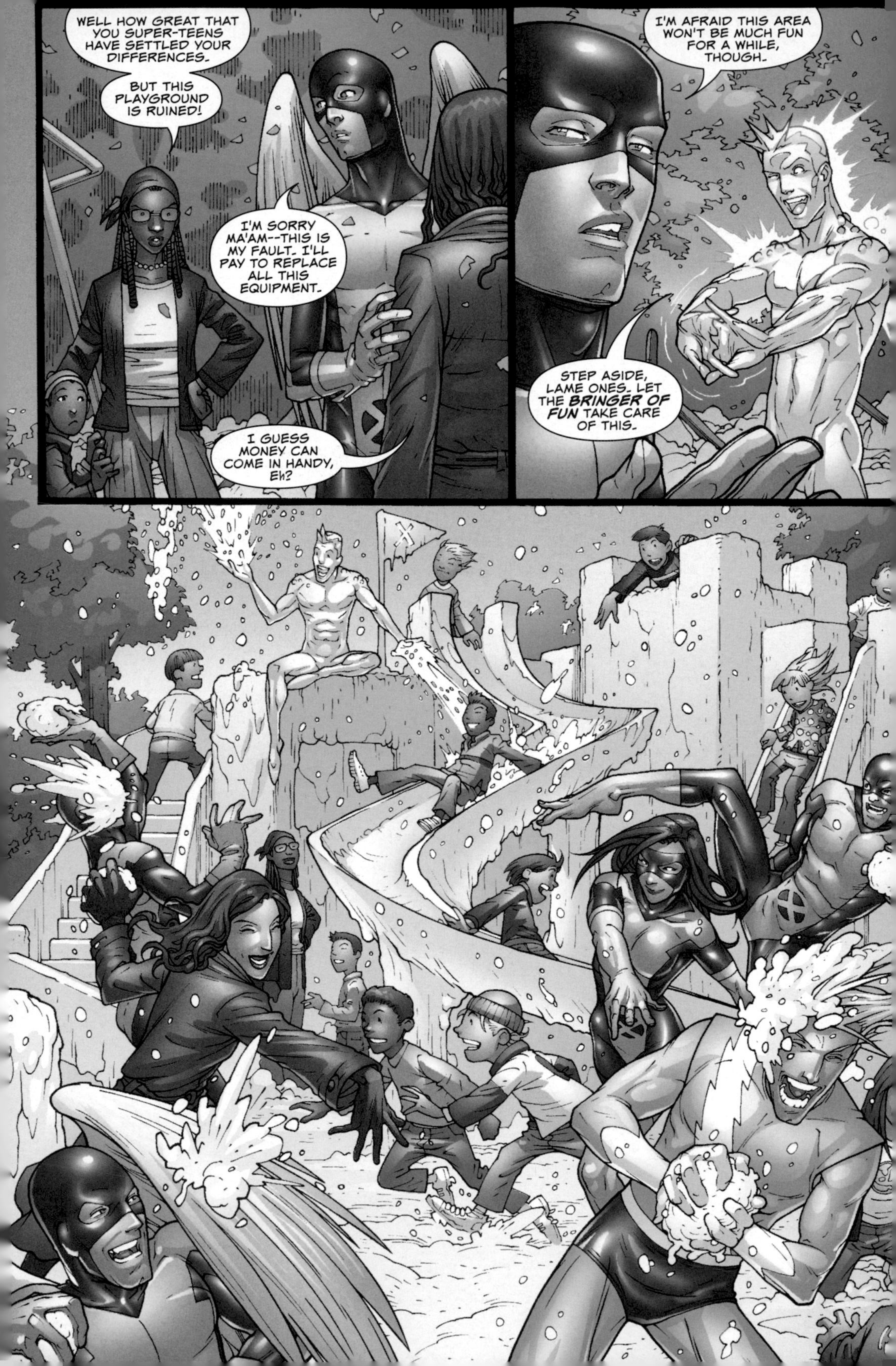
WELL HOW GREAT THAT YOU SUPER-TEENS HAVE SETTLED YOUR DIFFERENCES.
BUT THIS PLAYGROUND IS RUINED!
I'M SORRY MA'AM--THIS IS MY FAULT. I'LL PAY TO REPLACE ALL THIS EQUIPMENT.
I GUESS MONEY CAN COME IN HANDY, EH?
I'M AFRAID THIS AREA WON'T BE MUCH FUN FOR A WHILE, THOUGH.
STEP ASIDE, LAME ONES. LET THE BRINGER OF FUN TAKE CARE OF THIS.

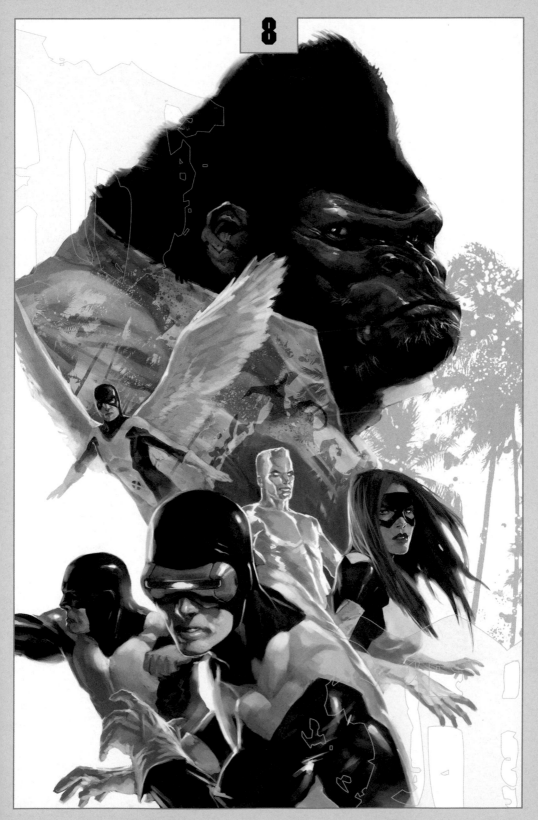

THE NEXT STEP IN HUMAN EVOLUTION HAS ARRIVED—HOMO SUPERIOR. MANKIND ISN'T SURE WHETHER THIS REPRESENTS HOPE FOR THE FUTURE...OR THE END OF THE HUMAN RACE. IN A PRIVATE SCHOOL IN UPSTATE NEW YORK, ONE BRILLIANT MUTANT IS TEACHING A GROUP OF FIVE SUCH GIFTED STUDENTS WHAT THEY'LL NEED TO SURVIVE IN THIS NEW WORLD. THESE ARE THE UNTOLD STORIES OF PROFESSOR XAVIER'S FIRST CLASS OF X-MEN!

XAVIER'S SCHOOL FOR GIFTED YOUNGSTERS

PROPERTY OF:

Professor X

HEADMASTER

Ah what a class. If I may pat myself on the back for a moment, I did quite well in choosing students. My only regret is that I still had to print a run of 1000 yearbooks despite having only five students.

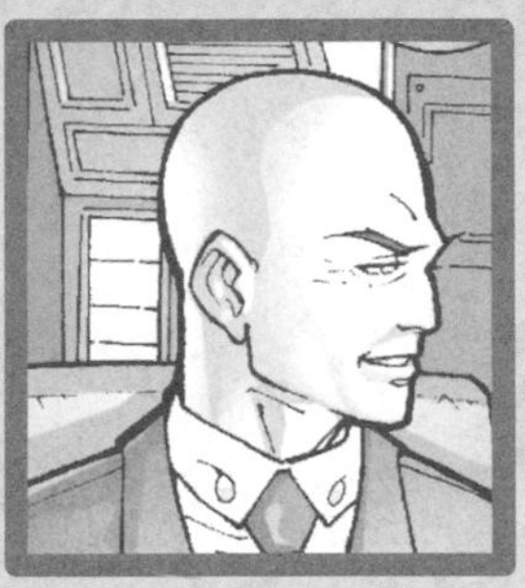

PROFESSOR CHARLES XAVIER

Jean. Of this first class, she gives me the most pride... and the most trepidation. She is potentially the most powerful mutant alive, by my reckoning, and I'm not sure any human is ready for such power. The school has given her the best that it could however—peers she loves. I hope that will make the difference.

Scott. Exceptional field leader. I often wish that he could see the team as people as well as he sees them as weapons. Still, that discipline is what will keep them alive, so I can hardly complain.

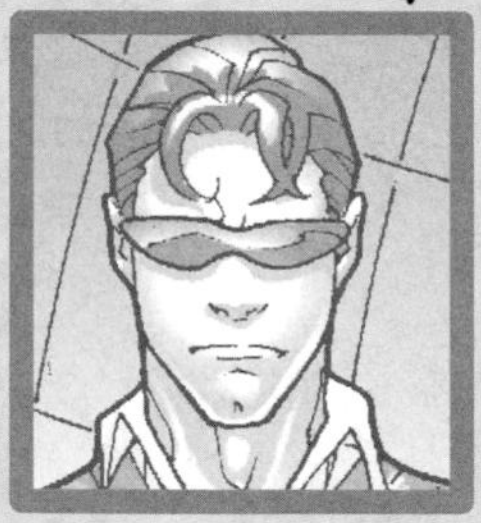

SCOTT SUMMERS
"CYCLOPS"

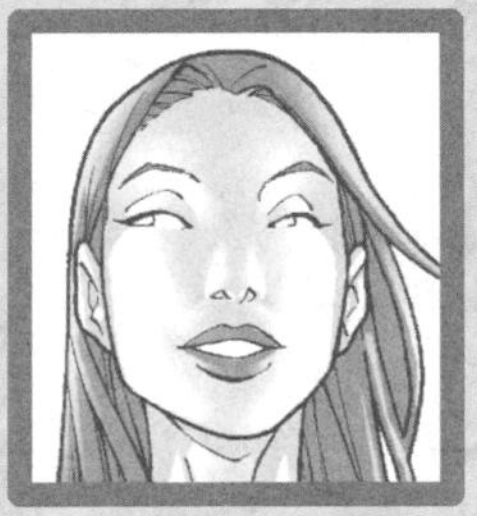

JEAN GREY
"MARVEL GIRL"

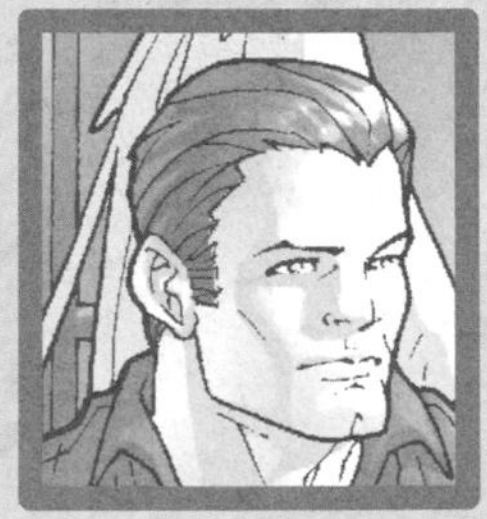

HENRY "HANK" MCCOY
"BEAST"

Henry. It is very hard to look at him and not see myself as a younger man. Not that I'm that much older, of course. His mind will be a driving force in the future of mutantkind, I am sure of it.

Warren. Impetuous, easily distracted, and a bit arrogant, Yet if all mutants could be like him rather than insecure, self-loathing and paranoid, I would be happy indeed.

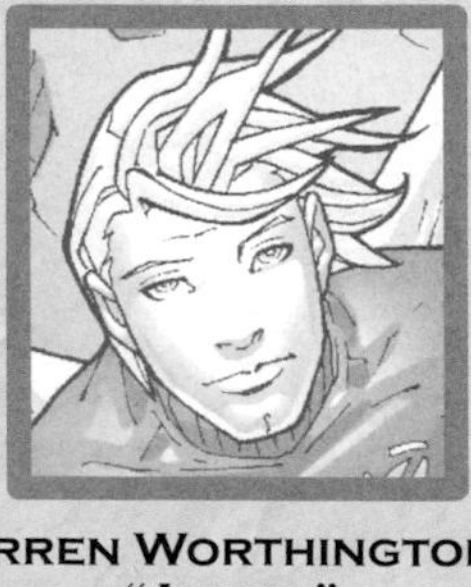

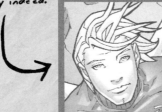

WARREN WORTHINGTON III
"ANGEL"

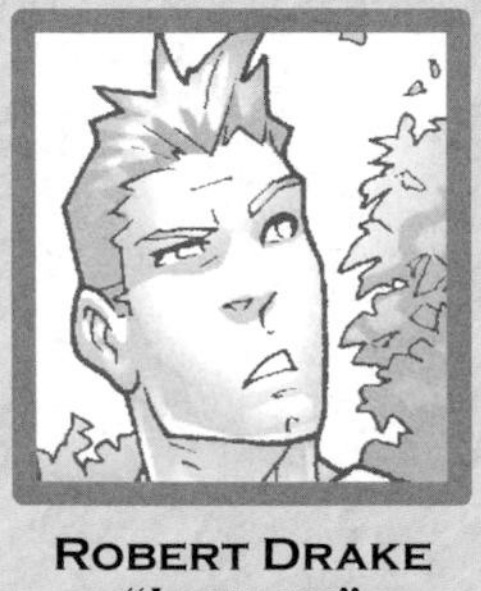

ROBERT DRAKE
"ICEMAN"

Robert. Somehow seems to grow younger ever day. I doubt I wou be much different if I could make snow, though.

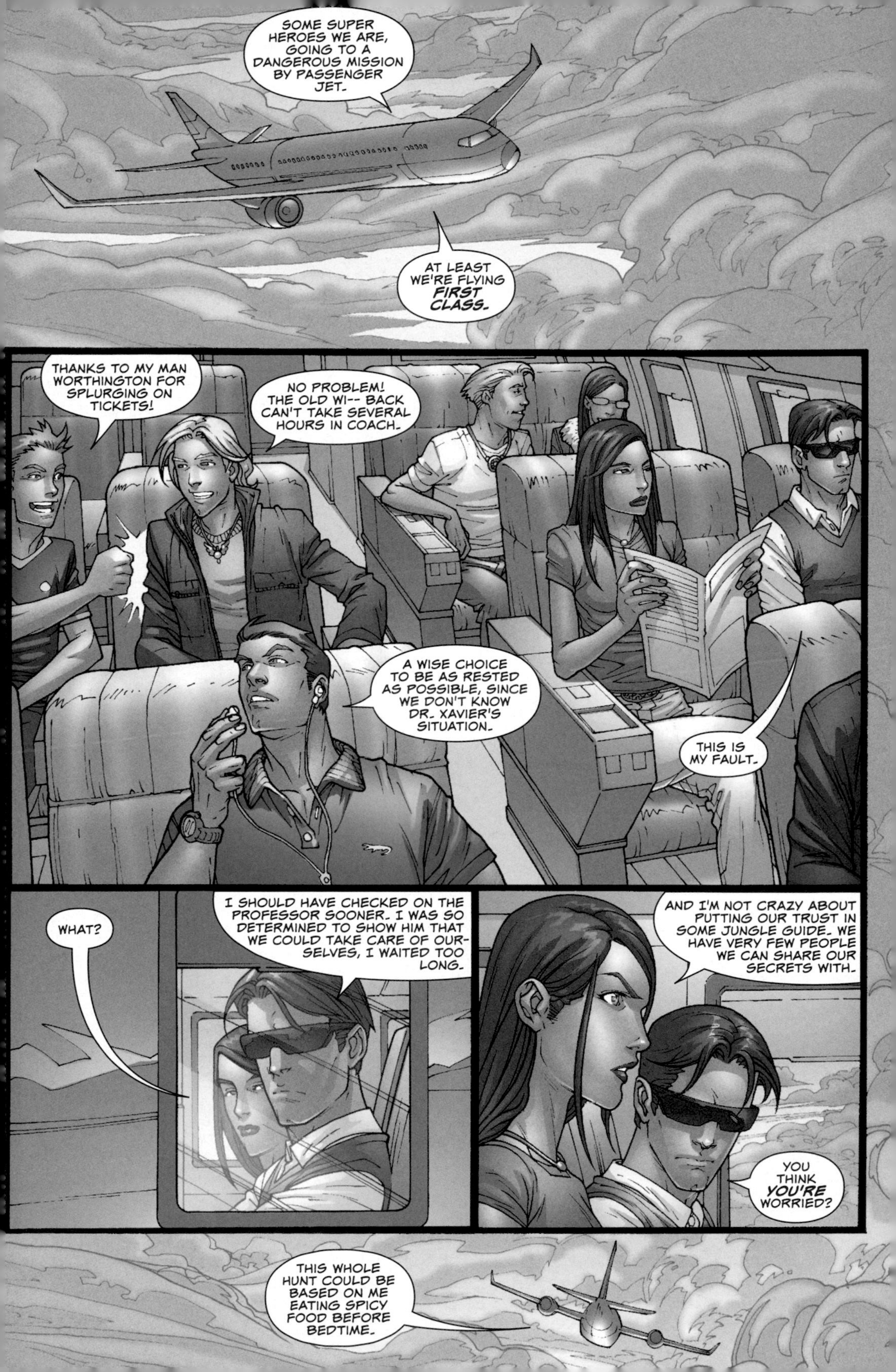
SOME SUPER HEROES WE ARE, GOING TO A DANGEROUS MISSION BY PASSENGER JET.
AT LEAST WE'RE FLYING *FIRST CLASS.*
THANKS TO MY MAN WORTHINGTON FOR SPLURGING ON TICKETS!
NO PROBLEM! THE OLD WI-- BACK CAN'T TAKE SEVERAL HOURS IN COACH.
A WISE CHOICE TO BE AS RESTED AS POSSIBLE, SINCE WE DON'T KNOW DR. XAVIER'S SITUATION.
THIS IS MY FAULT.
WHAT?
I SHOULD HAVE CHECKED ON THE PROFESSOR SOONER. I WAS SO DETERMINED TO SHOW HIM THAT WE COULD TAKE CARE OF OURSELVES, I WAITED TOO LONG.
AND I'M NOT CRAZY ABOUT PUTTING OUR TRUST IN SOME JUNGLE GUIDE. WE HAVE VERY FEW PEOPLE WE CAN SHARE OUR SECRETS WITH.
YOU THINK *YOU'RE* WORRIED?
THIS WHOLE HUNT COULD BE BASED ON ME EATING SPICY FOOD BEFORE BEDTIME.

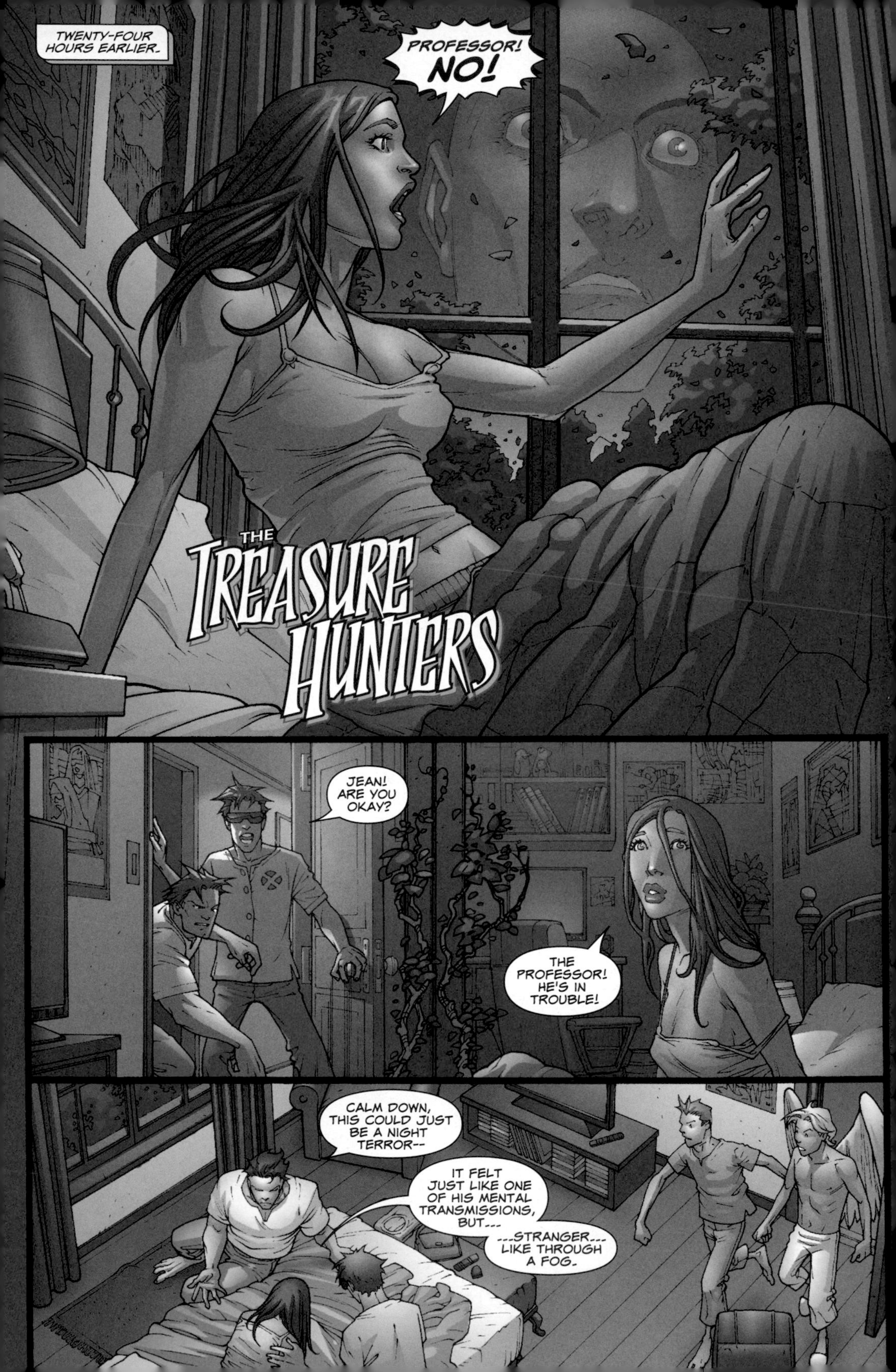
TWENTY-FOUR HOURS EARLIER...
PROFESSOR! NO!
THE TREASURE HUNTERS
JEAN! ARE YOU OKAY?
THE PROFESSOR! HE'S IN TROUBLE!
CALM DOWN, THIS COULD JUST BE A NIGHT TERROR--
IT FELT JUST LIKE ONE OF HIS MENTAL TRANSMISSIONS, BUT...
...STRANGER... LIKE THROUGH A FOG...

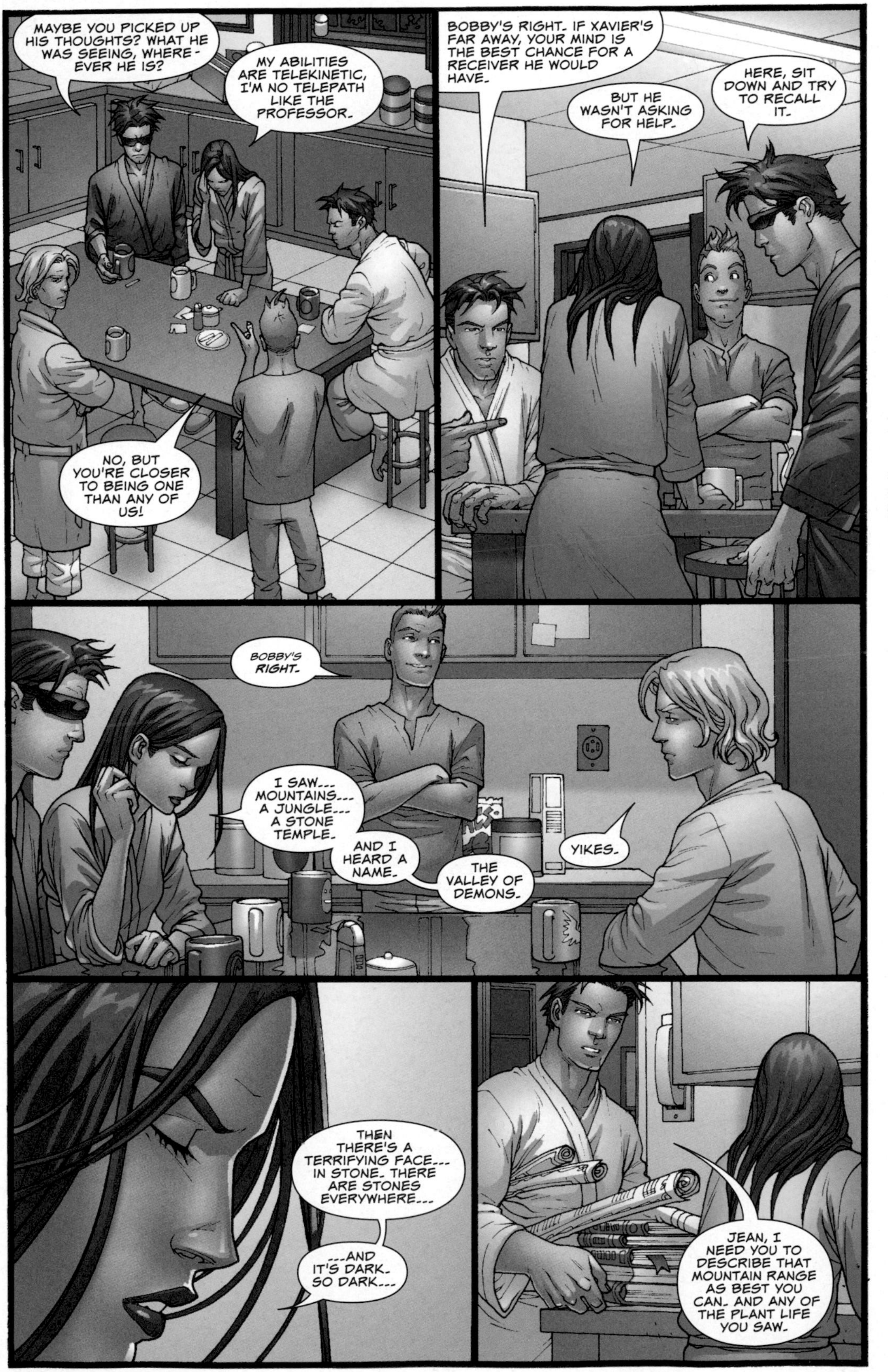
MAYBE YOU PICKED UP HIS THOUGHTS? WHAT HE WAS SEEING, WHERE-EVER HE IS?
MY ABILITIES ARE TELEKINETIC, I'M NO TELEPATH LIKE THE PROFESSOR.
NO, BUT YOU'RE CLOSER TO BEING ONE THAN ANY OF US!
BOBBY'S RIGHT. IF XAVIER'S FAR AWAY, YOUR MIND IS THE BEST CHANCE FOR A RECEIVER HE WOULD HAVE.
BUT HE WASN'T ASKING FOR HELP.
HERE, SIT DOWN AND TRY TO RECALL IT.
BOBBY'S RIGHT.
I SAW... MOUNTAINS... A JUNGLE... A STONE TEMPLE.
AND I HEARD A NAME.
THE VALLEY OF DEMONS.
YIKES.
THEN THERE'S A TERRIFYING FACE... IN STONE. THERE ARE STONES EVERYWHERE...
...AND IT'S DARK. SO DARK...
JEAN, I NEED YOU TO DESCRIBE THAT MOUNTAIN RANGE AS BEST YOU CAN. AND ANY OF THE PLANT LIFE YOU SAW.

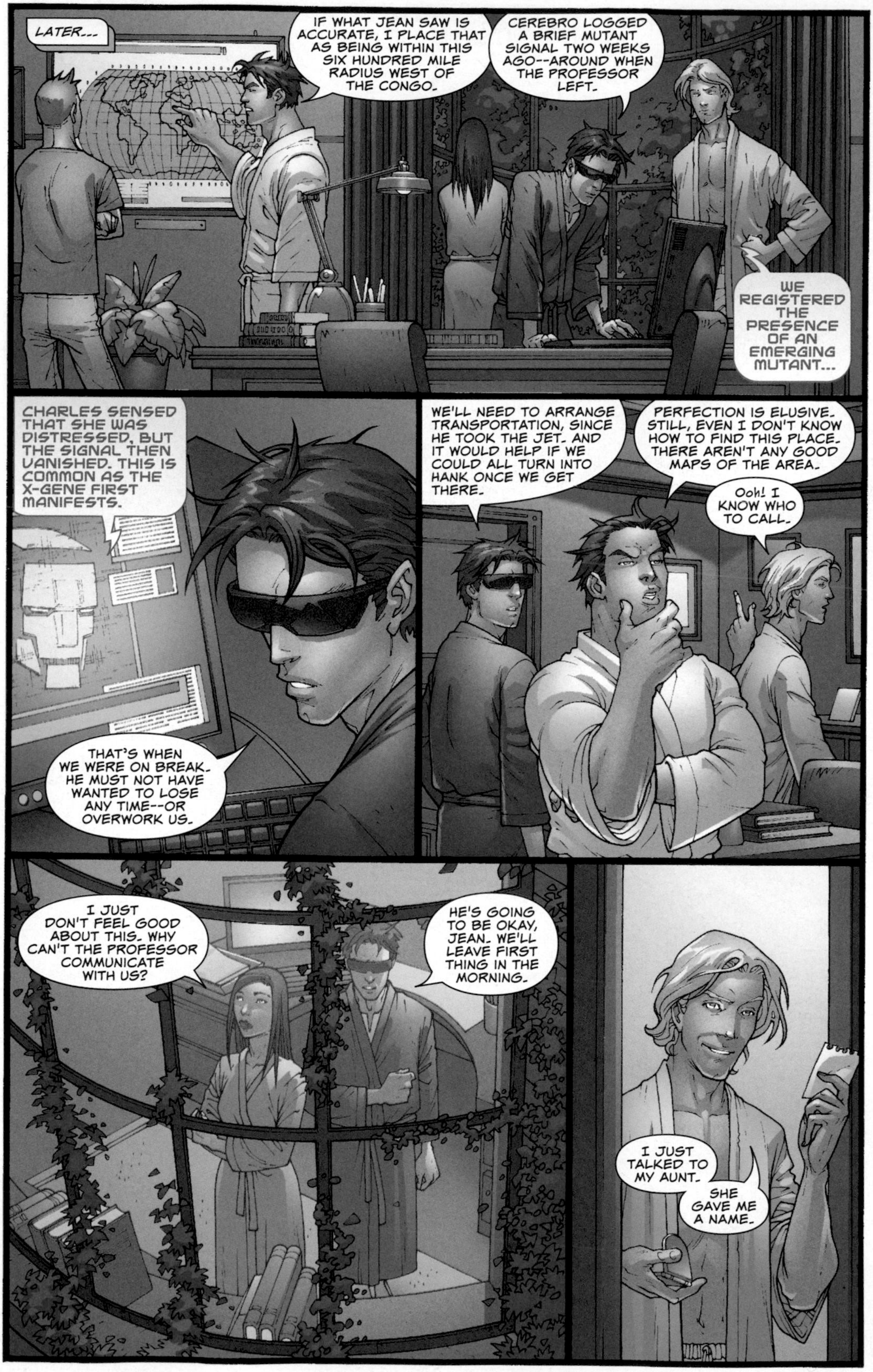
LATER...
IF WHAT JEAN SAW IS ACCURATE, I PLACE THAT AS BEING WITHIN THIS SIX HUNDRED MILE RADIUS WEST OF THE CONGO.
CEREBRO LOGGED A BRIEF MUTANT SIGNAL TWO WEEKS AGO--AROUND WHEN THE PROFESSOR LEFT.
WE REGISTERED THE PRESENCE OF AN EMERGING MUTANT...
CHARLES SENSED THAT SHE WAS DISTRESSED, BUT THE SIGNAL THEN VANISHED. THIS IS COMMON AS THE X-GENE FIRST MANIFESTS.
THAT'S WHEN WE WERE ON BREAK. HE MUST NOT HAVE WANTED TO LOSE ANY TIME--OR OVERWORK US.
WE'LL NEED TO ARRANGE TRANSPORTATION, SINCE HE TOOK THE JET. AND IT WOULD HELP IF WE COULD ALL TURN INTO HANK ONCE WE GET THERE.
PERFECTION IS ELUSIVE. STILL, EVEN I DON'T KNOW HOW TO FIND THIS PLACE. THERE AREN'T ANY GOOD MAPS OF THE AREA.
Ooh! I KNOW WHO TO CALL.
I JUST DON'T FEEL GOOD ABOUT THIS. WHY CAN'T THE PROFESSOR COMMUNICATE WITH US?
HE'S GOING TO BE OKAY, JEAN. WE'LL LEAVE FIRST THING IN THE MORNING.
I JUST TALKED TO MY AUNT.
SHE GAVE ME A NAME.

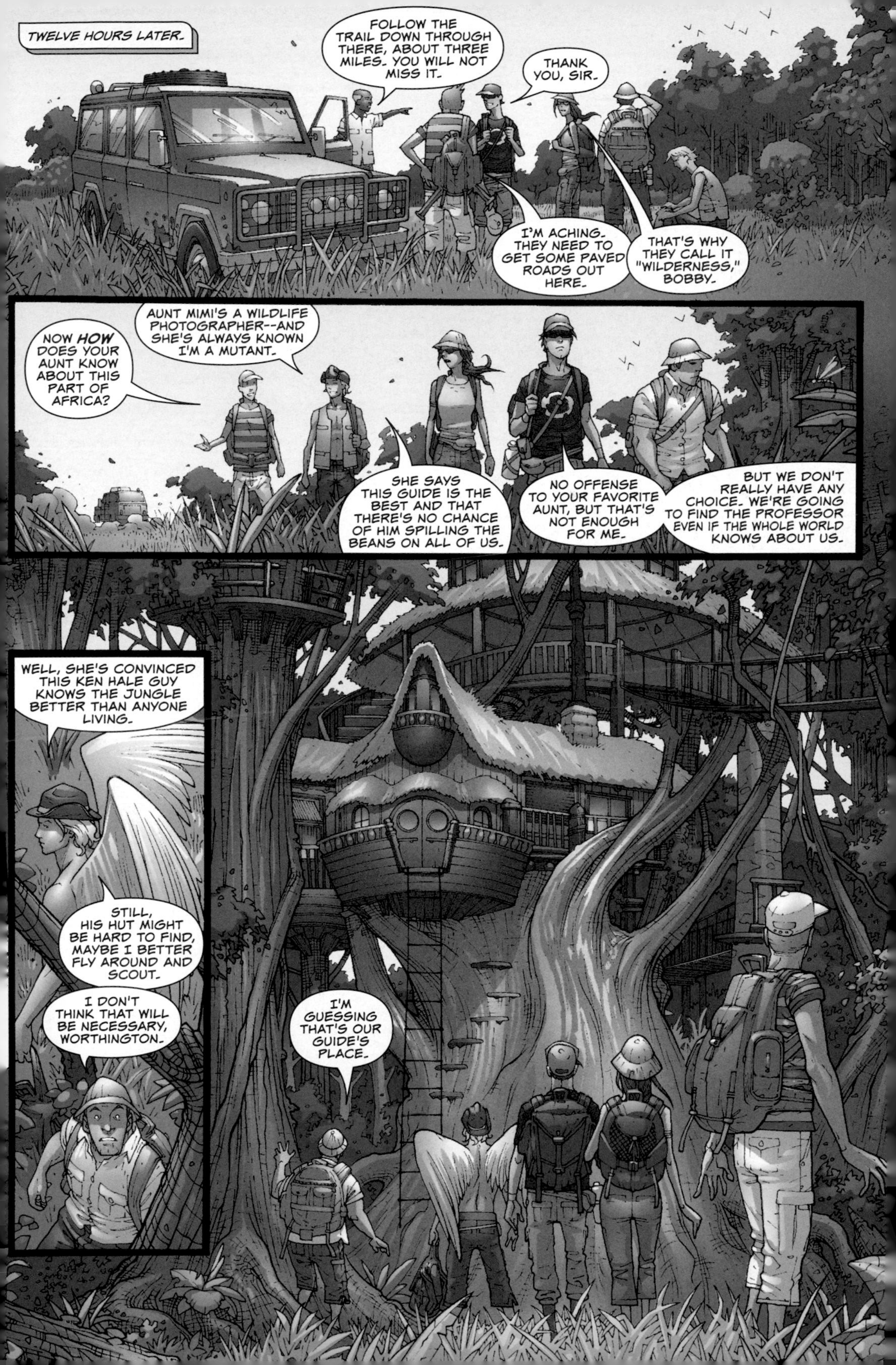
TWELVE HOURS LATER.
FOLLOW THE TRAIL DOWN THROUGH THERE, ABOUT THREE MILES. YOU WILL NOT MISS IT.
THANK YOU, SIR.
I'M ACHING. THEY NEED TO GET SOME PAVED ROADS OUT HERE.
THAT'S WHY THEY CALL IT "WILDERNESS," BOBBY.
NOW HOW DOES YOUR AUNT KNOW ABOUT THIS PART OF AFRICA?
AUNT MIMI'S A WILDLIFE PHOTOGRAPHER--AND SHE'S ALWAYS KNOWN I'M A MUTANT.
SHE SAYS THIS GUIDE IS THE BEST AND THAT THERE'S NO CHANCE OF HIM SPILLING THE BEANS ON ALL OF US.
NO OFFENSE TO YOUR FAVORITE AUNT, BUT THAT'S NOT ENOUGH FOR ME.
BUT WE DON'T REALLY HAVE ANY CHOICE. WE'RE GOING TO FIND THE PROFESSOR EVEN IF THE WHOLE WORLD KNOWS ABOUT US.
WELL, SHE'S CONVINCED THIS KEN HALE GUY KNOWS THE JUNGLE BETTER THAN ANYONE LIVING.
STILL, HIS HUT MIGHT BE HARD TO FIND, MAYBE I BETTER FLY AROUND AND SCOUT.
I DON'T THINK THAT WILL BE NECESSARY, WORTHINGTON.
I'M GUESSING THAT'S OUR GUIDE'S PLACE.

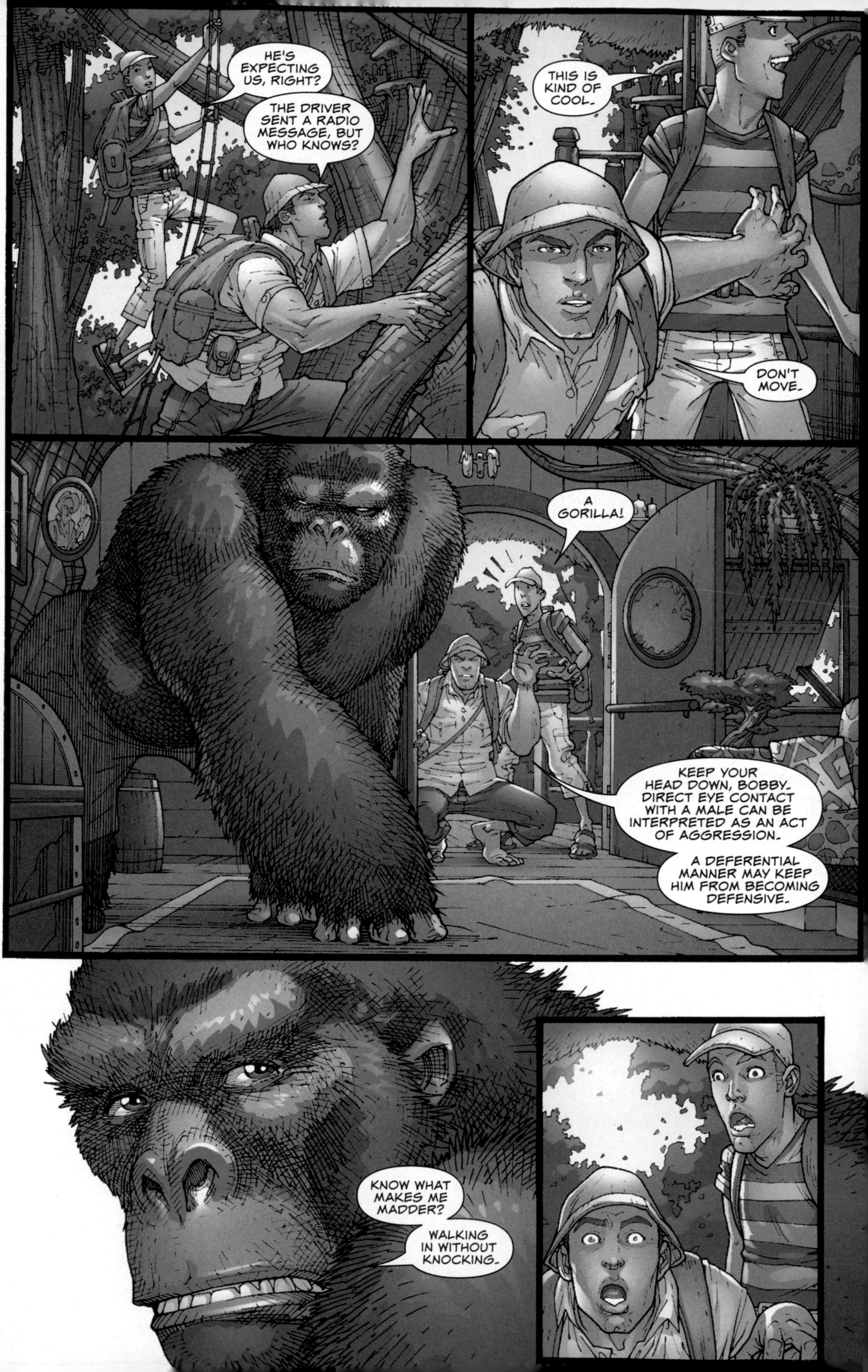
HE'S EXPECTING US, RIGHT?
THE DRIVER SENT A RADIO MESSAGE, BUT WHO KNOWS?
THIS IS KIND OF COOL.
DON'T MOVE.
A GORILLA!
KEEP YOUR HEAD DOWN, BOBBY. DIRECT EYE CONTACT WITH A MALE CAN BE INTERPRETED AS AN ACT OF AGGRESSION.
A DEFERENTIAL MANNER MAY KEEP HIM FROM BECOMING DEFENSIVE.
KNOW WHAT MAKES ME MADDER?
WALKING IN WITHOUT KNOCKING.

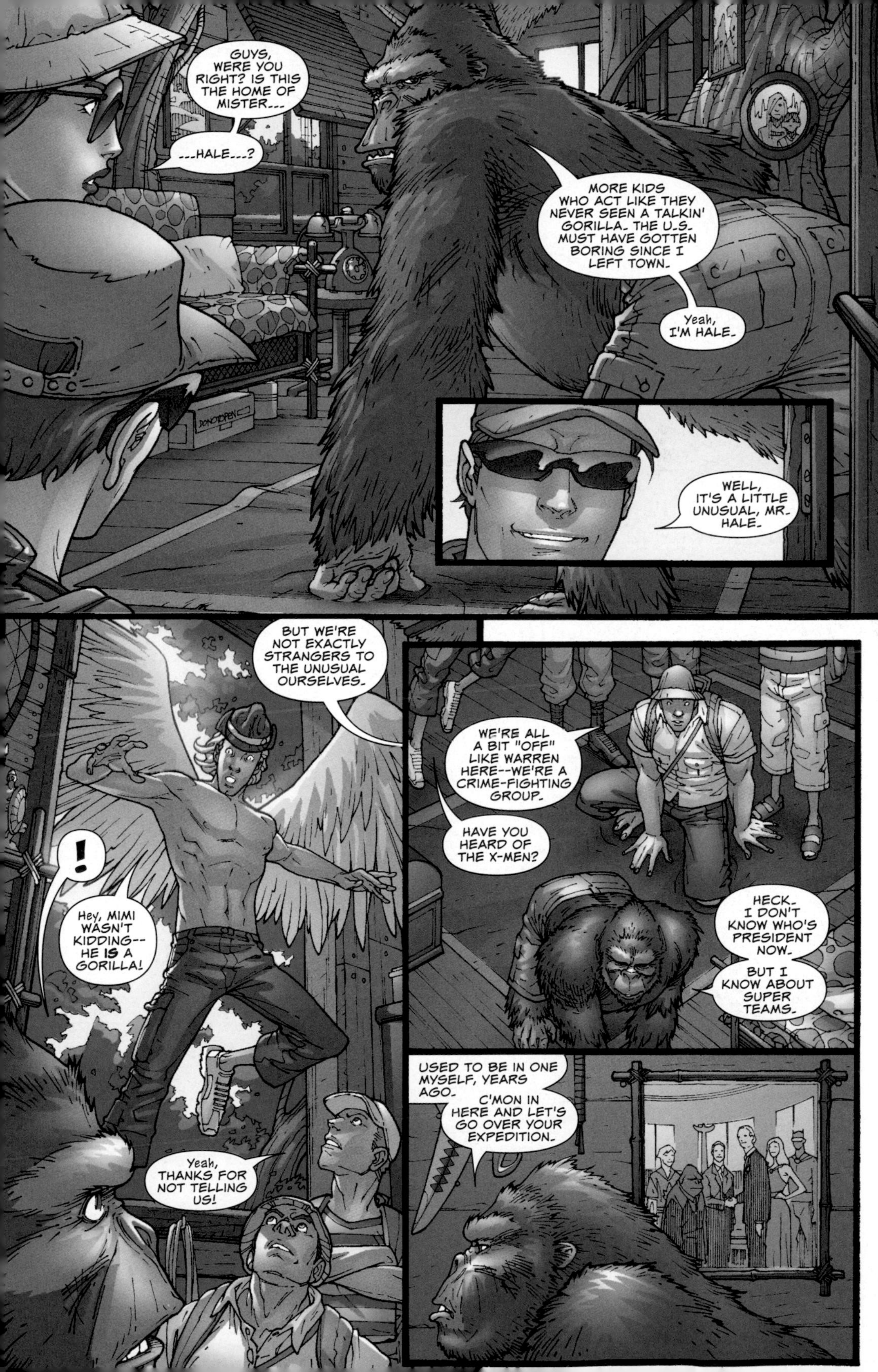

GUYS, WERE YOU RIGHT? IS THIS THE HOME OF MISTER...
...HALE...?
MORE KIDS WHO ACT LIKE THEY NEVER SEEN A TALKIN' GORILLA. THE U.S. MUST HAVE GOTTEN BORING SINCE I LEFT TOWN.
Yeah, I'M HALE.
DO NOT OPEN
WELL, IT'S A LITTLE UNUSUAL, MR. HALE.
BUT WE'RE NOT EXACTLY STRANGERS TO THE UNUSUAL OURSELVES.
!
Hey, MIMI WASN'T KIDDING--HE IS A GORILLA!
Yeah, THANKS FOR NOT TELLING US!
WE'RE ALL A BIT "OFF" LIKE WARREN HERE--WE'RE A CRIME-FIGHTING GROUP.
HAVE YOU HEARD OF THE X-MEN?
HECK. I DON'T KNOW WHO'S PRESIDENT NOW.
BUT I KNOW ABOUT SUPER TEAMS.
USED TO BE IN ONE MYSELF, YEARS AGO.
C'MON IN HERE AND LET'S GO OVER YOUR EXPEDITION.

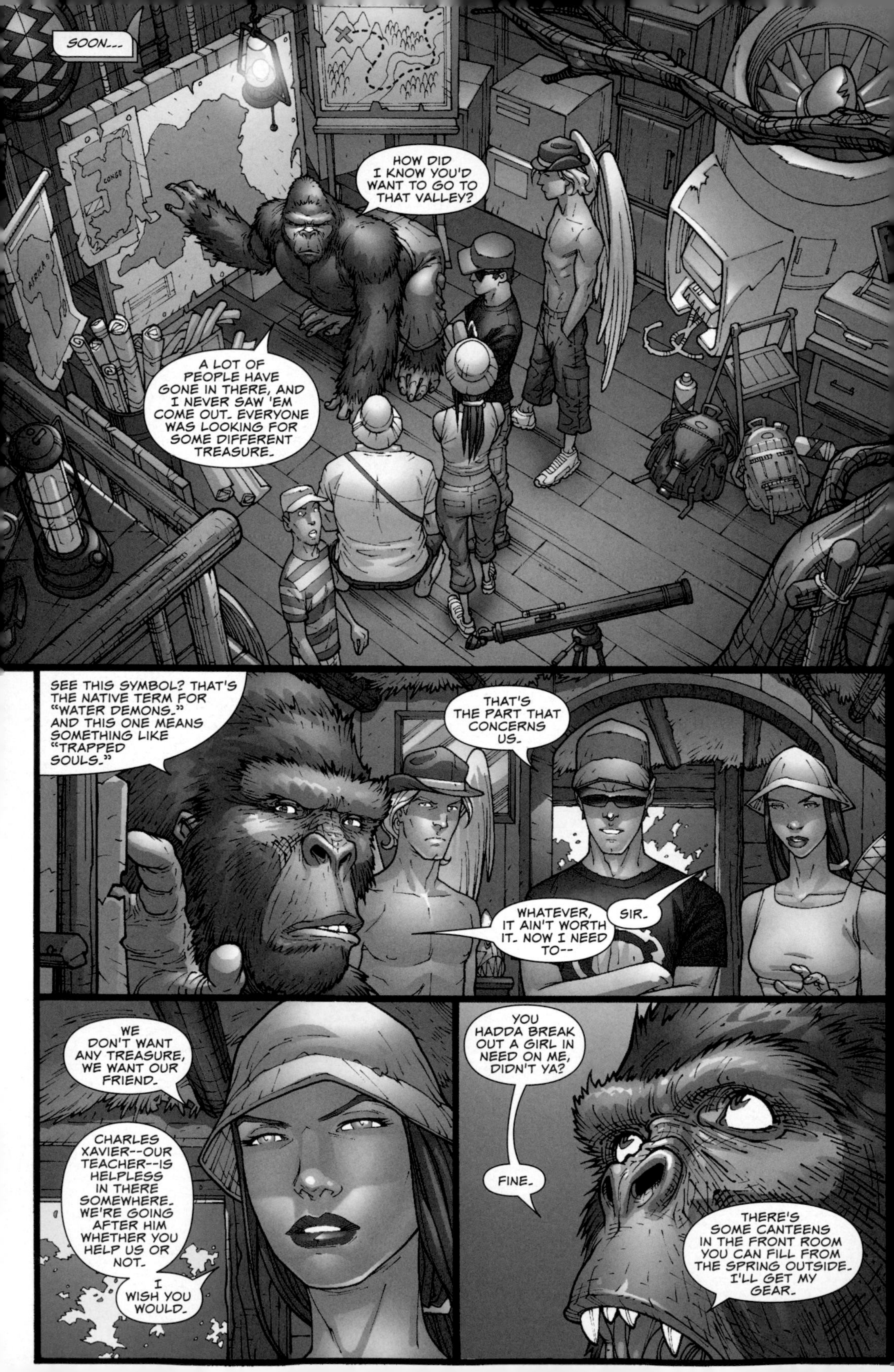
SOON---
HOW DID I KNOW YOU'D WANT TO GO TO THAT VALLEY?
A LOT OF PEOPLE HAVE GONE IN THERE, AND I NEVER SAW 'EM COME OUT. EVERYONE WAS LOOKING FOR SOME DIFFERENT TREASURE.
CONGO
AFRICA
SEE THIS SYMBOL? THAT'S THE NATIVE TERM FOR "WATER DEMONS." AND THIS ONE MEANS SOMETHING LIKE "TRAPPED SOULS."
THAT'S THE PART THAT CONCERNS US.
WHATEVER, IT AIN'T WORTH IT. NOW I NEED TO--
SIR.
WE DON'T WANT ANY TREASURE, WE WANT OUR FRIEND.
CHARLES XAVIER--OUR TEACHER--IS HELPLESS IN THERE SOMEWHERE. WE'RE GOING AFTER HIM WHETHER YOU HELP US OR NOT.
I WISH YOU WOULD.
YOU HADDA BREAK OUT A GIRL IN NEED ON ME, DIDN'T YA?
FINE.
THERE'S SOME CANTEENS IN THE FRONT ROOM YOU CAN FILL FROM THE SPRING OUTSIDE. I'LL GET MY GEAR.

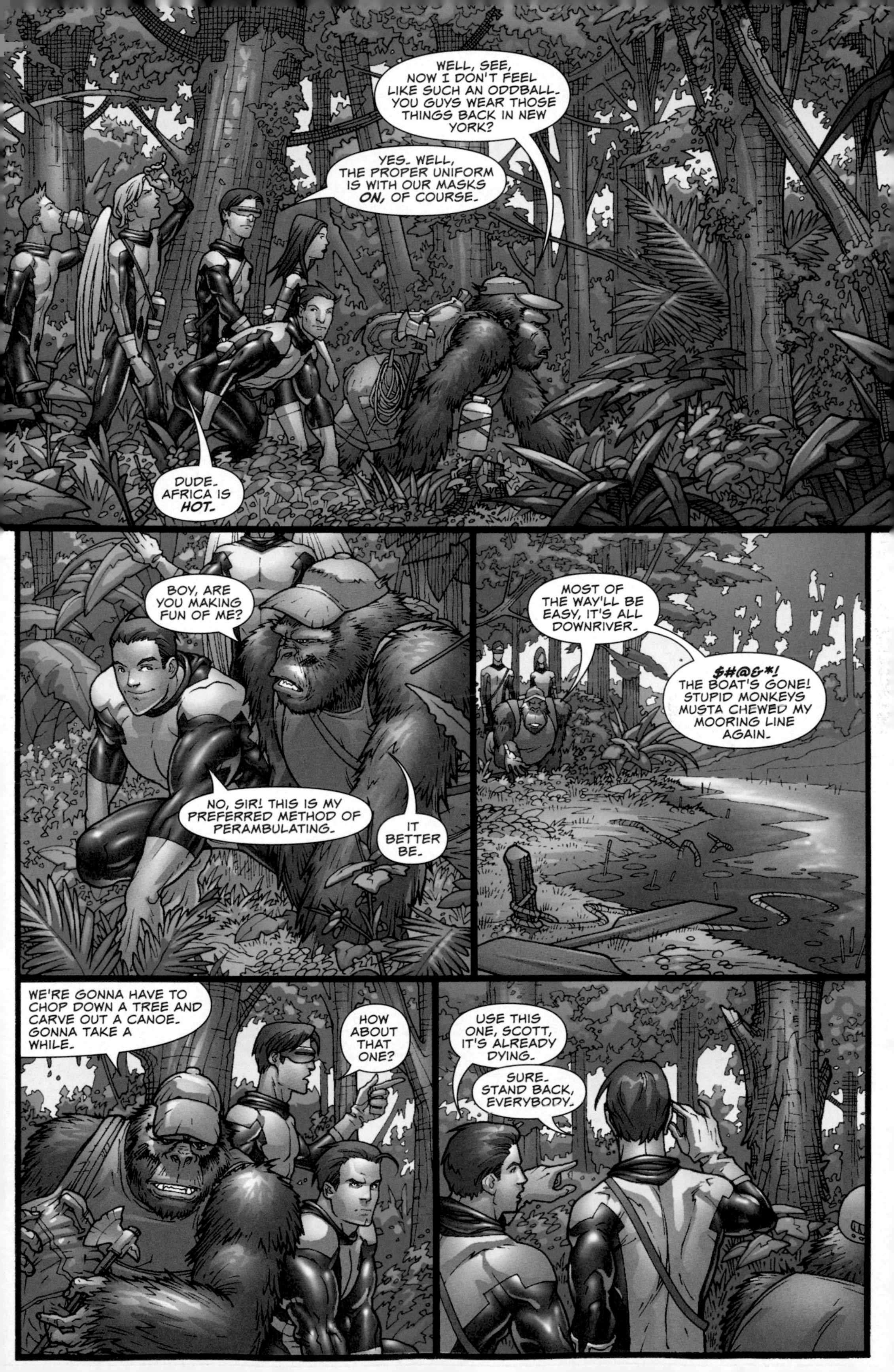
WELL, SEE, NOW I DON'T FEEL LIKE SUCH AN ODDBALL. YOU GUYS WEAR THOSE THINGS BACK IN NEW YORK?
YES. WELL, THE PROPER UNIFORM IS WITH OUR MASKS ON, OF COURSE.
DUDE. AFRICA IS HOT.
BOY, ARE YOU MAKING FUN OF ME?
NO, SIR! THIS IS MY PREFERRED METHOD OF PERAMBULATING.
IT BETTER BE.
MOST OF THE WAY'LL BE EASY, IT'S ALL DOWNRIVER.
$#@&*! THE BOAT'S GONE! STUPID MONKEYS MUSTA CHEWED MY MOORING LINE AGAIN.
WE'RE GONNA HAVE TO CHOP DOWN A TREE AND CARVE OUT A CANOE. GONNA TAKE A WHILE.
HOW ABOUT THAT ONE?
USE THIS ONE, SCOTT, IT'S ALREADY DYING.
SURE. STAND BACK, EVERYBODY.

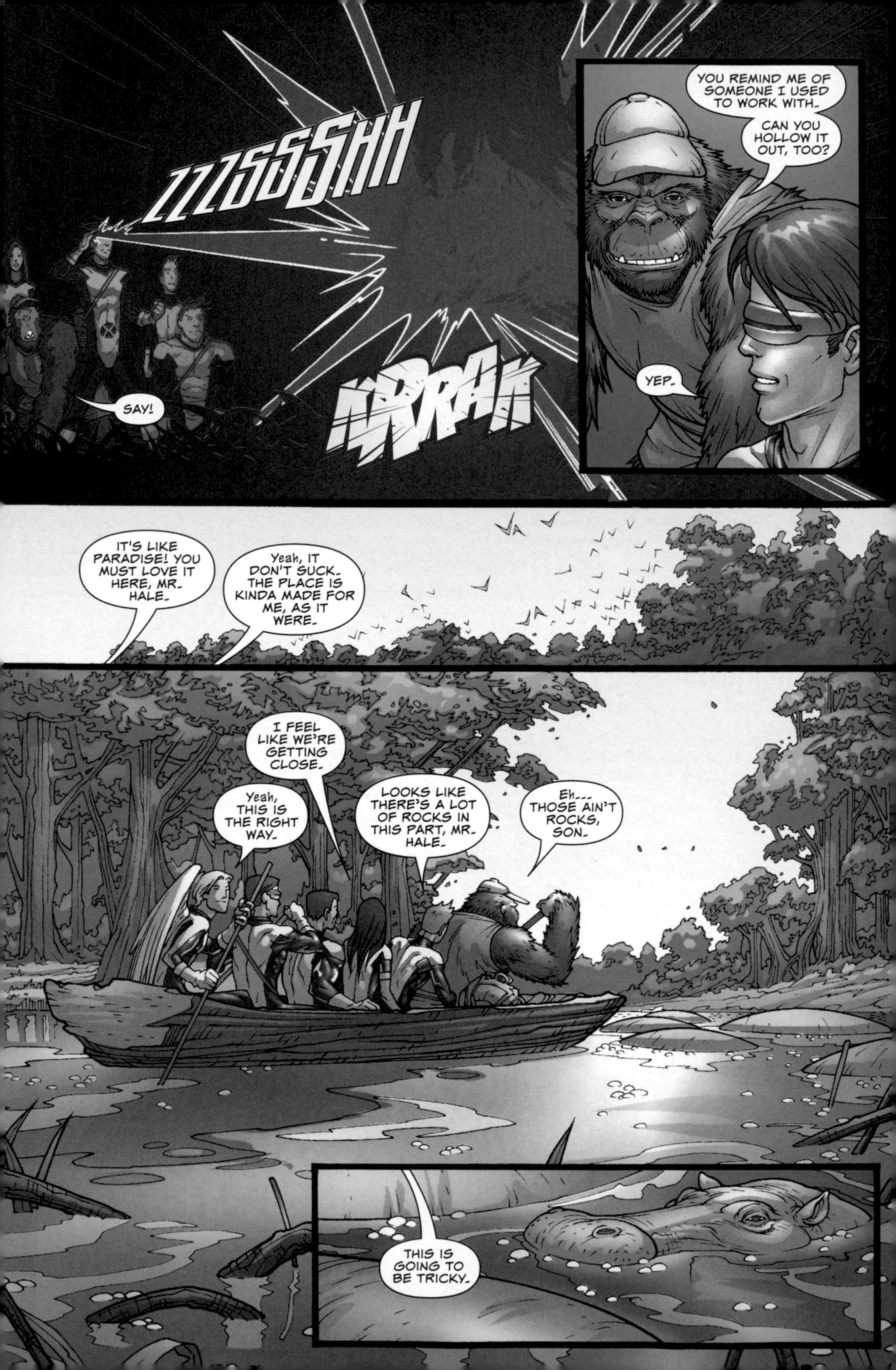
ZZZSSSSHH
SAY!
KRRAK
YOU REMIND ME OF SOMEONE I USED TO WORK WITH.
CAN YOU HOLLOW IT OUT, TOO?
YEP.
IT'S LIKE PARADISE! YOU MUST LOVE IT HERE, MR. HALE.
Yeah, IT DON'T SUCK. THE PLACE IS KINDA MADE FOR ME, AS IT WERE.
I FEEL LIKE WE'RE GETTING CLOSE.
Yeah, THIS IS THE RIGHT WAY.
LOOKS LIKE THERE'S A LOT OF ROCKS IN THIS PART, MR. HALE.
Eh... THOSE AIN'T ROCKS, SON.
THIS IS GOING TO BE TRICKY.

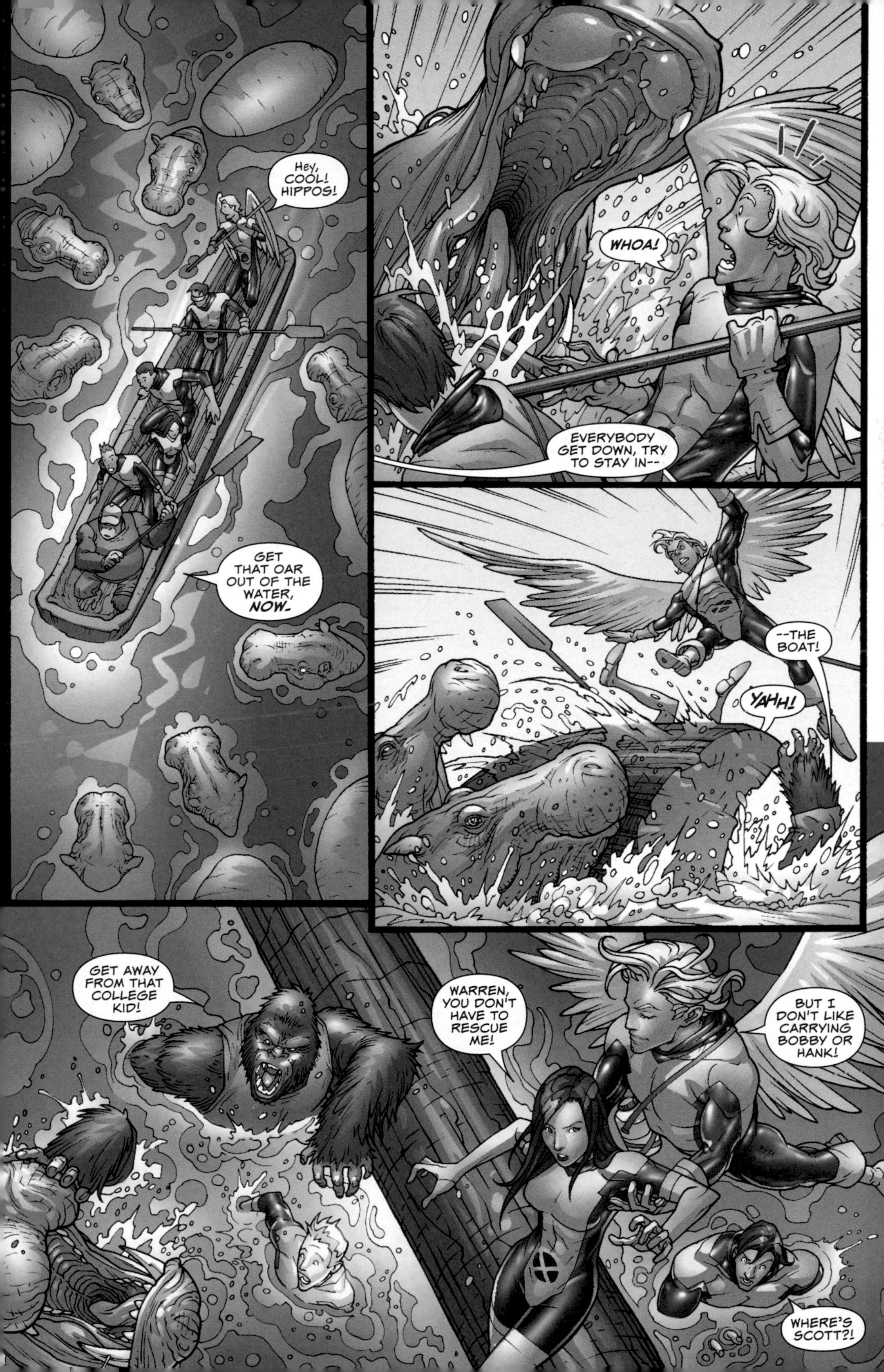
Hey, COOL! HIPPOS!
GET THAT OAR OUT OF THE WATER, NOW-
WHOA!
EVERYBODY GET DOWN, TRY TO STAY IN--
--THE BOAT!
YAHH!
GET AWAY FROM THAT COLLEGE KID!
WARREN, YOU DON'T HAVE TO RESCUE ME!
BUT I DON'T LIKE CARRYING BOBBY OR HANK!
WHERE'S SCOTT?!

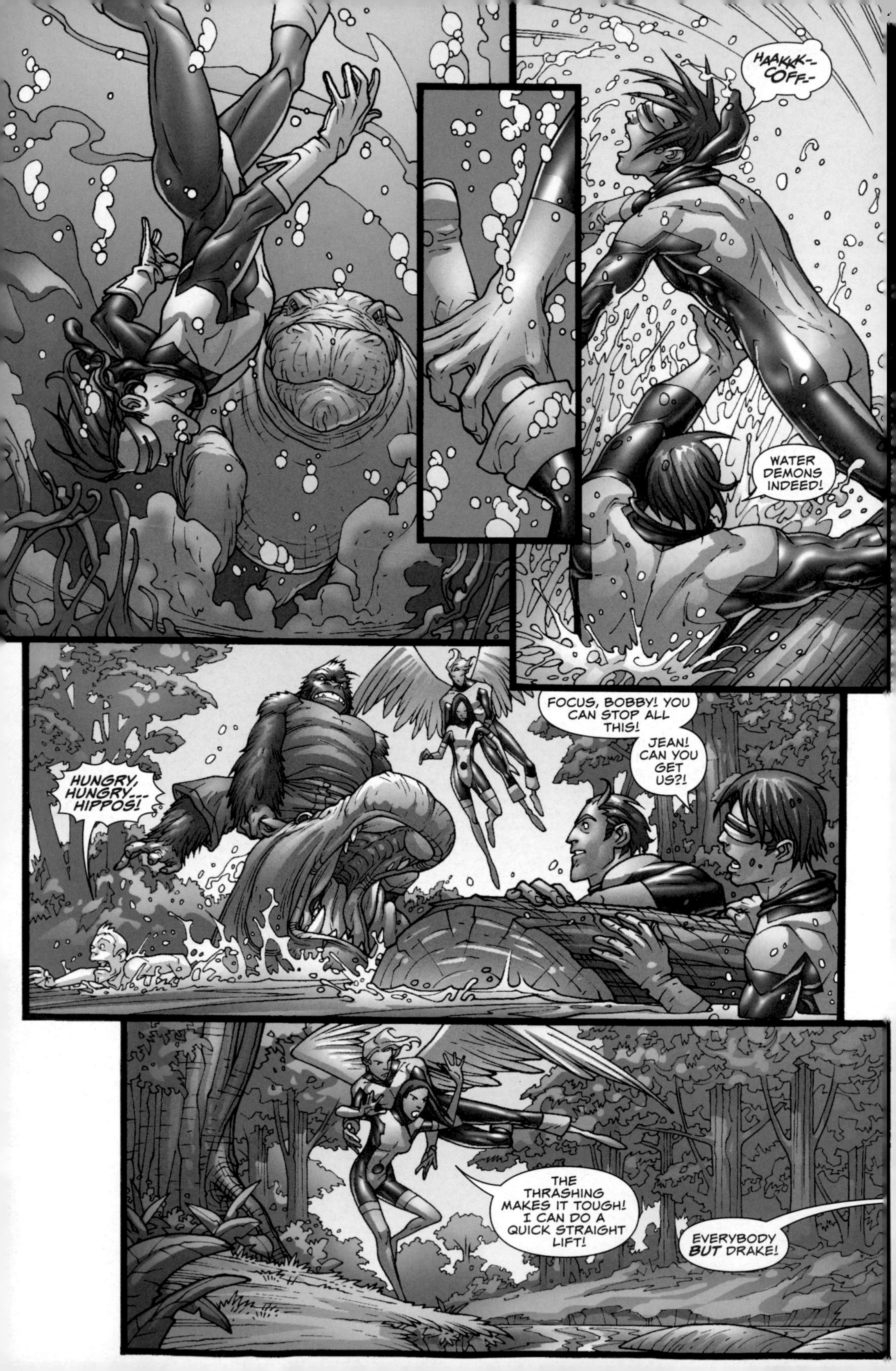
HAAKKK--COFF--
WATER DEMONS INDEED!
HUNGRY, HUNGRY... HIPPOS!
FOCUS, BOBBY! YOU CAN STOP ALL THIS!
JEAN! CAN YOU GET US?!
THE THRASHING MAKES IT TOUGH! I CAN DO A QUICK STRAIGHT LIFT!
EVERYBODY BUT DRAKE!

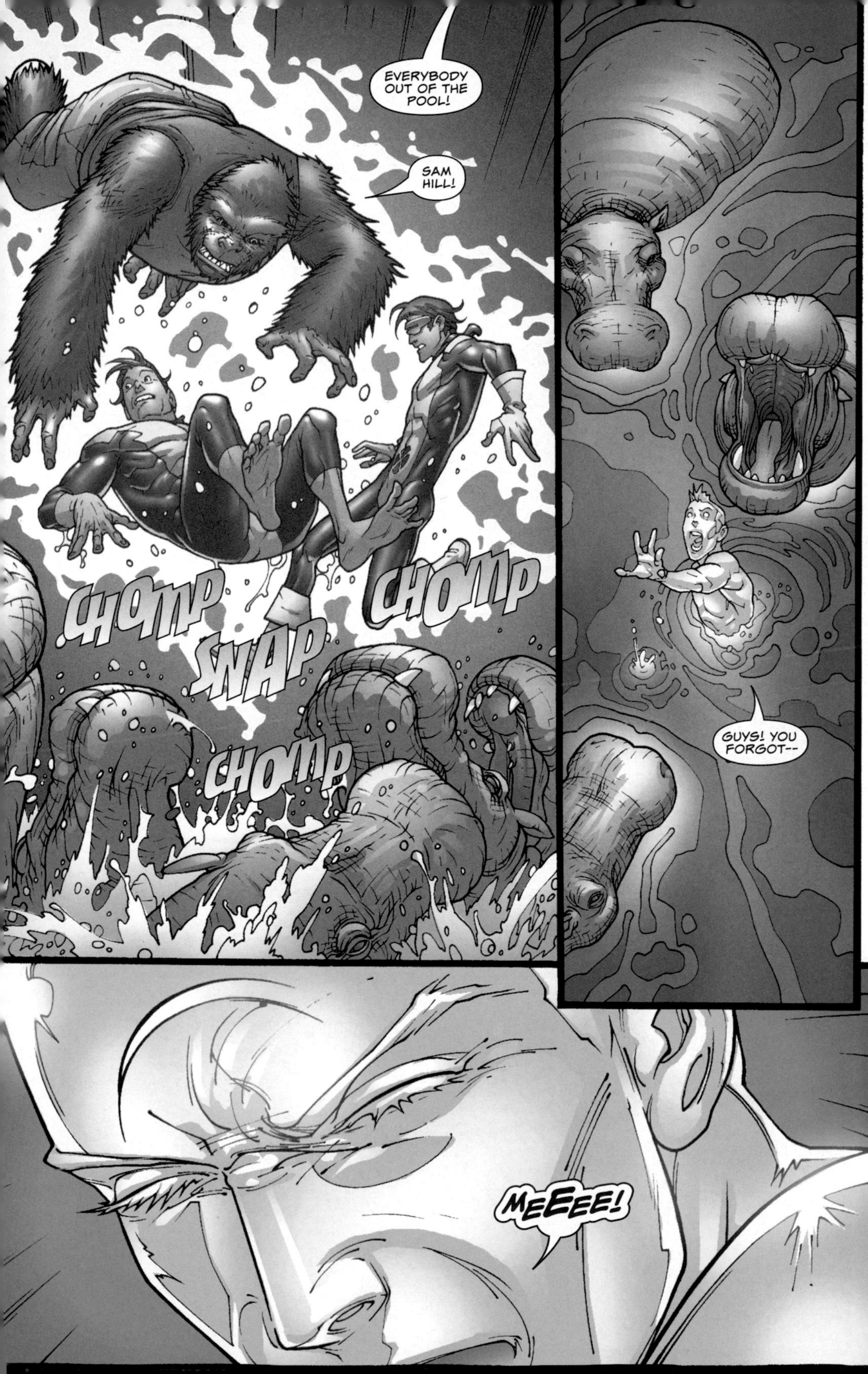
EVERYBODY OUT OF THE POOL!
SAM HILL!
CHOMP
SNAP
CHOMP
CHOMP
GUYS! YOU FORGOT--
MEEEE!

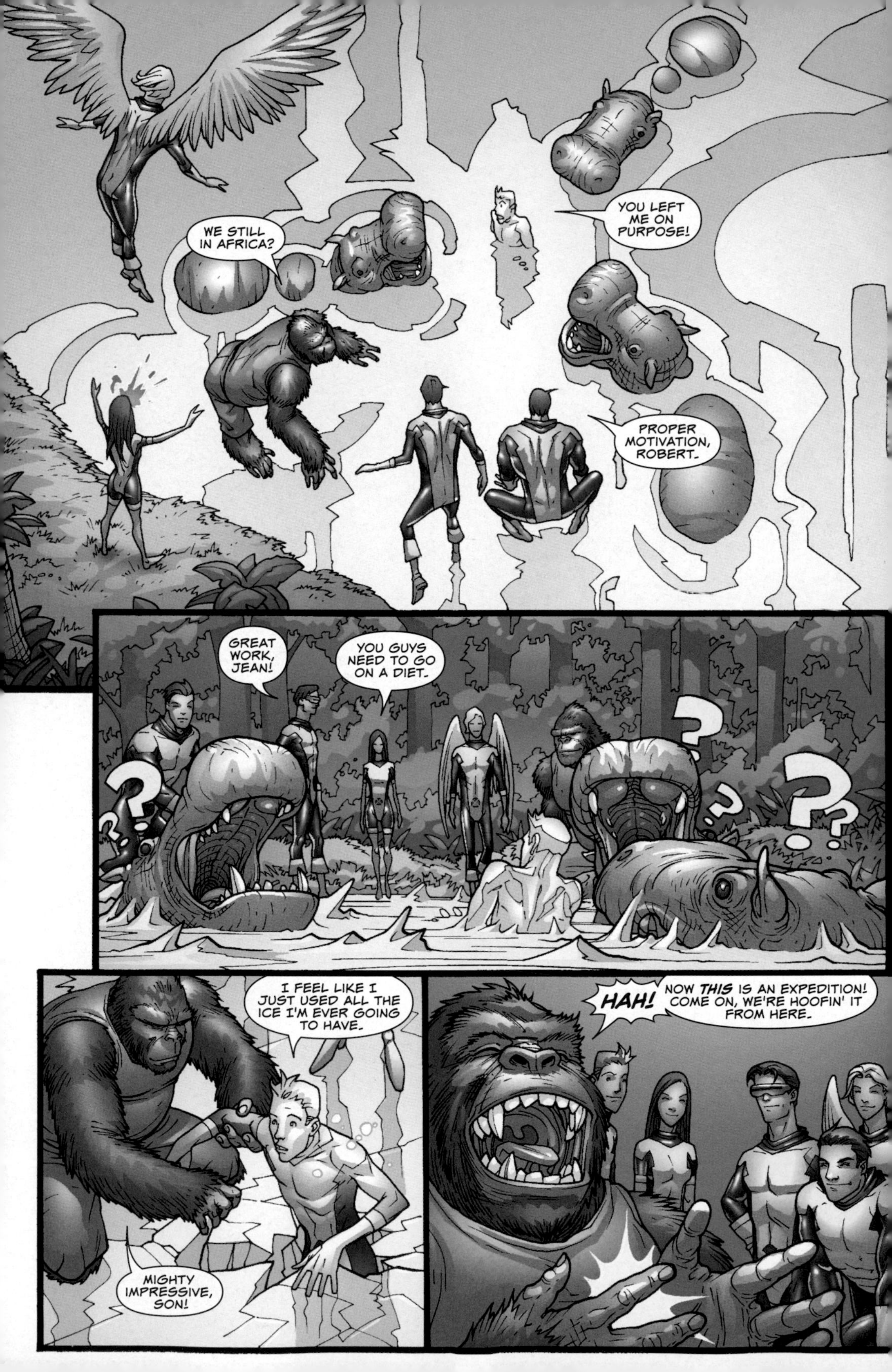
WE STILL IN AFRICA?
YOU LEFT ME ON PURPOSE!
PROPER MOTIVATION, ROBERT.
GREAT WORK, JEAN!
YOU GUYS NEED TO GO ON A DIET.
I FEEL LIKE I JUST USED ALL THE ICE I'M EVER GOING TO HAVE.
MIGHTY IMPRESSIVE, SON!
HAH!
NOW THIS IS AN EXPEDITION! COME ON, WE'RE HOOFIN' IT FROM HERE.

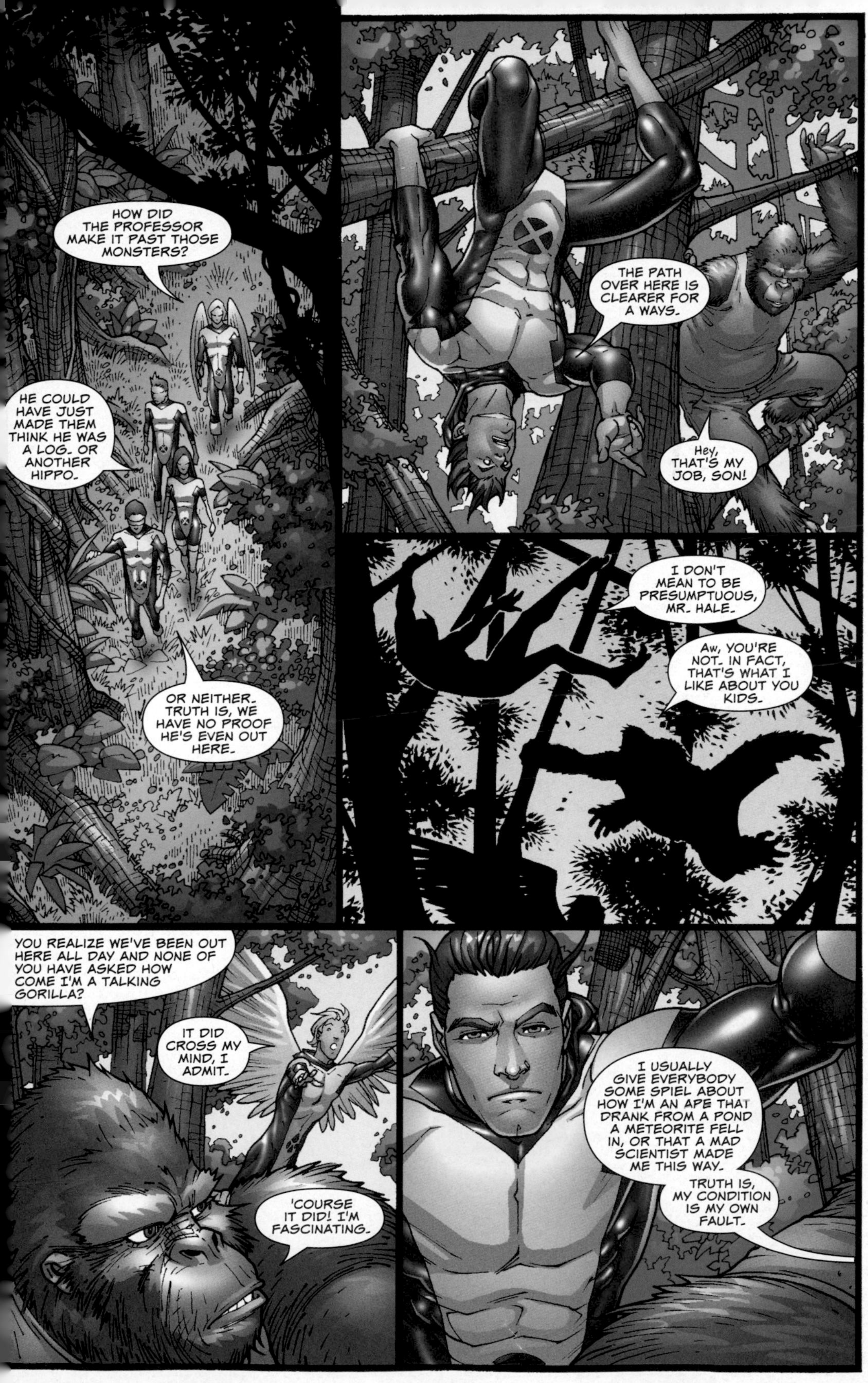
HOW DID THE PROFESSOR MAKE IT PAST THOSE MONSTERS?
HE COULD HAVE JUST MADE THEM THINK HE WAS A LOG. OR ANOTHER HIPPO.
OR NEITHER. TRUTH IS, WE HAVE NO PROOF HE'S EVEN OUT HERE.
THE PATH OVER HERE IS CLEARER FOR A WAYS.
Hey, THAT'S MY JOB, SON!
I DON'T MEAN TO BE PRESUMPTUOUS, MR. HALE.
Aw, YOU'RE NOT. IN FACT, THAT'S WHAT I LIKE ABOUT YOU KIDS.
YOU REALIZE WE'VE BEEN OUT HERE ALL DAY AND NONE OF YOU HAVE ASKED HOW COME I'M A TALKING GORILLA?
IT DID CROSS MY MIND, I ADMIT.
'COURSE IT DID! I'M FASCINATING.
I USUALLY GIVE EVERYBODY SOME SPIEL ABOUT HOW I'M AN APE THAT DRANK FROM A POND A METEORITE FELL IN, OR THAT A MAD SCIENTIST MADE ME THIS WAY.
TRUTH IS, MY CONDITION IS MY OWN FAULT.

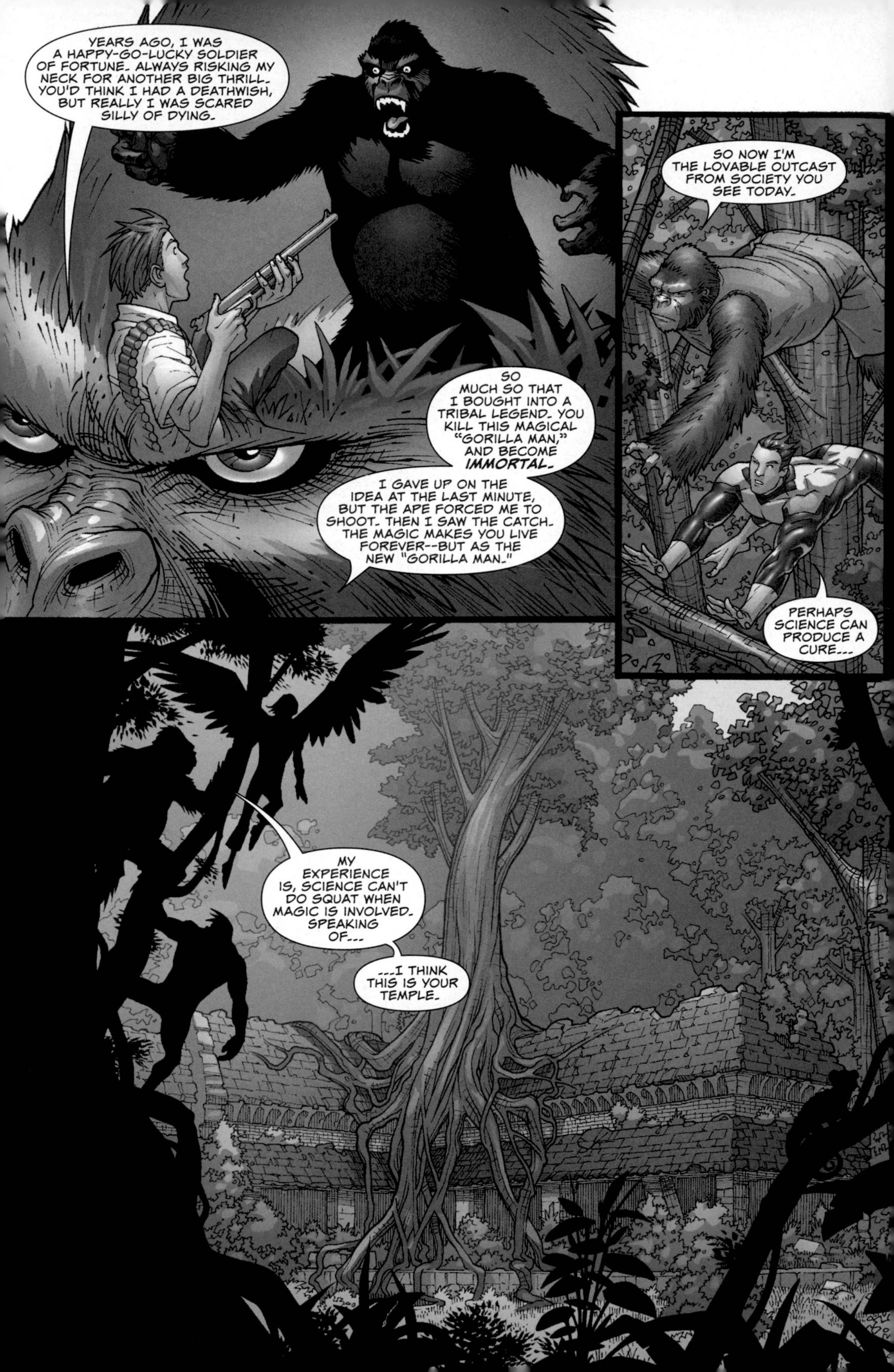
YEARS AGO, I WAS A HAPPY-GO-LUCKY SOLDIER OF FORTUNE. ALWAYS RISKING MY NECK FOR ANOTHER BIG THRILL. YOU'D THINK I HAD A DEATHWISH, BUT REALLY I WAS SCARED SILLY OF DYING.
SO MUCH SO THAT I BOUGHT INTO A TRIBAL LEGEND. YOU KILL THIS MAGICAL "GORILLA MAN," AND BECOME IMMORTAL.
I GAVE UP ON THE IDEA AT THE LAST MINUTE, BUT THE APE FORCED ME TO SHOOT. THEN I SAW THE CATCH. THE MAGIC MAKES YOU LIVE FOREVER--BUT AS THE NEW "GORILLA MAN."
SO NOW I'M THE LOVABLE OUTCAST FROM SOCIETY YOU SEE TODAY.
PERHAPS SCIENCE CAN PRODUCE A CURE...
MY EXPERIENCE IS, SCIENCE CAN'T DO SQUAT WHEN MAGIC IS INVOLVED. SPEAKING OF...
...I THINK THIS IS YOUR TEMPLE.

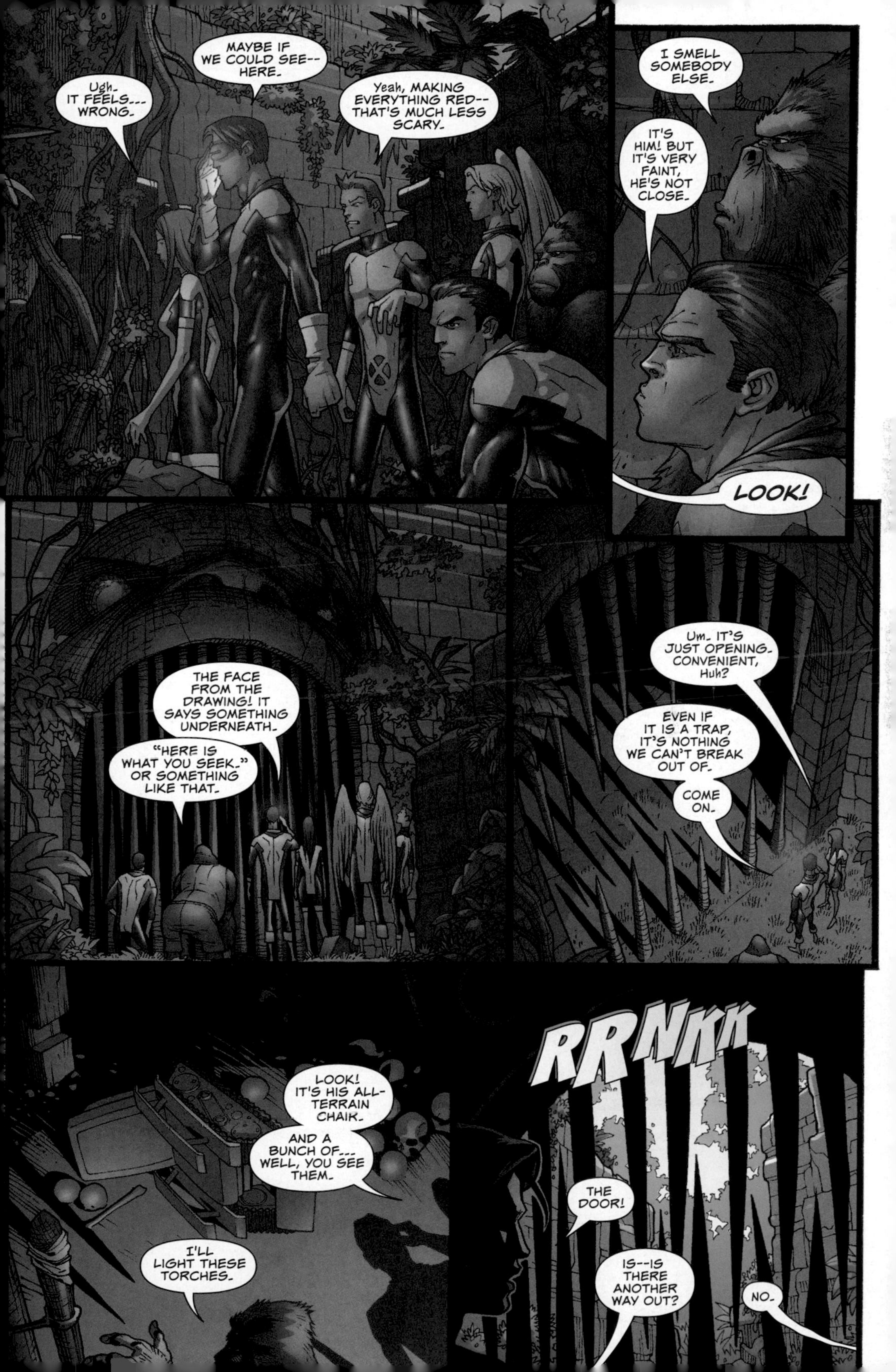
Ugh. IT FEELS... WRONG.
MAYBE IF WE COULD SEE-- HERE.
Yeah, MAKING EVERYTHING RED-- THAT'S MUCH LESS SCARY.
I SMELL SOMEBODY ELSE.
IT'S HIM! BUT IT'S VERY FAINT, HE'S NOT CLOSE.
LOOK!
THE FACE FROM THE DRAWING! IT SAYS SOMETHING UNDERNEATH.
"HERE IS WHAT YOU SEEK." OR SOMETHING LIKE THAT.
Um. IT'S JUST OPENING. CONVENIENT, Huh?
EVEN IF IT IS A TRAP, IT'S NOTHING WE CAN'T BREAK OUT OF.
COME ON.
LOOK! IT'S HIS ALL-TERRAIN CHAIR.
AND A BUNCH OF... WELL, YOU SEE THEM.
I'LL LIGHT THESE TORCHES.
RRNKK
THE DOOR!
IS--IS THERE ANOTHER WAY OUT?
NO.

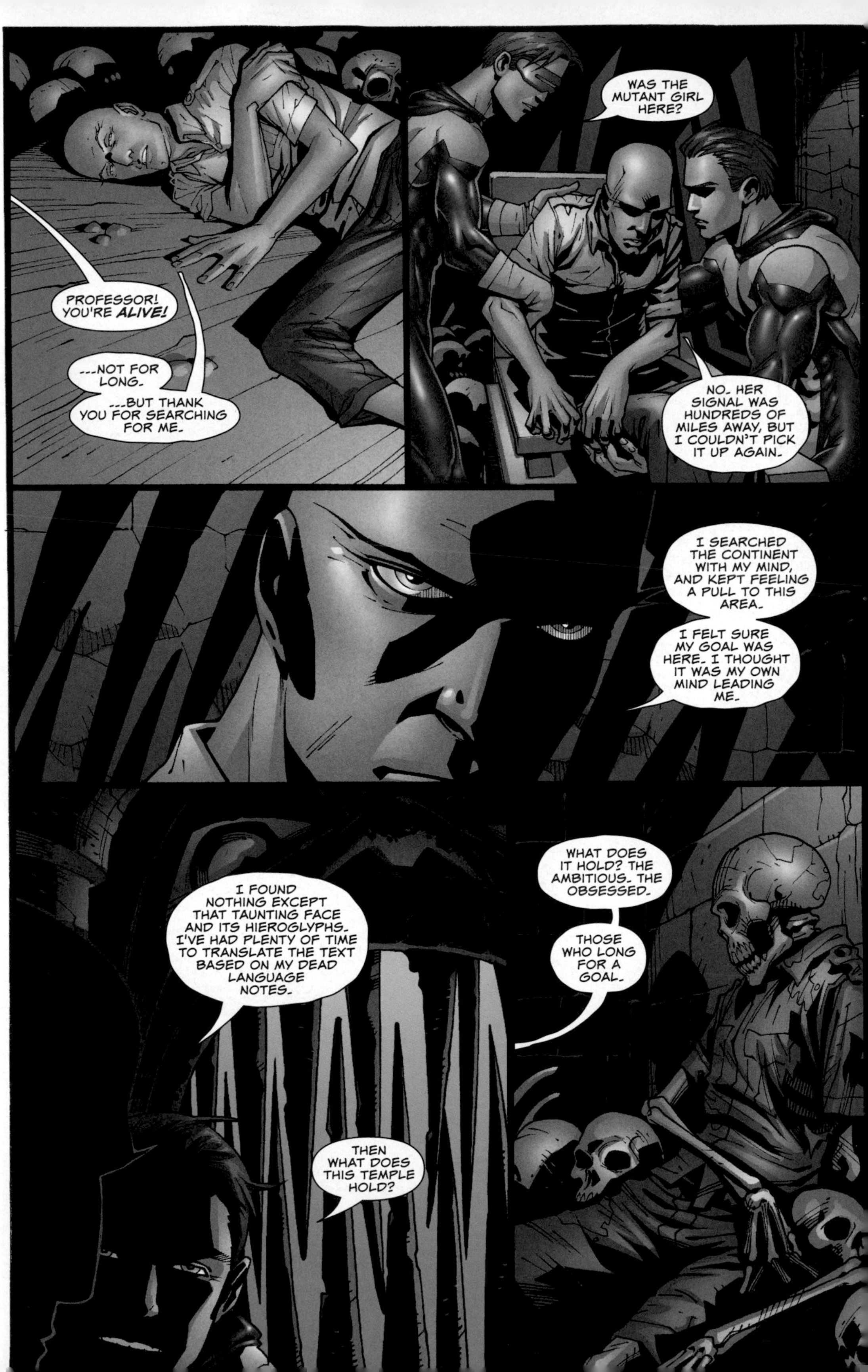
PROFESSOR! YOU'RE *ALIVE!*
...NOT FOR LONG.
...BUT THANK YOU FOR SEARCHING FOR ME.
WAS THE MUTANT GIRL HERE?
NO. HER SIGNAL WAS HUNDREDS OF MILES AWAY, BUT I COULDN'T PICK IT UP AGAIN.
I SEARCHED THE CONTINENT WITH MY MIND, AND KEPT FEELING A PULL TO THIS AREA.
I FELT SURE MY GOAL WAS HERE. I THOUGHT IT WAS MY OWN MIND LEADING ME.
I FOUND NOTHING EXCEPT THAT TAUNTING FACE AND ITS HIEROGLYPHS. I'VE HAD PLENTY OF TIME TO TRANSLATE THE TEXT BASED ON MY DEAD LANGUAGE NOTES.
THEN WHAT DOES THIS TEMPLE HOLD?
WHAT DOES IT HOLD? THE AMBITIOUS. THE OBSESSED.
THOSE WHO LONG FOR A GOAL.

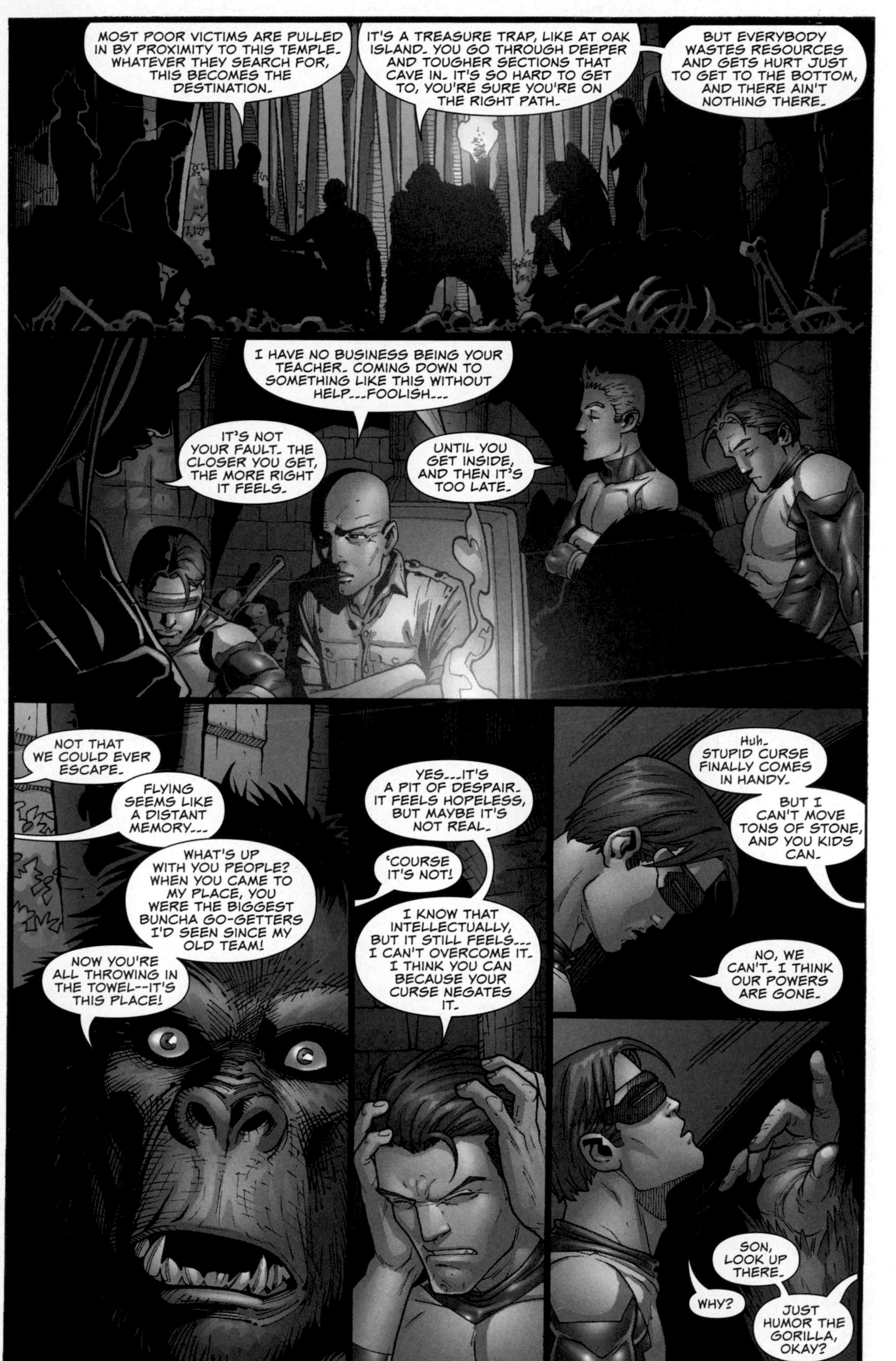
MOST POOR VICTIMS ARE PULLED IN BY PROXIMITY TO THIS TEMPLE. WHATEVER THEY SEARCH FOR, THIS BECOMES THE DESTINATION.
IT'S A TREASURE TRAP, LIKE AT OAK ISLAND. YOU GO THROUGH DEEPER AND TOUGHER SECTIONS THAT CAVE IN. IT'S SO HARD TO GET TO, YOU'RE SURE YOU'RE ON THE RIGHT PATH.
BUT EVERYBODY WASTES RESOURCES AND GETS HURT JUST TO GET TO THE BOTTOM, AND THERE AIN'T NOTHING THERE.
I HAVE NO BUSINESS BEING YOUR TEACHER. COMING DOWN TO SOMETHING LIKE THIS WITHOUT HELP...FOOLISH...
IT'S NOT YOUR FAULT. THE CLOSER YOU GET, THE MORE RIGHT IT FEELS.
UNTIL YOU GET INSIDE, AND THEN IT'S TOO LATE.
NOT THAT WE COULD EVER ESCAPE.
FLYING SEEMS LIKE A DISTANT MEMORY...
WHAT'S UP WITH YOU PEOPLE? WHEN YOU CAME TO MY PLACE, YOU WERE THE BIGGEST BUNCHA GO-GETTERS I'D SEEN SINCE MY OLD TEAM!
NOW YOU'RE ALL THROWING IN THE TOWEL--IT'S THIS PLACE!
YES...IT'S A PIT OF DESPAIR. IT FEELS HOPELESS, BUT MAYBE IT'S NOT REAL.
'COURSE IT'S NOT!
I KNOW THAT INTELLECTUALLY, BUT IT STILL FEELS... I CAN'T OVERCOME IT. I THINK YOU CAN BECAUSE YOUR CURSE NEGATES IT.
Huh. STUPID CURSE FINALLY COMES IN HANDY.
BUT I CAN'T MOVE TONS OF STONE, AND YOU KIDS CAN.
NO, WE CAN'T. I THINK OUR POWERS ARE GONE.
SON, LOOK UP THERE.
WHY?
JUST HUMOR THE GORILLA, OKAY?

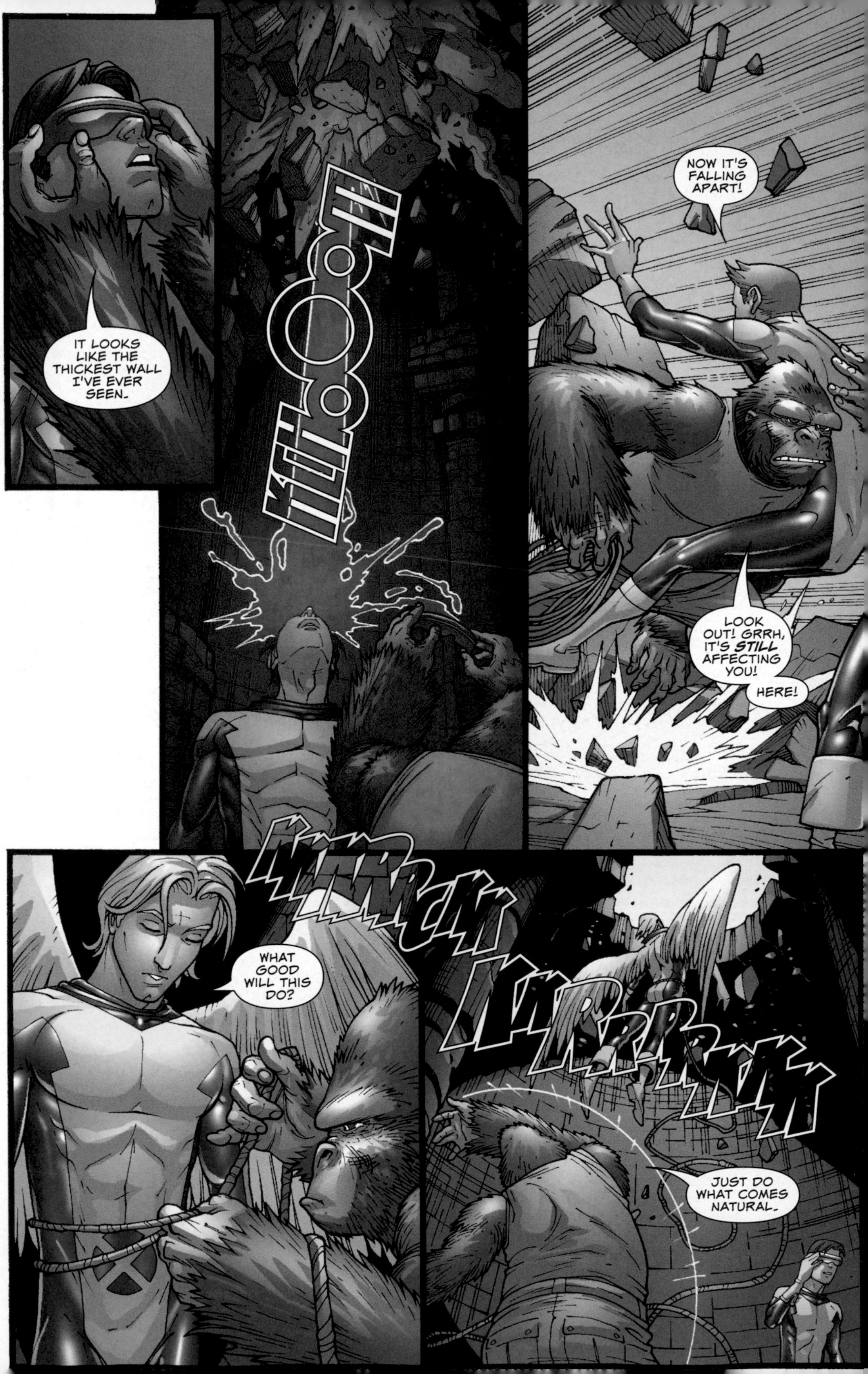
IT LOOKS LIKE THE THICKEST WALL I'VE EVER SEEN.
NOW IT'S FALLING APART!
LOOK OUT! GRRH, IT'S STILL AFFECTING YOU!
HERE!
WHAT GOOD WILL THIS DO?
JUST DO WHAT COMES NATURAL.

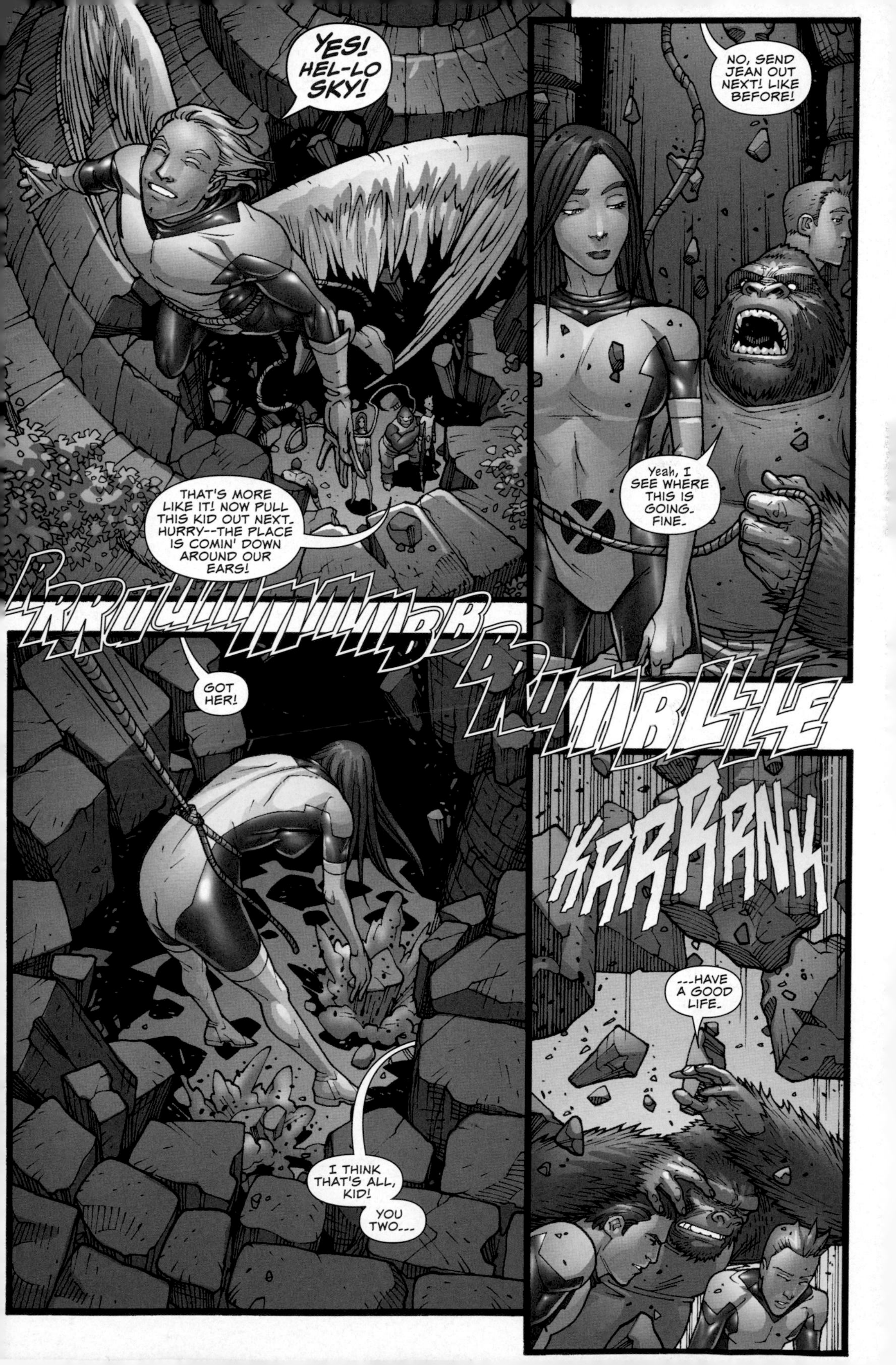
YES! HEL-LO SKY!
NO, SEND JEAN OUT NEXT! LIKE BEFORE!
Yeah, I SEE WHERE THIS IS GOING. FINE.
THAT'S MORE LIKE IT! NOW PULL THIS KID OUT NEXT. HURRY--THE PLACE IS COMIN' DOWN AROUND OUR EARS!
GOT HER!
I THINK THAT'S ALL, KID!
YOU TWO---
KRRRRNK
---HAVE A GOOD LIFE.

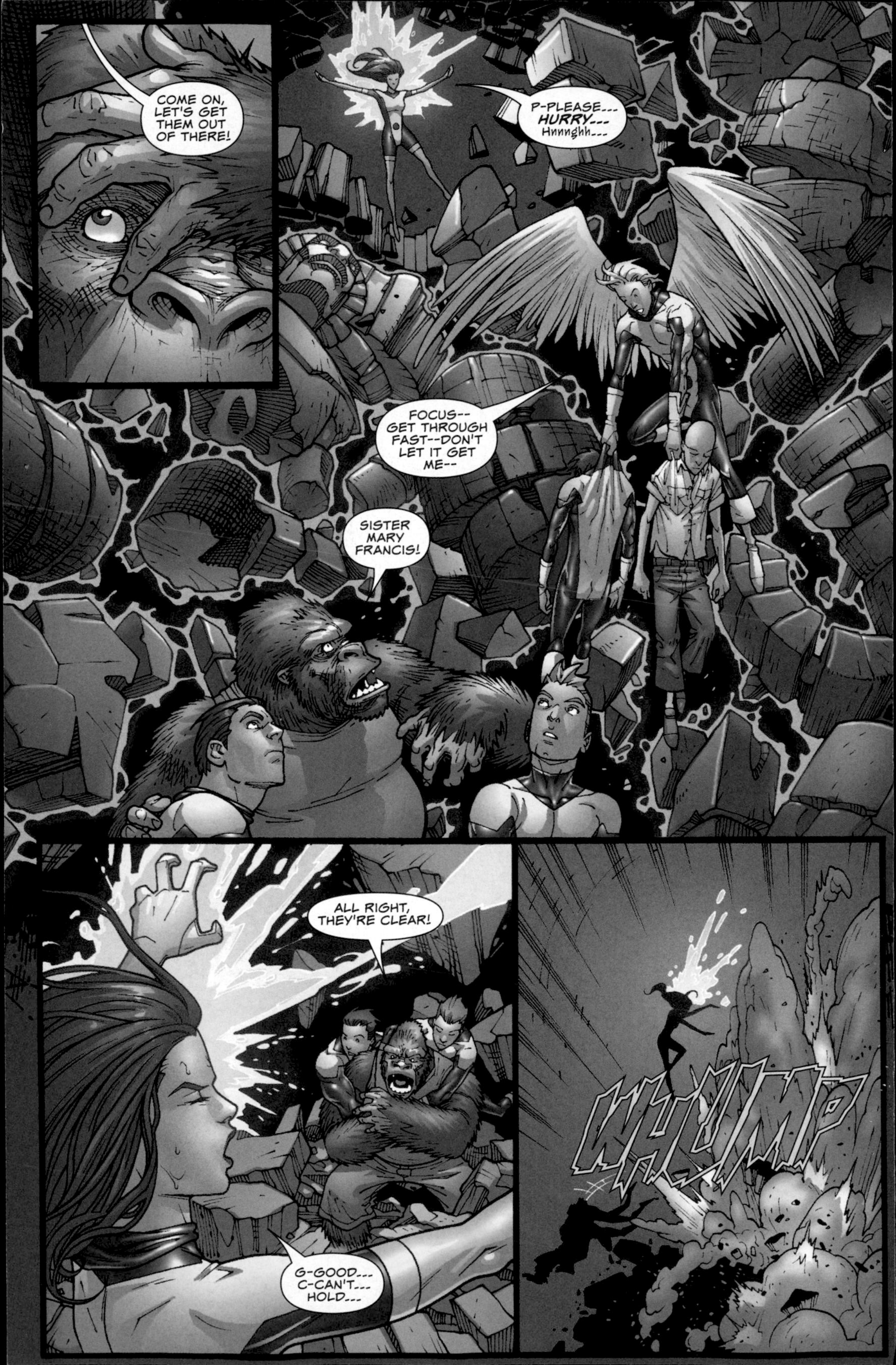
COME ON, LET'S GET THEM OUT OF THERE!
P-PLEASE--- HURRY--- Hnnnghh---
FOCUS-- GET THROUGH FAST--DON'T LET IT GET ME--
SISTER MARY FRANCIS!
ALL RIGHT, THEY'RE CLEAR!
G-GOOD--- C-CAN'T--- HOLD---
WHUMP

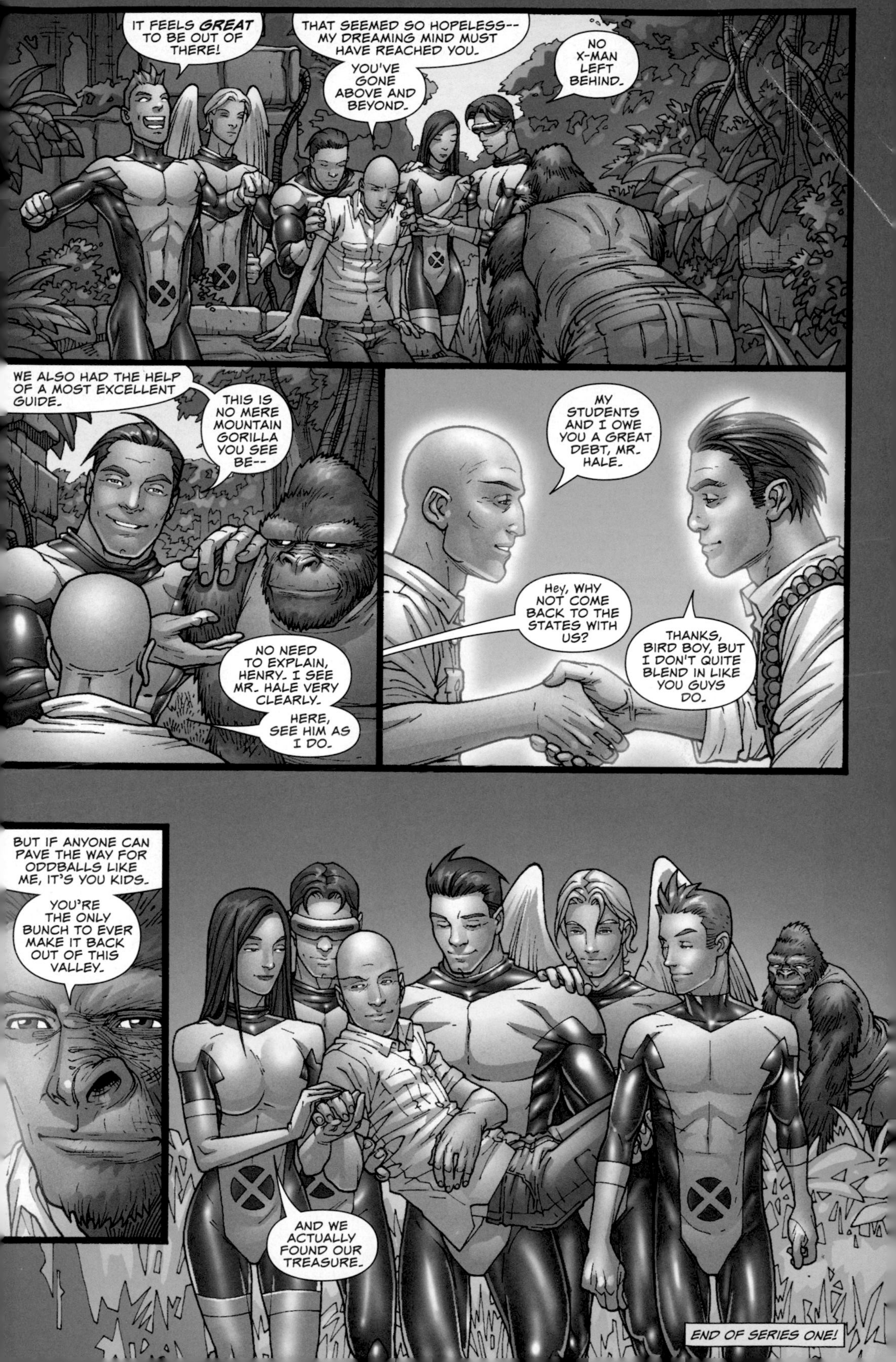
IT FEELS GREAT TO BE OUT OF THERE!
THAT SEEMED SO HOPELESS-- MY DREAMING MIND MUST HAVE REACHED YOU.
YOU'VE GONE ABOVE AND BEYOND.
NO X-MAN LEFT BEHIND.
WE ALSO HAD THE HELP OF A MOST EXCELLENT GUIDE.
THIS IS NO MERE MOUNTAIN GORILLA YOU SEE BE--
NO NEED TO EXPLAIN, HENRY. I SEE MR. HALE VERY CLEARLY.
HERE, SEE HIM AS I DO.
MY STUDENTS AND I OWE YOU A GREAT DEBT, MR. HALE.
Hey, WHY NOT COME BACK TO THE STATES WITH US?
THANKS, BIRD BOY, BUT I DON'T QUITE BLEND IN LIKE YOU GUYS DO.
BUT IF ANYONE CAN PAVE THE WAY FOR ODDBALLS LIKE ME, IT'S YOU KIDS.
YOU'RE THE ONLY BUNCH TO EVER MAKE IT BACK OUT OF THIS VALLEY.
AND WE ACTUALLY FOUND OUR TREASURE.
END OF SERIES ONE!

XAVIER'S SCHOOL FOR GIFTED YOUNGSTERS

PROPERTY OF:

KEN HALE,
Bachelor of Science in Kickin' Butt

HEADMASTER

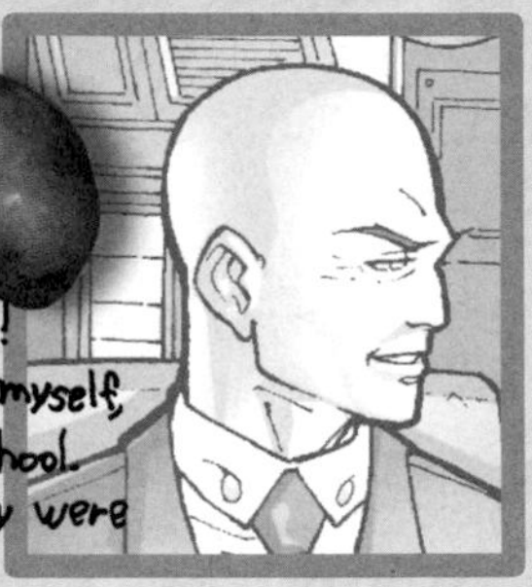

PROFESSOR CHARLES XAVIER

Hey, the kids sent me a yearbook--nice! Always thought about going to college myself, but I could barely sit still through high school. I guess I learned some stuff while they were here. Does that make me an X-Ape?

The Professor was pretty wiped out when we met, so I didn't get a real take on him. But he seemed okay for an egghead.

This guy is wound a little tight, but for a kid, he's all business on a mission, and I like that. Reminds me of my old boss, Jimmy Woo. (if Jimmy could knock down trees with his eyes. In that respect, he reminds me of that nutty robot.)

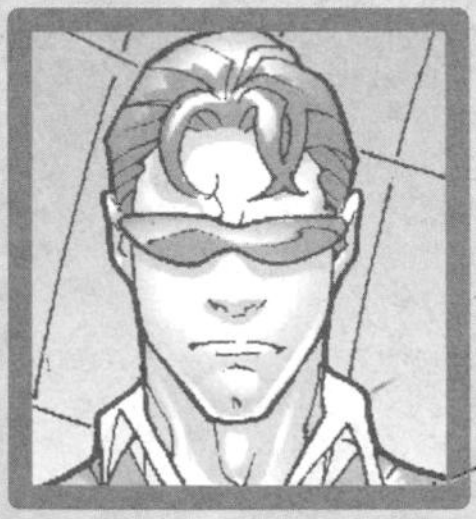

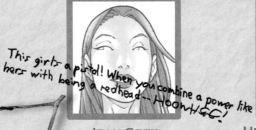

SCOTT SUMMERS
"CYCLOPS"

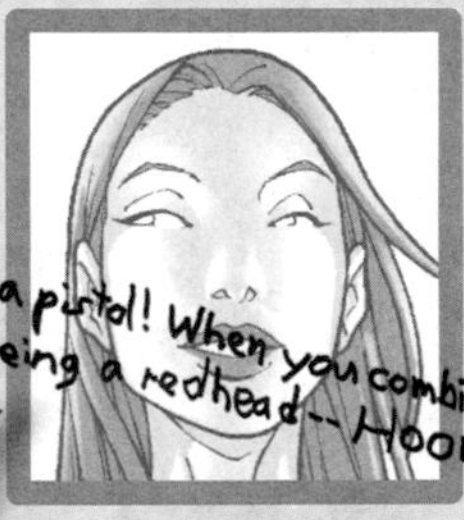

This girl's a pistol! When you combine a power like hers with being a redhead--HOOWHEE!

JEAN GREY
"MARVEL GIRL"

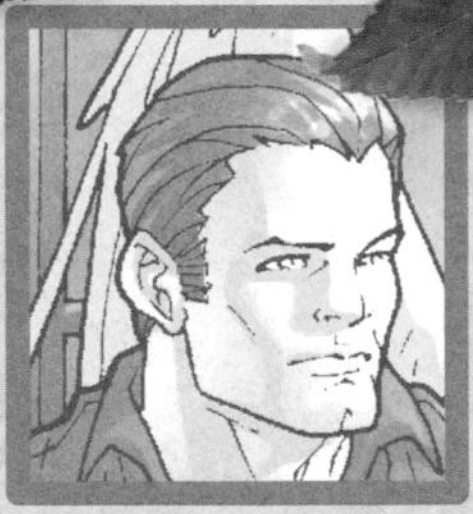

HENRY "HANK" MCCOY
"BEAST"

Needs to pipe down some, but he's a good kid. Got a whole lecture on African flora and fauna while we were out, like I needed it. Least I know the real names for things now.

See, if I could have picked my curse, it would have been to be more like a bird than a gorilla. Man, it must be great to fly without a plane!

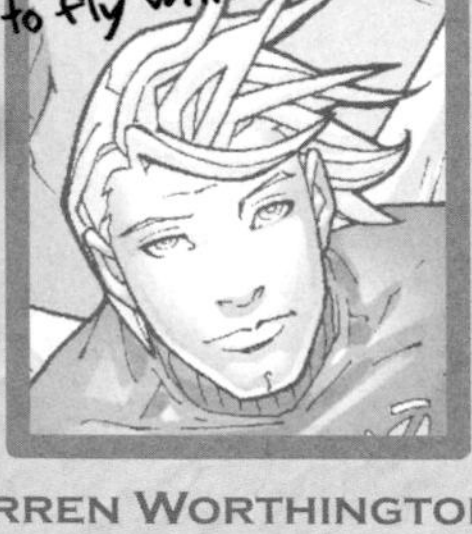

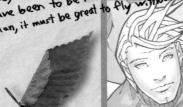

WARREN WORTHINGTON III
"ANGEL"

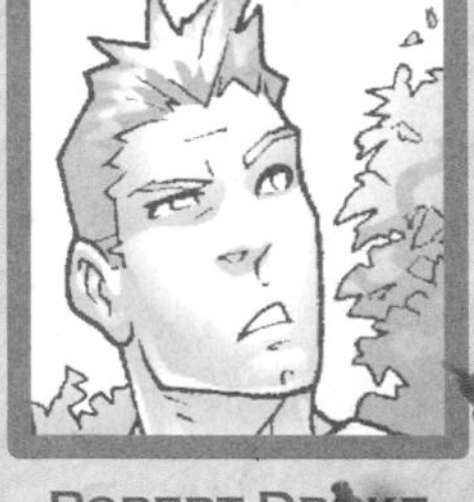

ROBERT DRAKE
"ICEMAN"

A couple of times I was ready to throw this kid to the lions, but I gotta admit, I wasn't any better when I was his age. Heck, worse.

SPECIAL

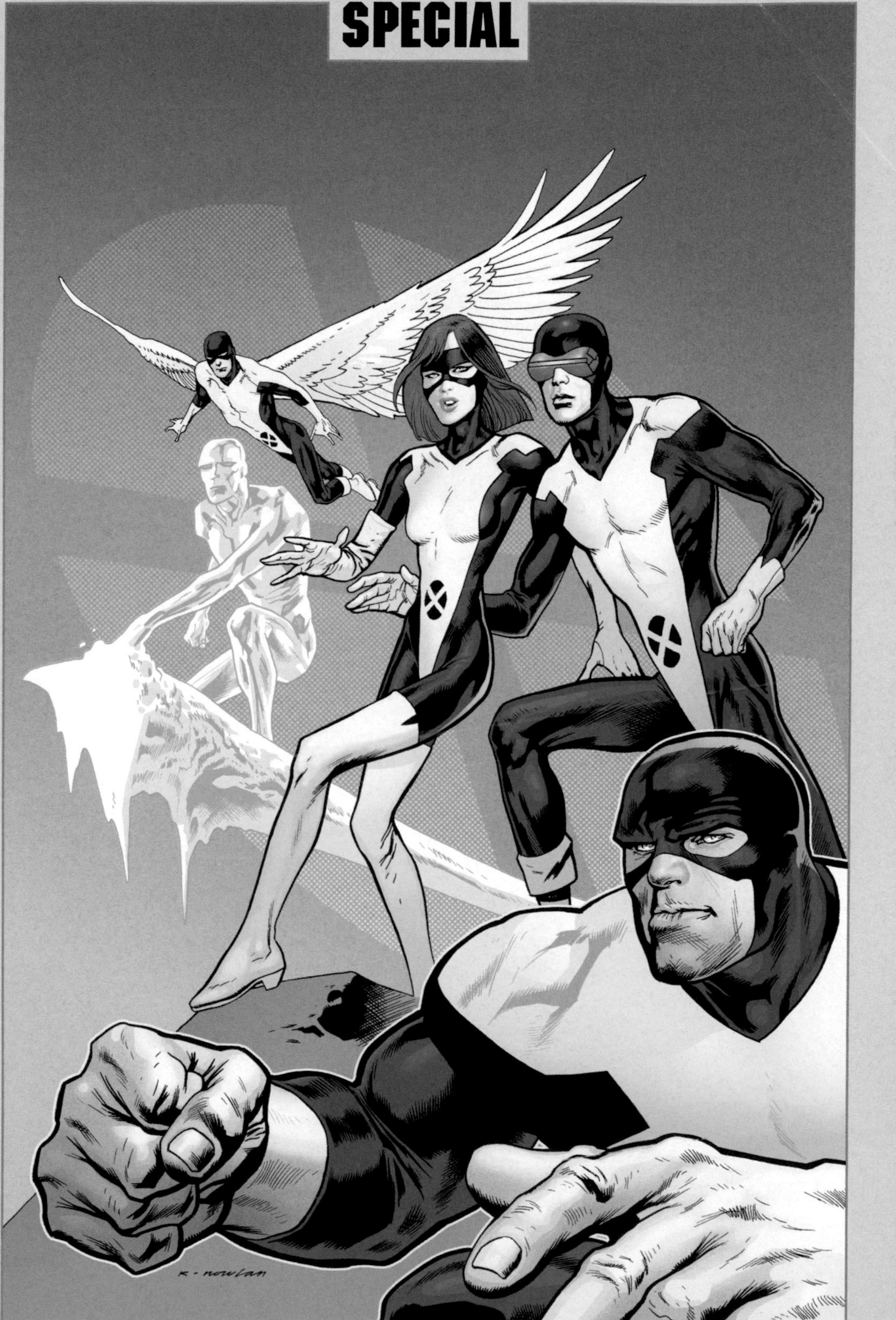
K. Nowlan

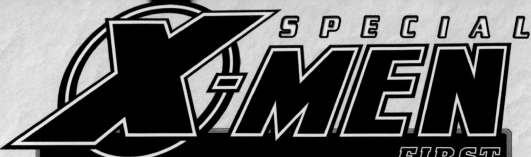

X-MEN SPECIAL
FIRST CLASS

"THE MUSEUM OF ODDITIES"
WRITTEN BY JEFF PARKER
ART AND LETTERING BY KEVIN NOWLAN

"THE SOUL OF A POET"
WRITTEN BY JEFF PARKER
PENCILS BY NICK DRAGOTTA
INKS BY MIKE ALLRED
COLORS BY LAURA ALLRED
LETTERING BY BLAMBOT'S NATE PIEKOS

"A GIRL AND HER DRAGON"
WRITTEN BY JEFF PARKER
ART BY PAUL SMITH
COLOR BY PETE PANTAZIS
LETTERING BY BLAMBOT'S NATE PIEKOS

"THE KEY"
"MEN FEAR THE BLOB"
"THE MENTAL MIGHT OF MARVEL GIRL"
WRITTEN BY JEFF PARKER
ART AND LETTERING BY COLLEEN COOVER

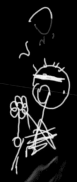

COVER BY KEVIN NOWLAN
PRODUCTION -- BRAD JOHANSEN
ASSISTANT EDITOR - NATHAN COSBY
EDITOR - MARK PANICCIA
EDITOR IN CHIEF - JOE QUESADA
PUBLISHER - DAN BUCKLEY

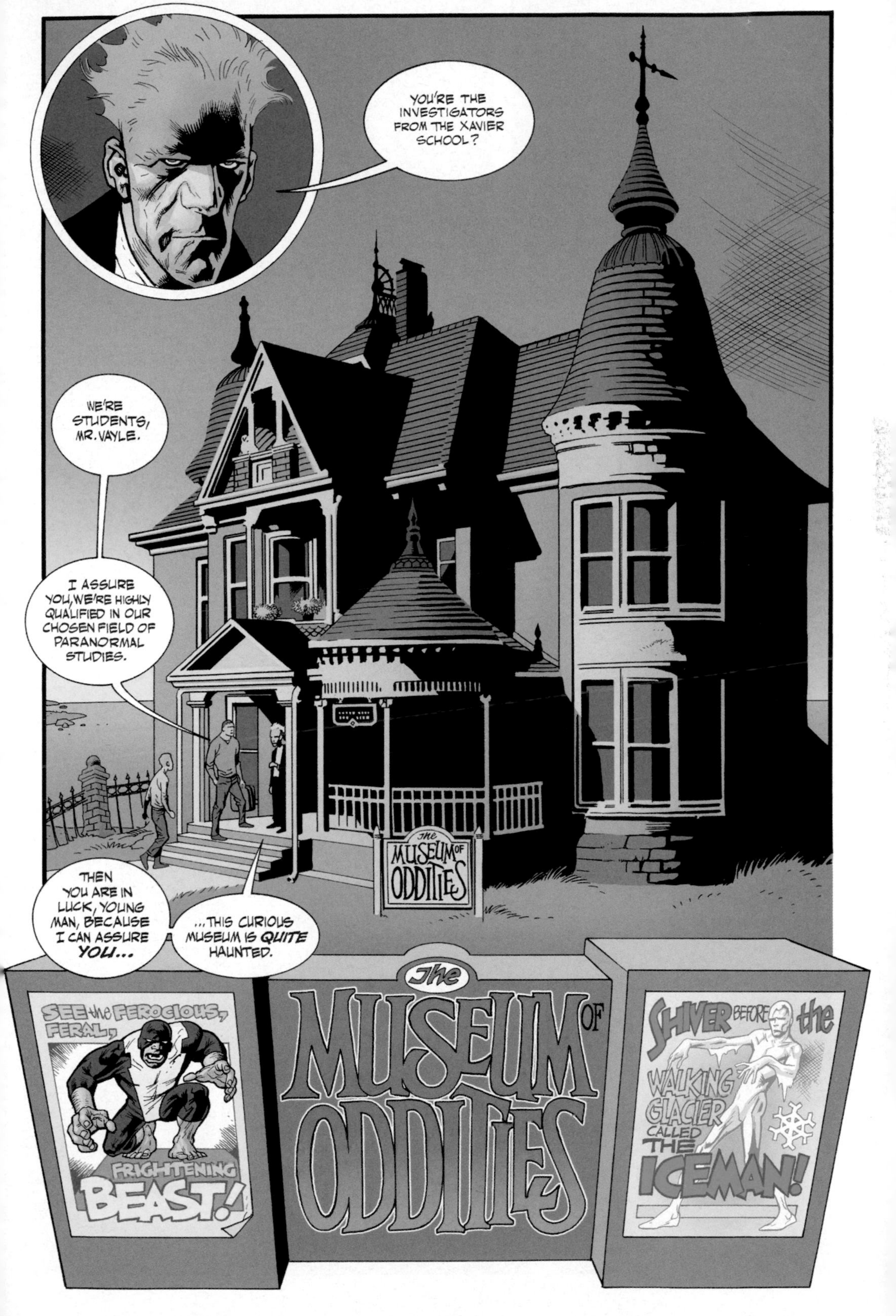
YOU'RE THE INVESTIGATORS FROM THE XAVIER SCHOOL?
WE'RE STUDENTS, MR. VAYLE.
I ASSURE YOU, WE'RE HIGHLY QUALIFIED IN OUR CHOSEN FIELD OF PARANORMAL STUDIES.
THEN YOU ARE IN LUCK, YOUNG MAN, BECAUSE I CAN ASSURE YOU...
...THIS CURIOUS MUSEUM IS QUITE HAUNTED.
The MUSEUM OF ODDITIES
SEE the FEROCIOUS, FERAL, FRIGHTENING BEAST!
The MUSEUM OF ODDITIES
SHIVER BEFORE the WALKING GLACIER CALLED THE ICEMAN!

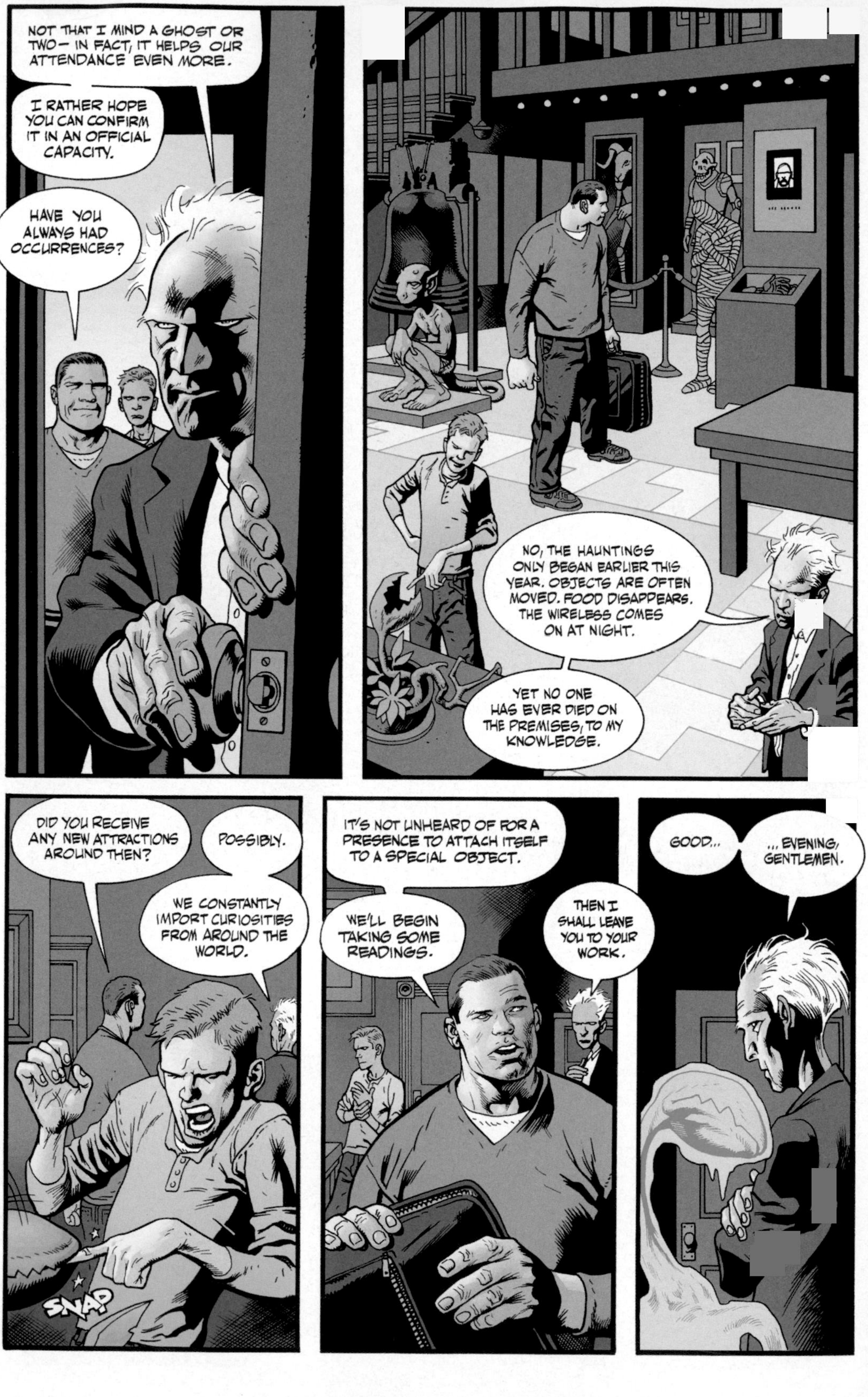
NOT THAT I MIND A GHOST OR TWO— IN FACT, IT HELPS OUR ATTENDANCE EVEN MORE.
I RATHER HOPE YOU CAN CONFIRM IT IN AN OFFICIAL CAPACITY.
HAVE YOU ALWAYS HAD OCCURRENCES?
NO, THE HAUNTINGS ONLY BEGAN EARLIER THIS YEAR. OBJECTS ARE OFTEN MOVED. FOOD DISAPPEARS. THE WIRELESS COMES ON AT NIGHT.
YET NO ONE HAS EVER DIED ON THE PREMISES, TO MY KNOWLEDGE.
DID YOU RECEIVE ANY NEW ATTRACTIONS AROUND THEN?
POSSIBLY.
WE CONSTANTLY IMPORT CURIOSITIES FROM AROUND THE WORLD.
SNAP
IT'S NOT UNHEARD OF FOR A PRESENCE TO ATTACH ITSELF TO A SPECIAL OBJECT.
WE'LL BEGIN TAKING SOME READINGS.
THEN I SHALL LEAVE YOU TO YOUR WORK.
GOOD...
...EVENING, GENTLEMEN.

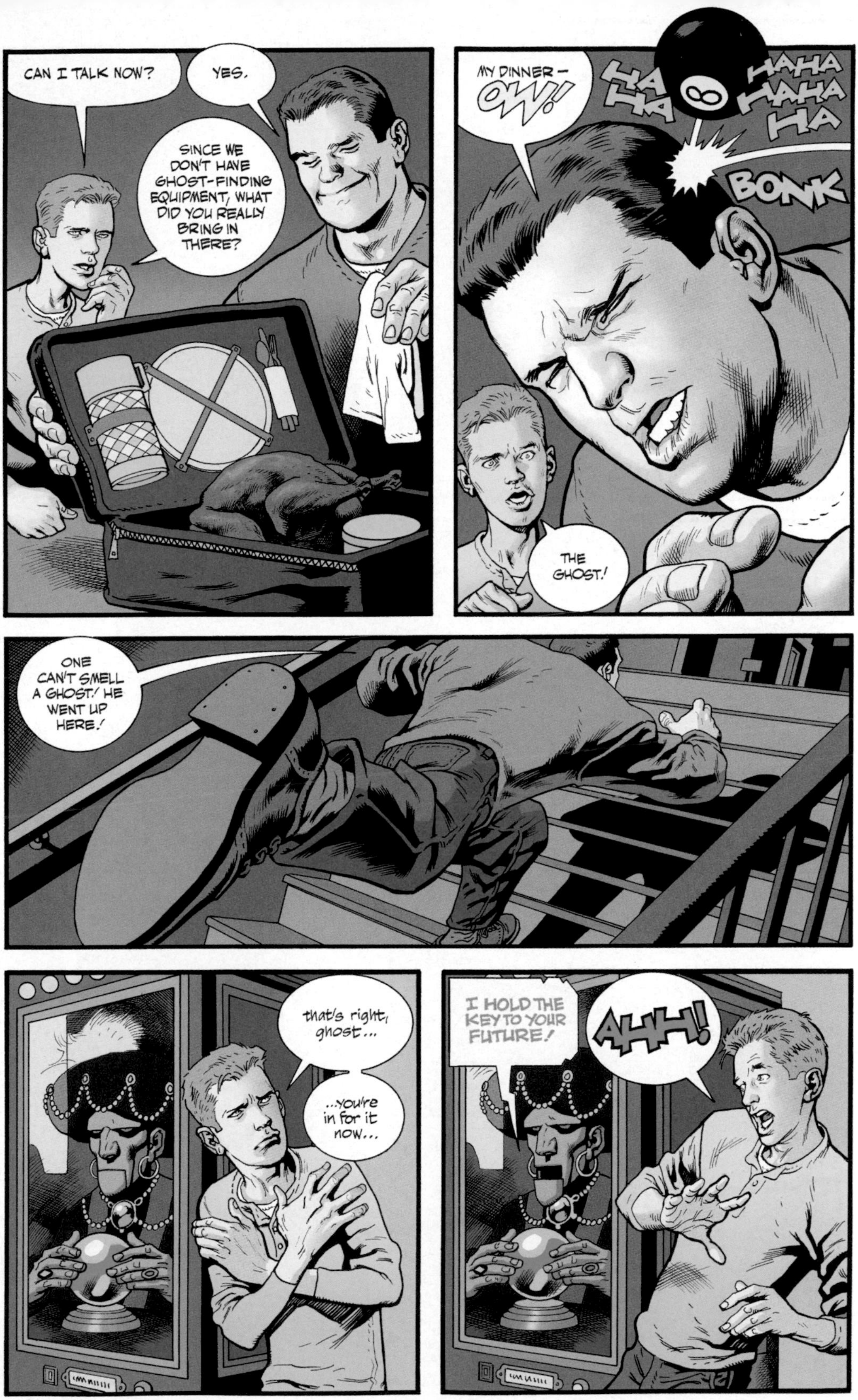
CAN I TALK NOW?
YES.
SINCE WE DON'T HAVE GHOST-FINDING EQUIPMENT, WHAT DID YOU REALLY BRING IN THERE?
MY DINNER – OW!
HA HA
HAHA HAHA HA
BONK
THE GHOST!
ONE CAN'T SMELL A GHOST! HE WENT UP HERE!
that's right, ghost...
...you're in for it now...
I HOLD THE KEY TO YOUR FUTURE!
AHH!

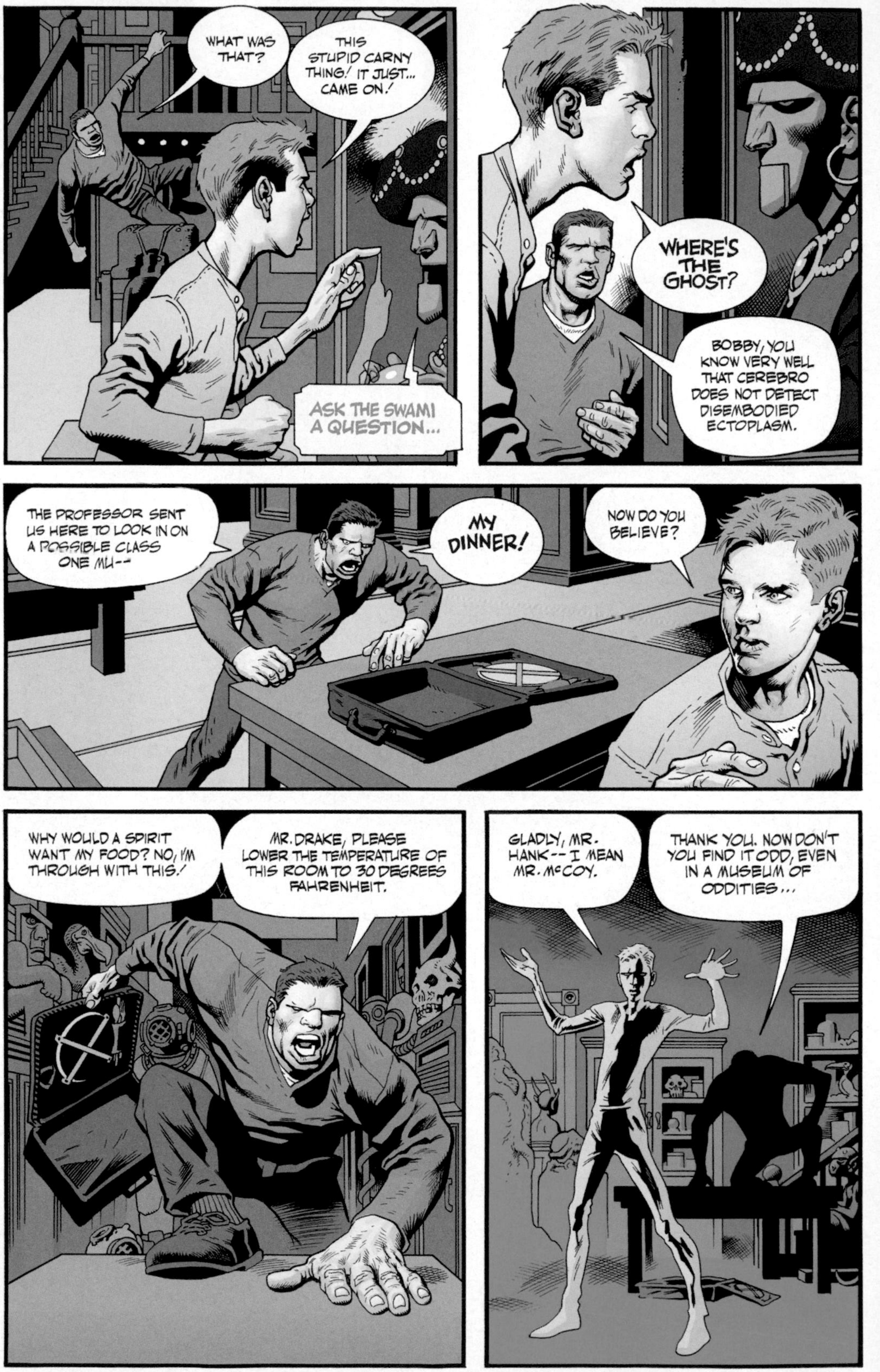

WHAT WAS THAT?
THIS STUPID CARNY THING! IT JUST... CAME ON!
ASK THE SWAMI A QUESTION...
WHERE'S THE GHOST?
BOBBY, YOU KNOW VERY WELL THAT CEREBRO DOES NOT DETECT DISEMBODIED ECTOPLASM.
THE PROFESSOR SENT US HERE TO LOOK IN ON A POSSIBLE CLASS ONE MU--
MY DINNER!
NOW DO YOU BELIEVE?
WHY WOULD A SPIRIT WANT MY FOOD? NO, I'M THROUGH WITH THIS!
MR. DRAKE, PLEASE LOWER THE TEMPERATURE OF THIS ROOM TO 30 DEGREES FAHRENHEIT.
GLADLY, MR. HANK-- I MEAN MR. McCOY.
THANK YOU. NOW DON'T YOU FIND IT ODD, EVEN IN A MUSEUM OF ODDITIES...

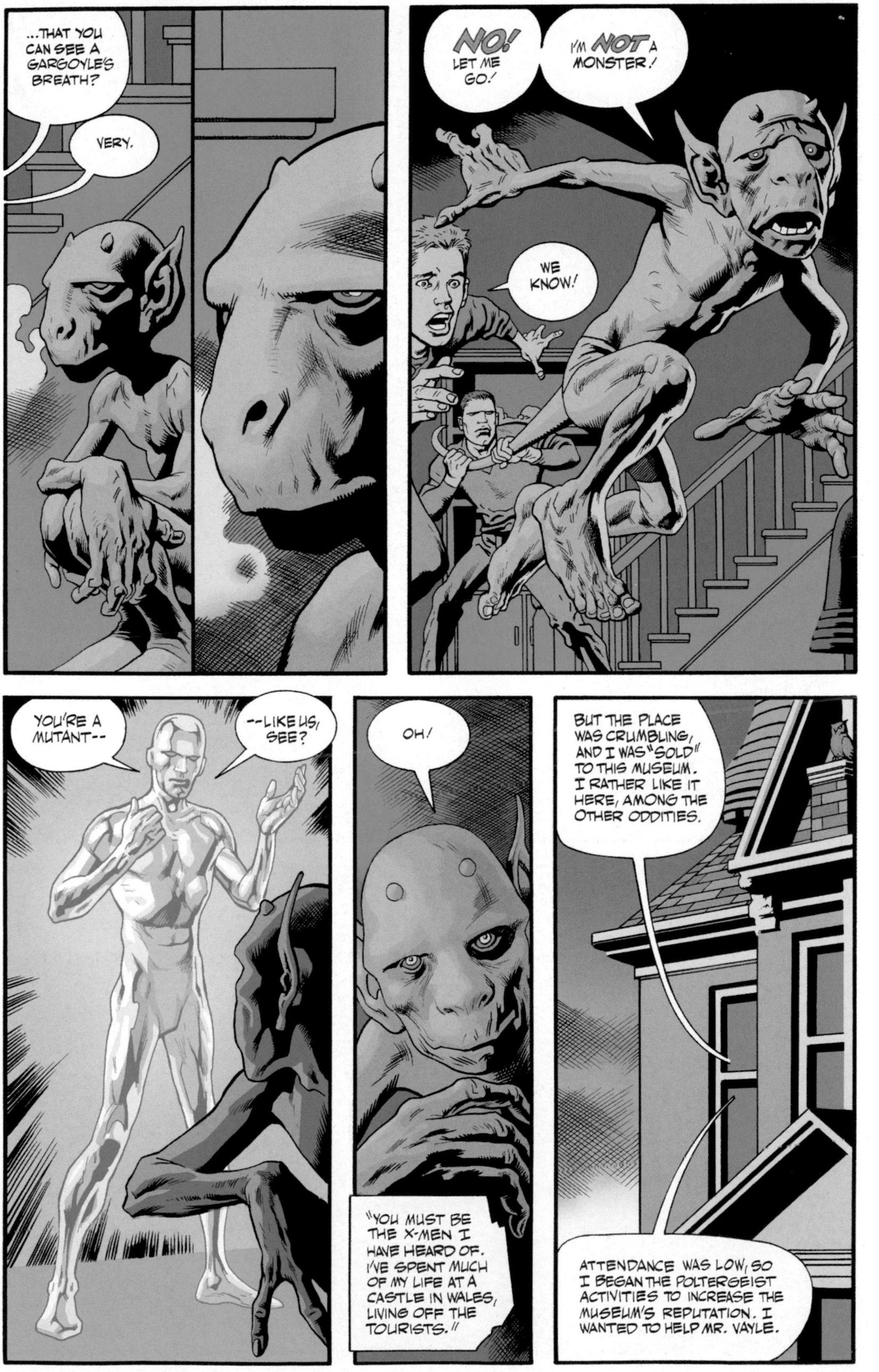

...THAT YOU CAN SEE A GARGOYLE'S BREATH?
VERY.
NO! LET ME GO!
I'M NOT A MONSTER!
WE KNOW!
YOU'RE A MUTANT--
--LIKE US, SEE?
OH!
"YOU MUST BE THE X-MEN I HAVE HEARD OF. I'VE SPENT MUCH OF MY LIFE AT A CASTLE IN WALES, LIVING OFF THE TOURISTS."
BUT THE PLACE WAS CRUMBLING, AND I WAS "SOLD" TO THIS MUSEUM. I RATHER LIKE IT HERE, AMONG THE OTHER ODDITIES.
ATTENDANCE WAS LOW, SO I BEGAN THE POLTERGEIST ACTIVITIES TO INCREASE THE MUSEUM'S REPUTATION. I WANTED TO HELP MR. VAYLE.

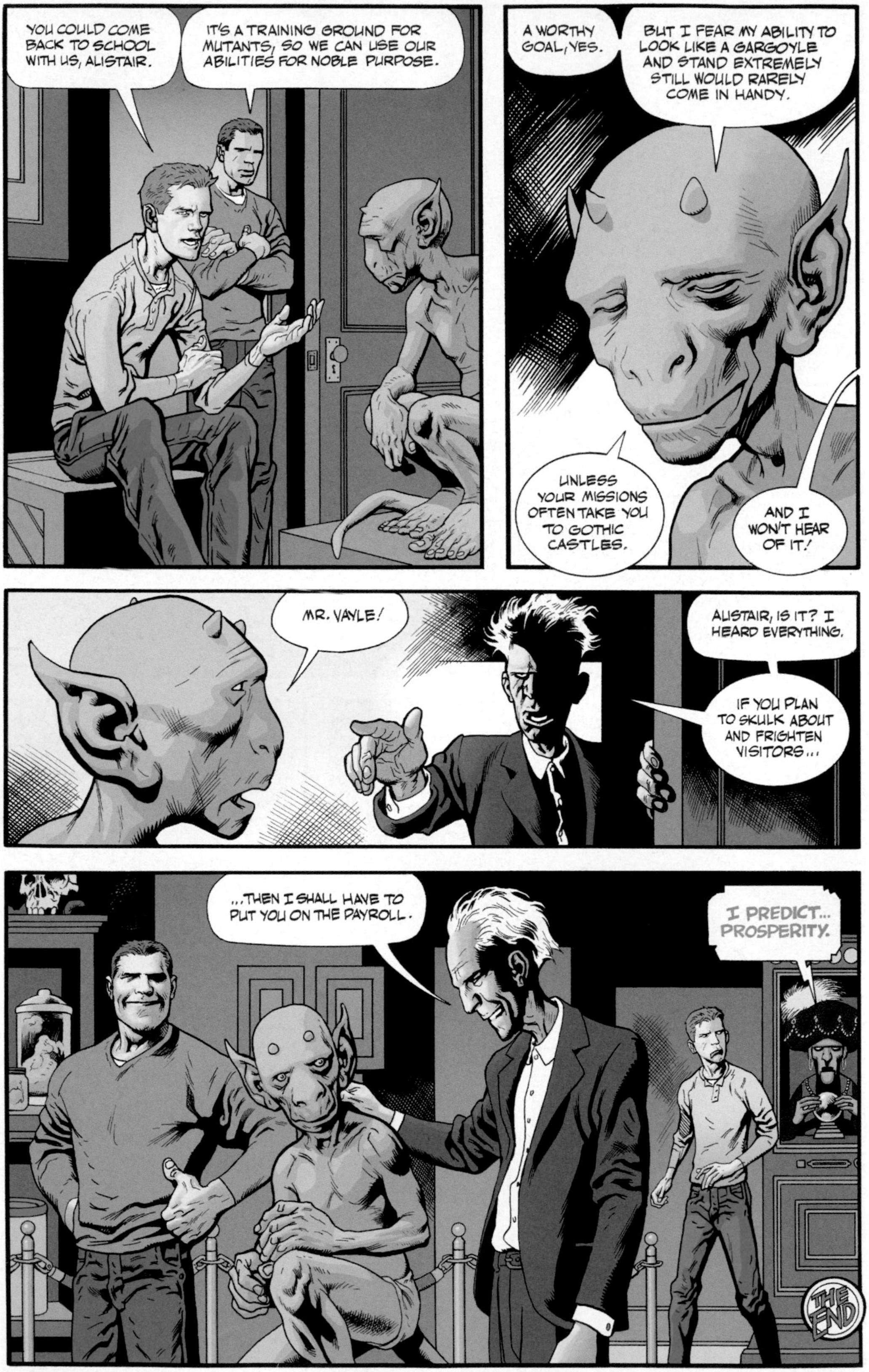
YOU COULD COME BACK TO SCHOOL WITH US, ALISTAIR.
IT'S A TRAINING GROUND FOR MUTANTS, SO WE CAN USE OUR ABILITIES FOR NOBLE PURPOSE.
A WORTHY GOAL, YES.
BUT I FEAR MY ABILITY TO LOOK LIKE A GARGOYLE AND STAND EXTREMELY STILL WOULD RARELY COME IN HANDY.
UNLESS YOUR MISSIONS OFTEN TAKE YOU TO GOTHIC CASTLES.
AND I WON'T HEAR OF IT!
MR. VAYLE!
ALISTAIR, IS IT? I HEARD EVERYTHING.
IF YOU PLAN TO SKULK ABOUT AND FRIGHTEN VISITORS...
...THEN I SHALL HAVE TO PUT YOU ON THE PAYROLL.
I PREDICT... PROSPERITY.
THE END

MAGNETO
IN "THE KEY"

This is the cafe Xavier's young mutants frequent.

And here I shall persuade them to join *MY* select group of mutants, the *BROTHERHOOD!*

COFFEE A GO GO

Blast. I've been here for *hours.*

They must be out doing "good". Now even I, as *homo superior,* must bow to the whims of nature.

The bathroom is locked.

I know! But fat chance getting these snotty hipster baristas to give ya the key!

Yeah, I think the college guy is into me. Gives me chills sometimes, though.

RESTROOM KEY

TIPS

How...?

Simplicity itself...

When you're the LORD OF MAGNETISM!

MEN

EMPLOYEES MUST WASH HANDS
LAVOS LOS MANOS

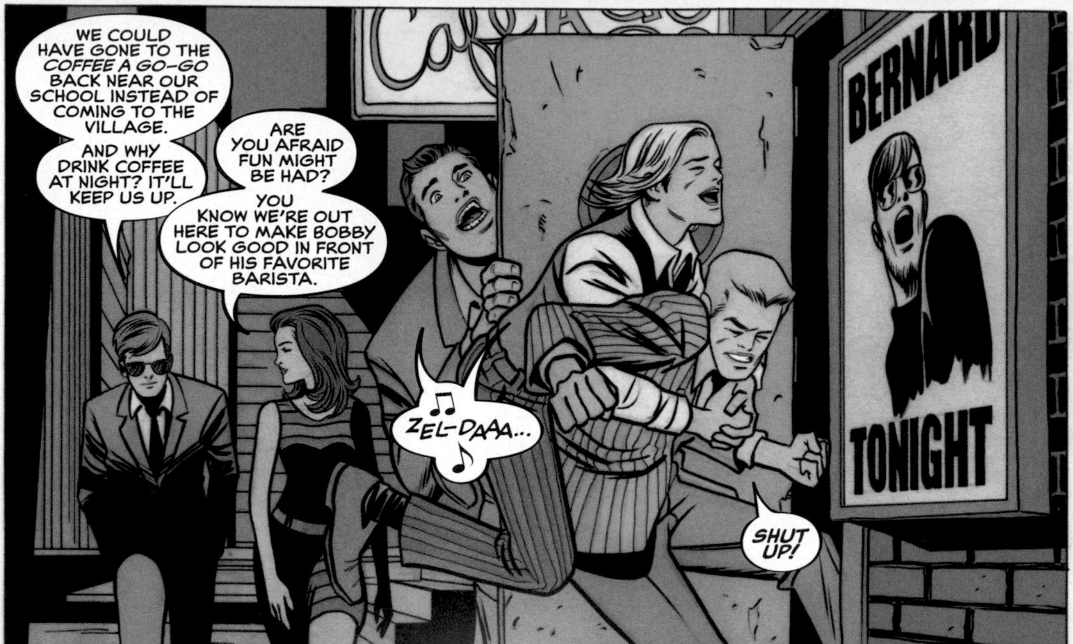
WE COULD HAVE GONE TO THE *COFFEE A GO-GO* BACK NEAR OUR SCHOOL INSTEAD OF COMING TO THE VILLAGE.
AND WHY DRINK COFFEE AT NIGHT? IT'LL KEEP US UP.
ARE YOU AFRAID FUN MIGHT BE HAD?
YOU KNOW WE'RE OUT HERE TO MAKE BOBBY LOOK GOOD IN FRONT OF HIS FAVORITE BARISTA.
ZEL-DAAA...
SHUT UP!
BERNARD
TONIGHT

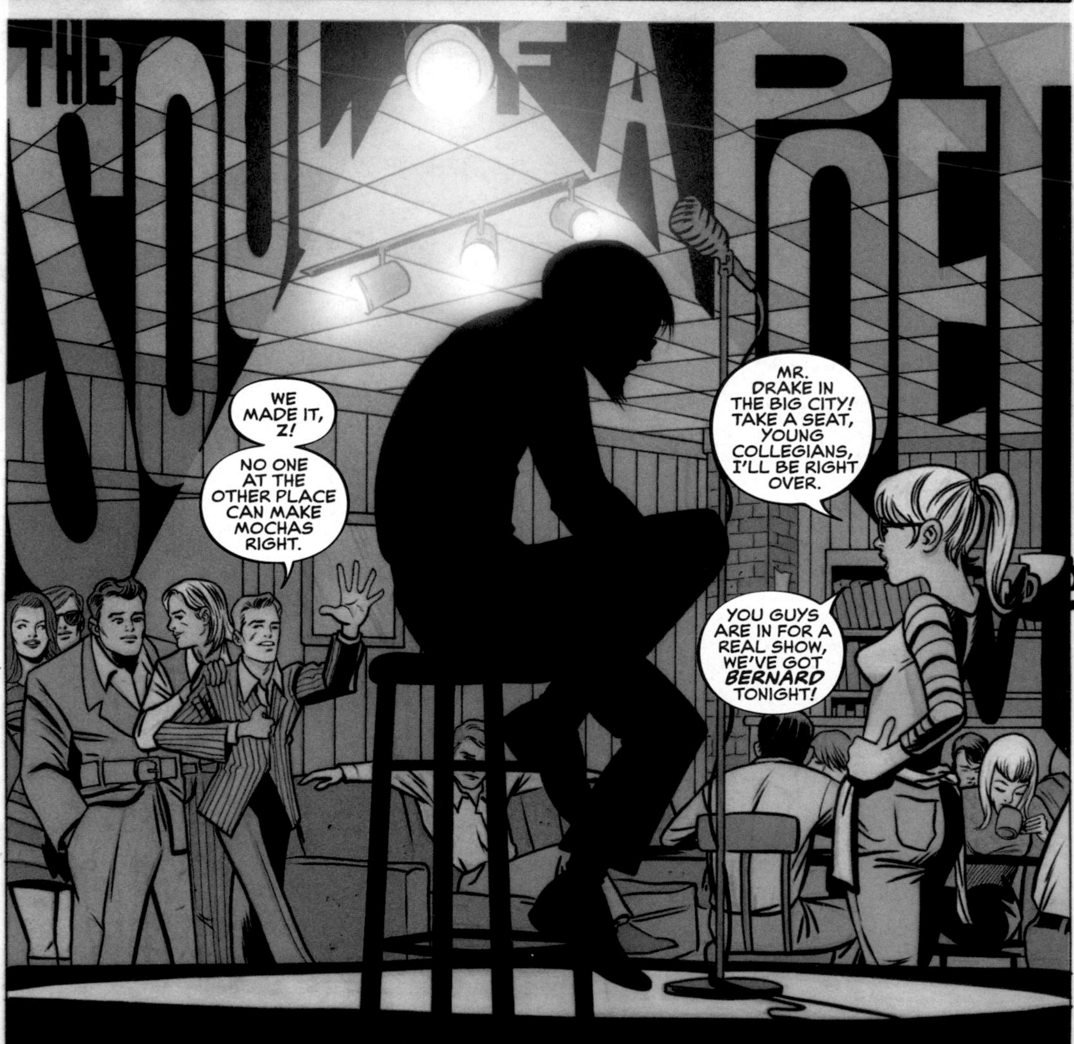
THE SOUL OF A POET
WE MADE IT, Z!
NO ONE AT THE OTHER PLACE CAN MAKE MOCHAS RIGHT.
MR. DRAKE IN THE BIG CITY! TAKE A SEAT, YOUNG COLLEGIANS, I'LL BE RIGHT OVER.
YOU GUYS ARE IN FOR A REAL SHOW, WE'VE GOT ***BERNARD*** TONIGHT!

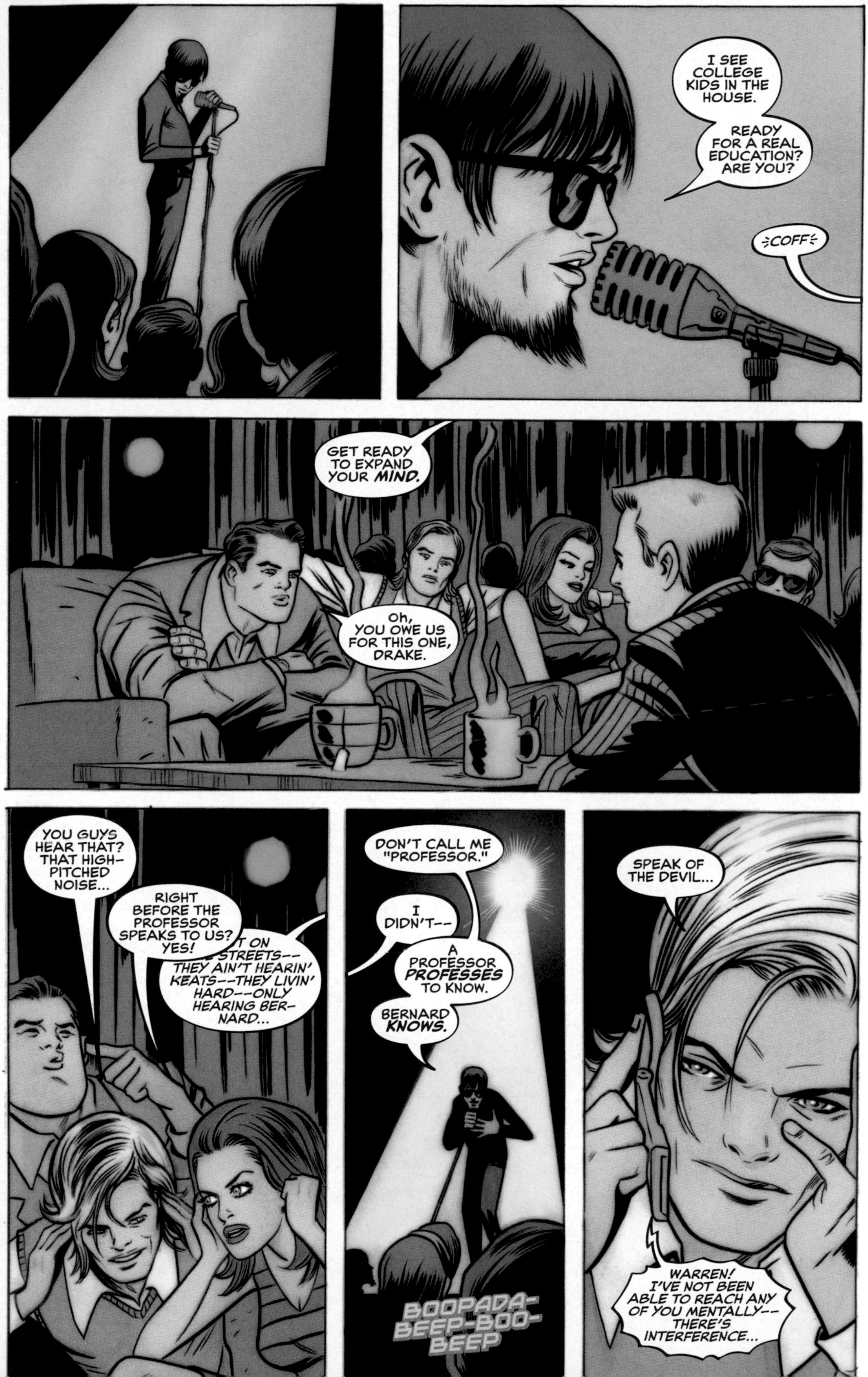
I SEE COLLEGE KIDS IN THE HOUSE.
READY FOR A REAL EDUCATION? ARE YOU?
COFF
GET READY TO EXPAND YOUR MIND.
Oh, YOU OWE US FOR THIS ONE, DRAKE.
YOU GUYS HEAR THAT? THAT HIGH-PITCHED NOISE...
RIGHT BEFORE THE PROFESSOR SPEAKS TO US? YES!
THEY AIN'T HEARIN' KEATS--THEY LIVIN' HARD--ONLY HEARING BER-NARD...
DON'T CALL ME "PROFESSOR."
I DIDN'T--
A PROFESSOR PROFESSES TO KNOW.
BERNARD KNOWS.
BOOPADA-BEEP-BOO-BEEP
SPEAK OF THE DEVIL...
WARREN! I'VE NOT BEEN ABLE TO REACH ANY OF YOU MENTALLY--THERE'S INTERFERENCE...

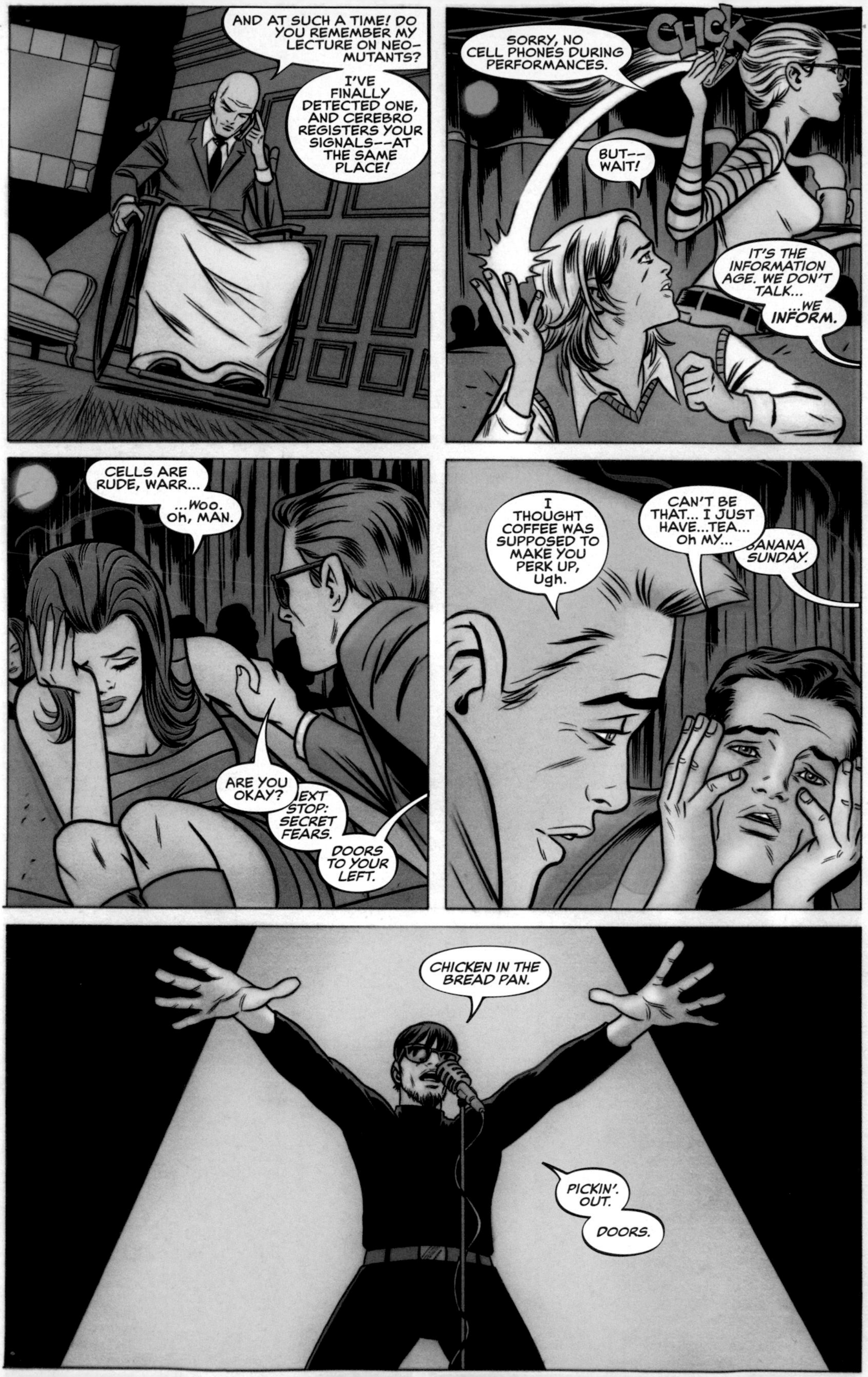
AND AT SUCH A TIME! DO YOU REMEMBER MY LECTURE ON NEO-MUTANTS?
I'VE FINALLY DETECTED ONE, AND CEREBRO REGISTERS YOUR SIGNALS--AT THE SAME PLACE!
CLICK
SORRY, NO CELL PHONES DURING PERFORMANCES.
BUT-- WAIT!
IT'S THE INFORMATION AGE. WE DON'T TALK... ...WE INFORM.
CELLS ARE RUDE, WARR...
...WOO. Oh, MAN.
ARE YOU OKAY?
NEXT STOP: SECRET FEARS.
DOORS TO YOUR LEFT.
I THOUGHT COFFEE WAS SUPPOSED TO MAKE YOU PERK UP, Ugh.
CAN'T BE THAT... I JUST HAVE...TEA... Oh MY...
BANANA SUNDAY.
CHICKEN IN THE BREAD PAN.
PICKIN'. OUT.
DOORS.

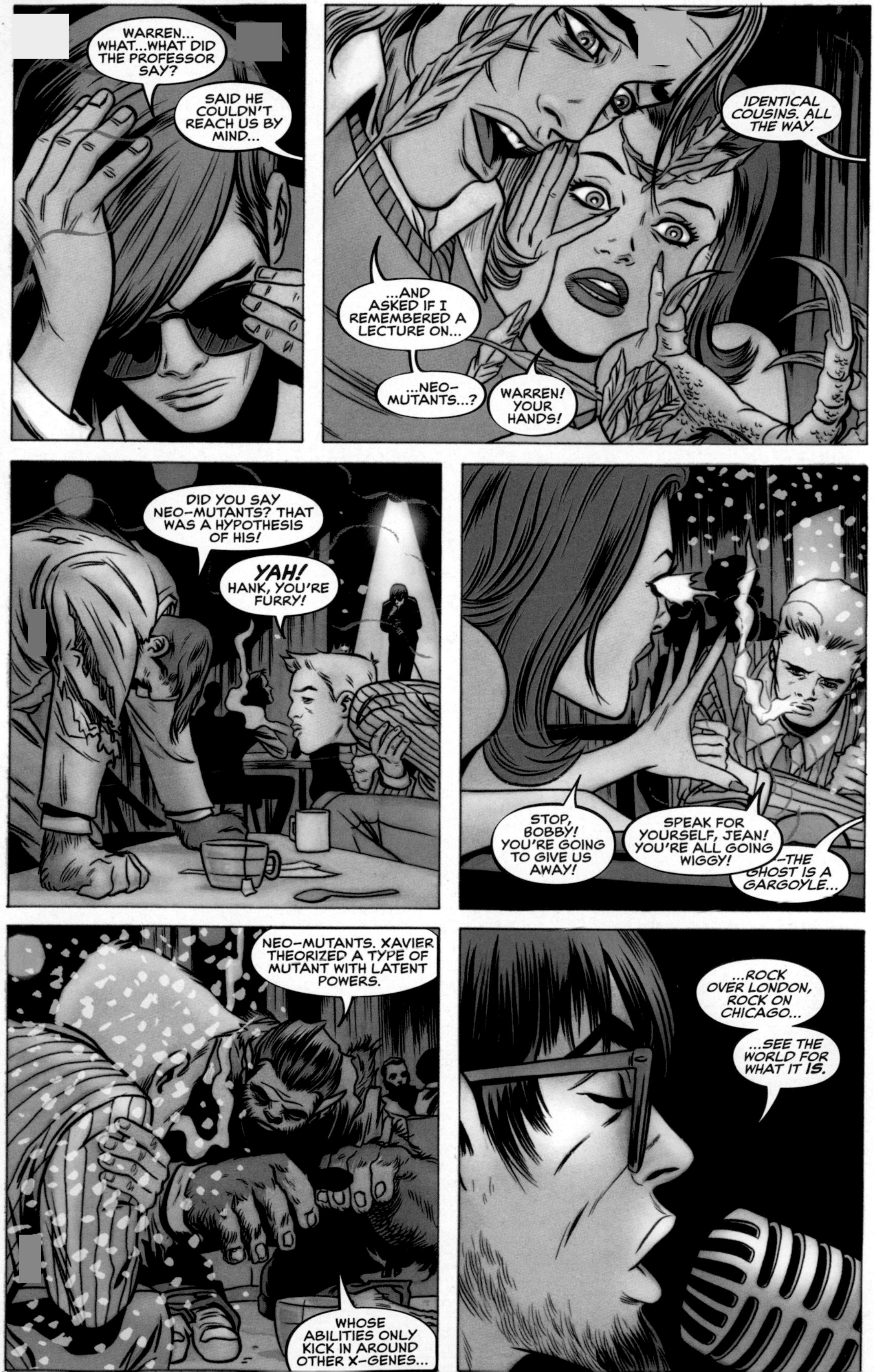

WARREN... WHAT...WHAT DID THE PROFESSOR SAY?
SAID HE COULDN'T REACH US BY MIND...
IDENTICAL COUSINS. ALL THE WAY.
...AND ASKED IF I REMEMBERED A LECTURE ON...
...NEO-MUTANTS...?
WARREN! YOUR HANDS!
DID YOU SAY NEO-MUTANTS? THAT WAS A HYPOTHESIS OF HIS!
YAH! HANK, YOU'RE FURRY!
STOP, BOBBY! YOU'RE GOING TO GIVE US AWAY!
SPEAK FOR YOURSELF, JEAN! YOU'RE ALL GOING WIGGY!
—THE GHOST IS A GARGOYLE...
NEO-MUTANTS. XAVIER THEORIZED A TYPE OF MUTANT WITH LATENT POWERS.
WHOSE ABILITIES ONLY KICK IN AROUND OTHER X-GENES...
...ROCK OVER LONDON, ROCK ON CHICAGO...
...SEE THE WORLD FOR WHAT IT IS.

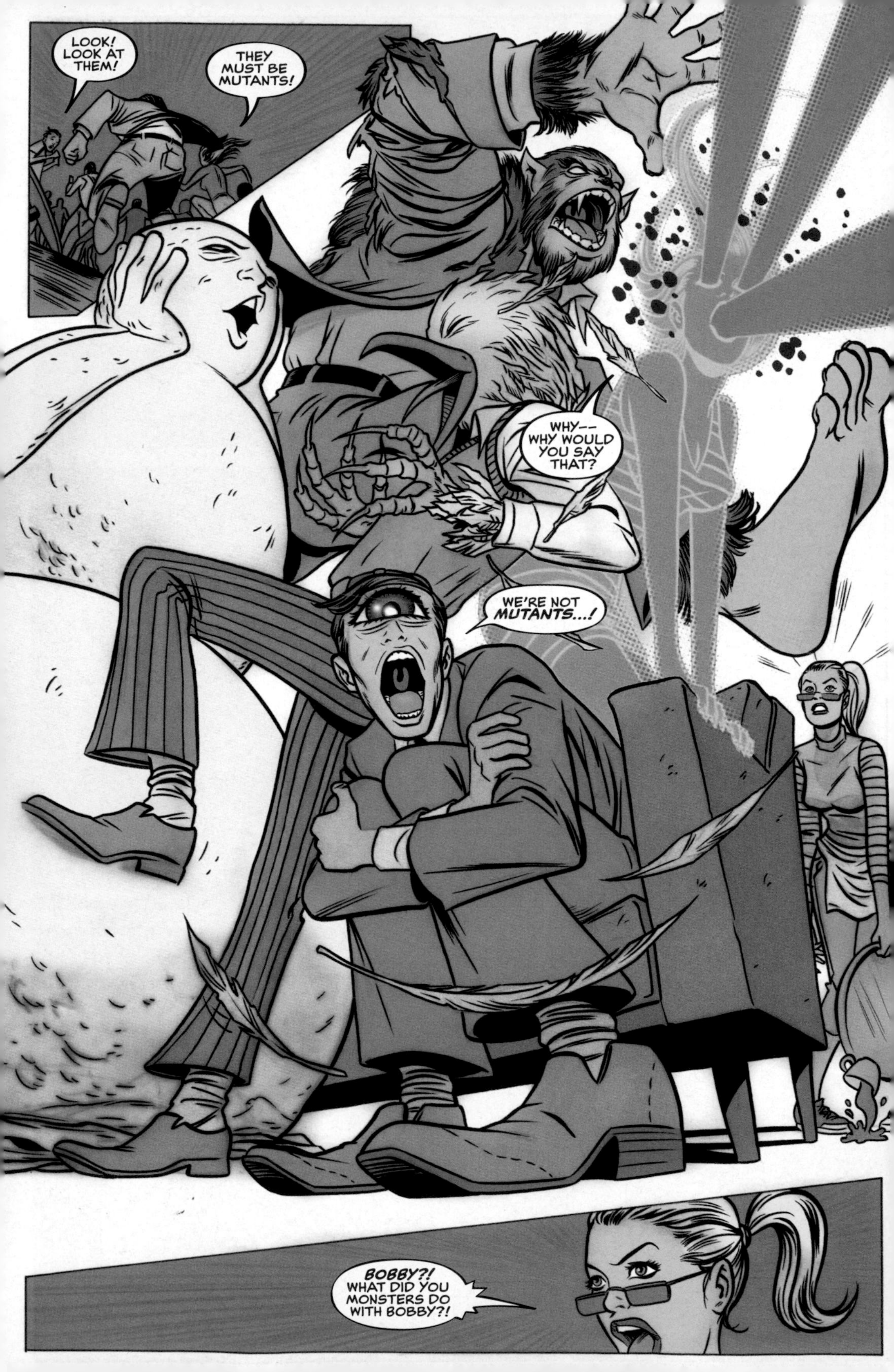
LOOK! LOOK AT THEM!
THEY MUST BE MUTANTS!
WHY-- WHY WOULD YOU SAY THAT?
WE'RE NOT MUTANTS...!
BOBBY?! WHAT DID YOU MONSTERS DO WITH BOBBY?!

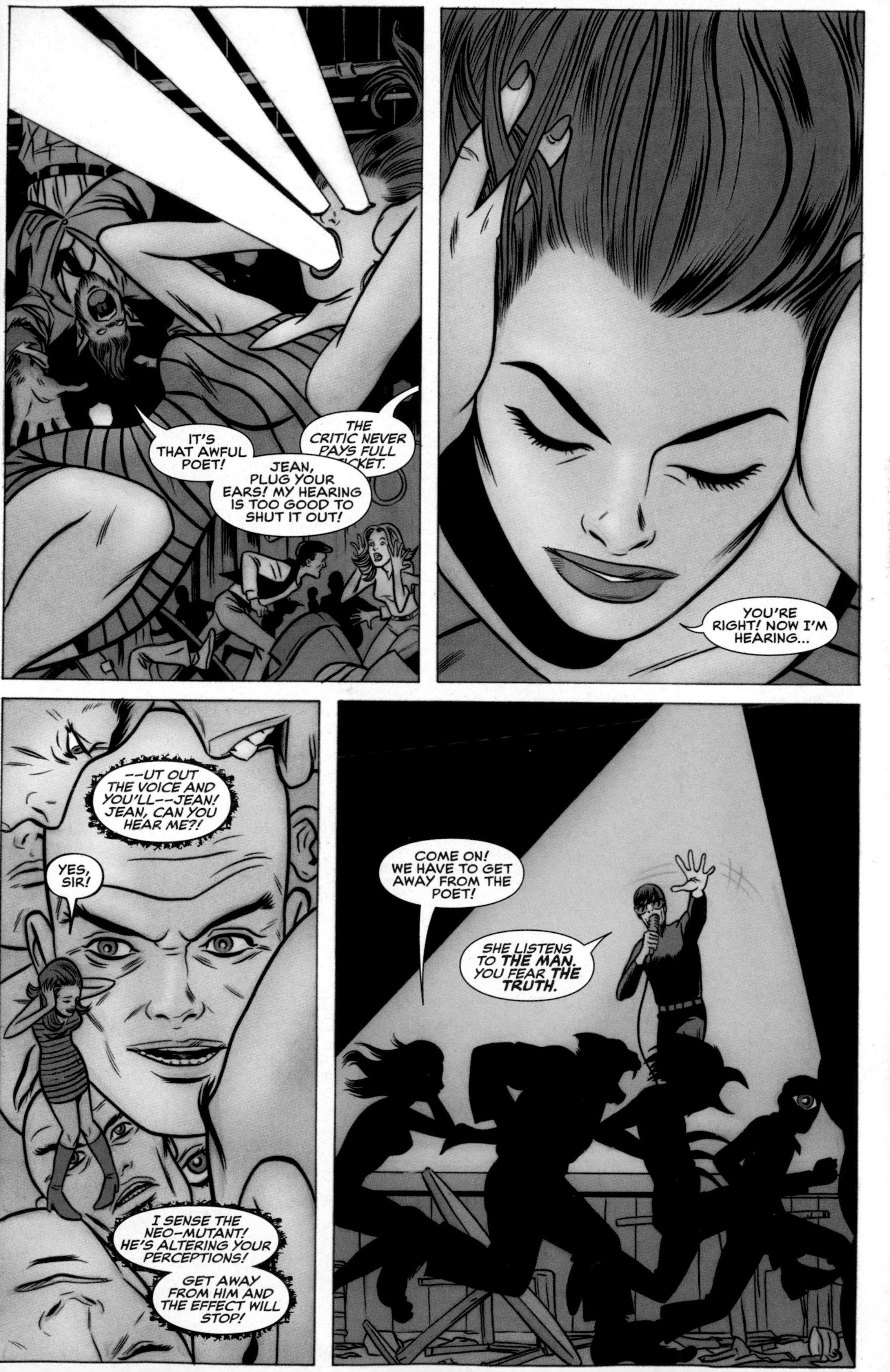
IT'S THAT AWFUL POET!
THE CRITIC NEVER PAYS FULL
JEAN, PLUG YOUR EARS! MY HEARING IS TOO GOOD TO SHUT IT OUT!
YOU'RE RIGHT! NOW I'M HEARING...
--UT OUT THE VOICE AND YOU'LL--JEAN! JEAN, CAN YOU HEAR ME?!
YES, SIR!
I SENSE THE NEO-MUTANT! HE'S ALTERING YOUR PERCEPTIONS!
GET AWAY FROM HIM AND THE EFFECT WILL STOP!
COME ON! WE HAVE TO GET AWAY FROM THE POET!
SHE LISTENS TO **THE MAN.** YOU FEAR **THE TRUTH.**

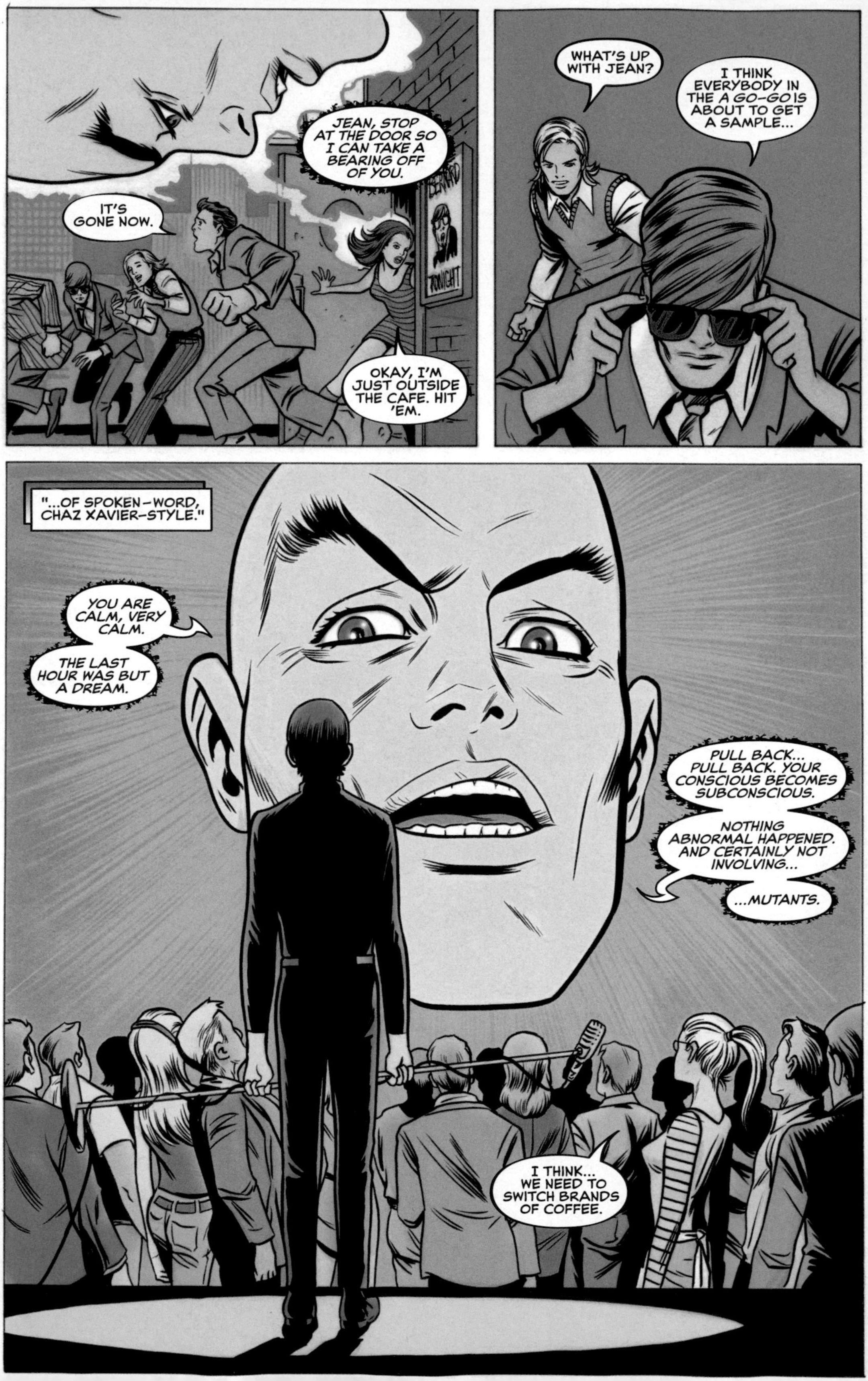
JEAN, STOP AT THE DOOR SO I CAN TAKE A BEARING OFF OF YOU.
IT'S GONE NOW.
OKAY, I'M JUST OUTSIDE THE CAFE. HIT 'EM.
WHAT'S UP WITH JEAN?
I THINK EVERYBODY IN THE A GO-GO IS ABOUT TO GET A SAMPLE...
"...OF SPOKEN-WORD, CHAZ XAVIER-STYLE."
YOU ARE CALM, VERY CALM.
THE LAST HOUR WAS BUT A DREAM.
PULL BACK... PULL BACK. YOUR CONSCIOUS BECOMES SUBCONSCIOUS.
NOTHING ABNORMAL HAPPENED. AND CERTAINLY NOT INVOLVING...
...MUTANTS.
I THINK... WE NEED TO SWITCH BRANDS OF COFFEE.

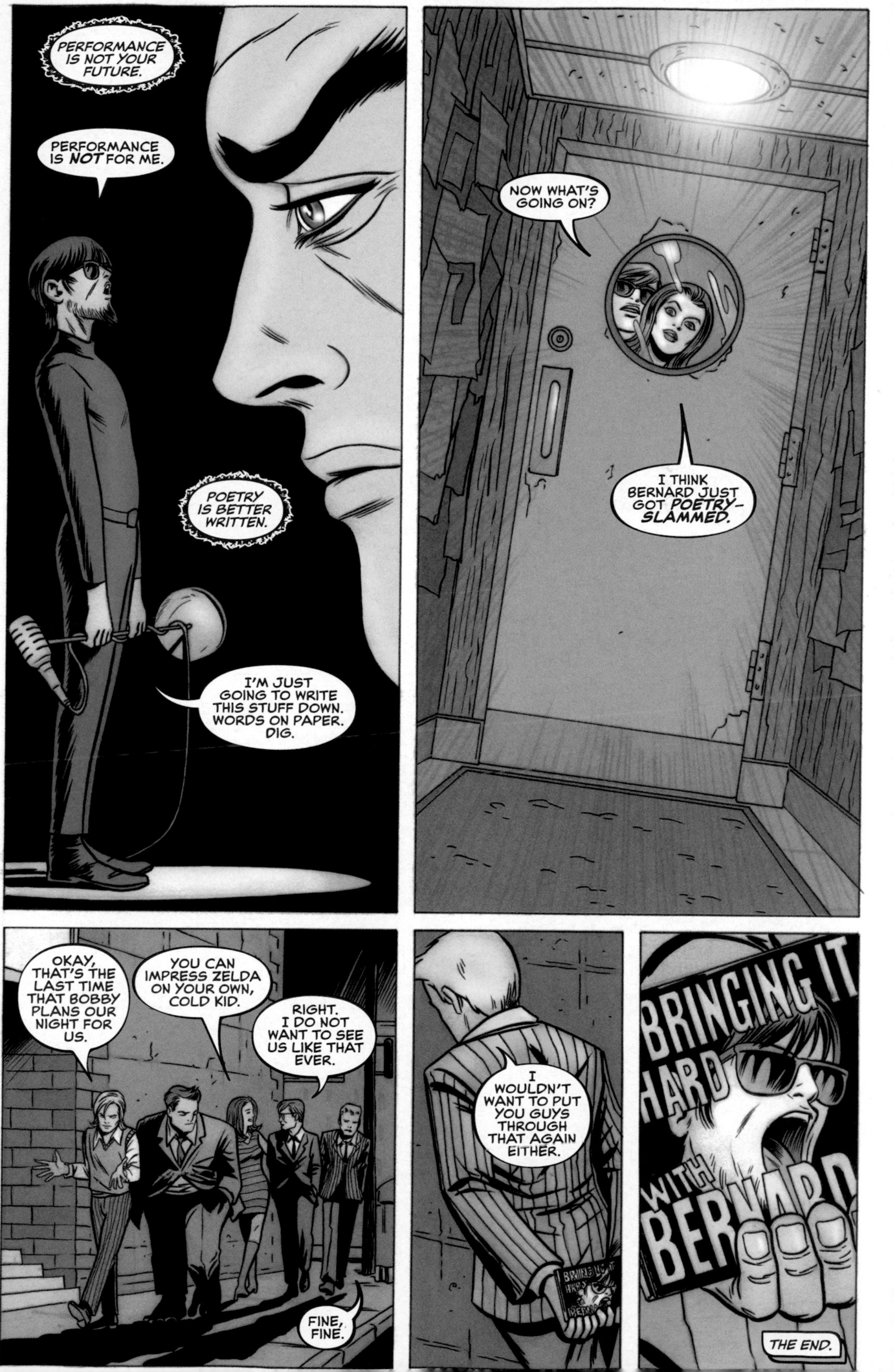
PERFORMANCE IS NOT YOUR FUTURE.
PERFORMANCE IS NOT FOR ME.
POETRY IS BETTER WRITTEN.
I'M JUST GOING TO WRITE THIS STUFF DOWN. WORDS ON PAPER. DIG.
NOW WHAT'S GOING ON?
I THINK BERNARD JUST GOT POETRY-SLAMMED.
OKAY, THAT'S THE LAST TIME THAT BOBBY PLANS OUR NIGHT FOR US.
YOU CAN IMPRESS ZELDA ON YOUR OWN, COLD KID.
RIGHT. I DO NOT WANT TO SEE US LIKE THAT EVER.
FINE, FINE.
I WOULDN'T WANT TO PUT YOU GUYS THROUGH THAT AGAIN EITHER.
BRINGING IT HARD WITH BERNARD
THE END.

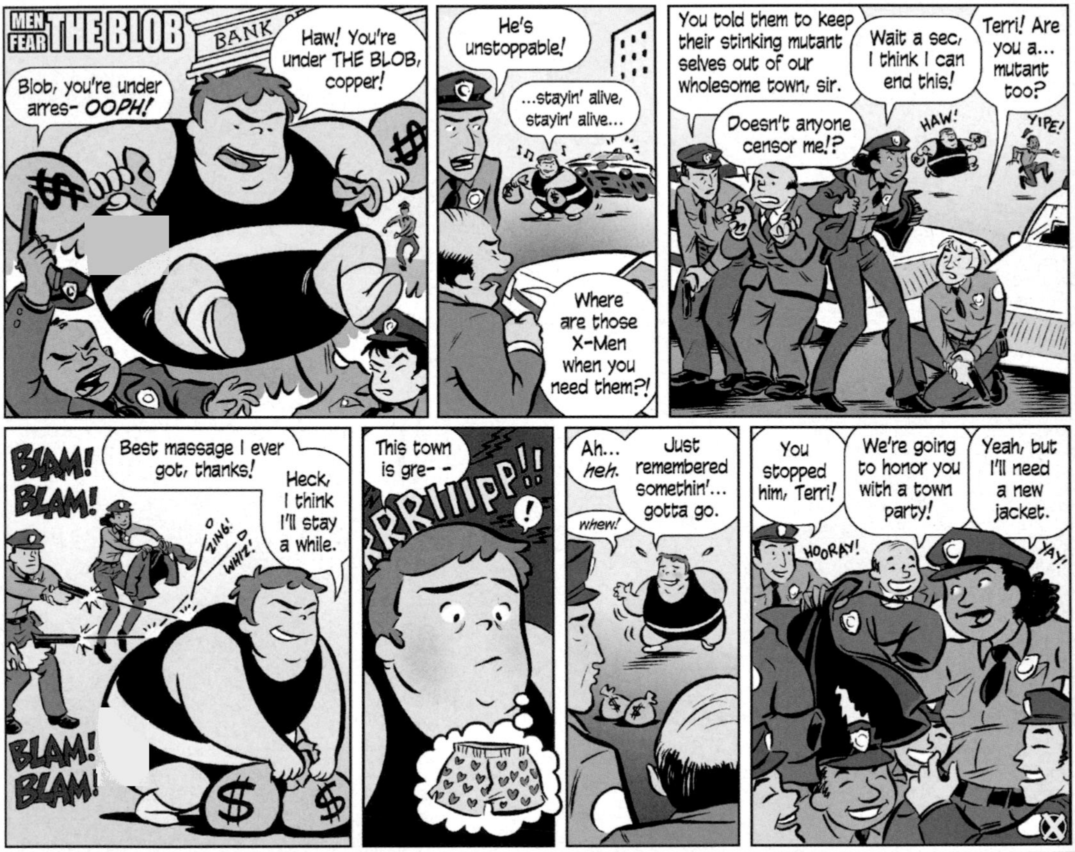
MEN FEAR THE BLOB
BANK
Blob, you're under arres- OOPH!
Haw! You're under THE BLOB, copper!
He's unstoppable!
...stayin' alive, stayin' alive...
Where are those X-Men when you need them?!
You told them to keep their stinking mutant selves out of our wholesome town, sir.
Doesn't anyone censor me!?
Wait a sec, I think I can end this!
HAW!
Terri! Are you a... mutant too?
YIPE!
BLAM! BLAM!
Best massage I ever got, thanks!
Heck, I think I'll stay a while.
ZING!
WHIZ!
BLAM! BLAM!
This town is gre- -
RRRIIIPP!!
!
Ah... heh.
Just remembered somethin'... gotta go.
whew!
You stopped him, Terri!
We're going to honor you with a town party!
Yeah, but I'll need a new jacket.
HOORAY!
YAY!

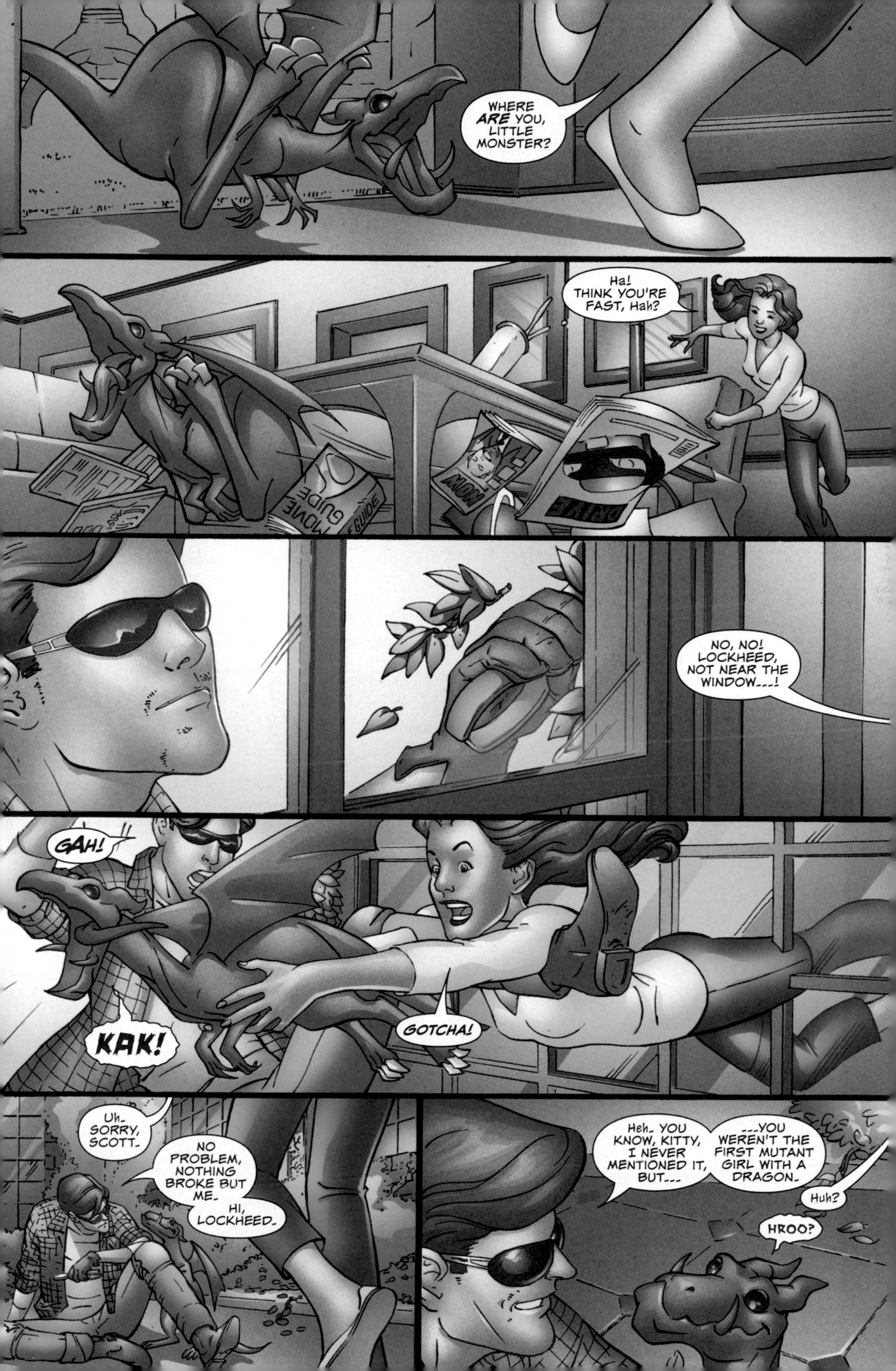
WHERE ARE YOU, LITTLE MONSTER?
Ha! THINK YOU'RE FAST, Hah?
MOVIE GUIDE
NOW
DRIVE
NO, NO! LOCKHEED, NOT NEAR THE WINDOW...!
GAH!
KAK!
GOTCHA!
Uh. SORRY, SCOTT.
NO PROBLEM, NOTHING BROKE BUT ME.
HI, LOCKHEED.
Heh. YOU KNOW, KITTY, I NEVER MENTIONED IT, BUT...
...YOU WEREN'T THE FIRST MUTANT GIRL WITH A DRAGON.
Huh?
HROO?

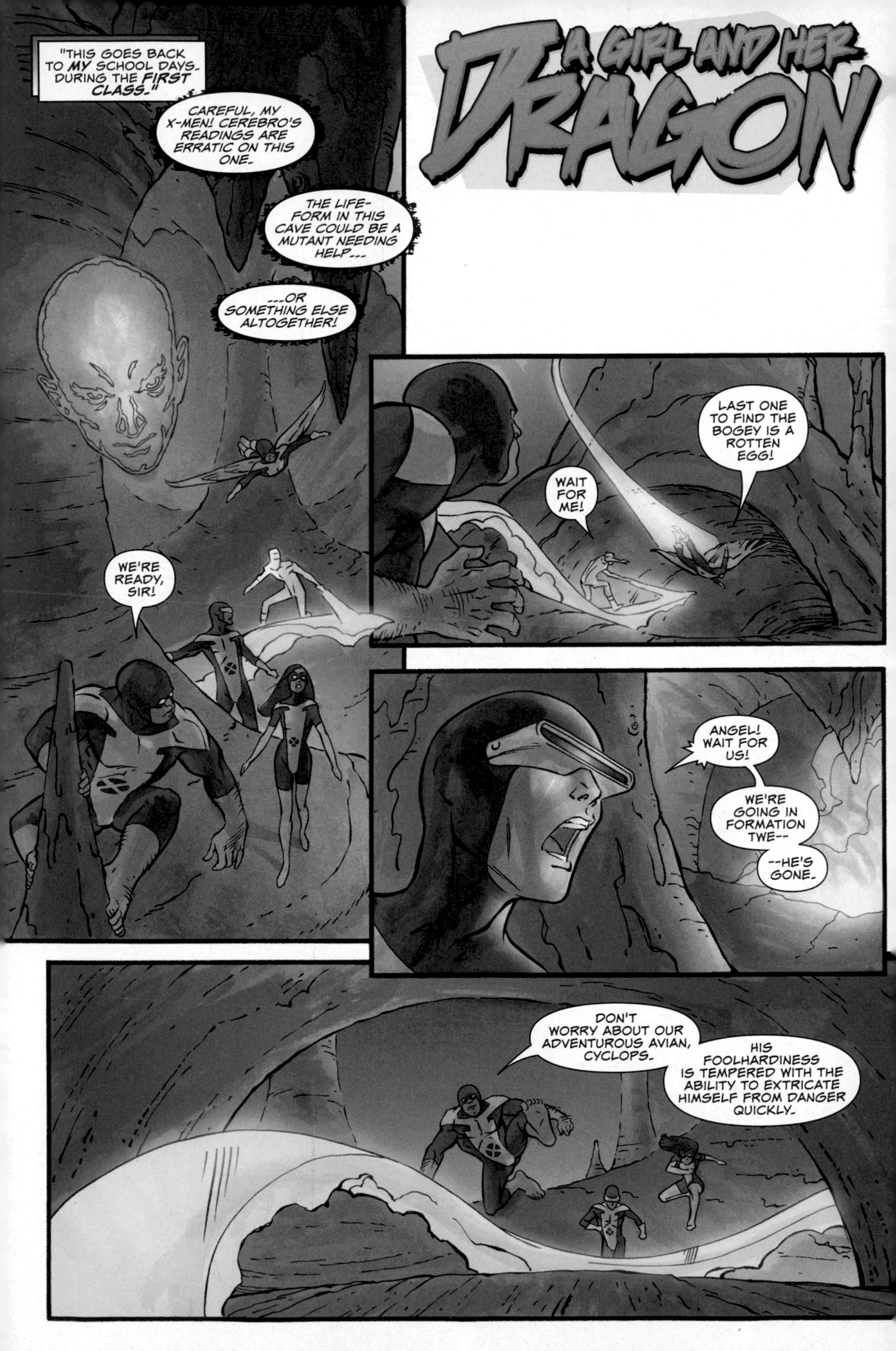
A GIRL AND HER DRAGON
"THIS GOES BACK TO MY SCHOOL DAYS. DURING THE FIRST CLASS."
CAREFUL, MY X-MEN! CEREBRO'S READINGS ARE ERRATIC ON THIS ONE.
THE LIFE-FORM IN THIS CAVE COULD BE A MUTANT NEEDING HELP...
...OR SOMETHING ELSE ALTOGETHER!
WE'RE READY, SIR!
LAST ONE TO FIND THE BOGEY IS A ROTTEN EGG!
WAIT FOR ME!
ANGEL! WAIT FOR US!
WE'RE GOING IN FORMATION TWE--
--HE'S GONE.
DON'T WORRY ABOUT OUR ADVENTUROUS AVIAN, CYCLOPS.
HIS FOOLHARDINESS IS TEMPERED WITH THE ABILITY TO EXTRICATE HIMSELF FROM DANGER QUICKLY.

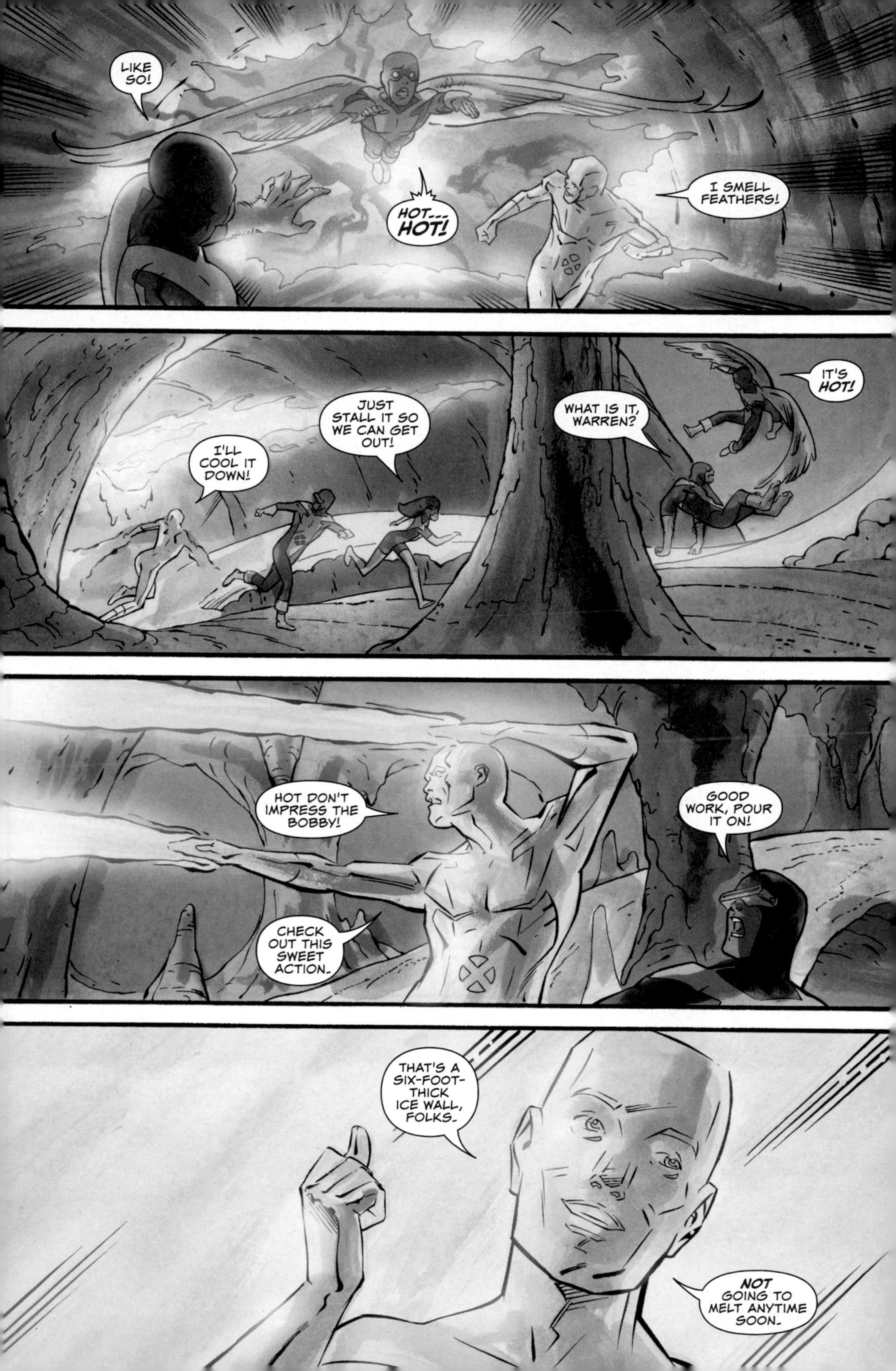
LIKE SO!
HOT--- HOT!
I SMELL FEATHERS!
I'LL COOL IT DOWN!
JUST STALL IT SO WE CAN GET OUT!
WHAT IS IT, WARREN?
IT'S HOT!
HOT DON'T IMPRESS THE BOBBY!
CHECK OUT THIS SWEET ACTION.
GOOD WORK, POUR IT ON!
THAT'S A SIX-FOOT-THICK ICE WALL, FOLKS.
NOT GOING TO MELT ANYTIME SOON.

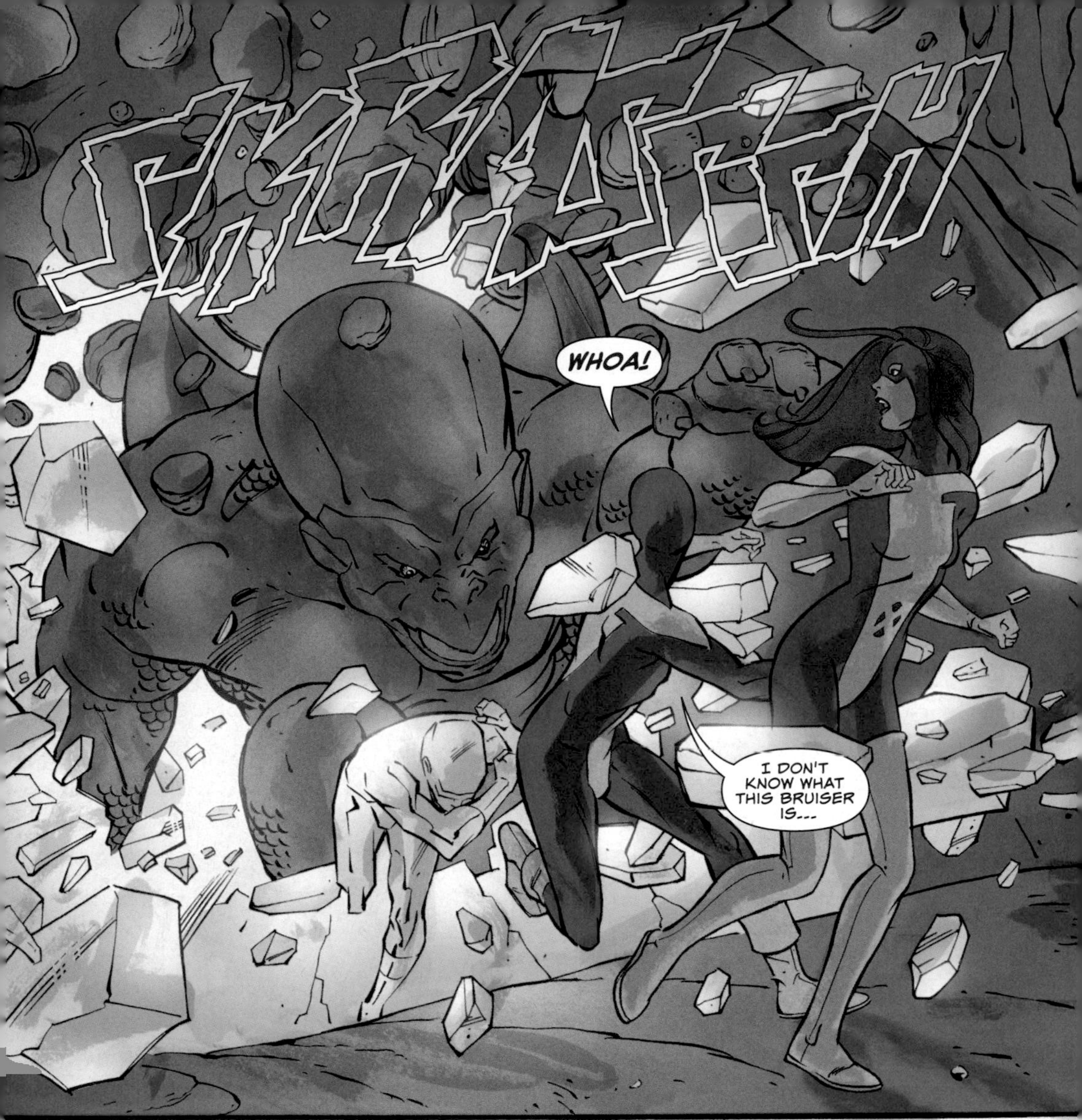
WHOA!
I DON'T KNOW WHAT THIS BRUISER IS...

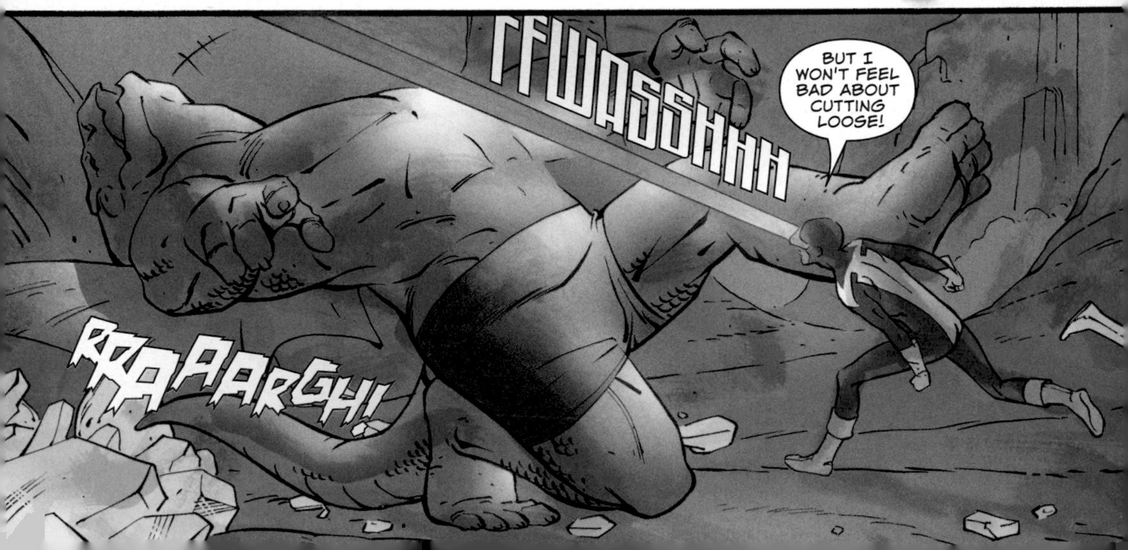
BUT I WON'T FEEL BAD ABOUT CUTTING LOOSE!
RRAAARGH!

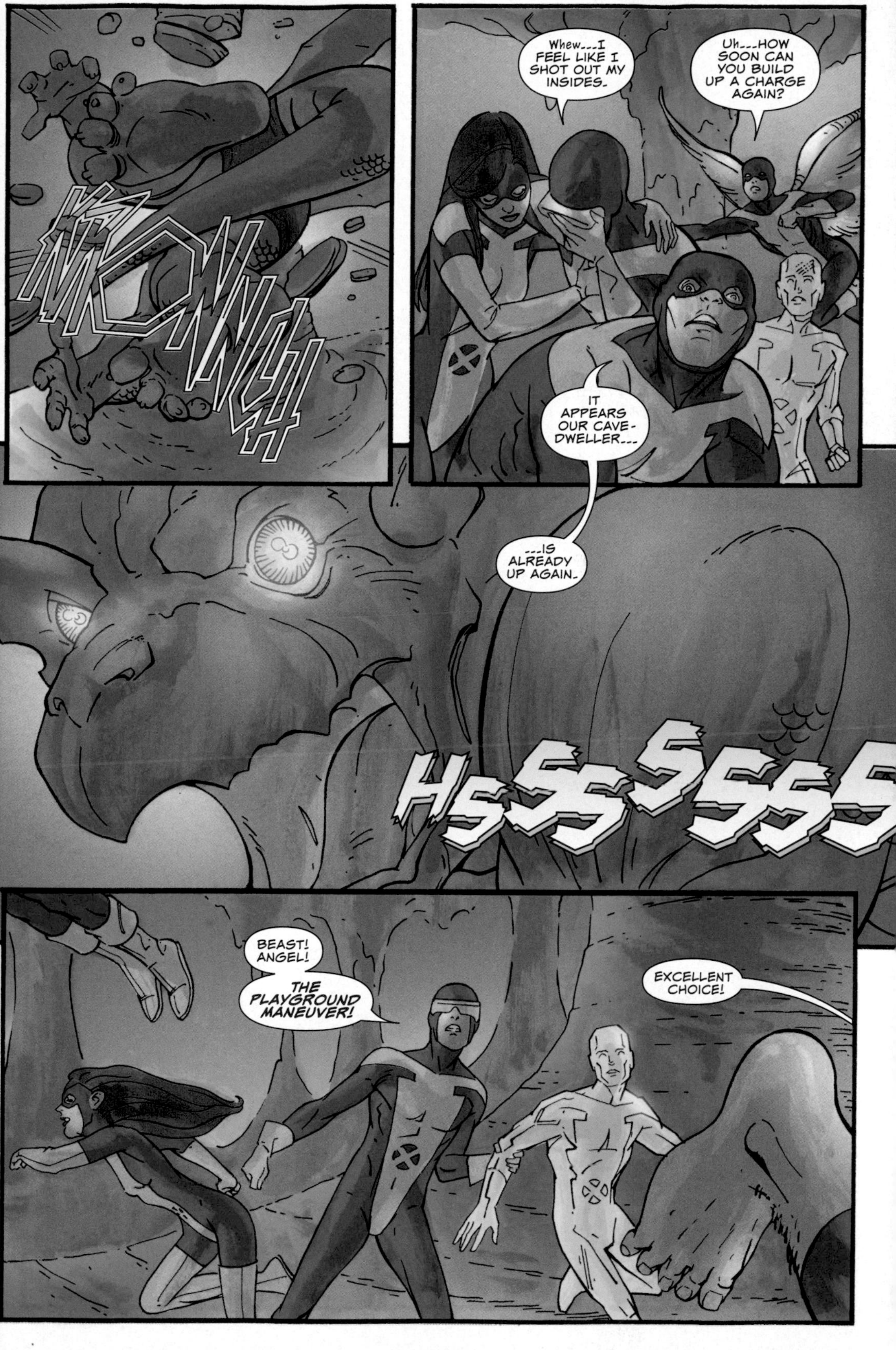
KRONNCH
Whew...I FEEL LIKE I SHOT OUT MY INSIDES.
Uh...HOW SOON CAN YOU BUILD UP A CHARGE AGAIN?
IT APPEARS OUR CAVE-DWELLER...
...IS ALREADY UP AGAIN.
HSSSSSS
BEAST! ANGEL!
THE PLAYGROUND MANEUVER!
EXCELLENT CHOICE!

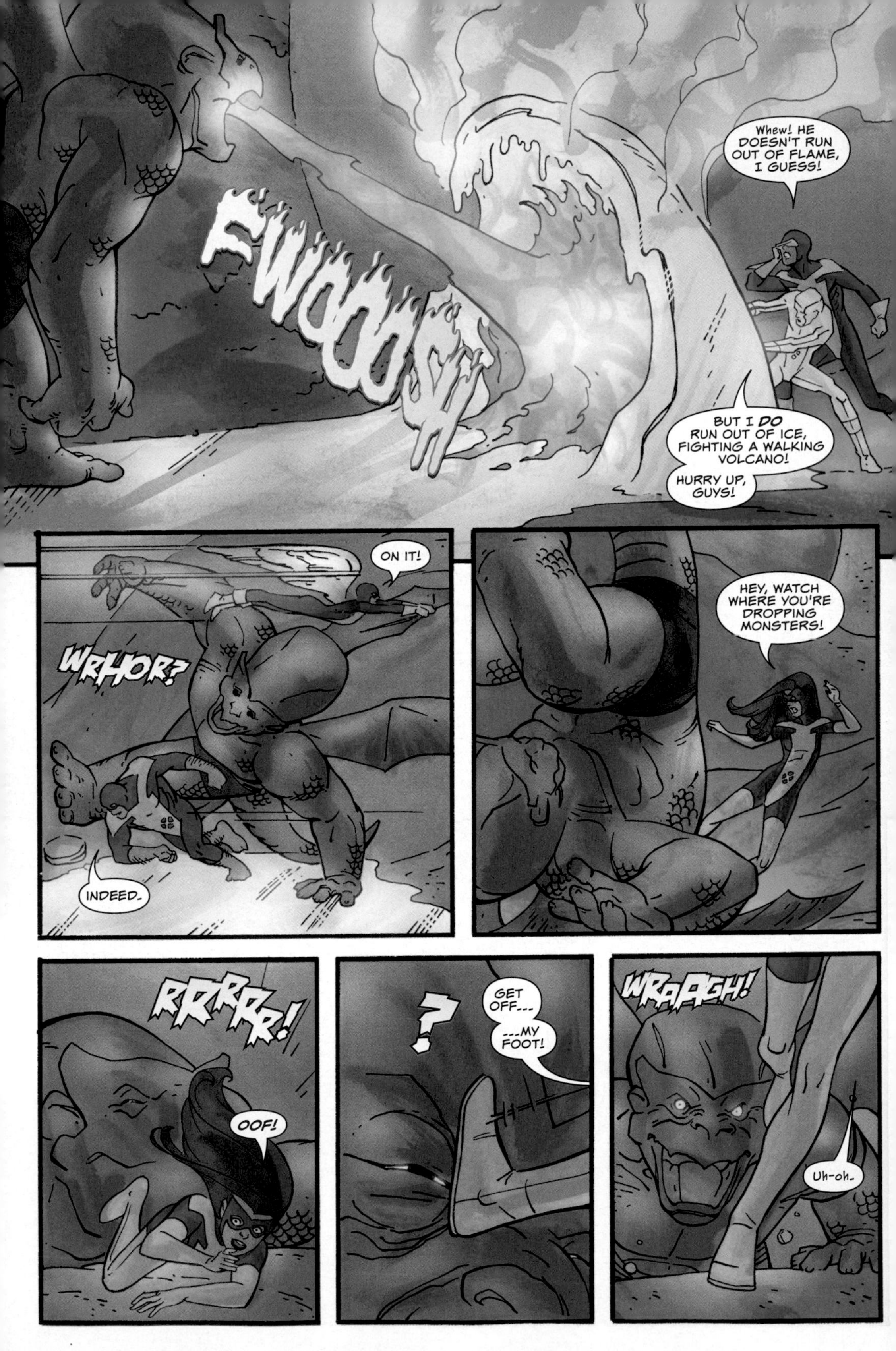
FWOOOSH
Whew! HE DOESN'T RUN OUT OF FLAME, I GUESS!
BUT I DO RUN OUT OF ICE, FIGHTING A WALKING VOLCANO!
HURRY UP, GUYS!
ON IT!
WRHOR?
INDEED.
HEY, WATCH WHERE YOU'RE DROPPING MONSTERS!
RRRRR!
OOF!
?
GET OFF---
---MY FOOT!
WRAAGH!
Uh-oh.

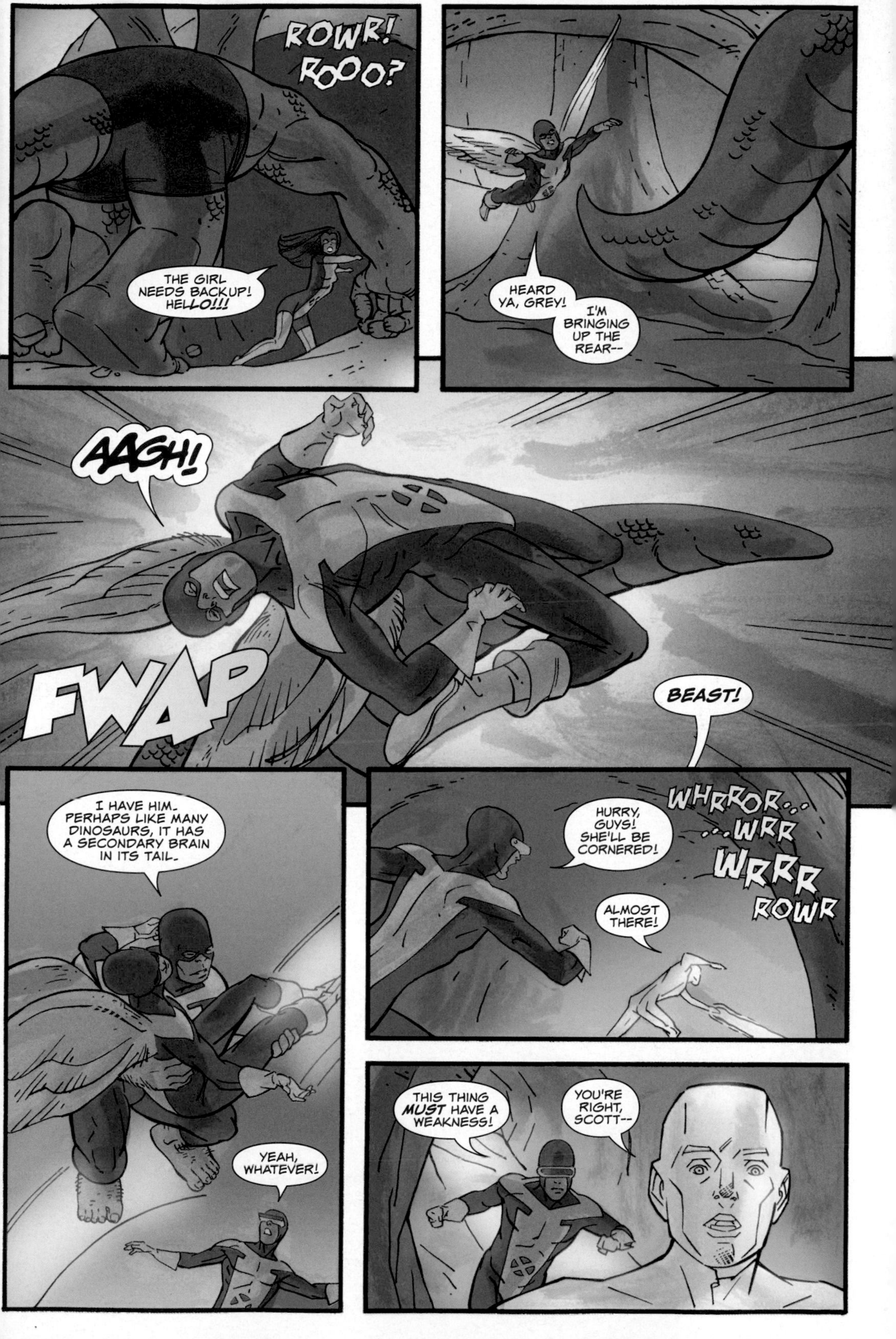
ROWR! ROOO?
THE GIRL NEEDS BACKUP! HELLO!!!
HEARD YA, GREY!
I'M BRINGING UP THE REAR--
AAGH!
FWAP
BEAST!
I HAVE HIM. PERHAPS LIKE MANY DINOSAURS, IT HAS A SECONDARY BRAIN IN ITS TAIL.
YEAH, WHATEVER!
HURRY, GUYS! SHE'LL BE CORNERED!
WHRROR... ...WRR WRRR ROWR
ALMOST THERE!
THIS THING MUST HAVE A WEAKNESS!
YOU'RE RIGHT, SCOTT--

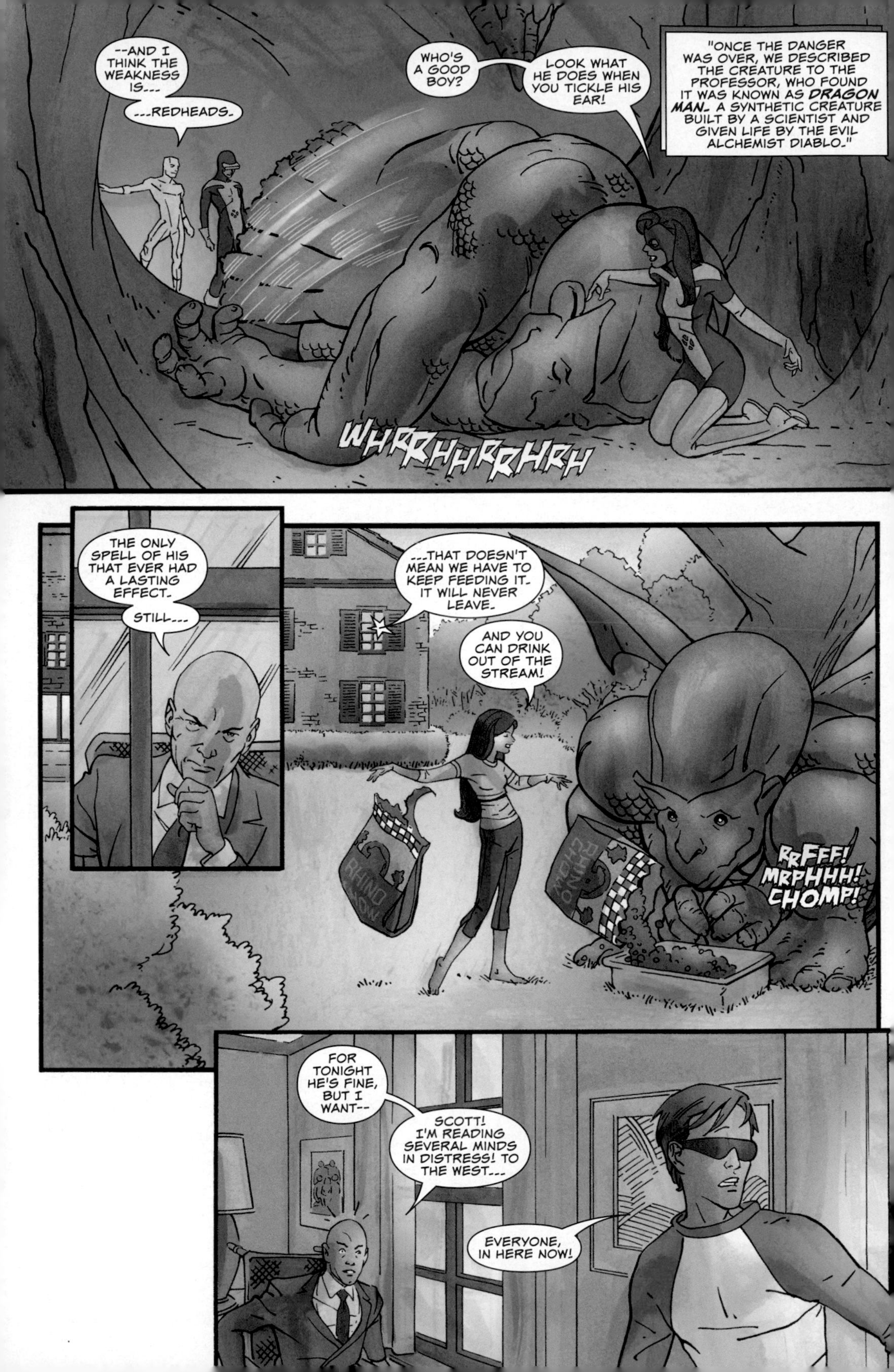
--AND I THINK THE WEAKNESS IS---
---REDHEADS.
WHO'S A GOOD BOY?
LOOK WHAT HE DOES WHEN YOU TICKLE HIS EAR!
"ONCE THE DANGER WAS OVER, WE DESCRIBED THE CREATURE TO THE PROFESSOR, WHO FOUND IT WAS KNOWN AS DRAGON MAN. A SYNTHETIC CREATURE BUILT BY A SCIENTIST AND GIVEN LIFE BY THE EVIL ALCHEMIST DIABLO."
WHRRHHRRHRH
THE ONLY SPELL OF HIS THAT EVER HAD A LASTING EFFECT.
STILL---
---THAT DOESN'T MEAN WE HAVE TO KEEP FEEDING IT. IT WILL NEVER LEAVE.
AND YOU CAN DRINK OUT OF THE STREAM!
RHINO CHOW
RHINO CHOW
RRFFF! MRPHHH! CHOMP!
FOR TONIGHT HE'S FINE, BUT I WANT--
SCOTT! I'M READING SEVERAL MINDS IN DISTRESS! TO THE WEST---
EVERYONE, IN HERE NOW!

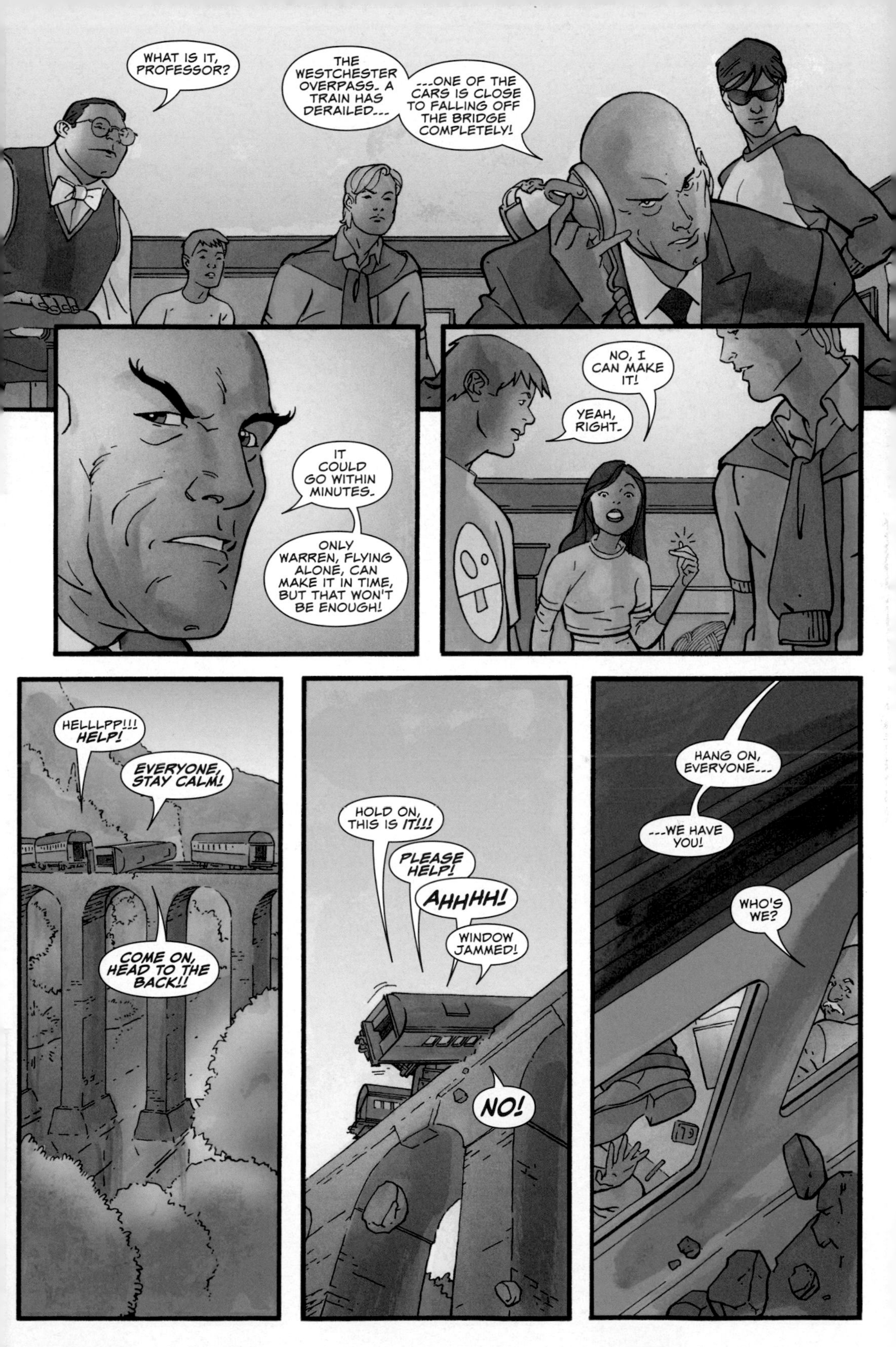
WHAT IS IT, PROFESSOR?
THE WESTCHESTER OVERPASS. A TRAIN HAS DERAILED...
...ONE OF THE CARS IS CLOSE TO FALLING OFF THE BRIDGE COMPLETELY!
IT COULD GO WITHIN MINUTES.
ONLY WARREN, FLYING ALONE, CAN MAKE IT IN TIME, BUT THAT WON'T BE ENOUGH!
NO, I CAN MAKE IT!
YEAH, RIGHT.
HELLLPP!!! HELP!
EVERYONE, STAY CALM!
COME ON, HEAD TO THE BACK!!
HOLD ON, THIS IS IT!!!
PLEASE HELP!
AHHHH!
WINDOW JAMMED!
NO!
HANG ON, EVERYONE...
...WE HAVE YOU!
WHO'S WE?

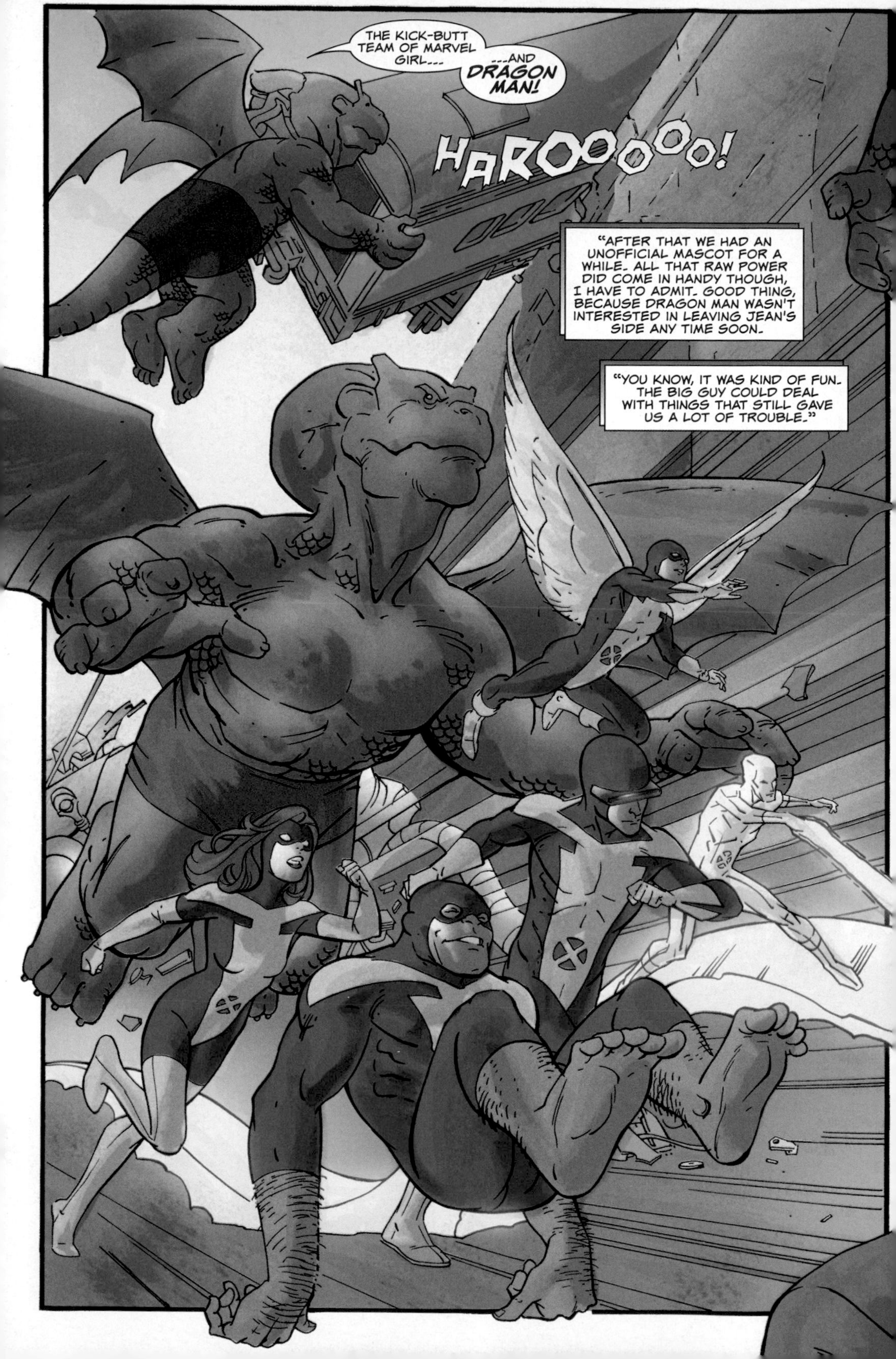
THE KICK-BUTT TEAM OF MARVEL GIRL---
---AND DRAGON MAN!
HAROOOOOO!
"AFTER THAT WE HAD AN UNOFFICIAL MASCOT FOR A WHILE. ALL THAT RAW POWER DID COME IN HANDY THOUGH, I HAVE TO ADMIT. GOOD THING, BECAUSE DRAGON MAN WASN'T INTERESTED IN LEAVING JEAN'S SIDE ANY TIME SOON.
"YOU KNOW, IT WAS KIND OF FUN. THE BIG GUY COULD DEAL WITH THINGS THAT STILL GAVE US A LOT OF TROUBLE."

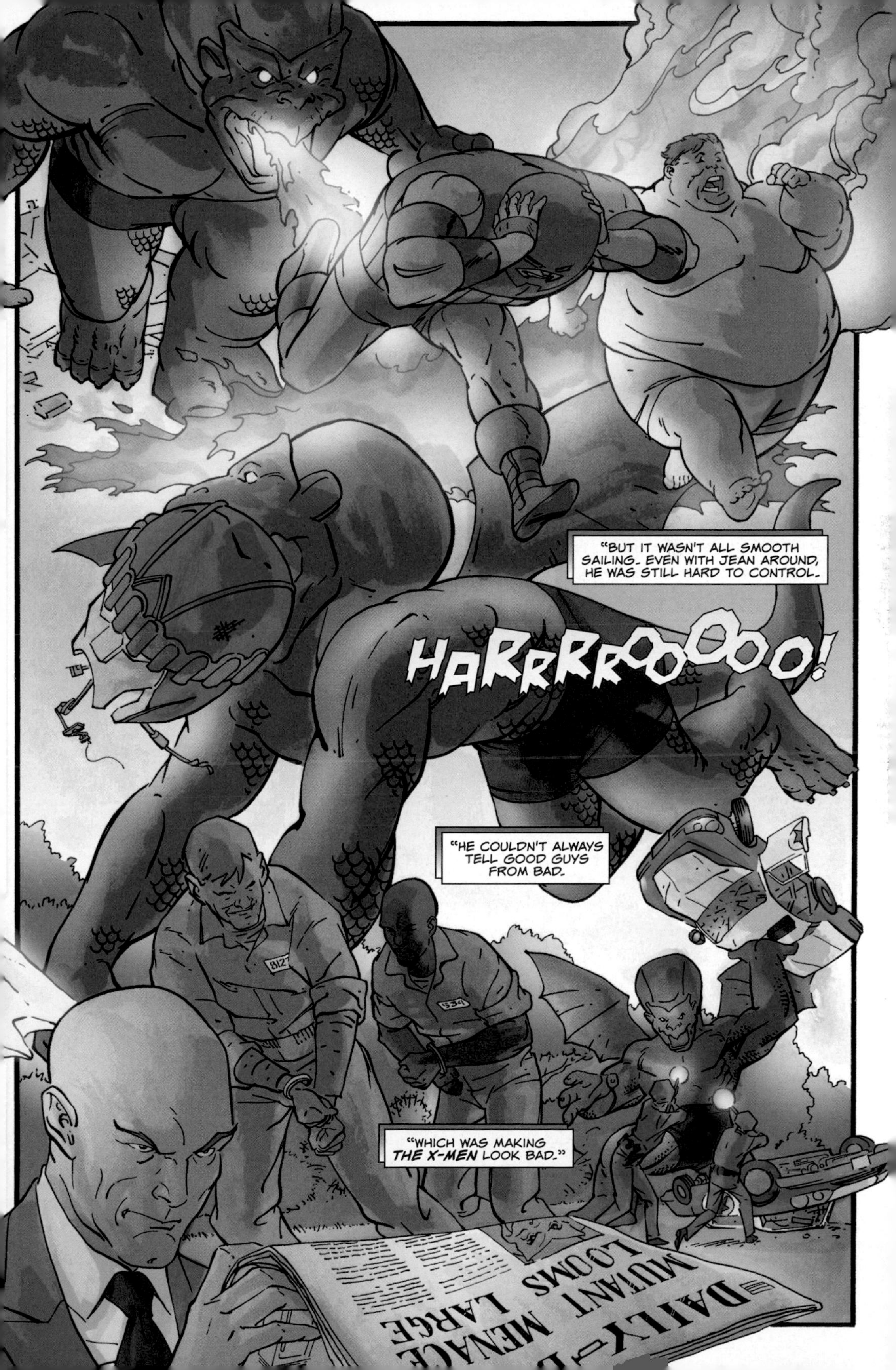
"BUT IT WASN'T ALL SMOOTH SAILING. EVEN WITH JEAN AROUND, HE WAS STILL HARD TO CONTROL.
HARRRROOOOOO!
"HE COULDN'T ALWAYS TELL GOOD GUYS FROM BAD.
"WHICH WAS MAKING *THE X-MEN* LOOK BAD."
DAILY
MUTANT MENACE LOOMS LARGE

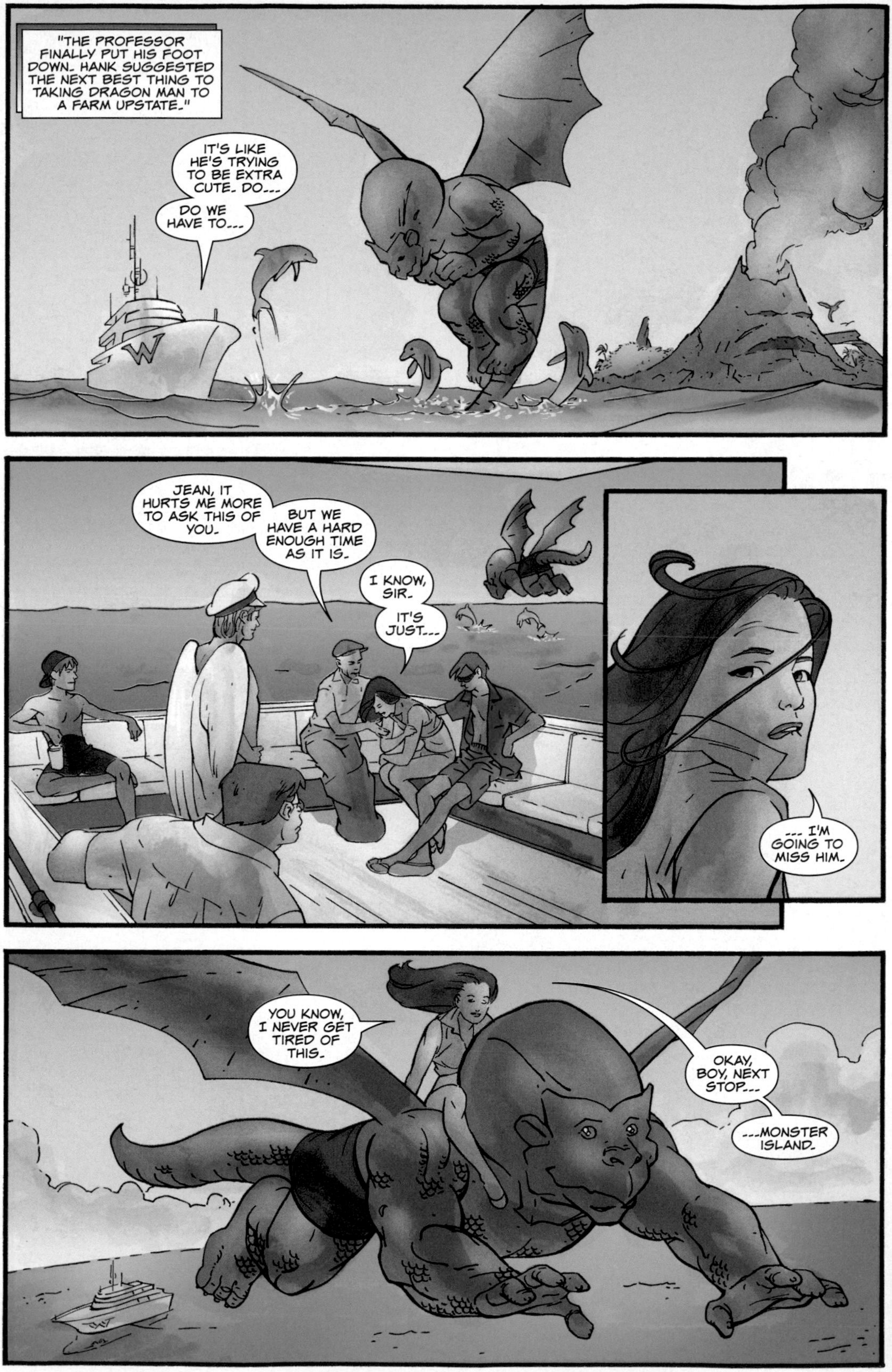
"THE PROFESSOR FINALLY PUT HIS FOOT DOWN. HANK SUGGESTED THE NEXT BEST THING TO TAKING DRAGON MAN TO A FARM UPSTATE."
IT'S LIKE HE'S TRYING TO BE EXTRA CUTE. DO...
DO WE HAVE TO...
JEAN, IT HURTS ME MORE TO ASK THIS OF YOU.
BUT WE HAVE A HARD ENOUGH TIME AS IT IS.
I KNOW, SIR.
IT'S JUST...
...I'M GOING TO MISS HIM.
YOU KNOW, I NEVER GET TIRED OF THIS.
OKAY, BOY, NEXT STOP...
...MONSTER ISLAND.

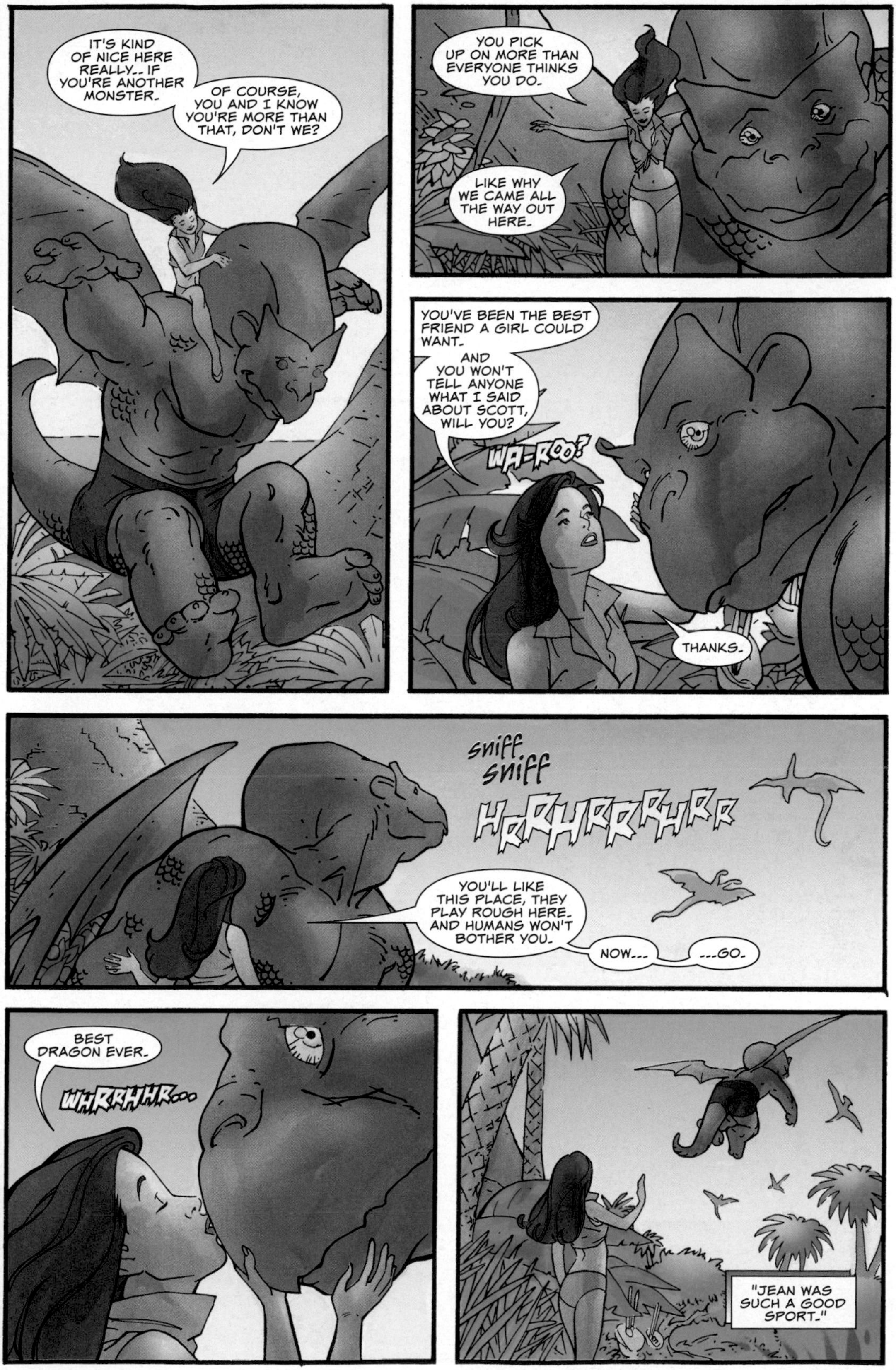
IT'S KIND OF NICE HERE REALLY... IF YOU'RE ANOTHER MONSTER.
OF COURSE, YOU AND I KNOW YOU'RE MORE THAN THAT, DON'T WE?
YOU PICK UP ON MORE THAN EVERYONE THINKS YOU DO.
LIKE WHY WE CAME ALL THE WAY OUT HERE.
YOU'VE BEEN THE BEST FRIEND A GIRL COULD WANT.
AND YOU WON'T TELL ANYONE WHAT I SAID ABOUT SCOTT, WILL YOU?
WA-ROO?
THANKS.
sniff sniff
HRRHRRRHRR
YOU'LL LIKE THIS PLACE, THEY PLAY ROUGH HERE. AND HUMANS WON'T BOTHER YOU.
NOW...
...GO.
BEST DRAGON EVER.
WHRRHHR...
"JEAN WAS SUCH A GOOD SPORT."

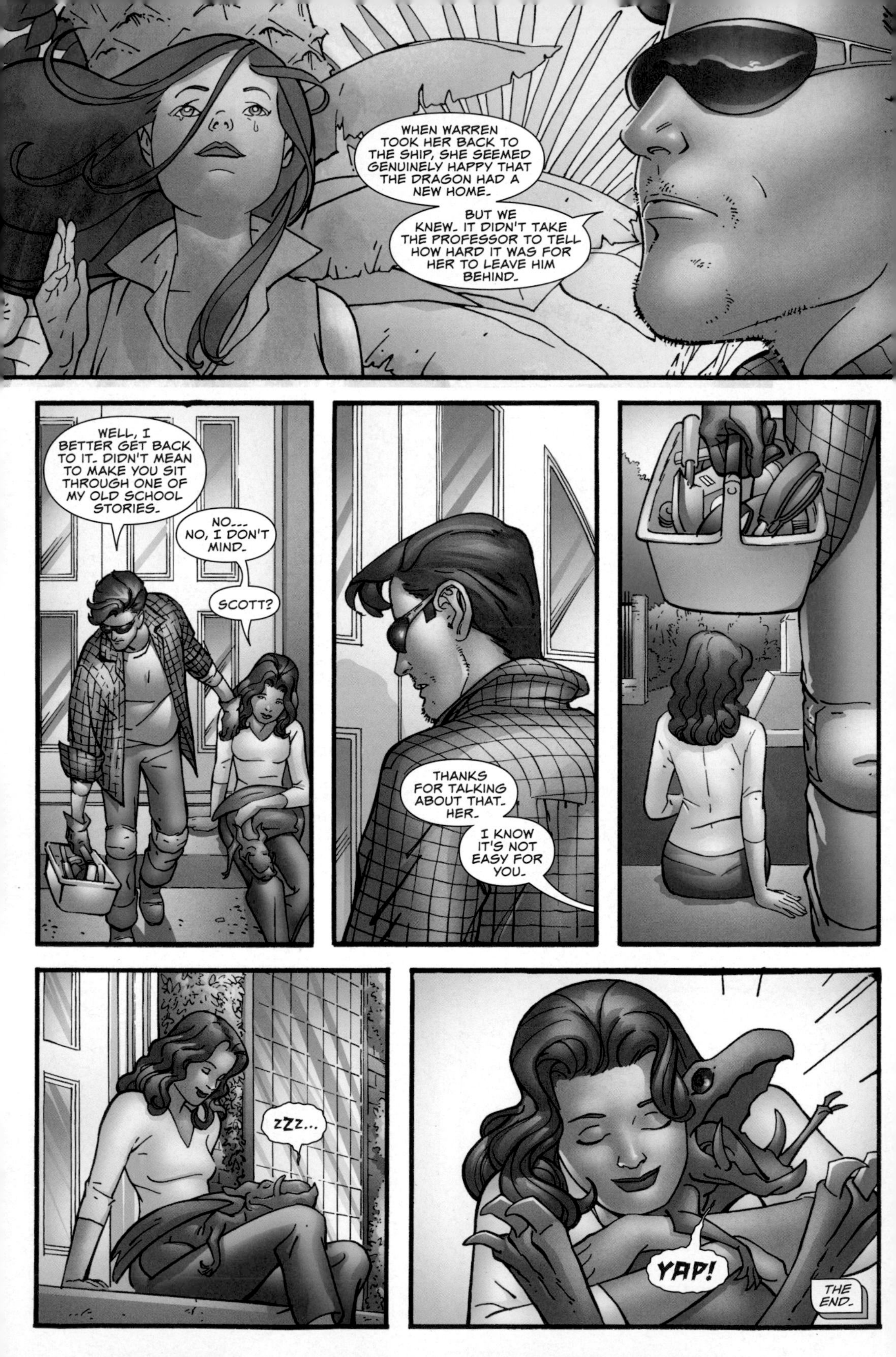
WHEN WARREN TOOK HER BACK TO THE SHIP, SHE SEEMED GENUINELY HAPPY THAT THE DRAGON HAD A NEW HOME.
BUT WE KNEW. IT DIDN'T TAKE THE PROFESSOR TO TELL HOW HARD IT WAS FOR HER TO LEAVE HIM BEHIND.
WELL, I BETTER GET BACK TO IT. DIDN'T MEAN TO MAKE YOU SIT THROUGH ONE OF MY OLD SCHOOL STORIES.
NO... NO, I DON'T MIND.
SCOTT?
THANKS FOR TALKING ABOUT THAT. HER.
I KNOW IT'S NOT EASY FOR YOU.
ZZZ...
YAP!
THE END.

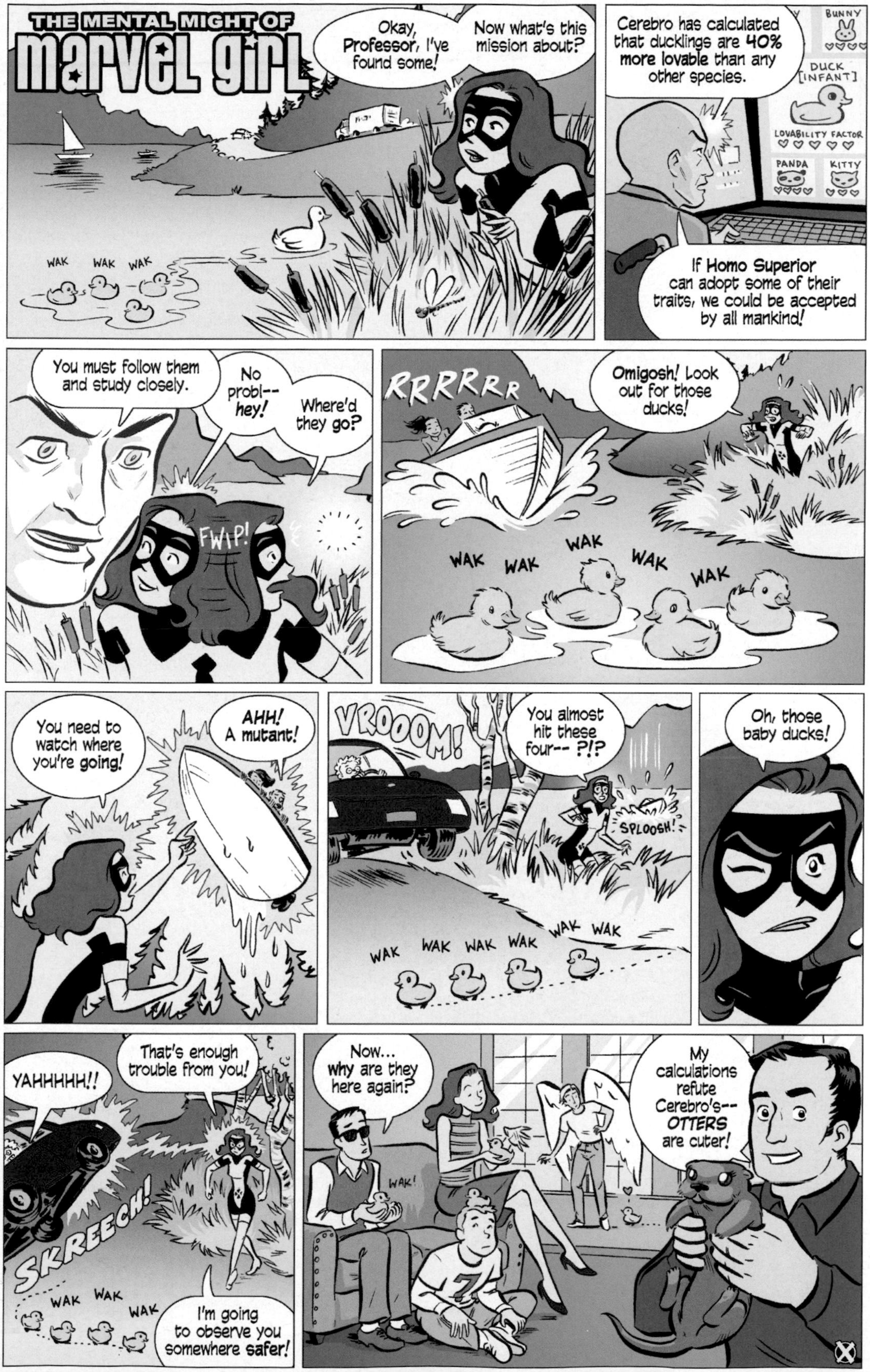
THE MENTAL MIGHT OF
marvel girl
Okay, Professor, I've found some!
Now what's this mission about?
WAK WAK WAK
Cerebro has calculated that ducklings are 40% more lovable than any other species.
BUNNY
DUCK [INFANT]
LOVABILITY FACTOR
PANDA
KITTY
If Homo Superior can adopt some of their traits, we could be accepted by all mankind!
You must follow them and study closely.
No probl-- hey!
Where'd they go?
FWIP!
RRRRRR
Omigosh! Look out for those ducks!
WAK WAK WAK WAK WAK
You need to watch where you're going!
AHH! A mutant!
VROOOM!
You almost hit these four-- ?!?
SPLOOSH!
WAK WAK WAK WAK WAK WAK
Oh, those baby ducks!
YAHHHHH!!
That's enough trouble from you!
SKREECH!
WAK WAK WAK
I'm going to observe you somewhere safer!
Now... why are they here again?
WAK!
My calculations refute Cerebro's-- OTTERS are cuter!

PROFESSOR X

nature. He entered Bard College in New York at age 16 and earned his bachelor's degree in biology within two years. He was then accepted into the graduate-studies program at England's prestigious Oxford University, where he earned degrees in genetics and biophysics. There,

Charles met and fell in love with a young Scotswoman named Moira Kinross. Their passionate discussions on the subject of genetic mutation gave way to an equally passionate romance, and they planned to marry. Their only obstacle was Moira's former boyfriend, Joe MacTaggert,

REAL NAME: Charles Francis Xavier

KNOWN ALIASES: Professor X

IDENTITY: Publicly known

OCCUPATION: Mutant rights activist, geneticist, teacher, formerly adventurer, soldier

CITIZENSHIP: United States of America with no criminal record

PLACE OF BIRTH: New York City, New York

MARITAL STATUS: Single

KNOWN RELATIVES: Brian Xavier (father, deceased), Sharon Xavier (mother, deceased), Cassandra Nova (sister), Kurt Marko (stepfather, deceased), Cain Marko (Juggernaut, stepbrother), David Charles Haller (Legion, son)

GROUP AFFILIATION: X-Men (founder)

EDUCATION: PhDs in genetics, biophysics, psychology, anthropology, and psychiatry

HISTORY: Charles Francis Xavier was born the son of nuclear researcher Brian Xavier and his wife, Sharon. Following her husband's accidental death, Sharon married Brian's colleague, Kurt Marko. Cain, Kurt's son from a previous marriage, came to live at the Xavier's Westchester mansion shortly thereafter. A cruel and spiteful boy, he bullied his new stepbrother, and his father secretly beat him as punishment. Charles felt his sibling's pain first-hand thanks to the emergence of his mutant telepathic powers. Following their mother's death, a fire in the family home took Kurt's life, leaving the stepbrothers alone.

By the time he graduated high school, Charles was completely bald as a side effect of his mutant

HEIGHT: 6'

WEIGHT: 190 lbs

EYES: Blue

HAIR: Bald (blond in childhood)

DISTINGUISHING FEATURES: Paraplegic

POWERS & ABILITIES:

STRENGTH LEVEL: Before being injured, Professor X possessed the normal human strength of a man of his age, height, and build who engaged in regular exercise.

SUPERHUMAN POWERS: Professor X is a mutant who possesses vast psionic powers, making him arguably the world's most powerful telepath. He can read minds and project his own thoughts into the minds of others within a radius of approximately 250 miles. With extreme effort, he can greatly extend that radius. Professor X can also psionically manipulate the minds of others, for example to make himself seem invisible and to project illusions. He can also induce temporary mental and/or physical paralysis, loss of particular memories or even total amnesia. Within close range, Professor X can manipulate almost any number of minds for such simple feats. However, he can only take full possession of another being's mind one at a time, and he can only do so if he is within that being's physical presence.

Furthermore, Professor X can project powerful mental bolts of psionic energy enabling him to stun the mind of another being into unconsciousness. These bolts only apply force upon other minds; they do not inflict physical damage. Professor X can also sense the presence of other superhuman mutants within a small radius of himself by perceiving the distinct mental radiations emitted by such beings. In order to detect the presence of mutants beyond this radius, he must amplify his powers. He often does this by using first Cerebro and more recently Cerebra, devices that are sensitive to that portion of the electromagnetic spectrum that contains mental frequencies.

Professor X can project his astral form, the sheath of his life essence, onto abstract dimensions congruent to our own known as astral planes. There, he can use his powers to create ectoplasmic objects. He cannot engage in long-range astral projection on the Earthly plane.

SPECIAL SKILLS: Professor X is a leading authority on genetics, mutation, and psionic powers, and has considerable expertise in other life sciences. He is also highly talented in devising equipment for utilizing and enhancing psionic powers.

SPECIAL LIMITATIONS: Part of Professor X's spine is shattered, thus confining him to a wheelchair.

FIRST APPEARANCE: *X-Men Vol. 1 #1* (1963)

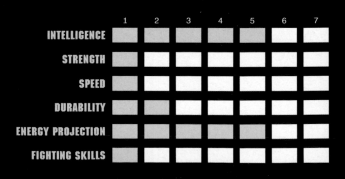

	1	2	3	4	5	6	7
INTELLIGENCE							
STRENGTH							
SPEED							
DURABILITY							
ENERGY PROJECTION							
FIGHTING SKILLS							

JEAN GREY

a lance corporal in the Royal Marines and a bully, just like Cain. In Joe's eyes, Charles was a good-for-nothing intellectual, so Charles enlisted in the military after completing his studies at Oxford to validate himself in terms his rival would understand.

Charles quickly became something of a legend in the area of search and rescue thanks to his mutant abilities. Attached to the same unit as his stepbrother, Charles was present when Cain deserted under fire during a mission in Asia. Following him in the hope of convincing him to return to their unit, Charles witnessed Cain's discovery of the mystical Ruby of Cyttorak and his transformation into the superhuman Juggernaut. Charles escaped the subsequent cave-in, mistakenly believing his stepbrother was dead.

Charles later traveled to Israel, where he befriended a fellow drifter named Erik Magnus Lehnsherr, the mutant who would become his greatest enemy: Magneto, self-styled master of magnetism. Whilst Charles optimistically believed that humans and mutants could coexist, the Jewish Magnus foresaw mutants as the new minority to be persecuted and hunted because of their differences.

Charles returned to America and resumed his studies of mutation. It was not long before Professor John Grey, a friend of Charles' from Bard College, brought his young daughter Jean to Charles for help. Jean had been traumatized when she telepathically experienced the death of a friend. Charles aided in her recovery, and in the ensuing years trained her to use her mental powers. Charles later met with Fred Duncan, an F.B.I. agent investigating the growing number of mutants. Charles told Duncan of his plan to locate young mutants and enroll them in a school using his ancestral mansion home as a base to train them to use their powers for humanity's benefit. Over the following months, Charles used the mutant-locating computer Cerebro to assemble his original group of students: Cyclops, Iceman, Angel, Beast, and Jean Grey, who took the name Marvel Girl. He dubbed his students the "X-Men," because each possessed an "extra" ability that normal humans lacked.

REAL NAME: Jean Grey

KNOWN ALIASES: Marvel Girl

IDENTITY: Secret

OCCUPATION: Student, adventurer

CITIZENSHIP: United States of America with no criminal record

PLACE OF BIRTH: Annandale-on-Hudson, New York

MARITAL STATUS: Single

KNOWN RELATIVES: John Grey (father), Elaine Grey (mother), Sara Grey (sister, deceased), Gailyn Bailey (niece), Joey Bailey (nephew), Paul Bailey (brother-in-law)

GROUP AFFILIATION: X-Men

EDUCATION: Enrolled at Professor Xavier's School for Gifted Youngsters

HISTORY: The younger daughter of history professor John Grey and his wife Elaine, Jean Grey was 10 years old when her mutant telepathic powers first manifested after experiencing the emotions of a dying friend. Her parents took her to be treated by Professor Charles Xavier, who erected psychic shields in Jean's mind to prevent her from using her telepathic powers until she was mature enough to control them.

Eventually, using her telekinetic powers, Jean was a founding member of Xavier's team of mutant trainees the X-Men as Marvel Girl.

HEIGHT: 5'6"

WEIGHT: 115 lbs

EYES: Green

HAIR: Red

SUPERHUMAN POWERS: Jean Grey possessed telepathic powers allowing her to read minds, project her thoughts, and mentally stun opponents with pure psionic force,

among other talents. She also possessed telekinesis, allowing her to levitate and manipulate objects and others.

As Phoenix, Jean possessed total telekinetic control of matter at the molecular level.

FIRST APPEARANCE: *X-Men Vol. 1 #1* (1963)

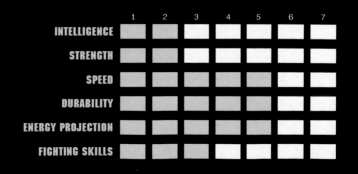

	1	2	3	4	5	6	7
INTELLIGENCE							
STRENGTH							
SPEED							
DURABILITY							
ENERGY PROJECTION							
FIGHTING SKILLS							

ANGEL

REAL NAME: Warren Kenneth Worthington III

KNOWN ALIASES: Angel

IDENTITY: Secret

OCCUPATION: Student, adventurer

PLACE OF BIRTH: Centerport, Long Island, New York

CITIZENSHIP: United States of America with no criminal record

MARITAL STATUS: Single

KNOWN RELATIVES: Warren Kenneth Worthington Sr. (grandfather, deceased), Warren Kenneth Worthington Jr. (father, deceased), Kathryn Worthington (mother, deceased), Burtram "Burt" Worthington (paternal uncle), Mimi (maternal aunt)

GROUP AFFILIATION: X-Men

EDUCATION: Enrolled at Professor Xavier's School for Gifted Youngsters

HISTORY: Warren Kenneth Worthington III was born into an extremely wealthy family in Centerport, Long Island. As a child, young Warren often concerned his parents, Warren Kenneth Jr. and Kathryn, by climbing high up into trees and onto their mansion's roof, seemingly unafraid of heights. Eventually, Warren was sent to a prestigious East Coast boarding school where he roomed with Cameron Hodge, who would soon become his best friend.

While attending school, the life of young Warren changed forever when one day he sprouted wings from his shoulder blades. At first easily concealed, the abnormal appendages reached full size within months. Initially alarmed, Warren soon grew to relish the freedom of flight. Still, he strapped the wings tightly to his back to avoid suspicion. Warren was forced into action when fire struck his dormitory. Donning a blond wig and long nightshirt to conceal his identity, he delivered the students inside from certain death. Eyewitnesses claimed the students' savior was an "angel."

Despite the obvious risks — exposure, loss of social standing, or even death — Warren would not be grounded. Shortly after saving his classmates, he took up life as a costumed crimefighter in New York City, using a gun filled with pellets of knockout gas to defeat criminals. The nocturnal activities of this so-called "Avenging Angel" drew the attention of Professor Charles Xavier. Warren became a founding member of the Professor's X-Men, a handful of troubled teenagers learning to control their strange powers and fighting to preserve Xavier's dream of peaceful coexistence between humans and mutants.

HEIGHT: 6'

WEIGHT: 150 lbs

EYES: Blue

HAIR: Blond

DISTINGUISHING FEATURES: Large feathered wings with 16' wingspan

POWERS & ABILITIES:

STRENGTH LEVEL: Angel possesses the normal human strength of a young man of his age, height, and build who engages in intensive regular exercise. His wings can create enough lift to enable him to carry aloft at least 500 pounds in addition to his own body weight.

SUPERHUMAN POWERS: Angel's natural wings span 16 feet from tip to tip, and fold themselves against his back when not in use. Fully feathered like a bird's, the wings have a very flexible skeletal structure, enabling him to press them to the back of his torso and legs with only the slightest bulge visible under his clothing. His entire anatomy is adapted for flight: His bones are hollow like those of a bird; his body is virtually devoid of fat; he possesses greater proportionate muscle strength than a normal human; his eyes can withstand high-speed winds; and a special membrane in his respiratory system allows him to extract oxygen from the air at extreme velocities and altitudes.

Angel flies by flapping his wings, as a bird does. Though he generally flies below the height of clouds at 6,500 feet, Angel can reach a height of 10,000 feet with little effort. With severe strain he can reach the highest recorded altitude of a bird in flight -- African geese at 29,000 feet above sea level -- but he can only remain that high for several minutes. He can fly non-stop under his own power for a maximum of approximately twelve hours. Contrary to some reports, he cannot make a transatlantic flight solely under his own power.

FIRST APPEARANCE: *X-Men Vol. 1 #1* (1963)

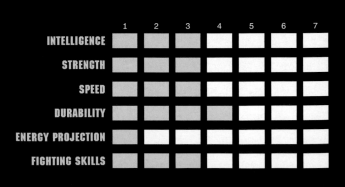

	1	2	3	4	5	6	7
INTELLIGENCE							
STRENGTH							
SPEED							
DURABILITY							
ENERGY PROJECTION							
FIGHTING SKILLS							

BEAST

REAL NAME: Henry "Hank" P. McCoy

KNOWN ALIASES: Beast

IDENTITY: Secret

OCCUPATION: Student, adventurer

PLACE OF BIRTH: Dunfee, Illinois

CITIZENSHIP: United States of America with no criminal record

MARITAL STATUS: Single

KNOWN RELATIVES: Sadie McCoy (grandmother), Edna McCoy (mother), Norton McCoy (father), Robert McCoy (uncle)

GROUP AFFILIATION: X-Men

EDUCATION: Enrolled at Professor Xavier's School for Gifted Youngsters

HISTORY: While working at a nuclear power plant, Norton McCoy was exposed to massive amounts of radiation that affected his genes. As a result, Norton's son, Henry "Hank" McCoy, was born a mutant who showed the signs of his being different from birth with his unusually large hands and feet.

As a youth, Hank's freakish appearance was the subject of much ridicule from his classmates, earning him the nickname of "beast." However, one classmate, Jennifer Nyles, came to know the real Hank after he began tutoring her in biology. On the night of the junior prom, Jennifer insisted that Hank accompany her as her date, and stood up for him after he was teased.

In his senior year, Hank's superhuman agility and athletic prowess earned him recognition as a star football player. During one game, Hank easily stopped a trio of robbers who were attempting to escape across the football field. The villain named the Conquistador noticed his efforts, kidnapping Hank's parents in an attempt to coerce the young mutant into working for him. The X-Men soon arrived and defeated the villain, and Hank was invited by Professor Charles Xavier to join the team of teenage mutant heroes and enroll in the Xavier School for Gifted Youngsters. Unable to resist the temptation of a private institution that could offer him limitless academic opportunities, Hank accepted.

HEIGHT: 5'11"

WEIGHT: 402 lbs

EYES: Blue

HAIR: Brown

DISTINGUISHING FEATURES: Unusually large hands and feet

POWERS & ABILITIES:

STRENGTH LEVEL: The Beast possesses superhuman strength enabling him to lift/press approximately two tons under optimal conditions.

SUPERHUMAN POWERS: In addition to his superhuman strength, the Beast possesses superhuman agility, endurance, and speed, despite his bulk. He possesses the agility of a great ape and the acrobatic prowess of an accomplished circus aerialist. His physiology is durable enough to allow him to survive a three-story fall by landing on his feet without suffering any broken bones or sprains. The Beast's legs are powerful enough to enable him to leap approximately 15 feet high in a standing high jump, and around 25 feet in a standing broad jump. He can also run on all fours at approximately forty miles per hour for short sprints.

The Beast can crawl up brick walls by wedging his fingers and toes into the smallest cracks and applying a viselike grip on them, as well as walk a tightrope with minimal effort. He is adept in performing complicated sequences of gymnastics such as flips, rolls, and springs, and can also walk on his hands for many hours. Further, his manual and pedal dexterity are so great that he can perform multiple tasks such as writing with both hands at once or tying knots in rope with his toes.

The Beast possesses enhanced senses, the ability to secrete pheromones to attract members of the opposite sex, as well as a slight healing factor that allows him to regenerate minor wounds and recover quickly from minor ailments such as colds. The Beast also possesses catlike night vision.

SPECIAL SKILLS: Hank has extensive knowledge of genetics, biochemistry, and a variety of other scientific fields. Hank is also an accomplished keyboard player.

FIRST APPEARANCE: *X-Men Vol. 1 #1* (1963)

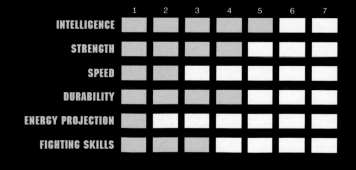

	1	2	3	4	5	6	7
INTELLIGENCE							
STRENGTH							
SPEED							
DURABILITY							
ENERGY PROJECTION							
FIGHTING SKILLS							

CYCLOPS

REAL NAME: Scott Summers

KNOWN ALIASES: Slim, formerly Slym Dayspring

IDENTITY: Secret

OCCUPATION: Student, adventurer

PLACE OF BIRTH: Anchorage, Alaska

CITIZENSHIP: United States of America with no criminal record

MARITAL STATUS: Single

KNOWN RELATIVES: Philip Summers (grandfather), Deborah Summers (grandmother), Christopher Summers (Corsair, father), Katherine Anne Summers (mother, deceased), Alexander Summers (Havok, brother), Jack Winters (Jack O'Diamonds, former foster father)

GROUP AFFILIATION: X-Men

EDUCATION: Enrolled at Professor Xavier's School for Gifted Youngsters

HISTORY: Scott Summers was the first of two sons born to Major Christopher Summers, a test pilot for the U.S. Air Force, and his wife, Katherine. Christopher was flying his family home from vacation when a spacecraft from the interstellar Shi'ar Empire attacked their plane. To save their lives, Katherine pushed Scott and his brother, Alex, out of the plane with the only available parachute. Scott suffered a head injury upon landing, thus forever preventing him from controlling his mutant power by himself. With their parents presumed dead, the authorities separated the two boys. Alex was adopted, but Scott remained comatose in a hospital for a year. On recovering, he was placed in an orphanage in Omaha, Nebraska.

As a teenager, Scott came into the foster care of Jack Winters, a mutant criminal known as the Jack O'Diamonds. After Scott began to suffer from severe headaches, he was sent to a specialist, who discovered that lenses made of ruby quartz corrected the problem. Soon after, Scott's mutant power first erupted from his eyes as an uncontrollable blast of optic force. The blast demolished a crane, causing it to drop its payload toward a terrified crowd. Scott

saved lives by obliterating the object with another blast, but the bystanders believed that he had tried to kill them.

Winters sought to use Scott's newfound talents in his crimes, and physically abused the young boy when he initially refused. However, Scott's display of power had attracted the attention of the mutant telepath Professor Charles Xavier. Xavier rescued Scott from Winters' clutches and enlisted him as the first member of the X-Men.

HEIGHT: 6'3"

WEIGHT: 195 lbs

EYES: Brown, glowing red when using powers

HAIR: Brown

DISTINGUISHING FEATURES: None

POWERS & ABILITIES:

STRENGTH LEVEL: Cyclops possesses the normal human strength of a young man of his age, height, and build who engages in intensive regular exercise.

SUPERHUMAN POWERS: Cyclops possesses the mutant ability to project a beam of heatless, ruby-colored concussive force from his eyes, which act as interdimensional apertures between this universe and another. Cyclops' body constantly absorbs ambient energy, such as sunlight, from his environment into his body's cells, which allows him to open the apertures.

SPECIAL LIMITATIONS: Due to a head injury, Cyclops is unable to shut

off his optic blasts at will and must therefore wear ruby quartz lenses to block the beams.

PARAPHERNALIA: The visor Cyclops wears to prevent random discharge is lined with powdered ruby quartz crystal. It incorporates two longitudinally mounted flat lenses that can lever inward providing a constantly variable exit slot. The inverted clamshell mechanism is operated by a twin system of miniature electrical motors. As a safety factor, there is a constant positive closing pressure provided by springs. The mask itself is made of high-impact cycolac plastic. There is an overriding finger-operated control mechanism on either side of the mask, and normal operation is through a flat micro-switch installed in the thumb of either glove.

FIRST APPEARANCE: *X-Men Vol. 1 #1* (1963)

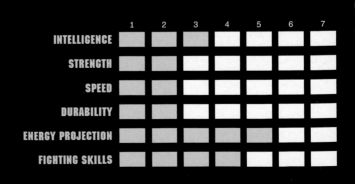

	1	2	3	4	5	6	7
INTELLIGENCE							
STRENGTH							
SPEED							
DURABILITY							
ENERGY PROJECTION							
FIGHTING SKILLS							

ICEMAN

REAL NAME: Robert "Bobby" Louis Drake

KNOWN ALIASES: Iceman

IDENTITY: Secret

OCCUPATION: Student, adventurer

CITIZENSHIP: United States of America with no criminal record

PLACE OF BIRTH: Fort Washington, Long Island, New York

MARITAL STATUS: Single

KNOWN RELATIVES: William Robert Drake (father), Madeline Beatrice Bass Drake (mother), Mary (cousin), Joel (cousin), Anne (aunt)

GROUP AFFILIATION: X-Men

EDUCATION: Enrolled at Professor Xavier's School for Gifted Youngsters

HISTORY: Bobby Drake discovered his mutant power to create ice while in his early teens, yet kept his condition hidden from everyone but his parents. Initially, Bobby was unable to stop feeling cold and shivering, but soon managed to keep it under control. When a bully named Rocky Beasely and his friends attacked Bobby and his then-girlfriend, Judy Harmon, the youngster panicked. To save Harmon, Bobby temporarily encased Rocky in ice, thus revealing his abilities for all to see. Believing the boy to be a menace, the townspeople organized a lynch mob. They broke into Bobby's home and overpowered him, but the local sheriff took the teenager into custody for his own protection. Meanwhile, the situation had come to the attention of Professor Charles Xavier, the telepathic mentor of the team of teenage mutant super heroes known as the X-Men.

Professor X dispatched his first X-Man, Cyclops, to contact Bobby. Cyclops stole into the jailhouse as planned, but the two began fighting when Bobby refused to accompany him. Caught by the lynch mob, Cyclops and Bobby were about to be hanged when they broke free. Professor X used his mental powers to stop the townspeople in their tracks and erase their memories of Bobby's powers. A grateful Bobby then accepted Xavier's invitation to enroll at his School for Gifted Youngsters and took the codename Iceman. Though

initially granting him a snow-like form, Bobby soon learned to increase his degree of cold control, resulting in an ice-like, almost transparent form.

Hated and feared by humanity, the X-Men honed their amazing abilities while standing in defense of a world pushed to the brink of genetic war by a handful of mutant terrorists. Iceman, the team's youngest founding member, became known as the comedian of the group. Regardless, he pulled his weight and worked well with the rest of the team.

HEIGHT: 5'8"

WEIGHT: 145 lbs

EYES: Brown

HAIR: Brown

DISTINGUISHING FEATURES: Can sheath his entire body in solid ice.

POWERS & ABILITIES:

STRENGTH LEVEL: Iceman possesses the normal human strength of a man of his age, height, and build who engages in intensive regular exercise. In his ice form, Iceman is able to augment his strength to superhuman levels, the full extent of which is as yet unknown.

SUPERHUMAN POWERS: Iceman is able to lower his internal and external body temperature without harm to himself, thereby radiating intense cold from his body. He is able to reach -105 degrees Fahrenheit within a few seconds, and is immune to subzero temperatures around him.

Iceman can freeze any moisture in the air around him into unusually hard ice, and thereby form simple objects such as slides, ladders, shields, and bats. He can also augment his ice form with extraneous moisture to enhance his strength and durability.

FIRST APPEARANCE: *X-Men Vol. 1 #1* (1963)

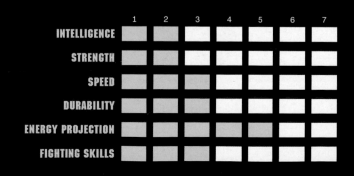

	1	2	3	4	5	6	7
INTELLIGENCE							
STRENGTH							
SPEED							
DURABILITY							
ENERGY PROJECTION							
FIGHTING SKILLS							

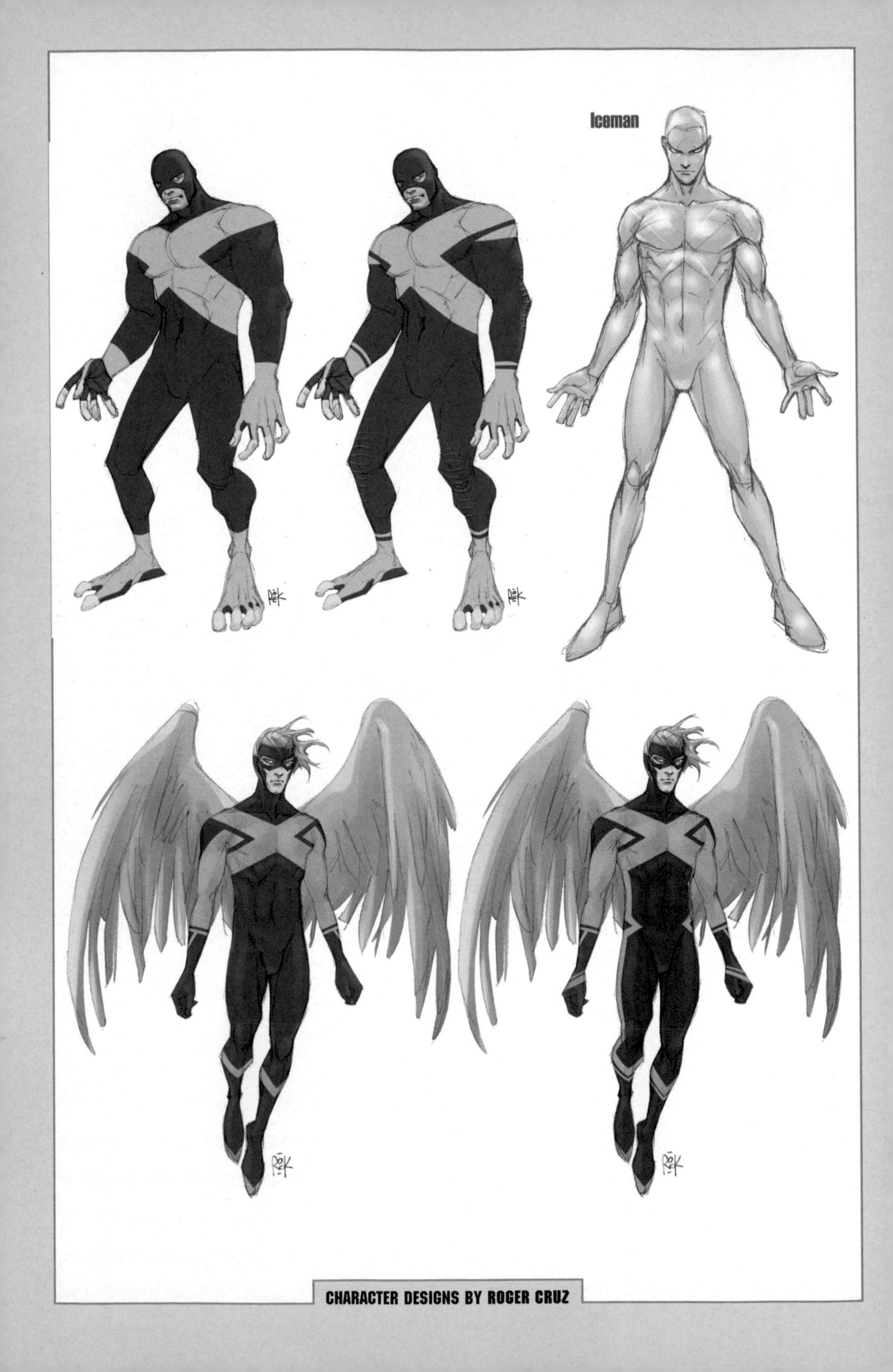
Iceman

CHARACTER DESIGNS BY ROGER CRUZ

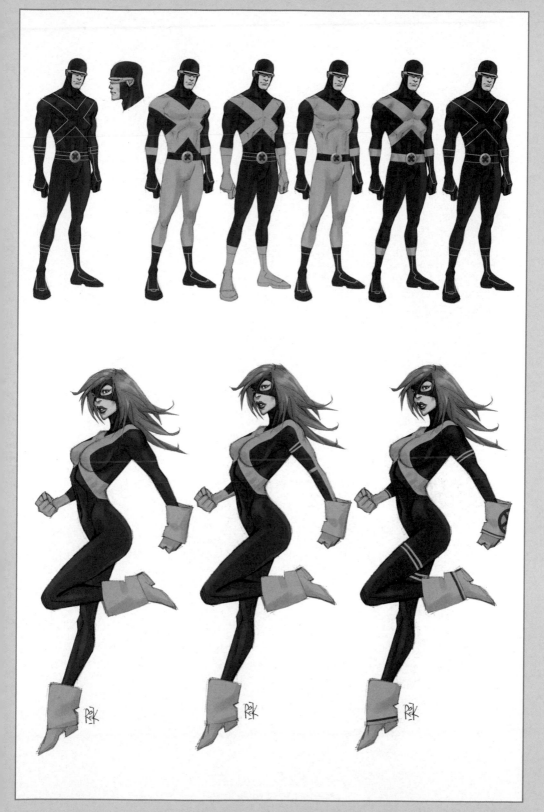

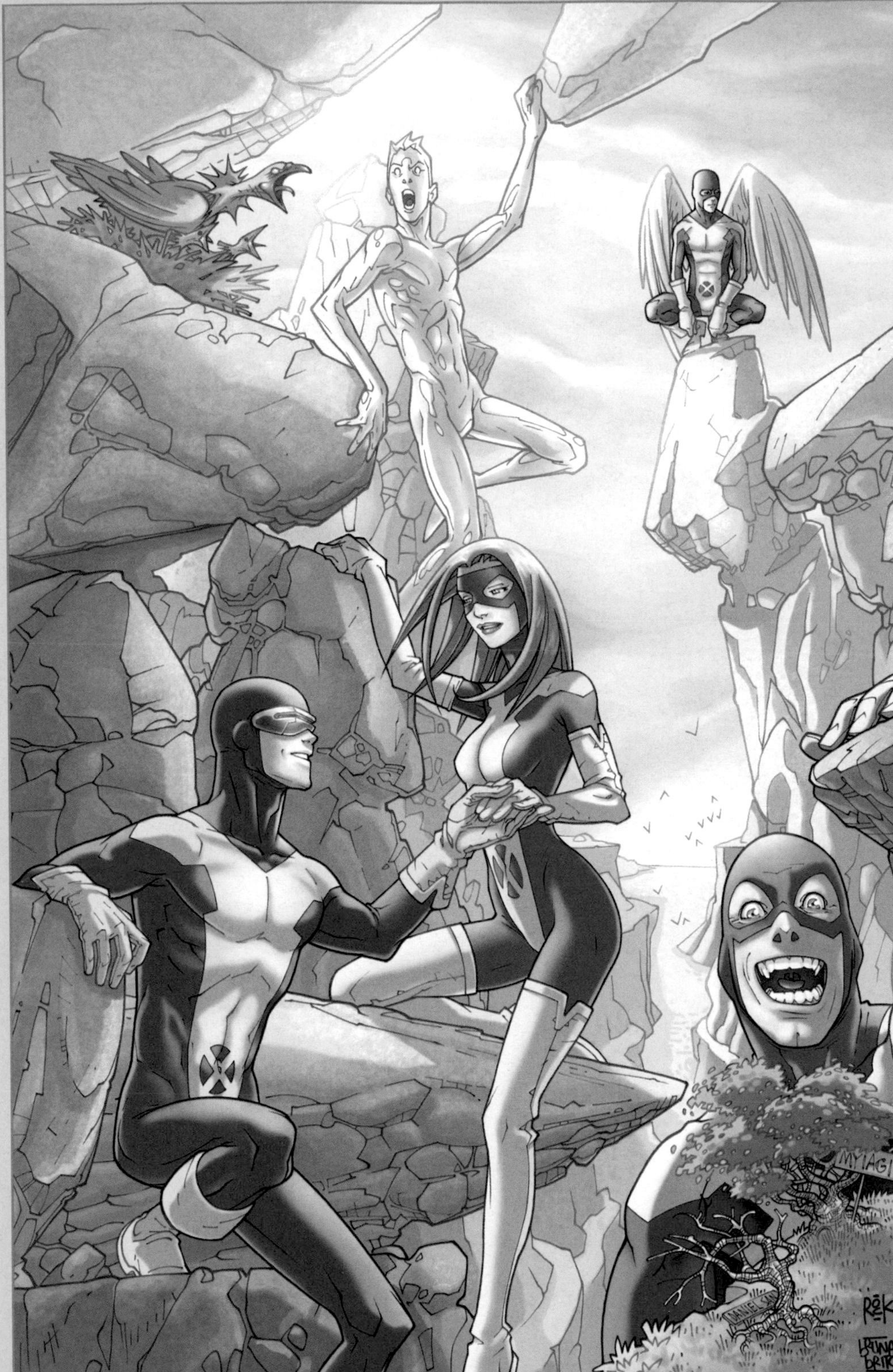
MYIAGI

UNUSED PINUPS BY ROGER CRUZ

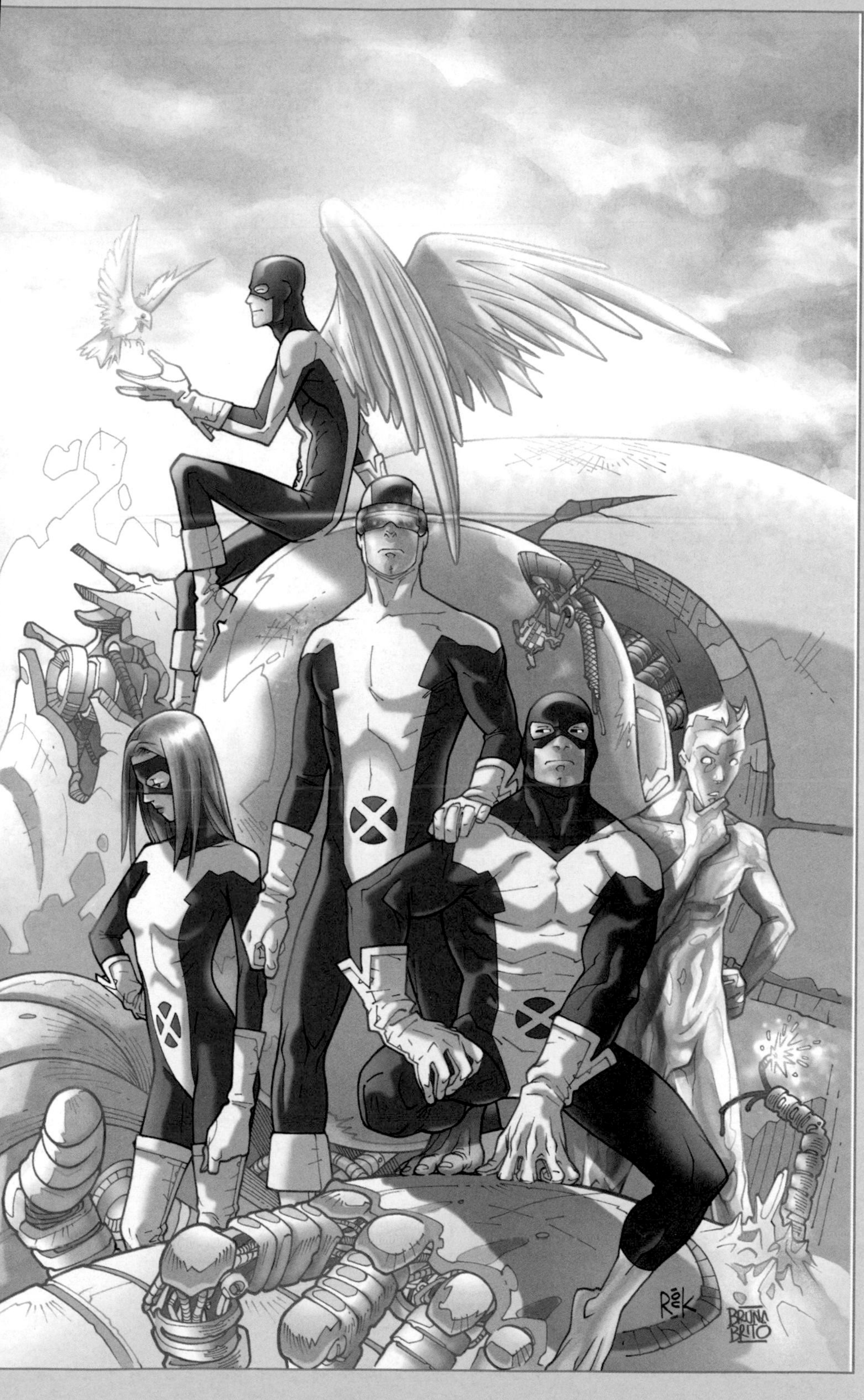
BRUNA BRITO

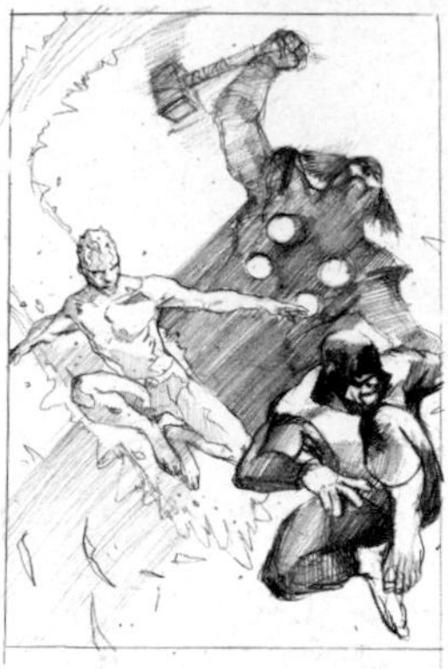

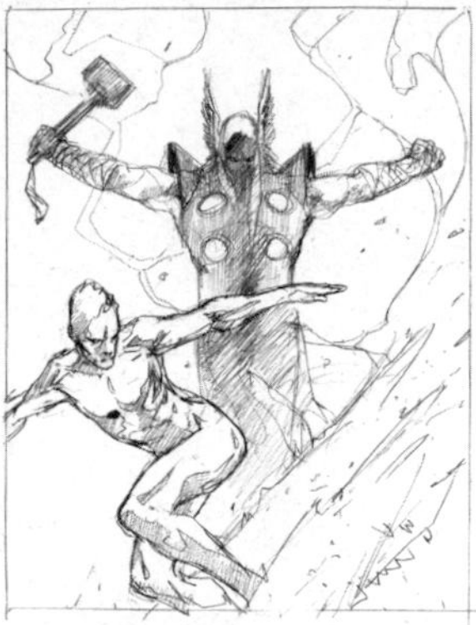

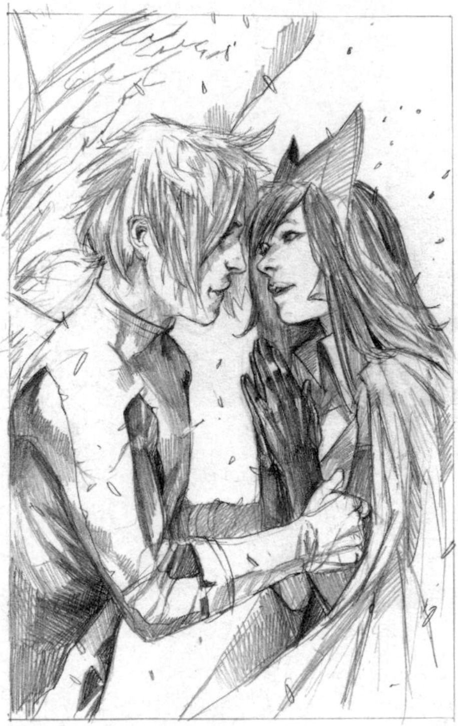

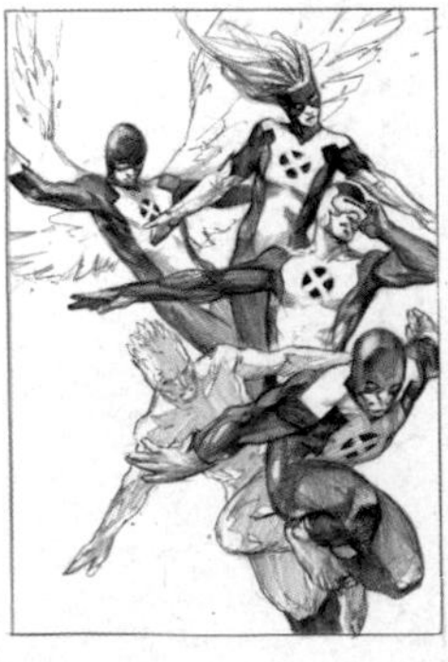

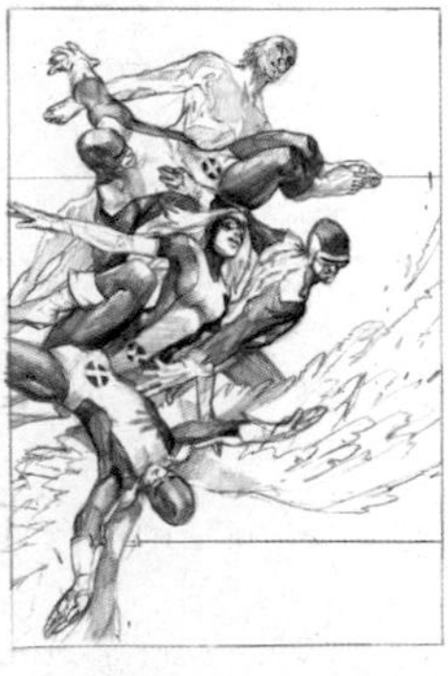

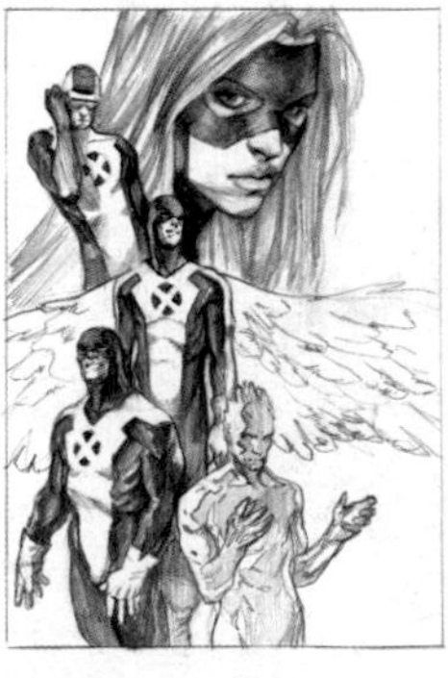

COVER SKETCHES BY MARKO DJURDJEVIĆ